Chimera's Cradle

CHIMERA'S CRADLE

Brian Stableford

LEGEND

Published by Legend Books in 1997

1 3 5 7 9 10 8 6 4 2

Brian Stableford has asserted his right under the Copyright, Designs and Patents
Act, 1988 to be identified as the author of this work

First published in the United Kingdom by Legend

Legend Books Limited
20 Vauxhall Bridge Road, London, SW1V 2SA

Random House Australia (Pty) Limited
20 Alfred Street, Milsons Point, Sydney,
New South Wales 2061, Australia

Random House New Zealand Limited
18 Poland Road, Glenfield
Auckland 10, New Zealand

Random House South Africa (Pty) Limited
Endulini, 5a Jubilee Road,
Parktown 2193, South Africa

Random House UK Limited Reg. No. 954009

A CIP catalogue record for this book
is available from the British Library

Papers used by Random House UK Limited
are natural, recyclable products made from wood grown in
sustainable forests. The manufacturing processes conform to
the environmental regulations of the country of origin

ISBN 0099443716

Typeset by Deltatype Ltd, Ellesmere Port, Cheshire
Printed and bound in Great Britain by
Mackays of Chatham PLC, Chatham, Kent

Part One

Across the Rim,
Captives of Fate and Fortune

The place where humans first came into the world was named Idun by the people of the ship, in memory of a place which never was but was remembered and revered nevertheless. The people of the ship built a city there, but their sons and daughters were not permitted to live long in the city.

'You must go forth into the world and multiply,' the forefathers said to the people of the world. 'You must go to every region which will support you: to every forest, every plain and every seashore. You must build cities of your own wherever you can, and protect them as best you can against corrosion and corruption. Where you cannot build cities you must follow other ways of life, but you must leave no land alone, even in the farthest reaches of the world, for the purpose of human life is to fight evil wherever it may be found.'

When the city of Idun crumbled into dust, as the cities of the world are ever wont to do, the forefathers made no attempt to rebuild it. To their remaining sons and daughters they said: 'Go follow your brothers and sisters into the regions of the world, for we have other work to do here before we leave. Where there was a city we shall make a garden, but it will be a garden of poisons. Do not forbid your descendants to visit this garden, but bid them beware of it, for they will be wise to avoid it for many generations.'

The garden of Idun became the source of many evil and dangerous things, for which reason the people of the world called it Chimera's Cradle, but they also named it the Navel of the World, to remind themselves that they too were chimerical beings.

The best of the new chimeras spawned and cradled in the garden followed the people of the world as they dispersed themselves through the forests and the plains, but the worst of them tainted the region around the garden.

The people of the world complained of this injustice, but to no avail. 'Even that which has never been known before may yet be created,' the loremasters said, 'but it cannot be designed. The cradle in which it will be hatched and nourished must give birth to evils too, but in the end evil will be defeated and Order will prevail.'

The people of the ship gave what earthly gifts they could to

2

the people of the world, but the most precious gift of all was one they did not have to give, and that was an incorruptible stone. Aboard the ship, there had been many kinds of stone that were incorruptible there, but corruption had no dominion aboard the ship and incorruptibility was easily achieved. In the world, alas, corruption reigned supreme.

'The war against evil will be hard fought in the world,' the loremasters told their sons and their daughters, 'but war is the mother of all weapons, and the war against evil is the mother of the weapons by which evil shall one day be defeated. There is as yet no incorruptible stone in all the world, but it will not always be so. We have planted the garden of Idun so that the incorruptible stone might one day be born from the Pool of Life, nourished by milk and blood. When that day comes, your children's children must seize and use the stone, and turn the evil of corrosion to the good of inscription.'

The Lore of Genesys

I

ANDRIS MYRASOL AWOKE feeling that his body did not quite belong to him – or that it was protesting against his ownership, on the grounds of long and intolerable abuse. The feeling would not have been so bad had he not suspected that he had indeed suffered a partial loss of control over the empire of his flesh.

He lay quite still, trying to recover as much self-possession as he could. He was relieved to discover that his tenure within his aching body seemed a little more comfortable and a little more secure than it had been the day before.

Perhaps, this time, I'm really getting better, he thought. *Perhaps I'm on the mend at last.* It was not so much an estimate of probability as an expression of hope.

He knew that he had been ill for a long time, although he couldn't put a number to the days of his affliction. Even before Philemon Taub and Venerina Sirelis had given him the purified Spirit of the Waters to drink he had been sick for days. He had sometimes felt quite well, but he knew now that he hadn't actually been well since the night Shabir's raiders had spirited him away from Aulakh Phar's wagon. Since then, periods of delirium had alternated with irregular intervals in which his body and mind had functioned almost normally.

The draught Philemon had given him to drink, promising that it would make him better, had served instead to redouble his confusion. Andris wasn't sure how many days had passed since the battle at the Community's house. His short-term memory had become awkwardly unreliable, although he remembered everything that had happened to him before he first ventured into the Soursweet Marshes with what seemed like perfect clarity.

I will get better, he assured himself, trying to muster the

4

power of positive thinking. *I have to. I can't afford to be ill while we're still in danger.*

Without opening his eyes or bestirring himself more than was strictly necessary Andris took census of his recovered faculties. He twitched his fingers and toes, one by one, and was relieved to find that he could feel the presence of every single one of them. His body didn't seem unusually lumpen; nor did his thinking seem unbearably sluggish.

Having counted his physical and mental assets he attempted to count his circumstantial blessings. That was a trickier task by far.

At least I'm still alive, he thought. *Considering that I've recently crossed the greater part of the Soursweet Marshes while I was out of my mind and tackled a horde of giant Serpents two at a time, armed only with a broken banister rail, that's really quite surprising. Given that I've also been caught up in a nest-war while wandering around the deepest chambers of a dragomite hive – not to mention being kidnapped by a fear-crazed general – I think I can safely say that just being alive is firm evidence that I'm on a lucky streak. Nor am I alone in my plight. Princess Lucrezia is on my side now, and Ssifuss seems to be intent on sticking with us . . .*

It took him a moment or two to recall the names of his other companions, but he did it. *As for Venerina Sirelis and the boy,* he went on, *they're two pairs of hands if nothing else – and her brain may have some useful knowledge in it, if only we can separate the authentic wisdom from all the deist claptrap with which it's confused . . .*

He opened his eyes then, to find that he was lying on his back, looking up at the stars.

Never having been much of an astronomer Andris couldn't tell the difference between these stars and the ones which shone over Ferentina. To him, one flamestar looked very much like another and the silvery bed of light in which they sat, compounded out of the light of millions of more distant suns, was just a background. He had never tried to educate his eyes in the subtle business of measuring the slight differences of colour and intensity which allowed the flamestars to be individually identified, nor had he tried to memorise the patterns which they formed; he was a mapmaker not a navigator. Even so, he knew that this was the southern hemisphere of the world, and that the stars at which he was staring were strange; some, at least, must be stars which he had never set eyes on before he crossed the Dragomite Hills.

I'm an adventurer, he thought, *maybe even a hero. I'm a soldier of fortune, as bold and brave as any. At least, I think I am. Is that three blessings? It's the sort of thing that would count as a blessing in most people's reckoning, isn't it?*

He didn't actually want to make up the other side of the mental balance sheet by enumerating his problems, but he couldn't help himself. No matter how lackadaisical his short-term memory had become, his troubles could hardly be ignored.

He and his companions were stuck in the middle of a hostile wilderness with a large force of mounted men and giant Serpents less than ten hours behind them. They had very little water, even less food, and only one good knife between the five of them. What was more, when Rayner had climbed a steepletree last evening to see what lay to the east he had reported that there appeared to be another large party following a nearly parallel but slightly convergent course. Those travellers too were probably hostile – or at least, they had to assume so, until they found good reason to think otherwise. As if even that weren't enough, Andris couldn't help adding to the list the fact that he still had no way of knowing whether Merel Zabio was alive or dead, or whether she had made it to Salamander's Fire if she were alive, or whether he would ever be able to get there to meet her even if she had.

'Are you awake, Andris?' The whispered words cut into his reverie suddenly enough to make him start in spite of their careful softness. He inferred that the others must still be asleep, and that the princess didn't want to wake them. He looked round to face her. His eyes had adjusted well enough to the darkness but she was sitting in the starshadow of a reef of dead rock and he couldn't see her features clearly.

He remembered, vaguely, that they always made camp on outcrops of dead rock, although such expanses had become more difficult to find of late; the strange living rocks which Venerina Sirelis called flowing stones were very common hereabouts, and wherever they were not, the ground was equally inconvenient by virtue of the profusion of spiky cacti and the rigid shoots of some unusually aggressive species of tree. Thorny bushes of the kind which had made crossing the Soursweet Marshes such a nightmare still contrived to surround every muddy ditch and lakelet with a dense defensive wall.

'What time is it?' Andris whispered. It seemed easiest to answer Lucrezia's question with a question, given that any reply at all would constitute an affirmative response.

'I don't know,' Lucrezia admitted. 'I haven't got used to these southern stars yet. A few hours past absolute midnight, but a while before dawn. We stopped early – you were on the point of collapse again, I think. Do you remember yesterday at all?'

Andris tried to remember, but he was a little wary of identifying the last day he could dimly remember as 'yesterday'. He was uncomfortably aware of the fact that he'd fallen into the unfortunate habit of losing whole days, sometimes two or three at a time. He sat up, stretching the muscles in his back.

'How long is it since Rayner spotted the other caravan?' he asked cautiously.

'That was the day *before* yesterday,' she told him, with a slight sigh.

'That's what I thought,' he lied. 'So we're still heading south?'

'A little to the west of due south,' she told him. 'Venerina's convinced that the other caravan is a second party of slavers. It might intend to link up with the one that sacked the Community, or might simply be heading for the same destination, but either way we'll have to make our move very soon. We don't have any choice.'

Andris wondered whether he ought to know what Lucrezia meant by 'our move'. While he was trying to remember Lucrezia moved closer, her features emerging from the starshadow. Her face was haggard, and not just from lack of sleep. She'd never been plump, but she'd lost the adequately fed appearance she'd had when Andris had first encountered her in the depths of the dragomite hive. She was pale and drawn now, almost to the point where she could have passed for an amber instead of the golden she was. Her eyes glittered as if they were afire, even in the starlight. She certainly didn't look like a princess any more. Her hair was as filthy as a common vagabond's, and so were her clothes.

While they had both been guests in the huge house on the

shore of the Lake of Colourless Blood Lucrezia had been clean and neat and thoroughly composed, but that had been several days ago – at least four, maybe even six or seven, depending on how many he'd mislaid while his mind went awandering.

'We need you, Andris,' she said plaintively. 'We don't stand any real chance of pulling this off without you. With all due respect to Ssifuss and his assiduous archery practice, you're the only real fighting man we have – and you're worth two or three of the ordinary kind. You have to pull yourself together. Venerina says that you can do it. She says that it really wasn't a powerful dose of the drug they gave you, and that all the poisons had been carefully extracted from it. She says you shouldn't be like this, even if the poisons of the marsh had affected you much worse than they seemed to have done.'

'She doesn't know anything about it,' Andris muttered defensively. 'I'm different – not like the people of the Community. I don't know what's happening to me, but it's certainly not what she expected.' He knew that he was no closer to being a deist now than he had been before, but he was equally certain that the process of *becoming* which had begun as soon as he had been put to sleep by Shabir's raiders was still continuing, still groping towards some unimaginable conclusion.

'You don't have to be so defensive,' Lucrezia said. 'I'm different too. Their precious Spirit of the Waters couldn't get into me at all. Serpent's blood is my curse.'

'Is that why we're still heading west of south instead of southeast?' he asked uneasily. 'Is your Serpent's blood drawing you to the Silver Thorns and the Gauntlet of Gladness, in the hope that you might follow it to the Navel of the World? Is *that* your plan, now?'

'You know it's not,' she told him – but she didn't sound certain.

'You'd better remind me,' he said, wondering why it was so difficult to admit that he couldn't remember. It wasn't his fault, after all.

She reached out to touch him lightly on the shoulder, as if to soothe his smouldering ire. 'You weren't entirely with us,' she conceded. 'Maybe we were a little too discreet while we were still working it out. Venerina was afraid that we might not be able to trust Ssifuss any longer.' She glanced sideways, presumably towards the place where the Serpent lay sleeping.

'Why shouldn't we trust Ssifuss?' Andris asked warily. So far as he knew, they had no reason not to.

'I'm sure we can,' Lucrezia said. 'He seems to be just as frightened of the company behind us as we are, perhaps more so. He says that he never believed in giant Serpents – thought they were just monsters of legend. Mossassor evidently thought differently, and Ssifuss is beginning to wonder what else Mossassor might have been right about. All that means little or nothing to Venerina, though – she's scared, and understandably so, given what's behind us.' Andris understood the significance of Lucrezia's decision to use 'he' rather than 'it' in referring to the Serpent – but he also understood Venerina's anxiety.

'Ssifuss doesn't seem to feel any kinship with the giant Serpents,' Andris said.

'He certainly doesn't,' Lucrezia agreed. 'In fact, he seems to think that you're perfectly wonderful because you killed so many of them.'

'So the giant Serpents and their human allies who are still chasing us are catching up,' Andris said, just to make sure that he had it right, 'and their friends aren't very far behind. That's why we have to make our move soon.'

'I'm still not sure they're actually *chasing* us,' Lucrezia told him cautiously. 'They're certainly heading south, with as much speed as they can muster, but it's possible that they're taking their prisoners to some unknown destination behind that wall strung out along the southern horizon, and have no idea that we're ahead of them. We have to hope so – we need every advantage we can get.'

'What wall?' Andris wanted to know.

'Not a *real* wall,' Lucrezia said patiently. 'I don't know what else to call it, though. We only got a glimpse before the sunset turned it to shadow. Maybe it's the Silver Thorns, if the Silver Thorns are just another kind of steepletree.'

Andris furrowed his brow. 'How many days is it since we ditched the boat?' he asked.

'Six.'

'Then it must be at least six days more to the Silver Thorns, if my maps are trustworthy,' he told her. 'It's probably more like eight or ten – I don't suppose we've made as much headway as we might have.'

'Whatever the line on the horizon is,' she said, 'we'll get there tomorrow. All I know for sure is that it's big – and it stretches a long way east and west.'

'That's not possible,' Andris told her. 'There's nothing of any significance marked on that part of the relevant map. You must remember – you did see the map I drew for Fraxinus. The colours were all wrong, but the scale was right. It's a good twelve to fifteen days' march from the southern edge of the marshes to the Silver Thorns, and the Nest of the Phoenix is beyond them.'

'In that case,' she said, 'either the men who made your map didn't consider the feature important, or it wasn't there when they made the map. Venerina says that she's heard of something called the Great Reef, and that this must be it – she's heard it rumoured as a place where food and water can be found, fairly safe in itself although the land beyond is treacherous in the extreme.'

'There was nothing called the Great Reef on the map I was taught to draw,' Andris told her stiffly.

'When the landscape changes, people have to invent new names,' the princess said mildly. 'You only have to stand up to see its jagged rim black against the stars – but you'll have to wait for dawn to estimate its true nature and magnitude. By then, we ought to be very close to it – we have to get there with several hours to spare. Venerina reckons that the creatures that destroyed the Community will be making straight for water, and the fact that the other party is aiming the same way adds strength to the conclusion. We have to get there first. You have to pull yourself together, if you can. We'll only get the one chance.'

'One chance to do what?' he asked warily. 'I'm sorry if I've heard it before, but I just can't . . .'

'We have to try to take the prisoners back,' she told him flatly. 'I think we can do it, if we're clever enough.'

Somehow, the fact that she was talking in a confidential whisper made the words sound even more extravagant than was warranted by their meaning. Andris pondered their implication, wondering if there was some other vital fact that he'd forgotten. 'How many prisoners did they take?' he asked.

'Ssifuss estimated that there were about forty.'

Andris tried to remember how many marauders had attacked the Community, and how many giant Serpents he was said to have killed, but Lucrezia didn't wait for him to ask. 'We think there might be as many as fifty men with them,' she said. 'There are no more than a dozen giant Serpents, perhaps less than ten. They have three wagons with about a dozen men riding in them, and about fifty horses all told. If the other horsemen Rayner spotted really are the second half of their raiding party, and if they manage to join up before they get to the Reef, you can probably double those figures.'

'There are only five of us,' Andris pointed out, 'and we haven't a single decent weapon, unless you count the Serpent's bow and spear. I know he's been practising bowmanship, but . . .' He trailed off as he realised why the fact that they had to be heading for a water-source was so important. The princess was a witch, after all, and she still wore her own armoury about her waist. 'The prisoners will have to drink too,' he pointed out, after a slight pause. 'If you poison the water – assuming that you have enough poison to make sure that it won't be so diluted as to become harmless – you'll kill the prisoners too.'

'There are different kinds of poisons,' she told him. 'Even the most powerful – the ones that can stand the greatest dilution, that is – don't necessarily kill. You surely learned *that* in the marshes. We don't need to inflict mortal damage or induce paralysis – we only have to weaken them. Four humans and a Serpent can do a lot against a temporarily disabled army, if they pick their moment carefully enough.'

Four humans and a man-sized Serpent against fifty or a hundred men, plus ten or twenty giant Serpents! Andris thought. *Some plan!* 'I'm glad you've worked it all out with such minute accuracy,' he observed drily. 'The wondrous detail of it makes a nice match with its scrupulous sense of fair play.'

'They attacked the Community without warning,' Lucrezia reminded him, although she must have known that his mention of fair play hadn't been in the least serious. He'd lived far too long to worry about fair play in matters of mortal combat, even where witchery was involved. 'They came to take prisoners, but they weren't squeamish about killing those who resisted them. We're entitled to use any and all means to free the people they captured – and we surely owe it to Venerina and her followers to try. I know I tried to warn you against the deists when they were plotting to feed you that potion, but the fact remains that they did save *our* lives. If it weren't for them, I'd certainly be dead – and in all probability, so would you. We can't run away from this. It's not just that we don't have any supplies to run with – we have a debt to repay.'

Andris didn't question her moral calculation. The Community *had* saved their lives. There *was* a debt which ought to be honoured, if there was a chance to honour it. He licked his lips and looked up at the starry sky again. 'Will Ssifuss agree to this?' he asked.

'I think so,' Lucrezia said. 'He's stayed with us this far – I think he'll agree that we don't have any choice but to strike while we can.'

'If it goes wrong,' Andris dutifully pointed out, 'it's likely to go *horribly* wrong. If even a few of them don't drink deeply enough from your poisoned pool, they'll take us apart. Given the odds, the probability is that either we'll end up prisoners ourselves, or we'll be dead.'

'I know that,' the princess replied. 'Even I don't yet know how good a witch I really am . . . but we can't simply turn away and head for Salamander's Fire. Maybe you weren't in any fit state to agree yesterday, but you are now. You have to play your part in this, Andris. Without your speed and strength, we don't even stand a slim chance.'

I wouldn't be here, Andris thought, *if this apprentice witch hadn't wanted to practise her witchcraft on me back in Xandria.* But he knew that was irrelevant now. He couldn't go back and start all over again. He had to start the rest of his life from where he was, no matter what condition he was in.

'I'm beginning to remember a little more about yesterday, now,' he said, hoping that saying it might make it true. 'It wasn't a good day, was it?'

'No,' she said, 'it wasn't. The scraps we had to eat tasted foul and the water we sipped wasn't much better. Our clothes and boots are worn out, and the ground is littered with creatures avid to grab us by the ankles with jaws of stone. If you hadn't got such big feet . . . well, no matter. We got through yesterday, and we'll get through tomorrow – but we *will* have to fight. We don't have any option.'

12

'No,' Andris said, flexing his fingers as if to test their strength. 'I don't suppose we do.'

2

When the first bright rays of daylight breached the eastern horizon Lucrezia stopped walking. She lifted her eyes from fearful contemplation of the ground that lay ahead of her marching feet. She was curious to know what the many hues of dawn would do to the palisade of shadow that was lurking about the southern horizon, awaiting their approach.

The near-white gleam of starlight was quickly consumed by the profound blue which crept from horizon to horizon, brightening all the while – but it was the ground rather than the distant barrier which was immediately transformed by colour and clarity. The ominous pools of shadow which she had been carefully skirting metamorphosed into crudely patterned and darkly coloured masses of various shapes and sizes. For a moment or two, while her eyes adjusted, they did indeed seem to be *flowing* – but as soon as the apparent metamorphosis of the terrain was complete they settled once again into stern solidity. If they *did* flow, they flowed exceedingly slowly.

The crowns of the trees were wider hereabouts, and much greener, although the trees themselves were widely spaced. Beneath the spreading branches pools of shadow still remained. The trees bore no fruit, and very few birds gathered in their foliage; those which could be seen were presumably hunting for insects.

Lucrezia pulled her makeshift hat on to the top of her head and secured it as best she could. There was little need as yet for its protection, but it was part of the ritual of greeting the day. Venerina Sirelis was doing likewise; she too had paused and Rayner with her.

Andris Myrasol and Ssifuss had drawn some way ahead, having only just become aware that their companions had paused. Now they came to a halt and looked back inquiringly, their actions and their manner mirroring one another in a faintly absurd fashion. Lucrezia wondered whether the two of them might qualify as a pair of sorts, physically mismatched as they were. She looked past them at the landscape which awaited them, and the barrier which marked its limit.

Stretching as far as the eye could see to the west and the east, but curving away to the south as it faded towards either extremity, was the jagged silhouette of what Venerina had called the Great Reef. It was now easy enough to see that it was far more like the edge of a forest than a manufactured wall, although its 'foliage' was very strange. There was little green in it, and just as little of the purple which unearthly vegetation often wore in place of green. Its dominant colours were shades of brown and grey, but there *was* silver there, and the silver did indeed seem to take the form of needle-like tips like those the steepletrees had, which might easily have been called thorns by mapmakers in search of evocative labels. Not all the colours were metallic, though; there were reds and blues promiscuously dotted about the heights, glinting in the sunlight as if they were polished.

Lucrezia compared the bulk and extent of the barrier with her memory of the Great Wall of Xandria. The Great Wall required the constant labour of many hundreds of men to maintain its strength, but this was a living thing which renewed and repaired itself. She couldn't yet make an accurate judgment as to the distance or the scale of what she could see, but she knew that if it really did curve away to form a closed circle, as it appeared to do, then the space it enclosed must be at least as large as the entire province of Xandria, and a thousand times bigger than the city which bore the same name.

She also remembered the barricade which the men of the Nine Towns had built out of bones and the body-parts of dragomites. In terms of its colours what lay ahead of them was not so very dissimilar; that wall too had been dominated by browns and greys, with very little green to be seen. There, however, the similarity ended. The barricade warning dragomites and mound-women to turn back from the narrow land had been a sad and dull affair, with very little lustre left upon the plates of dragomite chitin which provided most of its mass. Rot had already begun to work upon it, in all its myriad ways. This barrier was lustrous still, and in some strange way it seemed more alive than the fertile fields of Xandria or the Forest of Absolute Night.

If the taller entities making up the wall *were* trees, Lucrezia decided, they were certainly not the kind of trees which had leafy crowns. Their coiling branches had a distinct coppery sheen, and the highest of all seemed to be almost bare, save for the reds and blues which dotted them. The lower ones, by contrast, were elaborately dressed in filmy cobweb-like drapes that might have been lazy parasites.

'There,' said Venerina Sirelis, pointing with a quivering finger. 'Where the twisted dendrites grow exceedingly tall and the lesser growths show the most luxuriant colours. That's where we'll find the water. That's the gateway for which our enemies are aiming, and the breach where we'll turn the tables on them.'

Lucrezia couldn't help glancing behind her, but the enemies in question were nowhere to be seen. The terrain was not level enough, and there were too many trees, to allow her an uninterrupted view northwards – but Lucrezia did not doubt that the enemy was still there, patiently tracking them.

'It won't be easy,' Lucrezia said, looking ahead again to where Andris Myrasol and Ssifuss were retracing their most recent footsteps, impatient with their companions' decision to pause. 'With Andris still in a daze and hardly a serviceable weapon between us . . .' She stopped, because there was no point in spelling it out.

'The Spirit of the Lake is with us still,' Venerina assured her, trying with all her might to summon up the last reserves of her determination, 'and it hasn't yet released our pursuers. They still carry the marsh's poisons within them – even the Serpents. You had medicines for your own relief, and we gave you more, but they have none. They will be weary, thirsty and vulnerable.'

Lucrezia looked at poor Rayner, who seemed as weary and vulnerable as any man could possibly be, for all that the Spirit of the Lake was supposed to be working with him rather than against him. She knew that he could hear every word of the conversation, and thought it best to conserve what hope he had. *We don't know what medicines they might have,* she thought, but she did not say it aloud.

16

'What's wrong?' Andris demanded.

'Nothing,' she replied. 'Go on – we're following.'

The amber didn't press the point; he simply turned round again. Ssifuss hesitated a moment longer, waiting to see that the laggards did indeed begin to walk again. They were in single file now, with Andris in the lead. It was a good formation, allowing everyone except the leader to have a course through the maze of living rock mapped out for them – and Andris was, after all, a mapmaker by vocation.

Lucrezia tried to gather her strength and resolve, at least to the level which she had attained during her brief but comfortable sojourn in the Community's house, but she wasn't sure that she could do it.

When she had travelled south from Xandria with Hyry Keshvara it had seemed that her only real enemy was discomfort – that if only she could accustom herself to life without the routine luxuries of King Belin's Inner Sanctum all would be well. No matter how uncomfortable she had actually become in Hyry's company, while subsisting on inferior food and suffering all the aches and pains which biting insects and blistered feet could inflict, she had never let go of the conviction that the price of adventure was worth paying. That conviction had been shaken by the massacre of Djemil Eyub's men in the Forest of Absolute Night, and by her subsequent involvement in a dragomite nest-war, but it had held. There had been time enough to test her resolve to destruction while she and her companions were wandering in the Soursweet Marshes, but she had spent the greater part of that time in helpless delirium.

The last few days had, alas, been very different, and much more difficult.

While the five of them had moved steadily southwards, ahead of the strange company that had destroyed the Community, Lucrezia's faith in the great adventure had slowly ebbed away. The ambition and fervour that had fuelled her escape from Belin's citadel now seemed manifestly foolish. She found herself facing all kinds of awkward questions which she could not refuse to hear. What goal could she possibly entertain now, save to escape with her life? What end could possibly be worth seeking, except safety? What merit was there in curiosity, given that curiosity continually led her into extreme danger?

She wished that she had someone with whom to discuss these questions, but she had lost Hyry Keshvara and Ereleth too. Andris was inclined to argue such matters along brutally simple lines that seemed unable to recognise or properly comprehend the kind of impulse which had driven her out of the Inner Sanctum, while Venerina Sirelis had her own very different way of looking at things – with which Lucrezia could not begin to sympathise.

The situation might have been slightly more bearable had she not been inclined to blame herself for the myriad misfortunes which had brought all this about. She, after all, had prevented Hyry Keshvara from joining up with Carus Fraxinus at the planned time. Had it not been for her escape neither Ereleth nor Dhalla would have left the citadel – and had she not been captured by dragomites . . .

At that point, however, the threads of possibility became far too tangled to be followed much further.

All in all, things seemed much worse than she had ever imagined possible.

Mere walking had now become so burdensome that Lucrezia wondered whether she would ever recover the state of health she had enjoyed in Xandria. She felt as if the life were draining out of her. She almost envied Andris Myrasol the strange state of mind into which he had recently been slipping every time he settled into a pattern of repetitive action. His manner was by no means as mechanical now as it had been while he rowed the boat in which they had escaped from the Community's house, but he was not yet the man he had been in the Dragomite Hills, when he had saved her from the rogue dragomite. He was recovering, but he seemed to spend by far the greater part of every day in deep retreat within some private realm of the imagination.

They walked for three hours more before Ssifuss caught up with Andris and tapped him on the shoulder to call a halt. The amber consented meekly. The Serpent still had a little water left in its pack, which it doled out with scrupulous even-handedness when Lucrezia and the other two caught up.

'Musst take care,' Ssifuss advised them, as they found safe places to sit and threw themselves down. 'Ssome sstone ssingss not dangerouss, but not eassy to tell. Besst be ssafe.'

Lucrezia nodded dutifully to acknowledge the Serpent's

warning. She watched Rayner's eyes darting fearfully from side to side as he measured the distance separating him from the nearest 'sstone ssingss'. The boy's trepidation was understandable; he had come close to losing a finger because he had been unable to believe that the stones could close their traps quickly enough to catch him.

'How much do you know about these stony creatures?' Lucrezia asked Venerina Sirelis, who had sat down close beside her. 'There's nothing like them in Xandria.'

'Very little,' the deist replied. 'They're rare in the marshes – invaders, not part of the great organism whose heart is the Lake of Colourless Blood. Sometimes they lurk at the bottom of shallow pools, masked by mud, and they can even be seen in the shallows of the lake occasionally. They seem to feed by absorbing detritus. Their surfaces are sometimes pockmarked by little pitfalls which might trap insects and worms, but I never saw one with pitfalls big enough to catch a man's foot until I came here. Travellers have always told tales of huge ones which can open great jaws to either side of a sleeping man while he beds down on what he mistakes for inert rock, but I never took such tales seriously.' She glanced at Rayner as she spoke, but the boy wouldn't meet her eye.

Lucrezia had examined a few of the flowing stones during previous periods of rest, mildly intrigued by the intricate designs which were outlined there as if by a stone-carver's chisels, but Ssifuss wasn't expert enough in the use of human language to offer an elaborate account of what it knew about them. It had told her that the stony ones were avid to trap and immure anything living, and that creatures sometimes emerged from the living stone, but nothing else.

'It's said that the worms which emerge from the stones aren't worms at all, but spores of stone-creatures,' Venerina added. 'Philemon would know.' The deist fell quiet after that; she was still grief-stricken by the loss of Philemon.

'The living walls of dragomite hives must be distant kin to such creatures,' Lucrezia said thoughtfully. 'Andris saw a chamber where one such wall was covered with diffuse but seemingly human flesh, which gave every appearance of being alive. Perhaps crude pitfalls are the least of the dangers we have to fear – some of these creatures might be capable of subtler forms of capture and absorption. The great majority seem to be capable of very limited deformation, but there may be others lurking among them which are softer and far more flexible.'

'God's creatures take many forms,' the older woman said dully. 'His pattern is infinite in its complexity.'

'Did the Spirit of the Waters tell you that?' Lucrezia retorted tartly. She had grown tired of that kind of airy statement before the deists had persuaded Andris to drink Philemon's unfortunate brew, and she found it difficult to tolerate now.

'The Spirit of the Waters needs no words,' Venerina replied, as if speaking by rote. 'We who have accepted it feel the singularity of creation directly. We are fully conscious of being a tiny part of the Community of the Lake, and of the World, and of the Great Scheme which extends from star to star to the farthest reaches of the universe.'

'Ereleth taught me the secret of a drug with a similar effect,' Lucrezia riposted drily, 'but witches consider it a device to make men mad. Having seen what your potion has done to Andris, I'm inclined to trust the lore of witchcraft rather than your fanciful faith.'

'You can't understand,' the other woman countered defensively. 'There is something in you which resists the Spirit of the Lake. Whether it be witchery or Serpent's blood I cannot tell, but if you were only capable of surrender you would not need argument to convince you of the reality and authority of God. The fact remains that you are as much part of His pattern and His purpose as I am.'

'I'll try to be glad of that,' Lucrezia said. She made an effort to dampen the hostility which threatened to infect the remark but she couldn't resist her own flight of fancy and went on. 'I suppose that if we need a way to imagine the universe entire, we might do worse than to think of it as a dragomite hive writ enormously large, pumping out eggs of a billion different kinds from all manner of worldly womb-walls.'

The deist was obviously unhappy about this characterisation, but made no protest. She was interested in these matters too. 'Do you remember what the Serpent said about him and his erstwhile companion being *of the same earth*?' she asked. Like Andris and Lucrezia she had taken to referring to the Serpent as *he* even though she knew that it was sexless.

Lucrezia remembered the remark well enough. She had suggested that it probably meant that Ssifuss and Mossassor had been born from the same clutch of eggs, which might have been laid in soft sand like a turtle's. She was quick to guess the alternative that Venerina was about to suggest.

'You think it might mean that they were birthed from a living wall something like one of these stone creatures? It's possible. Each of these sculpted spores might undergo a slow metamorphosis, like an adult moth formed within a chrysalis of stone, eventually pulling itself free – detaching itself in much the same way that the head Andris carries in his pack detached itself from the wall of the dragomite queen. Will you ask him, or shall I?'

'The Serpent likes your friend far better than the rest of us,' the deist said, slightly put out by the fact that Lucrezia had anticipated her. 'If there's prying to be done, the amber's the one to do it.'

'If that half-human head which gave itself to Andris were merely one of a hundred different kinds of growth,' Lucrezia mused, following the train of argument further, 'the dragomite queen might have other ways of producing young than churning out eggs. When the winds of change begin to blow, as they did for the dragomites when the hills were blighted – or when some seed of upheaval is sown, as it was by the nest-war – there might be creatures remotely akin to dragomite queens which react far more productively than the queens were able to.'

'Perhaps,' Venerina agreed, refraining from adding any pious comment about the infinite ingenuity of God.

'Mossassor told Hyry Keshvara that *paedogenesis* is the key to what is happening to the world,' Lucrezia added. 'Aulakh Phar explained the word's meaning with reference to flies that breed as maggots for many generations while food is abundant at a single location, but must then set forth on a quest for new resources as winged flies. Perhaps the dangerousness of the stone-creatures is not that their traps might swallow men whole, but rather that they may change into a deadlier form if and when the whim so takes them ... as it may be taking them now. Perhaps they grow tired, eventually, of generating tiny flies and humble worms. Perhaps *all* of these nests of darkness are cradles for chimeras, as the dragomite hive was in its own peculiar fashion.'

21

'We had better hope not,' Venerina told her. 'Were even a few of them to rise up as a company of golems, we'd be hopelessly outnumbered.'

'What's a golem?' Lucrezia asked. 'I've never heard the word.'

'It's in the lore,' the older woman told her, 'but only in a tale – the tale of a magician who moulded a man out of mud to protect his neighbours against the persecutions of a tyrant, then let it lapse into inertia when its task was done. The mud-man had no name of his own, but was called a golem – as if there had been golems before and might be again.'

Like Andris, I dare say, Lucrezia thought. *You tried to turn him into a deist, but you turned him into mud instead.*

'They do not tell that tale in Xandria?' Venerina asked curiously.

'Not within the citadel,' Lucrezia admitted. 'It sounds like the kind of tale the common folk might tell, casting men of my father's kind in the role of persecutor. Checuti would know if it is known in Xandria at all.'

She chewed her lip, trying to restore the softness and moisture to it, but it was a hopeless task. She wondered what had become of Checuti after they had been separated in the marshes. Was it possible that he was still alive? If Andris had been able to cross the marshes on foot, carrying her in his arms, Checuti surely could have come out safely on horseback, no matter how itchy his limbs became.

She had not realised until she formed the thought how keenly she wanted Checuti to be alive. She was so far from home now that she did not want to lose anyone who might be numbered – even by virtue of an optimistic count – among her friends.

22

3

NOT LONG AFTER the fading of the twilight on the second day of their journey the horse which Jacom Cerri had plundered from Amyas's devastated wagon train broke down. He tried to coax it back to its feet but he knew enough about horses to conclude that the task was fruitless. Eventually, he cut the animal's throat.

Had it happened a day earlier Jacom would have half expected his companion to leap upon the dead horse and make a meal of it, but he had had ample opportunity to study the manticore's habits by now and he knew that although the creature had the body of a tiger he did not have a tiger's dietary habits. Manticores seemed to prefer their meat cooked, as befitted creatures who could speak the human language as well as any human, and who called themselves by names like those which humans wore.

The manticore which had captured Jacom – or saved his life – called himself Kasdeja. Jacom had not yet managed to find out much more than that, but he had tried to make the most of his powers of observation. The monster's huge mouth was equipped with teeth similar to his own in all but size, which offered further confirmation of the hypothesis that his diet was similar to his own. The conclusion had given Jacom some slight cause for relief. If a tiger's body did not give rise to a tiger's appetites, he reasoned, then a scorpion's sting need not be correlated with a scorpion's aggression.

By virtue of its strangeness, the manticore's sting seemed to Jacom far more threatening than the huge claws which the creature could unfurl from his awesome paws. The claws could easily have ripped Jacom apart, but they seemed almost ordinary by comparison with the awful talon mounted at the end of the chimera's segmented tail.

'Should I butcher the horse?' Jacom asked his captor. 'Will we need its meat?' He knew nothing at all about the territory that lay ahead; the manticore had told him their journey would last several days, but had said very little about the nature of the ground they must cover. The creature had no conspicuous difficulty with human language, and had taken care to display that fact when first approaching him, but once Jacom had agreed to be taken wherever the manticore wanted to take him, Kasdeja had lapsed into a frustrating taciturnity. This was his first real chance to find out more.

'Take the best meat,' Kasdeja instructed him bluntly.

Jacom didn't mind being give orders, but he couldn't shake off the uncomfortable feeling that there was an element of mockery in the way the manticore addressed him. Perhaps that was inevitable, given that the manticore's face was a manifest travesty of a human face, writ too large upon the monster's heavy head.

Jacom fetched a skinning knife from his pack and set to work, hoping that he could create an impression of thorough competence – although this was one aspect of his military training that he had not previously been forced to put into practice. While he had been with Fraxinus's caravan and Amyas's miniature army there had always been others ready and willing to carry out this kind of labour.

'This will slow us down,' Jacom observed, while he plied the knife.

Kasdeja had crouched down to watch him work, like some huge ungainly hunting dog. 'It doesn't matter,' the manticore told him. 'The ground ahead is no good for horses.'

'We've been fortunate to bring it so far without one of the figured stones grabbing a hoof,' Jacom agreed. 'They're so solid and so slow that they seem utterly harmless, but I know they're not. Amyas warned me about them.'

The manticore made no comment.

'Exactly what sort of bad ground lies ahead?' Jacom asked. He looked towards the west as he spoke, but there was little to be seen by starlight except a ragged confusion of shadows.

'You'll see soon enough,' the manticore replied lazily.

'How close are we to Chimera's Cradle now?' Jacom asked, remembering that the manticore had recognised the phrase when he'd used it before. 'Andris Myrasol's map showed something called the Silver Thorns, and the Gauntlet of Gladness running through them. Then there was something called the Nest of the Phoenix surrounding the Navel of the World. It was shaped like a ring.'

'I've passed through the Silver Thorns,' Kasdeja admitted. 'Forests of that kind are safe enough if you're careful, but best avoided nevertheless.'

'They must have been around for a very long if they're known to the lore our forefathers made,' Jacom said ruminatively. 'What about the other names – do they mean anything to you?'

'It's not our ground,' the manticore said evasively. 'There is a ring of sorts, at the war's rim. You'll see that too.'

'What's the *war's rim*?' Jacom demanded.

'You'll see,' the manticore repeated, with ostentatious weariness. 'You'll have plenty of time for talk, if all goes well. Don't be afraid.'

Jacom didn't know whether the creature was teasing him with its evasiveness, or whether it didn't know what answers to give him. The horse's carcase was skinned now and the stink was appalling. The dead animal's blood had clotted somewhat, but there still seemed to be an ocean of red stickiness covering flesh and ground alike. His hands were covered in gore. The raw meat wasn't easy to cut, even with a steel blade. Lustrust had taken its toll of the once sharp edge.

'How did you learn human language?' Jacom asked. 'Who taught you?' Even if he learned little or nothing, he thought, conversation would take his mind off the nastier aspects of his work.

'I learned as I grew, as you did,' the manticore told him, as if it were obvious. It *wasn't* obvious; Jacom had no idea whether the creature had been born from the womb of a female of its own kind or had stepped full-grown from the face of some gargantuan figured stone. He had no reason to assume that the reproductive system of manticores fit the pattern of earthly life, and plenty of reasons to think that it might not.

'How many years does it take a manticore to grow?' Jacom asked. 'A human is full-grown in seven or eight.'

'I'm nine years old,' Kasdeja told him.

'Have you brothers and sisters?'

'All manticores are brothers,' the creature informed him. 'My only sisters resemble *your* kind, and I've brothers of your kind too. We're not so different, you and I.'

Jacom weighed the implications of this as carefully as he could while he stripped the horse's haunches of good meaty muscle.

'Dragomites have sisters that resemble my kind too,' Jacom observed. 'How closely they're akin to me I wouldn't know. I don't even know how closely I'm akin to giants. I'm only a simple soldier after all – but you knew what I was when you chose to take me prisoner, didn't you?'

The crouching manticore made no response to that. He wasn't easy to provoke. He yawned capaciously, but he wasn't sleepy or bored – just relaxing while he had the chance.

Having stripped as much lean meat as was convenient from the dead horse's rump and withers Jacom looked around for material to build a fire. He couldn't salt the meat, so the only way he could preserve it was to cook and smoke it. The manticore watched him incuriously.

'It must be a great inconvenience not to have hands,' Jacom observed. He uprooted several fern-like plants whose foliage had been dried out by drought; the brittle fronds would serve as kindling.

'My sisters and their two-legged brothers have hands,' the manticore observed negligently. 'We have claws and stings. Together, we have what we need.'

Jacom had to wander further afield in search of more substantial wood, and then he had to use his knife to cut what he could. It was some time before he was able to resume the interrogation, and by then he had formulated a plan of sorts.

'I suppose,' he said, 'that your kind are the dragomite warriors of your particular community: the fearsome guards whose job it is to intimidate potential enemies, and fight them if necessary. Whatever you might mean by the *war's rim* it's obvious that you're at war with those creatures that attacked Amyas's company. Your officers are doubtless the ones who have hands.' He said *officers* rather than *masters* because he was an officer himself, and could not help but wonder whether his status had been relevant to his selection for the mysterious mission on which he and his captor were now embarked.

'We aren't like dragomites,' Kasdeja said. It was a less

revealing response than Jacom had hoped for, but he was determined not to be put off.

'Of course, dragomite warriors remain mere creatures of instinct,' he went on. 'Partnership with humans has augmented the native intelligence of their queens, but they're not intelligent themselves. You certainly are – unless it's simply the fact that you can talk that makes you seem so. I suppose it's possible that you have a limited range of responses. Perhaps you just parrot the words *you'll see* and *you'll find out* whenever you're out of your intellectual depth.'

'Perhaps,' agreed the manticore, with what sounded suspiciously like tolerant amusement.

Jacom felt miserably inadequate to his task. Surely Carus Fraxinus or Aulakh Phar – or even Hyry Keshvara – could have got far more out of the manticore than this. He brought matches from his pack, wrinkling his nose as he realised that it might have been more sensible to build his fire at a greater distance from the butchered horse. He wondered, belatedly, how far the scent of blood might drift on the all but windless air. He had had the opportunity to observe that packs of hellhounds gave the manticore a wide berth, but there might be even worse things abroad in this blighted territory than hellhounds. Kasdeja had waited until the humanoid creatures that had attacked Amyas's company had gone before he came to take Jacom prisoner.

'I've heard that there are people with Serpent's blood who are drawn to the Navel of the World in times of upheaval,' Jacom told the manticore, as he fanned the tentative flames of the newly lit fire. 'It may be mere superstition, of course, but if it were true you wouldn't have to range far and wide in search of men like me. You'd merely have to sit and wait, and let them come to you.'

'It's not that easy,' Kasdeja admitted, scratching behind his right ear with a surprisingly delicate movement of an absurdly large claw.

'I suppose not,' Jacom agreed. 'Competition must be quite fierce, with hordes of creatures like the ones that attacked us riding hither and yon across the land. Except that they didn't seem very interested in prisoners.'

'They were killers,' the manticore said. 'You might see more of that kind – and worse, too. It might not be easy to get back to our own ground.'

'So why bother?' Jacom demanded. 'Why come so far in search of me – or someone like me? What use am I to you, or to those who sent you? What do you want me *for*?'

'You'll be told in due time,' was all the manticore would say – but he hesitated before saying it, as if he had almost said more.

'You're *not* stupid, are you?' Jacom said, with a reckless lack of tact. 'You really do have a mind of your own. Your head is human inside as well as outside. At any rate, it's at least as human as the head which Andris Myrasol brought out of the dragomite hive. Unearthly, but human . . . if that makes any sense at all. I met a Serpent once who thought that human beings were a disease, a sickness of the world that ought to be shaken off. I never thought to ask him whether he meant to include dragomite-women and other human-seeming creatures born of alien flesh . . . or of alien *ground*. Exactly what kind of war are you and your brothers fighting, Kasdeja?'

For a moment, Jacom thought that the manticore was going to say 'You'll see' again – but this time the hesitation was sufficient to alter the response.

'You're inquisitive,' the creature observed, 'and impatient.'

'It's a habit we true humans have,' Jacom said. 'Aren't you inquisitive too?' He was astonished when the question brought a slight frown to Kasdeja's normally placid features.

'In our way,' the manticore replied.

Jacom knew that it might be a revealing remark, in spite of its evasiveness – if only he could work out what it might reveal. 'How does your way differ from mine?' he was quick to inquire.

'*We* are all of one mind,' Kasdeja replied, in a way which reminded Jacom very forcibly of the mound-woman Jume Metra. 'All our lore is borrowed,' he added, 'but we are faithful to it nevertheless. You have lore that your forefathers made, but you go your own ways. We are the future in the making, while you are mere relics of the past.' The last sentences were spoken as if they were being quoted, but they were not taken from any lore that Jacom recognised.

Jacom had no idea what to make of this strange speech, and he wished that he could pass the puzzle on to someone with a wiser head – but he was alone now, with little prospect of ever seeing

28

Carus Fraxinus or Hyry Keshvara again. He felt in desperate need of the perfect question, which might serve to elicit a proper explanation, but Kasdeja had come to his feet again and was already turning away, as if he regretted having said so much.

'Perhaps you have more in common with the humans who live with dragomites than with my kind,' Jacom said hurriedly. 'I've been into the depths of a nest, where I met a human drone – and one of my companions spoke at length with a half-human queen.'

While he said this Jacom tried to follow the manticore's eyes with his own, and hold his gaze; but the smoke from the fire was beginning to sting his eyeballs and he knew that he ought to be hurrying to gather more substantial fuel.

'That's good,' Kasdeja said distantly. 'My brothers and sisters will be interested to hear it.' As he spoke, though, he moved further away, leaving Jacom to make what he could of what had already been said.

Jacom had never made overmuch effort to commit the lore of Genesys to memory, but he had been reminded of its gist often enough these last few tendays. The people of the ship had built a city which had crumbled into dust, and then had built a garden in its stead: a garden of poisons which was the source of many evil things, but which they called the Navel of the World as well as Chimera's Cradle.

How does the next passage go? he asked himself, wishing that he had paid better attention to his tutors in those long-gone days when he had thought such things utterly irrelevant to his own life and prospects. *They too were chimeras, isn't that it? 'They' being the people of the world. And then . . . the best of the new chimeras followed the people into the forests and the plains . . . but the worst of them tainted the lands around the garden. Does that mean that Kasdeja and his kindred are among the worst of the things which Chimera's Cradle produced? Is the war he talks about a war between haphazard armies of chimeras, some of which are sent forth to kill anyone they may encounter, while others take prisoners? But what is the prize for which they make war . . . and how long has the war been raging . . . and how long will it last?*

The next passage in the lore of Genesys, Jacom felt sure, was the one which talked of incorruptible stone, and called it 'the most precious gift of all' – but what that had to do with anything, he couldn't imagine. Mossassor – the Serpent who did *not* think that humans were a disease afflicting the face of its world – was also searching for a garden, but seemed to have no better idea than the princess or the queen what might be found there, or why it might be worth searching for. How could any of this make sense?

'You don't understand this any better than I do, do you?' Jacom called after Kasdeja. 'You're doing what your lore requires, but you don't understand why it's required. You feel compelled, but you don't know why. You don't even know whether you *ought* to know why – because you don't know how much has been forgotten, in the course of the last hundred generations. We all have *that* in common, don't we? Humans, Serpents, Salamanders and all the monsters of legend. We all have our lore, but we've all lost the logic that governed its making.' He felt very proud of himself for having formulated this profound, if rather bitter, insight. He wished that he had a better audience to marvel at his wisdom, so that he could demonstrate to at least a few of those who had long thought him stupid that he was nothing of the sort.

'You seem well enough acquainted with the limits of *human* ignorance,' the manticore replied, with what seemed to be an attempt at crushing sarcasm, 'but things aren't as simple as you think.'

'No,' said Jacom, who preferred to take the enigmatic remark as proof that he was in the right. 'I don't suppose they are.'

The night was darkening steadily as patchy cloud spread slowly across the sky from the south, but the unshadowed stars were very bright. As Jacom gathered more fuel for the fire he had little difficulty avoiding the stone-creatures that were liberally scattered about the terrain. Woody vegetation was not very abundant, but he found the dead husks of a number of gourd-like plants, which were easy enough to carry back to the fire provided that he was careful of the brittle spikes that studded their surfaces.

'Is it only human prisoners you're after?' he asked, when he had settled to his work again and Kasdeja had condescended to come back to the fire. 'Will your brothers bring Serpents too? Will they bring Salamanders, if they can?'

'My brothers will bring Serpents if they can,' Kasdeja told him brusquely. 'Most Serpents have forgotten how to fly, and the ones which have not are best avoided, but the Salamanders have remembered. The Salamanders will come by themselves, as they always have.'

Jacom had never seen a Salamander, but he had heard reports and rumours of their stoutness and stolidity. He had never heard any rumour that they could fly.

'If they can fly, they'll doubtless find the journey much easier than we will,' Jacom said. 'I fear that I can't walk half as fast as you.' He had had ample time to observe that the manticore was easily capable of matching the pace and stamina of a trotting horse.

'Can you ride without a saddle?' the manticore asked him.

'I've never tried,' Jacom replied. 'There's no need for anyone to ride bareback in a civilised nation like Xandria. Even if I had, I doubt that the experience would have prepared me to ride a manticore – if that's what you have in mind.'

'We ought to try,' Kasdeja said. 'The land without the rim is dangerous enough, and the grounds within are worse.'

'Are there many other monsters there who'd be pleased to relieve you of your prize?' Jacom wanted to know.

The manticore didn't answer in words, but Jacom assumed that his silence was affirmative.

'Doubtless there are creatures even more monstrous than you,' Jacom said. 'Will you fight to keep me, if you have to?'

'Were it not for my sting and my strength, you'd be lost already,' his captor assured him. 'I'll keep you from harm if I can.'

Jacom didn't doubt that it was true, but it certainly wasn't enough to make him like or trust the monster. He silently reserved the right to make his own decisions about what company he'd rather keep, should he ever have the opportunity to make a choice.

Even so, when he finally laid himself down to sleep, he felt safe knowing that the manticore sat silently on guard – and he felt that he had had a profitable day, in terms of the only calculus left to him for measuring his fortune: the calculus of understanding.

4

ANDRIS MOVED BACK to the place where Lucrezia and Venerina Sirelis were deep in conversation, feeling slightly annoyed that the princess had made no effort to involve him. Was he no longer good enough for her to confide in, now that she had found another mother-substitute?

'That reef thing isn't on my map,' he said, almost plaintively, as he squatted down. 'If the silver-tipped columns are the Silver Thorns, they've vastly expanded their range since our forefathers made their maps.'

'We're beyond the authority of your map now,' Lucrezia told him, 'and beyond the authority of the lore too. The world is different now.'

Ssifuss had followed him; when he sat down the Serpent craned its long neck, leaning over his shoulder in an oddly intimate manner. Its hood was fully extended, like some kind of strange headdress, and its forked tongue flicked back and forth across its thin lips.

'Iss not good,' Ssifuss said, waving a hand to indicate the territory which lay ahead of them. 'Iss not good at all.'

The words echoed one of Mossassor's favourite formulations, but the tone was markedly different. Mossassor had always sounded mournful when it deemed something 'not good'. Ssifuss sounded urgently anxious. It was possible that the implication was misleading, but Andris didn't think it was. He had an awful suspicion that the Great Reef might not be a convenient place to mount an ambush and overturn odds of ten or twenty to one.

'Why not?' Lucrezia asked. 'What's dangerous about it?'

'Everysssing,' said the Serpent. 'Here, iss only sshallow sstoness. Ssere, I ssink, sshall find *real* dwellerss in deep.'

Andris had never heard the phrase before but he saw a reaction in Lucrezia's eyes which suggested that she had. It was of her, rather than the Serpent, that he asked: 'What are the dwellers in the deep?'

'Jume Metra once said something about them,' she explained. *There will always be dwellers in the deep.* I assumed at the time that she was referring to dragomite queens but it looks as if there are other life forms in the world akin to dragomites but not the same.'

Andris picked up the inference readily enough. If dragomite queens were only one of many kinds of life which dwelt beneath the world's surface, mazy with living corridors, what might their hugest and strangest cousins be like? He looked up at Ssifuss, but before the Serpent could add anything Lucrezia spoke again.

'We know that the world is also hollow,' she said pensively.

'What's that supposed to mean?' Andris asked her. The words emerged from his parched throat more harshly than he intended.

'I don't know,' she replied. 'It's something else Jume Metra said. I thought she meant *her* world – the little world of the hive. Perhaps she didn't. Perhaps she really did mean *the world*. Perhaps the whole thing's alive – and the Silver Thorns are merely the giant hairs set about the lips of its mouth . . . or of its birth canal.'

She didn't laugh, although she seemed to mean it as a joke. Neither did Andris. What he had seen in the dragomite nest had ruined his sense of humour regarding alien systems of reproduction. Again he looked at Ssifuss, but Ssifuss hesitated before speaking; it was doubtful that the Serpent had understood more than half of what Lucrezia had said. When it did speak, it was only to say: 'Musst move. Need water ssoon.'

Andris made every effort to concentrate his mind as they set off again, fearing that he might otherwise lapse back into virtual automatism. He focused his attention on the strange landscape which lay ahead of him, and told himself that he must at least maintain a proper internal dialogue, even if his companions were too tired for actual talk.

He realised as they came closer to it that the Great Reef was much more complicated than it seemed. The tallest parts, whose topmost reaches formed the jagged rim of the apparent palisade, were more varied than distance had made them appear. The ones which Venerina Sirelis had called 'dendrites' were indeed somewhat tree-like, but only insofar as they had branches. Nothing could be seen of their basal stalks, which were hidden by extensive undergrowth, but the major elements of their 'crowns' extended outwards in helical coils, sprouting tightly wound sub-branches. The branches were the colour of a bronze's skin, except where they were interrupted by gourd-like bulges, which ranged from near-white to near-black through all the intermediate shades of grey. These were occasionally studded with lumps of indigo or dark red and the lower ones were festooned with lacy creepers. Occasionally, these branches looped around other tall structures which grew more straightly: abrupt spires like rigid rat's tails. The spires were not only topped with silver but liberally decked with what looked at this distance like silvery hairs.

They must be the Silver Thorns, he thought. *Perhaps they still reign supreme in some region within the interior of this strange rim, as my map promises – and perhaps they still stand guard about the Gauntlet of Gladness, whatever that is – but here they keep abundant and strange company.*

There were other tall structures whose tips were visible in the confusion, some of which looked like giant fans and others like the unfurled wings of huge birds of prey. Their bases too were as yet indistinguishable amid a confusion of squatter entities. Most of these resembled giant mushrooms with multicoloured caps, some of them as slender and as widespread as parasols while others were uncomfortably reminiscent of giant penises. Many seemed to be encaged or overdraped by coloured nets, but whether these were parasitic growths or merely parts of the exotic organisms Andris couldn't tell.

He lengthened his stride slightly to bring him level with Ssifuss. 'It's certainly the weirdest thing I've ever seen,' he said, but the Serpent didn't know what 'weird' meant. 'Strange,' he said, instead. 'Very strange.'

'Sstrange ground,' the Serpent replied dolefully. 'Iss alwayss bad, worsse now.'

'Why is it worse now?' Andris asked. He knew that some kind of upheaval in the world's affairs was under way – Carus Fraxinus had told him that, back in Xandria, and the news had been echoed by everyone he had met since, but no one seemed to have any but the vaguest idea of what might be involved. 'Is

Lucrezia right? Is there something being born from the very bowels of the world – the monstrous offspring of your mysterious dwellers in the deep?'

'Cannot know how many are dwellerss in deep,' the Serpent said. 'Cannot know how deep. Are many earss, but cannot know what liess *below*. Only know ssat ssingss *come out* – only myss to tell uss what. Mossassor ssought myss true. I ssought not, but now . . . ssingss *do* come out. Are giantss – not know what elsse. Iss ssame for you, no?'

'I suppose so,' Andris conceded. 'Ereleth certainly thought that there was truth in some of our myths, and Fraxinus too. The only trouble is, we've forgotten most of the stories, and the ability to separate truth from fiction. Neither Ereleth nor Fraxinus had the least idea what's happening, really.'

'Uss too,' said Ssifuss. 'But if Mossassor iss right, musst ssearssh for garden. Iss *important*.'

'Is that what you've decided to do? You're going in search of the garden of Idun, as Mossassor intended?'

The Serpent shook its scaly head, letting its forked tongue flicker back and forth across the dry rim of its mouth. 'Musst find Mossassor, if I can,' it said. 'Firsst musst find water, perhapss food. Ssen . . .'

The creature seemed to be looking at him expectantly, waiting for him to supply the rest of that particular sentence. It wasn't too hard to guess why.

'Then we try Lucrezia's plan,' Andris said. 'I don't know how good her witchery is, but I guess we do have to try it. Without weapons and horses we can't go anywhere in a hurry. She and I have a debt to repay. You do understand debts, I suppose?'

'We undersstand debtss,' Ssifuss agreed. 'Musst fight – but not eassy. You know ssey are not humanss? Not Sserpentss, not humanss. Ssomessing elsse. Ssomessing sstrange.'

'I wasn't sure,' Andris said. 'What are they, then, if they're not men and not Serpents? Why did they attack the Community and take those prisoners? Where are they going, and why?'

'In ssere,' Ssifuss said, presumably in reply to the final question. 'Don't know why. Are not of ssame ground ass uss. Ssome may look like uss, but different. Iss not good. Ssomessing wrong, ssinsse *long* ago. Disseasse of ground. Bad disseasse. Iss bad for Sserpentss – humanss too.'

Andris remembered Hyry Keshvara saying that Ssifuss had once thought that human beings were a kind of disease afflicting the world. Obviously the Serpent had now reached the conclusion that there were even worse diseases, requiring more urgent attention.

'This *ground* you keep talking about – the one you and Mossassor are both from,' Andris said, trying once again to penetrate the enigma. 'That's some kind of living thing, isn't it? I know you don't like it being compared to the dragomite queen, but it does have something in common with these *dwellers in the deep*, doesn't it? Is it where you come from when you're born?'

Ssifuss shook its head again, but the gesture wasn't a flat refusal to respond; the Serpent really did seem to be searching for words that would serve as an explanation. 'Not *come from*,' it said. 'Not like ssingss behind uss – not at all. Yess, iss living. Iss where we *go*. Iss tie whissh bindss uss. Iss *ourss*. Humanss have nossing like it.'

Andris would certainly have pursued the point further, although Ssifuss seemed to have done its best, but his head was beginning to ache in the heat of the climbing sun, and he began to feel a little dizzy. He put his hat on, but it was far too ragged to be fully effective.

Ssifuss, observing his distress, evidently thought it best to abandon the conversation. The Serpent moved in front of him again, so that it could keep careful watch on the 'flowing stones' which littered the approach to the Great Reef. Andris let it go on; if pain were the price of maintaining his concentration it might not be worth paying.

Andris forced himself to continue marching with military regularity. He kept his head as still as he could and his eyes fixed in a forward direction. He knew that he might fall back into a trance as a result, but he felt that he had to hold himself rigid and maintain the purposefulness of his movements lest he lose his grip on himself altogether.

Andris had seen the reefs of the Slithery Sea and could understand well enough why someone had attached the same word to the formations he was studying now. A talkative sailor had once explained to him that the sea-reefs were made by tiny animals related to those which equipped themselves with shells. Rather than surrounding themselves with impenetrable suits of armour the reef-creatures preferred to erect bulbous stalks, coiling towers or fan-like arrays that bore them up from the seabed towards the subsurface layers of water, which were teeming with the tinier creatures on which they fed. Armed with this intelligence Andris had taken the trouble to marvel at the strange undersea forests which sprang up in quiet lagoons and extended in vast ribbons along the shorelines of certain islands, following the contours of the shoreline.

The same sailor had explained that as the world turned the sun's gravity tugged the waters of the Slithery Sea, westwards while it set and eastwards while it rose, moving the sluggish waters back and forth through all the living sieves that the reef-creatures maintained. It was easy enough to see the similarity between the structures that the reef-creatures erected and some of those which lay before him now: the same kinds of stalks could be seen and the same kinds of fan-like and globular growths. There were many other shapes too, but it was easy enough to imagine those as parasites upon the reef, added on to the basic structure.

Andris knew, however, that the similarities between the territory which lay ahead of him and the reefs of the Slithery Sea raised more questions than they answered. What sailor had come this way to observe the coincidence and name the reef? If those strange stalks had been erected by the labour of relatively tiny creatures located at the end of every branch, what did the creatures feed on? There was no life-laden layer of the air waiting high above the desert to be plundered by careful predators. Nor were there tides in the air to draw any such prey conveniently back and forth.

Somehow, though, it all had to make sense. There had to be a pattern in it – some kind of *plan*. Andris had not needed the potion Philemon Taub had brewed to tell him that. He had known it while he was wandering in the marshes, delirious with the stings of countless thorns. He had known it even before that, although he had never quite contrived to subject the knowledge to careful contemplation. Now, he thought that if only he could put the pieces of the puzzle together in the correct order he might be able to figure out what kind of 'disseasse' the world was suffering from, and why it had flared up again after a long quiescence.

We think of ourselves as individuals, he reminded himself, *but there's a sense in which we're not. Each and every one of us is a world of sorts, full of tinier creatures that live within us in varying degrees of amity and enmity. Within our bodies there is ceaseless competition and ceaseless collaboration, which affects our consciousness as well as our physical being. We are constantly subject to invasions, some of which the community of our being repel and some of which – willingly or under duress – we accommodate.*

There's also a sense in which the whole world is an individual, although we're far too tiny to perceive its individuality. What seems to us to be a ceaseless riot of competition has grander patterns and greater cycles. Even the universe entire has a scheme of sorts – whatever errors the deists may make, they're surely right about that – but it's the world which concerns us now. The world must have its own life cycle, and this must be part of it. Earthly life forms are born, they grow, they mate, they produce offspring, and in the fullness of time they die – but unearthly life works to a different pattern, or at least has other patterns available to it. Serpents hatch from eggs, it seems, and lay eggs too – but they don't mate, and they stand in some mysterious relationship with living ground.

He told himself that he ought to be saying all this to Lucrezia and Venerina Sirelis, asking them to help him unriddle it, but he couldn't make himself turn round. He knew that he was slipping away again, but for the moment that seemed the lesser of two evils. In any case, he felt oddly sure that if he could only get his state of mind exactly right he would *see* the pattern, not in the way that Venerina Sirelis claimed to see it – as if it were a God – but in a truer way that would properly satisfy his hunger for an explanation. With the Spirit of the Waters to help him, he felt sure that he could do it.

Perhaps the individual that is the world undergoes periodic metamorphoses, as an insect does, he thought. *If so, perhaps these metamorphoses have a profound effect upon all the tinier creatures which are parts of its grander design or passengers within that design. In the northern lands, humans have suc-ceeded in subjugating the soil to their own purposes, but everywhere south of the Forest of Absolute Night unearthly forms maintain their own problematic empire. Humans are*

38

*impotent to resist the changes which overtake these regions –
and so, it seems, are the Serpents and Salamanders, who are the
unearthly counterparts of human beings.*

*And yet, if the lore of Genesys and Ereleth's secret command-
ments can be trusted, it seems that our forefathers intended us to
take action in response to the kind of changes which are
happening now, and to play an active part in their unfolding.*

And while these thoughts preoccupied his stubbornly intro-
verted consciousness Andris dutifully and mechanically followed where Ssifuss led, along a course which became more
convoluted with every hour that passed – but still brought him
ever nearer to the great enclosure where all the answers to all his
questions might be hidden.

5

WHEN THEY REACHED the edge of the Great Reef Lucrezia saw that they were still at least a kim away from the most expansive of the giant dendrites. The tallest of the jutting steepletrees that she had tentatively identified as Silver Thorns was even further away, perhaps beyond the dense thicket of the Reef itself. The going was more difficult than it had been on the plain because there were countless massive objects to be skirted as well as a profusion of ominous entities that seemed best avoided.

Lucrezia drew level with Ssifuss and Andris. Ssifuss paused readily enough, but Andris had slipped back into a daze. Lucrezia had to catch his arm and yank it hard. Once she had gained his attention the amber stopped but it seemed to require a considerable effort before he could focus his eyes and his ears. By the time she was convinced that he was fully conscious again Venerina and Rayner had closed up on them. They all looked around curiously.

Lucrezia observed that most of the flowing stones which thrived hereabouts did not lie flat on the ground. Instead, they formed parasitic plaques upon the solid faces of the fan-like reef-creatures and the sprawling caps of the 'mushrooms', or thick-stranded webs suspended between the branches of tree-like structures.

'Dangerouss,' the Serpent said, pointing at a particularly ornate web made up of seemingly delicate crystalline threads. 'Don't toussh.'

'Have you seen them before?' Lucrezia asked.

The Serpent shook its head. 'Have lore. Warnss againsst ssoft sstoness. Sssticky oness more dangerouss sstill, I ssink.'

Lucrezia took the inference that not all the creatures related to the flowing stones were solid and awkward. Some were 'soft' and some were 'sticky', and this made their ability to absorb things more dangerous to passers-by. Andris nodded his head to show that he understood, but he still seemed a little absent-minded to Lucrezia. The Serpent must have agreed with her judgment; it made the slight spitting noise it employed to indicate impatience and frustration.

'It's all right, Ssifuss,' Lucrezia said reassuringly. 'We do understand. I think Andris can hear you well enough.'

Venerina and Rayner were looking about themselves with anxious awe, but they made gestures to inform Ssifuss that they had taken its warning to heart.

Ssifuss was not convinced. 'Musst be careful,' it said to Andris, plucking at the amber's ragged sleeve by way of emphasis. 'When we climb, *musst not toussh.*'

Andris finally managed to form a word. 'Climb?' he queried.

'It's all right, Ssifuss,' Lucrezia said again. 'I'll do the climbing, for now. Andris isn't up to it yet – and he's probably too heavy anyway.'

Andris took this as an insult, and he made an evident effort to collect himself. He moved away from the Serpent's insistent fingers and looked down at his companions.

'I'm fine,' he lied. 'If there's climbing to be done, I can do it.'

Lucrezia didn't bother to press the point. 'First we need to locate the water-source,' she said to everyone. 'It shouldn't be hard, but now we're in amongst these things we need a higher vantage point to see exactly how the land lies. If we can get high enough, we ought to be able to make a better estimate of our enemies' strength and the time of their arrival – we have to know whether the two parties have fused into one yet. It might also be useful to know what lies to the south – even if we decide to come out this way in order to go east in search of Fraxinus, we'll have to penetrate the heartland eventually. If those copper-coloured branches are strong enough we might be able to climb suffi-ciently high to see halfway to Chimera's Cradle. I might, anyway – I'm probably light enough to get all the way to the top even if Andris isn't.' When the amber opened his mouth again, as if to protest, she quickly added: 'You've lost some weight, but you're still more than twice as heavy as I am.'

'I can climb,' Rayner put in. 'I'm nearly as light as you are, and far stronger. Better let me do it.'

Lucrezia frowned, although the comparison was fair enough. 'We'll *both* go,' she said insistently.

Ssifuss held up its hand, spreading its fingers in what was presumably intended as a placatory gesture. Rayner shrugged his shoulders, as if to say that he hadn't intended to start a quarrel.

Lucrezia looked up at the copper-coloured branches which spiralled upwards from the compound boles of the tallest dendrites. They had a metallic lustre, but she knew that might be mere appearance cloaking a very different texture. Where they jutted above the mushroom-like forms clustered about the bases of the dendrites they were thicker than a man's thigh, but higher up they thinned out to the width of a slender arm. It was impossible to judge how strong or brittle they might be.

She took heart from the observation that there was movement to be seen in the branches. Birds were fluttering back and forth, and she could hear the muted hum of insect wings. At least some of the creatures which coiled around the coppery branches were capable of movement, sliding along as if they were slender worms following the grooves of a wooden screw – but whether they *were* worms, or snakes, or unusually active creepers she couldn't tell.

'That one looks as sturdy as any,' Venerina Sirelis said, indicating an exceptionally tall structure some three or four hundred mets away, whose topmost extremities were almost as high as the ones much further in. 'The webs seem to cluster in the lower branches, and it looks easy enough to climb to a safe height.'

'Let's take a closer look,' Lucrezia said, moving off as she spoke. For once, Ssifuss and Andris were both content to let her go by and to bring up the rear. She was careful to watch where she walked as she negotiated a route to the base of the massive dendrite, and equally careful to avoid touching anything, so far as was possible. She couldn't avoid all contact with the clustering mushrooms, though. Their teguments didn't feel like fungal flesh; they were much harder, like seasoned wood or shell. She soon overcame the worst of her apprehension, although she took Ssifuss's advice and stayed well clear of the crystalline cobwebs. She didn't see anything that looked sticky.

When she eventually reached the base of the dendrite Lucrezia found seven separate stalks combined into a thick trunk, each of which branched five or six times as it climbed into the sky. In addition to the bulbous structures swelling the branches at irregular intervals – most of which were bigger than a man's head – each growing shoot terminated in a small spheroid body that looked remarkably like a giant eyeball, with a shiny black patch for a pupil.

As Venerina had observed, the parasitic structures that resembled calcined spiderwebs only afflicted the lower branches, and it seemed easy enough to negotiate a way past them.

Lucrezia tested the strength of the branches extending from the knotted bole and found them very solid indeed. It was difficult to guess the carrying capacity of the thinner branches higher up. Andris made his own test, outreaching her by half a met and more.

'It does feel more like metal than stone,' Andris observed. 'Perhaps the colour really is bronze – but there's not a trace of greenrot or bluerot. Did you ever see a metal tool so clean and uncorroded?'

'It's not incorruptible,' Lucrezia told him. 'Do you see the black streaks there and there? That's *some* kind of rot. But you're right – I never saw a tool so clean, or a stonemason's work as free from stonerot as the hardest of those stone-creatures seem to be. Corruption doesn't seem to have the power here that it has back home.'

'I'm not so sure of that,' Andris demurred. 'I wonder whether the opposite might be the case: that stonerot's empire is so insidious hereabouts that it extends way down into the bowels of the earth. The Dragomite Hills were merely the tips of much bigger structures buried underground; these may be similar.'

'*Dwellers in the deep*,' she muttered, although he must have had the phrase already in mind.

'Iss true,' Ssifuss observed. 'Ssome sstone ssingss go deep. Very, very deep. Ground *iss* disseassed, I ssink.'

'This may look rather like a sea-reef,' Andris went on, still trying to prove to his companions that he was in full possession of his faculties again, 'but it's not. Maybe those things really are the eyes of some vast stony worm, whose body lies beneath us – and maybe all of this is merely its outer skin.'

43

'We'd better get on with it, Lucrezia,' Rayner said, already beginning to haul himself up into the lower branches, dutifully steering clear of the webs. Lucrezia felt a slight pang of satisfaction at the sound of her name. Andris would almost certainly have said 'highness'.

The boy had meant what he said about his ability to climb and his strength. He made rapid progress.

Lucrezia made as if to follow, wriggling free as Andris dropped a heavy hand on her shoulder with the intention of holding her back. 'You're the witch,' he reminded her crossly. 'If you fall, we're all lost. I ought to go.'

'Rayner's right,' she told him. 'This is a job for the lightest among us. I'll go carefully – trust me.'

It seemed that he did trust her, because he let her go.

Rayner had a head start and the agility of youth on his side – Lucrezia judged that he couldn't be more than five years old. She tried as hard as she could to catch up with him but she was never really in the race – and it *was* a race, because the boy obviously didn't want to be beaten. Lucrezia let him go, refusing to hurry. She wanted to be as sure as possible that each new handhold would support her weight.

Any birds that had been perching in the upper branches were long gone by the time Rayner reached their domain, but the worm-like creatures wound around the curving limbs were in no hurry to get away. Rayner took the Serpent's warnings seriously enough to give them a wide berth but Lucrezia was moved by curiosity to take a closer look. They were longer than she had thought at first, many extending to four or five mets. She could not detect any sign of eyes or a mouth at either end and their bodies were ornamented with all kinds of ridges and hairy excrescences, so she could not think of them as snakes or worms. Some of the shapes jutting out of their bodies looked very similar to those sculpted on to the surfaces of the flowing stones, so she could not help but wonder whether they might be more closely related to those kinds of creatures than to the plant and animal species with which she was familiar, although they were certainly capable of more rapid movement. Lazy they might have been, but when she approached too close they spun away with remarkable velocity.

By virtue of the pauses she made to study the dendrite's lesser

44

companions Rayner drew further and further ahead of Lucrezia. When caution regarding the strength of the thinner branches finally made her hold her position the boy was waiting ten or twelve mets above her, jauntily perched on a curving stem no thicker than his forearm.

'Look!' Rayner said, as soon as he saw that Lucrezia had paused.

He was pointing back the way they had come. Their followers were distant, but clearly visible; Lucrezia could pick out the three wagons and the winding column of marching prisoners. It was just about possible to distinguish the giant Serpents from the mounted men, but Lucrezia didn't have time to attempt a count before Rayner pointed in another direction, saying: 'And there!'

Lucrezia shaded her eyes against the rising sun as she looked eastwards, and saw something else moving just below the horizon. She squinted, trying to make out more detail, but they were too close to the limit of her vision. If they were mounted men – and she was reasonably sure that there were mounted men among them – it was impossible to estimate their number. The second party was still a considerable distance behind their more immediate pursuers, and it seemed obvious that the two bands would not meet up with one another before they reached the Reef.

Was that good news, Lucrezia wondered, or did it spell disaster? Did it imply that no matter how successful they were in taking action against the first party of slavers, they would still face a desperately hard battle against the second? Or might it be possible, after all, that the second group was *not* merely the second half of a greater force? Might they, in fact, be enemies of the creatures which had attacked the Community – and allies, therefore, of Lucrezia and her companions?

The princess tried to compare the distances which separated her station from the two approaching companies, but it wasn't easy. Nor was it easy to judge the pace of their approach. Her impression was that the party travelling from the north would arrive three or even four hours ahead of the other if both maintained their present pace, but that wasn't a comfortable interval if both parties were indeed enemies. She bit her chapped lower lip gently, wondering how this updated information might affect the plan which she and Venerina Sirelis had cooked up between them.

Then, rather belatedly, she turned her head to look behind her, at the territory which lay to the south.

She heard Rayner call out 'I see water!' but she didn't turn to look where the boy might be pointing. Her attention had been caught and held by something else.

The Great Reef was indeed a mere reef, not much more than a kim deep, and from her present vantage point she could easily see past the taller dendrites to the terrain beyond. It was obvious at first glance that the land which lay within the Reef's curving rim did not in the least resemble the plain which they had just crossed.

The most vertiginous landscape Lucrezia had ever seen was that of the Dragomite Hills, which had been all steep slopes and crooked spires; she had seen few others with which to compare it, but she had felt fairly safe in the assumption that it was an epitome of exoticism she was unlikely to encounter again. The landscape within the curved rim of the Reef was not quite as precipitous as that of the Dragomite Hills, but it seemed equally extreme in its strangeness, and perhaps more so. It was gathered into a veritable riot of ridges and fissures, with a multitude of low conical hillocks richly dressed in exotic vegetation. There were emerald greens enough to be seen to suggest that there might be at least some earthly plants here, but there were far more purples and blues. There were very few coiling dendrites like those which thronged the Reef, but there was a plethora of spiky plants of the kind Venerina had called steepletrees, including a number of those whose gleaming tips – often gathered in rows, like the upraised spears or half-pikes of a platoon of Xandrian foot-soldiers – demanded that they be recognised as Silver Thorns. By far the greater number of the steepletrees hereabouts were not in the least silvery, however; most were black or blue.

All of this was astonishing, but Lucrezia had not expected to see anything familiar, and she was not unduly dismayed by the peculiarity of the landscape. There was, in fact, only one aspect of the panorama which seemed to be utterly out of place.

Although its beginning was lost in the tangled mass of the Reef, there extended into the alien wilderness a winding but insistent road, as dull and grey as any highway in Xandria. Many of the road's curves were hidden as it followed the contours of the tufted hills or wound around clumps of ragged spines, but Lucrezia could see enough of it to guess that it extended southwards as far as the eye could see, and perhaps much farther. It seemed to be heading, as directly as was feasible, for the Navel of the World.

In terrain which Ssifuss believed to be highly dangerous, the presence of such a thing seemed paradoxically alluring, all the more threatening by virtue of the enigmatic welcome it seemed to be laying out.

Why in the world would there be a road here? she asked herself. *Who could have made it – and for whose convenience? Does it guide those who use it to Chimera's Cradle or to some other place – and do those who go south along it ever return?*

MUCH TO HIS relief, Jacom wasn't compelled to ride bareback. Although Kasdeja was considerably stouter than the horse he had previously ridden the girth required only slight modification before the saddle, stirrups and saddlebags could be fitted to his back. The bridle was ruled out by purely practical considerations, although Jacom didn't suppose for one moment that Kasdeja would have consented to wear any such contraption had that not been the case.

The manticore's mane was shaggy enough to provide ample handholds and Jacom soon became used to the awkward feel of it. He also became used to the creature's rank body odour, which overpowered the stench of the smoked meat in his pack.

'What would King Belin give for a troop of such cavalry?' Jacom murmured, as they moved off across the plain. As soon as he had mounted he realised that his position gave him readier access to the manticore's ear than he had had while he rode by the other's side; the fact that the manticore had to reply without turning its scornful eyes upon him was an added advantage.

'If a king had manticores to command,' Kasdeja retorted drily, 'they'd not need riders – but we are not like dragomites or hellhounds. We do not hunt in packs.'

'Nor do we,' Jacom replied, 'but that doesn't prevent our banding together with common purpose.' After a pause, he said: 'King Belin keeps a company of giants, ostensibly as guards for the Inner Sanctum of the citadel, but actually to maintain a symbolic presence at the heart of his empire. They're content to serve, although no man could ever compel one to do what she didn't consent to do. I dare say that he would welcome a company of manticores in much the same spirit.'

'Manticores do not seek masters to serve,' Kasdeja told him, as he trotted over the barren ground, contemptuously ignoring the slight threat which the figured stones posed to his enormous paws.

'No?' said Jacom. 'I thought that you were taking me to meet your masters.'

'I am no more a slave than I am a killer,' the manticore informed him haughtily.

'Well,' Jacom said, 'I've already been part of an enterprise which included Serpents and dragomites as well as a giant and a witch. I dare say that I could be part of one that included manticores, if there were reason enough. Whether you're a partner or a hireling, you seem to be part of some greater company, on whose behalf you and your brothers are searching out new recruits of several different kinds.'

Kasdeja didn't rise to the proffered bait in the way Jacom had hoped, but he did allow himself to be drawn into a discussion. 'Was the giant a human or a Serpent?' he asked. It was the first time the creature had shown any evident curiosity, and Jacom felt a slight surge of triumph and expectation. Fraxinus would surely have been proud of him – and the princess too.

'A human,' he answered, resisting the temptation to add *of course*. 'Why? Are you anxious to collect one? You'd not find it easy – I dared not take a stand against you with no weapon but a sword, but Dhalla would certainly have done so, and I'd not know which of you to bet on were the two of you to fight it out.'

'What ground are human giants from?' Kasdeja wanted to know. 'Is it within the war's rim?'

'I believe they come from the desert lands in the eastern reaches of the Xandrian empire,' Jacom said, refusing the temptation to play the same tantalising game as his captor. 'Many tales are told about their origins in the citadel, but most derive from lewd speculation. The fact that they're all female prompts all kinds of crude rumours regarding the methods by which they might reproduce. If an all-male company of manticores were to be attached to Belin's army, there'd probably be similar jokes about *their* parentage and habits.'

'What do the giants have to say about it?'

'Nothing, so far as I know,' Jacom replied. 'I dare say they think it best not to dignify such scurrility with a response, although my erstwhile companion Princess Lucrezia believed that there was a significant mystery there, linked to the enigma of Serpent reproduction.' He might have said more but he left it there, hoping that the manticore might pick up the thread and cast some light upon the mysteries in question.

'What you call desert lands may be more fertile than you think,' was what Kasdeja actually said, in gnomic fashion. Jacom felt sure that there was a void of understanding which even the individuals he was now being taken to meet had not contrived to fill.

'What kind of humans are the brothers and sisters who taught you their language, Kasdeja?' he asked, as he crouched a little lower in the saddle. 'Were they born from eggs, like dragomite-women, or born from a womb as I was?'

'What does it matter?'

'I'm curious to know,' Jacom said, still thinking that the princess would have wanted him to pursue the point, and would have complimented him on any progress he might make. 'Did you hatch or were you born, Kasdeja? Were you ever an infant, or did you emerge from some monstrous figured stone, fully formed as you now are?'

'Every living thing is born after its fashion,' the manticore replied, with a slight stiffness that suggested he had taken offence, 'and every living thing has an infancy of sorts. One hatches from an egg or a chrysalis, one squirms free from the belly of another or from some glutinous bubble in the earth. All things change as they grow, some more than others. You might think me strange, Jacom Cerri, but this is my world as well as yours, and your kind have no other now.'

I have stung him! Jacom thought, without the least repentance. *Somehow, I have injured his pride.* Seeking to follow up this unexpected advantage he thought hard about what to say next. He was aware, in doing so, that of all the members of Carus Fraxinus's expedition he was perhaps the least fitted for this task, but even that gave him a slight thrill of excitement. It had always seemed to him that Ereleth, Phar and the princess had considered him little more than a fool, the unworldly son of a fruit farmer, and he had always resented it. Where were they now, while he rode full tilt towards the Navel of the World on a manticore's back? At best, they were at Salamander's Fire, hundreds of kims behind him; at worst . . . well, that hardly bore consideration.

'The man who led our expedition across the Dragomite Hills insisted that we were all on the same side, whether we knew it or not,' Jacom told the manticore. 'He saw nothing unthinkable in the prospect of forging an alliance with Serpents and dragomites – in fact, he was eager to do it. He didn't believe that intelligent beings could ever be natural enemies, condemned by fate to a war of annihilation. Were he here, he'd greet you as a potential friend and ally, a conscript to the great conspiracy of intelligence in the war against ignorance – but I'm a little more cautious than he, and I'm not so sure that alliances can easily be forged between humans and other kinds of being, whether we have a language in common or not.'

'You might yet be surprised,' Kasdeja replied, with a slight touch of malice, 'by your own capacity to form alliances.'

'Is that a threat?' Jacom said. 'If so, I'd like to hear it stated clearly.'

'Don't be afraid,' the manticore said, not for the first time. 'If we win through to our ground, no harm will come to you. Ours is a better garden than the one you call Chimera's Cradle, even for humans. I do not know why, but I am sure of it. Our ground can offer you more than the ground your forefathers made.'

'Incorruptible stone?' Jacom guessed, remembering his reflection on the lore of Genesys.

The sound Kasdeja made deep in his throat might have been a laugh. 'Nothing is incorruptible,' he said, 'nor does it need to be. Life is what matters. What our ground offers is the future.'

'Our lore calls incorruptible stone the most precious gift of all,' Jacom said uncertainly. He recalled what the manticore had said about being *the future in the making*, but not quickly enough to substitute a question about what might be implied by an offer of the future.

'Your lore is misconceived,' the manticore told him. 'You will learn better soon enough – and I mean no threat in saying so. Believe me, you are more fortunate by far that you have ended in our custody than you would have been had you sought out any other entity within the rim. Be silent now – I must watch the ground.'

Although the stars were shining brightly enough between the scattered clouds it was difficult for Jacom to keep close watch on the terrain they were covering, and he had all but ceased to try.

Although the figured stones still mingled with many kinds of bushes and cacti, as well as the ramrod-like stems of the floater-plants, Jacom had become so accustomed to the landscape that he had settled to ignoring its tedium. As soon as Kasdeja drew his attention to the matter, however, he became aware of a subtle difference in the manticore's gait which suggested that something significant had changed.

Kasdeja was no longer following a dead straight course, and one or two of his changes of direction were quite abrupt. Jacom tried to figure out what it was that the creature was avoiding and why, but the patches of ground they were skirting seemed more deeply steeped in shadow than anything else in their environs. Eventually, he gave up the attempt to solve the problem by observation.

'Are these pools of water that you're skirting,' he asked, 'or are they a more dangerous kind of flowing stone?'

For a few moments it seemed that the manticore was determined to ignore him, but then the creature let out a rumbling sigh. 'Not liquid,' Kasdeja replied, 'but pools of a sort. Next time we pause to rest, be sure to stay clear of them. They can suck you down in minutes, and even my strength might not be adequate to pull you out again.'

'Some kind of living quicksand, then,' Jacom concluded. 'Softer and more ravenous cousins of the figured stones.'

'These are small enough,' the manticore added, as if by way of concession, 'and we could probably get free of them without undue difficulty were I to put a foot wrong, but some of those within the rim are a different matter. There, *everything* is alive, no matter how inert it may seem. Everything is part of something vaster, although the connections which bind the units together may be far from obvious, and you must assume that *everything* is ravenous until it proves otherwise. You must take this warning seriously – and although we shall not go that far, you might care to know that the so-called cradle at the hub of the great wheel, which your reckless ancestors made, is the most dangerous ground of all.'

'To you, perhaps,' Jacom said.

'To *you*,' Kasdeja insisted. 'My brothers and I know these places, so far as they can be known, and you must trust me. I would not like to lose you, and if you stray from my side you're likely to be lost – if not to the kind of raiders you met on the road then to something worse. Such things could cause me trouble were they numerous enough, but they have sense enough to stay clear. You must have sense enough to stay close to me, lest the ground itself should swallow you at a gulp.'

Jacom wasn't entirely sure how seriously to take this, and he suspected that the creature might be lying to keep him docile, but he knew that it would be foolish to risk any reckless move. Whatever else was false, the manticore was the one who knew the territory.

He could see a jagged edge of shadow looming up on the horizon now, which was presumably the 'rim' of which the manticore spoke. In spite of the burden on his back and the care he was taking to avoid the living quicksands, Kasdeja was still covering the ground so quickly that they would be there in less than two hours.

'Will we pause to rest soon?' Jacom asked. 'I don't like to complain, but you're somewhat broader in the back than any horse I've ever ridden and my legs feel as if they're being ripped apart.'

The manticore made a slight sound which might have been a gesture of contempt, but all he said was: 'Soon enough.'

Andris Myrasol would have made a far better manticore-rider than I ever shall, Jacom thought. *Dhalla would have made a better one still, had a manticore been willing to take her aboard. Giants might almost have been made with manticore-riding in mind.* The last observation was, however, far too close in implication to all the stupid dirty jokes which the citadel guard told about and against their supposed allies, and Jacom retained enough of his native prudishness to discontinue the train of thought.

At least he seems anxious for my safety, he mused instead. *He certainly intends to deliver me to his mysterious siblings in good condition. The question is, what use do they intend to make of me thereafter? He instructs me not to be afraid, but he will not give me any real grounds for confidence. Does that mean that he is deceiving me, and that he is carrying me to my doom? Or should I read more into the fact that he took care to capture me alive, and seems anxious to preserve me against the dangers which still threaten us?*

'You'd better hold tight,' the manticore said, the voice cutting rudely into his reverie. 'Not all my adversaries have sense enough to avoid me.'

Jacom jerked his head up to see what had occasioned this new warning, seizing the manticore's mane more firmly with both his hands as he did so. The manticore's night vision must have been better than his own, because he could see nothing at all in the shadows that lay ahead but the slightest hint of movement. Something was there, but he could not tell what or how many.

'Am I so valuable a prize?' he muttered, as he strove with all his might to see what must be there to be seen, and managed to pluck a few fugitive shapes out of the near-black background.

'They're killers, not collectors,' the manticore replied. 'Don't look to them for help or rescue – they'll tear us limb from limb and eat us up if they have the chance.'

Jacom's suspicion that this judgment might be less than completely honest did not last long. As clearly discernible shapes finally began to materialise within his field of view he felt a horrid thrill of fear.

He had been half expecting to see a company of mounted men – or half-men – like those he had fought before, but the five creatures that were waiting for them weren't in the least human. They looked like huge flightless birds, although they seemed to have scales instead of feathers. They were close enough already for him to see sharp white teeth within their great beak-like snouts: teeth which caught the light even better than the flinty scales which covered their bodies.

'Hold tight and duck down!' Kasdeja instructed him, as the flock came forward to meet them.

The logic of the command was clear enough; without the sword that Kasdeja had told him to throw away there was nothing Jacom could do but keep the inconvenience of his presence to a minimum. The knife he had used to skin the horse was no use at all in a fight like this, and nor was any part of the exhaustive training he had received in the Arts Martial.

When he saw the flaring eyes of the creatures that were coming for him, and the poses they struck with their out-stretched claws, Jacom ceased to worry about what might await him within the rim; his only thought was the hope that he might live to find out. He gripped the mane of his own monster more tightly still, and held himself as low as he could – but he kept his fearful eyes open, and prayed that the manticore could use his sting with absolute precision.

55

7

THE GREAT REEF offered no shortage of hiding places but Lucrezia did not find the choice an easy one. On the one hand, they had to be far enough away from the pool where their enemies would presumably make camp to be in no danger of premature discovery. On the other, they had to be close enough to act swiftly and efficiently if and when they received confirmation that their plan was taking effect.

The poison with which she had spiced the pool was not one which would stupefy their enemies, but it ought to make their muscles relax to the point at which they would find it impossible to use their weapons, or even lift their arms in their own defence. None would die of its effect – nor any of the prisoners who would be forced to share it – but with luck it would render every last one of them vulnerable to casual dispatch by blade or bludgeon. The only problem was the dosage; the pool was probably deep enough to dilute the drug into ineffectiveness if it were stirred too vigorously, and she had to hope that the newcomers would drink swiftly and deeply. She also had to hope that the giant Serpents would have thirsts to match their size.

Eventually, she settled with Andris and Ssifuss in the hollow of a globular structure whose once active parts seemed to have been dead for a long time, although rot had not yet crumbled them to dust. The outer wall of the husk was ornately decorated with all manner of patient parasitic growths but the interior was relatively unsullied, and would have been purely white but for the shadows cast by the sunlight creeping through a thousand pores and crevices.

The floor of the hideaway was comfortable enough to accommodate the three of them and their meagre possessions – not quite so meagre now, for they had collected as many gourd-like objects as they could in order to store a good supply of fresh water before Lucrezia had poisoned the pool.

They had not had time to make any similar effort in respect of food, although Ssifuss had fired off a single arrow at a big bird which had refused to be intimidated by their nearness. The abundant practice the Serpent had put in while crossing the Soursweet Marshes had refined its skills sufficiently to grant it a success of sorts, but the bird had contrived to dislodge the arrow from beneath its wing and had made its escape. It had seemed highly probable that it would not get far, but they had not had time to chase it and the likelihood was that some other predator or scavenger had seized the opportunity by now. At least the arrow had not been lost.

Ssifuss was still a little restless as they settled to wait, but if it felt that there would have been time for more adventurous hunting it was cautious enough to say nothing about it. Lucrezia, for her part, did not expect that they would be waiting for long; she expected news at any minute.

Rayner had proved his agility sufficiently to be given the spying commission that he ardently desired, and he had been set on the north side of the pool, with instructions to climb as high as he could without being seen, in order that he might keep watch on the other approaching company as well as the men and monsters who had sacked the Community's house. Venerina Sirelis had also asked to be placed as an observer in order to make what efforts she could to enumerate and identify the prisoners, and she had been set to wait on the nearer side of the pool, so that she could bring that intelligence back to Lucrezia, Andris and Ssifuss.

While they had been active in making their preparations the time had passed quickly enough, but once they had nothing to do but sit and wait it began to hang heavily on Lucrezia's consciousness. All the anxieties she had so far contrived to suppress now flooded into her tired mind. What if the combination of powders she had prepared was too quickly diluted by diffusion into the hidden depths of dark water? What if the first drinkers – be they men or horses or giant Serpents – should show such immediate evidence of having been drugged that the rest paused before drinking and mounted an immediate search of the area? What if the drug had the desired effect but left too little time for the destruction of the first company before the others arrived to relieve it? What if the drugged prisoners could not be moved to a safer pace before the mysterious members of that second party made their appearance?

'How do you feel now, Andris?' she asked the amber, not so much because she was in doubt about his fitness for the coming conflict as because she felt in dire need of distraction.

'I can play my part,' he assured her, in a tone that was sombre but stern. He was gnawing his lower lip and there was a distinct frown on his face. It was plain to see that he had been engaged in serious cogitation – a habit of which he had not seemed overly fond before they entered the poisoned marshes, but which now seemed to be in danger of taking him over completely.

Although a little hard thinking could hardly do the amber any harm, Lucrezia couldn't help missing his former jauntiness and exaggerated self-confidence. That self-assertive pride had been rooted in the smugness he felt by virtue of having forged an intimate alliance with his cousin, and might well have been judged excessive by an objective observer, in view of the girl's plainness and lack of accomplishments. Perhaps it was not entirely surprising that he had lost it. Even so, she would have been very glad to see it now.

'I wish you hadn't consented to take that damnable drug of Philemon Taub's,' she said, with feeling. 'If you'd just held off for half an hour . . .'

'It's not the drug,' he said. 'At least, I don't think so. It might not have done me any good, but its effects didn't stop me fighting my way out of the house when it came under attack, or hauling that rowboat across the southern reaches of the marsh with all possible speed. It didn't deliver the kind of immediate revelation that Venerina and Philemon promised me, but I believe that I really am getting closer to an understanding of what's going on. I know it doesn't really make sense, but the so-called Spirit of the Waters really does seem to be pressing some kind of enlightenment upon me.'

'I'd rather you were able to concentrate on the matter in hand,' Lucrezia told him, 'at least for now.'

'That's exactly what I'm doing,' he said. 'I'll kill those monsters that sacked the Community readily enough – but I hope to keep one or two of them alive long enough to tell me what *they're* doing.'

Lucrezia had a suspicion that she had already found out what the giant Serpents and their allies were doing – or, at least, where they were going.

'That causeway I saw extending towards Chimera's Cradle looks for all the world like an artefact,' she said, 'although I don't see how it can possibly be the work of human hands if this place is as dangerous as Ssifuss thinks. The people who raided the Community for prisoners must be intending to use it. I don't know who they are, but it's obvious that they've been roving far and wide in search of captives.'

Andris had evidently been pondering the matter too. 'We've called them slavers,' he said pensively, 'but we have no real reason to think that they seized Venerina's people as slaves. No one would go into the Soursweet Marshes without a very strong motive . . . and if raiders like these went there, they must have gone in other directions too. The existence of the second company surely proves that. Some must have gone towards the river towns, others towards Salamander's Fire. If the second party are fetching another slave-train from Shabir's realm there might be a third and a fourth too. We could be in deep trouble even if your crazy plan comes off – and so might anyone else trying to cross the plain.'

She knew that he must be thinking about Carus Fraxinus – and Merel Zabio.

'It's not a crazy plan,' she informed him stiffly. 'It's a perfectly sane plan. It's the only chance we have, given our number and our lack of resources, and it really is a chance.'

'I'm not worried about the plan itself,' Andris assured her, with a dismissive flick of the wrist. 'I don't mean any insult. Anyhow, it's a lot less crazy than the trick I tried to play on Shabir's army when I told him that your witchery could spread plague throughout its ranks. It's just that killing these semi-humans and their tame Serpents might not be enough. We really do need to find out exactly who they are, and exactly what they're trying to do. We already know that there's a second horde mere hours behind the first, and we need to know whether there are any more behind that one.'

'We might manage that as well,' Lucrezia told him, although

she wasn't particularly confident. 'If we can kill all the ones who can still move, there might well be a few rendered utterly helpless by the drug, who'd be available for interrogation.' *Except*, she thought, *that there might not be time. Time is the real enemy – or the worst.*

Andris shrugged his shoulders. It was obvious that he was deeply troubled, and not by any mere matter of tactics. At one time he had been blithely immune to the mysteries which obsessed Ereleth and Carus Fraxinus, but now they had taken possession of him he was making up for lost time. He had changed, and she could not tell how profound the change was. Perhaps the effect of the Spirit of the Waters would wear off now that the marshes were so far behind – but perhaps it wouldn't.

'Tell us about the giant Serpents,' Andris said, not to Lucrezia but to the Serpent which sat nearby, patiently listening to their anxious exchanges. 'Tell us why you never believed in them – and why you're willing to take arms against them now.'

Ssifuss moved its head slightly from side to side, but the gesture wasn't a refusal. It seemed to be thinking hard, trying to find the words.

'Giant Sserpentss bad,' it said finally. 'Very bad. Monssterss. Lore ssayss *be afraid*. Ssought ssere wass no need. Wass wrong. Are Sserpentss, but not *uss*. Musst desstroy, like disseasse.'

'Like a disease?' Lucrezia echoed. 'You keep saying that – but exactly *how* are they like a disease?'

Ssifuss thought long and hard about that one too, but the answer it eventually came up with was distinctly oblique.

'Many Sserpentss ssink humanss a disseasse,' it said eventually, tactfully refraining from reminding them that it had been numbered among the many only a few days before. 'Ssomessing ssat doess not *belong*. Ssomessing ssat poissonss land, desstroyss ssat whissh is *ourss*. Landss norss of foresst are very *sstrange* to uss. Mosst Sserpentss *hate* humanss, sstay away from ssem . . . but no one ssayss fight, no one ssayss Sserpentss sshould try to *cure* disseasse. Lore ssayss wait, let time heal. Lore ssayss time *will* heal, but not *how*. Many Sserpentss ssink *heal* meanss all humanss die but Mossassor ssink anosser way. Mossassor ssink humanss and Sserpentss one day come togesser, not ass ssame ssing but of ssame earss. No word, but ssink ssomessing like *brosserss*. Not like ssat wiss giant Sserpentss. *Not* brosserss, never can be. *Bad* disseasse. Doess not belong. *Ssreat* to everyssing we have, everyssing we are.'

Lucrezia was impressed by the effort that Ssifuss put into the formulation of this speech, which was by far the longest it had ever attempted while in their company. She believed that it represented a dramatic shift in the Serpent's attitude, signifying its acceptance of the fact that it now considered itself to be on their side, a full partner in their enterprise. On the other hand, she couldn't make head or tail of the supposed explanation.

Andris must have been equally at a loss, but he was ready enough to take the matter further. 'What you're saying,' the amber said, 'is that Mossassor believed that humans and Serpents might one day enter into a mutually beneficial relationship, but that Serpents and giant Serpents could never do that?'

'Yess,' Ssifuss replied. 'Ssink sso.'

It wasn't a very helpful answer – but human wisdom was equally cryptic. If the esoteric lore which went under the name of the Apocrypha of Genesys was what it pretended to be, then some kind of debt was owed by humans to Serpents because of something that had happened long ago, in the garden called Idun, and humans ought to regard both Serpents and Salamanders as potential allies in the great game of life – perhaps potential 'brothers', whatever Ssifuss intended to imply by his use of that word. On the subject of giant Serpents, however, even the Apocrypha of Genesys was stubbornly silent. Ordinary humans and human giants seemed to have no trouble at all in co-existing peacefully, but Serpents evidently had a very different view of their own legendary kin.

'What I saw can't really be a road, can it?' Lucrezia said, although she was perfectly prepared to believe that it was.

Ssifuss made no reply; whatever Serpent lore had to say about soft and sticky stones it evidently said nothing about roads to Chimera's Cradle. It was Andris who took up the thread. 'The waterhole can't be their final destination,' he said, with a shrug of his shoulders. 'They're going somewhere much further in. If the Gauntlet of Gladness marked on my map provided a safe corridor through the Silver Thorns, there might be others.'

'All bad ground,' Ssifuss said. 'Dangerouss.'

'Not bad enough to deter giant Serpents,' Andris pointed out, 'nor their human companions. If they've brought their prisoners this far, they must have somewhere to take them to, and a safe route by which to reach their destination – a route fit for the use of men and giant Serpents alike.'

Before Ssifuss could reply to that Venerina Sirelis slipped through the narrow crack which had given them access to the shell-like entity's interior.

'They're at the waterhole now,' she said. 'Not all of them, alas. The wagons are coming more slowly, and there must be at least a dozen men with them as well as the prisoners. The riders and the giant Serpents have hastened ahead. Doubtless they will fall upon the water with all the avidity we anticipated, Serpents and men alike . . . and they'll be suffering obvious effects before the rearguard arrives.'

Lucrezia knew that this was bad news. In this instance, division of the enemy's forces was no aid to conquest. She saw that Andris was cursing beneath his breath, keeping silent only because the die had been cast and there was no backing out. However inconvenient the disposition of their enemies might be, they had to fight.

'Did you count them?' Lucrezia demanded.

'Men, nineteen; Serpents, eleven,' Venerina replied, without hesitation. 'That's the advance party. Another twelve men with the wagons, at least, and forty-some prisoners. None of the prisoners seems very young or very old, although there might be some who couldn't walk in the wagons. They've been poorly fed, but they may well be strong. The Spirit of the Waters will help to sustain them.'

Lucrezia knew that Venerina was being determinedly optimistic, searching for any factor which might make the odds against success less steep – but nineteen plus twelve was only thirty-one, which was fewer than they had earlier estimated. The news *was* good, even if the twelve turned out to be a slight underestimate.

'We'll have to take the first group very quickly,' Andris murmured. 'Thirty is few enough throats to cut, if they are indeed rendered helpless.'

What he left unsaid was that a further twelve or fifteen throats would be very difficult to cut, without any such advantage.

'We can't wait,' Lucrezia said, feeling that she must take the lead, since she alone could judge the efficacy of her witchery.

'We must strike now, to give us the best interval before the wagons arrive. We can't wait for them to fall. Helplessness will overcome them quickly enough as we move in.' There was no way she could be certain of that, but she had to say it anyway.

No one attempted to contradict or question her, but she knew that their silence did not mean that they had no doubts. They understood well enough that dissent would serve no purpose.

As they moved out of their shadowy hiding place the brilliant sunlight dazzled Lucrezia's eyes, and made her wish that they had the softer light of night to shadow their activities. She braced herself nevertheless and took care to remember that she had killed before, with all the calm and callous efficiency of a trained witch.

I must do what is expected of me, she told herself, *and I ought to hope that I will one day be able to tell the tale to Ereleth, so that she might be proud of her pupil.* She was uneasily conscious, though, of the way that the 'must' of the first resolution had softened into the 'ought to' of the second.

8

A NDRIS KEPT HIS HEAD well down as he crept towards the pool where the enemy was gathered. Lucrezia and Venerina Sirelis were making their way forward to his left, while Ssifuss was on his right. He wondered how close they would have to get before they could make an accurate assessment of their adversaries' condition.

When the Community's house had come under attack Andris had been in no fit state to study its attackers, and such attention as he had been able to pay had been concentrated on the monstrous Serpents. Despite the abundance of available cover and the fact that they had placed no sentries it was not easy to look them over now without running the risk of being seen, but he made what observations he could as he moved forward, knowing that every item of information as to their means of defence might be precious.

The horsemen were ill-dressed by any standards, their shirts and trousers being very ragged and badly tailored. The only remarkable thing about their raiment was that it appeared to be cut from some kind of scaly skin marked somewhat after the fashion of a Serpent's. This curious echo of their monstrous companions made them seem all the more monstrous themselves. Their saddles and tack seemed to be of a markedly higher standard than their clothes, but Andris was inclined to suspect that the only credit they deserved on that score was recognition of their talents as thieves. He knew that the marauders had come to the Lake of Colourless Blood from the west, so it was highly unlikely that they had plundered their mounts from the men of the river towns, but the animals were similar in build to those used by Shabir's cavalry and the tackle was similarly metal-poor.

He was glad to note that their weapons were also primitive.

Their chief armaments were clubs, and such blades as he could see were made of stony substances rather than steel. He did not doubt that these daggers could inflict considerable damage with their points, but at least they were not swords – nor, he assumed, were they poisoned. He and his companions had all the advantages on this score, of course; he had the spear which Ssifuss had given him, while the Serpent had a quiverful of arrows, and Lucrezia had anointed them all. Venerina had their one remaining knife, which was similarly doctored, but it was too small to be a very useful weapon; she and Lucrezia would have to snatch up more effective instruments as soon as they could.

He had very little time to judge the matter, but it did seem to Andris that the marauders were men of few words, although that might have been an effect of their evident fatigue. Despite that fatigue, he judged that they had never intended to stay very long at the pool. They were making no attempt to set up a proper camp, and had not even bothered to unsaddle their horses. He guessed that they had merely paused to rest the horses and renew their water supplies, and were bent on continuing through the Reef with as little delay as possible.

When he was less than twenty mets from the pool he saw that Lucrezia's witchery was beginning to take effect, at least on the men and their mounts. Several of the horses had begun to stagger drunkenly, and he could see the expressions of astonishment on the faces of the men who tried to respond to their distress. He saw one man go down, then another – but no one cried a warning, and there were others still kneeling at the poolside, making cups of their hands.

At least half the giant Serpents were drinking too, having lowered themselves on to their forelimbs as if they were four-legged beasts – but the ones which had resumed a standing position, towering above their lesser companions, showed no sign of disability as yet.

Andris's brief and surreptitious observations did not allow him to deduce the exact relationship between the Serpents and their human companions. The Serpents seemed even more taciturn than their allies and he never saw one of them speak, either to a human or to another of its own kind. He couldn't be certain whether they were equal partners in the enterprise or mere hunting dogs. If the party had an overall leader he could not immediately tell which man or creature it might be, and there was no time for more scrupulous observation. There was something about the way the humans moved around one another that reminded him of the dragomite-women who had accompanied Fraxinus's caravan through the southern reaches of the Dragomite Hills, but he knew that he might be superimposing that impression on what he saw. Because he knew that some seeming humans were not born from human wombs he was disposed to hope that these might be among them. It would make killing them a little easier.

Despite the fact that no one howled a warning or barked an order, once alarm began to spread among the company its members were quick enough to realise their danger. None, however, leapt immediately to the conclusion that they were under attack; their panic didn't send them scrambling for their weapons. They were more inclined to stare at their hands and stamp their feet, in the hope of bringing a proper vigour back to their limbs. Those bunched around the pool were looking up, but none bounded away or spat out water. They had not connected what was happening to the slaking of their thirst.

There was no sign of the wagons, but Andris knew that they could not be very far away. He measured the distance which separated him from the nearest of his enemies, and tried to gauge whether any of their weapons would be more use to him than the spear which Ssifuss had given him. He could not see one that would be easy to pick up when he ran forward, but he had to hope that Lucrezia and Venerina might have better luck. The Serpent undoubtedly had the best weapon, provided that it really had mastered the art of archery – but it remained to be seen how many arrows it could fire before one of its targets got too close.

While he tensed himself, ready for the charge, Andris saw that the giant Serpents were drawing into a huddle, reaching out to one another as if for reassurance. If it was instinct that drew them, the instinct was poor, for they could not make good use of their lashing tails while they were so close together – especially in the position they had unthinkingly taken up, with a wall-like structure to one side of them and two of the broad dendrite boles unfavourably close. Like their human allies they were now in obvious distress, but they had not yet turned to pick up their weapons. The advantage of surprise still lay with the ambushers.

'Now!' Andris cried, launching himself forward.

An arrow flew past him through the air, close enough to make him flinch slightly, although it was only the thought of the poison on its tip that made him do so. It struck one of the giant Serpents squarely in the chest, biting deeply into the flesh. The monster looked down in astonishment, and even though it did not fall Andris felt a rush of delight.

Another arrow followed the first, aimed at a different individual. It struck behind the shoulder, with just as little immediate effect, but it was a second hit.

Andris levelled his lance before him but the humans at which he aimed it had time to see him coming and were very anxious indeed to get out of his way. He could see the horror on their faces as they tried to leap aside and realised that their limbs were not responding as they should. They managed to shift themselves, but they were lurching and falling to either side. Some grabbed for weapons, but could not rise with them. He made no immediate contact as he carved the air with the head of the spear, but he was not displeased by the effect of his lunges, for they sent men tumbling left and right.

Rather than run among them while they might trip him and drag him down, Andris stopped short and paused to pick up a heavy club that lay beneath his feet. He took the club in his right hand and shifted the spear to his left. His battle plan now was simple enough: aim high with the club, to crack heads; aim low with the spear, to slash tendons and leg muscles.

He could not see Rayner or Venerina Sirelis but he saw Lucrezia move forward to his left. While he had charged she had crept, and she was scooping up a knife with a longer blade than the one Venerina had. She paused long enough to pick up a second, and to dip the points of both blades into one of the pouches that was open at her waist, before hurling herself into the attack. It was a good decision – she had not the muscles to wield a heavy weapon in imitation of her friend Dhalla, but she had the deftness of hand necessary to make a pair of lighter blades bear bloody fruit.

Having no illusions about the burden of expectation he was carrying, Andris did not tarry long among the stricken humans.

He smashed the heads of three who still had strength to raise their bodies from the ground, and slashed the throats of two who writhe like worms towards his boots. He made straight for the place where the giant Serpents had congregated, swiping sideways as he went. The monstrous Serpents separated as he came, but he didn't mind that – it would give Ssifuss targets at which it might fire without running any risk of felling its allies.

Andris knew that according to Lucrezia's count he had already disabled or killed five of the giants while they were fully alert and armed, so he knew that they were sluggish even at the best of times. He could see now that at least half of them were sorely troubled by the poison they had drunk, and all his apprehension seemed to have vanished under pressure of the surge of adrenalin which carried him forward. He lashed out at the monsters' heads, with spear and club alike.

Arrows were still arriving with mechanical regularity as Ssifuss methodically emptied its quiver. Even those which struck squarely did no lethal damage instantly, but they added to the creatures' confusion as well as their distress. When Andris first came within the range of their groping hands not one of the eleven had so far fallen down, but only four had taken up weapons and the remainder were not reaching out with any authentic purpose.

Andris was a very tall man, but the Serpents loomed over him nevertheless. He was also a very strong man, but the monsters had tough hides and tougher skulls, and their wrath-inflated hoods were all spread wide. He felt like some waspish insect charging into the midst of a company of sharp-eyed birds, but he had a waspish pride in the power and poison of his sting. The spear cut three of them about the neck before its progress was decisively interrupted, but he continued to lash out with the club. It wasn't easy aiming upwards, and he landed no blows as instantly crushing as those with which he'd felled the humans, but he felt jaws crack and throats give way beneath his blows.

He had pulled the spear back, to stab instead of slashing. One of the monsters tried to grab the haft, but failed. The Serpents' scaly teguments were difficult to cut – even a steel blade would not have carved their flesh with overmuch ease – but every blow he landed did some damage nevertheless, and he was landing them faster than he could count.

68

Still, however, they would not fall – even the ones with poisoned arrows buried in their breasts.

For a few awful seconds, Andris thought that he had played himself for a fool – that his sting was not so powerful, after all, and that they would reach out and tear him apart as if he were indeed merely some annoying insect. Doubtless they would have, in different circumstances, but when they tried to reach out for him they did so very clumsily indeed, as if they were groping in the dark with limbs enfeebled by fever and age. As he danced before them with an agility that belied his hunger and his fatigue they could not catch him and they could not swat him.

The huge Serpents wore no clothes save for loincloths of the kind that Ssifuss wore. They had neither belts nor harnesses, and thus no weapons ready to hand. Two or three of them turned away, looking for spears or cudgels, but most of them simply tried to use their hands. They had a long reach, especially when they leaned forwards, but their forelimbs were not nearly as powerful as their legs, being much slimmer in proportion to their bodies. Andris had only to make reflexive parries with his two weapons, cutting the tensed fingers and bruising the slender wrists.

Meanwhile, the arrows were still flying, although Andris knew that the supply must be running very low. Now, at last, the giants began to fall as the poisons they had drunk and the poisons in their cuts began to take effect.

Andris continued to use the cutting edge of the spearhead against fingers and forearms when defence was necessary, and against breasts and calves whenever there was space to attack. His club bruised heads and elbows with what must have been numbing effect.

Despite their initial failure to grab him or dispossess him of his weapons, the Serpents might still have turned the tables on Andris had not reinforcements arrived. Just as it seemed that the six or seven still standing might combine their efforts well enough to overwhelm him, however, a much lither Serpent appeared to harry its lumpen kin. Ssifuss now had a good metal blade, albeit a short and slender one, which it plied as avidly as it had emptied its quiver.

If the giant Serpents were astonished to see one of their own kind set against them they gave no visible or audible sign. Four turned away from Andris to face the newcomer, but that gave Andris all the space he needed to strike out this way and that at the ones which still faced him. He saw one adversary fall, then another, and although he knew that his thrusts had not put them down unaided he felt a great surge of exultation. This, he thought, must be how the heroes of romance and legend felt as they slew firedragons and manticores.

Andris dropped the club in order to grip the spear with both hands. He swung it with all his might in a horizontal arc, aiming below the level of the last pair of clumsily grasping hands. It made very solid contact with the exposed belly of his assailant, and he promptly swivelled on his heels to offer the same service to one of those which had turned towards Ssifuss.

Ssifuss had been tumbled over by a blow from one of those massive tails and was dazed by it. The giant which towered over its smaller kin would have smashed its skull had it been allowed a further second in which to complete the stroke, but Andris was there to intervene. The blow never fell.

Andris slammed the head of his spear into the giant's neck, with the cutting edge levelled to slice the throat and arteries. The creature was abruptly thrown back, as much by its own convulsive reaction as the force of the blow; its club flew away to one side.

Ssifuss wasted no time in scrambling to its feet and laying its hand on a weapon. Andris and Ssifuss were side by side now, and their remaining opponents were swaying like drunkards on the point of collapse. The two of them struck out in unison. The blows they struck had an immediate and powerful effect; one by one, the giants went down, and those which came to take their place fared no better.

All the giants that had been hit by the arrows Ssifuss had fired, even glancingly, had now been felled. The sum of Lucrezia's poisons had taken full effect. If there were any among them which had not drunk from the water it made no difference now. Andris was buffeted about the head by one stray arm, but it did not even stagger him. By the time one of the huge creatures finally managed to hit him with a blow from its tail and knock him sprawling the battle was all but won.

A lashing tail struck Ssifuss too, but the smaller Serpent was using its own tail as if it were an extra leg and was sufficiently well-braced to score its enemy's tail very deeply even as it was bowled over. The poison on Ssifuss's blade could not take effect immediately, but Andris knew as he watched the red blood gushing from the giant's wound that the stroke would be mortal. He could afford to turn part of his attention back to human enemies now, although he found that there were precious few of those within reach.

As Andris moved back and forth across the battlefield he had to avoid a rushing foot and then a reaching hand but the last two giants were now so slow and awkward that they could offer no threat. He was able to snatch up the spear again and stab with it: once, twice, thrice. Ssifuss had moved back slightly and the two remaining adversaries were coming after Andris but they seemed utterly impotent, nothing but huge targets waiting to be ripped apart.

Andris did no ripping, but the head of the spear inflicted three more deadly cuts before it broke and sent him scampering for a replacement. By the time he had laid his hand on one there was only one giant standing, and Ssifuss was standing firm against its last lurching rush. The huge Serpent fell on top of the smaller, but it did fall, and Andris knew that Ssifuss was sufficiently robust to survive the impact, provided only that it did not nick itself with its own blade.

Andris lowered the weapon he had raised in readiness to a height where it might be employed against mere human enemies, but there were none to be found.

The stench was appalling, but there was very little sound. There had been very few howls of anguish, hardly any screams of pain. It was as if the poisons had robbed their victims of the ability to protest against their fate. There was surely some justice in that; these were creatures which attacked without ceremony, and there was nothing to regret in their dying.

For a moment, Andris gloried in the thought that it was finished, and that the contest was won – but then the first of the wagons arrived, just a few awkward minutes too soon.

9

JACOM KNEW THAT he could take no useful part in the coming conflict, but he was not in the least reassured by the thought that his role was to hold tight to Kasdeja's mane. No matter how fearsome the enemy might be, he would far rather have had a sword in his hand. The only good remedy he knew for fear was violent action; time to think was no luxury when life and death hung in the balance.

As the five bird-like creatures closed in on the lone manticore Jacom perceived that they were actually reptiles. He guessed that they must be closer kin to crocolids than they were to the flightless fowl that were kept for their eggs and their meat by some of the smallholders on his father's estates. The web-footed legs on which they stood could have passed for those of a wading bird but their upper limbs were less like wings than they had seemed at first glance.

Jacom had never had been able to understand why flightless birds retained their useless wings instead of modifying their upper limbs to some other purpose. These creatures seemed somewhat better designed; although he could not divine the purpose of the 'wings' – cloak-like flaps of flesh attached to the upper limbs – the arms themselves terminated in claw-like hands of a surprising delicacy. Those hands, he saw to his astonishment, were clutching weapons: needle-sharp daggers which looked as if they were made out of black glass. He had seen similar ones in the hands of a few of General Shabir's men.

The sight of these armaments frightened him more than the sight of the rows of sharp teeth which decked the creatures' crocolidian snouts and marked them as specialist carnivores. The teeth only testified to the beasts' probable ferocity; the hand-held daggers testified to their probable intelligence. Kasdeja had already spoken contemptuously about the likely level of that intelligence, but he had only a single sting, no matter how much venom might be stored therein. While Jacom sat astride his back the manticore would not be able to make the best use of his own dagger-like claws.

If I only had my sword, Jacom thought, *I might be of some help, however slight. As things are I'm a definite hindrance.* It was not his fault, of course, but the prospect was no less alarming for that.

The five reptiles seemed respectful enough of the manticore's fighting ability, but they moved as if to form a pentagon around him, arranging themselves for a simultaneous assault. They danced backwards and forwards as Kasdeja swayed this way and then that, carefully keeping out of the range of his sting. There was nothing impatient in the way they executed their manoeuvre, and this added to the impression that they were thinking beings.

Jacom saw that Kasdeja's retaliatory strategy was to try with all his might to keep empty ground behind him. He also saw that there was a possibility that the awkward terrain could be turned to their advantage. The attackers were unable to complete their pentagon because the manticore took his stand near a shallow pit brimming with some dark and glutinous substance of which the reptiles were manifestly afraid. Thanks to Kasdeja's stern warnings Jacom knew well enough what danger the reptiles faced. He knew too, though, that taking up a position so close to the edge of ground that was avid to seize him and suck him down was a ploy that might backfire on the manticore. Kasdeja's movements would be limited too; he could not make evasive moves in that direction lest his own hind legs should slip into the muddy maw.

In the beginning, at least, the manticore's tactics proved sound. The reptiles were as careful of the pit as they were of their adversary's sting, and they were forced by its proximity to keep closer formation than they would have liked.

Kasdeja lowered his rump and raised his head, so that he could support himself on one forepaw and raise the other one high, with its claws splayed to slash and rake. Jacom was very glad that he had the saddle and stirrups to help him cling on; had he been forced to ride bareback he'd have no confidence at all in his ability to maintain his station.

73

Kasdeja's reach was greater than Jacom had expected and he deduced that the articulation of the manticore's shoulders must be unusually flexible, but the reptiles were as careful to stay out of striking range of the claws as they were to avoid the scope of his sting. Indeed, they were so very careful that for a full minute and more after Kasdeja had chosen his ground they dithered impotently, searching for some further advantage of position that proved impossible of attainment. While he observed this cautiousness Jacom almost began to hope that the attackers might think better of the fight and let the matter drop – but that, apparently, was not their way.

When they sought to end the impasse the reptiles acted in unison, although none had made any visible or audible signal. They closed in rapidly, their elongated heads arrowing forward with mouths agape. Their little hands reached out to stab at the manticore's face with their pointed daggers.

Kasdeja's sting lashed out at the reptile to the far left of the array. The threatened creature was quick to bring its arm around in front of its ducking head, so that the cloak-like membrane suddenly became a shield. Jacom wondered whether that was its sole function. The manticore's sting bit into the membrane and whipped away again. The reptile seemed quite satisfied with this result and immediately unveiled its face to strike again.

It seemed, for the moment, that the manticore's raking claws had done far more damage than its sting, for their tips had caught no less than three of the reaching heads, taking out the left eye of one monster and bloodying the snouts of the other two. The three mouths had snapped shut without pinching anything at all. The fifth reptile was the first to inflict retaliatory damage; its jaws clamped shut on the manticore's neck, not ten sems from Jacom's clutching hand – but Kasdeja's mane was so thick and wiry that the digging teeth could not draw blood, and might not have punctured the skin at all. Jacom heard a hiss of breath as Kasdeja reacted to the contact, but there was no pain in it.

The beast which had bitten the manticore paid dearly for its limited success; the tail which had lashed out to the right now lashed back as if it were a whip. This target was in no position to bring up a protective cloak, because its hands were reaching out in the hope of delivering stab-wounds to the manticore's shoulder. The sting struck the creature on the back of the head, where the skull articulated with the vertebral column, and the reptile screamed in agony as it jerked convulsively backwards, its locked jaws pulling out a liberal clump of Kasdeja's hair.

'Hang on!' Kasdeja yelled, as the heads wounded by its flailing claws refused to withdraw. Jacom, having some inkling of what was to come, moved his grip a little wider before clutching the coarse hair with every vestige of his strength.

As the reptiles pressed home their imagined advantage Kasdeja rocked back on to his huge hind paws and rose up into a rampant stance, lashing out with both forepaws at once. Perhaps the attackers had not thought that he could do that with a rider on his back, or perhaps the relatively trivial wounds the manticore had so far inflicted had confused their reactions, but their groping snouts and reaching arms wavered uncertainly. Their co-ordination had broken down.

Had the four creatures which were still capable of it organised their moves skilfully they might have dealt a mortal blow then. The manticore's neck and breast were exposed as he brought his two sets of claws into simultaneous play – but two of the reptiles had snatched their stilettos back as they brought their defences up against the lashing sting, and the other two were moving at cross-purposes.

Things now began to happen so quickly that Jacom couldn't see the various strikes that Kasdeja made. His face was too closely pressed to the back of the manticore's head and he would in any case have only been able to look one way. He felt his mount's shoulders heave as both forelimbs lashed out, and he knew that the sting was whipping out again and again with seemingly impossible speed, but he saw very little of what happened to the attackers until Kasdeja sank again on to all fours. Even then, Jacom's first instinct was to look behind him, to see how close he had come to being tumbled from the creature's back straight into the dark ooze that would have swallowed him up.

The rim of the pit was mere sems away from the rearmost of the manticore's huge paws, but the paw was on solid ground and the joints of the hind leg were set firm.

By the time Jacom looked forwards again, two of the reptiles were already fleeing, at what seemed to him an astonishing pace. They were matching strides with uncanny precision as they disappeared into the shadows of the Great Reef. The other three lay dying, their bodies twitching uncontrollably in the grip of the sting's poison while their wide-open mouths tried, without much success, to raise screams of agony. The sound they actually contrived was a murmurous wailing whine.

Kasdeja reached out with one forelimb to sweep one of the stricken creatures sideways and back, tumbling the body into the waiting pit. The reptile was obviously lighter in the frame than its bulk suggested, for it was easy enough to shift. It thrashed around as the black ooze seized it, but the thrashing only made it sink all the faster. Jacom was in no doubt that it was being actively and avidly swallowed up.

Kasdeja carefully picked his way between the two remaining reptiles, keeping a cautious eye on each of them lest either should contrive a last convulsive thrust.

'Are you badly hurt?' Jacom asked, as soon as they were clear. He was looking down as he spoke at the manticore's left flank, where dark blood was leaking, staining the tawny fur red.

'It's nothing,' Kasdeja assured him.

'You were right,' Jacom told him. 'They should have had the sense to stay clear.'

The manticore wasn't interested in compliments. 'We must be more careful within the wheel's rim,' he said. 'There are too many blind corridors and narrow crevices therein. Killers like those prefer to fight in the open, but they have brothers too.'

'What were they?' Jacom asked, still waiting for his heart to cease its anxious hammering. 'I never heard of anything like them.'

'If you want to name them, feel free,' Kasdeja replied. 'It is enough that they are killers, and that is probably *all* they were.'

'Like dragomite warriors, you mean?' Jacom said uncertainly. 'Bred for nest-war: shock-troops sent forth to hunt and destroy. But they had hands, and weapons. They must be more intelligent than dragomite warriors.'

'I doubt that they had speech or lore,' Kasdeja replied, 'and their instincts betrayed them in forcing them into a duel with a manticore – unless it was you who drew them, not I. Had they not seen you on my back, friend, perhaps they'd have steered clear.'

Jacom took due note of the remarkable fact that the manticore had called him friend, but thought that it was probably meant sarcastically. 'Why would they take such risks to kill a mere human?' he asked, that being the greater puzzle.

'There are things in this world that do not like your kind – but there are also things which like your kind so well that they cannot bear to see you in other hands than theirs. I cannot tell which they were, but it's possible they came from your ground – produce of what you call Chimera's Cradle.' This suggestion seemed to be intended sarcastically too, but there was an underlying sobriety which took the edge off the remark, as if Kasdeja knew of sinister implications which might be opened up by that possibility.

'If they come from the place which my forefathers made,' Jacom said carefully, 'I doubt they'd be shaped to a purely murderous purpose. Our lore bids us to be generous, even to creatures very different from ourselves.'

Kasdeja was unimpressed by this. 'For what purpose was the army to which you recently belonged formed and drilled?' the manticore asked. 'Not to hunt dragomites, I think – and certainly not to hunt manticores. It seems that you are not overly generous, even to your own kind. Chimera's Cradle gives birth to creatures not unlike myself, and others even stranger. I do not say that it *did* produce those killers, but I do say that it could and would.'

'I cannot believe that the plan our forefathers made included creatures such as those,' Jacom replied, as steadily as he could. 'If it did, they would surely be accounted in the lore. I don't understand what kind of war is going on beyond that curious wall, but it seems obvious to me that those things were enemies of humankind, and of Chimera's Cradle.' *On the other hand,* he added silently, *the fact that you fought them, even if it was on my behalf, doesn't make me confident that you're properly entitled to call me friend.*

'Change and circumstance make strange alliances,' the manticore assured him. 'Be glad that you didn't slip when I had to stand erect. I couldn't have saved you if you'd fallen on the dark ground – had I tried, you'd probably have been torn in two.'

'I must beware of being too valuable a prize, then,' Jacom retorted, thinking that it was his turn to indulge in a little sarcasm. 'It would be a sad and silly fate to be ripped apart by rivals trying to claim me, or trying to ensure that if they cannot have me no one else shall.'

'You're not such a great treasure as all that,' the manticore assured him sardonically, but he did not go on to offer any more accurate or informative judgment of Jacom's worth.

They were now on the point of entering the strange 'forest' which Kasdeja called the war's rim, and Jacom looked about curiously, wondering whether the 'trees' that seemed to be sculpted out of stone and metal were really alive.

If I were the princess, or even the worldly-wise merchant, he thought, *I might be far more valuable than I am – but I'm only a humble captain of the guard, exiled for my incompetence. I should not be here at all. This may be the kind of fate that awaits those cursed with Serpent's blood, or those with Salamander's fire burning brightly in their capacious hearts, but it ought not to be happening to a fruit-farmer's son.*

Jacom knew that if ever he returned to tell this tale in Xandria, no one who had known him before would believe it. He could not blame them for that; if ever he returned to Xandria, even he might have difficulty believing that all this had not been some nightmarish dream.

'Would you abandon me for a better prize if one were to be offered?' Jacom asked. 'How would you decide between one human and another?'

'Don't worry about that,' the manticore advised him. 'Now that I have you, and have spilled blood to hold you, I'll certainly not let you go. You're safe with me.'

Jacom wished that he had the wit to determine whether the last sentence was a lie or not – and what it might signify, in either case.

10

LUCREZIA WAS DISMAYED to discover, almost as soon as the battle had been joined, that she had lost her appetite for murder.

As Ereleth's apprentice, she had been schooled from an early age in the attitudes of mind appropriate to a poisoner, which she had carried effortlessly into adolescence. It was her duty and function as a witch-princess to know many ways in which people might be done to death, and to have no compunction at all in the exercise of her Art. In the citadel of Xandria she had killed for the sake of study and practice, without a qualm, and had not anticipated the slightest difficulty in carrying forward her vocation. The first time she had been forced by circumstance to use the Art in self-defence – when she and Hyry Keshvara had been stalked by robbers in Khalorn – she had risen to the challenge with uninhibited ferocity, and had taken her success as confirmation of her aptitude.

Unfortunately, much had happened between then and now.

She had watched helplessly while Jume Metra's warrior-women slaughtered Djemil Eyub's men, for no good reason. She had watched helplessly while dragomites slaughtered one another in the Corridors of Power, for no very evident reason. Helpless yet again, she had seen very little of the battle at the bridge when Checuti's bombs and Dhalla's spear had helped a handful of dragomites to rout an army – but she had seen its aftermath. She had walked across the corpse-strewn battlefield, whose sights, sounds and stink had assaulted her senses with mocking effrontery, and she had known full well that it had all been unnecessary. Had General Shabir shown an atom of common sense, all that bloodshed could have been avoided. It *should* have been avoided; it had been nothing but waste and futility.

Violent death no longer seemed to her to be a matter of artistry and necessity; it had become a black farce devoid of any sense at all. She could not help but see the present conflict in the same light. Why had these monstrous fools attacked the Community? Why had they brought death and destruction to a place of peace? Why had they forced such wrathful retaliation?

It was all just waste: waste and futility.

She went about her business nevertheless. She had no option. She wished that she were able to feel better about it, but all her wrath had gone into the planning and the recognition of necessity. She couldn't feel anything now, except for a grasping nausea which teased and squeezed her guts. She couldn't feel the desperate stimulation of fear, let alone any finer kind of exhilaration.

Perhaps, she thought, *in spite of all Ereleth's hope and confidence, I'm not cut out for witchcraft.*

Once she had crept out of her hiding place, however, she wasted no time in moving as unobtrusively as she could towards the nearest group of packs set down by the men clad in Serpent-skin. She was seen before she got there, but not so quickly that the men who had seen her could move to intercept her. One or two tried, but they were already losing control of their limbs. Most were far more alarmed by the sight of Andris, who bounded out of ambush with such bold ostentation that he seemed more giant than man.

She had a pouch open, ready to anoint the tips of any weapons she seized, but she knew that it would not turn the crude daggers into magical killing machines capable of striking men dead at a touch. The first law of witchcraft declared that the poison was the dose, not the substance, and she knew that the dose might well become inadequate to kill after the first solid strike. That didn't matter; her first task was not to kill but to disable. She had to make sure that any human enemies who were not yet paralysed by the drug she had put into the water could not take any useful defensive action. Her aim was to slash as many throats and eyes as she could, as quickly as she could. That was what she did, although it took a certain fierceness of concentration to refrain from turning to see how Andris and Ssifuss were faring in the fight against the giant Serpents.

Their human enemies were still clustered about the pool and

about their luggage, so there was no shortage of targets at which to aim, and Lucrezia whipped her weapons back and forth, scoring the flesh of their naked faces. She certainly blinded more than one, and caught several more about their throats and shoulders, but it was difficult to judge whether they would have gone down anyway as a result of the poison already inside them.

Rayner and Venerina engaged themselves at first in similar business, but she soon lost sight of them among the densely packed reef-structures.

Three of the men among the group she attacked had had sufficient presence of mind to arm themselves and to make efforts in their own defence, but the arms they had reached for were all heavy weapons – clubs and javelins – and they did not have sufficient command of themselves to aim or swing them properly. With knives they might have done far better, but they evidently used their knives for eating rather than fighting and not one of them tried to bring a blade into play. Lucrezia lost one of hers when it was torn from her grasp by a flailing arm, but she held the other. It was metal, presumably looted from the Community, and although lustrust had eroded its edge it did its work.

She avoided a few more palsied limbs which reached out for her as easily as she evaded the lamely hefted clubs and spears. She sustained no harm at all while she hacked and slashed her way through the crowd. She knew well enough that her training in witchery did not give her a charmed life but as she swayed back and forth, sometimes surrounded by three or four lurching bodies, it almost seemed as if some external force were forbidding them to lay a hand on her.

Lucrezia never had to chase after her victims; once she was in the fight they came to her, stupidly tripping over their stricken companions as they fought for space. She was nimbler by far, but even she found it politic to move backwards and sideways as the writhing forms accumulated, groping for her legs. She tried to pick up another knife but it was swept away as she reached for it and she had to be content with the one she had, which was vivid red with the blood of a dozen different enemies.

Still she felt nothing but nausea; still she thought nothing but what a stupid, ridiculous waste it was to have to deal in destruction on this appalling scale.

She had lost all track of time when the first of the wagons arrived. She had no idea how many men she had cut or how long it had taken her; she wasn't even sure whether the fact that they were still coming at her in that lumpenly clumsy manner meant that there were more than she had thought, or whether they stubbornly kept getting up again when they had been felled.

When the wagons did arrive, however, the balance of opportunity was shifted suddenly and significantly.

The men driving the carts had heard the sounds of battle while they were still some way off and their best weapons were already in their hands. *These* men were not in the least befuddled; they were not even as tired as their unlucky companions had been.

If there had been four men with each wagon there would have been a full dozen to face, and that would have been too many, but Lucrezia realised that the members of this particular company had been too enthusiastic to get to the water. There were now only five or six men actually riding the three wagons. There must be at least as many more hurrying the prisoners along in the rear, but they would be several minutes behind and she felt certain that Venerina Sirelis would already have moved to tackle them, to the best of her ability. Nor would the three wagons arrive as a united force, because the tangled 'undergrowth' of the Reef would not permit the vehicles to keep close enough company. They were already strung out.

The first pair of adversaries to leap down from their perches had Lucrezia squarely in their sights, and when they came towards her they evidently supposed that she had no chance of standing up to them – but while they were running Rayner burst out at them from behind a fan-shaped wall to the right, carrying a stolen spear in his right hand. The two men ought to have realised then that they might be in trouble, but they seemed astonishingly casual as they paused and closed ranks. Perhaps they could not believe that they had no helpers ready to hand, or perhaps they thought that a young woman and a mere boy were incapable of doing them any harm – but whatever the reason, their response to the two-pronged attack was recklessly careless.

One of the newcomers carried a lance, the other a mace, but neither seemed to be certain how to use his weapon or which of their immediate adversaries to use it on; while they hesitated, Rayner launched his spear, which lodged in the thigh of the man with the lance. The other swung his weapon back and forth, as if trying to knock Lucrezia's blade out of her hand. Lucrezia dodged it easily enough but Rayner, carried further forward than he had intended by the violence of his rush, failed to avoid the backswing.

The boy took a nasty blow on the hand but the impact jarred the attacker too. Lucrezia didn't hesitate to launch herself forward. Her target reached out to fend her off with his free hand, but he misjudged the danger and she ducked under the reaching arm, bringing her knife up into the man's groin.

His scream seemed to cut through her, twisting the knot in her gut, but she felt no thrill of alarm or exultation.

This time, the knife stuck hard. As the man went down it was twisted out of her grip. When she struggled free and skipped away from her writhing victim – who was disabled but not unconscious – she was empty-handed. Rayner, meanwhile, was grappling with the man he had speared.

While Lucrezia was still looking around for another blade the next two newcomers were already arriving. These two had seen what had happened and learned from it. They were in no danger of being instantly outflanked.

Lucrezia could see Andris out of the corner of her eye, his tattered clothing drenched in blood that she hoped was not his own, but there was no sign at all of Ssifuss and the limping amber was more than a dozen mets away.

While she was still looking wildly about, cursing the fact that no suitable weapon was within reach, Rayner was clubbed to the ground by the angry fist of the man he had hurt. Lucrezia had no alternative but to snatch up exactly the kind of weapon she didn't want and couldn't use to its best effect: the mace which had been carried by the man she had crippled. It was far too heavy for someone of her light build, and was in any case designed for use by a mounted man who only had to strike downwards. She gripped it with two hands and prepared to make what defence she could as the man who had felled Rayner stumbled towards her, bleeding from the thigh but still wielding his spear. She could see the smile which betrayed his belief that one blow would disarm her and another would cleave her skull. She felt a pang of regret for her broken fingernails, which had once been shaped into weapons capable of carrying poison but had long since had to be bitten down so as not to hinder the everyday use of her hands.

Her attacker swung his spear, aiming not at her but at the weapon in her hands. She made no effort to parry the blow, but moved backwards as lightly as she could, avoiding the swing. She knew that she would be lucky to take one more step like that without tripping over a body or colliding with something solid, but she dared not look round to see how the ground lay. The man with the spear was still hobbling forward, again extending his weapon for a telling blow.

There's nothing I can do, she thought. *Brute force is all that he needs.*

The spearhead swung once more, but this time the move was a feint, and as soon as she moved to avoid it the swing became a thrust, striking through her guard. She had no alternative but to jerk backwards very sharply, and this time she did trip.

It would not have been so bad had she been able to fall to the ground, because she turned as she fell and would have come down on her side, but her head collided with something very solid, and the stabbing pain blinded her momentarily. She tried, even so, to squirm away, thinking that if she only kept moving she might avoid a lethal blow of the spear.

Nevertheless, she didn't understand why no lethal blow came until her sight cleared and she saw her attacker spitted on a lance which a charging Andris Myrasol had thrust clean through his belly from kidney to navel.

'Get up!' the amber howled at her. She felt the force of his wrath but couldn't resent it. It was easy enough to see that even though the blood which drenched him was not his own he was at the absolute limit of his strength.

There were more men coming now, and there was no one to face them but Andris, unless she could get to her feet. There was still no sign of Ssifuss, and Venerina Sirelis was nowhere in sight; Rayner, she felt sure, was in no shape to rise from the ground.

She fought the pain in her head, gritting her teeth against its insistence and trying with all her might to will it away. It seemed to work, within limits. She did get up, and felt nothing worse than an uneasy swimming sensation as she tried to focus her eyes and her thoughts.

There was an awful interval, which must have lasted for at

84

least four seconds, when the three men who were now running towards them could have killed them. Had the attackers only had the sense or the discipline to concentrate all their attention on that one vital task, the opportunity was clearly there – but they had neither. They wasted time in looking wildly and fearfully about, utterly unable to comprehend what had happened and was still happening.

Lucrezia could see the mortal terror in their eyes, and understood that they were half unmanned already.

Whatever manner of men they were, she inferred, they clearly had not imagination enough to encompass this kind of disaster, nor intelligence enough to tell them what needed to be done. Perhaps they guessed that what had happened to their companions involved witchcraft, but if so they had a common man's notion of witchcraft, all superstition and exaggeration. They did not know what kind of thunderbolts they might expect, and their terror was not the ordinary terror of fighting men engaged in a game of mutual butchery.

Any pride Lucrezia might have felt in consequence of this realisation was undermined by the observation that their looks of mortal dread were not directed at her at all, but at her companion.

These men had kept close company with giant Serpents, but all they knew of half-giant ambers they had learned when they attacked the Community. There they had seen him assault their monstrous companions and slay near half a dozen of them; now he had appeared again, when least expected, evidently having slain a dozen more. It was Andris Myrasol they took for a magician, not Lucrezia; it was Andris Myrasol's presence which horrified them into near-helplessness.

While the amber screamed at her again, desperately conscious of the fact that he needed her help, the enemies which might have killed them both were half paralysed by terror, unable to take advantage of the opportunity to cut him down.

She moved towards him, and heard his sigh of relief.

As soon as she was steady on her feet, Andris thrust a club – lighter than the one she had dropped – into her hands. For himself, he took up the spear which the man he had spitted had been carrying. He was given not only the space to complete these manoeuvres unchallenged, but the time to make his weapon ready and to choose uncluttered ground on which to stand.

Their enemies simply watched him do it, not one of the three daring to be the first to come forward. Had they followed their instincts, they would undoubtedly have run, but whatever else they had forgotten they had not forgotten that there was nowhere to run to. They stayed where they had paused, stranded by their inadequacies.

It was not until Andris took a menacing step towards them that desperation forced them to do what cunning should have made them do far sooner. They rushed him – but it was too late.

Because they were three and Andris was one they might still have been able to overwhelm him even now, but they never believed that they could win. They thought themselves already beaten, and they were. Unlike the man who had come after Lucrezia, knowing that he had every advantage of strength and skill, they were not smiling. Their mouths already wore a sterner kind of rictus that Lucrezia had seen before, in the faces of worn-out slaves used by Ereleth for the purposes of demonstration.

She went forward in step with the amber, aware that she had not the strength required to wield her weapon well, but knowing too that any blow she managed to strike would probably be deadly. The slave-drivers hadn't realised that she was the witch who had planned and orchestrated this slaughter, but that didn't matter at all.

No one turned a weapon on her, and none of the blows the three men aimed at Andris struck home with any real effect. He was already battered and bruised, and he took at least two more bruises, but he smashed his spear into two helmeted heads with more than sufficient force to drop the men like broken dolls. Lucrezia crippled the third with a blow to the knee before the amber finished him off.

They both looked round for other enemies in Serpent-skin, but there were none to be seen. Instead, she saw bronzes wearing the light clothing of the Community. They had no weapons but they were free. Venerina Sirelis had played her part, and had done what she had set out to do. It was all over.

Lucrezia was still standing upright, very defiantly, when Andris fell to his knees. All the strength had ebbed out of him, and his glazed eyes seemed to be staring through the world into some further infinity.

'We did it,' Lucrezia said, wincing as she let her defences down and the pain flooded back into her head.

'At times, my lady,' the amber whispered, as he looked up at her from beneath half-lowered eyelids, 'I wish that I had taken your father's generous offer of a lifetime's enslavement to the royal stonemasons. I know now the value of a safe and ordered life.'

Lucrezia sat down beside him, and put her throbbing head in her hands. 'But we did win,' she muttered, unsure as to which of them she was trying to convince. 'We paid them what we owed them, and the spoils are ours.'

She tried as hard as she could to sound like a true witch-princess, of whom Ereleth would have been mightily proud, but she was uncomfortably certain that she lacked the necessary conviction.

Andris felt utterly drained, and in no way adequate to the work that remained to be done. He was acutely aware that the prospect facing them now that they had won the fight was still exceedingly problematic, by virtue of the fact that it wasn't *the* fight at all, but only the first phase. Another and more difficult conflict was yet to take place.

He was now one of fifty rather than one of only five, and his side now had arms approximately equal in number and kind to those carried by the enemy they had still to face, but the next battle would be no mere formality. There could be no question of disarming the greater part of the second force with poison. The evidence of the first massacre could not be concealed; as soon as the second party came to within a hundred mets of the pool they would know that something terrible had happened. The stink would tell them that, even before they caught sight of a single corpse or splash of blood.

The fight he had just undertaken had been a mere matter of kill or die; however difficult it had been it had been perfectly simple. Now the air was as heavy with unanswered questions as it was with the foul odour of blood and spilled guts, and Andris felt those questions crowding in upon his weary mind.

'I'm sorry, Andris,' Lucrezia said, with genuine sympathy, 'but you have to get up. We still don't know for certain what manner of men or monsters the second company might contain, but we can be sure they'll be here before nightfall. We have to make haste.'

Andris was kneeling on the ground, with his buttocks resting on his ankles; even so, the angle at which he had to look up in order to meet her dark eyes was not steep.

'Haste will not be easy to make, my lady,' he said, 'unless you have witchery with which to breathe strength and skill into the prisoners. They never supped your poisoned water, but if appearances can be trusted they're terribly weak.' He looked around as he spoke; the truth of what he had said was unfortunately obvious. The people who had been captives of the men in Serpent-skin and their giant companions were delighted to have been released, but they were not in good condition. They needed rest and they needed food, but they would hardly have time to drink from the gourds that Venerina Sirelis was passing among them before she was urging them on to make preparations for the next crisis.

'The chance to exact vengeance puts strength into any heart,' Lucrezia told him, although he knew full well that she had learned the lesson from legends and romances rather than experience. 'With luck, we'll have a real fighting force by the time the hour arrives when we'll have to defend ourselves. In the meantime . . .'

She broke off as Venerina Sirelis approached them.

'Rayner's dead,' the older woman said unceremoniously. Her face and voice were drained of all emotion. 'The Serpent's hurt, but only slightly. Someone will have to climb, to take stock of what approaches.' Andris knew that by 'someone' she meant Lucrezia.

'I'm sorry,' Lucrezia said, presumably referring to Rayner. 'I'll go.'

Venerina didn't reply. The arithmetic of the case was simple enough: one life lost; more than forty saved – for the moment, at least. Even so, the loss of the boy was hard to take.

Andris was uneasily aware of the fact that they still had no idea what the prisoners had been saved from, let alone what they had been saved for. Venerina obviously intended to take them back across the wilderness of figured stones and into the marshes, to reclaim and repair their home, but that might not be easy to do if there were more marauders abroad between the Reef and the Soursweet Marshes – and there was a division of the spoils yet to be negotiated. If the second battle went as well as the first there would be wagons enough to be easily divided, but there would doubtless still be room for dispute over solid supplies. The water which they had removed from the pool before Lucrezia poured her poisons into it was by no means a huge stock – especially now that there were so many mouths to consume it. Andris presumed that the drinking water would be safe again eventually, but time was pressing and might not cease its pressure for a long while.

'You must make a careful count of the approaching company,' Venerina told the princess. 'We can't hope to surprise them as we did these, but with better numbers and better arms we ought to be able to set a different kind of ambush. God willing, we'll destroy them as utterly as we destroyed their fellows.'

Venerina didn't seem to care that any prisoners the second party had – assuming that they were indeed a second party of slavers – were unlikely to have come from the Community. It was hatred rather than fear that moved her now. Andris had always thought that deists were meek, and she had certainly seemed gentle enough before the marauders came, but she was all righteous wrath now.

'We might do better to run,' Andris pointed out, although he knew that the suggestion would not be welcome. 'They'll find trouble enough when they arrive to find their friends slaughtered and the pool poisoned.'

'Which way were you intending to run?' Venerina wanted to know.

'Eastwards,' Andris told her, knowing what her reaction would be. She had only one direction in mind, and that was north.

'They'd certainly chase us,' Lucrezia pointed out. 'The wagons can only make slow headway within the Reef, and the horses attached to the wagons are the only healthy beasts we have. Their horsemen could move much faster. We can't move out of the Reef to the north because we'd be in clear view, and the ground to the south looks treacherous, save only for the strip that looks like a road – which leads in the wrong direction.'

Andris frowned at her, but he understood why she felt committed to supporting Venerina Sirelis. He had no intention of making an argument out of it. When she saw that, she walked away in search of a suitable dendrite to climb. Her clothes were caked with blood but she didn't seem to notice, let alone care. His own were in a worse state, but there seemed little point in trying to do anything about it.

'I have to ready my people for a fight,' Venerina said flatly.

'The only choice to be made is where to take our stand. When it's over, we'll go home.'

The deists desired nothing save to be left in peace to continue their mysterious communion with the Spirit of the Lake; that was the whole of their reason for being. They were prepared to dare anything, and to risk everything, in order to secure themselves against further interference.

'If ever we have the time,' Andris said to her, 'you must explain to me exactly what it is that your God has supposedly revealed to you. Your attempt to have Him reveal it to me directly has gone awry. In the meantime, though, we need explanations of some simpler matters.'

'Ssifuss is already doing what he can in that regard,' Venerina told him. 'You left at least two of the monstrous Serpents crippled but conscious. I doubt that you'll be able to question any of the humans who drank of the poisoned water, but you might find a living man among those who arrived with the wagons. While I see to the prisoners you might as well investigate the possibility of conducting an interrogation – but remember that there's much to be done and little time in which to do it.'

Andris raised a weary hand in acknowledgement of these instructions, and lifted himself slowly to his feet. Surveying the scene of carnage from his full height, he realised that searching among the fallen for someone who could talk was going to be a horribly unpleasant task, but he consoled himself with the thought that Ssifuss was the one who had to try to get some sense out of the giant Serpents.

The last three men he had faced had all been slain, as had the one he had spitted on a lance. It didn't take him long, however, to find another who was not yet dead. To judge by the man's wounds he had little chance of recovery, but there was life enough left in him to permit a certain degree of leverage should he prove untalkative.

Andris hoped that it would not be necessary to descend to such crudities. Although many years had passed since he could properly consider himself a prince he still liked to think of himself as a fastidious man; he had never tortured anyone in his life.

He began by making the man as comfortable as possible and

91

fetching him water to drink. He also gave him time enough to study his surroundings, so as to understand the full horror of what had happened.

'The world is hostile enough by itself,' Andris said, 'without our making enemies of one another. As you can see, I'm a man of the far north who has travelled halfway across the known world in order to be here, and I've seen a great deal of fighting on the way. I've never yet seen any that wouldn't have been better left undone. My name is Andris Myrasol – will you tell me yours?'

The man looked up at him, an unfathomable expression on his face. He seemed to be a golden rather than a bronze, but his complexion was ruddier than any Andris had ever looked upon before, at least at this close range. His eyes were dark but his hair was a curious coppery colour.

'Circumstance alone has made us enemies,' Andris pointed out. 'I know nothing about you, nor you of me. There is no long-standing hatred between us, but you attacked the house whose owners had taken me in without warning and without reason. This is the outcome of your own strategy. I would like to know why. I don't say that you owe it to me to explain, but I would be very interested to learn. Who are you? Where have you come from? Where were you going, before you were interrupted by the backlash which your own actions provoked?'

The stricken man stared up into his face. His eyes were very dark – even darker than Lucrezia's – and it was impossible to read anything into their disconcerting stare. For a moment, Andris wondered whether he might be incapable of speech – whether, in fact, he might be a mere animal in human guise.

'Where were you going?' Andris repeated, in a harsher tone which implied that his patience was at an end, but there was no reply, nor even a flicker of understanding.

Andris was almost convinced that the golden could not understand him, and wondered whether there were humans in the world who knew no language save for that which was used by giant Serpents. To make certain, though, he reached out to touch the man's thigh, which had been savagely torn by a blunt blade.

'Tell me,' he said, trying to sound as menacing as he could.

The wounded man's resolve collapsed under the threat.

'Water,' he murmured, just loud enough to be heard.

Andris took a drink from the gourd he had brought, then held it out to the wounded man, but he would not release it when the man reached up. 'Where do you come from?' he demanded. 'Where were you going?'

The stare became bleaker still, the expression on the red-gold face more sullen. For a few seconds, he hesitated, but then he muttered a single word. The word was *garden*.

'A garden,' Andris echoed, moving the rim of the gourd to the thirsty lips. 'Do you mean the garden mentioned in the lore of Genesys? The garden of Idun?'

The wounded man drank before answering. Then he whispered a few more words. Andris was almost sure that they were *garden of poisons*. It was impossible to judge whether the man was really incapable of saying more, but he seemed to be on the point of lapsing into unconsciousness.

'*Where there was a city we shall make a garden,*' Andris quoted from the lore of Genesys, '*but it will be a garden of poisons. Do not forbid your descendants to visit this garden, but bid them beware of it .*. . Is that the garden you mean?'

The man inclined his head slightly; Andris took it for an attempted nod.

Tiredly, Andris went on. '*We have planted the garden of Idun so that the incorruptible stone might one day be born from the Pool of Life, nourished by milk and blood. When that day comes, your children's children must seize and use the stone, and turn the evil of corrosion to the good of inscription.* Even Serpents know about the garden, it seems – there is one with me now who set out reluctantly to search for it. Will the road beyond the Reef lead us to it?'

The man contrived a faint smile in response to that, as if to say: *Yes, but you'll follow it to your doom.*

Andris reached out to place a huge hand around the man's scrawny neck, but then thought better of it; a strangling hand was no aid to conversation. He moved the hand down until it hovered above a slit in the man's Serpent-skin tunic, above a gash in his belly. 'I could haul out your intestines inch by inch,' Andris pointed out. 'I could drape them all over that stony tree whose protruding roots I used to pillow your head. On the other hand, I could leave you what little comfort remains to you as your life drains away. I could leave you this water, to drink at your leisure. I am essentially a tender man, in spite of my great height, but I've been too badly battered and bruised by your Serpent friends to be overly scrupulous. If you want to be let alone, tell me what I want to know; if not, you might yet live for days, *and all of it in mortal agony.*'

The light which flickered briefly in the dark eyes was angry and resentful, but the man had too much sense to be a hero now.

'Garden needs flesh,' he muttered. 'Some seeds will only grow in *human* flesh. Need people.'

Andris knew that he ought not to be astonished, and that he really might have guessed this particular secret, but he was convulsed by surprise nevertheless, starting back in sudden revulsion. Water spilled out of the gourd, and the wounded man watched the droplets fall.

'I see,' Andris said, no longer needing to feign the menace that was in his deceptively soft tone. 'Perhaps you are acquainted with the bronzes who crossed the Dragomite Hills to trade deadly seeds in the Forest of Absolute Night. I suppose I ought to be pleased to find pieces of the puzzle falling into place at last – but *why* are you searching for living men to supply these homicidal seeds? Are you servants of the giant Serpents, or are they *your* instruments of terror?'

Again the man reached for the gourd; again Andris would not let him take it.

'All servants,' the man replied, his voice hissing between his bloodstained teeth. 'All serve, or feed the garden. All obey.'

'And who, exactly, are the masters you obey?' Andris demanded.

All the man could produce was a hissing sound. It was impossible to tell whether it was an unnaturally protracted and strangled S, or a word in the Serpents' language, or merely the air expressed from failing lungs. If the man was feigning his inability to answer he was doing a good job, but Andris wasn't about to let him get away with it. He gave the man another sip of water, and then placed his arm on the man's abdomen, ready to squeeze.

'No!' the man begged. 'Ssssalaaaa . . .'

'Salamander?' Andris guessed. 'You mean that your masters are *Salamanders*?'

There was no mistaking the urgent shake of the head; it was a clear denial. 'Ssa . . . man's *fie*', the broken voice contrived to say.

'Salamander's Fire?' Andris echoed. 'You surely can't mean the *place*? What do you mean, *Salamander's Fire*?' His own voice had a hint of anguish now. If Merel Zabio had survived the battle of the bridge, Salamander's Fire was where she would be headed for – where he and Lucrezia would be headed for, if they escaped their present predicament. He didn't want to hear ominous news of Salamander's Fire.

Again, though, the man was shaking his head violently. 'Not *place*,' he gasped. 'Thing *itself*.' He must have seen that Andris didn't understand, and must have feared the consequences of that misunderstanding, because he was quick to try again. '*Ground*,' he said. 'Earth. Fire. *Life*.'

Andris shook his head, and saw the other's dark eyes flare in terror. The bronze made one last attempt, but he could only manage an ambiguous syllable: '*Wooo* . . .' The syllable went on for some time before it drained away; the wounded man tried desperately to draw air back into his lungs, and screwed up his face as he realised that he could not do it.

'Womb,' said Andris, realising at last what the other was trying to say, and what it might mean. 'You're not human at all, are you? You're like the dragomite-women, born from some deep and soggy figured stone: a stone which can produce monstrous Serpents as easily as it produces counterfeit people. Giants, no less – with Salamander's fire burning in their hearts. And somewhere even deeper down . . . are there drones, too? Heads with brains inside . . . brains which have at least an inkling of what all this is about, even if you don't?'

He stopped, realising that the guesswork was running away with him and getting out of hand. He needed more information, not flights of fancy.

'Why?' he asked. 'Why grow the thorn-bushes at all? What use is the poison their flowers produce?'

The wounded man couldn't speak, but he contrived to shake his head while he tried to draw breath. Andris remembered something Jume Metra had said. *We are all of one mind.* The mound-queen had said the same, according to Lucrezia. The individual served the mysterious purpose of the whole, without

95

questioning, without even considering the possibility of questioning. Only the drone who had called him brother had spoken as an individual, and even the drone had done so mockingly.

'I need more,' Andris said, but he knew even as he said it that he wasn't going to get more. Either he had misjudged the extent of his informant's injuries, or these half-human folk were less robust than the members of the species they mimicked.

The man clad in Serpent-skin clothing had given up his fight to draw breath. He was dead.

'Never mind,' Andris muttered, speaking only to himself. 'There'll be more of you along in a matter of hours. Next time . . .'

'MAKE SURE YOU have a good supply of water,' Kasdeja advised Jacom before they left the strange forest of crystal and stone which encircled the lands surrounding the Navel of the World. 'These primitive creatures hold their supplies in pools which anyone may plunder, but the dwellers in the deep are more careful hoarders and their wells are hard to tap.'

'I've crossed the Dragomite Hills,' Jacom reminded the manticore, as he carefully filled his waterskin from the murky ditch that ran between two snaky figured stones, 'and I've been into the depths of a dragomite mound. I know a little about the kind of creature you're talking about.'

'You know a *little*,' the manticore agreed, 'but you'd best heed my warnings nevertheless.'

'I'd know a good deal more if you'd only condescend to tell me,' Jacom retorted, backing away from the stones whose mouths – although they had not moved perceptibly – seemed to be reaching out for his vulnerable hands. 'Perhaps even that wouldn't be enough, but I'd rather have the benefit of whatever preparation you can offer before I meet your masters. I might be more useful to them in consequence – perhaps more useful than you, given that I have hands and you have not.'

'Hands don't make masters,' Kasdeja replied. 'You've just seen proof of that. Killers have hands, the better to hold daggers with. You're a killer yourself, are you not?'

Jacom sighed as he climbed back into the saddle on the monster's back. 'Neither does a stern determination to keep secrets make a man into a master,' he riposted. 'I know a great many men in Xandria who think it does – loremasters and guildsmen, fortune-tellers and healers – but they're wrong. They believe that their particular lore makes them better than their fellows, and they hoard it like misers, sorely jealous of any item that might accidentally escape, but in every case the most jealously guarded secret of all is the vast extent of their ignorance.'

The manticore moved out of the shadow of the petrified forest, choosing his ground with care. The sun was still visible above the western horizon, but nightfall was close. They had rested for a while in the relative safety of the Reef, nursing their cuts and bruises, but the manticore still gave the impression that time was of the essence. There had been a sense of urgency even in his rest and recuperation; he had been gathering his strength for the final stage of their strange journey.

The darkening ground over which they passed seemed almost featureless by starlight save for deep fissures which crazed it. The manticore avoided these where practicable, although he was not averse to jumping their thinner extensions. This was more a corridor than a plain, though; fifty hundred mets to either side of their course the terrain was much more ragged. It reminded Jacom of the Dragomite Hills, but only because there were as many slopes and spires. This landscape would have to be melted down, its spires reduced to stumps and its sharp edges corroded to shapelessness, before there was any real resemblance. Even in the dimming evening light he could see that the slopes hereabouts were a riot of sculptured faces and well-cut facets: an infinite wilderness of broken statues and shattered glass.

'Are these cracks in the ground like the grooves etched into the figured stones?' Jacom asked his mount. 'Are they pitfalls and gin-traps set out to catch unwary passers-by?'

'There are few *unwary* passers-by in these lands,' Kasdeja told him. 'The cracks would certainly swallow up anything that came their way, but the dwellers in the deep aren't lazy predators relying on that kind of bounty for their nutrition. The crevices let in air and water, but they're also a kind of defence.'

The places where Kasdeja's huge paws fell seemed solid enough to Jacom, although he took it for granted that there would be more glutinous ground nearby which the manticore was careful to avoid. He tried to imagine what might lie beneath the surface, but he had only the single example of the dragomite mound to guide his speculations, and there did not seem to be any 'crops' growing on the surfaces of these vast structures, nor any workers to tend and harvest them. If there were monsters lurking in the depths – and he did not doubt for a moment that there were – they did not care to show themselves at present.

He could not help but think of the chamber where he and Andris Myrasol had seen walls plastered with an inchoate mass of human flesh, as if a dozen people had been spread like soft cheese on a slice of bread. He wondered whether that might be the fate awaiting him. The 'ground' which had spawned Kasdeja clearly had some reason for wanting visitors from outside – just as the princess and the queen had reasons for wanting to serve as visitors – but he could not begin to imagine what purpose could be fulfilled by any such meeting. He tried to take heart from Kasdeja's denial that these bulky cousins of the figured stones were not reliant for their nutrition on grinding up the travellers they trapped in their crannies and culverts.

'I could name men who'd think it an enormous privilege to take a ride like this,' Jacom said, for want of anything better to say. 'I only wish that I could trade places with one of them.'

'I dare say he'd be better company,' Kasdeja told him drily. 'Don't underestimate yourself – and don't terrify yourself by conjuring up unnecessary nightmares. Once we reach our destination you'll be safe from murderous attacks like those you've recently faced. What will happen to you thereafter I can't say for certain, but you'll be far safer there than you were where I picked you up. You should be grateful to me. I could have taken another in your place.'

'One human's much like another, I suppose,' Jacom said. 'The men who are trying to defend the Last Stronghold against all manner of brutal enemies may have bronze skins, and they may have lost more of the lore than we've managed to preserve in Xandria, but they're no different from the men of my homeland in any fundamental sense.'

'That might be true,' the manticore said, 'but you can't judge by appearances. Not everything which looks human *is* human, and no one knows how many kinds of human there are. Who knows what treasures might be lurking deep inside you, unsuspected even by you?'

'One of the men I could name who'd gladly take my place is Aulakh Phar,' Jacom said. 'He was ever inclined to explain anything and everything by reference to tiny creatures living inside us: bacteria, viruses and countless tiny worms which supposedly live in our blood and in our guts, in our bones and in our brains. He held them responsible for all disease and much of our well-being too. The lore is entirely on his side, I know, but how can anyone possibly know what lies beyond the power of the eye to see? To me, it all smacks of superstition.'

'You'll forgive me,' Kasdeja said, 'if I'm not inclined to trust the judgment of a man who didn't believe in manticores two days ago, when it comes to defining matters of superstition.'

Jacom did indeed forgive him that. In other matters, too, he was no longer inclined to trust his own judgment. The casual scepticism which had been so easy to maintain in the ordered world of his father's estates and the even more ordered environment of the Xandrian army did not seem so apt in a place like this. If the world itself had giants lurking beneath its skin, why should he not have creatures of a different kind beneath his own?

He wished that Aulakh Phar were with him now. He was sure that the old man could do a far better job of winkling information out of the evasive manticore. That was the least part of his reason for wishing it, though – the greater part by far was the desperate loneliness that seemed to be growing with every giant stride Kasdeja took into the gathering night. Jacom felt in dire need of the boost to his courage that familiar company would have provided. Merel Zabio might have been as useful as Phar on that score, perhaps even more so. Hyry Keshvara would have been more useful still, and the princess . . .

He checked himself there. To wish that the princess might be in this kind of predicament merely so that he might have the benefit of her company was surely a failure of duty, and he still wished to think of himself as a dutiful man. He had to cling to that, else what would be left of him but raw fear? While he could hang on to the notion of duty there was still an atom of heroism within him: a precious spark of glory that might yet carry him through his awful adventure.

The thought that he was being taken into the heartland of an alien wilderness where even the ground was unsafe to tread, without any plausible hope of ever getting out again, was hardly conducive to a keen awareness of duty but that wasn't the point. A sense of duty wasn't something that waxed and waned with shifting fortune; it was something a man had to maintain no matter what. If his situation favoured fear and bitter regret regarding all the things he had never done – not to mention those he had never attempted and never dared – that was all the more reason to use duty as a suit of armour, a foil against fate.

As the last rays of the blood-red sun seeped over the western horizon, showing through the jagged line made by the tops of the distant rim's tallest dendrites, the terrain over which the manticore was trotting seemed to become even more malign. The uncertain light of the flamestars exaggerated the unevenness of the ground, conferring an uncanny quality on all its meandering ridges and squat mounds. Dying sunlight limned the dark maw of every pit and fissure, emphasising the blackness of the shadowed depths within. Starlight had not the strength to reveal much colour, but Jacom could still see that there were many subtle shades of brown, green, silver and blue to either side of their course. He knew that the brown was not the healthy brown of a horse's coat, nor the green the healthy green of unripe wheat. The silver was not the gleam of freshly minted coin and the blue was certainly not the placid blue of the Xandrian sky. Everywhere he looked there was a frightful confusion of sinister hues, becoming ever more ominous as they faded – and not one of them could be reckoned comforting in its familiarity.

I mustn't think of it as a desert, Jacom advised himself, *nor even as the hide of some vast chimerical creature. There are many individuals here, although I can't tell how many they are or how large each one might be. They huddle together like dragomite queens, filling all available space and co-opting all available matter, in ceaseless competition with one another. They're greedy by nature, not merely for air and water and whatever nutrition fuels the fires of their alien life, but for other things. Some, at least, are greedy for human and other beings: for Serpents and Salamanders and giants. There are some such beings, it seems, which are very anxious indeed to indulge that greed, and others anxious to prevent them. Kasdeja calls it a war, but it is not the kind of nest-war which nearly swallowed me up before. I suspect that these dwellers in the deep are even more powerful and far more puzzling than dragomite queens.*

He remembered what Kasdeja had said about Salamanders delivering themselves to whatever fate awaited him, but he also had the legend of Princess Lucrezia's Serpent's blood in mind, and the strangely intense curiosity which drove Carus Fraxinus – and the Salamander's fire which Dhalla claimed to feel in her heart, quietly burning.

The fact that I seem to have none of these things, Jacom told himself, *need not necessarily mean that I lack any such secret; it might only mean that I have never learned to recognise or identify it, or that it is one which has no counterpart in consciousness. After all, Andris Myrasol thinks of himself as a perfectly ordinary man, although he clearly is not, and Hyry Keshvara doubtless thinks of herself as a perfectly ordinary woman, although it is easy to see that she is very exceptional indeed. And what of Checuti, that remarkable aggregation of paradoxes? Why did I tell the manticore that all humans are very much alike when I might equally well have said that they are all very, very different?*

The force of this argument was somewhat undermined by Jacom's awareness that other people had always thought him stupidly ordinary, and that his disagreement with the judgment had always lacked true conviction, but he insisted on following the train of thought regardless. It was, after all, he who had been chosen by the manticore as a man worth kidnapping to the borderlands of the Navel of the World. His capture might have been a matter of mere convenience, in that the attack on Amyas's caravan had left him alone and vulnerable, but if the manticore had not thought him worth taking the creature surely had the power and the ingenuity to have gone in pursuit of worthier prey.

Should I hope with all my heart that Merel and Aulakh Phar made it safely through to Salamander's Fire? he wondered. *Or is it permissible to hope that they too might have been captured by one of Kasdeja's brothers, so that we might be reunited to face adversity together? Would it be too wild a hope to wonder whether Andris Myrasol or Hyry Keshvara might have met a similar fate?*

The last thought provoked questions worth posing aloud. 'How many manticores were sent to scour the lands beyond the wheel's rim?' he asked Kasdeja. 'How many men like me will they bring back to their nesting ground?'

'I have a hundred brothers,' the manticore reported, tacitly inviting covert comparisons with the number of King Belin's wives and daughters, 'but many remained behind when some were sent forth. I might be sent out again and again while the time is right. There'll be other humans awaiting you when we reach our destination, and there might be more arriving in time. You'll not be alone.'

So I'm free to hope, Jacom concluded. *I'm free to keep on hoping that whatever befalls me, my friends might yet arrive. After all, Carus Fraxinus still had his wagon when I saw him last, and every intention of making his way to Chimera's Cradle by way of Salamander's Fire. In order to achieve that aim he'll have to pass this way himself, no more than a few kims to either side of our present course. I have a duty to him as well as to myself, if there's anything I can do to prepare the way for him.*

His brave reverie was interrupted by the sight of something looming up against the starry sky, which he could make out even though his light-adapted eyes had only just begun to make sense of the twilight's confusing shadows.

'What's that dark mass on the horizon?' he wanted to know. 'The one that's eclipsing the stars in the north-west?'

'It's a forest of sorts, made up of jutting stems tipped with silver,' Kasdeja told him. 'We call them Silver Thorns.'

Do we, indeed? Jacom thought, resisting the temptation to say: *So do we.* He remembered the words scribbled on Andris Myrasol's map. 'Is the Gauntlet of Gladness beyond them?' he asked lightly.

Kasdeja was unimpressed by his casualness. 'We'll leave the Gauntlet of Gladness to the use of those for whom it was intended,' he said. 'You might think it safe, and you'd doubtless find protectors waiting for you there, but we're heading for ground that's less treacherous by far. Whatever your lore might tell you, the Gauntlet is a road of no return. Your chances are better with me. Can you make out a conical form which lies some way to the south of the Thorns? That's where we're bound. The tip of its shadow should be discernible now.'

'Just about,' Jacom confessed.

'You'll see it more clearly when we're closer – that's just the top of it. Its lower slopes are gentler.'

Jacom observed that the silhouetted cone did not come to a

sharp point; it was flattened, as if it had been levelled off – or as if it had internal slopes as well as outer ones.

Perhaps it is the mouth that will swallow us up, Jacom thought. *Like one of these great cracks which we're avoiding as best we can: one more pitfall, no less dangerous for being borne aloft like the topmost entrance to a dragomite mound. But I have gone into such a mouth before, and willingly. I have the courage for it, if not the wisdom. I will go into it boldly, no matter what awaits me there.*

He was not entirely certain, however, whether it was the dutiful soldier in him that was speaking, or the humble fool.

13

HAVING SPENT SO many hours in the roof garden of the Inner Sanctum where King Belin kept his wives and daughters Lucrezia was not unused to heights. Nor was this the first time she had climbed one of the coppery dendrites. She was surprised to find, however, that the absence of poor Rayner made a considerable difference to the experience. The fading light was no help; although the setting sun still provided light enough to see it was not the all-revealing blaze of noon.

The feeling of isolation which came upon her as she made her way into the realm of slender branches and snake-like creepers was curiously disturbing. The lower-lying structures which made up the bulk of the Reef had acquired a hostile aspect, the fan-like growths having the appearance of undulating blades while the spikes protruding from globular formations seemed to be patiently awaiting the opportunity to impale her should she make a false step.

On the other hand, the horrid stench which could not be escaped at ground level could not extend its offensiveness to her present elevation, and it wasn't too difficult to find a vantage from which, even when she looked down, the vast majority of the corpses were hidden.

She saw immediately that the second company was now within three kims of the edge of the Reef. More leisured study assured her, however, that its progress was so slow that it probably would not arrive for more than an hour. She couldn't count the mounted men with absolute accuracy but she estimated that there were about thirty, plus a dozen giant Serpents afoot. The slight hope she had carefully nursed that the second company might not be of the same kind as the first was crushed by the sight of the monstrous Serpents. Like the first group, this one had three supply wagons – and like the first, it had a column of prisoners roped together. They too numbered at least thirty.

But we are more than forty strong now, she thought, trying to conserve a healthy measure of hope, *and we are armed as well as they are. If Venerina's people can fight as well as pray, and if we can choose the ground on which we fight, the giant Serpents might not prove too powerful an enemy . . .*

She paused as her scanning eye caught sight of something else: a movement on the horizon directly behind the approaching column.

'*That* we could well have done without,' she murmured aloud. 'Two slave-trains is more than adequate; three is a ridiculous superabundance.' She squinted hard, trying to make out more detail, but the moving objects were so far away as to be mere dots, and the ebbing of the light made it difficult to resolve any vestige of shape. It took her a full two minutes to obtain an impression of their number, size and speed, and even then she couldn't be sure that her judgment was sound.

She could see no wagons, and she was fairly confident that the more distant company consisted entirely of men on horseback, but what manner of men they might be she had no idea. They were certainly travelling faster than the company they were following, but it was obvious that they couldn't possibly catch up before the nearer group reached the Reef. The probability was that they would be two or three hours behind – but that might still be in plenty of time to get involved in the conflict, even if the battle were to commence as soon as possible. If the battle had been fought to an end, and if her own side had been victorious, the prospect of having to fight *again* was as absurd as it was intolerable.

Was it possible, she wondered, that the third company might be friends instead of enemies? Might they be chasing the slavers rather than following in their footsteps?

There was not time, alas, to get a clearer sight of them. Night was on its way. The third force could only be reckoned an unknown. She bit her lip in vexation. It was all too much: complication piled on complication, with no end in sight.

Lucrezia squinted as she scanned the rest of the horizon, from the north to the east to the south and finally to the west, but she didn't know whether to be relieved that she could see no other sign of movement on the ground. The eastern sky was dotted with what looked like little balloons, reflecting back the ruddy light of the sun which lay opposite them, but they were drifting northwards on a gentle breeze. To the far south there was a greyish ribbon, presumably made up of the tall growths which Andris Myrasol had taken for the Silver Thorns, but it was too far away to allow her to make out much detail.

The territory between the Reef and the grey ribbon looked uglier in this light than it had before. It was shadowed now, its broken slopes seeming even crazier. The huge dark tracts which mottled it refused to reflect the eerie awkward light, while the spiky growths and tinier stone-creatures reflected it all too well. From this height, and with the sun at this angle, most of the stony areas north of the Reef had a uniform sheen, as if they had been polished, but the things within the Reef had not. Its brighter parts were fragmented into countless fugitive glints and scintillations, while the deep fissures which ran hither and yon between them made it seem as if the earth had insufficient substance to fill the space allocated to it. The darker tracts seemed far more sinister, given the warnings Ssifuss had issued against all things soft and sticky.

The 'road' which she had noticed before cut the landscape cleanly in two although its route was winding. She couldn't see every one of its twists and turns but she was reasonably sure that it was continuous and unbroken. Given the nature of the landscape, it was easy to believe that nothing could be continuous without deliberate contrivance – but it was very difficult to believe that mere men could have made a road across such alien terrain.

She was on the point of descending, fearing that someone in the approaching company might catch sight of her, when she realised that the road-like ribbon was not unique. At the very limit of her vision away to the west there was a second winding lane, whose surface caught the rays of the setting sun like a thread of firelight.

She reasoned that if the Reef were indeed a great circle running all the way round the Navel of the World, then the two 'roads' might be reckoned drunken spokes of a vast wheel. If there were two, there might well be more. Was the enigmatic Gauntlet of Gladness one of them? Was it shown on the amber's map to indicate a safe passage through the Silver Thorns? If so, why were no others marked? Was it because no others were safe? Or was it because none had been evident in the long-gone days when the dendrite-rimmed wheel had been much smaller than it was now?

There were more important questions to address at this point, so she let those lie unanswered as she made her way down through the languidly curling branches to the stouter boughs, and then to the ground. Andris and Venerina were waiting anxiously for her report.

'The second company is not the last,' she told them. 'I suppose we might hope that they are being pursued by vengeful foes, but we certainly can't take it for granted. If that *were* the case, we'd be sensible to delay the business of fighting till the others arrive – but if not, we ought to make haste. We have no more than an hour to make up our minds.'

They both considered the possibilities. The expression of perplexity on Andris Myrasol's face testified to the difficulty he had in unravelling them. 'We're certainly due a change of luck,' he said. 'If these hive-men have been raiding in the Nine Towns they might well have invited pursuit from the remnants of Shabir's militia. It would be ironic, I suppose, to find ourselves united with such men against a common enemy – but we can't risk everything on the possibility that they might be allies rather than enemies.'

'It would be as great a risk to fall upon the newcomers as soon as they arrive,' Venerina said, with a sigh. 'My people are not fighters, and they've suffered a great deal during the trek across the plain. I wish I could say that they're ready for a battle, but they're not.'

'I wish I could say that I'm ready for a battle,' Andris said sourly, 'but there isn't a man in the world could keep on killing giant Serpents no matter how many came against him. How many are there?'

'Twelve,' Lucrezia said.

His only response was to shake his head sadly.

Venerina said nothing too, but it was obvious from her expression that she didn't think a second fight could be won if it were fought now. She hadn't asked Lucrezia whether the prisoners taken by the second party included members of the

Community, and Lucrezia wouldn't have been able to give her a certain answer, but they both knew that it was unlikely. Venerina's righteous wrath had subsided with the residue of excitement that the battle had left. Now, perhaps understandably, she was allowing herself to be tempted by the possibility of saving her own people and leaving the others to their fate. Shame made it impossible for her to voice any such suggestion in front of those who were not part of the Community and yet had made heroic efforts to save its people, but there was no doubt that her heroism had proved a perishable commodity. What Andris had told them about the fate which had awaited the captives made it more difficult still for Venerina to take back her commitment, but it was clear to Lucrezia that the released prisoners were not the only ones unready to fight.

'It's also conceivable that the third party might not have anything at all to do with the people they're following,' Lucrezia observed thoughtfully. 'They might be other men in search of Mossassor's fabled garden, or other witch-folk possessed of Serpent's blood.'

'This is typical, isn't it?' the amber complained. 'Every incident that happens only adds to our confusion; every item of information that we learn only adds to the mystery.'

'At least we know that we've nothing to lose by fighting the men in Serpent-skin to the death,' Lucrezia said. 'Unless, of course, you'd deem it poetic justice were I to be captured and fed one of those seeds I once intended to feed to you.'

'I wouldn't,' he replied flatly.

'Did you find out anything more from the other survivors?' Lucrezia asked. 'Did Ssifuss get anything out of the giant Serpents?'

'Nothing,' the amber admitted. 'A handful of the false humans are still alive, crippled by the poison they drank, but we dare not let them live any longer. By the time they can answer questions they'll also be ready to fight again, and we can't risk their friends releasing them in exactly the same way that Venerina released their captives. Ssifuss seems to have got no replies at all from his wounded cousins, and he still isn't sure whether or not they were capable of speech.'

'This isn't helping,' Venerina said. 'We have less than an hour to take our position. We need to decide.'

But how many of us get to vote? Lucrezia wondered. *And how do we settle any disagreement?*

'We need to intercept them before they get to the waterhole,' Lucrezia said. 'It's the only chance we'll have to take them by surprise.' As soon as she voiced the opinion, however, she could see that it would not prevail.

'We can't,' said Venerina flatly. 'There's not enough ground. Even if they send no scouts ahead of them, we'd have to attack the head of the column while the rear wasn't even in the Reef. In any case, we need more time to gather our strength. The water's still dangerous – and even if it weren't they'd not trust it. We have to withdraw, and use the wagons to build a defence. Let them come to us, if they will.'

If they will! Lucrezia thought. *She hopes they won't. She wants to give them the chance to pass by, so that she can take her people home. Except, of course, that there's a third company yet to come.*

'*Is* there enough ground?' she asked Andris.

He shook his head. 'The stink is drifting in the air,' he said. 'I doubt that we could fall upon them before they took alarm even if we had the strength to do it. We're still the weaker force, highness. I've been watching the liberated prisoners – they've hardly strength to loot the battlefield, let alone fight a war. Venerina's right – for the time being, we have to withdraw. If that means the enemy redouble their strength, so be it. It's a risk we have to take.'

Lucrezia knew that Andris was no coward, and that he would have no sympathy for Venerina's sudden loss of heart even if he understood its cause. If he said there was no alternative, that was exactly what he meant.

'Where do we build our defence?' she asked.

'My people have found a place,' Venerina told her. 'It's not far away but it's far enough; we have time to get the wagons there, and there's a route which isn't too difficult. By the time they're ready to come at us, we'll have a virtual fortress to defend.'

Lucrezia met the amber's eyes again, questioningly. He looked back, not happily but without the least hint of intimidation.

'Ssifuss says the same,' Andris said. 'He's gathering his arrows, and anything else he can find.'

'All right,' she said. 'If it's settled, it's settled.'

Venerina immediately turned away and started issuing orders to the liberated prisoners. Andris stayed where he was.

'Do you remember what Philemon Taub told you?' he said.

'He told me that I mustn't follow the urging of my Serpent's blood,' she said, knowing immediately what the amber meant. 'He told me that if I did, it would cost me my life. But as I understand it, the garden these creatures were headed for isn't the forefathers' Idun – it's part of the poisoned ground neighbouring Idun that's mentioned in the lore. Philemon was warning me about unspecified dangers, and now we know what some of those dangers are, but none of that affects the essence of our mission.'

'*The essence of our mission?*' Andris repeated incredulously. She had to admit, when she heard it spoken in that kind of tone, that it sounded ridiculous as well as pompous.

'There isn't time for this, Andris,' she said. 'When we know whether we're going to live or die there might be time, but there isn't now.'

'But I think I'm beginning to understand,' he complained. 'I think I know what this is all about.'

You don't even have the words you'd need to think about it, she retorted, but had the sense to do so silently. *Aulakh Phar might be able to understand, or Ereleth, but you and I can't.* Aloud, she said: 'That's good. Let's hope that you and your understanding survive the night. For now, let's get these wagons loaded and on the move. If we're not going to prepare a hot welcome for the enemy, let's at least make sure that we're out of the way when they realise what happened to their predecessors.'

14

IT MIGHT HAVE been better, Andris thought, had the night been cloudy. It was always easier to lie low in deep darkness, when searchers would be compelled to use lanterns.

The taller entities which formed the thicket of the Reef cast eerie starshadows in every direction as they interrupted the light of the flamestars, but when the whole sky was alight from horizon to horizon nothing could stop its frail but insistent luminosity creeping into every covert and cranny. He knew that he was probably far less easily visible than he felt, but still he felt exposed – a lumpish target waiting for the whirr of an arrow or the thud of a javelin.

The scouts sent out by Venerina Sirelis had found an adequate location for the wagons they had appropriated, although it had required heroic efforts from everyone concerned to plot a viable route through the Reef and then to move the carts through the narrow gaps between the stony outcrops. They had been able to place the three as sides of a square whose fourth element was supplied by an unusually large and solid coralline fan. The ground before the mighty fan had been virtually clear for twenty mets or so, save for a mazy array of shallow ridges whose more ominous crevices they had carefully filled in with litter, cemented with stonemason's yeasts discovered in one of the wagons.

The square formed by the wagons filled in slightly more than half the clearing, but there was clear ground around them and clear air above them; there was no way that attackers could come at them from above. Andris had stationed himself in the lower branches of the nearest dendrite so that he could keep watch on the likely routes by which men or monsters might approach from the direction of the poisoned pool.

By now, he knew, the second column must have established

their camp, presumably not far from the pool. He tried to imagine what their reaction might have been to the discovery that the area was littered with fresh corpses. Their first thought, of course, would be that their counterparts must have been overwhelmed by a larger and much stronger force. Unless they were utter fools, however, they would pause to wonder whether the water of the pool could be trusted, and would surely make tests before drinking deeply. Exactly what those tests would tell them Andris wasn't sure. It was possible that the water, if sufficiently stirred, would be drinkable again by now.

Once they had discovered that the water had been drugged, the newcomers would know that low cunning had made a considerable contribution to the massacre of their allies – but they would still suspect that their enemies might have been numerous even before their ranks were swelled with liberated prisoners. Provided that they had the same sense of discretion as true humans, they ought not to be thinking in terms of aggression and revenge. They ought, in fact, to be making fearful plans for their own defence – plans which would be more fearful still if they knew that they were being followed in their turn . . . unless, of course, they knew for sure that the followers were friends.

Unfortunately, as Andris was only too well aware, the men clad in Serpent-skin were *not* true humans, so there could be no certainty in his estimation of their likely attitudes. Nor had he any clearer idea now than Lucrezia had had when she made her report as to the identity of their pursuers.

Andris felt in desperate need of a long night's rest, and he clung to the hope that the newcomers might at least wait for daylight before taking any action. Bright as the starlight was, it was still mere starlight, and the floor of the Reef was as full of shadows as any maze of back streets in any city he had ever visited. Even people who hated the glare of noon, and were in the habit of snatching no more than two or three hours' sleep in the midnight so that they could enjoy the tenderness of starlight to the full, knew that shadowed places could be direly dangerous.

The muted sound of voices that filtered up to his ears from below told him that Venerina Sirelis was deep in conversation with her sentries. He hoped that she was educating them in the arts of battle rather than the politics of retreat, but he would have preferred it had they kept silence. Although the Reef was by no means quiet by night, being inhabited by various kinds of chirping and croaking creatures, the racket they made was not the kind which could obliterate the distinctive timbre of human voices. The Reef was abundantly equipped with natural baffles which interrupted the passage of sound, but the wagons were no more than half a kim away from the pool. The possibility of voices being overheard by a roving scout was yet another which they had to minimise as best they could.

Andris, who had been a lone wanderer for half a lifetime, was reasonably adept at the business of self-distraction and self-amusement. He had plenty of things to think about, including the slowly gathering theories which he had tried unsuccessfully to confide to Lucrezia as the sun set. He felt, however, that he required a rest from that kind of brainwork almost as urgently as he required a rest from the ceaseless toil of fight and flight, so he took refuge in reflections of a more relaxing kind. He imagined a conversation between himself and his cousin.

Where shall we go when this is all over? he asked her. *Now that we have seen and understood so much of the world, we ought to be able to select the kind of place in which we'd be content to settle down.*

He didn't doubt for a moment that Merel would want to settle down. She might not have grown as tired of the nomadic life as he had, but she was a woman – and, he thought, a far more *womanly* woman, in spite of the fact that she was no great beauty, than Hyry Keshvara or Princess Lucrezia.

Xandria's my homeland, she replied, *and it has the considerable advantage of being the most civilised place in the world. The city itself isn't a comfortable place to be, and it's not a good place to be poor, but there are coastal towns along the southern shore of the Slithery Sea which are very pleasant indeed. Honest coin can be earned there, even by men whose lack of useful lore is only compensated by brutish strength.*

You'd make a labourer of me, would you? he said teasingly. *Perhaps I'd be better as a sailor on a trading ship, taking long and leisurely voyages through the Thousand Isles. The pay would be mediocre, but I could have a girl in every port.*

Golden girls aren't so fond of ambers, she told him. *They think of them as darkland barbarians. The girls of the Thousand*

Isles don't dream of great hulking creatures like you – they prefer slim and clever goldens who have useful lore and witty tongues. If you told them you were a mapmaker they'd laugh, and think you a fool or a charlatan. You're an acquired taste, Prince Myrasol, and I'm the only one who has so far acquired you. Better be grateful for that.

Oh, I would, he assured her, unable to prevent himself from adding: *If only I were sure that you're still alive.*

I could say the same about you, she replied, *but I have every confidence in that. You're a hero now, for sure, and heroes always win through their trials and tribulations to reclaim their chosen mates. All the best stories reach that kind of ending.*

In a story, Andris pointed out, *the teller always has absolute power. Even if the story is an old one that's been handed down from generation to generation since the days of the ship that sailed the dark between the stars, the teller is still in control. All that needs to be done to make sure that it works out properly is for the teller to say so. If it needs a miracle to make it happen, the teller only has to say 'and then there was a miracle'. Such power, like any other power, corrupts its users and its instruments alike. Tellers become increasingly unscrupulous, hearers become ever more demanding in their expectations. Real life isn't like that. When a man gets a blade in his guts or poison in his belly it does him no good to look up at the sky and say, 'I'm a hero, where's my miracle?' That's what's wrong with Venerina's way of interpreting the scheme of things, you see – having glimpsed a greater pattern she construes it as a kind of tale and feels compelled to invent a teller with both the power and the intention to make it come out right, but that's not the way things are. It wouldn't be like that even if there were a tale, and a teller to shape its end. If the world were a tale, it'd be an enigmatic and deceptive one, and if the tale had a teller, he'd just be some ancient blind man reciting something he learned by rote in his distant youth, without any understanding at all.*

I think you're contradicting yourself, Merel observed, in the irritating way she sometimes had when she felt compelled to bring him down to earth from some uncontrolled flight of fancy, *and even if you aren't, you seem to have forgotten that all this is just a tale whose teller is you. I'm not really here at all.*

I know, he said. *That's the trouble, you see. I can conjure you up with no effort at all, and while you're here you'll say anything and everything I want to hear – but as soon as I stop telling myself the story, it's back to the stress and the strife of the struggle for survival.*

And the awful allure of alliteration, she observed, although the real Merel would never have said any such thing and probably wouldn't have known what alliteration was. It was more the kind of remark that Lucrezia would have made.

Andris put a stop to the reverie at that point, wishing that it hadn't left a slightly sour taste in his mouth.

He saw movement in the distance, and pressed himself to the branch on which he was lying, trying to make himself less conspicuous. The shadows of the higher branches would make it very difficult for any observer to pick him out – especially given that so many of the other branches were home to parasitic hangers-on – but his sheer bulk might attract suspicion.

The creature which had moved was also trying to be inconspicuous, clinging to the darker shadows and moving with circumspection, but it had even less advantages in that regard than he. While he had only to remain still, the other was on the prowl – and while he was only half a giant, the other had a very full stature indeed.

Andris watched as the giant Serpent came closer and closer. Its approach was slow and hesitant, interrupted by many wary pauses, but by luck or judgment it maintained a course that would inevitably bring it into confrontation with the wagons.

Andris didn't waste time wishing that he had a bow and a quiver of poisoned arrows. He had already seen the limited effect such darts had on creatures like this, and he knew that a single scream of terror or alarm would be enough to tell the men and monsters by the pool that there were enemies in this direction, not very far away. Had the scout been human Andris would have started making hopeful plans for his quiet interception, but a creature like this could not be stifled by a big amber hand about the throat. Although he had killed more of these monsters in a few days than any responsible tale-teller would have imagined credible, Andris had no delusions about his ability to tackle this one.

The creature paused again, thirty mets away. It was still clinging to the shadow of one of the smaller and more convoluted dendrites. The sound of whispered voices was still reaching Andris's ears, but the Serpent probably couldn't hear them. On the other hand, from where it was standing it could almost certainly see the canopy of one of the wagons.

Andris waited to see what the monster would do, not knowing whether to hope that it would come further forward – thus endangering itself as well as him – or that it would turn back, contenting itself with the duty of carrying the news that an unknown enemy of unknown strength was camped here.

The Serpent seemed to be in just as much doubt. It took a couple of hesitant steps forward, its beady eyes gleaming as they caught a glimmer of starlight, and then stepped back again. Andris could not tell whether he had been seen or not.

Seconds went by while the Serpent considered the situation. Andris held his breath for a while but had to let the air out of his lungs before the giant moved again. When it did, it was to move forward, and Andris got ready to jump down, convinced that he would have to rouse his companions for a fight. The Serpent had only taken three tentative steps, however, before the sound of a drum cut through all the slighter sounds of the skeletal forest.

Three beats were followed by two, and then the whole was repeated. It must have been a recall signal, because it stopped the giant Serpent in its tracks, and immediately caused it to turn back. It retreated with far greater alacrity than it had shown in advancing, and Andris judged that the creature must have been every bit as relieved to hear the summons as he was.

As soon as it was gone, Andris made his descent. He looked towards the wagon where Venerina Sirelis was waiting, but after a moment's hesitation he swung himself into the wagon where Lucrezia and Ssifuss were supposed to be asleep. He was not surprised to find that they had not, in fact, laid their heads upon their pillows. They reacted to his arrival with urgent alarm.

'It's only me,' he reassured them. 'They know where we are. They can't know how few we are, or whether we're all gathered here, but we've been spotted. The question is, what will they do about it – and when?'

'They don't seem to be the kind of people who send out messengers and negotiators,' Lucrezia said. 'I think they'll send more scouts to figure out our numbers, and then try to surround us. Maybe we should make our move now.' He could tell that she wasn't sure what *our move* might or ought to mean; the uncertainty was evident in her voice.

'There's nowhere to run to and we haven't the numbers required to surround *them*,' Andris reminded her. 'If they want to come at us, we'll have to let them come, in their own time.'

'Iss right,' Ssifuss agreed. 'Iss nossing elsse to do.'

'They *will* come,' Lucrezia said grimly. 'No matter how they weigh up the dangers, they're going to figure that they don't have any alternative either.'

Andris knew that she was probably right; having sent out scouts to hunt for them, and having found them, the raiders would surely decide that they had to take the risk of attacking – but when?

'I'd better spread the word,' he said, making every effort to keep his tone neutral. 'We may not have much time.'

The expression in Lucrezia's eyes seemed to say: *When will it end?* He hoped that the expression in his own didn't seem to say: *When we're dead.*

15

'YOU'RE SAFE NOW,' Kasdeja told Jacom. 'From now on, you can walk. Get that saddle off my back and throw it away. Carry what you can and leave the rest.'

There wasn't much left to throw away. They'd eaten the last of the food and there was hardly enough water in the skin to wet his lips. Jacom took the saddle off the manticore's back, figuring that he was probably as glad to see the last of it as Kasdeja must be.

It seemed to Jacom that 'climb' might have been a more apt description of what lay ahead of him than 'walk', but the slope which lay before them wasn't nearly as sheer as the precipitous sides of a dragomite mound. As he tried to measure the height of the hill he judged that any difficulties he encountered would be caused by its smoothness rather than its steepness.

They had already ascended to an elevation some fifty or sixty mets clear of the level of the plain. Jacom had a better view of it from here than he had had from the Reef or from his seat on the manticore's back. Although the early part of the night had been clear the after-midnight sky was steadily filling up with dense grey cloud. The light wasn't gone yet but it was very poor.

The dullness of the darkening night seemed to de-emphasise the sullenness and the awkwardly fragmented nature of the terrain. The cracks and fissures didn't seem so obvious now, and the subtle differences in texture between the solid ground and the more glutinous patches were harder to make out. Had he not known about its chaotic colouring Jacom might have thought it hospitable enough.

To his surprise, he caught sight of something moving in the distance – several somethings, in fact. They must have been animals of some considerable size, bigger than the manticore and by no means as nimble. They were the first living creatures bigger than a dammer that he had glimpsed since the manticore had chased away the dagger-wielding reptiles. Whatever the creatures were, they were moving towards the Reef.

'Big brothers of yours?' he asked, pointing out the moving shadows.

'No kin of mine,' the manticore replied. 'That's hostile ground. The war's dangerously close in that direction.'

When they had crested a ridge not long after sunset Jacom had made out a strange line which ran almost straight across the landscape. Although it was impossible to be sure, it seemed to him that the creatures must be following that line.

'Was that a *road* I saw over there while the stars were still bright?' he asked incredulously. 'Are they following it to the hub of the wheel?'

'You might call it a road,' Kasdeja told him laconically. 'Not built by men, of course, nor the labour of any other hands. Think of it as a great crumpled spike, if you will, or a unicorn's horn: something hard and inert, driven through the great morass to provide a conduit for emissaries less clever than myself. My own ground has no need to waste energy or materials in the construction of such highways, but Chimera's Cradle has long extended the Gauntlet of Gladness and others have followed the example.' Now that its destination was at hand the creature seemed far more willing to talk.

'Is *that* what the Gauntlet of Gladness is? A spiny conduit through the Silver Thorns, extended by the creature whose navel lies in the Nest of the Phoenix?'

'Your mapmakers must take responsibility for their own names,' the manticore answered.

And for their faith in the power of the garden their forefathers built to maintain the geography they described, Jacom added, for his own benefit. *If there is still a navigable route through the Silver Thorns, it can't be maintained without cost. No safe passage could be maintained in land like this, where the very rocks are alive, without determined effort.*

Aloud, he said: 'What names do *you* attach to such things?'

'I've heard it called a pseudopod,' the manticore admitted, 'but that's just another label, invented for convenience.'

'By whom?' Jacom wanted to know.

'You'll find out soon enough,' Kasdeja countered, reverting to type – but then, as if by way of apology, he went on. 'As I say, the entity you call Chimera's Cradle extends more than one of them along ridges of dead ground where conflicts are deadlocked and its adversaries have claimed others – but no one who sets out to travel any such road can be certain of reaching his destination. It's safer by far to ride a manticore, I can assure you of that.'

'I'm tired of being grateful,' Jacom told the creature. 'I didn't ask to be brought here.'

'You have hopeful friends following in your wake,' Kasdeja reminded him. 'If they believe that all they need to do is follow the map you described to me, they'll be unpleasantly surprised. Nothing is constant here but change, and every ground is treacherous. What your lore calls Salamander's fire can illuminate – but it can also burn.'

'Very poetic,' Jacom remarked, knowing that he must sound churlish.

'Don't be afraid,' Kasdeja said, his voice remaining light in spite of Jacom's rudeness. 'I dare say that you're safer now than any man within forty days' ride . . . perhaps safer than any others in the world.'

'So you say,' Jacom countered.

'I do,' the manticore retorted. 'It's the truth, as far as I can judge it.'

If I were to make any effort to defy the fate to which he is bent on delivering me, Jacom thought, *I would have to make it now. But have I any other choice except death? Are there really fates far worse than that – and if there are, was what I saw in the dragomite mound an instance of one?*

The hesitation was pointless; he had no reasonable alternative but to keep going and to find out. He began to walk up the slope, doing his best to match strides with the manticore.

The surface of the conical hill was not at all like that of a dragomite mound stripped of its fungal crops. Those denuded mounds had reminded him of great heaps of birdshit dried and hardened by the sun – an impression much enhanced by the stink of rot which lingered in every narrow valley, immune to any but the fiercest wind. This hillside seemed more like a heap of freshly gathered fruit which had contrived to fuse into a single mass of flesh with a uniform rind. The texture of the 'rind' reminded him of an orange, although the colour was wrong; it was wrinkled in much the same way, but slightly polished, so that any advantage which the unevenness gave to climbers was cancelled out by slickness.

The rain began to fall before they were more than halfway to the flattened rim above them, which Jacom estimated to be sheltering a crater no more than a few hundred mets in diameter. There was no sign of lightning – for which he was glad, given that he seemed to be nearing the highest point for many kims – but the rain fell steadily and forcefully, soaking him to the skin within minutes. The uniform which Amyas had given him at the inn south of Antiar was threadbare now, hardly more than a patchwork of rags and tatters, and it became even less shapely as the rain plastered it to his skin.

There was no point in asking Kasdeja whether it might be worth seeking shelter until the rain slackened; unlike a dragomite mound this hill had no multitude of tunnels offering entry to its labyrinthine interior.

The rainwater made the slick surface more slippery than before, but Jacom wasn't greatly afraid that a fall would do him irreparable harm; he was sure that the slope was gentle enough not to send him rolling all the way down to the quicksands which formed a kind of moat around it.

'Why is there a single entrance, set so high?' Jacom asked his companion. 'If the body of this unimaginably vast creature lies mostly underground, surely it could provide portals at the foot of the slope – portals that could be opened and closed at will if permanent entrances would expose it to the danger of invasion.'

'Could you open extra mouths in your belly or the soles of your feet, if you happened to think it convenient?' Kasdeja asked, but it was not an honest argument and Jacom knew it. He was not the kind of being which could absorb others into its flesh, nor the kind which could give birth to all manner of fleshy chimeras, nor the kind which could extend 'pseudopods' for many kims across the barriers of dead rock which separated one earth-giant from another. He let the matter lie, though – the rain had dampened his enthusiasm for that kind of combative probing.

He stumbled, but was quick to extend his hands to interrupt the fall. He managed to cling to his position even though his boots lost their immediate purchase. Ten steps later he slipped again, and this time he did slide back a couple of mets, taking some skin off the heel of his left hand and the front of his right knee. Kasdeja seemed to be ready to leap after him and extend a helpful paw, but having seen what the unfurled claws mounted on those huge hairy pads could do Jacom was not in any hurry to accept such aid.

The weather had been so hot for several days that he had looked forward to the possibility of rain, thinking that an interval of cool wetness might be very welcome, but he was soon heartily sick of having his clothing cling so soggily to his torso. The chill which the cool rain imparted to his flesh never felt comfortable, immediately becoming one more irritation. There was no alternative but to go grimly on and on, trying to reach the rim of the hill as soon as possible.

As his body seemed to grow heavier Jacom's steps shortened, and he continued to lose ground by small slips. His objective seemed to be no nearer when he peeped upwards from beneath his sodden eyebrows, but Kasdeja gave no sign of impatience.

Eventually, Jacom felt that he could go no further, although the rim was now no more than three hundred mets away. He sat down, clasping his hands about his bowed head.

Kasdeja didn't complain. Indeed, he took the trouble to squat down in his sphinx-like fashion upslope of Jacom, providing a certain amount of shelter from the water coursing down the smooth hillside.

Visibility was very poor now because of the rain which filled the air above the cracked plain, and although it was probably an optical illusion it seemed to Jacom that the flat underside of the cloud-layer was much closer to him than it was to the land from which they had climbed. That terrain now seemed almost as featureless as the black cloud; the Silver Thorns were lost in the murk, the straight 'road' and its shadowed travellers completely hidden. The fissures which streaked the surface seemed to have drawn in upon themselves – as, perhaps, they had.

'I'd far rather it had rained while we were down there,' Jacom remarked, 'and that the sun had saved itself for the climb. The slope would be easier if it were drier, and from way up here we might be able to see all the way to the rim.'

'If the sun were blazing,' Kasdeja opined, 'you'd be complaining of dehydration – and there's nothing much to see out there, even on the clearest day.'

'From the top,' Jacom said, the thought occurring to him for the first time, 'I'd be able to look the other way. I'd be able to see into the Nest of the Phoenix. I'd be able to see Chimera's Cradle: the garden of Idun and the Pool of Life itself!'

'You still might, if the clouds allow enough starlight through,' Kasdeja told him. 'Most of what you might want to see is concealed even in the brightest light, but you'll have other chances to look out in that direction if you want to. You'll even have companions who can explain what you can see better than I. For now, the object is to get to the top and descend again. As soon as you feel rested, we must go on.'

Jacom removed his protective hands and tilted his head back, letting the rain wash his face and fill his mouth. He had often been thirsty these last few days, and had always had to be careful to conserve what water they had; the present superabundance seemed somehow insulting – as if fate and the world were mocking him.

I've beaten them all, he said to himself, determined to mock a little in his turn. *I've beaten Carus Fraxinus and Aulakh Phar, Hyry Keshvara and Princess Lucrezia. Maybe I haven't reached Chimera's Cradle, but I'll be able to look into it. I've achieved the almost-impossible while they're still strung out between the war's rim and Salamander's Fire, if they're alive at all. They reckoned me among the least of the members of their expedition – a mere hired sword – but I've ridden and supped with a manticore, and I've climbed a hill which stands on the threshold of the Navel of the World. What would Lucrezia think of me now, if she knew that I had done all that?*

He had to frame the last sentence carefully, in order to avoid the phrase 'if she could see me now'. He was well aware that he must be a sadly bedraggled figure, in spite of all his undeniable achievements.

'I'm rested,' he said to his protector. 'Let's go.'

This time, he was content to follow the manticore, and Kasdeja was content to let him, glancing back every now and then to make sure that he was still there. Jacom put one foot in front of the other with stubborn determination, and every time he stumbled or slipped he got back to his feet again, ignoring the blood that now flowed sluggishly from the heels of both his hands, and the sharp pain of the bruises on his knees.

He simply kept going, until he reached the top. By then, the sky was beginning to clear again. The storm was over and the starlight was getting brighter by the minute. From where he stood he could see almost nothing of what lay beyond the further rim of the crater – but that didn't matter, for the moment. The first item of curiosity which needed to be settled was what lay within the crater.

He had half expected a funnel of some kind, narrowing to a central pit, but in fact there was a fairly abrupt downslope of no more than twelve or fifteen mets, and then a miniature plain covered in dense vegetation whose nearer reaches resembled a thicket of tall but silky reeds. There was no sign of any entrance to the interior of the hill, although the thicket might have hidden half a hundred. Beyond the reeds he could see what looked like the crowns of earthly trees, and between the trees he could see conical structures that might have been the roofs of circular huts – or stony domes like those he had occasionally seen on the plain below.

'I want to walk around the rim,' Jacom told Kasdeja. 'Before we go down, I want to walk to the far side and look out towards the Navel of the World.'

Kasdeja must have been expecting the demand. 'If you still have the strength,' he said. 'Lead, and I'll follow. Be careful you don't slip – the heads of those reeds are thorny.'

Jacom had stood on the highest sentry-stations of the citadel of Xandria, looking out over the Slithery Sea or the southern fields, thinking himself on top of the world. At another time, he had stood at the foot of the giant trees of the Forest of Absolute Night – which grew somewhat taller than the walls of the citadel – and had thought the top of the world unreachable. Now he was higher up than the tallest trees of the forest, with the starlit and cloud-strewn sky almost close enough to touch, or so it seemed.

As he set off along the narrow pathway which comprised the crater's rim, he felt that he was on a tightrope suspended above the dark entirety of creation. He felt that he was about to look into the heart of Genesys itself, still beating despite being beset

125

by a host of stony predators eager to consume its flesh. The fact that it was night and not day, and befuddled night at that, could not obliterate the worth of that achievement.

Whatever happens later, he told himself, *no one can take away this moment of success – not even the mighty King Belin, who sent me to this exile. However far I fall, I've been to the top of the world.*

16

LUCREZIA CROUCHED DOWN so that she could peer through the narrow gap she had opened between the wooden side of the wagon and the canvas awning which covered its cargo. Her position was awkward, requiring her to hold her muscles tautly, but she dared not relax lest tiredness should get the better of her. She knew that the alarm would be raised immediately once their enemies were sighted but she didn't want to wake up into a battle. She could have stayed awake without keeping watch on the Reef, but while her eyes were open she couldn't bear to direct her gaze anywhere else.

The light was poor because the southern half of the sky was filled with lowering cloud, but the northern half was still bright. She knew that it must be raining at Chimera's Cradle, but there was no noticeable wind to blow the rainclouds this way and no immediate prospect of losing the light entirely.

There were six others in the wagon with her, all of them ex-prisoners of the giant Serpents and their not-quite-human companions. They had been fed from the rations stored in the wagons and given unpolluted water to drink but they could hardly be described as fighting fit. They had been marched across difficult terrain for several days and they all had very sore feet. Some of them had suffered so many minor injuries that they could hardly lift a spear, and they were all close to exhaustion. They were, however, more than willing to fight. They had no wish to be captured again, and they were enthusiastic to exact a measure of revenge against creatures of the kinds that had subjected them to their ordeal. Venerina had told them what Andris and Ssifuss had learned from the adversaries they had interrogated about the fate to which they were being delivered.

The man who was stationed next to Lucrezia had seen Andris Myrasol kill one of the giant Serpents while making his escape from the Community's beleaguered house. He was taking what heart he could from this memory.

'If they come,' he whispered to her, 'they'll be as tired as we are. Not as footsore, perhaps, but thirstier. Their weapons are no better than these, and they can't have any great advantage in numbers.'

Lucrezia knew that he was trying to reassure himself and his companions, so she took care to agree with his estimation, but she didn't attempt to draw the conversation out. She and he both knew that when the enemy attacked, the giant Serpents would be the biggest problem. It was one thing for Ssifuss and Andris to shoot and stab them while they were befuddled, or for Andris to tackle them one or two at a time in the confusion of a mêlée, but this was different. This time, their enemies had all the time in the world to position their available forces and plan the attack.

How much difference that would make she couldn't tell, but she was already regretting the decision to delay matters rather than laying an ambush and settling the matter as soon as possible.

Vigilant though she was, it wasn't Lucrezia who caught sight of the first sign that the attack was beginning; someone further along the line whispered: 'Look to the right!'

At first, she saw nothing, but then she caught a fugitive glimpse of reflected light. The light flickered oddly, and for a second or two she couldn't understand why – but then she realised that the hidden flame whose light was reflecting from one of the fan-like arrays was no mere candle.

'It's fire!' the whisper came again. 'They're going to try to burn us out!'

The voice had guessed right, but no panic spread. Lucrezia knew that it wouldn't be as easy as it sounded. Anything thrown at the canvas would simply rebound; the tough fabric wouldn't catch light easily even though it was tinder-dry. Nor would the wood flare up, even if a firebomb actually came to rest against a wheel.

Unfortunately, the attackers had a better plan than simply hurling firepots. She saw one of the giant Serpents emerge from cover, holding a javelin in its huge hand. There was something burning behind the head of the weapon. The creature came three paces forward, measuring its stride. Someone fired an arrow, but it only struck a glancing blow as the Serpent hurled the javelin with all its might. The head of the spear bit into the wooden side of the wagon, which was slightly softened by rot. It bit deep, and although the nearest man was quick to reach out with his own spear, using it as a lever in the hope of dislodging the burning shaft, he could not possibly have been quick enough. *Now* the missiles came: pots full of oil, thrown to catch the sputtering flame.

'Put the fire out!' someone cried – but they had no water to spare for dousing fires, and as the pots shattered against the side of the wagon the oil caught alight, splashing the great wheel and the lateral timbers.

Now there were more Serpents moving at the edge of the clearing, similarly armed with spears. Lucrezia didn't doubt that they were making the same move against each of the three wagons. Arrows flew from the defensive formation, but Lucrezia knew that unless the defenders could snuff out the fires their improvised fortress would rapidly become a death trap.

She heard the dull sounds made by the spears as they struck home, but none was close to her station. She heard yelps of wrath and pain as defenders reached out with cloth-bound hands to smother the burning chaff behind the spearheads, but more firepots were already flying across the open space in long low curves. The throwers had to expose themselves to arrows, but the giant Serpents could throw spears and pots much further and harder than any human and they were not easy targets. The arrows which struck them were poisoned, but they had not drunk bad water and Lucrezia didn't see any of them fall.

The trails of burning oil which the pots spilled after landing looked feeble enough, and had there only been three or four the defenders might have coped, but the attackers knew that they had only a few minutes to attain their objective and they flung dozens of the missiles. They must have used up their entire supply of cooking oil as well as their lantern fuel, but they contrived to spread so much in such a brief interval that the fire leapt gladly from one trail to another – and all the trails led to the wagons.

Defenders were beginning to jump down, hoping to beat out the flames, but the Serpents still had spears and many other missiles; these began to fall in a steady rain, and whenever the humans were hit – if only by a lump of stone – they were knocked down.

At least their instruments are primitive, Lucrezia thought. *If they had plastic and the wit to make the kind of bombs that Checuti made, they'd smash the wagons in no time.* It was cold comfort, though; primitive instruments were effective in a situation like this, and the defenders had no plastic of their own with which to retaliate.

There were no more firepots to hurl now; the attackers had run through their stock, but Lucrezia could see flames licking at the wood and canvas of all three wagons and she could measure the panic spreading through the ranks as cries of alarm turned to cries of terror. There were human throwers in company with the Serpents now, and ample light by which to see them, but the burning oil was releasing clouds of smoke which threatened to obscure them.

Lucrezia remembered feeling grateful that the dark clouds to the south had shown no sign of moving northwards, and understood how foolish that gratitude had been. Heavy rain would have made a mockery of the attackers' strategy. She wished that she had a bow, so that she might join in with the men who were trying to fell the throwers, but she knew that she could not have hit anything. She also knew that the poisons with which she had anointed the defenders' blades might now be a danger to friends as well as enemies as the defenders tumbled out of the wagons in disarray.

Fortunately, the fire was not spreading so quickly or burning so hotly that there was a mad scramble to get out. She could hear the sound of Venerina's voice commanding order in one of the other wagons. 'Be careful!' she cried to her own companions. 'There's time enough to go one by one!' She took it for granted that they must certainly go, for the fire was burning along the whole length of the cart by now, licking greedily at the wheels and taking hold of the flanks. The released prisoners were letting themselves down at the front as well as the back but the rear egress was easier and that was the way she moved, carefully making sure that the tip of her spear came nowhere near human flesh.

The smoke was worse than the heat, but it was not yet

choking. She put her hand to her mouth, but it was a token gesture.

Two of the men squealed as they stepped across fiery pools and were burned, but the screams had as much impatience in them as pain; they had taken boots from their fallen captors to replace their own, and they had a measure of protection even against flames. Their real problem was deciding which way to go. Most moved instinctively into the protected space within the square, where the burning wagons would form a wall between them and their enemies, and no one was instructing them otherwise; but Lucrezia knew that hot air rises and that a space surrounded by fire generates a wind sucking the smoke and flames inwards. She knew that if she went the other way she would be silhouetted against the fire, but she guessed that the attackers must have thrown almost everything they had to throw by now, and that the fight would be hand to hand from now on.

Lucrezia was able to judge her descent cleverly enough not to dip her feet in burning oil, but that was only the first phase of her predicament. Once out in the open she saw at a glance that the burning oil was distributed far too widely, amid too much potential fuel, for there to be any hope of smothering it and saving the wagons. In any case, the attackers were coming forward now to take full advantage of their opening. Cries of alarm from the men who had already jumped down were needlessly calling attention to the new danger.

The horses saved by the ex-captives, which were tethered within the square formed by the wagons, were extremely distressed by the way that fire was building up all around them, and their panic was making things even more difficult for those who had fallen back within the square. Lucrezia saw that she and the others who had come forward were too few as yet to form any kind of defensive line in front of the sea of fire but there were a dozen voices raised urging others to come out in support.

The newcomers had obviously decided that all-out attack was their only option, even though they had had no accurate idea of the odds. They came from all sides now, with the same furious recklessness their allies had employed in attacking the Community. Lucrezia imagined that they must be delighted to find such a ragged and ill-formed line before them.

A few of the charging men were mounted, in order that they could use their weapons as they had been trained to do. That might not have been an advantage had the defensive line been stronger; the weapons arrayed against the horses were spears, and the animals knew enough to be wary of charging spears. The members of the Community were aware that a solid line of spears was a good deterrent, and they made what haste they could to form one, but it was too late.

Lucrezia stabbed at the neck of one of the horses as its rider urged it forward. The horse reared up – probably more afraid of the fire behind her than the spearhead – and the rider tumbled from its back. She felt a thrill of exultation as the horse turned and bolted, bowling over two of the men who were coming forward on foot behind it, but it was far too small a victory to turn the tide of the battle, which was definitely running against her own side.

She could see a pair of giant Serpents lumbering behind the disconcerted men, and her heart sank. She looked around for support and shouted for it, but such was the noise that her cry was probably lost in the confusion. More men were coming forward now but still they could not form a proper line. No one who emerged from the square confined by the burning wagons dropped back again, and no one was fool enough to run further forward, but there was simply not enough time to make a formation. The attackers came against them with renewed enthusiasm, confident of victory.

Lucrezia had no alternative but to concentrate all her efforts on survival. As the attackers hurled themselves upon her she stabbed with the spear, wielding it in desperate imitation of the moves she had seen Dhalla and her fellow giants make as they went through their drill in the courtyard before the Inner Sanctum of the citadel. Two men fell, having recklessly run right on to the poisoned tip, but others were warier and her nearest allies were too far away to collaborate with her in confounding them.

While her adversaries paused to organise themselves Lucrezia looked from side to side in the hope of finding friends. She saw other attackers falling, some bearing spearpoints down with them. She knew that they were finished, but she saw that their falling created gaps for those pressing behind them. The giant

Serpents were now beginning to lash out with the long cudgels which they carried, and she saw defenders falling too. Then her own assailants pounced, and she had to lunge with the spear again.

Her adversaries were well enough prepared to evade the initial thrust, but as she swung the weapon sideways she caught one man on the side of his head and knocked him down. Alas, the reaction of the blow was so jarring that the shaft stopped still, and another attacker swung his mace so powerfully against it that it was torn from her hands.

Lucrezia had a knife in her belt but it was a tiny thing, hardly more than a claw. She was quick to seize it with her left hand while her right dug into an open pouch to fetch out a fistful of powder. This she hurled into the eyes of the man who was set to stab her in the heart, and she was sufficiently quick-witted to sidestep the right way as he blundered on ineffectually. She tried to stab the next man who came at her, but she didn't have the necessary reach; he wasn't tall but he had long arms and his knife was larger than hers.

His blade wasn't metal and it wasn't poisoned, but it was sharp. She felt it slice her right ear and score her shoulder. She was momentarily amazed by the fact that there seemed to be no pain – it was as if the shock of it had forbidden all other sensation – but she knew that she had been hurt and hurt badly. She knew that the next few seconds would certainly be her last unless she could produce some wonderful trick with which to save herself. She struck out at the man who had cut her, moving within his reach now that his dagger had done its work. She slammed her own blade into his belly but couldn't get out of the way as he threw his arms around her.

They fell together.

He wasn't a big man but he was heavy enough to knock the breath out of her. The fall drove the dagger even deeper into his guts and tore the wound wide open. She felt the wet warmth of his blood and guts flooding over her. The stink was overpowering. He was still moving, but without any purpose. She managed to roll him sideways to bring herself clear of his weight.

Had her other attackers waited they could have killed her with ease then, but they had not. Having seen her fall they had moved on and no one was now within striking distance. *Now* the pain came, drawing a line of agony from her temple to her shoulder. Her arm suddenly felt useless, as if the nerves connecting its sinews to her brain had been switched off. She clutched at it with her good left hand, looking wildly around.

She remembered regretting that she had played no active part in the battle of the bridge, and knew now how stupid that kind of regret was.

She backed away from the smoke-filled arena where the fight was raging, but she could feel the fierce heat of the fire consuming the wagon. It was all ablaze now, a wall of flame. She looked to her left and to her right; there seemed to be no space at all into which she might retreat.

Still the attackers kept coming, although more and more were falling as they met sterner resistance. One of the giant Serpents went down, spitted by a spear-thrust, but it had already struck back at the man responsible, breaking his skull with an urgent sweep of its own blunt weapon.

Lucrezia ran for the only gap she could see, with no thought in her head but to get away from the carnage. One of the attackers came after her but someone else moved to intercept him; her would-be assailant ran on to the tip of the man's dagger. She never saw the face of the deist who had saved her but she saw his blade turn from the breastbone of the man he had killed for her, slipping between the ribs on the left-hand side, cutting out a mortal wound. The shock and the pain curled the half-man up, preventing the completion of his counterstrike.

For a fleeting second Lucrezia wondered whether she ought to pick up the stricken man's weapon, but she ran on past instead without ever making a conscious decision to do so.

Yet another man came after her, but he never reached her because someone struck him down from behind. She had come to the rim of the clearing by now and she had a few precious seconds of breathing space. She was frightened of moving into the shadows cast by the Reef-structures, lest more enemies were lurking there, so she looked back. Unfortunately, her hesitation left her within range of one of the Serpents, which lashed out at her with its cudgel. She ducked under the blow, feeling a surge of satisfaction as the weapon cut the empty air above her head, then had no choice but to take the available cover and she dived into the shadows, still clutching her right arm.

The Serpent lashed out at her again and she ducked lower still as the head of the creature's cudgel whizzed by. This time the clubhead had insufficient momentum to carry it harmlessly past and it fell upon her neck, knocking her down as she lunged forward. As the new pain surged through her, contesting with the old, she felt sure that the bones in her spine had been cracked – but no great damage could have been done, for she was able to roll over as she fell and scramble for cover as the giant lurched after her.

Had it been able to pursue her she would surely have been killed, but she had rolled under the branches of a spiky dendrite and the Serpent stumbled back again as it pricked its arms. It must have been persuaded that the glancing blow had done enough damage, for it turned away immediately.

Lucrezia rolled clear, and came to her feet again. Her movements seemed terribly ungainly, but her feet carried her into the shadows. There was starlight enough to get some idea where she was going, and for a few moments she thought that she had got clean away, but then she ran straight into another giant Serpent. This one had already fallen, stung by at least one poisoned arrow, but it wasn't dead. Even as it lay dying on the ground it reached out for her.

She leapt sideways and its groping hand clenched empty air, but she cannoned into a coralline wall. Had the impact jarred her right shoulder the pain would surely have been unbearable, but it was her left that suffered. The reflexive lunge was the Serpent's last purposive thrust, but as soon as she rebounded from the wall its thrashing tail caught her from behind and threw her back into it. This time she cracked her head, and the blow knocked her sick.

She staggered away, but she no longer knew where she was going.

Lucrezia fell to one knee, fighting stupefaction. Before blood trickled into her eyes and forced her to close them she saw that she had gone back the way she had come instead of plunging further into protective darkness.

The battle was still going on. She was lost in a mad confusion of bodies, no longer able to figure out who were friends and who were foes. The light seemed to have got much worse because of the smoke billowing from the blazing wagons.

I mustn't fall! she thought. *Whatever happens, I mustn't fall.* She blinked furiously, trying to clear her eyes.

Unfortunately, mere resolution wasn't enough. She couldn't blink away the blood, and as soon as she rose from her kneeling position her senses reeled. She exerted every effort to stay where she was, but her body would not respond.

She felt herself falling, very slowly. When she hit the ground the impact felt strangely muffled but once she was prone the dizziness went away and she didn't lose consciousness. It would have been far more comfortable if she had, for there seemed to be nothing to be conscious of save for her agony.

17

WHEN THE FIRST FLAME flickered into life Andris was startled by a shock of guilt. He had heard indistinct sounds of movement beneath the lower boughs of the dendrite in which he was stationed but he had taken them for the usual animal rustlings; there had been nothing to warn him that much larger creatures were on the march.

He opened his mouth to call out a warning but he realised that there was no longer any point in so doing. At least some of the enemy had already worked their way past him and to shout now would give his own position away – nor would it serve any useful purpose, given that the spark must have caught the attention of the sentries on the wagons.

Within five seconds the strangling of the impulse was justified; the alarm was raised.

Andris couldn't see at first what the flame was for; it was briefly eclipsed by a huge body and then reappeared close by the wagons. Not until the first oil-pot shattered and the flame blossomed into vivid fire did he realise what the attackers' plan must be.

Still he did not know what to do; he could hear no more sound below him than he had heard before. He didn't know whether the enemy knew his position and were giving him a wide berth or whether they were employing unnatural stealth in moving men and Serpents to all sections of the wide perimeter from which they would unleash their assault on the wagons. He knew that if he could take them in the rear while their attention was focused on the wagons he might be able to do a good deal of damage, but the timing of his assault would be crucial. If he descended to ground level too soon and found himself surrounded he would be brought down quickly enough; if he left it too long it might cost the lives of some of those he was anxious to help.

While he hesitated he was stricken by an odd combination of sensations, arising from his puzzlement as to what the men in Serpent-skin were trying to do. On the one hand, he couldn't see how it made sense for the giant Serpents and their allies to hurry into an all-out assault on an enemy of unknown strength without even waiting for daylight and he cursed them on that account for their recklessness. On the other, he had been half convinced all along that this was exactly what the enemy would do, and on that account he cursed himself for his own unreadiness. Both these curses were, however, distinctly half-hearted. Although it seemed to him that life had developed a furious perversity, which involved hurling one unnecessary misfortune after another at everyone who was associated with him, he found himself unable to get unduly worked up about it.

Andris knew that he could stay where he was and remain reasonably safe from harm – and he knew, too, that a sensible man of Checuti's stripe would probably do exactly that. If he were to play any substantial part in the fight, however, he could not maintain his coign of vantage; he had no ready supply of missiles to rain down on the marauders from above.

It was a straightforward choice between fight and flight, and he had already committed himself to fight.

Without any substantial pause for thought, he made his descent, hoping that he might arrive at ground level just in time to take the first wave of attackers from the rear.

With the aid of two saws borrowed from the captured wagons Andris had cut a branch from one of the dendrites which was as long as he was tall and as thick as his wrist. He had placed this where he could easily snatch it up, and he did so now with alacrity. The eyeball-like globule at its tip would serve as a very adequate clubhead, but his initial intention was to use the weapon two-handed, like a quarterstaff. It was very heavy, and he knew that it would tax the strength of his arms, but its solidity was welcome, giving him full confidence that any enemy he struck squarely – even if it were a giant Serpent – would be crippled by the blow.

Unfortunately, there was no enemy immediately to hand. He could hear the sound of horses whinnying now, but it was impossible to judge their direction against the background noise of shouts and screams that was swelling ominously in the direction of the wagons. There were shadows everywhere around him, and even though his eyes were accustomed to the conditions he was confused by the chaotic play of the fragile starlight.

The strange automatism which had seized him during his first skirmish with the giant Serpents seemed to have entirely loosed its grip on him, but Andris felt no particular awe at the prospect of meeting such adversaries again. Nor did he feel any particular fear, nor even any great excitement. He simply held his weapon ready as he looked to left and right, and then moved forward in the direction of the fighting.

He thought that his way was clear, but it wasn't. As he made to pass between two stony pillars the head of a massive club came zooming into the gap, aimed at his skull. Had he not had the quarterstaff at the ready he would not have been able to evade the blow, but he had turned it almost to the vertical, with the 'eyeball' upwards, and he only had to adjust his grip slightly to intercept the other weapon and turn its thrust aside.

The force of the clash told him immediately that it was no human hand that had struck out at him. It was a giant Serpent – and a giant Serpent which must have lain in wait for him, knowing exactly which way he would come.

He realised, belatedly, that the enemy *had* seen him, and marked his position. Not only that, but they had marked what manner of man he was, and adjusted their strategy accordingly. He cursed the incompetence which had let him be discovered as he danced backwards, expecting that the Serpent would come out of hiding to pursue him, and give him a chance to aim a killing blow at its head.

Alas, it did not. It moved to be visible, but it was content to station itself in the gap through which he had tried to go, blocking it off. He guessed without having to look round that it wasn't alone, and he was already ducking in anticipation of another thrust.

He couldn't tell how many ambushers the enemy had set to lie in wait for him, nor what manner of creatures they were, but he knew that he had been caught on bad ground and that it would be direly difficult to find a defensible station. Had he only stayed by the compound trunk of the great dendrite he could have placed his back to it, but it was too late now. Shadowy forms were coming at him from that direction, and from others too.

Andris threw himself into the fray with a kind of resignation, which accepted that life had become a simple matter of doling out injury until the moment came when he was prevented from so doing. Survival was the only issue at stake; the battle in the clearing could be none of his affair until he had saved himself. He lashed out at men on foot and oversized Serpents with even-handed generosity, knowing that they were at least four in number and that four too many.

They scattered before his thrusts, but not like skittles. He couldn't hit them while he had to cover so much ground so quickly. He felt big and clumsy; it seemed absurd to be surrounded by so many enemies and not to be able to fell even one of them. They made no mistakes in judging his reach, and they were clever; this was nothing like the fight he had been in the day before, nor any other he had experienced lately. These imitation men and their monstrous companions had judged him accurately, and had made plans to counter his strength.

A missile soared past his ducking head, and another hit him on the thigh. He was surprised to find that it was neither a spear nor an arrow, either of which might have set him up for the kill. It was only a lump of rock, and another was already hurtling at him. None of the shadowy forms came forward to grapple with him.

He was hit again, this time on the upper arm, but again it was only a lump of stone and not something more dangerous. The blow was bruising, but by no means crippling. He refused to flinch or modify his guard, and was able to strike the next one out of the air with the end of his staff. Then he moved forward rapidly, trying to carry the fight to his adversaries. He lashed out and at last made contact, once and then again.

How much damage his blows had done Andris could not accurately estimate, but it was certainly far less than he had tried and intended to do. He had become so accustomed to duelling with giant Serpents that he was mildly surprised when none went down before his assault – but then they came at him, rushing in concert, men and Serpents together. He bludgeoned one of the two humans to the ground, but he couldn't move swiftly enough to get clear.

The crowded spikes and stems of the surrounding reef-structures caused almost as many problems for Andris as they did for the Serpents. The Serpents couldn't bring their massive tails into play, but he couldn't land a solid blow on their hands, let alone their heads. Counting the one who had struck at him first they were three in number, and he knew that three would be enough to fell any human in the world, except perhaps a real giant.

With survival still in mind he looked about for a possible way of escape, but there was none.

I'll smash a skull or two, at least, he thought, but they didn't need to be able to read his mind to be wary of that. He lunged at them but they parried his thrusts. They too had survival very much in mind, and they took no risks as they moved to contain and confine him, pressing inexorably forward.

By now, he felt sure, the defenders must be spilling out of the wagons in panic. The attackers must be spread rather thinly around the makeshift fortress, and he wondered if his best chance might be to move in the direction of the fighting, in the faint hope that his adversaries might be distracted or even attacked from behind. Alas, even the man he had hit was getting to his feet now and the cordon that had been thrown around him showed not the slightest sign of breaking.

He launched himself into another furious attack, and this time he killed the dazed human who had survived his first blow, but the others defended themselves with practised efficiency. He couldn't land a single useful blow on any of the Serpents, and he felt that he had almost used up his last reserves of strength.

He snatched up the club which the fallen man had carried, and hurled it with all his might at the nearest Serpent, but it bounced off the monster's upper leg with as little effect as the rock which had earlier struck his own thigh.

Andris knew that he had no alternative but to make one last desperate attempt to burst through the shrinking cordon, so he followed the club with a charge, using his staff as if it were a lance aimed at the Serpent's belly. It refused to be intimidated, swinging its own club to turn his thrust aside. He continued regardless, cannoning into the massive creature.

The giant Serpent was heavier than he was, and it had a tail with which to brace itself; he could not bowl it over and it was he who took the worse shock from the impact. Sheer inertia carried him forward. He tripped over the monster's splayed foot, but that saved him from a blow aimed from the side and he found himself rolling, bound for an empty space beyond the cordon. Alas, he had neither the time nor the muscular co-ordination to make that ground; he was intercepted by the well-aimed blow of a Serpent's tail, and thrust by its force into collision with the braced tail of the Serpent into whose all too solid body he had earlier cannoned.

He was mildly astonished that he was given time to get up, but his attackers seemed to be more intent on surrounding him again than they were on finishing him off. As soon as he stood up, however, he was caught by another calculated blow, which ripped his weapon right out of his hands.

He moved aside reflexively as one of the knob-headed clubs which the Serpents carried struck out at the side of his head. He knew there was no weapon nearer than the one that had been torn from his grasp, and so he went after that one – but he knew as he lunged that he couldn't possibly reach it.

He had time to think, however, that there must be some method in the way his enemies had tackled him, with clubs instead of spears and lumps of rock instead of blades. He had seen them fight that way before, at the Community's house, and he had realised afterwards that they preferred to stun their enemies if they could, so that they might take their full quota of prisoners. They had laid a trap for him, but they had laid it very carefully indeed – and now that he realised the precise extent of their care he felt the first real flicker of dread. He had not known before exactly why these imitation men were so keen to take prisoners, but he knew it now; he had forced the information out of a dying man in an unkind manner, and now the memory returned to haunt him.

He never saw the object which collided with the back of his skull with an awful solidity, and couldn't tell whether it was a clubhead or a tail. The blow didn't knock him out, but it knocked him over.

He didn't try to get up again, contenting himself with wriggling across the ground towards the makeshift quarterstaff. He was desperate to lay his hand upon it, knowing that it was his one and only chance, but he never got to it. He did not feel the blow which put an end to his long and arduous campaign, and never had the chance to cry out against the horror of his fate.

18

JACOM STOOD ON the rim of the crater, momentarily heedless of the pouring rain, staring in the direction of the Navel of the World. Kasdeja waited a few mets away, relaxed and patient. The northern sky was empty of cloud and the flamestars shone brightly there, but the light was by no means good even for the dead of night.

In the west he could just make out a plateau whose top seemed to be very pale. Had he had the advantage of daylight the whiteness would probably have been vivid, and he might well have been able to make out a certain amount of detail, but in the present circumstances it was no more than a dim blur, partly shrouded in mist. There was, however, a single shape which stood out over the rest, reflecting the starlight with unusual precision. It might have been the tip of a cone but it put him uneasily in mind of the point of a dagger.

To the north of the lone peak, a little closer to his present position, there was another raised area; its walls were not so sheer as those of the plateau and its elevation was not nearly as high as his present station but it had its own defences in the form of a ragged rampart that might have been a miniature version of the Great Reef. Into this natural stockade ran the road-like ribbon he had glimpsed from much lower down, although he could not see from here what kind of a gateway lay at its terminus. There was abundant vegetation within this protected area too, but there were darker colours mingled with the green, including the purples which Jacom had learned to associate with unearthly vegetation. As with the plateau, the cloud and rain blurred all matters of detail, although there were no mists adding to the confusion.

To the south there were further hills clustered together, these rather more reminiscent of dragomite mounds although their slopes were decked in brown, almost as if each one bore a healthy mane of coarse hair. This area had a protective rim too but it was not a high wall, merely a vitreous circle of grey and black which might or might not have been alive. Jacom suspected that it *was* alive – and, indeed, that everything hereabouts was alive according to the patient fashion of the figured stones.

'Which one is Chimera's Cradle?' Jacom asked the manticore. He remembered Andris Myrasol's map well enough, but he wasn't certain exactly where he stood, and the forest which the Silver Thorns allegedly formed to either side of the Gauntlet of Gladness was lost in the murk which still cloaked the northern horizon in spite of its cloudlessness.

'The white plateau topped by the pyramid,' Kasdeja replied. 'The garden within the palisade to the north of it is where thorn-bushes grow into the flesh of living hosts, who grow to believe that they are oracles. Had you seen its emissaries you might have taken them for true humans, but the illusion could not have been long sustained. In any case, they keep company with giant Serpents.

'The ground to the south is dangerous even to me. Perhaps the half-humans who attacked your company came from there, or the lizards which were foolish enough to attack me beyond the Reef, or perhaps both. There are other grounds, of course; the one your forefathers built is surrounded by defences and is not easy to reach today, if it ever was, although my brothers can do it. It sends forth emissaries, but they're not your kind – I don't know why. Nor do I know what capacity it has to resist invasion and corruption, from above or from below, or whether it has contrived to resist invasion and corruption in the past. When I say that it's your ground – *earthly* ground, as you would say – I speak of tradition, not of certain knowledge. If you and your kind still hope that the salvation of your petty empires will come from there, you will surely be disappointed.'

'And what will happen to our so-called petty empires if no salvation comes?' Jacom wanted to know.

'You needn't fear that your people will be wiped out,' the manticore told him. 'If that was ever a possibility, it cannot happen now. Some of your brothers and sisters are kin to Serpents and to Salamanders now – and to manticores too.'

145

'I'm not sure that I want to be kin to Serpents, Salamanders and manticores,' Jacom said, 'if it means that I'm reduced to the state of the people who consort with dragomites.'

'None of us can choose his brothers,' Kasdeja informed him soberly. 'Even the ground which shapes and nurtures us seems to be unable to *choose* the forms its offspring will take. The dwellers in the deep have no voices of their own; if they have their reasons they also keep their secrets, even from their children. Common minds cannot fathom those reasons yet, and perhaps they never will.'

'Is yours a *common* mind?' Jacom asked, knowing the answer already.

'Common enough,' the manticore told him, 'for all its seeming rarity.' It was nearly a joke.

'Are there any minds in all the world uncommon enough to understand the secrets yours has failed to fathom?' Jacom asked.

'I don't know,' was the only reply he got. He wondered whether a straightforward yes or a no would have been more comforting. Even if there were no understanding minds here perhaps there were a few in Chimera's Cradle, patiently tending the Pool of Life while they waited for the prophesied emergence of an incorruptible stone. Should he hope for that, for the sake of Fraxinus and Phar?

Jacom wondered what would happen if he were to leap from the crater's rim and run helter-skelter down the slope, heading for the mysterious plateau which lay half hidden beneath its own garment of cloud. He knew, however, that he couldn't possibly outpace the manticore. Kasdeja's conspicuously relaxed attitude signified that his appointed task was as good as complete. Neither killer nor saviour could reach Jacom now.

'Well,' Jacom said, turning back to face the interior of the crater, 'it looks as if the time has come for me to meet your makers. You'd better lead the way.'

'There's no need,' Kasdeja said. 'We'll part here, for now. Go down – and don't be afraid. Whatever happens, you will not die. Believe that, I beg of you.'

Jacom furrowed his brow as he tried to follow the exact implications of this peculiar plea, but he didn't hesitate. He stepped down from the rim of the crater, half sliding into the seemingly innocuous wilderness of silky grass. His intention was to strike out immediately for the earthly-looking trees and the conical structures that were mingled with them. There, if anywhere, he would find people like himself – and he had grown lonely for human company while the manticore carried him across the living face of this curious continent.

Almost as soon as he had set forth, however, he regretted his impetuosity. As he pushed with his arms to part the silky-haired stems of the reed-like plants his wrists and forearms were gripped tight. He felt lissom stalks coiling about his limbs, trapping him and rendering him helpless. He tried to struggle but it was useless; the stems wound around him all the more possessively.

Within seconds he had no freedom of movement at all. He was wrapped round from head to toe.

To his profound dismay, Jacom found that the silvery tresses which each stem wore at its crown were not delicate at all. They clung to his face like a mask, blinding him and sealing off his mouth and nostrils. Worse still, he felt the tips of the finer filaments digging into his flesh like a host of little needles.

He tried to fight but there was nothing at all that he could do – and he realised as his senses reeled that he was being drawn slowly downwards. His feet were being sucked into the depths of whatever living soil lay beneath the silken thicket. He remembered what had happened to the body of the killer that Kasdeja had kicked contemptuously into the slough by which he'd made his valiant stand.

Jacom expected to lose consciousness at any moment, and then to choke. There was a minute or two when his lungs protested agonisingly against their inability to draw breath, and the sensation was so acute that he longed for the *coup de grâce* which unconsciousness would deliver – but he didn't lose consciousness. Down and down he was drawn, and in the meantime the inquisitive needles dug deeper and deeper into his flesh. He could feel their progress, but there was no acute pain involved in the process. When his lungs relented in their painful rebellion, falling quiet within his breast, he felt oddly comfortable – and still in full possession of his faculties.

He began to see the sense in what Kasdeja had said to him; whatever happened to him now, he would not die. The entity that had swallowed him was not after meat; it wanted more of him than that.

Jacom's first reaction was to be thankful for the miracle of his continued consciousness, but he had spent too long in the company of Aulakh Phar, who had always tried as best he could to educate everyone within earshot as to the mysteries of his patchwork lore. The function of the lungs, he knew, was to extract oxygen from the air, which reddened the blood in his arteries while it was conveyed throughout his body to fuel the languorous fire that was life itself. He couldn't help supplying the argument that if his lungs were no longer delivering oxygen to his blood, then the needle-like fronds which had invaded his flesh must be doing so instead.

This was no miracle, nor was the guarantee of life which Kasdeja had offered him a guarantee that he would remain as he was. Again he remembered the living human flesh that had been smeared all over the walls of the dragomite queen's innermost chambers, and wondered whether *that* retained consciousness and the power of regret.

This awareness of the logic of his situation didn't make his descent any more comfortable. He was still blind and deaf, and the fact that every sem of his skin was so securely prisoned filled him with a nauseous claustrophobia – a purely psychological phenomenon but one which direly increased his anxiety and his distress. He felt sure that if he were to vomit up the unappetising contents of his stomach the result would be exceedingly unpleasant, all the more so by virtue of his apparent inability to choke on it.

He still had a sense of downward movement, although he wasn't sure that it was trustworthy. Despite his defiant conviction that he was more than mere meat he couldn't help imagining himself as an item of food passing down an extraordinarily convoluted gut towards a stomach far too resilient ever to vomit him up again. That image led readily enough to another in which he felt himself dissected, layer by layer and organ by organ, so that his brain and his bones might be carefully redistributed and realigned, while he remained conscious all the while of exactly who he was and what was being done to him. He wondered whether what he had seen in the depths of the

148

dragomite mound represented the ultimate in imaginable horrors, or whether there was something even worse.

The idea that he might be reshaped and reborn as a manticore, or a man with a monster's head, or a bird-like reptile, suddenly began to seem like relatively hopeful instances plucked from a vast spectrum of horrific possibilities.

He knew that he would have screamed had he been able to do it – but he also knew that once he had screamed he would have begun to shout, and that what he would have shouted would have been questions. No matter how extreme his terror was, it couldn't entirely displace his hunger to find some sense in this chaos of mysteries, and there was a crumb of reassurance to be found in the thought that if he were to fall to the very centre of the world he might at least discover an arena in which vital questions could and would be answered.

His panic began to ebb away.

Eventually, the sensation of descent ebbed away too, although that might have been mere illusion. He seemed to himself to be at rest, with his feet still pointing towards the inner depths and his head still nearest to the surface. His nerves became much steadier, and the horrid sensation of being completely enclosed began to seem slightly less oppressive.

He could no longer feel the slight but relatively painless pricking sensation which he had assumed to be the invasion of his flesh by the corporeal extremities of the giant in the hill, but he felt no sense of disconnection from his own body. He was not numb, and although he could not twitch his fingers he was sure – if only at an intellectual level – that they were still mounted on his hands, still inhabited by the essence of Jacom Cerri.

As his panic and discomfort faded, and time went by – measurable by the heartbeat which he could still feel in spite of the fact that he drew no breath – he was possessed by a feeling more akin to boredom than anxiety. He wanted something to happen, and did not feel capable of mustering overmuch patience to see him through the wait.

In desperation, he began to count his heartbeats, although he had no accurate idea whether they were eighty to the minute or a hundred and eighty.

He gave up counting somewhere around two hundred, when a brief flutter of panic returned, although he could not tell what had triggered it. It took him some time to realise that the grip upon him was relaxing, and that the gentle but insistent pressure on his skin was relenting by degrees.

Suppressing a paradoxical stab of fear that freedom might only be the freedom to asphyxiate, he waited to be let loose.

He nearly fell over when it became possible to do so, but he managed to catch himself and hold himself in a standing position. The ground beneath his feet seemed firm enough and very even, and when there was air to be breathed in it seemed almost intoxicating in its luxury; it was warm and moist and there was certainly no shortage of oxygen in it.

Light grew around him along with space: diffuse red light which was not as disconcerting as he might have imagined, given its vivid colour.

The light showed him that the chamber hollowed out for his convenience was some three mets by two and two high, without a single true right angle to be seen. At first sight the walls were plain and rather slick, unfortunately reminiscent in hue and texture of the bloodied entrails of some partly butchered animal, but his eyes had hardly had time to adjust to the return of sight before shapes began to emerge therein.

The shapes which showed themselves within the walls surrounding him were scrupulously human in design, and of a perfectly normal size. The faces which stared at him from every side – four in all – were the faces of ordinary men. They were somewhat reminiscent of Kasdeja's face, but they didn't make him feel as tiny as Kasdeja did. The ugly redness flowed out of them, leaving them bronze and then golden – as golden as he was himself. It was as if they were stepping out of the walls, released as full-grown adults from some great glutinous womb. Their emergence was certainly miraculous, but the miracle was in the walls, not in the faces. He was a creature of miracle himself now, was he not? He too had been drawn into the earth, united with the dweller in the deep which had no voice and whose reasons were inscrutable even to its children.

Jacom licked his lips, half expecting to find them slick with some disgusting fluid, but they were soft and quite dry.

I am brave enough for this, he told himself sternly, and discovered that it was true, at least once he had formed the words.

The human bodies were almost separate from the wall now; he was sure that they would be shaped exactly like common men, no matter how uncommon their minds might be. He was sure, too, that when they had stepped clear of the wall to meet him eye to eye they would reach out and touch him, and speak to him. The one thing he could not imagine was what they had to say to him, and why his replies might be of any interest to them.

'Well, you have me,' he said to the face which was in front of him, meeting its eyes as squarely as he could. 'I only hope it was worth the trouble your brother took in bringing me here.'

'Time will tell,' the other said, reaching out a hand to take Jacom's arm. 'At least, we must hope so.'

19

EVERY TIME LUCREZIA tried to force herself away from the ground her senses reeled and forced her down again. She found herself in the awkward and distressing position of being in full command of her faculties only if she consented to lie down, although command of her faculties was no luxury while all they had to tell her was that she was hurt. Oddly enough, although she knew that she was still losing blood, the pain of her wounds was becoming markedly less intense. She felt that she was gradually becoming *distanced* from her stubborn sensations, as if her mind were attempting to repudiate the body which had let her down.

In the meantime, the battle went on, but that too had become distanced. The open space before the burning wagon was no longer crowded; every now and again some dark shadow would loom up above her, passing from right to left or left to right, but the noise of clashing weapons was no longer close.

They've scattered into the Reef, Lucrezia thought. *Having lost their defence, they've broken ranks.* If only Venerina's people had been able to form a better defensive line, she judged, they might have repelled the attack, but they had not had enough stomach for the fight. Their brittle resolve had cracked and they had quickly turned tail, just as Shabir's men had at the battle of the bridge.

Was it all for nothing? she wondered. *Did Andris and Ssifuss slay a company of giant Serpents to release these people only for them to scatter at the first sign of new danger? Is this how they repay our heroism?*

Such bitter thoughts were hardly comforting, but they were easier to entertain than the fear of her own imminent death. She could not tell with any accuracy how badly she had been hurt but she knew that her wounds weren't trivial and there was no doctor within a thousand kims. She also knew that the fight was not finished yet. If the giant Serpents and their half-human allies had won it, they would be back to mop up the survivors. If she were allowed to live, she might yet end up feeding one of the monstrous plants which she had tried to cultivate in the roof garden of the Inner Sanctum.

She remembered the dog and the slave. There had been no indication that they had suffered terribly, but the sight of what they had eventually become had been as horrible as it was intriguing.

She tried to raise her head again, but she hadn't the strength. All she could do was flop over into a supine position, looking up at the clouds of smoke that were obscuring the stars. At least the heat was driving the smoke upwards now, sucking cleaner air in from the sides; breathing wasn't so very difficult.

Another shadow moved, coming towards her from the left. It was moving more steadily than others she had seen, in no particular hurry. It came to stand over her, looking down.

It was no one she knew, and for a moment she conserved the hope that it might be one of the men from the Community – but he was clad in garments which looked as if they had been cut from Serpent-skin, and she had to accept that he was not a man at all.

He was carrying a club with a stony head, in a relaxed fashion that testified to his lack of fear. He clearly believed that the battle was over and that he and his companions had won it. He looked down at Lucrezia, and she met his gaze.

He didn't speak. His eyes were quite steady as he appraised her situation. She considered the possibility of speaking to him, negotiating for her life on whatever basis came to mind, but she remained silent. She was, after all, a princess of Xandria. No matter how hard she had tried to put her rank behind her she could not bear the thought of begging, and she knew that whatever she said she would appear to be begging.

The imitation man raised his club to strike, measuring the intended blow with meticulous care. Lucrezia knew that it would be fatal; he had decided that she was too badly hurt to be of any use. She didn't flinch. She didn't even blink. She looked death in the eyes, with the pride of a princess.

Then the imitation man jerked convulsively, and she saw the

153

stern expression in his starlit eyes turn to shock. She knew that he had been struck from behind but she didn't know how until he fell forwards and she saw the fletchings of the arrow that had buried itself between his shoulder blades.

Ssifuss! she thought. Then she flinched as the creature's body landed on her own, falling across her thighs. She struggled to get rid of it, and he struggled too, for a few seconds, as he writhed against the pain.

It was another hand that rolled him away, in the end – and another hand, too, that finished him off with a swift stroke of a dagger. It was not a Serpent's hand; it was as human as the hand of the imitation man it had killed.

When Lucrezia recognised her deliverer she wasn't capable of feeling anything but bewilderment.

Jume Metra pressed her finger to her lips as she turned away from the body of the creature she had felled to see how Lucrezia was. She darted her eyes from side to side, straining to catch and analyse the sounds of the distant battle. The smoky haze that blurred the starlight was lightening now, and the mound-woman's features stood out clearly enough. The odour of burning that lingered upon the drifting air was blotted out by the stink of the shit that the dead man's bowels had released.

Two minutes and more passed, while Lucrezia obeyed Metra's instruction to be silent and Metra herself did nothing except to wipe her blade clean of blood, using the dead man's sleeve.

When Metra was finally satisfied that no pursuers had come after her, and that no one else was lurking nearby, she nodded.

'Can you get up?' she whispered.

'I don't think so,' Lucrezia said.

The mound-woman didn't seem surprised. 'Don't try,' she said. 'Help will come soon. Others ran away from us but were not all together – this one separated, may be others left behind. He didn't know that we had come.'

He wasn't the only one, Lucrezia thought grimly. 'I thought you were lost – dead in the marshes,' she murmured.

'Thought the same of you at first,' the dragomite woman replied. 'We knew you had no horses.'

'Who's *we*?' Lucrezia queried. She knew that Jume Metra and

154

her kind almost always used 'we' in preference to 'I', and she wasn't sure that the plural could be taken literally.

'Checuti found me,' Metra said, as if she couldn't quite believe it. 'Saved me. Then others found us, else we would both be dead – they told us you were alive. When they tried to bring us to their home we met others fleeing. They told us that many had been killed, many others taken. Many were hurt and needed time to recover, as we did. It was a bad time.'

'I can imagine,' Lucrezia whispered.

'Bad dreams,' Metra said, touching fingers to her forehead. 'We were very sick, but they gave us medicine.'

'Me too,' Lucrezia told her. 'I wasn't as badly affected as you, but I'd certainly have died in the swamp if Andris hadn't carried me to safety.'

Jume Metra's shadowed face showed little enough expression, but Lucrezia thought she could detect a flash of sympathy in the other's starlit eyes. 'All on the same side,' Metra said, as if she were admitting something she had not believed before.

Lucrezia knew that the admission covered everything that had come to pass in the marshes and thereafter. If Andris had not saved her, the people of the Community could not have saved Andris, and would not have gone to search for Metra and Checuti – and Metra could not have put an arrow in the back of the man who had been about to kill her. 'All on the same side,' Lucrezia echoed softly. 'Even Checuti.' She felt perversely proud of that, as if she were responsible for it – but Checuti had done as much for her, in Xandria.

Metra lowered her eyes. She knew what kind of debt she owed. 'Big Serpents and half-men had other prisoners too,' she said. 'Second company came between us.'

'You set out with the marsh-dwellers,' Lucrezia said faintly, trying hard to put all the pieces of the puzzle together. 'When you and Checuti were well enough you joined forces with the Community's survivors and set out after the raiders – but by that time *two* parties of raiders were ahead of you. Did you join them because you thought that Andris and I must be among the prisoners?'

'Were heading south in any case,' Jume Metra said defensively. 'Safety in numbers.' The mound-woman cocked her ear again, listening for danger signs, but the distant sounds of battle seemed to have dwindled almost to nothing.

Metra had kept her steel-bladed knife in her hand, ready for use, but she put it away in her belt now. 'Would not have attacked so soon,' she said, half apologetically. 'They were too strong, and had too many big Serpents. Must have known we were behind them, must have been frightened when they found other enemies already here.'

Lucrezia realised that the attack she and her companions had suffered had been an act of desperation rather than a calculated risk; the imitation men and the giant Serpents had been caught between the jaws of a fast-closing trap, and had not dared to wait. Now they had lost their prisoners, just as their predecessors had. Their garden would go short of fertile soil.

'They knew their only chance was to tackle the opposing forces one at a time,' Lucrezia whispered. 'They must have known how close you were, but they had to hope that you'd be too tired to take them in the rear as soon as they were committed to an all-out assault on us.'

Metra shrugged. 'Panic,' she opined. 'Is the same in nest-war. Great fear breeds action, never caution. Is probably safe now, but have to wait for help. Need two to carry you.'

Lucrezia moved slightly, testing the bloody wounds she had sustained. She still could not tell exactly how bad they were.

'Will I die?' she whispered, knowing that it was time to face the possibility.

Metra seemed to give the idea full and proper consideration, although she didn't touch Lucrezia's body. 'Don't know,' was her uncomforting reply. 'Must lie still.' She turned away again, as if to look for danger, although it was obvious that she was momentarily unable to meet Lucrezia's querulous gaze.

Lucrezia felt faintness rush upon her again as the mound-woman's ominous words took effect, but she fought against unconsciousness and won. She hoped that might be reckoned a good omen.

'What happened to your pack?' she asked, noticing that Metra was unencumbered and wanting to find a safer topic of conversation. She knew that the mound-woman would not have left her precious cargo of eggs to one side for any trivial reason.

156

'No more,' Metra replied, without turning round. 'Dead and rotted.'

The tone of her voice was neutral, but Lucrezia knew what a weight of implication the words contained. Jume Metra was now the last survivor of her hive, and the exceedingly slender – but nevertheless measurable – chance she had had of founding a new nest had now gone for ever. In a sense, she must consider that she herself was as good as dead and rotted, but she had continued to live, and to act, on behalf of a very different collective interest.

'I'm sorry,' Lucrezia said, knowing that it could not sound convincing.

Jume Metra only said: 'Someone coming.' She whispered the words but there was more hope in them than dread. She was expecting allies.

It was indeed an ally. Lucrezia recognised the shape of Checuti's head even before he knelt beside Metra to inspect her. She could see that he was glad to have found her alive – but she could also tell that he was anxious about her prospects of remaining so.

'My lady!' he said, trying to put on a light and bantering tone, as befitted his reputation. 'I'm glad to see that luck is still on your side. I had dared to hope that you might be among the prisoners we came to liberate, but I hadn't expected to find that you had already freed yourself and slain your captors. Is Andris with you, by any chance?'

She frowned at that. Should he not have known by now that Andris was with them? Where *was* Andris? Why had he not come to save her, instead of Jume Metra?

'I wasn't with the prisoners,' Lucrezia dutifully informed him, although she couldn't raise her voice above a whisper. 'We were here before them, and set an ambush with the aid of witchcraft – five of us against forty. We killed them all.'

The expression of astonishment which took possession of Checuti's features was a wonder to behold.

'And then you faced up to the second company?' Checuti said. 'You put us to shame, highness. Was Andris one of your five?'

Lucrezia frowned again. 'Isn't he here?' she asked. 'He should be hereabouts – and Ssifuss too.'

'I haven't seen either of them,' Checuti told her. 'Do you

157

suppose . . .?' He looked towards the burning wagons, which had now been reduced to ash and embers.

'Not there,' Lucrezia said. 'He was on sentry duty – Ssifuss too – but they gave no alarm. Andris thought he might have been seen earlier on, when the scout . . .'

She tried yet again to sit up but Checuti was quick to restrain her. 'Please don't move, my lady,' he said. 'Wait for a while, until another strong man comes. We'll need a litter of some sort, but we'll need woundglue first. We have supplies from the cellars of that remarkable house, and men who know the witchcraft of that accursed swamp, but you must wait until they come. They're still attending to the prisoners abandoned at the pool. Did Metra tell you that Keshvara is among them?'

'Hyry?' Lucrezia's heart leapt at the news. 'Hyry's alive!'

'Very much alive,' Checuti said. 'Weak, but not hurt.'

Metra seemed to be as startled by this intelligence as Lucrezia was. 'Didn't know,' she said, to explain why she had not broken the news.

'She was with the prisoners,' Checuti said, in case Lucrezia hadn't taken the information in the first time. 'They're mostly men of the Nine Towns. She must have crossed the entire Narrow Land after the battle of the bridge only to be captured in the far south. I haven't had a chance to talk to her at length but she says that Phar and Merel Zabio survived, and Jacom Cerri too.'

'Andris will be glad of that,' Lucrezia told him. 'Ssifuss too.'

Checuti pursed his lips when she spoke Ssifuss's name. 'Had the people I was with seen any Serpent,' he said uneasily, 'they'd have taken it for an enemy, irrespective of size.' He looked around, measuring the shadows and the density of the Reef-structures.

The night had grown a little darker, presumably because the pall of cloud which had blotted out the southern stars was drifting northwards. 'There's space out there for dozens to be hiding,' Checuti said, 'or lying exhausted, recovering their strength. It'll take until daybreak and beyond to figure out who's alive and who's dead. You must have endured a great deal these last forty or fifty hours, my lady.'

'You've no idea,' Lucrezia assured him.

A young bronze Lucrezia did not recognise – presumably a

member of Metra and Checuti's party – came to join them. He touched the thief-master upon the arm.

'Some fled,' he said. 'Perhaps half a dozen men on horseback and a few Serpents. There might be a few more in hiding hereabouts, so we'll have to remain on guard. If the ones who rode away still have prisoners with them there can be no more than two or three.'

Lucrezia was momentarily surprised to see Checuti treated as a leader, but she realised that it made sense. With Venerina Sirelis temporarily lost and Philemon Taub dead those who had survived the attack on the Community's house had had no leader of their own, and he must have been the one man among them with any experience of fighting.

'Fetch a doctor right away,' Checuti said, after nodding to signal that he understood what he had been told. 'This woman needs help. There's a female trader with the prisoners we've just set free – short hair, tough as ten of the likes of you. Tell her to come too, if she can; this is her friend.'

Her friend! Lucrezia thought. *Princess or not, I am Hyry's friend. I hope she thinks so too.* Yet again faintness tried to claim her, although she had not tried to move, and yet again she fought it. Jume Metra stood up uncertainly. 'Go,' Metra said to the bronze, as if the weight of her instruction could double the urgency of Checuti's command.

The bronze turned and ran into the shadows.

'It seems, my lady,' the thief-master said softly, 'that we are pawns in some intricate game which fate is playing with the world. A mere hundred days ago neither you nor I had any thought in our heads but to look after our own welfare and comfort – and look at us now! We are saving one another's lives with such mechanical regularity that we have become heroes out of legend. We are a thief without a stolen coin, a princess without a vagabond prince, a mound-woman without a nest, a trader without a trinket . . . and yet we are a company, closer to Chimera's Cradle than the fool who adopted us all into his quest for the place.' Lucrezia knew that he had left the pause because he did not know whether Andris Myrasol could be counted into their company or not. She also knew that he was trying to humour her, to lift her spirits a little with his wit and wordplay.

'I've lost a lot of blood, haven't I?' she whispered.

'You have Serpent's blood to spare,' he answered. 'Don't be afraid.'

'I won't,' she promised – but even as she promised it she lost her battle against the prowling darkness that so dearly wished to possess her.

The sight and sound of him faded away, and she wondered whether she would ever wake again.

20

ANDRIS KNEW THAT he was dreaming, but the last thing in the world he wanted was to wake up. Within his dream he felt safe, and relaxed. Within his dream there was space and time to do and say and think all the things that there had not been time to do and say and think while he was awake.

Awake he was continually beset by conflicts and crises; dreaming he had infinity for a playground and all eternity to spare.

For a while he talked to Lucrezia, although she was invisible. He could have seen her had he wanted to – indeed, he could have conjured up a whole landscape in which to place her – but he didn't feel the need. For now, he was only interested in making himself heard, and it didn't matter in the least how slight the presence of his audience was.

'I began to see it while we were in the marshes,' he said, 'but I didn't understand the full implications then. The potion Venerina gave me hasn't helped in the way she and Philemon thought it would, but I think I understand why that was. It's all a matter of scale, you see.'

He hesitated, but not because of any doubt as to whether she was listening or whether she was following the thread of his argument. She had no choice in such matters, being a mere figment of his dream. When he'd tried to pass on the produce of his supposed wisdom in the marshes she'd been unable to listen, and when he'd tried again while they were at the Community's house she hadn't quite been able to follow his thread, but she was perfectly able to listen and follow now.

'We think of ourselves as tiny beings and the world as a vast expanse,' he continued, 'some of whose territories we've tamed – but to the tiny creatures living in our bodies *we're* the vast expanses. I think the world is a good deal more peculiar than we suppose – and a good deal more peculiar than our forefathers supposed when they first established us here. I think they designed and prepared the lore according to a lot of presuppositions which turned out to be incorrect, and had to amend it in a hurry, turning it into an ungainly patchwork. I think the world is much more like a body than the forefathers thought – or, at least, that it has individuals within it of a magnitude that we can barely perceive, let alone comprehend.'

'Giants,' she whispered.

'Not exactly,' he demurred. 'What *we* call giants – whether they're human or Serpent – are almost as tiny as we are on the scale we have to try to think about. Even the dragomite queen – the whole interior of the hill, I mean, not that half-human creature sitting on that absurd throne – wasn't so very large. Even she was no more than an insect, and those stone-creatures we passed on the way here are little more than *bacteria* by comparison with the things I mean. I'm talking about creatures that can be as big as the entire Soursweet Marshes, or as big as the Forest of Absolute Night. *They*'re the dominant life forms on this world, not humans or Serpents or Salamanders . . . except, of course, that they're related in some peculiar way to the Serpents and the Salamanders . . . because the Serpents and Salamanders are among their countless offspring, although paedogenesis has helped them cultivate intelligence and win a measure of freedom. I don't mean they're the *children* of the dwellers in the deep . . . they're more like *spores*, if you can imagine spores which cultivate intelligence. The reason we can't see these incredibly huge beings, of course, is that they're mostly underground. In fact, they mostly *are* the ground.'

'But not Chimera's Cradle,' Lucrezia put in, to make it clear that she did know what he was talking about, and that she was more than capable of elaborating the scheme by herself. 'Chimera's Cradle is *our* ground – isn't that what Ssifuss said? Our *earth* – the earth the forefathers made, to produce that which is genuinely *earthly*.'

'That's right,' Andris agreed. 'When the forefathers lost their city, they had to build a garden – a garden whose construction required them to borrow something from Serpents and something from Salamanders: Serpent's blood, let's say, and Salamander's fire. But gardens grow slowly and humans age quickly, so whatever they planted couldn't be expected to bear fruit for many generations. And in the meantime . . .'

'In the meantime,' Lucrezia said, 'they left. They went away, and left us to it.'

'In the meantime,' Andris repeated, picking up the sentence she'd interrupted, 'the creatures that were already here reacted according to their own fashion to the usurpation of their privilege. A kind of war began: a slow, sporadic war extending over thousands of years. A war we can hardly imagine, let alone understand. A war which changed things in ways the forefathers couldn't have predicted. A war we're caught up in, without even knowing it.'

'We know it now,' Lucrezia contradicted him. 'Whatever we may have overlooked, we haven't overlooked that. We've been constantly in combat since the moment you set foot on the quay beneath the citadel wall, and it doesn't look as if it's going to let up for a moment. If we want to get to Chimera's Cradle, via Salamander's Fire or by any other route, we'll have to fight every step of the way. Didn't Philemon try to tell us that, when he warned us that we'd be in mortal danger if we didn't turn back? He didn't know, of course, that the mortal danger in question was about to reach out from the Great Reef, all the way to his own peaceful resting place.'

'He was right, in a way,' Andris said. 'We've placed ourselves in terrible danger . . . but we're here now, and there's no way back. The important thing is that we have a part to play in the world's brief crisis, if only we can figure out what it is. At least, the things within us have a part to play: your Serpent's blood and my Spirit of the Lake. We're just *caught in the middle*, between the very large and the very small . . . but that doesn't mean we're irrelevant. We have our own contributions to make, our own rewards to receive.'

'Where does the deists' God fit into it?' she asked.

'The deists would say that *we* fit into *Him*,' Andris told her. 'But God's just the name they give to the game of life – the game in which we're all involved, the play in which we all have our parts. What they really mean by God, although they don't see it that way, is merely the rules by which the game is played: rules that we don't make and can't alter. They weren't really *made* at all, not by a *maker* at any rate, but they are there and they do govern the limits of possibility. I understand much better now where those limits lie, and why. The Spirit of the Lake is helping me to do that. I'm not just Andris Myrasol, any more than you're just Princess Lucrezia. We have worlds inside us, inhabited by all kinds of unearthly species, some of which are stranger than we imagine . . . perhaps stranger than we *can* imagine, even if they help us.'

The dialogue ran out of steam then. He let it drift away, and dreamed a different dream. This one was more insistent, as if it were some alien entity forcing itself upon him rather than the creation of his own fertile brain.

He dreamed that he was tightly bound to a horse that was far too scrawny to carry a burden like him for any length of time. It was daylight, and the sun was uncomfortably bright; whoever had bound him hadn't taken the trouble to give him a hat. The terrain over which the horse was carrying him was within the great arc of the Reef; he was heading southwards along the 'highway' that Lucrezia had seen from the high branches of the dendrite.

He was in the company of seven mounted men and five giant Serpents. There were no wagons, and there were no other prisoners. It seemed that his captors had fled the Reef with but a single prize, and he was it. For a moment or two he felt perversely flattered, but then he realised that without adequate water supplies the raiders had had no choice but to abandon the prisoners they had brought across the outer wasteland. He could only qualify as some sort of consolation prize.

It was an uncomfortable dream, and Andris was glad when he was able to fold it away into the darkness and replace it with another leisurely dialogue. This time, he addressed himself to the head of the drone which he had brought out of the dragomite hive. He had talked to the drone before, in his dreams, and he had clung fast to it even in the extremity of his delirium after Ssifuss had reunited him with it.

'I'm sorry I haven't found an opportunity to equip you with a new body, Seth,' he said. 'I've been busy. Battles to fight, mysteries to solve.'

'That's all right,' the hive-man said. 'There's time yet.'

'I hope so,' Andris told him. 'I really do.'

'There's a long way to go,' Seth answered equably, 'but the time will pass quickly enough.'

'How much of this do you understand?' Andris wanted to know. 'What lore did you conserve, down in that strange cavern? You had secrets, I know – secrets which you kept from your sisters. How did you come by them? Who told them to you? How long have you kept them?'

'Only give me a voice,' said the drone, 'and I'll tell you everything.'

'You have a voice,' Andris pointed out. 'You're speaking to me now.'

'I need a voice of my own,' said the head, as if it ought to have been obvious.

'I think that's the problem,' Andris said. 'We all need voices of our own, but those of us who speak don't know, and those of us who know can't speak. The dwellers in the deep need voices of their own and minds of their own, but they only have creatures like us to help them. They have eyes and they have ears, but they have no voices and they have no minds. Imagine what it would be like if the invisible passengers in our flesh and our blood had mind and voices, but we had none.'

'I don't have to imagine,' Seth said. 'I've dwelt within the body of the dragomite queen since I first drew breath. She's just an insect, but she's a dweller in the deep nevertheless. Her kind may yet be winners in the game, inheritors of the world.'

'I don't think so,' Andris said.

'You don't *know*,' the head rebuked him. 'You hope, but you don't *know*. No one does. No one can.'

'No *one* can,' Andris agreed, 'but a legion might.'

He dreamed then that he was in a soft tomb made out of something warm and sticky – or perhaps it was a womb and not a tomb, or a cocoon and not a womb. Whatever it was he was sealed within it, unable to breathe, but not, strangely enough, unable to dream. He dreamed that a face hovered above him, intently looking down at him through the translucent membrane which imprisoned him.

Although he couldn't see it clearly, Andris judged that the creature was as tall as an ordinary man but a good ten sems shorter than him. Its features were reminiscent of the creature which had guided him through the depths of the dragomite hive to the secret chamber where the queen kept her human drones. Its eyes were large, dark and forward-looking. Its skin was dressed with polished scales. Its mouth was wide and its head was hairless. Its ears were rounded. Its blurred stare was unwavering but it didn't seem to be hostile; it gave the impression of solicitude, as if it were looking after him as well as at him. Andris would have spoken to it if he could, but in this phase of the dream he was mute.

He had no idea how much time went by while he was in the tomb – or the womb, or the cocoon – but he never grew impatient. The restfulness of it was pleasant.

In another phase of the dream he saw the garden, but he wasn't certain that the eyes with which he saw it were his own.

An unexpectedly sheer slope ran up to the crest of a hill, some fifty or sixty mets in extent. It was decked with at least two hundred bushes, although the sturdiest of them would easily have qualified as trees in the orchards of Ferentina. The smallest of them were built around the torsos of humans buried to the waist, but the tallest had lifted their victims – or their hosts – out of such captivity, so that their 'trunks' extended from the tips of their heads to a woody pedestal beneath their feet.

Each bush or tree had two main branches, based in the extended arms of its human element, but those main branches put out dozens of other sub-branches, and there were shoots extending in every direction from the breasts and shoulders of the imprisoned people. Every branch was decked with delicate spatulate leaves, and also with curved thorns, each as long as a sewing needle. The bushes bore flowers and fruits, too: flowers as white as stripped bone and fruits as red as human blood.

The bushes all had open eyes, and they stared upon the world with infinite patience, but their faces were ravaged by care. There was no agony in their expressions, but there was sadness.

There was not the slightest doubt that the hosts in whose flesh the plants were embedded were still alive, still conscious, still active in spite of their almost-stillness. They were anchored to the ground by invisible roots but they were not completely still. Their boughs were mobile, and they could turn their heads. They looked at him – or whoever owned the eyes through which he was privileged to look – as curiously as he looked at them. They moved their limbs, albeit without any great alacrity, stirring themselves as if some wayward breeze were blowing through their branches.

One of the nearest opened its mouth and called to him, 'Come here!' When he made no move – having no power of movement, so far as he could judge – half a dozen others began calling, their voices overlapping. Some said 'Come to me!' while others asked his name and one or two were content to offer words of welcome which seemed all the more sinister for their apparent sincerity.

The chimeras did not persist in their calling when he made no response; after a minute or two, silence fell again.

It was obvious that the gatherers tending the garden had been busy. He remembered that the time of troubles had begun some years before – long enough for someone to send seeds from the garden as far as Xandria. How many other gardens like this had its emissaries managed to plant in distant parts? Precious few, he thought, where there were men to root them out. No matter how poisonous those thorns were, nor how loudly those voices proclaimed the happiness of their condition, he knew that such things would not be tolerated in any land where he had lived – and he had crossed half the world since leaving Ferentina.

'I will not be part of this,' he said. 'I *will not*.'

'You are on our ground,' answered the nearest of the chimeras, which had been the first to ask him to come closer. 'You can neither run nor fight; the earth itself has hold of you. What will be, will be. You have but one choice, and that is to listen or to close your ears. You will be far more use to yourself, as well as to us, if you lend us your intelligence as well as your flesh. We have your flesh already, as I think you know.'

The dream form which Andris was inhabiting looked down at itself. It was standing on what seemed to be a carpet of soft moss, but he saw that the prints its feet made were more than two sems deep. It could lift its foot freely, for the moment, but when he asked himself where it might put the foot down while being sure that it could pick it up again, he understood what the chimera was saying to him. This place had already provided him with a second skin, which had laboured hard to keep him fed, watered and fit while the gatherers brought him here; it had been under no compulsion to release him at all.

'You're sick,' Andris said, although he could not tell what kind of voice it was he used to frame the words.

He realised, as the words fell upon the still air, that they were true. The garden *was* sick. The branches on the bushes were broken and bleeding; the petals of their flowers were torn. They felt no pain, but their sadness was real. They feared death. They feared extinction. They were caught up in a war which they were not winning.

'No,' he said, trying to raise the pitch and volume of his borrowed voice. 'I don't care. I have my own side in this, my own quest. I fought with dragomites, but I won't fight with you. I won't do it. I know I'm only dreaming, but I won't do that, even in a dream. I have my own life, my own ends. Whatever you might do to me, I'll never be part of this. Never.'

The chimeras stared back at him bleakly. Somewhere nearby, he felt sure, other eyes were staring at him with equal bleakness and equal curiosity. Seth was there too, but his eyes were still closed; like Andris, he was waiting, biding his time. Lucrezia had gone; Andris could no longer find the darkness where he had left her.

Andris wanted to go back to that darkness, but he couldn't.

His dream was turning into a nightmare, and the worst part of the nightmare was the rapidly growing suspicion that all of it was not a dream, and that perhaps the part of it which *was* a dream was not as important as the part which only seemed to be.

It wasn't difficult, once he had begun to think like that, to understand that when he woke from his dream – if he ever did – he would certainly find himself anchored to the earth, sprouting countless branches decked with poisonous thorns.

He wanted to cry out, but he couldn't. He wanted to run away, but he couldn't do that either. His dream, to the extent that it *was* a dream, held him more securely than any prison – and he knew that it would never let him go. From this particular nightmare, there could be no release.

Part Two

To the Gardens of Transformation, Prisoners of Mutation and Misfortune

The world of dreams will always be unquiet, for that is the nature of dreams. We are children of the world but we are also children of the world of dreams; its inquietude is the hope and urgency of our yearning hearts.

There are dreams which look back as if they were memories, but memories are not to be trusted, for they are subject to corruption and corrosion. The dreams which look back at paradise are lies, for there never was a paradise; there was only another world, which we have lost.

The best dreams are those which look forwards. The art of prophecy is more treacherous than the art of memory, but dreams may be treasured, kept safe from corruption and corrosion. Memories cannot be hoarded as treasure until the Pool of Life delivers incorruptible stone into human hands, but prophesies can be kept safe if only the dreams that they represent continue to command affection.

There is no destiny, for the future is as yet unmade, but our dreams will play their part in its making and they are to be treasured on that account. Unless we dream the best dreams of which we are capable, the future will be poorer than it might be. Nothing is written in the stars which says that humans will conquer each and every world on which they choose to dwell, and conquest itself might be an illusion, but wherever humans are they may remain, if only they can find a way.

Human beings should never be afraid or ashamed to dream, or to dwell in dreams. Whatever they may say in desperate denial, those human beings who cannot dream cannot live, now or in the future that is yet unmade.

The Wisdom of the Tree of Knowledge

I

LUCREZIA DRIFTED IN and out of consciousness continually, losing count of the hours and the days. She was aware of being lifted at regular intervals in order that cups might be put to her lips and spoons to her tongue. She drank and she ate, but she did so mechanically, without any involvement of intention.

She saw faces, and knew that she knew at least some of them, but she was incapable of conscious recognition and meaningful response. Words were often spoken to her, and she sometimes spoke herself, but the meaning of all these utterances evaded her sluggish mind and made none but the merest impact on her memory.

She felt a certain amount of pain, but it was always dull, and it seemed, somehow, that it didn't really belong to her. In fact, it seemed that nothing belonged to her any longer – neither flesh nor sensation had any sense of being hers. She was aware that time was passing, that events were occurring, but she was incapable of caring.

It was impossible for her to care, in any positive sense, whether life went on or not, but her flesh had a tenacity that her mind had not. Her blood had an energy and resilience of its own. While she floated in limbo, lost to all involvement and motivation, her blood renewed itself within her veins – and whatever secrets her blood held renewed themselves also.

There was no sudden awakening from this state; she recovered herself by slow degrees. An element of volition crept back into her sipping and her swallowing. She found herself able to put names – Hyry Keshvara, Checuti, Jume Metra – to the faces which still remained in orbit around her when all the others had gone. She was able to remember a little of what was said to her, and insert a little intelligence into her replies.

Still time passed: hours; days. Still she drifted back and forth, helplessly, between the world which was and the world which had only the substance of dreams.

Her dreams weren't unpleasant, but when she was capable of taking notice of them she felt a certain dissatisfaction with them nevertheless, because they were so obstinately backward-looking. She dreamed about the Inner Sanctum and Ereleth, not even about dragomites and battles, let alone about Chimera's Cradle and the other gardens within the Great Reef. Her dreams were dreams of escape, after their fashion, but as soon as she was sufficiently conscious of herself to pass judgment upon them she was careful to remind herself that the citadel and her education as a witch-princess had been the things that she wanted so badly to escape *from*.

Eventually, she escaped even from the Inner Sanctum of her dreams. The walls of indifference which had contained her for so long an interval were rotted away, but even then she couldn't simply step outside. First she had to sleep more deeply; then she had to awake, as she might have awakened on any other day, to find herself fully restored to the gorgeous and menacing world.

She found, once her head was a little clearer, that she was lying on a tolerable mattress, covered by a good blanket. She was dressed in a thin shift of some kind, which wasn't freshly woven by any means but felt as tolerably soft as the mattress did.

She was inside a confined space that was dimly illumined by the tiny flame of a thin candle; it reflected back off a canvas awning exactly like the one mounted on the wagon which had burned to ashes behind her when the giant Serpents and their monstrous companions had attacked.

There was someone lying beside her, fast asleep. As soon as she tried to move, though, the sleeper stirred and turned to face her. It was Hyry Keshvara.

When she saw that Lucrezia's eyes were open, the trader sat up. She shook off the burden of sleep with an alacrity that Lucrezia could only wonder at.

'Can you hear me, my lady?' Hyry asked, as if there were a possibility that Lucrezia might *not* be able to hear her.

'Yes,' Lucrezia said. 'I'm all right.' Some time passed before she could add: 'I know I haven't been, but now I am.'

Hyry took a little more convincing than that, but she was persuaded in the end. 'I had begun to fear that you might not recover fully,' the trader admitted. 'I wondered whether your mind would be permanently impaired, even though your flesh had healed.'

Lucrezia tried to sit up but couldn't do it. She could barely move her arm, but she contrived to reach up with her fingers to touch the place on her neck where that long and ragged wound had begun.

There was no scab that she could feel, and no pain either. If there was a scar, it was not obvious to the touch. She knew that she had been given something to make her sleep while her body mended. Hyry would not have had a drug to do that, nor knowledge enough to borrow one from Lucrezia's witch's pharmacopeia, so she must have been attended by a doctor — presumably one from the Community. She felt ravenous.

'You shouldn't have knocked me out like that,' she said, when she could form that kind of sentence. 'You should have let me stay awake.'

'You were unconscious long before the doctor reached you,' Hyry told her. 'We had to plaster your cuts with woundglue. The glue's anaesthetics helped to keep you under but the doctor thought it best to feed you additional dopeweed. At first, he thought you'd lost too much blood to recover, but you have a stubborn body, it seems. I don't think it was the doctor's ministrations that pulled you through, but it seemed wisest to follow his instructions, even after he'd gone. Checuti thought so too.'

While she was speaking, and without waiting to be asked, Hyry had fetched a stone bottle. It contained something stronger than water, although it quenched Lucrezia's thirst well enough. It took the sharp edge off her hunger, although she knew that she'd have to have solid food soon. In the meantime, Hyry studied her, evidently trying to work out whether she had, in fact, fully returned to the land of the living.

'How long has it been?' Lucrezia asked.

'Since the battle? Nine days. Venerina Sirelis and her people started the long march home four days ago. They left us a wagon and plenty of supplies. We've had abundant opportunity to make ourselves comfortable, although we've not been entirely undisturbed. There are predators in the Reef as well as birds and fervent creepers, and we're camped close to a good waterhole. Jume Metra's on watch. Checuti's sleeping in his own little nest.'

Lucrezia drank again from the bottle, glad that the liquid was warming as well as wet. She deduced that 'fervent creepers' must be the snake-like things that coiled around the upper branches of the dendrites, and was proud of herself for being able to make the connection.

'Anything solid?' she asked. 'To eat, that is.'

Hyry rummaged amid the clutter which surrounded them; it was difficult to judge its exact quality by candlelight, but Lucrezia found its bulk reassuring. After wandering through the marshes with a dwindling pack and then trekking south across the Plain of Figured Stones with nothing but her belt it was good to be surrounded by *things*. Hyry gave her something that was neither bread nor meat, but might have been a roasted creeper. Lucrezia didn't dare ask what it was; she simply set about chewing. The sensation was welcome and reassuring.

'What about Andris?' she asked, after a little while.

'No sign,' Hyry told her. 'Disappeared without trace – Ssifuss too. They might have been taken, but they're certainly nowhere near here, dead or alive. Venerina's people searched long and hard.'

Lucrezia needed more time to absorb the import of this news, but the pause wasn't as long and she was losing her enthusiasm for chewing more rapidly than she had imagined possible. 'Are you all right?' she asked eventually.

'I'm fine now,' the trader assured her. 'There was never anything wrong with me that food and rest couldn't cure. If it hadn't been for Checuti and Jume Metra, though . . . I gather that the bastards who grabbed me intended to feed me to one of those bushes I brought to you. Even Checuti and Metra might have been helpless if you and Venerina Sirelis hadn't taken out the first party and then embroiled my own captors in a fight.'

'It wasn't me,' Lucrezia said, in a voice which had sunk to a whisper. 'It wasn't Venerina either. We were there, but it was Andris and Ssifuss who disposed of the giant Serpents. Without them, we'd all be dead – or worse.'

'And it was thanks to your witchery that they had the chance,' Hyry added. 'We've heard the whole story. Without you . . . well, I'm very glad indeed to hear you speaking sensibly again.

174

Did Checuti tell you that Aulakh Phar is alive – or was when when I saw him last? Jacom Cerri too, and Merel Zabio. We were separated in Antiar, but I heard that they'd all gone south with a bronze named Amyas, with a small army for their protection.'

'Andris Myrasol would have been very glad to hear that news,' Lucrezia said, her heart fluttering at the thought of his probable capture.

Nine days! she thought. *Nine days must have been long enough to reach the garden for which they were heading – and if not, it's certainly a lead which can't be caught up now. Why has Venerina Sirelis gone north? Why didn't she repay the debt she owed to Andris?*

'Andris fought for Venerina Sirelis three times,' Lucrezia said aloud. 'On every occasion he faced enemies the like of which he'd never seen before – enemies that few other humans would have dared confront. At the house by the Lake of Colourless Blood he helped dozens to escape. The stand he took against the drugged Serpents did at least as much to secure our first victory here as my witchcraft. When the wagons were fired he could have retreated to the more distant branches of the dendrite but he must have come down instead, to do what he could to hold the Serpents at bay yet again. All of that he did while severely disconcerted by poisons, including some which Venerina deliberately gave him to drink . . . but you're telling me that she simply took her people home, leaving him to the mercy of his enemies.' It was a very long speech but she got through it.

'It wasn't as simple as that,' Hyry said uneasily.

'Wasn't it?'

'We don't know that he's alive even now,' the trader pointed out. 'At first, we didn't know whether he might turn up at any moment, and by the time we were certain that he wasn't in the vicinity the men and giant Serpents who'd fled the battle were long gone. If we'd chased after them, we'd have been risking everything we'd saved. If he was taken, he was taken across direly dangerous ground towards a destination where hundreds more men and giant Serpents might be waiting. Even if we'd thought we could catch up with them by launching an immediate pursuit, we'd have been fools to try it. Venerina Sirelis felt that her first responsibility was to her own people – that if she

175

couldn't guide the liberated prisoners home, the Community would be finished. She couldn't let the fate of one man stand in the way of securing the future of her own people.'

'If the Community can't honour its debts,' Lucrezia said harshly, 'what good is there in its survival?' It was petulance speaking, not common sense; she knew well enough that the Community had already saved Andris Myrasol's life once, and hers with it. What the amber had done thereafter was more than sufficient to cancel out his debt to Venerina, but the fact remained that he was only one man; Venerina must have had at least fifty to think about. When the balance of risk had been set against the balance of responsibility, there had only been one conclusion for the Community's leader to reach – and Hyry could not have persuaded her otherwise, even if she had wanted to.

'So we're a party of four,' Lucrezia said, after another pause. 'Just you and me, Metra and Checuti. Why aren't we headed for Salamander's Fire?'

'It seemed best to wait a while,' Hyry said. 'We all needed to recuperate; there was nothing lost by waiting for you to recover – and for a while we dared not move you. You have no idea how close you came to death, highness.'

'There are no highnesses here,' Lucrezia told her dully, 'and I believe I understand well enough how nearly fatal that neck wound was. I shed more blood than was left inside me.'

'Very nearly,' Hyry agreed. 'Without medical help, you'd be dead – and even with it, you needed more than common resilience. Now that you're recovered, we can make our plans. It'll soon be dawn – we can be ready to move in a matter of hours, if . . .' She left the sentence dangling.

'If what?' Lucrezia prompted, although she knew well enough what Hyry must mean.

'If we do intend to head for Salamander's Fire,' Hyry said, 'Checuti thinks it might be wiser – and safer – to work our way around the Reef to the point at which Carus Fraxinus is likely to arrive, if he's en route from Salamander's Fire to Chimera's Cradle. I know he said he'd wait there, but he's very likely to have given us up by now.'

Lucrezia found that she was finally able to raise herself on to her elbow. This enabled her to meet Hyry Keshvara's gaze in a more forthright manner. 'We can't do that,' she said, although she was uncomfortably aware of the fact that they might be unable to do otherwise. 'Venerina Sirelis might have abandoned Andris and Ssifuss, but we can't. Andris didn't abandon me when he had more than adequate reason to do so. Neither did Ssifuss.'

Hyry met her gaze squarely enough. 'You can't be serious,' the trader said flatly.

'Yes I can,' Lucrezia replied.

The trader seemed unworried by the contradiction; Lucrezia judged that Hyry must be taking refuge in the presumption that she was still ill, not quite herself. Privately, Lucrezia had to concede that four humans, equipped with one wagon and a handful of horses, could hardly hope to prevail even against half a dozen horsemen and a brace of giant Serpents, let alone any greater number. Chasing such a company all the way to its destination would probably be tantamount to suicide . . . even leaving aside the awkward matter of the nine days that had elapsed since Andris Myrasol had disappeared.

'We're on our own whatever we do next,' Lucrezia went on. 'We don't know that we can link up with Fraxinus again, whether we head for Salamander's Fire or stay close to the Reef, but we do know that our ultimate destination lies southwards, and that there's a road of sorts which leads that way.'

Hyry contented herself with a slow shake of the head. She might have said more, but she looked around instead as Checuti climbed up into the wagon.

'I heard your voices,' he said. 'Dawn's not far off. How are you, my lady?'

'Well enough,' Lucrezia told him. 'Hyry and I were just discussing the possibilities which lie before us, now that I'm recovered.'

Checuti must have heard some of what she'd said before making his presence known. 'I know that the call of your Serpent's blood is supposed to draw you in the direction of Chimera's Cradle, my lady,' he said, 'but the blood which flows in my veins – and probably that which flows in the veins of real Serpents – exercises no such insistence. Even Ssifuss, were he here, would presumably consider it wisest to try to link up with

Mossassor and Fraxinus before braving the journey to the Navel of the World.'

'If Fraxinus survived the Spangled Desert he'll probably still be waiting at Salamander's Fire,' Lucrezia said, although she didn't really doubt Hyry's judgment that he probably wouldn't be. 'It's a long way there and back again.'

'And all the evidence suggests that the terrain in between is becoming ever more difficult and dangerous,' Checuti agreed. 'That's why it's best to stay close to the Reef. Considering that you once intended to plant a thorn-bush in the amber's flesh yourself, highness, there's a certain irony in your present hankering to risk everything in a mad dash to save him from that fate, don't you think?'

'We've made a pact since I tried to buy Andris out of my father's prison,' Lucrezia pointed out. 'A pact which involves us all, including you. You might think that you made it under duress, but I gave you the antidote to my house-mother's cunning worm without asking a price. Can you really turn your back on Andris's plight so easily?'

'If there were any real chance of saving him,' Checuti countered, soberly and in all apparent honesty, 'I'd be enthusiastic to try, but without abundant help, as you know full well, there's no chance at all.'

Lucrezia's head had begun to ache now that she had raised it from its makeshift pillow, and she knew that logic was against her.

'I need fresh water,' she murmured. 'Please!'

'I'll get it,' Checuti said, raising a hand as Hyry moved to stand up. He left the way he had come.

'What about Jume Metra?' Lucrezia asked. 'Where does she want to go now?'

'I think she's decided to think of us as a kind of substitute nest,' Hyry replied. 'Without some kind of common enterprise to share she'd be unbearably lost, and I'm sure she'll consent to whatever the three of us decide. I can't tell how reliable she might be in future, though, if matters became further complicated. Were we to meet other dragomite-women, she might recalculate her loyalties.'

Lucrezia had nothing to say in reply that seemed worth the

178

effort of speech. She let her head fall back to the pillow, determined to lie there until Checuti brought the water.

'Better to rest,' Hyry said approvingly. 'Dawn's coming – we'll all feel better when it's light.'

Somehow, Lucrezia doubted it; she had a strange conviction that the way she felt right now was as good as she was going to feel for some considerable time to come.

2

ANDRIS CONTINUED TO dream, and to suspect that there was more to his visions than mere hallucination.

In one phase of his dream the soft mask that covered his face was carefully removed. It came away easily enough; it was sticky enough to cling momentarily here and there, but its removal caused him no pain at all. Delicate fingers deftly cleared the last remnants of it from the corners of his eyes before he lifted the lids.

His eyes were immediately drawn to the face that hovered above him, intently looking down at him. It was not a human face, nor a Serpent face, but it had a little of the human and the Serpent about it, although the earthly creature it most resembled was a frog. He had seen something like it before but for the moment he could not remember where. The dark eyes met his; reflected daylight made the polished scales of the creature's hairless head gleam and glisten. The gaze of the dark eyes was so steady and so contemplative that it seemed to define the creature's essence; whatever species it belonged to – or whatever combination of species – it was first and foremost a *Watcher*.

While Andris stared at it the Watcher moved back slightly, but it continued to meet his curious eyes. It never blinked, but now that he could see it clearly he observed that a transparent nictitating membrane occasionally flickered across the moist surface of each eye.

In a flash of inspiration, he remembered where he had seen other things like it: in the depths of the dragomite nest, and then again in the depths of the living Lake of Colourless Blood. It must be kin to the Serpents and the Salamanders, he decided: a third unearthly sentient species, somehow unmentioned in the lore. No sooner had he made that decision, however, than he began to doubt it. Perhaps it was not a distinct species at all.

Perhaps it was a chimera, patched together from several different kinds of flesh. Perhaps it was part-human, part-Serpent and part-frog. Such things were conceivable in this region of the world; indeed, there seemed to be nothing in these parts that was anything but an exotic compound of earthly and unearthly flesh.

Am I still dreaming? he wondered. *Could I think so clearly in a dream? Could I change my mind in a dream?*

'Where am I?' Andris asked, but he knew that it was a foolish question. Awake or dreaming, he already knew where he was. He was in the garden. The question he needed to ask was: *What am I, and what shall I become?*

When the Watcher didn't answer his unnecessary question Andris looked down at his own body. The upper part of it was still in the process of shedding its slowly disintegrating second skin. The translucent membrane was shrivelling readily enough, and he had not the slightest difficulty in using his hands to tear great lumps of it away from his breast and forearms. There seemed little point in wondering whether it had always been that disgusting shade of grey or whether that was merely evidence of its dying.

The lower part of his body had no such tegument. He had lost all contact with the lower part of his body, and it was invisible.

That settles it, he concluded. *I'm dreaming. No doubt about it. Dreaming.*

Because he was dreaming, and knew that he was dreaming, he knew that there was nothing unduly strange about the discovery that he had been buried waist-deep in the mossy soil. Nor was there anything very frightening about the conviction he felt that he had not merely been buried in the soil but eaten alive by it and gathered into its substance.

Because he was dreaming, and knew he was dreaming, there seemed to be no particular paradox in his acceptance of the fact that he no longer had legs, or genitals, or even a navel. He was one with the earth now. He grew out of the ground – and not as a plant might grow, embedded but still separate, but as an extension of the ground itself.

As a dreamer, he could accept such a fate with relative equanimity. It would have been very different, of course, had he been awake.

There was no sign yet of green shoots sprouting from his skin, but he knew that they would appear in time – and that they too would be an aspect of the ground, in no way foreign to his own adopted flesh.

Because he was dreaming, he felt no incongruity in the thought that he had been foolish to fear this possibility. Had Princess Lucrezia fed him the seed in the citadel of Xandria, he now realised, he would not have been colonised by something alien; he would merely have become something new – and although the soil of the Inner Sanctum's roof garden would have been nothing but soil, at least to begin with, it would in time have been drawn into the process of metamorphosis. That might, in fact, have been the true purpose of the experiment: to transform the man, *and then the ground*. The bronzes Hyry Keshvara had met in the Forest of Absolute Night had not told her that, of course. They had taken her for a fool, and the princess too. How many other fools might they have found, wandering in the unearthly forest without the benefit of darklander superstition and darklander fear of all things unfamiliar?

That was the trouble with traders, his dream-self decided. They had inquisitive minds; their native suspicion of the new and the strange had atrophied. They were prepared to *investigate possibilities*. They always wanted to know things that simpler men were determined *not* to know. Carus Fraxinus thought that his inquiring mind was a sign of intelligence and the spirit of civilisation, but it was really a kind of disease: an innocent invitation to doom and disaster.

'We are all *worlds*,' his dream self said to the Watcher, which listened attentively. 'We all have the means within us to transform the greater worlds in which we find ourselves. That's why we have to be very careful how we live our lives. We have to take care to hold that transformative power within ourselves rather than letting it out to enliven the ground on which we walk. Ssifuss was right after all, you see; humans *are* a kind of disease, or at least have the capacity within them to *become* the seeds of disease. Just as the diseases we catch can transform us, in all kinds of bizarre ways, so we can transform whole worlds. All we have to do is to become *active*, so that the potential which normally lies dormant within us can be released. As within, so without.'

The Watcher made no reply, but it was interested. It was listening.

Andris wondered, within his dream, whether he ought to ask for water with which to wash away the last remnants of the second skin, but when he ran his fingers over his bare forearm it seemed to be a good deal cleaner than it had been for many days, if not for years. He realised, somewhat to his surprise, that he didn't feel the least need of water to drink, nor food to eat. His mouth was moist and his stomach comfortable.

He felt a new and precious kind of freedom, which he had never thought possible while he had been condemned to inhabit his waking self. From now on, he was one with the ground. From now on, he would not need to eat and he would not need to drink. He had shed his old needs along with the false skin; he had new needs now, and new horizons of possibility.

Within his dream, he found no horror in the thought that his wandering was over. Within his dream, he knew that he had reached his destination – that this was what he had been seeking ever since he had left Ferentina.

'I am what I am,' he told the patient Watcher. 'I am what I will be, and there is no cause for regret or astonishment in that. This is my ground, for which I have been searching all my days. I am part of it now, and it is part of me. I'm not a disease. I might have been, had the princess given me the seed in Xandria, but not here. Here, the ground was ready to receive me. In coming here, I've come home. I'm not a wanderer any more. I'm not a stranger any more. No one else will ever mistake me for something I'm not. No one else will ever treat me with contempt because I don't look like them. I've lost the freedom to be hungry; I've lost the freedom to be tired; I've lost the freedom to be thrown in jail, bullied, blackmailed and abused. I've found the garden where I can safely rest. This is a dream, but it's a good dream and a healthy dream.'

The Watcher heard him, but it made no reply.

In spite of what he said to the Watcher, Andris was not without astonishment and he was not without regret, because he could see clearly enough that all was not well in the garden. The garden had been attacked, more than once. Its inhabitants had been brutalised, their branches broken and their blossoms crushed. The garden had been *hurt*, and the hurt was not ended yet.

Andris concluded that the time of troubles which had devastated the Dragomite Hills and made his adventure possible was not yet concluded; the fever that had come upon the living ground had yet to die down; death was still a possibility, as was permanent decay. Andris knew that because he was part of the garden now, his own life hung in the balance with the life of the garden, just as Seth's life had hung in the balance with the life of the dragomite queen.

Andris remembered that Seth had been only half a man, exactly as he was now, but that Seth had said something vitally important – something which he must continue to hold in mind whatever disconcerting phases of his dream he had yet to endure.

'The warriors may have told you that we are all of one mind here,' Seth had told him, 'but it is not so. They do not understand. We are not all of one mind, nor all of one body, no matter how things may appear.'

'I am one with the body of the garden,' Andris said, within the safety of his dream. 'I am one with the seed that grows within me: the seed that will make branches of my arms and lift me up to stand taller than any other; the seed that will make bloody flowers of my flesh. We are all of one body here, and must be all of one mind. How could it be otherwise? And yet . . . we are *not* all of one mind. I have my own mind – and so long as I am able to dream, I shall keep it.'

The only individual who actually heard this speech was the Watcher, but Seth was capable of speech while Andris had the power to dream his words, and it was Seth that replied, or seemed to. 'You're a man, Andris, as am I,' Seth said. 'We're brothers in blood and brain, and the dwellers in the deep can't take that away from us no matter what they do.'

Andris struggled to make sense of this dispute. For a giddy moment or two he wondered whose dream it was that he was dreaming, and whether he might, after all, be a mere figment of the imagination of some vast slumbering God.

'Change and decay in all around I see,' he whispered. 'O thou who changest not, *abide with me*.'

He felt a thrill of terror then, of purest nightmare. He knew that the voice which had seemed to be Seth's was really his own, and that some part of him was trying to warn the part of him that was trying so desperately to keep calm and to maintain order that calm was unjustified and that chaos had wormed its way into the very heart and soul of him.

He reached out with both his arms towards the silent Watcher.

'Bring me the head that I carried from the depths of the dragomite nest,' he said insistently. 'You must bring my brother to me, for I shall be only half a man without his company, without his balancing presence. *Bring me my brother's head!*'

The Watcher went away, for what seemed like a long time, while night fell and the stars came out, blurred by drifting cloud.

In the next phase of the dream, however, Andris held Seth's head cradled in his arm.

'Were she not so vast and imperious,' Seth told him, although his eyes and lips were still firmly shut and he was still no more than the *seed* of a man, 'any mother of *this* kind would be better called a slave than a queen. Her only desire is the survival of the ground; she cares not a whit for her own flesh, which has long since outgrown any capacity for self-awareness and self-protection. But you're a drone, as I am. You're mind and memory, lore and lust. You're my brother, whether you will say so or not. All men are brothers, who have the forefathers in common.'

In Ferentina, as Andris knew to his cost, brothers were often the deadliest of enemies, becoming murderers in matters of inheritance. That was the way things were done – in Ferentina. He knew now that there were a thousand ways men might live, although he had not seen a thousand in the course of his travels. Perhaps there were a million, or even more.

Perhaps a man *could* fuse with living ground, and remain a man. Perhaps . . .

He dreamed then that he felt the pricking within his flesh of a thousand thorns. He dreamed that his sinews were becoming creepers, that his blood was turning to sap, that his skin was becoming a crown of foliage, that his very thoughts were turning green. He dreamed, but he knew that there was more in his dream than mere fantasy.

We are at war, he thought. *We are all at war, whether we*

185

know it or not. The war is in our blood as well as in the world. As without, so within.

'What are you?' he said to the creature he had named the Watcher. 'Are you Serpent or Salamander, man or plant?'

The Watcher made no reply, but it continued to come to him again and again, to see what he was becoming and listen to his rambling. He had to make up replies on its behalf, just as he had made up replies for Lucrezia and for Seth. Fortunately, he had all the time in the world, and within his dream he had the authority needed for such work.

'What's the purpose of the garden?' Andris asked the Watcher. 'Why is the ground so avid to place its seeds in the flesh of living creatures? Why are the half-men and the giant Serpents sent out to the world beyond the Reef to search for victims?'

'That's a question which could be answered in many ways,' the Watcher replied, although it never moved its mouth and never made a sound. 'You might say that our purpose is simply to survive, in the only way that we can – but there is more to it than mere survival. Your lore tells you that, as does ours. You might say that we're at war, that we must fight for life as every living thing must, lest our ground be swallowed up by its neighbours and enemies – but there is more to it than a mere struggle for existence. You might rather say that we are players in a game of ceaseless change, bending our minds to the task of finding better ways to be, ever greedy for pleasure, power, wisdom and all the other things for which all active minds are avid. We have more in common than you may think, Andris Myrasol.'

Andris was not particularly surprised that the Watcher knew his name. After all, it was some temporarily alienated part of his own frightened mind that was speaking on the Watcher's behalf, and he knew his own name better than any other.

'I see that your gatherers have been busy,' Andris said, striving to keep his voice level as he looked down the slope at his new kindred. He had been placed higher than any other, and he knew that when he had grown tall enough he would be able to see the whole garden. 'I know this time of troubles has been brewing for years – long enough to send your seeds as far as Xandria, although none took root there. How many other gardens like this one have you managed to plant in distant parts, I wonder?

Precious few, I dare say. Wherever there are men to root them out, they will be rooted out, and where there are no men to offer fertile flesh, they can't be planted at all.'

That wasn't quite true, because he could see even from his present stance that not all the trees in the garden had human inhabitants; some had Serpents instead, and a few had features he couldn't recognise. He felt, however, that the principle held. Wherever in the world there were creatures like himself – creatures which had legs, and minds of their own – bushes of this kind would not be permitted to take root. Their insidious cause would be opposed as desperately and as implacably as the men of the Nine Towns had opposed the encroachment upon their territory of ambitious dragomites.

'No matter how poisonous those thorns are,' Andris continued, 'nor how loudly those voices proclaim the happiness of their condition, such things would not be tolerated in any land where I have lived.'

'The gatherers have not been as successful as we could have desired,' the Watcher replied mournfully, although it made no sound at all. 'The road to the lands where humans live is long and dangerous, and there are enemies even more fearsome than you to be faced. Most of these you see below you are products of our own earth, adding nothing and changing nothing. Ours was never the best ground, and we have cause for anxiety as to its future. The garden has been invaded, time and time again, by monsters bent on its destruction – you see the legacy of their visitations everywhere.'

There was no sign of any armed men or giant Serpents in the garden now. Their absence seemed at least as significant as their presence would have been. Even in a dream Andris was free to wonder whether the garden was undefended, and what might happen if it were invaded again by 'monsters bent on its destruction'.

'If you want questions answered,' the Watcher told him, 'you must ask them of another, but you must not expect her to know all the answers. We have a loremaster, but she is neither a guardian nor a guiding intelligence. If you want to know what you are and what you might become, you must ask someone who has a real voice, who can speak to you with words other than your own – but she can only tell you as much as she knows.'

'I understand that,' Andris murmured. 'The problem is: where do I find that someone? Whose is the one voice that the garden can offer, if you have none? When may I bring this languorous debate with myself to a sensible conclusion, and replace it with sensible conversation?'

'When you are grown,' the Watcher said. 'When you can turn your head to look behind you.'

It had not occurred to Andris until then that he could not turn his head, but now he discovered that it was true. Shoots had begun to burst from his flesh, and in winning their freedom had put an end to his. He could no longer reach out on his own account, although his arms were gradually straightening under pressure from within. Seth's head was no longer cradled in the crook of his elbow; it sat upon his palm now like some huge obscene fruit.

This is a nightmare, he told himself. *It seems to be a dream, but it isn't. It's a nightmare, and it's real – not in every detail, but in its essentials. I am at war here, for the tenancy of my soul. I've already lost my body; I mustn't lose anything more. Whatever becomes of my flesh, I must remain a man. If there's a voice to be heard, I must retain my own, else there will be nothing to say but 'we are all of one mind here'. I don't believe that's ever true; Jume Metra was a woman, not a dragomite. She was never entirely lost within her dream. I'm at war within myself, and I must win. No matter what confusion comes upon me, I must win. I mustn't lose myself within the dream that is flooding my veins, my nerves and my heart. I mustn't lose myself, not merely for my own sake but for the sake of what I'm becoming. Whether this be Chimera's Cradle or some mere echo of it conjured up by the unearthly inhabitants of the world, it's part of the same great game, and I'm still a player. Whatever happens, I must remain a player.*

'We are *not* all of one mind here,' he said to the Watcher. 'We are not, and never will be. The dwellers in the deep cannot win this war. They will never win it while men remain in the world.'

But the Watcher didn't know what he meant by that – and neither, at least for the time being, did he.

3

CARUS FRAXINUS TOOK a sip from the water bottle which he kept beside him on the bench whenever his turn came to guide the wagon. His wide-brimmed hat saved him from the worst effects of the sun's rays but dehydration continually sapped his strength and concentration.

He had thought while crossing it that the Spangled Desert must be the harshest and most disturbing environment in the world. The facets of its myriad dust particles, which scattered the sun's light and heat by chaotic reflection, had added an extra dimension of menace to its natural aridity. This realm had, however, come to seem worse still, albeit in subtler ways. Floater-plants and flowing stones were engaged in a careful but deadly war of attrition hereabouts. Instead of scattering the radiance of the sun, or soaking it up as earthly vegetation did, the stones and their stern enemies appeared to hold it in suspension, furnishing a layer of refined discomfort through which the wagon had to pass. The ornamented stones maintained a curious sheen, as if they had been varnished, and the ramrod-straight trunks of the burgeoning floater-trees were brightly polished, like dark glass in which strange liquid images streamed and fused.

The near-flatness of the terrain that lay between the clumps of trees was deceptively easy; in fact it demanded intense concentration from the driver of the wagon. The horses had cultivated skills of their own in avoiding the most obvious traps laid by the figured stones, and Fraxinus had taken care to fit them with heavier shoes before leaving Salamander's Fire, but the six with which they had set out – including the two which Aulakh Phar and Merel Zabio had brought – had once again been reduced to the minimum of four that was required to haul the wagon. Even the dragomite warriors had not escaped unscathed; only two of them remained now. It was as much by luck as by judgment that the human members of the expedition had suffered no serious injuries. In spite of the care they always took, no less than three of them had been seized by the foot at one time or another, and had been fortunate not to lose anything more precious than a carefully reinforced leather boot.

'Is it my imagination,' Fraxinus had asked Aulakh Phar after suffering a near escape of his own, 'or are these glorified paving stones becoming more active?'

'It's not your imagination,' Phar had confirmed pensively. 'Their bodies are indeed becoming more fluid, as can readily be tested by thrusting the blade of a knife into them. I think they're reacting to the invasion of the airborne spores. They've been peacefully passive for a long time, patiently hoarding reserves against the time when they'd need to mobilise their strength, but now they're responding to a challenge. That must be the pattern of these Times of Emergence. Some tiny trigger sets in train a whole series of responses, which gradually wake the very ground on which all livelier forms of life must walk.'

'Not so much a time of emergence as a time of swallowing up, then,' Fraxinus had opined, but now that he was privy to the secrets of Salamander's Fire he knew that what was swallowed up by some kinds of ground could re-emerge after a sleep of centuries, or of millennia . . . and he knew, too, that what emerged could be altered while it slept: subjected to some arcane alchemy of the flesh, by means of which the patient experiments of the living ground became incarnate in strange metamorphoses.

What would it be like, Fraxinus wondered, *to be swallowed whole by one of the true giants of unearthly life? If a creature the size of the citadel of Xandria – or, for that matter, the entire city of Xandria – were to gulp me down, not as food but as a curious kind of treasure, what would it feel like to be cocooned, human flesh united with alien flesh? Would it be a mere fall into unconsciousness, or would there be more to it than that? Would there be dreams, and would they be mine alone or something shared? And what, in the end, would return – if anything returned at all? If I were to be transmuted, Salamander-fashion, into some gaudy creature blessed with the power of flight, what would I remember of my former existence? Would I still think of myself as Carus Fraxinus, or would my inner being have been altered in concert with my flesh? Could I still think of myself as human, or would I have become an avatar of the fertile field which had incorporated me?*

His train of thought was interrupted when someone climbed over the backrest of the bench to sit beside him. Had it been Aulakh Phar he would have assumed that the other was coming to keep him company, but it was Merel Zabio, so he assumed instead that she felt the need to get away from the close company she had been keeping in the body of the wagon – which did indeed seem unreasonably crowded, even though Vaca Metra preferred to stay with her two remaining warriors and Dhalla rarely entered it. Since she had recovered from the wounds she had incurred at the battle of the bridge the giant had taken a strong dislike to all confined spaces, although she had of necessity been fully accustomed to them while she served as a Sanctum guard.

'Why did you let that pig Shabir come with us?' Merel asked. 'He'll betray us if he has a chance. Underneath his grudging politeness there's a hard core of hatred.'

Merel had not forgiven Shabir for separating her from Andris Myrasol, and probably never would.

'He might yet leave us, if our path happens to cross that of a company he'd prefer,' Fraxinus said equably, 'but if circumstances force him to stay with us I think he'll play his part. He's not an evil man – he did what he thought he had to do.'

'You should have left him to die in the desert,' Merel opined unrepentantly. 'You can't tame a snake with kindness.'

Thanks to his long and various experiences travelling beyond the borders of Xandria's empire Fraxinus had reason to think that the proverb she had quoted was overambitious in its claims – as indeed most proverbs were – but he didn't want to get into a discussion about the limits of folk-wisdom and the politics of snake-domestication.

'Shabir may yet be useful to us,' Fraxinus said instead. 'Whatever else he may be, he's a skilled fighting man, and that stubborn streak of his might be invaluable in a fight. So far we've only had to face hellhounds and lizardlions. Two dragomite warriors constitutes a force sufficient to intimidate most creatures of that scavenging kind, but if the Salamanders' lore can be trusted there'll be worse things ahead of us. Half-men, manticores and all manner of giants.'

'They couldn't know that,' Merel retorted. 'I don't pretend to understand the story they spun out so laboriously, but I do know that the Salamanders at Salamander's Fire only had legends to rely on, just as we do.'

Laboriously was certainly the operative word. Even with the aid of Mossassor and the Serpents which had long been resident at Salamander's Fire, it had not been easy for Ixtlplt and the 'wise ones' to explain what they knew – or thought they knew – about Times of Emergence. The languages of the three species had far too little in common. Fraxinus now thought that he had a reasonable grasp of the strange life cycles of Serpents and Salamanders, but their strange world views remained stubbornly difficult to comprehend.

'Legendary lore ought not to be despised,' Fraxinus told her gently. 'When the forefathers instructed us that the only sin is forgetfulness, they weren't talking about the everyday skills of potters and metalworkers. They were urging us to retain the knowledge that we couldn't use from day to day but might need once in every thousand years. I don't know how much we've lost while clinging on to such fragments as the *Apocrypha of Genesys* and Ereleth's secret commandments, but I wish we'd kept more.'

'If I understand Phar rightly,' Merel said, 'it's not just that this sort of thing happens only once in a thousand years, but that every time it happens it's different. According to him, we can't know which of our old bogeymen will come crawling out of their warm and stony graves, or what new ones might emerge along with them.'

'That's probably true,' Fraxinus admitted. 'But we have to try to understand the process. If possible, we also have to try to figure whether there's any underlying pattern in the evolution of new forms that might enable us to see where the whole thing might lead in times to come.'

'Process and progress,' Merel said. 'Aulakh told me.'

Aulakh was sometimes too glib for his own good, Fraxinus thought.

'He says that Salamander's Fire makes legends real,' the girl went on. 'He says the winged Salamanders aren't inheritors of hundreds of generations of tales told and re-told by unreliable tellers, and that what they brought out of the living stone was *memory* – clouded and refined, but memory nevertheless. Pity they can't talk, isn't it?'

Actually, the winged Salamanders *could* talk, at least in the sense that they could speak. They could pronounce words in the human and Serpent languages rather better than their lumpen kin, although it wasn't clear that they could import much meaning into their mimicry. Nor was it obvious that they could speak the language of their own kin with significantly greater competence. It was possible that they weren't intelligent at all – but they did have memories. They knew what they had been 'born' to do. They knew that they must fly to Chimera's Cradle in order to descend into the Pool of Life, and that they must in the fullness of time send emissaries back to fuse with the inner walls of Salamander's Fire. Whatever communication was involved in this, it had begun in the days of the forefathers, when a Salamander had brought to Idun the gift of 'a tree whose fruit had knowledge of another kind' and had received the recompense of 'a coin' it 'could not spend'.

The tree and the coin were, Fraxinus presumed, metaphorical, like the fire that 'burned bravely' in the depths of the Salamanders' own cradle of chimeras and in the hearts of human giants, not to mention the Serpent's blood which the forefathers had bought with promises, and which still flowed in some human veins. He understood the metaphors a little better now. The 'blood' which the forefathers had obtained from Serpents must have been their biological heritage; the key to their peculiar nature. The 'tree' which they had obtained from Salamanders must have been *their* biological heritage; the key to *their* rather different nature. The 'coin' which the forefathers had given to the Salamanders was something of their own heritage, but something metallic rather than organic; with that and the promises given to the Serpents the forefathers had tried to forge an alliance between the three species against something they saw as a common enemy: the true giants, which Mossassor had learned to call 'the dwellers in the deep'.

Aulakh Phar, being too glib for his own good, had reduced the matter to a much lower level of simplicity by saying: 'It's all to do with sex – and the unearthly world's lack of it.'

Fraxinus didn't realise how far he had drifted into his reverie until Merel said: 'It's going to be very dangerous, isn't it? It's been bad so far, but it's going to get even worse.'

'We really don't know,' he told her, 'but while we have two dragomite warriors and a giant we're far from defenceless – and good human fighters are valuable too. I'm as glad to have you with me as I am to have Shabir.'

'You never wanted me,' Merel opined. 'You only wanted Andris. I'm just a petty thief.'

'Aulakh assures me that you can handle yourself in a fight,' Fraxinus countered, 'and I know that you have as much fortitude as any of us. You're too stubborn to let fear or hardship get the better of you – you don't ever give in. You're worth your weight in good fresh steel, believe me.'

'If that means I'm entitled to a full share in any profit we get out of this, I'm grateful,' Merel retorted, with a gruff sarcasm which couldn't quite conceal the fact that his soothing flattery hadn't gone to waste. 'Unfortunately, my reckoning says that we're a very long way from breaking even.'

'Sometimes,' Fraxinus said, 'a merchant just has to keep going deeper and deeper into a deal, hoping that the eventual reward will pay back all the bribes he's laid out on the way.'

'What bribes?' she scoffed.

'Metaphorically speaking, of course,' he added.

There was a moment's diplomatic silence before she asked the next question, although he knew exactly what it would be.

'Do you really think there's a chance of our getting out of this with something worthwhile?' she asked, framing the question more subtly than was usual. The only 'worthwhile' thing on her mind, at present, was her pale-skinned cousin.

Fraxinus didn't answer. It wasn't that he didn't have an answer, but simply that his attention had been caught by movement in the distance. There were several extensive stands of floater-trees in the way, and the terrain was less even than he had lately become used to, but there was no doubt that a company of horsemen was approaching from the south-west. The horsemen must have seen the wagon at almost the same moment as Fraxinus caught sight of them, for the pattern of their movement immediately changed. One of the dragomites had seen them too, and had begun to draw nearer to the wagon.

Merel, realising that no further reassurances would be forthcoming for the moment, followed the direction of his worried gaze.

'They're just horsemen,' she said, shading her eyes with her hand and squinting against the awkward light. 'Not manticores, nor any other kind of monster. Maybe not enemies, this time.'

'Perhaps not,' Fraxinus agreed, but he wasn't sure. What the Salamanders had said about half-human beings spewed out by the monstrous entities that ringed Chimera's Cradle was no longer of merely speculative interest.

The riders were already moving for cover, aiming for the shelter of the densest cluster of floater-trees that lay within the horizon. Fraxinus tried to count them, but all he could be sure of was that they were at least a dozen strong. He was confident that the forces at his command could defend the wagon successfully against a force of twelve or fifteen horsemen, but it mightn't be an easy victory.

'If they *are* massing for an attack,' Merel observed anxiously, 'they can intercept us readily enough. The ground's not as flat as it was. If we try to run for it, we're sure to lose one of the horses before long – but if we decide to make a stand they can take all the time they need to make plans. *If* they're hostile.'

Ereleth leaned over Merel's shoulder to find out what was going on. Dhalla, who had been marching behind the wagon, came forward with her spear in her hand.

'Shall I find out who or what they are?' the giant asked, with an eagerness which suggested that she had been bored for some considerable time and was not averse to the prospect of a little action.

'No need,' Fraxinus said. 'I think they're about to tell us.'

From the clump of floater-trees in which the mysterious troop had taken refuge a single rider was emerging. He was carrying a pole or spear to which some ragged and faded garment had been attached, presumably to serve as a white flag.

While Fraxinus slowed the horses and brought them to a halt the lone rider moved towards them. He was not urging his mount to a gallop because he had to study the ground over which he came with all due care and attention, but he made reasonable progress.

Fraxinus had already drawn the optimistic conclusion that

the rider must be human, else he wouldn't know the meaning of a white flag, but his old eyes weren't up to the task of recognising the man before Merel Zabio did.

'Oh,' she said unenthusiastically. 'It's him again.'

'Who?' demanded Ereleth, whose own eyesight was long past its best.

'It's Cerri's man,' Dhalla said. 'That sly and stupid sergeant from the citadel. You said he'd hired himself out to the bronzes.' The last remark was addressed to Merel, who had last seen Purkin little more than fifteen days ago.

'He did,' Merel said, 'but I don't suppose he had any more intention of fighting their battles than we did. At least he's a trained fighting man. Can't have too many of those, can we?'

'Unfortunately,' Ereleth murmured, as she squinted hard into the heat-haze, 'he might not be coming to volunteer his fighting skills. The flag of truce says that he wants to talk – but if all he wanted was to re-enter our service he wouldn't need such apparatus, would he?'

'No,' said Fraxinus pensively, 'he wouldn't.'

4

L UCREZIA HARDLY NOTICED when the rain ceased its steady beat upon the canvas awning of the wagon. Hyry Keshvara had been telling her story, while Lucrezia listened with intense interest. Checuti and Jume Metra listened too, although they must have heard the bulk of it before, while they waited for Lucrezia to recover from her wound. Checuti was paying attention but it was impossible to judge the extent of Jume Metra's interest. The trader had already taken her audience through the long journey to Antiar in company with Tarlock Nath and Amyas, and had given them an account of her brief reunion with Sergeant Purkin.

'I was right about Nath wanting to get his family out of Antiar as soon as possible, with as much of his wealth as he could carry,' Hyry told them. 'The problem was that the city had become a barrel of plastic waiting for the fuse. While we'd been trudging south in that ramshackle haywain the cavalrymen who'd fled the battle of the bridge had been pouring southwards in their hundreds, albeit broken up into much smaller groups, not knowing whether or when they might be held accountable for their desertion. As well as paranoid Antiarians there were paranoid Ketherians, Mugolians and others from even further south passing through the town – and they all gravitated to the marketplace, where every rumour ran riot.

'Some of the rumours were true, of course. The bronze really was trying to recruit mercenaries to go to the aid of his own people in the far south. Others were utterly without foundation. Although they didn't know any names, some of the soldiers had got hold of the information that our party included a brace of witches, one a queen and the other a princess. Some said that it was their witchcraft that had settled the battle at the bridge by spreading panic, plague or Goran alone knows what. As you can imagine, the fact that Tarlock Nath was known to have brought back prisoners, including a mature woman who might or might not be the witch-queen and a young woman who might or might not be the witch-princess, was quickly stirred into the melting pot – as was the much more relevant suspicion that Nath was about to blow town with everything he could carry, leaving the people who had elected him to the Convocation to their own stew of troubles.

'Perhaps the old fool shouldn't have taken me to the market with him – but without being able to see what was being traded I could hardly give him my best advice as to what might be worth taking to Xandria. Perhaps it was unduly provocative to turn up with eight heavily armed bully boys, although he might very well have been torn to pieces if he hadn't. Anyway, when the word went round that he was there to pay extravagant prices for vital supplies, driving prices up while planning to turn traitor, the crowd very soon turned ugly.

'The rioters weren't united in any common purpose; maybe things would have gone in a more orderly fashion if they had been. I think some of the merchants and the better-off folk were more interested in me than in Nath, figuring that if I were so useful to him I might be just as useful to them, and they all had hirelings of their own. It was because of that, I think, that Nath and I were so quickly separated once the brawl actually broke out. If the first people who'd grabbed me had managed to complete their assignment I'd probably have been bounced into an almost identical situation, but when they ran into competition I was able to make a move on my own account.

'I knew that the one thing I had to lay my hands on was a horse, but in a situation like that everyone who has a horse clings on to it for dear life. As soon as I took off running I could see that the only way I was going to get a horse was to kill somebody – and that the risks involved in trying that would be considerable. I tried to make it back to Nath's house on foot, figuring that I needed to link up with Aulakh and Jacom – or, if I had to settle for second best, with Purkin's men. Unfortunately, there was a mob ahead of me, and it wasn't the kind of mob I could tack myself on to without being noticed. I didn't even have a knife, and I knew that the moment I got involved in any kind of fight I'd have locals swarming about me like angry bees, so I decided to go for the quieter streets and look for opportunities where tempers weren't running so high. Unfortunately, I was one against a whole town, and even though I was a golden among goldens, dressed in borrowed clothing, there was no way I could make myself inconspicuous.

'I knew it was only a matter of time before somebody hostile got hold of me, so I figured it was best to take the initiative. Given that I was a foreigner, it seemed only sensible to try to make common cause with other foreigners. I couldn't find any bronzes, but I did find a gang of Sabinalians who didn't have any idea what was going on. I knew by their colours where they came from, and I'd already figured out that the men from the southernmost of the Nine Towns must have been the most disaffected members of Shabir's army.

'I told the Sabinalians that the Antiarians had turned against the other townsmen and were hounding them out of town. It was so nearly true that I didn't have much difficulty convincing them. They didn't have horses but they did know where they could get aboard a boat. They didn't particularly want to take me with them even though I did my level best to convince them that I could be useful, but in the end I only had to screw one of them to get a passage, and once was enough to get me all the way to Tawil, where it seemed politic to quit their company.

'Tawil wasn't nearly as close to anarchy as Antiar had been, perhaps because the population was more or less united in recognising the necessity of holding their fields against the threat of the floater-plants. They still had some semblance of community and organisation, and they weren't unduly paranoid about strangers. It still seemed too dangerous to risk stealing a horse but I managed to pick up some money and some clean clothes without attracting any particular attention.

'I heard rumours about Amyas's caravan but by the time I got to the place where it was said to be it had already gone, and the resentments it left in its wake seemed more than likely to rebound on me. I got into a fight with some of the locals and I hadn't much choice about which way to run. I tried to go south but I was driven west, and it wasn't easy to stay ahead of my pursuers while I was still on foot. If it had been a little simpler I might not have been so careless, but as things were I practically ran straight into the giant Serpents and their semi-human companions. They gathered me in with insulting gratitude.

'While they were still trawling the environs of Tawil and Sabinal I figured that there must be a reasonable chance of getting away, especially if the townspeople managed to raise an army to send against them. I should have known that raising armies was something the locals were no longer capable of doing, but I clung to the hope while I could. At one point I thought the captive-takers might actually go after Amyas's company, but they had too much sense – it was much safer to pick up townsmen in threes and fours, without ever risking a real fight. By the time the long march south-westwards began I knew that there wasn't going to be any rescue.

'I tried to conserve my strength as best I could, but they were careful to let us become weak in spite of the walking we had to do. The horsemen killed a couple of troublemakers to make sure the rest of us stayed in line, but they didn't have much to worry about – the Tawilians and Sabinalians were so dispirited that they'd given up as soon as they were seized, terrified by the mere appearance of the big Serpents. In my younger days I might have contrived something, but I wasn't anywhere near my best, so I had no alternative but to play a waiting game ... never expecting, of course, that *you* might be somewhere up ahead, highness, lying in wait – or that Checuti might be falling in behind with a company of cavalry.'

'I've already told her, my lady, that she had it easy compared with us,' Checuti put in. 'I've told her the tale of how we crossed kim after kim of ground crawling with Shabir's soldiers, only to have to fight scores of crocolids and rapacious birds in the swamp while we were delirious because of all the poisons we'd imbibed.'

'I'm sure you maintained your usual scrupulous regard for accuracy,' Lucrezia said.

'Venerina Sirelis told us what happened after you arrived by the shore of the Lake of Colourless Blood,' Hyry said, 'but I'm even less sure about her scrupulous regard for accuracy than I am about Checuti's. I've met deists in Khalorn but these are different. When we parted company she left a message for me to pass on to you.'

'What message?' Lucrezia wanted to know.

'Apparently, Andris Myrasol demanded an explanation from her, which she never had time to give . . . and now never will: an explanation of exactly what it was that Philemon and she hoped to achieve by persuading him to drink some potion. Do you know what she meant by the Spirit of the Waters?'

Lucrezia nodded.

'She said: *Had I been able to explain more fully in words, I'd not have insisted on letting the spirit do its own work.* She claimed that she didn't know why the potion failed – she thought that the amber had already made his reconciliation with the marsh and the lake. She assumed that the only thing remaining was to let him see with the spirit's inner eye: to experience the form and mind of God. When I asked her what that was supposed to mean she said: *When the other senses have been educated God is manifest in all things; once His plan is known, everything can be seen to be a part of it.* She said that she knew well enough that many people can't accept the Spirit of the Waters, and she said she was very sorry that she was misled into the belief that Andris was one of those who could. She insisted that they meant him no harm – indeed, she was at pains to convince me that they meant to offer him the greatest gift they had. They thought that he would see and understand, that he would sense the connectedness of everything within and without the world and find his own true place within the great scheme. She said she hadn't lost hope that he might still find his way to the precious knowledge they sought to impart to him, if only he were still alive.'

'I doubt that he could take much comfort from a hope like that, if he *is* still alive,' Lucrezia murmured. 'Did she say why Philemon Taub told us that we mustn't go to Chimera's Cradle, if we valued our lives?'

'She told me to tell you that the true way lies through the waters, not through earth, fire or air,' Hyry said. 'She told me to tell you that your blood will betray you, if you let it. She wouldn't explain. I don't think she really knew what she was talking about. It was all just deist craziness.'

'The lake is alive,' Lucrezia told her. 'Like the dragomite queen. It seems that wherever there are unearthly organisms of that huge kind there are people living in association with them – people who've become assimilated into them. They all think that theirs is the only true way. There are more organisms of that kind crowded around Chimera's Cradle, and we're on the very edge of their realm. Some, at least, send forth expeditions in search of new blood. That's what was supposed to happen to you.'

'I'm grateful that you saved me from it,' Hyry said, with evident sincerity.

'We can't claim any particular credit for it,' Lucrezia answered wryly, 'given that we had no idea that you might be among the prisoners.'

'Yes we can,' Checuti said. 'The fact that our actions were magnificently noble allows us to claim credit for anything. You owe me your life, Keshvara, and I expect you never to forget it. One day I might require similar service.'

'We all played our parts,' Lucrezia pointed out. 'Had any element of the scheme failed all the others would have failed with it. Each of us needed the best endeavours of all the others ... and if anyone still owes anything to anyone it's Andris Myrasol we should be thinking about, because he's the one who presently stands in need of *similar service*.'

'I take your point,' Checuti said, equably enough, 'but if there's one lesson that stands out very clearly from Keshvara's account of her adventures, it's that we all have to respect the limits of possibility.'

Lucrezia opened her mouth to object, but she had got no further than the opening consonant of the word *but* when she was interrupted by a sudden crash. The wagon lurched under the impact, which was at the front end; it was as if something very heavy had fallen on to the driver's seat. Unfortunately, the flap of the canvas was still drawn tight against the rain which had stopped some time ago, and they could not see what was happening. Checuti and Jume Metra were quick to snatch up spears, but they all four backed away from the canvas, wanting to see what would come through it before lunging forward with the weapons.

Lucrezia watched with trepidation as the fingers of an unhuman hand reached through the gap in the canvas to fumble at the knotted strings which secured it. It was not a Serpent's hand, although the fingers were just as slender and just as deft.

The sight of the hand was enough for Checuti, who drew back

his arm in order to launch his spear like a javelin. Jume Metra braced hers defensively. As they made their preparations, though, the wagon gave a second lurch as something climbed on to its rear end. Another unhuman hand reached through the loose flap there to grab the end of the thief-master's spear and prevent him from releasing it.

This second hand *was* a Serpent's hand. It was, in fact, the hand of Ssifuss, who had apparently returned from wherever he had been just in time to prevent his friends taking precipitate action. Lucrezia was very glad to see it, but her gladness was all but lost in the confusion of the event.

'Iss good!' the Serpent said, sounding more like Mossassor than ever. 'Iss not enemy! Iss good!'

Lucrezia trusted the Serpent sufficiently to grab hold of Checuti's weapon herself, so that there was no possibility of his wrenching it free. Jume Metra hesitated a moment, but then lowered her own weapon.

The flap at the front of the wagon opened, and a face came through behind the hand. It looked more like a dragomite's face than a Serpent's: its eyes were huge in proportion to its narrow head, and it had palps about its lipless mouth. It also had antennae, although they were very much shorter than a dragomite drone's. The texture of its skin was not at all like a dragomite's, though; its scales were very bright, reflecting the dull daylight as if they were a host of tiny mirrors.

It spoke, but the words which spilled out of its mouth were like none that Lucrezia had ever heard.

'Iss *good*,' Ssifuss insisted. 'Iss myss, iss messsenger. Never sseen, never believed, but iss true. Mossassor . . .'

The mythical messenger interrupted the Serpent with a much more clamorous speech, whose sibilant syllables sounded just a little less alien. Lucrezia realised, with some astonishment, that the creature was trying to speak to Ssifuss in the Serpent's own tongue. Ssifuss listened, but seemed to be having great difficulty deciphering what was being said. When the newcomer fell silent, the Serpent remained awkwardly silent too.

'Well?' Checuti demanded. 'What did the damned thing say?'

'Not ssure,' Ssifuss replied, perhaps ashamed by its own inability to follow the speech aimed at it. 'Ssayss iss *true*

Ssalamander. Ssayss iss bound for garden. Ssayss humanss follow. *Ssink* ssayss Fraxinuss, but not ssure.'

The newcomer, seemingly impatient with this long process of translation, spoke again. This time, it seemed to be doing its best to speak the human language, with a vocal apparatus even less well-adapted to that task than Ssifuss's was. Had Lucrezia not been forewarned, she would not have been able to make any sense at all of the strange glissando, but having been primed by Ssifuss she felt sure that she could identify the syllables which the creature was trying to pronounce.

'Frax-inus,' it was almost certainly trying to say. 'Frax-inus . . . Frax-inus . . . *coming*. Go to *garden*. Go to *garden*.'

Alas, it was impossible to be sure whether what it said was an instruction, or merely a statement of its own intent.

5

ANDRIS DREAMED ON, but the dream retained its stubborn edge of reality. He came to understand that what he thought of as *dreaming* was simply an altered state of consciousness further disturbed by hallucinations of his own making. That knowledge had not quite lost its power to hurt him but he no longer reacted with uncontrollable horror to the thought that his actual flesh and blood really had been devoured by alien ground. He felt that he was beyond horror now, beyond dread and beyond any shock that might destroy his sanity – or at least, he had to hope so.

He knew that he was in the process of becoming something very different from what he had been before, but he also knew that some such change had begun to afflict him long before he had been brought to the garden. When he had first encountered the numbing poison that the men of the Nine Towns harvested from the Soursweet Marshes he had begun to acquire his new ability to dream at the edge of reality, and he had begun to make contact with something inside himself: something alien, and yet not *completely* alien.

Andris didn't know how this happened to him, and he certainly wasn't prepared to accept the deists' insistence that he had somehow been allowed to see and communicate with the God who was the sum of all creation and the dictator of its destiny, but he knew that his visions sheltered a hard kernel of truth.

He really had been brought to the garden.

He really had been incorporated into its living ground.

There were indeed tiny entities dwelling within him, meaning him no harm but not really part of him. Those entities had their own purposes and perhaps their own destinies – and those purposes had something to do with what was happening in and around Chimera's Cradle.

Andris devoted what attention he could to the study of the nature and progress of his slow metamorphosis, but it wasn't easy. It was difficult to maintain concentration, and there were always more delusions waiting to confound his attempted analyses.

He assumed that he must still be anaesthetised, but he couldn't tell whether it was a blessing or a curse.

Perhaps, had he not been cushioned against sensation, he would have been in excruciating agony while the seed within him organised its intricate interpenetration of his organs and his limbs.

Perhaps, on the other hand, it was the absence of any accurate record of sensation that was preventing him from being able to understand exactly what was happening to him and how.

The other alternative was that his inability to make conscious contact with the gradual transformation of his flesh was merely a side effect of no particular significance, a random whim of happenstance.

He found it exceedingly difficult to keep track of time. Sometimes he found the sun shining, while at other times he bathed in starlight, but he could not count the hours or reckon the passing of the days. He felt that he had been curtly detached from the principal yardstick that had served to measure out his previous existence. He continued to feel neither hunger nor thirst, and the absence of these familiar sensations collaborated in securing the empire of timelessness.

He knew that in his former existence he had not normally been conscious of the presence of his guts, save when they ached or demanded to be fed, but now that his most basic appetites had been cancelled out he wondered whether he was entitled to consider himself the same person he had been before. Given that he was not the same kind of person at all, should he not admit that Andris Myrasol was dead and think of his new being as something only now being born, something that required a new name?

That was a thought from which he shied away. He didn't want another name. He didn't want his old self to be obliterated. However much he changed, he wanted to retain his continuity as an individual.

He gradually ceased even to dream of being his old bodily self.

His memories of walking, sitting, climbing and lying down faded into virtual disuse, recalled only in brief and surprising spasms, but he clung nevertheless to the conviction that he was still the same individual, still the same Andris Myrasol.

He was not left entirely to himself. He was continually visited by the creature he called the Watcher, sometimes alone and sometimes in the company of others: usually humans, or things that looked like humans. These visitors sometimes spoke to one another, albeit briefly, but they only stared at Andris with appraising eyes, measuring the growth of the vigorous shoots which were springing from his shoulders and his torso.

Andris had nothing with which to compare the fervour of his hybrid flesh but he hoped that its progress might be unusually rapid. If he must become a tree, he decided, then he wanted to be an exceptional tree: a veritable prince among trees. He had, after all, been a veritable prince among men, although precious few of his fellows had ever acknowledged the fact.

If he must live the rest of his life as a part of the garden, he thought, then he wanted to be a special part, stronger, gaudier and more precious than all the rest.

'Was I really worth the effort your raiders expended in bringing me here?' he asked the Watcher at one point. 'Each group had forty prisoners before they met real resistance, but they lost them all and suffered terrible casualties. I was their only compensation, was I not?' He was hoping for an affirmative answer.

'Time will tell what you are worth,' the creature replied evasively – but he had supplied its reply himself, modestly rebuking himself for his own aspirations to grandeur. It was a habit he had always had.

Andris had other visitors too while he remained dazed and half paralysed: small birds, insects and even slow-moving snakes. All these, he observed, were tolerated by his neighbours, but there were other, far larger birds whose occasional tentative explorations met a more aggressive response. These vulturine creatures retreated in a hurry as thorny branches reached out to maul them. Once he saw one struck down, its body gradually sucked into the soil once it had stopped twitching. Although he had no confidence in his own ability to do likewise, having hardly begun to master whatever he now had instead of tendons and muscles, the larger birds steered clear of him. He noticed eventually that the only bushes they approached were those which had been broken and weakened to some degree; he concluded that their vulturine appearance was no mere coincidence.

Although the process of learning to use his new limbs was horribly slow Andris made more rapid headway in mastering his new voice. He knew that almost all of his remembered conversations had taken place entirely within his imagination, but he was certain that the tree-people could indeed speak, and must, he concluded, still have lungs of some sort within their bodies. Whenever the Watcher came close Andris would try to speak, and even though the creature never replied – except, of course, when he supplied the replies himself – he saw that it reacted with its eyes. How long it took him to raise the timbre of his new voice from a drunken whisper to something like its old strength and sureness he could not tell, but he did it. In the meantime, he continued to hold conversations of a less reliable kind with various figments of his questing imagination.

Seth continued to serve as a sounding board for his speculations, and was always ready to do so, now that he hung from one of Andris's branches like a pendulous fruit.

'I doubt that this is the kind of body you wanted when you quit the dragomite queen,' Andris said to the drone apologetically. 'I presume that you had had your fill of sharing. Still, it is a body of sorts, and there must be a possibility that it will give you the renewed life you wanted so badly.'

'Life is life,' the head replied, without moving its lips. 'Beggars can't be choosers. In any case, I might still get out of here; I've put down no roots.'

'You might need another brother to wander by and pluck you from my branch like a ripe apple,' Andris pointed out. 'You were exceedingly fortunate to discover one such passer-by in the depths of a dragomite nest, and you would be more fortunate still to find one here. The half-men who brought me here do not seem to be abundantly supplied with fraternal sentiment.'

'Others do come here, sometimes,' Seth pointed out. 'It seems that they come as invaders and destroyers, but they come nevertheless. While the ground is alive, there is hope – and we must hope that it remains alive in spite of the invasions that plague it. Were it to die and rot, we'd die and rot with it. Don't listen to promises of immortality, Andris – they're mere delusion.'

'I'm not sure that the dwellers in the deep do die,' Andris replied. 'I think they may swallow one another occasionally, just as they swallow lesser things, but I'm not sure that they die.'

'Nests do,' Seth said.

'Do they?' Andris countered. 'Do they really die, or are they merely absorbed, one into another, as queen fuses with queen?'

'Is there a difference?' Seth countered in his turn.

'I think there is,' Andris told him. 'I'm not sure that this war between the dwellers in the deep ought to be reckoned a battle for *survival*. It may be a war of *conquest*, in which the losers are absorbed into the bodies of the victors.'

'It's the same thing.'

'I'm not so sure. There's a passage about conquest in Fraxinus's beloved *Apocrypha of Genesys* which says that the idea of conquest is a delusion, like the idea of empire. I wish I could remember more of it. I suppose that I've been conquered, in a way – defeated and absorbed – but I don't *feel* that I've been defeated *or* absorbed. My body may be captive but my mind is still free . . . freer than before, in some ways.'

'That's possible,' Seth conceded. 'I'm the living proof of it. Perhaps your body isn't as securely trapped as it seems. You're still learning, after all, and still changing. Who knows what you might be capable of when you're finished? The ground itself may not know.'

'I'm not sure that the ground knows anything at all,' Andris admitted, but even as he said it he was trying to look back over a shoulder he no longer had, to see what – or who – might be behind him. He couldn't do it yet, but he felt sure that there would come a time when he could.

I dare say that the ground will have its say, if it can, Andris thought. *After all, we're of one flesh now, whether we like it or not. I'm just a drone now, like poor Seth. Would I be able to sever my own head, as he did, if I could only learn the trick of it – and had someone to take me in charge?*

'No matter what is done to me,' he said aloud, although he had lost sight of Seth and was now speaking to something far more diffuse and far less easy to imagine, 'I won't be part of *you*

209

if I can possibly help it. No matter how much of my flesh your seed consumes, no matter how much of your living soil oozes into my blood and my bones, I'll always be Andris Myrasol, Prince of Ferentina. You can make as many empty gestures of amity as you wish, but it will make no difference. *We are not of one mind.* Do you understand that? *We are not and never will be one and the same.*' He knew that it might not be true, and that he certainly couldn't make it true simply by saying it, but he felt compelled to say it nevertheless, in defence of his essential self.

'We do not even know if that is what we ought or need to be,' a female voice replied, in a curiously mournful tone, 'but if it is, you might be a fool to think that you'll have the choice.'

The speaker remained invisible. The Watcher remained visible, but the Watcher never spoke; the Watcher only watched – and listened.

More time passed, in the uncertain fashion which it now had.

Andris continued to grow. He grew tall, and he thought – or hoped, at least – that he was growing more extravagantly than any other chimera in the garden. The lower part of his body began to emerge from the ground again, but the legs that had fused to form the lower part of his trunk no longer seemed to be the legs they had been before, and his genitals had been reduced to a mere suggestive tumour.

As shoots sprang out of him in every direction Andris found it frustratingly difficult to see what was going on around him. Foliage which he could not quite bring himself to think of as his own obscured his view, to the point where he could hardly tell when some other humanoid being passed by, but in time he lifted his arms and his crown was elevated too. Once again, his sight cleared.

In the meantime, time must have passed: days and nights that he could not count.

He tried to content himself with the patient work of watching the leaves bursting from his branches. He studied the form and growth of the first white flower buds born amid the leaves, with as much interest as he could muster.

While his trunk continued to grow longer and stouter his upraised arms continued to lift the profusion of his branches upwards, clear of his head. He felt increasingly confident that he would be a giant among trees, as he had been a giant – of sorts – among men.

It was curious to watch branches which had begun to sprout ten or a hundred sems beneath his chin migrate by slow degrees until the lowest of them was twenty sems above the level of his eyes. The body that had enclosed the flesh of the plant while it germinated in his gut sometimes seemed to him to be enclosed in its turn, immured within the unearthly flesh of the tree, but he was gradually losing the last vestiges of his sense of separateness and he didn't know whether it was worth making an effort to cling on to that particular illusion. He was still capable of imagining that his familiar form was yet contained within the body of the tree, stretched and deformed but still in some vital sense recoverable, but he knew that his metamorphosis was more profound than that. He could imagine that his arms had become extraordinarily elongated, and that his head had sunk into his chest, but there seemed little point in any such pretence. He wondered whether it would be more sensible to try with all his might to adapt himself to his new form: to subject his new and unearthly flesh to the empire of his will.

By that means, he thought, he might be able to make the living ground part of him, instead of merely allowing himself to be part of it.

It seemed that such efforts didn't go to waste. Slowly, sensations of touch began to return to supplement sight and hearing. Pain came with them, but he wasn't afraid of pain; he was prepared to appropriate it, just as he appropriated the alien feelings that carried the hint and promise of new pleasures.

I've been a man all my life, he told himself. *I've been a soldier and a sailor, a labourer and an idler, a lover and a liar. If I had my time over I'd do everything differently. Who wouldn't? Who but an imbecile would say 'I'd do exactly the same thing again'? Any man worthy of the name would say 'I've already done that; this time I'll try something else'. Why shouldn't I be grateful for the opportunity to try something totally different? As long as I can be me, I can be anything at all, and if I have the chance to be a tree, I ought to try to be the finest tree I can. If I have to fuse with living ground, I ought to do it bravely. If I must become part of a dweller in the deep, then I must also ensure that the dweller in the deep becomes part of me.*

He said all this aloud to the Watcher, and the Watcher seemed to approve, although its frog-like mouth was incapable of feigning a smile.

Andris began to understand how it might have been possible for human beings to take up residence in the Corridors of Power and call themselves dragomites. He began to understand, too, how human beings living on the shore of the Lake of Colourless Blood might have welcomed the Spirit of the Lake into their own being, and tried to learn what it had to teach them about the game of life.

Even within his dream, however, he couldn't forget Merel – and while he couldn't forget Merel, he couldn't escape the occasional pangs of a sharp and poignant sense of loss. Sometimes, he longed to see her again; at other times he hoped that he never would. Sometimes, he wanted her to become part of the garden too; at other times, he hated himself for wishing such a fate upon her.

'This too is life,' he told himself and the Watcher. 'Life is full of doubts and conflicts. Whatever else life is, doubts and conflicts are part of its very essence. We are all at war, with ourselves as well as everything else. How else could we change, while retaining our continuity? There must be tension and strife within us, else we would be like the kinds of stones that do not flow and have no figures in their faces. When we are awake, as well as when we dream, we must have hopeful illusions to guide us and nightmares to spur us on.'

He had no idea how long it was since he had seen a real human being, but he felt that it was far too long. Loneliness afflicted him even in his new form, and it was loneliness for the company of his old kind – for the sound of familiar voices and the touch of familiar hands. He knew that he would be surrounded by others of his *new* kind until the day he died – or became something else again – but he couldn't believe that he would ever entirely lose that longing for familiar voices and familiar caresses, nor did he want to let it go.

Sometimes, he still lamented his fate, and could not condemn himself for doing so.

6

'I HOPED THAT IT would be you, sir,' Purkin said, relaxing in the saddle after positioning his mount very carefully. 'I'm very glad to see you. I knew that the wagons Amyas brought from the Nine Towns must be a way ahead of you, if you'd made it through the Spangled Desert, but I feared that you might not make it.'

You certainly did, Fraxinus thought, staring at the makeshift flag of truce. *You feared it enough to get the hell out at the first real sign of trouble.*

'He seems to make a habit of deserting his masters,' Merel murmured in Fraxinus's ear, too softly for Purkin to hear. 'Amyas was prepared to look the other way while Aulakh and I made our escape, but he was determined to hang on to his fighting men. Something must have happened since then.' She was stating the obvious.

'It's good to see you again, sergeant,' Fraxinus said, lightly enough. 'Is Captain Cerri with you?'

'No, sir,' Purkin replied. 'He was either killed or carried off, along with the greater number of my erstwhile companions-in-arms.'

'What happened?' Fraxinus asked anxiously. 'Aulakh Phar told me about your journey and its purpose, but he said that all was well when he left you.'

'All was far from well,' Purkin replied, his voice dry and bleak. 'The Last Stronghold, which we'd come so far to defend, was already beleaguered and close to collapse, although we didn't know it. We were attacked on the road by a horde of monstrous creatures which had animal heads set on human bodies. Those of us who came through the fight and fled towards the Stronghold were turned aside and scattered. Half a hundred riders came out, attempting to clear a way for us, but it was all for nothin'.

'I escaped with a few of my men and a handful of the bronzes. We were driven southwards, then west. We tried to link up with the others but it wasn't possible. These lands are full of enemies: beasts of many evil kinds and things which look like men but aren't. We had to lie low to avoid capture. We're only fourteen strong, and only five of those are citadel-trained. I – that is, we – decided that our best bet was to make our way back the way we'd come, to the Nine Towns. However badly things were goin' there, there's nothin' out here that offers any better hope, nothin' at all. Do you have some water, sir? I'm desperately thirsty.'

Fraxinus picked up the water bottle he kept by his side, made sure the stopper was secure, then threw it to Purkin. The sergeant tried to catch it but couldn't; he had to dismount to pick it up, but he'd placed his horse on safe ground and he had no difficulty recovering it. He drank from it gratefully.

'We're short of water ourselves,' Fraxinus said delicately. 'Food we have, because the dragomites are so adept at picking up floaters, but water is hard to find hereabouts.'

'Don't I know it,' Purkin replied, lowering the neck of the bottle from his lips. 'Must be water under the surface, given the way those rugged stalks spring up, but it must be buried deep. Saw rainclouds in the west last night, but the wind didn't bring 'em this way, worse luck. Did you find what you wanted at Salamander's Fire?'

'Answers to some of our questions,' Fraxinus replied in a neutral voice. 'The final answers are to be found at the Navel of the World.'

'That's where all the fake men are coming from,' Purkin told him warily. 'Not just fake men, either. Worse things even than that. The land to the south-west is direly dangerous. Saw some big birds headin' that way yesterday, all glittery in the sun, but mostly things are comin' the other way, runnin' or chasin'. Accordin' to Amyas, all this was human land once – Cities of the Plain had an empire just like Belin's. Now the Stronghold's gone it's all finished. If you ask me, sir, Xandria has cause to be thankful the Dragomite Hills are strung right across her southern borders. If it wasn't for that natural barrier, the land we call home would probably look just like this. It's time to go back, sir, if we still can. Answers ain't worth dyin' for.'

Fraxinus didn't bother to tell the sergeant what the 'big birds' had actually been. 'We can't go back,' he said soberly. 'Not to Xandria, nor even to the Nine Towns.'

'I think we can make it, sir,' Purkin countered. 'If we can't follow the river north we can follow it west – skirt the marshes, head for the Grey Waste. It'd be a long way round, but the amber's map showed the river curvin' northwards on the other side of the marshes. If we could get that far, we'd be goin' the right way. Even if we couldn't get through to Xandria right away we'd surely find other earthly land. Accordin' to Amyas, things like this don't last for ever. Bad times come, then fade away. We have to believe that people can live through these things, come out the other side, or we're lost. Way I see it is, if you can't hold what you have, you just have to give way and run.'

'I've noticed that you tend to see things that way,' Fraxinus retorted drily. 'Sometimes, you seem to run before it's strictly necessary.'

'If I'd run a bit sooner, I'd have more than five of my men left,' Purkin riposted. 'If I'd run when most of the lads ran, I'd be snug and safe somewhere in Khalorn. You didn't run, and you seem to have steered into just as much trouble as I did. You ought to come with us, sir, in my opinion. Some of my men – my new men, that is – might not like the idea of joinin' up with dragomites, but I c'n explain that they're tame enough. Together, we'd stand a much better chance of gettin' through, an' gettin' home.' His speech had become increasingly slurred as it drew towards its close, and Fraxinus could measure the other man's desperation in the abandoned consonants.

'You're welcome to join us,' Fraxinus said quietly. 'It's still a long way to Chimera's Cradle, but we'll get there. When we've found out what we need to know, we'll go back to Xandria.'

Purkin drained the last of the water from the bottle and looked around. Although he couldn't see the people inside the wagon, and had no way to estimate how many of them there might be, he must have known that everyone there was listening to his every word.

'You'd be crazy to carry on the way you're goin',' he said, in an unnecessarily loud voice. 'You came south to see what there was to see, but you've seen enough of it now to know that it's far worse than anythin' you expected. I don't know what answers you got in Salamander's Fire, but I'll lay odds they didn't make Chimera's Cradle sound any less dangerous than the rumours *I've* heard. Anyone with any sense would come with me – *anyone*, queen or thief, giant or merchant.'

Fraxinus noticed that the sergeant hadn't mentioned Serpents or dragomites. He had long felt secure in his authority over the ill-mixed expedition, at least since Ereleth had ceased to compete with him, but he knew that this was the first explicit threat he had faced. He also knew that he had no right to stop anyone who might decide that Purkin was correct. He glanced sideways at Merel, uneasily aware that she was filling her lungs, making ready to reply.

'We're crazy all right,' she called back waspishly, 'but we're not crazy enough to follow a leader like you.'

Fraxinus suppressed a smile, but he felt that he had to put up a better show than that to justify himself. 'It's not just curiosity that drives me on, sergeant,' he said. 'If we don't find out what's happening here, all human civilisation might eventually go the same way as the Cities of the Plain and the Stronghold you were brought to defend. You must see that mere defence isn't enough – as you say, this sort of crisis in the world's affairs has happened before, but it's made no impact on our lore. Perhaps, this time, Xandria will be left untouched – and I dare say you're not prepared to worry about what might happen next time, when our remote descendants will have inherited the world – but we can't be sure even of that. The effects have already spread as far as the Forest of Absolute Night. We need to know what's behind all this, if we can figure it out, and we need to make new lore that ensures it's remembered and understood. If we don't do it, who will?'

'If you *can't* do it,' Purkin retorted, 'you'll all die. I'm not ridin' into the jaws of a trap – I'm goin' home, if I possibly can. It'd be a lot easier if you were with me. If we were all together, we'd stand every chance. Separated . . .'

He left his listeners to form their own conclusions about that, delicately refusing to point out that a wagon and a giant would add far more to his resources than his ragged cavalry would add to Fraxinus's strength. Fraxinus knew, though, that the sergeant did have a point. There was unity in strength, and there was considerable danger in continuing the way he was headed.

'As it happens,' he said, 'I've one man here who might be interested in taking command of your troop. You never met him, but those of your men who come from the Nine Towns will know him well enough. General Shabir!'

Purkin's expression had already darkened before Fraxinus pronounced the name; it darkened even further when Shabir came to stand behind Fraxinus.

'They're *my* men now, sir – every one,' Purkin was quick to assert. 'Old ranks mean nothin'.' He didn't seem entirely confident of that, but he was clearly determined to play it that way.

'Are you interested in following a deserter halfway round the world, Shabir?' Fraxinus asked, looking at the man leaning over his shoulder. 'If you are, here's a recruiting sergeant who'd like to sign you up as a corporal.'

'Perhaps I should speak to the men who once served in my army,' Shabir replied, for Purkin's benefit. 'I dare say they'll have had their fill of this man by now, even if there's not an Eblan among them.'

Purkin obviously didn't relish that prospect, but he had a reply ready. 'Perhaps they'd rather go home with you than home with me,' he said, 'but the one place they won't go is the Navel of the World. They've had their fill of its produce already. Perhaps we might share our command, general – I know that my men will stay with me no matter what.'

For a fleeting second, Fraxinus thought Shabir might take up the offer, but too much had changed since the battle in the Spangled Desert. The general had heard what Purkin had to say and he'd already made his decision.

'Tell my men that I'm here,' the Eblan said. 'Tell them I'm not afraid of what lies ahead. Tell them that they're welcome to come with us, if that's their wish, but they must make their own decisions.' Having said that, he withdrew disdainfully into the body of the wagon.

'Does anyone else have a message for the sergeant?' Fraxinus called, permitting himself the luxury of a smile. He knew that now Merel and Shabir had declined Purkin's offer, there was no one else who would even contemplate it.

When no one replied, he turned back to Purkin and said: 'My offer's still open if you want to change your mind – if you or any of your men would like to join us.'

Purkin's expression was distinctly ugly; he evidently thought that he was being mocked and insulted, and he was not nearly so sure of the loyalty of his own men as Fraxinus was of his.

'You don't know what you're up against, Fraxinus,' the sergeant said. 'I've only seen the tiniest part of it, but I know that a giant and two dragomites aren't enough to see you through. There are whole armies up ahead of you, and even if they're not real humans they have horses and hands and weapons, and they ain't interested in talk and trading. If you don't turn away now, you're all goin' straight to your deaths. Believe me, I know.'

'What do you think Captain Cerri would do if he were in your place?' Fraxinus asked him. 'Or this Amyas, about whom Aulakh Phar has told me so much?'

'They're both dead,' Purkin retorted bitterly. 'I'm still alive. I think I'm entitled to be reckoned the better judge of acceptable risks, don't you?'

'No, I don't,' Fraxinus said. 'You can come with us if you want to. If you don't, you can look after yourselves – that's all there is to it.'

'It's not as simple as that,' Purkin shot back. He still had the flag of truce in his hand, seemingly unaware of the fact that it had branded him a potential enemy rather than a friend. He thought that he still had threats in reserve, but he didn't. His threat had already been perceived, and discounted.

'Yes it is,' Fraxinus insisted, packing all the resolution he could muster into the cold statement. 'You don't have the wherewithal to bargain with us. If you want to go on your way, I certainly won't stop you – but you made your offer when all my people could hear you. I wonder what response I'd get if I made mine when all *your* men could hear and judge for themselves.'

Purkin scowled. 'I ain't holdin' anyone by force,' he said unconvincingly. 'Anyone wants to join with you, good riddance – but I reckon they have too much sense.' He looked from side to side, his flickering glance taking in the giant and the two dragomites.

Fraxinus had no doubt at all that had the wagon been less well defended, Purkin would have had no qualms about leading his men to attack and plunder it. *Shabir is a better man than that,* he thought. *At least he did what he did at the bridge in the hope of inspiring his fellows, not merely out of fear and greed. This is the true enemy of us all: the individual who will contemplate and execute any treason in the name of survival.*

'Tell them anyway,' Fraxinus said mildly. 'We can't offer much in the way of food or comfort, but we hope to see some interesting sights – and we'd be very glad of an extra horse or two.'

'You're crazy,' Purkin said, not for the first time.

'It's a crazy time,' Fraxinus told him. 'In crazy times, only crazy men can hope to figure out what's going on.'

Purkin put his left foot in the stirrup and hauled himself up on to his horse's back. The animal whinnied a faint complaint, but it had been too well-schooled to rebel. 'If I ever get back to Xandria,' the sergeant said, 'I'll make sure they know what happened to you, and why. If your name's remembered at all, it'll be a warnin' against folly.'

'I'll be remembered,' Fraxinus told the sergeant, as the memory of his son's face became momentarily sharp. 'Even if no word ever gets back, I'll be remembered. Unless I'm much mistaken, you're already forgotten, and always will be.'

Purkin wasn't about to give up the last word. His parting shot, as he rode away, was: 'Don't bet on it.' It was a threat, but it was an empty one – or so, at least, Fraxinus hoped.

'We'll have to be careful now,' Ereleth said, as Fraxinus coaxed the horses forward again. 'You didn't have to annoy him quite as much as that.' Recalling her own attempts at diplomatic negotiation, Fraxinus thought this censure unwarranted.

'We'll have to be careful anyhow,' he said quietly. 'If he's right, we have enemies far more dangerous than him.'

'He is right, though, isn't he?' Merel said reflectively. 'We *are* crazy. I'm still hoping that Andris is alive, somewhere up ahead, but the rest of you . . . well, you don't even know what to hope for, do you?'

Fraxinus wished that he had a reply ready, but he hadn't. All he could say was: 'We need to know what's happening to the world. It's our world, after all. If we refuse to confront its dangers and its secrets, what are we? We need to know how we fit into the scheme of things, even if it turns out that there's nothing we can do to change it.'

It was the first time he had voiced that particular possibility, although it had always been at the back of his mind. Now that he had, he certainly didn't feel any better about it.

'They'll follow us,' Ereleth said. 'They'll track us, at least for a while, and they'll try to pick up the pieces if we meet trouble we can't cope with.'

'Perhaps they will,' Fraxinus said quietly, 'but if we do run into the kind of trouble we can't cope with, it really won't matter to us who picks up the pieces, will it?'

7

LUCREZIA WAS GLAD to step down from the wagon, which had suddenly seemed unreasonably confined with the winged creature peering in at one entranceway and the Serpent blocking the other. Ssifuss and the winged one had now moved away from the wagon into an open space and had drawn close to one another, jabbering away in two different tongues.

So far as Lucrezia could judge, the winged creature had little real understanding of the Serpent tongue, although it was certainly trying to pronounce words in that language. Ssifuss, in his turn, had only the most rudimentary understanding of the other syllables which spilled from the creature's mouth and could not begin to match them. She couldn't believe that their attempted communication would produce much real information.

Checuti led Lucrezia and Keshvara away to the far side of the wagon. Jume Metra followed them. 'Did you ever hear of anything like that before?' he asked them.

'Not unless it's a firedragon,' Hyry replied. 'Firedragons are supposed to have wings and bright scales, aren't they? If it can breathe fire, I suppose it will qualify.'

'It can breathe the word *Fraxinus*,' Checuti said. 'That's strange enough for me. Perhaps Ssifuss was mistaken about its claim to be a Salamander – perhaps what it was trying to say is that it's come from Salamander's Fire.'

Lucrezia had already deduced that the creature must have come from Salamander's Fire and that Fraxinus must therefore have reached that intermediate destination. The question of exactly what manner of creature it might be seemed to her to be a secondary issue. 'Go to garden' had been the real core of its message; the problem lay in deciding whether it was merely stating what Fraxinus intended to do or requesting them to do likewise.

'Perhaps the belief that firedragons breathe fire is just a mistake based on careless reportage,' Hyry guessed. 'Perhaps the first part of their name only signifies their origin. On the other hand . . . perhaps it *is* a Salamander – a kind of Salamander that only appears once in a thousand generations.'

'Paedogenesis,' Checuti said.

Keshvara had been the first to hear the word from Mossassor, and the first to interrogate Aulakh Phar about its meaning; she knew what Checuti was implying. She looked sideways at Lucrezia.

'If Mossassor meant what Aulakh Phar thought he meant,' she explained, 'the Serpents and Salamanders we know are really juvenile forms which have the ability to reproduce themselves without bothering with the final stage in their life cycle. It occurred to me to wonder whether the big Serpents accompanying the bronzes might be the true adults of the species, even though they seem less intelligent than their smaller brethren.'

'Did they seem very much less intelligent?' Lucrezia asked. She knew that Ssifuss hadn't managed to persuade one to speak, but she had been inclined to attribute that to obstinacy rather than incapacity.

'They did to me,' Hyry confirmed. She seemed slightly annoyed to have her judgment questioned. Having been their prisoner, the trader had had far more opportunity to observe the giants than Lucrezia. She waited for Lucrezia to nod her head before continuing. 'If you think in terms of maggots and flies, it's not so difficult to believe that something which looks like a bloated Serpent – as Salamanders do – might be able to metamorphose into something like that.' She pointed at the winged creature and paused again, waiting for further encouragement. The winged creature looked around when Hyry pointed, although it still appeared to be listening to Ssifuss. Lucrezia couldn't tell whether it understood what the Serpent was saying.

'Go on,' Checuti said.

'I think Serpents and Salamanders are both hatched from eggs laid in something akin to a dragomite nest,' Hyry went on, 'and I think Salamander's Fire is just a metaphor referring to whatever makes the nesting ground switch to pupation mode. I think Dhalla was told that she would sometimes feel it burning in her heart because she too is a product of a similar kind of nesting ground. We already know that such nests can produce human as well as unhuman offspring. I think Lucrezia's right. Our visitor is a Salamander flown from Salamander's Fire – a kind of Salamander which no one has seen for many generations.'

'If it was hatched out that way not long ago,' Checuti said pensively, 'I suppose the fact that it can speak at all might be reckoned a wonder. Even so, when I look at the winged thing and Ssifuss standing side by side I know which seems to me to be the adult and which the child.'

'According to Aulakh,' Hyry said, 'human intelligence depends on our being born immature. Our brains develop along with our learning, taking aboard the legacy of our formative experiences. Perhaps it's the same with Serpents and Salamanders – perhaps their intelligence arises out of their immaturity. Perhaps it's because they can breed as juveniles that they can pass on the legacy of their learning exactly as humans do, as lore passed from full-grown larva to part-grown larva. If the winged creature really is an adult, it might have carried through its pupation stage a certain amount of what it learned as a juvenile but not all of it. Perhaps it really is less intelligent than its juvenile equivalent.'

'Ssifuss thought that giant Serpents were mythical creatures,' Lucrezia put in. 'Now he knows they're not – and he knows that Salamanders have another form too.'

'Mossassor told me once that Serpents are good at forgetting because they have to be,' Hyry said. 'He couldn't explain exactly what it – I mean *he* – meant, but this must be part of it.'

Checuti was looking upwards now, his attention having been caught by something glimpsed between the curling boughs of the dendrites.

'Look!' he said.

Lucrezia craned her neck, moving her head slightly from side to side to cancel the effect of the obscuring pattern of the coiling branches and their intricate hangings. Three more winged creatures were descending towards the Reef. They flew with surprising grace, like great soaring birds rather than insects or bats, even though their wings were jewelled with multifaceted scales and framed by a fan-like array of bone-like struts. At this range their slender arms, held tight to their sides, were hardly visible at all, while their legs were clamped together to form a seamless rudder.

'Why are they going to the garden of Idun?' Lucrezia wondered aloud.

'They're not,' Hyry said. 'They're going to *a* garden, just as Mossassor was. I suspect they don't know where it is or why they're going, but they're following the dictate of some inner command. Perhaps that's what ordinary Serpents have to forget, in order to be free – except that when the time arrives, *some* of them have to remember . . . or can't help remembering, however dimly.'

'Mossassor said something about a *promise*,' Lucrezia reminded her. 'He wanted us to search for the garden *together*. Is that what the Salamanders want, too?'

Hyry was still following her own train of thought. 'The garden our forefathers built, after they tried and failed to build a city capable of standing firm against all kinds of rot, is only one of many now,' she said, 'even if it wasn't before. I suppose some will fly to one, others to another . . . and in the meantime, legions of half-men and adult Serpents are sent forth in search of other kinds of . . . other kinds of *what*, exactly?'

'Flesh?' said Checuti.

'Mind?' Lucrezia ventured – but she didn't think either of them had it right.

'They probably have no more idea than we have of what might happen to them when they arrive,' Hyry said. 'Even though this has happened before, it hasn't produced any lore that humans or Serpents have preserved, and I doubt that the Salamanders are very much wiser. At best, they too have their myths, which they've half forgotten, exactly as we have . . . because they ceased to trust them exactly as we did. If only *all* our ancestors had taken the trouble to *learn*, and to preserve their learning . . .'

'To do that,' Checuti pointed out, 'the people who went to the garden or gardens would have had to come out again, wiser than they went in. The same goes for Serpents and Salamanders.'

'Philemon Taub said that once we understood what it was

that was drawing us towards Chimera's Cradle, we'd understand why we mustn't go,' Lucrezia said. 'But *something* must be happening there – something vitally important. It's not just a matter of flesh being swallowed up. It's more to do with minds than meat . . . but I don't see how.'

'The problem is,' Checuti pointed out, 'that if your flesh gets swallowed up, your mind goes with it. What's vitally important to *me* is staying in one piece as long as possible; what's important to living hills and animate morasses is really no concern of mine.'

The winged Salamander that had landed on the wagon was rising into the air again now; it looked terribly ungainly as it flapped its wings with desperate energy, but the higher it went the more graceful it became. Ssifuss made his way back to join the waiting humans.

'Where have you been, Ssifuss?' Lucrezia wanted to know. 'Venerina's people have been gone for days – and you didn't need to hide from them in any case.'

The Serpent shook its head. 'Wassn't hiding,' it said. 'Followed Andriss. Ssey put in ssoft sshell but iss alive. Ssought might resscue, but too many, too careful. Ssought besst come back, get help. Iss dangerouss, but road iss good.'

Lucrezia was dumbstruck. Venerina Sirelis had been unwilling to chase after Andris even with a small army to help her, taking refuge in the plaint that no one even knew whether the amber was alive – yet a lone Serpent had gone after him. Having failed to find a good opportunity to take on the marauders single-handed, it had returned to get help – and this was the Serpent who had long considered mankind to be a blight upon the surface of its world!

'What did the flying creature say?' Checuti wanted to know.

'Ssayss iss true Ssalamander,' the Serpent repeated, with what sounded like sorrowful scepticism. 'Ssayss iss messssenger too, but hass learned few wordss. Ssink Fraxinuss iss moving, will pass to ssouss, don't know how long. Mossassor iss wiss him, giant too. Two dragomitess. Osser humanss, not ssure how many, ssink five. Musst be more ssan ssree, elsse eassy to ssay.'

Lucrezia was already counting up. 'Ereleth was with him after the battle,' she said, 'and so was one of the mound-women. Dhalla reached the far shore too, but no one else except

Mossassor. Jacom Cerri, Merel Zabio and Aulakh Phar must all have made it through to Salamander's Fire if there really are five other humans with him.'

'You're forgetting Sergeant Purkin and his men,' Checuti pointed out, 'not to mention the possibility that he may have encountered other humans. We can't be sure that any of Keshvara's erstwhile companions made it through.'

'Did your winged friend mention any other names?' Lucrezia asked the Serpent.

Ssifuss shook its head. 'Not good wiss namess,' it reported. 'Ssayss go to garden, but cannot ssay name. Doess not know one from anosser, I ssink. No matter. Musst follow Andriss now.' It wasn't clear to Lucrezia whether the last few words constituted a suggestion, a question or a declaration of intent.

'That would be a very foolish move,' Checuti said. 'If we wait for Fraxinus, we'll more than double our strength.'

'But Fraxinus isn't coming here,' Lucrezia pointed out. 'He's following the map Andris drew for him – he'll meet the Reef a long way from here, looking for the Silver Thorns and the Gauntlet of Gladness.'

'Then that's where we should go to meet him,' Checuti said positively.

'Musst go to Andriss,' said the Serpent, equally positively. 'Iss debt. Iss debt to Mossassor too, but wiss Andriss . . .' The creature failed to find the words it sought and settled for gestures instead, miming the hurling of a spear.

Lucrezia inferred that the Serpent felt that it owed its life to Andris because of the battle they had fought together, and that the obligation involved outweighed whatever debt it owed to Mossassor. Serpents clearly took matters of obligation very seriously indeed.

'By the time you got to him,' Hyry pointed out, 'he'd probably be sprouting thorns in every direction. Didn't he tell you where those raiders were taking their prisoners?'

All Ssifuss said was: 'Ssey go to garden.'

'However quickly we went after him,' Checuti countered, 'we'd need a virtual miracle to save him. Fraxinus must understand what's happening now, even though we can't quite grasp it – if Phar *is* with him, they've probably sorted out every last detail. I'd rather know what I'm walking into before I go on.'

Lucrezia bit her lip to save herself from retorting that he'd obviously rather not go on at all. 'Andris saved my life too,' she said to Ssifuss. 'Even though he knew what I once intended to do with him he fought with me and for me – for all of us – because he'd accepted that we're on the same side. We can't let him go to his death while there's a chance that we can prevent it.'

Hyry looked as if she wanted to repeat her claim that there wasn't anything anyone could do for Andris now, but she didn't dare. Her own life had just been snatched from the jaws of horrible disaster, and she must know how it would sound if she advocated leaving someone else to take her place.

Checuti knew it too, which was why he turned to Ssifuss. 'What exactly do you intend to do?' he asked.

The Serpent didn't hesitate. 'Go to garden,' it said. 'Find Andriss.'

'In that case,' Lucrezia said, feeling that equal decisiveness was called for, 'I'm going with you. Checuti, you and Hyry and Jume Metra can make your own choices.'

She hoped – but did not expect – that Checuti might respond by saying that of course he couldn't leave her. In fact, he waited to see what the others would say.

It was Jume Metra who spoke first. 'There are warriors with Fraxinus, perhaps a human sister. The nest is not yet dead.'

Hyry needed no further encouragement. 'You can't go with the Serpent, highness,' she said. 'It's suicide.'

For once, Lucrezia didn't feel any urge to object to the use of her title. 'You can't tell me what to do, Keshvara,' she replied, in exactly the kind of haughty manner that she had been trying for so long to discard, 'and if you meant what you said, you'd have a duty to follow me wherever I led.'

Hyry looked very unhappy at that, and Lucrezia realised that perhaps the trader did feel the urgings of exactly such a duty – not because Lucrezia was a princess, but because they had forged a bond of friendship while they came through the Forest of Absolute Night. 'This is madness,' the trader said.

'Iss not,' Ssifuss put in. 'Iss dangerouss, but road iss good. You ride, iss ssafe – ssafe ass Reef. Danger *everywhere*. If musst go on, besst go on *now*.'

Checuti had already made up his mind. 'You can take the

wagon if you want to, my lady,' he said. 'Metra and I will travel faster along the line of the Reef on horseback.'

'We don't want the wagon,' Lucrezia told him. 'We have to travel quickly too, if we're to have a chance of getting to Andris before his captors feed their deadly seeds to him.'

'You might already be too late,' Checuti pointed out.

'So might Fraxinus,' Lucrezia countered. 'This is the quickest way to Chimera's Cradle, and to the other gardens surrounding it. Ssifuss is right: if we have to go into this region eventually, we might as well go now, along a road which he's already tested.'

'Splitting up is the worst thing we can possibly do,' Hyry complained. 'We have to stay together, if we're to stand a chance of staying alive. I've only just found you all again – the last thing I want is to lose any one of you.'

'She's right, my lady,' Checuti said, still looking at Lucrezia. His voice was level but there was something in his eyes that looked suspiciously like amusement. 'You really ought to stay with us. We just spent a tenday nursing you back to health – what kind of gratitude would it display to march off straight into the jaws of death?'

'The kind I owe to Andris Myrasol,' Lucrezia retorted. 'The kind we *all* owe to Andris Myrasol.'

Checuti shook his head. 'I suppose it's not the first time,' he said, presumably remembering her impetuous dash from the safety of the Inner Sanctum. He turned to Jume Metra and said: 'We'd better start packing.'

Lucrezia looked at Hyry, who had yet to make a decision. Hyry looked away, refusing to make it. 'Whichever way we choose to go,' the princess said softly, 'we're still all on the same side, aren't we?'

Only one of them took the trouble to echo her words. 'All on same side,' it said. 'Iss truss. Iss truss now.'

Lucrezia could only hope that the Serpent knew what it was talking about, and that it might be right.

8

ANDRIS OCCASIONALLY DREAMED that he could still walk. He sometimes dreamed that he was walking through the garden, and that the tree-people turned to watch him pass by. He knew when this happened that it was merely a dream within a dream, in which his frightened mind looked backwards, trying to recapture some comforting vestige of his former existence, but he liked it nevertheless.

When he took brief refuge in such fantasies, many of the tree-people spoke to him, offering reassurances as to his fate and fortune. He was told over and over again that there was no need to be afraid, that all would be well, that no harm would come to him, that the best part of his life was yet to begin.

They even told him that he might be free again, one day – that what was adopted and adapted might one day be released, to take part in yet another Time of Emergence.

'The half-men sent out to fetch new blood are doubtless the offspring of those united with the ground,' Andris told them regretfully, 'but they are mere echoes of their forebears, nor are they truly free.'

It seemed to him that the greater number of the tree-people spoke as if they did not expect to believed, whether they were telling the truth or not. He was prepared to accept that they did believe what they said, but not that they had any real grounds for their belief. He thought that they sensed his scepticism. In any case, he always insisted that he was not afraid. He told them that he did not like the fate to which he had been delivered, but was *not afraid*.

He liked to think that he had moved beyond the reach of fear some considerable time before.

In his dreams-within-the-dream Andris was usually able to turn and look back at the faces which watched him pass, and meet their eyes. He could not help but be reminded of the human flesh which had been smeared over the walls of the dragomite queen's innermost chamber.

He had refused to look too closely at that display at the time, concentrating instead on the half-man whose head and shoulders had a more familiar appearance. Now, he was by no means certain that appearances could be trusted. Now he knew that there were many kinds of beings which looked human but had no particular loyalty to *his* kind. He had suspended judgment on the matter of what it meant to *be* human.

The human faces in the trees were mostly bronze or golden, and he felt no particular kinship with the one amber he could see in the distance. More than half of them were male, but the preponderance wasn't great. The apparent ages of the faces were only loosely correlated with the apparent ages of their vegetable parasites. Some of the largest and most luxuriant crowns were gathered about boles about half his own height, whose faces seemed to be no more than three or four years old; others, whose limbs were wide-spread and not in the least gnarled, displayed antique visages more like Aulakh Phar's.

There were always birds in the branches of the bushes, nibbling at the ripe red fruits which Andris had not yet grown. The bushes were selective in offering their bounty; they did not submit passively to any and all invasions. There were many kinds of insects but the ones to which the tree-people seemed most hospitable were big somnolent creatures like giant bees. Many of these were hovering about the flowers which still showed on some of the trees but had not yet come into bloom on his own spreading boughs. These were tolerated, if not actively welcomed, but most other insects were discouraged by dismissive gestures of the thorn-laden branches.

Andris couldn't be sure why some birds and insects were accommodated while others weren't, but he guessed that it had to do with their nature and origin. All these birds and these bees were probably the offspring of figured stones and their kin, perhaps of the dwellers in the deep themselves; their feeding was part of the complicated intercourse of the living grounds.

Andris was careful to study the power of movement which his neighbours had, and the manner in which they deterred and drove off unwelcome visitors. Many of the trees reached out to

230

his dream self as he passed them by, extending their outermost growing points as if to supplement their reassuring words with a gentle touch. Only one or two actually contrived to touch him, very lightly, although he made no conspicuous attempts to avoid such contacts.

Such imaginary walks always brought him back to the crest of the hill, but as he approached it his vision always became blurred; there was something there he could not yet see: a tree taller than all the rest.

It was his failure to make out this particular tree which reminded him, time and time again, that he could no longer walk because he no longer had legs. When he dreamed of walking, he was actually synthesising sensations from what he could see from his own fixed vantage point and he could not add into the dream information which he could not obtain: information as to what was *behind* his station. To find that out, he would have to master his new body sufficiently to twist his trunk and turn his head around.

He wondered whether this test had been set before him deliberately, as a lure to make him enter more fully into his new self.

If so, he thought, when he had returned from his most recent dream-within-a-dream to the honest nightmare of reality, *it's certainly working. I'm utterly lost in this wilderness of strange sensation, but I still have my curiosity. I experience everything as if it were a dream, because all the familiar props and sensations of my former consciousness are gone, but I cannot and will not deliver myself wholly to the seductive comforts of dreams-within-dreams. I want true consciousness back again. I want the best control I can achieve over my reconstituted limbs, however many they are and whatever strange sinews extend within them. I want to feel the new rhythms of my inner being, whatever fluids move through its vessels and whether or not I have a heart to force them. I want a new sanity to replace this awful madness. If I am a chimera, then a chimera I will be – but I must have clarity of mind. I must have the power of reason, or I am nothing.*

He didn't suppose for a minute that he was the first person to find himself in this predicament who had expressed such conviction, but he felt entitled nevertheless to think himself a hero.

Whenever the dream allowed, he concentrated all his efforts on the problem of exercising control over his new body. He moved his limbs, and exercised them constantly, and milked the pleasure of exercise as fully as he milked the pleasure of discovery. He became, by slow degrees, the kind of tree that could welcome some visitors and repel others – and found within the reconstruction of his aesthetic sensibilities the kinds of attraction and repulsion which allowed him to discriminate between the welcome and the unwelcome even before his buds had opened into flowers.

He also tried to move his head, but that was a much more vexatious task. He tried, above all, to twist his body round so that he might look behind him. He was sure that there was something there waiting to be seen; something he had glimpsed long ago, while lost in a deeper kind of dream, before his metamorphosis had properly begun.

In the end, he succeeded in turning far enough to look behind him – and immediately felt that his dream had entered another new phase, more important than any it had manifested before.

Behind him, there was another tree, taller than any he could see on the lower slopes. He knew as soon as he saw it that unless and until he outgrew it, this was the most powerful growth which the ground had produced: the pinnacle of its achievement.

Andris wondered briefly whether the seed of this spectacular tree might have been planted in the body of a giant, to nourish itself on the Salamander's fire which was supposed to burn in giants' hearts, but when he studied the female face engraved upon the massive trunk more carefully he decided that it couldn't be so. There was nothing of the broadness of Dhalla's features in the face, let alone her patience and placidity. This was a face of meaner proportions, in spite of the gargantuan girth of the bole with which its flesh was now fused.

Apart from the face, few traces of human form remained. In almost all the other bushes in the garden the outlines of shoulders, breasts, thighs and feet could still be seen, while the bronze or golden colouring of human skin still tinted the alien flesh with which the human was allied. Not in this case: the bole of this tree was a dark shade of brown he had never known to be associated with human skin, and its subtle contours held no echo of bulging hip or tapered ankle. Only the face was human, and even that was very darkly coloured, more black than bronze. So high were the eyes set that he had to bend his own crown back to meet the other's studiously mournful gaze.

The irises were as black as their pupils, magnifying the dolour of their expression considerably.

As soon as he was able to meet her eyes the other tree reached out to him; he felt the growing tips of her long and snaky branches touch the tender buds which sprouted from his myriad limbs. He refused to flinch as her naked thorns danced about his new extremities, without ever quite brushing them. He had thorns of his own now, as well as the buds which would become white flowers, but he made no threat of his own. There were no flowers left on her boughs, and the last few fruits which hung from them would soon be rotting on their stalks.

'Are you the queen of this strange hive?' he asked, although he wasn't sure whether he was really speaking, or whether his words were merely one more confabulation in an endless riot of imagined conversations. 'Was it you who dispatched hordes of monsters to sweep down on peaceful households, taking humans prisoner so that their living flesh might play host to the unearthly?'

'Your living flesh has played host to the unearthly since the moment of your conception,' the other replied. 'Had human flesh not made its pact with the unearthly, your ancestors would have died out within a few generations of their invasion. You have as much of the unearthly in you as any of your kin, Andris Myrasol – don't think because you have grown used to walking on your own feet that you're any less of a chimera than anyone here.'

Andris wondered whether the fact that she had pronounced his name proved that her speech was simply one more delusion.

'I might have looked like half a giant,' he said warily, 'but I wasn't. I simply grew taller than the average. I can assure you that I was fully human.'

'And I can assure you that none of your kind is more *fully human* than I am,' the tree retorted, but without any real aggression. 'The unearthly is always with you and within you; it

233

could not be otherwise. Your ancestors believed that they had tamed the unearthly and reduced it to mere instrumentality, but it was never so and never could have been.'

'As you know my name,' Andris said, 'may I know yours? Or have you forgotten the name you had before you turned into a thing of thorns and flowers?'

'You mistake my origin,' she told him. 'I was delivered from this ground; there is no new blood in me. If I ever lived as you have lived I have forgotten who and what I was . . . but I do have a name. Call me Arilla.'

'What is going on here, Arilla?' Andris asked urgently. 'I know that the garden is merely a facet of the outer skin of some unearthly creature made of fluid stone, which extends deep into the crust of the world. I know that there are others – perhaps many others – clustered hereabouts. Are they contesting to reclaim the ground that my forefathers claimed for their own, and the garden the forefathers built for the benefit of human-kind?'

'They're no more avid to reclaim that ground than they are to devour one another,' Arilla told him, in a curiously wistful voice. 'If the Serpents' lore can be trusted, things must have been different once – but even if there is more to that lore than myths and fantasies, the coming of your forefathers must have changed everything. If human lore can be trusted, the people of the ship intended to impose their own kind of order on the world, but they failed once and nearly failed a second time. Instead of order, they brought chaos – or the threat of it, at least. Yes, this is a battleground, and the place you call Idun lies close to its heart . . . but we cannot tell how many enemies we have, nor what resolution of the conflict might be possible, now or in the far future. The greatest enemies of all are our ignorance and our lack of understanding; in that, at least, I am not so very different from your free-living kin.'

My free-living kin! Andris thought. *She might have said 'not so very different from you', but I am part of her garden now; she and I are 'we'. She does not speak as Jume Metra spoke: she uses the word 'I' freely enough . . . but what, exactly, does she mean by it?*

The drooping branches whose tips had rested lightly on his own extremities withdrew now. He watched their lissom movements, knowing that he had a long way still to go in mastering his new limbs and their capacity for purposive movement. He was strong but graceless; she seemed somewhat less sturdy but far more comfortable in herself – but perhaps that was partly illusion, born of the knowledge that she was female.

'If this living ground can produce its own human bodies to fuse with its monstrous flowers,' he asked, 'why do you need to send so-called messengers out into the world to kidnap more?'

'The ground needs new blood,' Arilla replied. 'It is the one thing that can help it grow, and grow stronger. It is the one thing that can sustain us in the battle which we have been fighting since time immemorial. It wasn't *you* we needed – not the consciousness which you think of as your *self* – but the things which are inside you: the unearthly things to which you play host, just as the ground plays host to creatures like you. You live very rapidly by comparison with the creature of which I am a part, but the things which are tiny parts of you live more rapidly still, and change more rapidly too. Can you understand that?'

Andris found, slightly to his own surprise, that he had no difficulty at all in understanding it. Had he not been seeing it, in his mind's eye, ever since he entered the Soursweet Marshes? Even before that, Aulakh Phar had told him that there were countless tiny creatures living inside his body – that he was a world of sorts himself, playing host to an unimaginable number of little passengers, which operated independently of his animating intelligence. He had known it even before he brought it to the level of immediate consciousness; of course he understood it.

'I have a life of my own,' he said pensively. 'So, I dare say, have the creatures which dwell within me. I cannot imagine that they have any greater desire than I to be mere parts of some huger entity.'

'It isn't a matter of desire,' Arilla said. 'It's a matter of destiny.'

But there is no destiny! Andris objected. He didn't say it aloud but he was insistent nevertheless. *That's a saying even in my homeland – and the blind beggar had a fuller version of it. 'There is no destiny: the future cannot be foreknown but the human mind is pregnant with many designs . . .'*

'Don't be afraid,' Arilla told him, echoing the sentiment of her strange siblings. 'This is no misfortune. It wasn't your mind that

235

was needed by the Mother of Serpents, but she has it now – and you should be glad of that, because she has no intention of destroying it. I understand your anxieties and your fears, but you'll come to understand that they're misplaced. I can't promise you safety from injury and pain, for killers have already visited the garden and will surely come again, but you and I are beyond the reach of death. I *can* promise you the possibility that you might live a longer and a richer life here than you ever imagined possible when you walked upon your silly legs . . . and the prospect of another life beyond this one.'

There was an echo of the deists' hopeful faith in that 'promise', but Andris remembered that Seth had told him not to believe promises of immortality. Had Seth been made promises of that kind, when he first rebelled against his nature and his queen? 'I fear,' he countered, 'that you and I might have different notions of what constitutes death, and the ability to live beyond its reach . . . and we certainly have different notions of what might constitute a richer life.'

'You'll learn better,' Arilla said, as her image began to blur and fade out. 'When you have become what you're now in the process of becoming, you'll see things more clearly.'

He didn't know whether the blurring meant that he hadn't managed to turn round at all, but it seemed likely. He fought against it, possessed by a fervent desire to be done with dreams and dreams-within-dreams. It was now time, he thought, to put such artifice behind him and come into his new heritage, whatever it might be . . . but darkness drew him in even before she had finished speaking.

He found himself confined again within a dream-within-a-dream, but this time he was running instead of walking.

He was running as fast as his silly legs could carry him, but he was going nowhere, because there was nowhere to go.

This uncertainty must end, he told himself. *It must end soon, else I shall go mad.* But he could only hope that he wasn't mad already.

9

THE WARRIORS WITH unhuman heads became visible with the first light of dawn, as they had doubtless intended. There had been no sign of anything amiss while the wagon rolled patiently towards the shadowed horizon by starlight, but the wind had been blowing from the north-east, carrying away the kind of information which Vaca Metra's dragomites might have picked up. Now that daylight had banished the darker shadows from the plain the mounted men could not remain hidden any longer, and they had evidently calculated the effect of their appearance.

Fraxinus immediately reined in the horses, leaving Merel Zabio to carry the bad news back into the body of the wagon while he began to count the enemy. The largest party was directly ahead, numbering at least forty – they were too tightly bunched for him to make a more accurate count. That main group was flanked by two others, each of which had moved further forward so as to form an angle of forty-five degrees with the stationary wagon and their own companions. These groups were not so tightly bunched and Fraxinus was swift enough in eye and mind to count thirty-two to the left and twenty-four to the right.

Once they had displayed themselves the warriors were content to remain still for a while. Although they had obviously had intelligence of the wagon's approach they had had no opportunity to examine Fraxinus's party in detail, and he wondered what conversation might now be passing between them as they studied the two dragomite warriors and the giant.

'I suppose we should be grateful to Sergeant Purkin for warning us,' Fraxinus murmured, as others pressed in behind him to take stock of the situation, 'but I'd be a good deal happier if his guardsmen were here to form a rearguard.'

'We have been in this situation before,' Ereleth muttered. 'We faced as many in the Spangled Desert, and we defeated them with ease.'

'You had four dragomites then instead of two,' Shabir put in. 'My men were near exhaustion, and the ground was against us.'

'The ground is against *them*,' Fraxinus said. 'It may look flat but it's littered with figured stones, which pose far more danger to ridden horses than to nimble and well-practised dragomites or a giant's booted feet. Nor can they be skilled riders, as your men were. I wish they knew how easily we had won that other battle; it might make them sensibly wary. As it is, they may be too stupid to be scared.'

'They may be too stupid to feel anything at all,' Shabir opined. 'They may have human arms and legs, but they have the skulls of mere monkeys.'

'That says nothing at all about the quality of their brains, alas,' Ereleth put in. 'Do you think they have sufficient command of human language to parley?'

Shabir made a disgusted sound at that, but Fraxinus couldn't tell whether it was intended as an expression of scepticism or whether the general was remembering the time when *he* had thought to gain a crucial advantage by deceptive negotiation.

'Ask Merel to make a white flag and pass it forward,' Fraxinus said. 'There's no harm in trying, I suppose – but whoever carries it must be careful. I won't order anyone to do it and I'd have some trepidation about doing it myself.'

'Anyone who tried it would be a fool,' Shabir said, seemingly considering himself an expert in such judgments. 'If they have even a few bows and arrows they'd have every chance to shoot an envoy down. You'd have to uncouple a horse from the wagon or go out on foot – either of which would be a direly dangerous move, in the circumstances.'

'He's right,' said Ereleth. 'Best to wave the flag and let them respond, if they've a mind to. Let them send emissaries to us, if there's any scope for negotiation.'

Once, Fraxinus would have argued that there had to be room for negotiation in any situation, human affairs and human ambition being what they were, but he knew now that the assumptions a man might take for granted even in the uncivilised borderlands of Xandria's empire did not apply in this mad realm. What the Salamanders had told him had been amply backed up by direct observation and by Purkin's story. However little sense there might be in random slaughter there seemed to be whole species hereabouts which were exclusively devoted to that pastime: creatures whose sole reason for being was to kill everything that their kin could not make captive.

Merel passed a white flag forward and Fraxinus stood up on the driver's bench, lifting it high above the level of the wagon's canopy to catch the rays of the morning sun.

There was no answering movement in the party which blocked their course.

'They're still taking stock of the dragomites and the giant,' Shabir said. 'If they have intelligence and the power of communication, they're busy formulating a strategy. They're not taking the slightest notice of the flag.'

'There's no sign of anyone or anything behind us,' Merel Zabio said, relaying news from Mossassor. 'If Purkin's men were still dogging our footsteps during the night they've either lost a lot of ground or found some cover somewhere.'

Dhalla came to stand by the side of the driver's bench. She was wearing light armour fashioned from plates of dragomite chitin, which she had made for herself using the carapaces of their erstwhile companions; she must have collected it from Mossassor as soon as the situation became clear.

'If we go forward they'll come at us from three directions,' the giant pointed out laconically. 'Better to choose left or right and charge one of the flanking groups, holding back a single dragomite to cover our rear. If they scatter, we can keep on going; if not, we'll have to slaughter them, then turn to face the rest.'

Fraxinus looked past the giant at the dragomite which Vaca Metra was riding. The mound-woman could have shouted and been heard, but she chose instead to signal with her hand, gesturing furiously.

'The poorer ground lies to the right,' Fraxinus deduced. 'That's the way they'll expect us to go. They'll probably retreat, trying to draw us into treacherous territory.' He acknowledged the warrior-woman's signals, then indicated in his turn that Dhalla and the wagon would go to the left, and that Vaca Metra's warrior should go the same way while the other

dropped back. He knew that Metra could convey that instruction from where she was.

'Shabir – you and Mossassor had best arm yourselves with
bows and go to the rear,' Fraxinus continued, in the same
controlled tone. 'Aulakh, can you come forward to stand behind
me?'

'I'm already here,' Phar replied.

Fraxinus saw no reason to pause any longer; he laid down the
useless flag. He took one last look at the enemy forces, then
jerked the reins of the leading horses and urged them on with the
whip, then hauled them round to the left, aiming the wagon's
course directly at the party of thirty-two horsemen. Dhalla
broke into a run, her huge stride taking her ahead of the horses
while they were still building up pace, but not ahead of Metra's
dragomite warrior, which was capable of prodigious speed over
short distances.

The cavalrymen had obviously prepared for this possibility.
The band towards which they were headed immediately formed
into ranks, making ready to face the giant and the dragomite.
The smaller band began to move at an angle, trying to get round
to a position from which they could come at the left flank of the
wagon. The largest group charged without delay, coming at the
wagon from the right.

Fraxinus saw immediately that the horsemen had intelligence
enough to have given some consideration to the matter of
fighting dragomites and a giant. They had calculated, rightly,
that Dhalla was by far the most dangerous of their opponents,
and that they must fell her with arrows if they could. Like
Shabir's army before them, however, they had obviously
overestimated the damage that their arrows might do.

Having noted her armour, their bowmen deliberately fired
low, at Dhalla's hips and thighs, and two or three arrows
actually stuck in her flesh, but Fraxinus knew by now that they
could not penetrate deeply enough to slow her down. The half-
humans had underestimated her stride and her reach, too, and
the realisation that their first assault had had no effect must have
been quickly followed by the realisation that they had lingered
too long in her path. The giant already had her javelin extended
as though it were a battleaxe, and its steel head cut into them like
a scythe. She even had the temerity to aim high, to strike at the

men and not the horses, making the assumption that the latter would eventually become the welcome spoils of victory.

The horsemen fared better against the dragomite, having calculated the range and power of its jaws far more accurately than their fellows had calculated Dhalla's reach. They knew that if they attacked in close and careful formation the jaws could only strike one way at a time, leaving the thorax on the other side temporarily exposed to a well-judged spear-thrust. Indeed, Fraxinus saw that they had skill enough as riders to execute the move, at least in the first instance. They might well have succeeded in incapacitating the warrior with a single strike had it not been for the rider on its back, but Vaca Metra was an expert in such calculations as this, and knew exactly what her objective was.

The spearman charged with the task of wounding the dragomite was tumbled from his saddle by a well-aimed arrow. Once he was gone from the formation confusion took over; as the huge jaws cut the legs from three horses, spilling wounded men in all directions, any chance the horsemen had of regrouping was utterly lost.

Fraxinus had just enough time to note both these circumstances before looking to his own situation, but he had none at all to track their aftermath. The riders knew exactly how to stop the wagon and they also knew that there was nothing at all that Fraxinus could do to prevent them, provided that they were quick enough and sure enough.

They came in rapidly, leaning from their own mounts to hack and chop with blades and lances; one of the lead horses was injured almost immediately but the wagon careered onwards, carried forward by its momentum. The broken-legged horse had no alternative but to stay on its remaining feet, bound to the wagon's extended shaft by its harness, but the wagon lurched and yawed and began to judder as acceleration turned to deceleration. Fraxinus fought with the reins, determined to control the vehicle's path as it began to skid sideways.

Aulakh Phar was on the bench beside Fraxinus now, lashing out with a pike which had once belonged to Jacom Cerri's men, but it was an unwieldy weapon even for the strongest of men and Phar's thin arms could not keep hold of it once it collided with a target.

Fraxinus ducked as a light spear soared over his head and disappeared into the wagon, but he was quick to raise his head again as the taut rein pulled him upright. He was still fighting for belated control of the wagon when something hit him from the side, knocking him over and sending poor Phar reeling backwards.

For a moment or two Fraxinus kept hold of the reins, but he had to let them go as they threatened to pull him off the bench and under the wagon's wheels. He grabbed for the edge of the bench, intent on holding fast to it, but a long arm snaked about his neck, informing him that the attacker who had leapt from his horse had been as lucky as he. At any moment he expected to be stabbed or pulled down to the ground, but the arm lost all its power, and he knew that someone else – presumably Ereleth – had stabbed first, with deadly effect. He was able to continue clinging to the wooden platform, shrugging off the body of his assailant.

The wagon was slowing to a halt now, and the dead weight of the injured lead horse was dragging so badly that there was no hope of getting it moving again, even to manoeuvre it into position. Fraxinus raised his head, determined to see what was happening, but found that there seemed to be enemies on every side. A sea of horrid, bestial faces was crowding him in. He couldn't work out how there could be so many, given what he had seen of Dhalla's success and Vaca Metra's competence.

Ereleth thrust a weapon into his hand, trying to make sure that he grasped the hilt. 'Be careful!' she screamed into his ear, which he took to mean that the blade was poisoned and that he had to make very sure that its witchery was not turned against his allies. He dared not stand up on the bench, but he moved to one side of it, reaching out as best he could so that the tip of the sword was well away from his own flesh and that of his friends.

There was too much movement and too much confusion to allow him a calculated thrust, but Fraxinus felt the blade make contact once, then twice. He concentrated all his attention on the business of holding tight to the hilt, so that the weapon would not be torn from his grasp.

There still seemed to be enemies everywhere, cutting at him in return, but the impression was momentary. He ducked under one spear-thrust, flinching at a slight contact, but when he looked up again, anxiously, there was no spearman to be seen. He could hear Dhalla's voice rising in a ululating cry of triumph as she swept away the men who had come to kill him. For a fleeting second, his eyes met hers, but she was already looking beyond him, pointing with her bloody spear.

'Here they come!' cried a high-pitched voice from the rear – Merel's, he assumed, although its rawness rendered it unrecognisable. 'Twice as fast and twice as many!'

This, he realised uncomfortably, must be the second wave – with a third yet to come. In a way, it was a mercy that there was no interval left for calculation, and nothing to be done but to raise his sword ready to wreak what havoc he could. The battle-fever coursing through his veins had reached the pitch now where nothing mattered but action, and he drew himself upright as determinedly as any hardened warrior could have done, ready to lash out with all the force and fury he could muster.

Astonishingly, however, the fight was over within a matter of seconds. Having arrived at the wagon only to find the giant and the two dragomite warriors still standing, and seemingly unconquerable, the second group of riders evidently did not think it worth their while to make any serious engagement with Fraxinus and his fellows – who were, after all, armed with good steel and fighting from a sturdy platform. The horsemen swept past, not even troubling to fire more than a few arrows. Those with spears kept hold of them, obviously anxious to save them for another day.

Fraxinus found it no easier to take an accurate count of them as they rode away than it had been before the attack, but it was easy enough to count the fallen and the dead they had left behind once they had regrouped and ridden southwards at full gallop.

While the dragomites finished off the wounded with relentless ease Dhalla made what effort she could to gather the riderless horses. Fourteen of the creatures had fallen and a dozen more galloped off, but she gathered seven in.

'Save one of the riders alive!' Fraxinus shouted to Vaca Metra. 'Let's find out whether they can speak, and what they have to say if so.'

Vaca Metra raised a hand to signal that she had heard and understood him. The warrior she was riding immediately became more discriminating in the use of its bloodstained jaws.

Fraxinus discovered that he was bleeding from the head. As soon as he reached out to touch the wound it began to smart, but it was no more than a graze.

'Let's hope they have sense enough to leave us alone now,' Ereleth said, without much confidence. 'In fact, let's hope they spread the word throughout this vile land that we're more to be feared than anything else it may contain. I've had my fill of battles now.'

'So have we all,' Fraxinus said, 'but I fear that the dwellers in the deep have not. It appears that they've been fighting, in their own peculiar fashion, since the ship that brought our ancestors here touched down. It's possible that if they can't find a settlement, they'll fight until only one of them remains, and all the world becomes its flesh and shell.'

'I'm not sure that I care overmuch whether they're one or many,' Ereleth muttered. 'The secret commandments to which I'm heir seem more and more like an invitation to suicide with every day that passes.'

'Unfortunately,' Fraxinus said tiredly, 'the fate of our own species will surely depend on the outcome of the struggle. If we have any power at all to affect its outcome, the fate of all our children's children may depend upon it.'

Ereleth might have pointed out that she had no children of her own, being a witch-wife, but she said nothing. She was a house-mother, at least, and all Belin's children had been partly in her charge. She knew what was at stake, and she knew the meaning of duty; without the obligations of her position, she would have been nothing at all.

'We haven't seen the last of them,' said Aulakh Phar. 'I doubt that they'll attack us in the open again, but I can't believe they're the kind to give up.'

'Neither are we,' Fraxinus reminded him. 'Neither are we.'

10

LUCREZIA WAS RELIEVED to discover that appearances had not been deceptive and that Ssifuss's judgment had been sound. The 'road' which led towards the centre of the Reef's great circle was far from straight and far from flat, but it was solid. It was also wide enough to permit two horses to ride abreast without the least danger that either would stray on to more dangerous ground.

She was very glad that there were, in fact, two saddled horses to ride abreast behind the Serpent which led the way. Had Hyry Keshvara decided to go with Checuti and Jume Metra her own resolve might have been tested to the limit. Hyry was paying her back for forcing the split by retreating into the same mood of sullen disapproval that had possessed her while they had ridden from the environs of Xandria to the Forest of Absolute Night, but Lucrezia had every confidence that the trader's wrath wouldn't last long.

They had a second set of horses walking abreast behind them, obediently following Hyry's leading-rein. They were small animals by comparison with the ones in Belin's stables and poorly trained, but they were tough and docile. They were capable of carrying a good load and they consented to do so, albeit with some ill grace. The trader had taken full advantage of their willingness in making up the packs which sat on their backs.

The terrain was by no means lifeless, nor was its life confined within the living ground whose many different aspects were arrayed to either side of the road. Lucrezia saw birds in the branches of all the spiry and spiky trees which jutted from the ridges, and she saw animals too: agile lizards and scaly rats. She was interested to see that their peregrinations were not confined to the tree-like structures; they walked upon the ground too, although they picked their way carefully. It was obviously not the case that every sem of the surface was dangerous – in fact Ssifuss had revised its earlier judgment on the basis of its recent experience, informing its companions that in many respects the ground within the Reef seemed to be easier to negotiate than the ground without.

'Little flowing sstoness full of little pitss,' the Serpent had observed. 'Big oness have fewer and eassier to ssee. *Ssoft* ground more dangerouss, ssome iss . . . *fluid?*'

Lucrezia had confirmed that 'fluid' was the right word – and she had already had occasion to note that Ssifuss was right. The only creatures she had seen in the process of being sucked into the surface were those that had strayed on to ground so treacherous as to be reckoned a kind of quicksand. Even that kind of ground posed little or no problem to some of the native creatures; the little lizards seemed to be fast enough to run across such morasses without sinking.

Ssifuss had given them a further warning about sleeping, telling them that even the harder ground could allow things to sink into it if given long enough, but it had also assured them that if they were careful they would have plenty of time to react to any such threat. Lucrezia knew that the consequent unease would make it difficult to rest, but she was prepared to meet the challenge.

Some of the plants which grew to either side of the road looked very much like earthly plants to Lucrezia, but even those which were unmistakably unearthly often gave the appearance of being invaders, things which did not entirely *belong*. She concluded that if she and her companions were indeed travelling across the 'skin' of some incredibly huge figured stone then it was a skin which played host to a great abundance of parasites and hangers-on, including some species which might well have strayed from the earthly garden of Idun.

Aulakh Phar had told her once that the living surface of human skin was concealed behind a thin wall of dead cells, and that every pore and wrinkle of that mask was crowded with invisible creatures, both earthly and unearthly. When he had said it she had remembered the little weeds growing in the crevices of the Sanctum walls and the discolouring patches of stonerot which dappled the inner walls of the citadel. It was oddly reassuring now to be able to see similar discolouring patches on the roadway beneath her horse's hooves and on the flat surfaces of the great mosaic which stretched unevenly from horizon to horizon. If there were dozens of species of stonerot patiently corroding the skin of the giants that wrestled one another for possession of the ring within the Reef then this strange empire could be no more invulnerable than the supposedly impossible empire of Xandria. Furthermore, if the gentle but insidious corruption of stonerot made no distinction between the works of men and the most monstrous natives of the world, then there must be a degree of common cause between them.

The enemies of our enemies may not be numbered among our friends, Ereleth had quoted to her once while teaching her the lore of witchery, *but if we are clever we can usually make them our instruments.* Stonerot, it seemed, was the enemy of everything that was *built*, whether it was built by stonemasons with the aid of their clever yeasts or built by the dwellers in the deep to serve as their natural armour. It was not much of a revelation; didn't the *Lore of Genesys* insist, above and before any of its other insistences, that corruption and corrosion were the ultimate enemy of *everything*, the handmaidens of Chaos itself?

Lucrezia wondered whether the dwellers in the deep might see things the same way, if they could 'see' anything at all. If they had intelligence of some kind – even borrowed intelligence, like the intelligence of the mound-queen in a dragomite nest – might they too not recognise that the ultimate enemy was rot? Could that be why they sent emissaries out to seize captives? Could that be why they exercised some subtle attraction upon certain Serpents and humans? Might they be in search, however blindly, of some precious alliance between different kinds of flesh that might lead them to a crucial victory over the forces of corruption and corrosion? Did they too believe, however unthinkingly, that the enemy of their enemy might serve as their instrument if not their friend?

According to the lore, she thought, *it was the worst produce of Chimera's Cradle that poisoned the land around the garden of Idun. The people of the world complained about it, but the loremasters told them there was no other way. In the end, they said, evil would be defeated and Order would prevail. In the end, the Pool of Life would give birth to incorruptible stone. The living ground must hunger for that even more than we do, because the living ground needs incorruptible stone for its armour and its structure while we only need it to secure our city walls . . . and for inscription.*

Lucrezia had never quite understood why the lore was so insistent about the worth of inscription – after all, humans had their lore, and they already had all kinds of things to write on – but as she tried to 'read' the secrets which might or might not be inscribed on the skin of the giant she finally saw the point of the lore's promise. As things stood, no written message survived for long, whether it was scribbled on parchment or hewn in stone. It might last for days in the former case, years in the latter, but in either case the labour involved in copying and copying again was too burdensome to preserve a message for ever. Because of that, all information was subject to corrosion and corruption. The lore was leaky; it suffered continual and irrevocable losses. Only 'incorruptible stone' offered the hope of permanence: a means of anchoring knowledge so that its foundations would never be destroyed.

She understood, too, that such an evolution would not simply offer an opportunity to human beings. Serpents and Salamanders could use it too – and so could all the creatures which looked like humans, Serpents and Salamanders but were in fact the offspring of the dwellers in the deep. Serpents, she had been assured, were 'good at forgetting' because they 'had to be'. Perhaps the same was true of all the monstrous kindred of dragomite queens and flowing stones. Perhaps they too were 'good at forgetting' while they lay virtually inert for centuries – and perhaps they too might benefit from a method of inscription.

She turned to Hyry Keshvara, but the dour expression on the trader's face reminded her that there was bridge-building to be done before such topics of conversation could be raised.

'I'm sorry, Hyry,' Lucrezia said. 'I know you wanted us to stick together, but it takes two to make an insoluble disagreement. Checuti could have come with us. He *should* have come with us. If his only interest was saving his own skin he could have gone back to the lake with Venerina Sirelis.'

'You don't have to apologise,' Hyry told her. 'I made my own choice. I'm not under your command, *highness*. I never was.'

'In that case,' she said, 'why sulk?'

Hyry scowled. 'This is just the way my face sets when I'm tired,' she said. 'The ugliness is inbuilt – it's not an expression of opinion.'

Lucrezia didn't know how to reply to that and she thought it best not to press the point. 'I'm glad you came with me,' she said. 'If you'd refused, I might have backed down. I don't mean to insult Ssifuss, but I'd have felt as if I were alone if I were without human company – and this is no sort of adventure to undertake alone.'

'If I'd known that,' Hyry said wryly, 'I might have chosen the other way. If Checuti had known it, he'd certainly have told me – but he was glad when I elected to go with you, because it saved his conscience from the burden of sending you off on your own. He placed you in my charge once before, if you remember – he must have seen some vestige of maternal sentiment in me that I had not suspected. He does have a conscience of sorts, albeit a rather perverse one. I hope he enjoys the company of the mound-woman – if anyone can seduce her, he can.'

'If his mind had been on seduction,' Lucrezia said, 'he'd surely have gone with Venerina. It can't be Ereleth's charms which are drawing him back to Fraxinus.'

'I suppose not,' Hyry replied. She seemed slightly surprised that Lucrezia had contrived that kind of reply; perhaps she thought that the Inner Sanctum had been secure even against the corrosions of innuendo.

'Anyhow, Ssifuss seems to have been right,' Lucrezia said. 'The road's good. It was built to allow the passage of whole troops of mounted men. I see no reason to doubt that it will see us safe to the garden at the region's heart.'

'Nor I,' said Hyry. 'But what will we do when we get there, if the amber is beyond help?'

'We'll be a great deal closer to Chimera's Cradle,' Lucrezia pointed out.

'But we'll have no road to take us *there*,' Hyry replied. 'We're more likely to find impenetrable barriers in our way. If there's a road which leads directly to the heart of Idun, it's most likely to be where Myrasol's map marked it out, even though thousands of years have passed and the Reef has vastly expanded its circumference.'

Lucrezia had no argument to deploy against that, so she moved the conversation in another direction.

'This living ground must have a mind, of sorts,' she said. 'Most of its creatures may be slaves of instinct, far less intelligent than free-living men and Serpents, but they have a definite purpose. They took you prisoner for a reason, and there was more to that reason than providing fodder for a carnivorous plant.'

'I wish I were sure of that,' the trader said, reaching up to shade her eyes from the sun as she looked ahead. Such tree-like entities as there were to either side of the road immediately in front of them were not tightly clumped, nor were they closely gathered about the edge of their path. There was, by contrast, something like a forest looming on the horizon.

'We're not the only ones going this way,' Lucrezia pointed out. 'The winged Salamanders are capable of speech, and presumably of reason, but they're intent on going into the heart of the living land, searching for gardens. When Mossassor first found you he was delighted by the prospect of making some such common cause with you.'

'And you have Serpent's blood, while Ereleth has her secret commandments,' Hyry added. 'I know all that – and I know that everything unfolding hereabouts is following some kind of scheme. It's more like the scheme which tells an egg how to grow into a chicken than the kind of scheme that men like Fraxinus and Checuti hatch in order to enrich themselves, but it's a scheme nevertheless and we're part of it now whether we like it or not.' While Hyry was speaking she swatted at a number of insects buzzing about her face, contriving to keep most of them at bay, but Lucrezia saw one settle on the trader's neck, apparently unnoticed. She moved her horse closer and reached out with her own hand to brush the insect away. When it went, it left a little spot of red behind.

'We're thinking beings,' Lucrezia said. 'We're not condemned simply to be parts of the scheme. If we can only understand it, we might acquire the power to alter it.' She ran her hand over her own neck as she spoke, anxious lest she too might have been surreptitiously bitten. Her fingers crushed an unwary insect, and when she brought them back she saw that the smear of its broken body was red with her own blood. She told herself that it was only a gnat-bite, no worse than dozens she had suffered while travelling south from Xandria, but she knew that her supplies of balm had run very low.

'We might not,' Hyry said, blandly countering her argument. 'We might only have a bitter lesson to learn about the folly of our ambitions, and the ambitions of our race.'

'You don't believe that,' Lucrezia said.

'It's not a matter for belief,' Hyry retorted. 'While all possibilities are open, all must be considered.'

The Serpent walking ahead of them was also surrounded by flies but Lucrezia saw that it was making no attempt to shoo them away. She remembered that Ssifuss had suffered far less from scratches when they were in the Soursweet Marshes; a Serpent's scaly skin obviously provided better protection from minor abrasions and intrusions. While she watched the dance of the tiny insects, however, she noticed that Ssifuss was also attended by larger ones with coloured wings, whose unsteady flight reminded her of the pretty butterflies that had once been frequent visitors to her roof garden. They, at least, seemed utterly harmless, and when she saw that one had settled on the Serpent's bare shoulder she was not in the least alarmed – until her eyes travelled down the shoulder blade to the small of the Serpent's back, where she saw a patch of colour which didn't quite fit into the pattern of its scales. She might not have attached any significance to it had she seen it before, but she noticed now that it had something in common with the pattern on the butterfly's wings.

She rode forward, and tried to brush the insect from the Serpent's shoulder. It didn't take flight, and when she tried to pluck it off its slender stick-like body broke away from the 'legs' which had already attached themselves to the Serpent's scales. The delicate wings crumpled and cracked, and Lucrezia wiped the crushed remains from her fingers as Ssifuss reached up to feel the place where the creature had rested.

'There's another on your back,' Lucrezia said. 'That one's solidly embedded, wings and all. It's that awkward spot you can't reach with your own hands, but I can scrape it off if you like.'

'Pleasse,' the Serpent said.

She had to dismount to do it. She was able to scrape a little of the alien substance off, but most of it was so firmly attached to the scaly skin beneath as to seem a natural part of it.

'It's not just the ground we have to watch out for,' Lucrezia observed anxiously. 'If we don't come to the alien flesh, it will come to us. It might take a lot longer to devour us that way, but if these things can fuse with our flesh . . . maybe they can even lay eggs or distribute spores throughout our bodies.'

'We don't know that they can,' Hyry put in.

'Iss no pain,' Ssifuss reassured her. 'Iss like marssh. Little sstingss. Nuissansse, no more.'

'That's what I'm worried about,' Lucrezia said. 'I could easily have died in the marshes. What started as a nuisance eventually became a full-scale disability. If it hadn't been for Andris . . .'

She stopped because she saw the irony in that. If it hadn't been for what Andris had done for her in the marsh, carrying her to safety in spite of his own condition, she wouldn't be here now. She would have been able to go with Checuti and Jume Metra. Were they any safer, though? Could anyone be reckoned safe, once they had set foot on the uncertain surface that masked the dwellers in the deep?

'People can be transformed from within,' she said in a low voice. 'We know that. I've seen it happen. The seeds that were reputed to come from Chimera's Cradle were the lure which set this whole adventure going. We have to be careful – you most of all, Ssifuss, given that so little of your skin is covered.'

'Can't go back,' was all the Serpent said in reply.

It was true, and they all knew it. There was no point in turning round; whatever the dangers were, they had to be faced. If their bodies could be invaded by tiny things that had the power to change them, the probability was that the process had already begun.

'There's always danger of infection,' Hyry said. 'Always and everywhere. We have to rely on our bodies to fight the invaders off . . . with a little help from medicines. You're a witch, highness, as well-equipped as anyone to resist such pollution.'

'So I am,' Lucrezia agreed, hauling herself back into the saddle. 'But let's be careful anyway – as careful as we can.'

Ssifuss set off again, the blemish on its back which had seemed utterly insignificant before now standing out like a warning beacon as the princess brought her horse into step with Hyry's, a few paces behind him.

II

TIME PASSED AND the flowers that grew on Andris's limbs opened to the sun. They were larger and whiter than the flowers which still showed on some of the other tree-people. Each one had seven soft petals extended in a hemisphere with an undulating edge.

At the heart of each flower was a splash of red from which a waxy style and a cluster of anthers sprouted; somewhere deep within the hidden organs of the flower there were glands which leaked sweet nectar. When the bees came to gather that nectar they tickled his delicate flesh, but it was not an unpleasant sensation.

While he had been lost in the dream Andris had almost forgotten what an unpleasant sensation felt like. It was as if the changing of his body had dulled his capacity to feel pain almost to the point of annihilation, at least for the time being. There was much to be glad about in that – after all, he had felt more than his fair share of pain lately – but it worried him more than a little. The spectrum of petty pains was, after all, part of the apparatus which defined his being and shaped his life.

As soon as he became anxious about such matters, however, he found a way to soothe his anxiety. He discovered that he had only to think about Merel's loss and Rayner's death, or even about Shabir's treachery and Ereleth's tyranny, to conjure up distress and focus its effect. It was not physical pain but it was certainly pain, and it sufficed to define and give form to his own particular being.

While he could still hurt himself with bad memories, he was Andris Myrasol, with all that implied. Changed as he was, he remained in all the most important respects Andris Myrasol, Prince of Ferentina, mapmaker and vagabond, half-giant and hero. For the time being, at least, he could cling to all of that.

The next time he was able to turn his body far enough to look into Arilla's eyes he had his questions ready. He still couldn't keep count of the days, nor had he succeeded in submitting many other aspects of his confusion to the stern discipline of consciousness, but he felt much more confident that he could identify that which was real within the riot of hallucination. He knew how to proceed, or thought he did.

He asked her whether she had any ambition to walk and travel abroad as the garden's gleaners did.

'None,' she replied.

'But it must be possible, must it not?' he challenged her. 'The living ground has the power to shape its many children according to its whim. Were it to draw us back into its body it could surely spit us out again in any form it chose. It could confer mobility on you as easily as it robbed me of mine. Are you not in a position to direct its efforts? Are you not its empress, its guiding intelligence?'

'Even if I were,' she replied, 'I would no more have the power to direct my own transformations than you have. When you were a man you could not demand of your body that it reshape itself as a Serpent. In any case, I have no authority here – and you must not expect to acquire any of your own, no matter how tall you grow.'

'You have a voice,' he pointed out. 'Whatever you have forgotten of the lives you lived before this one, you have retained far better powers of speech than your sullen kin who brought me here.'

'I have a voice,' she agreed. 'We all have voices, although some of us have all but forgotten how to use them. Alas, they are our own. The dweller in the deep has no voice at all. If it is capable of thought and purpose, ambition and calculation, it does not confide in us. It is mute. So far as we know, the ground does not choose the forms which it emits, nor when to emit them. We are part of it; its needs are our needs and its destiny is our destiny – but all we know is what we infer and what we remember, and we know how memories fade. We know what we are, and what we will become. You will know it too, in time.'

I ought to hope that all this is true, Andris thought. *I ought to hope that it is not some fantasy conjured up by my lonely mind. But in either case, I must keep asking questions. I must maintain*

255

my pursuit of understanding, because that is the one thing I can and must keep, whether I have arms and legs or not. It is the one thing that can never be taken away from me by any metamorphosis, and while I have it I am still Andris Myrasol, lover of Merel Zabio, friend of Carus Fraxinus and Princess Lucrezia of Xandria.

'Are the giant Serpents and their human-seeming kin produced as ready-made adults,' he asked, 'already capable of thought and speech?'

'They are,' Arilla told him. 'I cannot speak for other gardens, but there is no infancy here.'

'Those powers of thought and speech must be bound up with other memories,' he said, as much by way of speculation as interrogation. 'Like the tiny figured stones which litter the plain to the north of the Reef this ground must first take in that which it eventually releases. Their bodies may be changed, but if they are capable of thought and speech the giant Serpents and the half-men must retain some consciousness of their former existence, even if they are four or five generations removed from it. Does it seem to them that they have awakened from a long sleep? Or does it merely seem that they have moved from one phase of a dream to another? *You* must have been human once, or half-human, no matter how little you remember of that life.'

'I have memories,' she told him, a little uneasily, 'but no certainty that the memories are anything more than phantoms. You will understand, in time. You are one of us now.'

What she meant by her remark about the possibility of her memories being phantoms, he supposed, was that she had no real reason to believe that she was not a composite individual, equipped with a crude patchwork of skills and resources long since divorced from the individuals whose legacy they were.

'I suppose it's conceivable,' he admitted, 'that a creature like this might build the power of speech and thought into individuals grown from seed – but without a network of experiences, how could the words acquire meaning?'

'I dare say that I have been reproduced more or less intact from another age,' she said, although her tone suggested that she would not be unduly disappointed should she ever be forced to a different conclusion, 'and that whatever happens to me now I will be reborn yet again, if not as a creature of my present kind then in some other form. If so, then so will you – but that does not mean that we can ever be anything more than mere bystanders in the war between the dwellers in the deep. We are pawns in a game whose rules we do not know and cannot deduce.' Clearly, she too had been troubled by the enigmas which now troubled him, but she gave the impression of having given up trying to solve them some time ago.

'Somebody must know the rules,' Andris asserted. 'If the most powerful players of the game are mindless, blindly exercising some innate but haphazard creativity, can the rules by which they operate be so difficult to determine? If there are a dozen dwellers in the deep, or a hundred, and if every one of them has gathered in a rich harvest of memories and minds, the combined power of those minds must surely be adequate to figure out the logic of the situation. Even if there is not a single one of the dwellers which has acquired a mind and voice of its own, surely there must be one whose intelligent instruments have discovered the pattern of their moves, the nature of their competition and the end of their struggle.'

'Perhaps there is,' she replied listlessly, 'and perhaps not.'

He could not be satisfied with that, and he pressed her further, but in the end he had to answer his own question. He wondered whether that made it more probable, or less, that he was really alone in his dream, filling the void with strange hallucinations because he could not bear his awful isolation.

'Creativity cannot be random else nothing would come of it but chaos,' he argued, for his own benefit. 'The mingling of human and vegetable flesh may be a kind of confusion, but chaos it is not. There is method in this, even though there may be no conscious plan. If we can only discover what that method is, we might have the chance to exert the authority of our own intelligence. There is no certainty that we can, and no certainty that understanding would empower us, but we do have to try, do we not? What else is there for us to do?'

'We may wait,' Arilla told him.

He wasn't satisfied with that either. 'You have the power of thought and the power of speech,' he told her. 'Whether the ground which gave birth to you has any intelligence of its own or not, you have yours and ought to defend it. If you have forgotten, you must try to remember; if you do not understand, you must try to work it out; if you have no ambition, you must find one . . . else you will lose even that which you have.'

'I have no power beyond the ability to move my own branches,' she told him plaintively. 'Even my mobile siblings are beyond the reach of suggestion or persuasion, having needs written into the fibres of their being which they must fulfil. We have the power of speech, but we do not need it. You will understand this, in time. You are one of us, heir to our nature and heir to our destiny. Only have patience, and you will find peace. The troubles which concern you now will dissolve away.'

That made him angry, although he could see a certain irony in the fact. It was too late for him to say that he had no wish to vegetate, to become a mere plant basking in the sun's rays.

'*Were* you once a human being like me?' Andris asked her, with a little more asperity than was warranted. 'What do you remember about the life you led then? Is it then that you were named Arilla? Try to remember, I beg you.'

'I have no memory of living anywhere but here,' she told him. 'So far as I know, I am entirely a product of the living ground – but I cannot know for sure that my memories of another kind of life have not been lost, or erased, or surrendered. It makes no difference. It doesn't matter. All that matters now is what we are. You must accept that, and adapt to it.'

'Perhaps I must,' he admitted, 'but I doubt that I shall ever agree with you as to what kind of adaptation is necessary or desirable.' He felt strangely heroic in saying this, although he knew that must be a flattering illusion of his dream state. She wouldn't reply to the accusation without further prompting.

'Do you have dreams?' he asked.

'Too many dreams,' she told him.

'Dreams which must reflect and recall an earlier period of activity, long before this one,' Andris guessed confidently. 'Your intelligence must have lain dormant for a very long time, stored and preserved in some manner within the body of the living ground. Perhaps it changed in the process. Perhaps you *let* it change. Perhaps you didn't cling hard enough to your sense of self: your name, your nature, your purpose. You might have

258

remembered everything, had you only tried hard enough. You might have accomplished something, had you only tried.'

'It doesn't matter what might have been,' she told him, but he didn't believe her.

'I wish I could see the sense in all this,' Andris complained. 'It *must* make sense, somehow. If only I could see . . .'

'You are unduly impatient, Andris,' Arilla told, with a hint of bitter contempt. 'You have not yet learned that days and years do not matter – that *centuries* do not matter – to beings like us. Nor do memories and ambitions. We are trees now; we have no choice but to live as trees.'

Is that treasonous voice really the voice of another, he asked himself, *or is it the voice of my own doubts, which only seems to be coming from behind me?*

'Perhaps the years and the centuries do matter less to beings which are effectively immortal,' he conceded. 'I dare say that the players in this game and the warriors on this battlefield have all the time in the world to reach the climax of their story. Perhaps *we* do not matter at all, except that we carry tiny things within our flesh and blood which the living ground needs . . . but still, we are here. We are what we are, and what we are is what we make of ourselves. Trees may have no choice but to live as trees, but I am human and if I must be a tree I must be a *human* tree. If I am to be a tree, and be reborn again and again as a tree, then I must at least aspire to be a special tree, a unique tree . . . a Tree of Knowledge. Perhaps I will fail, but I must try. I must cling to every last vestige of memory, every last sinew of reason. Am I not a hero, after all?'

'It does not matter what you *were,*' Arilla insisted, 'and you still do not know what you are fated to become. You would do better to let the questions die now, for they will certainly die in time.'

She was telling him, in effect, that his curiosity was unanswerable, and that it would fade away with his dreams once he had adapted himself to his new way of life – but Arilla did not seem to Andris to have adapted herself so cleverly or so happily, no matter how many times she had been consigned to the sleep of centuries.

'I know a man named Jacom Cerri,' Andris said, 'whose reaction to any deep matter is to shrug his shoulders, as if to say:

Who knows? Why should we care? I'm not like him. I think even he would rather have offered a better answer than he did, if he had only known how.'

'Perhaps no one knows how,' she told him. 'Perhaps no one ever will.'

Andris was forced to turn round again then, because it was too uncomfortable to hold himself twisted. He wondered why he had been positioned so that she was behind him. Had she determined that, or had it been an accident of chance? Or was it all a symptom of his self-inflicted madness, a contortion of his own sick mind?

He was tempted to lapse into the luxuriously calm sleep of which he was now capable, whose extraordinary peace he was still learning to savour, but something held him back. He had to concentrate hard to figure out what it was, but he did so.

He realised that he could hear the distant sound of voices raised in alarm.

Even his nearest neighbours were becoming agitated, and they were beginning to call to one another in great anxiety, begging for news. He parted his burgeoning foliage so that he might look out over the hill from his high vantage point.

He saw exactly what he had feared to see.

The signs had always been around him that the garden was sometimes invaded by enemies far worse than the vulturine birds, and he had always known that this war gave rise to conflicts in which any bystander might easily be injured or killed. He didn't know whether he was fated to be a bystander for ever or whether he was a potential player, but it was obvious that he had no choice as to his involvement or the side on which he must fight. This, at least, was neither dream nor madness; *this* was perfectly real.

The garden was under attack yet again, and he had not the slightest doubt that its attackers would tear him apart if they got the chance. Perhaps it would not hurt his arboreal self as badly as it would have hurt had his human body been torn limb from limb, but it would certainly hurt – and whether he was potentially immortal or not, there was no doubt at all that he could still meet a violent death.

'Even as trees we must fight,' he murmured, 'and if we must

fight, should we not fight for everything we hold dear, everything that is precious to us? If we must fight, should we not fight for *ourselves*?'

There was no answer, but he needed none. He knew that he was right. He knew that the truth was self-evident. The only question was whether he would be able to do it.

12

OUT OF THE seven horses which Dhalla had managed to secure, only five were usable. Three of these had to be pressed into immediate service drawing the wagon; the other two were hitched at the rear, along with one of the original team which had only been slightly hurt. The new animals were of poorer quality than the old and Fraxinus now had cause for sharp regret that Purkin had proved so obdurate. Xandrian horses were far better equipped to haul the wagon than those now charged with the task.

While Aulakh Phar and Merel Zabio set about stripping the best meat from the dead horses Fraxinus and Ereleth went to the place where Vaca Metra stood guard over one of their attackers, which she had commanded the dragomites to spare. It was the first time Fraxinus had got a clear sight of one of the bestial faces, and he could not suppress a quiver of horror as it looked up at him from unhuman eyes.

Its dark brown forehead and cheeks were hairless, but a rim of bushy hair ran from its temples to its chin. Its nose resembled a pig's snout. The teeth within its mouth were a peculiar dark yellow colour. There was no trace of fear in the stare which it directed at him from beneath its slightly lowered eyelids. Its eyes were charcoal-black and utterly anonymous.

'If you can speak,' Fraxinus said, 'you'd better do so. If you can't or won't we'll kill you now – but if you can, and if you know anything that we might want to learn, you have a chance to live.'

The creature's expression changed slightly, as if it had understood him, but it made no other response.

'If that's a stubborn refusal,' Fraxinus said, 'it's a very foolish gesture.'

'Cut his throat,' Metra advised carelessly.

'I doubt that it's a *he*,' said Ereleth, kneeling down so that she could poke the point of her knife at the groin of the light tunic which was the creature's only garment. The creature moved a hand as if to protect itself, while Vaca Metra shrugged, to signify that such nice distinctions were irrelevant to her.

'Speak if you can,' Fraxinus said, but still the creature stared back at him, insultingly resolute.

There seemed to be no good reason to refrain from giving the order for the half-human's execution, but Fraxinus hesitated. He would far rather learn what the creature knew, if it knew anything at all. He was still hesitating when Merel called out to him: 'Fraxinus! It's Dhalla!'

Fraxinus was quick to turn, but Ereleth was quicker. They were in time to see the giant, who had already fallen to her knees, topple slowly over, with hardly the strength to break her fall with her hand as she tumbled face forwards.

Since she had recovered from the wound she sustained at the battle of the bridge Fraxinus had fallen into the habit of thinking of the giant as an invincible foe; it was only now that he realised she could not have gone into the heart of this skirmish without sustaining multiple wounds.

'Poison!' hissed Ereleth. 'Those arrows must have been tainted!'

'I doubt it,' Fraxinus said, as he broke into a run, leaving Vaca Metra to carry out her own suggestion. 'More likely loss of blood.'

The giant was still conscious when they reached her side, but she was obviously in pain. Her face was contorted and her breathing very laboured. She was clutching at her left breast with her right hand, and for a moment Fraxinus thought that a spearhead must have gone clean through her armour and her ribs, but Ereleth knew better.

'It's her heart!' the witch-queen said. 'I've seen this before, in the citadel.' She was already scrabbling at her belt, searching for one of her many pouches. Fraxinus and Merel stood clear, allowing Ereleth to kneel beside the giant's head.

'Don't try to swallow,' the queen said, as she tried to force something between Dhalla's clenched teeth. 'Let it under your tongue, and leave it to dissolve there. *Open up*, for Goran's sake.'

It seemed to Fraxinus that Dhalla had to fight for the strength of will to open her own mouth, but she did it and Ereleth's hand forced whatever medicine she had found into the giant's mouth. There was no immediate effect, and Fraxinus could not help looking in the direction in which their erstwhile attackers had ridden off, to check that they could not possibly have seen the giant fall. They were still visible in the distance, but they were moving away, and they had gone too far to be able to see anything clearly.

'It seems that the Salamander's fire in her heart is beginning to burn out,' Ereleth said, looking up at him. 'You were right, Fraxinus – it isn't poison. It's age.'

'Age?' Fraxinus echoed, still confused by the tide of events. 'How old can she be? When was I right?'

'When you explained to me, in your all-wise merchant's manner, why a giant would need a heart more powerful than a mere increase in size could procure,' Ereleth told him, taking the last question first. 'She's ten years old – not much older than Merel, I dare say, but giants don't live as long as common women. They continue to grow, you see, until they reach the limit of their hearts' capacity. They never lose their courage or their strength, but the fire they feel burning in their breasts is muscular strain. She'll live, for now – but she'll need a long rest before she's fit to fight again, and her next battle-fury might be her last.'

It took Fraxinus a moment or two to remember the conversation to which Ereleth was referring, which had taken place as they made their way into the fringes of the Spangled Desert. He had argued that Dhalla must be a chimera of sorts. 'You didn't seem to agree with me at the time,' he observed, but he remembered well enough that he and the witch-queen had been spiky antagonists then, not much given to agreement.

'It didn't take much thought to realise that you were right,' she conceded now. 'I'm a southerner myself, and I'd never heard anything but rumours concerning the origins of Belin's giants when I was wedded to him as his witch. I knew better than to trust the filthy and fanciful stories that were whispered in the Inner Sanctum behind cupped hands, but I saw giants sicken and die in the course of their service. I made my inquiries of those who had first-hand knowledge, and drew my own conclusion. I doubt that any giant ever lived half as long as I have, even if she refused to exercise her strength as Dhalla has these last few tendays. Had the merest taste of her fighting skill not put those ghouls to flight, she'd probably be dead by now.'

Fraxinus looked sharply at Shabir, who had come to stand nearby, half expecting him to express the opinion that he'd be a far happier man had this happened before his capture in the Spangled Desert. Fortunately, the general had learned enough diplomacy to hold his tongue; now that he had thrown in his lot with Fraxinus he had as much cause as anyone to hope that the giant might see them safely to Chimera's Cradle.

Fraxinus was grateful to see that the medicine Ereleth had fed to Dhalla was having an effect already. The expression of strain had gone from the giant's face and she put her hand to the ground as if to push herself up into a sitting position.

'Wait!' Ereleth told her. 'A few minutes more – then walk slowly to the wagon. Lie down for a while.'

Fraxinus caught the witch-queen's eye, and moved his head to indicate that she should follow him as he moved away.

'I know,' she said, before he could frame the question. 'We may need her again soon enough. We're still a long way from Chimera's Cradle and those monsters may be back again. Even if they have the wit to stay clear of us there are doubtless more, and worse, lurking beyond the horizon. Humans seem to be on the point of extinction hereabouts, and that couldn't have been contrived by cavalry of *that* sort. I'll give Dhalla the best advice I know and instruct her to conserve her strength as best she can, but if there comes a time when she must hurl herself into a fray as desperately as that she'll be likely to fall at any moment.'

Vaca Metra joined them then. There was fresh blood on her knife, from the throat of the creature which couldn't or wouldn't talk, but that wasn't what she had come to report.

'One of the warriors has a broken leg,' she said. 'The wound isn't mortal but it won't mend. It can still fight, and it can still keep up with the wagon, but we shouldn't send it scavenging for food.'

She didn't add *and next time three or four horsemen come at it all at once, it will be finished*, but Fraxinus could draw that inference for himself. His heart sank. He had thought that they had come through the fight unscathed, but in fact they had nearly lost two of their three most formidable fighters.

'We might have gained half a dozen horses,' he murmured, intending the words for Ereleth's ears alone, 'but we lost too much in winning them.'

It was Ereleth's turn to stare into the distance, at the point on the horizon where the retreating host could still be dimly seen. 'If they have any intelligence at all,' she said, 'they won't come back. There's easier prey around, if they have sufficient power of self-determination to be selective.'

Fraxinus guessed what she meant. 'Purkin,' he said. 'If only the surly fool had condescended to add his troop to ours, we might have stood them off more easily – indeed, they might never have taken the chance of attacking us.'

'He'd only have run,' Ereleth said. 'Once a deserter, always a deserter. He wouldn't rejoin us because he couldn't look us in the eye, not because he was utterly determined to go back to the river towns.'

'I'm not so sure of that,' Fraxinus said, though not in any brazenly contradictory fashion. 'He really was frightened. He's faced those things before, as part of a considerable force of well-armed soldiers. I think he really was desperate to get back to a town, where he'd be among the kind of men he understands: the kind of men who hate and fear *all* chimeras.'

Ereleth had already turned away from him to minister to Dhalla again. Fraxinus went to help Merel, who was loading plunder into the back of the wagon while Aulakh Phar looked on. He told them the news.

'The new horses are poor quality,' Merel told him gloomily. 'They've been ridden too hard and too far, ill-fed and ill-used. Those creatures never made these saddles, nor the weapons they wielded – all this is stolen. Even the meat's poor.'

'And I've no preservatives worthy of the name,' Phar said. 'We'd better cook it soon and eat as much as our bellies will carry. Rot'll take the rest in double-quick time.'

'It could have been worse,' Fraxinus said, desperate to rebuild morale. 'Had they been better spearmen they'd surely have skewered at least one of us, and had they been better riders even Dhalla and the dragomites might not have cut such an easy swathe through them. They had only the rudiments of both skills, but we must be careful not to underestimate them.'

'Why did they attack us at all?' Merel wanted to know. 'Why are they roaming the land with stolen horses and stolen weapons, with no thought in their animal heads but to kill and keep on killing? It makes no sense.'

'Not to us,' Fraxinus conceded. 'But there's a logic in it somewhere, if only we can work it out.' He looked at Phar before adding: 'They're sexless, as you would doubtless have predicted.'

'Keshvara said that some of the Serpents consider us to be a disease,' Merel recalled. 'Perhaps these creatures agree.'

'Perhaps they do,' Phar agreed. 'Remember, though, that no Serpent or Salamander has so far raised a hand against us. A Serpent saved all our lives in the Dragomite Hills and the Salamanders of Salamander's Fire were as hospitable as they could be. So far, we've had far more to fear from creatures of our own kind than creatures of any other – and even these were half-human, though they must have been forged by something akin to Salamander's Fire. If we've learned one thing in the last forty days, it's not to judge too quickly who our worst enemies might be.'

By this time Merel had registered the second part of Fraxinus's observation. 'Why did you expect that they'd be sexless?' she asked Phar. 'They're human from the neck down.'

'Sex was an evolutionary afterthought on this world,' Phar told her. 'Things were different on the world that gave birth to our remotest ancestors – the world we still remember in our most intimate dreams, according to the *Apocrypha of Genesys*. Most, if not all, earthly species use sexual intercourse as a way of shuffling the genes which make us what we are, forever producing new combinations. I think it has something to do with the fact that the remoter ancestors of all earthly life evolved in the sea. It made perfect sense for every species to produce sperms which could swim to the eggs they had to fertilise – and our nearer ancestors kept the basic system when they emerged on to land, modifying it to suit their new ways of life. Here, though, life must have begun on and under the surface of the land and it found other ways of varying the blueprints which produced many-celled creatures. The basic model of unearthly reproduction isn't sperms-and-eggs; it's . . . well, think of it as flies and figured stones.

'Humans and earthly animals produce new individuals which recombine characteristics selected from our fathers and mothers, and any new variations are relatively slight, but unearthly life can produces chimeras. It's much more versatile than earthly life, but that versatility has penalties as well as advantages. Complex earthly life forms have mostly given up on asexual reproduction, except for plants which grow from clippings, but unearthly ones use asexual reproduction as a matter of routine for dozens or hundreds of generations, punctuating it at infrequent intervals with bouts of chimerical recombination. The bouts indulged in by most important unearthly entities – which are vast collectives, whose elements might be regarded as parts of a whole rather than autonomous individuals – are timed to coincide, resulting in Times of Emergence which occur at intervals of hundreds or even thousands of years.'

Merel couldn't follow that, although Fraxinus could see that she was trying as hard as she could. 'Are these unearthly things that look like men *all* sexless, then?' she asked, trying to stick to matters she could understand.

'Almost all,' Fraxinus told her. 'Some, like Dhalla, retain secondary sexual characteristics but don't actually reproduce by mating. It's not impossible that there are some which are perfect mimics, able to interbreed with true human beings . . . thus, in effect, qualifying as true human beings themselves even though some among their ancestors might not have been human at all.'

'As soon as the first earthly species were co-opted into the system of chimerical reproduction,' Phar continued, still attempting to equip her with a fuller and more sophisticated understanding, 'the distinction between earthly and unearthly life effectively broke down. Ever since then, there's been a gradual process of fusion going on – gradual, at any rate, according to our time-scale, although it only displays itself at widely spaced intervals, in orgies of creativity.'

Merel salvaged one item of information which she could readily accommodate to what she already knew. 'That's what all the talk of Serpent's blood and Salamander's fire is about,' she said. 'If the thing which produced *those*' – she pointed at one of the half-human corpses – 'can also produce humans which can mate with real people, their descendants would be part-unearthly. Princess Lucrezia's Serpent's blood must come from an unhuman ancestor, just like Dhalla's Salamander's fire.'

Fraxinus was quick to sound a cautionary note. 'We've no way of knowing that for sure. It might be just a legend.'

'The one great mystery that's left, you see,' Phar went on, in his own stubborn fashion, 'is how the crossing over was possible in the first place. If earthly life and unearthly life began in such drastically different fashions, using entirely different biochemical systems, how were the two ever able to get together? How was it that the things from which all these chimeras are presently emerging were ever able to incorporate our biochemistry into their own? The people of the ship can't have expected that, but if we're remembering the lore rightly, they found out about it soon enough. After that, they remade their plans . . . but what *we* inherited was a botched job, all makeshift provisions and hopeful improvisations.'

'Actually,' Fraxinus said, 'the more important mystery is to do with future prospects rather than remote beginnings. The point is, what will the end of all these confusions be?'

'You mean, can we take control of it?' Merel said. 'Can we do what the Salamanders have done and tame the living ground?'

'If only they had,' Phar said, with a despairing shake of his head. 'We've already achieved the kind of limited domestication that the Salamanders have at Salamander's Fire. That's how Dhalla's loremasters produce giants. The trouble is that the biggest players in the game are still running wild, and getting wilder all the time. Control would be a fine thing, but our descendants might have a hard enough time just surviving. Opinions seem to differ as to how hard they'll need to fight.'

'Whose opinions?' Merel wanted to know, looking from Phar to Fraxinus and back again.

'What Aulakh means,' Fraxinus said gently, 'is that we don't really know whether it would count as a terrible tragedy if the fusion of earthly and unearthly life continued to its terminus. If the world still had human beings, how much would it matter if they all had unearthly blood in them, and mixed ancestry?'

Merel looked suitably astonished. 'You mean,' she said, 'how much would it matter if those *things* – and others like them – were the only kind of humans left in the world?'

'What I mean,' Fraxinus said patiently, 'is that we've no way of knowing for sure that that isn't already the case – or that even if it isn't, whether it would make any very significant difference if it were to *become* the case.' He wished that he'd been able to phrase it better, but Merel had followed the thrust of his argument well enough. Her astonishment was turning to puzzlement as she began to consider this remarkable proposition.

Dhalla was on her feet again now, with Ereleth hovering beneath her elbow, as if ready to help support her. Fraxinus almost raised a smile at the thought of a stick-like creature like Ereleth helping to support something as massive as a giant. The witch-queen's solicitousness was strangely touching, though, and Dhalla seemed gravely grateful for it. Instead of moving towards the wagon, as Ereleth was urging her to do, the giant extended her right hand to point at the horizon a few degrees south of due west.

'More,' she said, in a clipped fashion, almost as if she were afraid that an extra syllable might cause her heart to seize up again.

Fraxinus climbed on to the wagon and stood on the driver's bench to gain the benefit of its height. He shaded his eyes against the sun's glare and studied the tiny dots moving at the limit of vision, blurred by the hazy air rising from the sun-warmed rocks of the plain.

'I don't think it's a substantial force,' he said tiredly, when he was certain that what he saw wasn't merely the head of a long column. 'But we'd better be ready, just in case. Let's make what haste we can.'

He was well aware, however, that haste would not be easy to make, and the thought of falling short of their objective now, when they had come so far and fought so hard, brought an awful bitterness into his throat.

This was not at all what he had hoped for when he first brought his wagons out of Xandria, and it was a great deal worse than anything he could have expected.

13

Ssifuss stopped rather abruptly but Lucrezia had no need to tug on the reins. Her mount came to a halt without any prompting at all, and had to be urged forward in order to bring her to a position directly to the Serpent's left. Hyry's horse dutifully went to the right.

They had come to the crest of a shallow hill, whose ridge had hidden the ground beyond from their inquisitive view while they toiled up the slope. They could see now that the lie of the land was not quite as straightforward as they had anticipated. In the shallow vale below them the 'road' forked into two, and each of its divisions ran into the thick forest of needle-like spires whose clustered tips they had already seen.

By standing briefly in her stirrups Lucrezia was able to confirm that there was even higher ground behind the spires, whose slopes were decked by yet another 'forest' of darker and more uncertain forms. She didn't doubt that there was a way through that forest too, and perhaps more than one, but she was by no means as sure as she had been that the right path would be easy to follow, even if they could identify it.

'The horsemen who bore Andris away must have taken one of these roads,' Lucrezia said, as she urged her horse downhill towards the fork, overtaking the Serpent. 'They must have left some sign of their passage. If we follow their lead, we'll surely be on the right track.'

'Perhapss,' Ssifuss said, resuming his mechanical stride.

'The traces they left might not be easy to see,' Hyry called to the Serpent, although she was content to remain a few discreet paces behind. 'A few of the men who captured me had horses with iron shoes, which must have been stolen from the men of the river towns, but others had mounts that were unshod. They might not have scarred the ground – and however hard it seems, this isn't inert stone; its slow flux could easily erase the evidence of their passing.'

Lucrezia saw no point in further speculation when the matter could so easily be put to the test. She urged her mount forward and rode ahead to the place where the hardened strip divided; there she dismounted. In the acute angle formed by the parted roads there was a substantial pool of water, to which her thirsty horse inevitably went. She followed it and took hold of its bridle, holding it back until she had dipped her hand in the pool and sniffed her damp hand.

There seemed nothing amiss, and she knew that if the road were intended for the use of men, horses and giant Serpents it would make sense to make provision for them. She let the animal drink; it did so gratefully. She cupped her hands and took a drink herself before letting go of the bridle and walking away to make her inspection.

It was immediately obvious, as Lucrezia moved from one divergent road to the other, that Hyry's judgment of the roadway's ability to resist marking was unwarranted; there were marks aplenty. Unfortunately, *both* forks showed discreet signs of recent use. She wondered whether that meant that they were equally safe, or equally unsafe.

Ssifuss came to stand beside her, removing the straw hat which protected its hairless head from the glare of the sun as it knelt down to study the ground. She saw that the mark on the Serpent's back where the 'butterfly' had fused with its skin had faded somewhat – but that its discolouration had also broadened, as if it were a patch of stonerot slowly extending its empire across the surface of a wall. She touched her own neck and cheek, where she had now accumulated three small bites, and looked at her wrists, where there were a further four. The swellings were tiny and no more than slightly itchy, certainly no worse than the first few scratches she had collected in the Soursweet Marshes, but she didn't dare take as much reassurance from that as she would have liked.

Hyry left her own horse and the two pack-animals at the waterhole, and was then prompted by Lucrezia's example to begin an inspection of her own skin. As her fingers probed a rip in her left trouser-leg she cursed.

'What is it?' Lucrezia asked anxiously.

'Only a tacktick,' Hyry replied. 'I'll need a flame to force it to withdraw, though – I don't want to leave the head behind.'

Lucrezia took a match from one of her pouches and looked around for a suitable surface on which to strike it. It failed to catch light, smearing its phosphorous head all over the scaly skin of the spiky 'tree'. The second one caught, though, and she held the flickering flame to the bloated tacktick while Hyry held the edges of the ripped cloth apart. The tacktick dropped away, the stolen blood within its body sizzling.

'Do you want some salve for that?' Lucrezia asked, referring to the bleeding wound.

'It'll be all right,' Hyry assured her gruffly. 'I'm used to *that* sort of thing.'

Ssifuss had finished its inspection. 'Ssat way,' it said, as it walked to the pool to quench its thirst. It was pointing to the left-hand path.

'Why do you say that?' Lucrezia asked.

'Ssmellss better,' Ssifuss replied.

'Do you mean that you think you can detect some residual scent of the men who took Andris?' Hyry said sceptically.

Ssifuss shook its head. 'Not ssat,' it said unhelpfully. 'Ssome-ssing elsse.'

'What?' Hyry wanted to know.

The Serpent shook its head again. 'Don't know,' it said. Lucrezia took this to mean that it didn't know the human words it would have needed to construct an adequate explanation.

Hyry shook her head but didn't press the point. She went to the pack-horses and began detaching the waterskins from the bundles draped over their backs.

'*They* don't seem unduly distressed,' the older woman said to Lucrezia as she pointed to discolouring patches on the flanks and withers of both animals. While they trailed in the rear there had been no one to drive the flies away and the whisking of their own tails had been slightly inhibited by the bulk of the packs they carried. Lucrezia went to examine the places where the 'butter-flies' had fused with their skins – or at least with their slightly shaggy coats – and observed that Hyry seemed to be correct; the horses showed no sign of distress even when the patches were touched.

'Which way do you think we should go?' Lucrezia asked Hyry, who was busy filling the waterskins and bottles.

'I don't suppose there's anything that smells like food, is there?' the trader called to Ssifuss. 'The stuff we've got left is just about inedible.'

The Serpent didn't answer.

'Well,' said Hyry, 'one way looks as good as another to me. If the left-hand way smells better, let's take it.'

'There are birds about which might make good eating,' Lucrezia observed, 'but it's not safe to step off the road to chase them – or even to fetch them if Ssifuss could shoot one down with his bow. Somewhere up ahead there must be sources of food. The things that look like humans must eat like humans, and giant Serpents probably have giant appetites. Maybe the forest has fruit trees as well as these hideous spiky things.'

'Why should the road divide, though?' Hyry asked pensively, as she replaced waterskins. 'It can't be a means of confusing travellers on the road, no matter how it looks to us. There must be some other logic to it – perhaps there's more than one place to which the creature's minions must go . . . or more than one place from which they come.'

'I don't know,' Lucrezia said. 'You're right, though – we might as well let Ssifuss have his way if we've no better means of deciding.' She looked at the Serpent again, but Ssifuss had nothing more to add. She sniffed the air herself, trying to figure out what Ssifuss might have detected. The warm breeze was by no means free of scents, but the faint odours meant nothing to her. A cloud of little flies was already beginning to form around her, and she moved away from the pool. 'We might be insects ourselves, making our way across the surface of a giant pincushion,' she observed.

'I'm glad to say that I've had very little to do with pincushions,' Hyry remarked. 'I've never kept close company with seamstresses.'

'It was difficult to avoid such contact in the Inner Sanctum,' Lucrezia retorted, wondering why she felt so embarrassed about it. 'As an apprentice witch I had far better things to occupy my time than mere finery but I'd more sisters than I could count, and few of them had any but the least useful kinds of lore to keep them occupied. I suppose it was a silly comparison, though – no

274

pincushion I ever saw had pins with such ornate shafts, nor a thousand spiderwebs spun between the pinheads.'

'I don't think they're spiderwebs, highness,' Hyry said, looking up into the canopy of the strange forest at the grey threads which hung there in great profusion, like the torn and soot-stained remnants of lace curtains that had been caught in a fire. 'At least, if they *are* spiderwebs I'm not looking forward to meeting the spiders.'

Lucrezia returned to her horse, picking up the trailing bridle before setting her foot in the stirrup. The horse moved away slightly, but it had been well enough schooled by someone, somewhere, to quell its own instinctive resistance. She let Ssifuss take the lead again, and followed the Serpent without waiting to see whether Hyry intended to ride alongside her. The separated strands of the highway were not quite as wide as the single lane had been, so it would have been more difficult to ride two abreast.

As she passed between the first pair of towering spikes Lucrezia saw that the road became narrower still as it wound its way between the structures. Although they tapered to a sharp point the bases of each spire were bulbous, and Lucrezia could not help thinking of them as great eggs – eggs for growing the heaviest kind of lances with which her father's cavalry were equipped. Because they stood so straight and so sheer they didn't cut off the sun's light the way a real forest would have done, and the threads which cluttered the canopy weren't too densely clustered hereabouts, but even so there were shadows every-where, mottled in unexpectedly gaudy confusion. The silvery spires were by no means mirror-bright but they did reflect light in every direction, breaking up the shadows in all manner of complicated patterns.

The further they went into the forest the stranger the shadows became. The canopy above their heads became gradually thicker, and Lucrezia saw slight signs of movement within it, but the biting flies were much less common here. The few 'butter-flies' she saw were white, and they showed no conspicuous indication that they were attracted to the hides of Serpents or horses. The road became narrower the further they went, and Lucrezia snagged the sleeve of her shirt on a sharp branch which

275

stuck out from a nearby tree like a steel spike. Had the sleeve not been so loose she might have sustained a bad cut.

Lucrezia turned in the saddle to tell her companion to be careful, but she should have been more careful herself. While her head was turned she ran into some kind of thread which had been trailing across her path, invisible in the awkward light. It was neither stout enough nor taut enough to unhorse her but it clung firmly enough to her hair to yank her head back, causing her twisted neck some discomfort – and when it broke loose from its nearer mooring, the loose end somehow contrived to wrap itself around her shoulders.

The thread was sticky, and when Lucrezia tried to use her fingers to get rid of it the coiling strand clung to them. It fell lightly about her shoulders as the horse continued its forward plodding, and proceeded to wind itself around her neck.

It seemed a slight enough nuisance at first, so Lucrezia didn't immediately try to stop her mount. Instead she contented herself with waving her arms about, trying to dislodge the coiling thread. She broke it again and again but all the separate pieces clung to her clothing and her flesh, and as she was carried further forward she made contact with another thread, and then another.

When Ssifuss turned to see what was happening and let loose an inarticulate cry of warning, it was far too late.

By the time she actually brought her horse to a standstill, Lucrezia had half a dozen threads wrapped around her neck and her chest, tangled in her hair and her clothing. Nor did coming to a halt contrive a crucial interruption of the process, for the trailing ends of further threads seemed now to be seeking her out, drifting towards her from either side and slipping down from the spiny boughs which arched over the road.

The princess opened her mouth, intending to call out a further and more urgent warning to Hyry, but that was another mistake; the filmy strands were even more eager to seize her tongue than they had been to cling to her clothing. One thread was tightening about her throat, choking her and strangling the cry of alarm before she could vent it. While she tried, more threads worked their way into her open mouth, clinging like recalcitrant hairs to the roof of her mouth. Others were touching her eyes, making her squeeze them shut.

In no time at all – or so it seemed – the princess was gagging and retching, trying desperately to catch her breath and draw air into her lungs. She could not do it. Within a matter of minutes, she felt herself falling into unconsciousness – and she couldn't free her hands to take tighter hold of her horse's rein, in the hope of saving herself a bruising fall.

14

THE BATTLE HAD only just begun to spill from the 'forest' of spiky growths which surrounded the garden into the protected area, but Andris knew that it must have been raging for some considerable time. He didn't know how thick the protective forest was, nor how well-equipped it might be with pitfall traps and other defences, but he understood that it must have been constructed with cunning and strength enough to withstand any commonplace invasion, or the garden would not still be here. This, evidently, was no ordinary invasion.

The creatures which were leaping from the trees were reptiles of a sort – moulded, he supposed, from crocolid flesh or something like it – but they had been reshaped somewhat after the fashion of the big grey birds which had visited disaster upon his unhappy excursion through the Soursweet Marshes. He couldn't believe that they could actually fly for any distance, because they were too large, but as they descended to the ground, furling the great horny flaps which connected their wrists to their thighs, he judged that they must be capable of prodigious gliding leaps.

He guessed that they must have come through the petrified forest without touching the treacherous ground, and that their thick scaly skins had protected them from any assaults and snares which the crowns of the trees had been able to mount. Andris had no confidence that the stout thorns and grappling branches of the half-human bushes would prove to be a significantly better defence.

The invading creatures had claw-like hands which clutched pointed daggers made of some glistening non-metallic substance, but these were not their best weapons. Their mouths contained long rows of sharp and ugly teeth, and their elongated necks gave them the capacity to strike out with their heads much as the grey birds had. They had long tails, too. These had nothing like the mass of giant Serpents' tails, but they were nevertheless capable of striking blows as well as serving as supportive limbs if the need arose. The living ground might have been able to seize and hold them if they had rested too long upon it but their movements were fast and frenetic, and they were not being caught and held.

Andris had watched battles before, but he had never been forced to do so while knowing that he could not move. He could no more run away than he could charge into the fray – and it would take a terrible effort even to turn to see what was behind him.

'Do you see them, Arilla?' he called, although he could not look at her.

'I see them,' she replied. 'Don't be afraid. They're flimsy creatures, easy enough to tear apart. If nothing worse comes in their wake, we'll be safe.'

This seemed to Andris to be reckless optimism, or a downright lie. He could not imagine that she would lie for his benefit, so he assumed that she must be trying to reassure herself.

The reptiles had roundly webbed feet like those of the Watcher, and the end of each tail also had a spreading membrane. Andris immediately saw the logic of this design. The ground within the garden might be firmer than that in the forest, but it was probably capable of easier deformation; these monsters had been carefully adapted to move on all kinds of living ground, always provided that they need never be still. They had been made for their present purpose: to destroy the conscious products of enemy ground.

That realisation was cause enough for fear, but Andris also found cause for a certain grim elation. If warriors were coming to kill him, and those like him, then he and they must be of some particular importance in the scheme of things. Whatever Arilla said or thought, he and individuals like him had some definite and continuing significance in the game whose moves were being played out here.

For the moment, at least, there was not the slightest sign of any weakness in the invaders' strategy. As they leapt from the trees they came down dancing, hopping feverishly one way and another. They were pursued and harried by an opposing force which presently outnumbered them by at least two to one, but their crazy movement was by no means purely defensive. The great majority of those opposing them were humans and human-sized Serpents armed with spears, who were far smaller than the invaders and could not match their reach; the giant Serpents who formed the minority were very much slower and could not match their agility. The primary purpose of the reptiles' frenzy was to hack and slash at the chimerical bushes with deadly effect, on a cut and run basis. That was what they had come to do, and what they intended to do no matter what forces were ranged against them.

At first glance Andris counted sixteen of the marauders, but within a few minutes a dozen more appeared, and no more defenders followed them. That hardly mattered; had there been a hundred defenders, of whatever kind, they would not have been able to destroy or contain so many rampaging reptiles.

So great was the advantage that the invaders seemed to have as they continued to spill out into the garden that Andris feared they might be unstoppable. The spears hurled by their smaller assailants seemed to be rebounding even when they hit, implying that the monsters' scaly hides were tougher than they looked. The attempts made by the giant Serpents to block their way seemed ludicrously clumsy and ineffectual.

Having slain such giants himself, Andris couldn't believe that fearsome creatures like the crocolid-birds had anything much to fear from them. Indeed, had the fight been on open and solid ground, the reptiles might have made short work of all the Serpents and the spearmen – but it was not. The ground was not *quite* solid, and it was cluttered with sedentary guardians more fearsome by far than the garden's mobile forces.

The first time Andris saw one of the invaders caught and held by the branches of one of the tree-men he realised how vital it was that they kept moving. The chimera in question had to suffer the assaults of two black daggers and the fearsome teeth, but it was able to use its branches to shield its human face. As soon as the reptile was hard held it was possible for one of the giant Serpents to bring its strength to bear. The giant thrust with its spear with power enough to penetrate the armoured hide, then reached out with its arms to tear its enemy's membranous wings and break its long-boned arms.

After that, the bleeding but still living bush was easily able to wrap its limbs about the dangerous head, rendering it harmless.

This is a suicide mission, Andris thought. *Clever as they are and powerful as they are, they would need to come in their hundreds to have any chance at all of fighting their way to the top of the slope. All they can do is lash out, cutting and maiming . . . but even if they kill half the chimeras in the garden they will only have inflicted scratches on the ground itself. They're like dragomite warriors: expendable units of some greater whole – but they can't possibly win this nest-war. Although the trees have been hurt before the ground itself is healthy and strong, not plague-ridden and decaying.*

Now *he* was being recklessly over-optimistic. A new party of reptiles was already tumbling from the forest, and there were no more men or Serpents to harass them – nor were the tree-men finding it easy to catch them. Andris wondered whether there might, after all, be hundreds of the invaders still to come. In any case, how could he take any comfort from the conviction that the living ground could not be killed? *He* could be killed – and it was the murder of creatures like him that was the evident objective of the attack.

The lower slope of the garden was now so crowded that the reptiles were getting in one another's way. He saw two of them cannon off one another, knocked down while they were still confused by giant Serpents; then he saw lesser assailants leap to plunge spears into the softer parts of their bodies.

The battle was spreading out sideways now that the forest-wall had been breached and a passage of sorts opened within it. Three other reptiles were seized and held by animate bushes, stabbed and raked by countless thorns – but the bushes sustained terrible damage in return and dozens of their kin were being slashed and wounded without being able to win any substantial compensation at all.

Had the reptiles concentrated their attention on their more active assailants they might have slaughtered them wholesale, but their preference for inflicting damage upon the bushes cost them dear as the men and the Serpents regrouped and began to direct their attacks a little more efficiently. Andris wondered why the attackers didn't tackle their enemies in rigorous order, felling the giant Serpents first and then tidying up the humans and human-sized Serpents; the bushes which were their primary targets could not run away, after all. He reasoned, however, that they simply did not have the time: that every moment they spent on dangerous ground without striking out at their main targets was reckoned to be wasted.

The living ground did not have elasticity enough to open up and swallow them whole, but it was now reacting to every footfall, and Andris saw that the craziness of the reptiles' dancing was not entirely due to their own agility. They were constantly being thrown off balance by the subtly shifting ground, and although they had little difficulty spreading the front of their collective assault to either side they were presently making little headway up the slope.

They cannot kill the ground itself, Andris thought, forcing himself to make a calm and considered assessment of the situation – because there was, after all, nothing else he *could* do. *That could only be done with weapons much subtler than these. There must be some significant reward in what they are actually doing, though. If they're trying to hurt us they must be attacking the intelligence the ground has adopted, the lore and wisdom it has accumulated. That lore and wisdom must, therefore, have some value over and above the worth of any tinier creatures that we carry in our flesh. Does that prove that these attackers have been dispatched by a guiding mind, which knows what it is doing and is capable of planning – or is it simply one more blind move in a game played by automata, one more deadly reflex of a sightless and thoughtless giant?*

There were no more reptiles descending from the trees now; it seemed that they did not number hundreds after all, but their mobile adversaries were very thinly spread. Even though the attackers couldn't or wouldn't pause to concentrate on the elimination of the imitation men and the lumbering Serpents the defenders were going down one after another, cut and broken by casual slashes of the daggers or by reflexive bites.

This time, Andris had cause to regret that the giant Serpents were not nearly as fearsome as they looked, for he could see that they were all but lost. Their smaller siblings were faring even worse; less than twenty were still standing. Andris saw the Watcher struck down, arterial blood spouting from a horrible wound in its neck, and felt a particular pang of regret. Somehow, he felt that he and the Watcher had unfinished business, or at least that its vigilant presence in so many of his troubled dreams represented a puzzle to be solved.

Now, at last, the invaders were beginning to make rapid progress up the slope. The bushes past which they moved had been devastated by their attacks, and it was difficult to conserve the hope that more than a few had been able to protect their vulnerable human parts.

There were only two dozen reptiles dancing now, but the mobile forces arrayed against them had been so badly depleted that they were doing their lethal work with greater efficiency than before. Those which were caught and held by the tree-men they attacked were no longer being speared by willing helpers; they had to be stabbed and strangled by the thorny branches themselves, and the struggles in which they were engaged were often so bloody that they seemed highly likely to result in mutual destruction.

The battle was much closer now; Andris knew that it would certainly reach and engulf him. There were eight or ten reptiles within fifty mets, any one of which might turn its fury upon him. These were noticeably more adept than their kin at the work of cutting, biting and tearing. Now that they had come so far up the slope they were converging again, but they were not coming close enough to one another to risk accidental collisions. Andris knew that he would have to grapple with at least one of them – and he knew, too, that no matter how much work he had put into the exercise of his limbs he was woefully ill-equipped to do battle.

The mobile defenders were still falling, one by one, struck down with casual contempt. All the tree-people had to look to their own protection now, and the movements of their branches were becoming increasingly frenzied as fear and desperation took hold. If they believed that they would be reborn no matter what happened they were certainly not sufficiently sanguine in that belief to let themselves be torn apart without a fight. Whatever memories and dreams they had preserved, and whatever self-regarding instincts they had lost, their present lives were very precious to them.

Andris saw that many of the squatter tree-people were trying to hold their branches in, to bunch them up as much as they could so as to hide their faces behind shields studded with countless thorns, and he also saw that the strategy was inadequate. The reptiles were too adept at slashing and biting, and they ruthlessly scythed the thorny cages apart.

The invaders were winning now, although the quivering ground was still treacherous enough to tip them over if they lost their balance – and once they fell they could more easily be seized by questing branches, then held in such a way as to minimise the damage their teeth and weapons could do. The marauders had lost more than half their number, but they were still too many.

Andris had not realised how content he had become to be half a plant until the frustration of not being able to bound down the slope and hurl himself into the battle boiled up into a veritable rage. He became conscious that his multitudinous limbs were already moving, reaching out in anticipation of the time when one of these enemies might finally arrive to wrestle with him. He knew that he ought to be afraid, because all his fighting reflexes were geared to the possession of two arms and two legs, but he was not. He was ready to fight, with whatever resources he had, and he was *avid* to fight – for himself, and for the garden. He had made no conscious decision to accept his adoption by the ground, or to begin thinking of the other tree-people as his siblings, but circumstances had defined them thus, and he had no doubt at all that these marauding reptiles counted as deadly enemies.

Sooner than he had expected, his chance arrived. As they came closer to the crown of the hill the reptiles became increasingly anxious to reach it, and hardly paused at all as they cavorted past bush-men whose thoughts were concentrated entirely on defence.

Two came at Andris at once, with murderous intent, and he reacted in kind. It occurred to him as he did so that in the uneducated eyes of his assailants he must seem no different from his much older neighbour. In focusing their attention on him they were probably responding to some innate inclination to risk everything in order to destroy the most valuable individuals the garden held.

'And am I not the best?' he shouted gleefully, as they closed in on him and came within the compass of his countless arms. 'Was

284

not the seed they gave me grown in superhuman flesh? If I am not yet the Tree of Knowledge, I may surely be the Tree of Death!'

15

Fraxinus was reluctant to call a halt but he was left with no alternative. They had kept on going long into the midnight and at least one of the horses pulling the wagon would have broken down had they been asked to go forward another kim. He had no way of knowing exactly what the shadows looming over the western horizon signified, given that nothing was marked on Andris Myrasol's map, and he did not want to approach too close without getting a clearer sight of what lay ahead. He did have a reasonably clear idea of what lay behind him – but however menacing that enemy might be, it was an enemy that had been defeated once and had not so far risked a second engagement. He knew that not everyone would agree with his calculation and he was prepared to meet the inevitable objections.

'If we settle here till dawn,' Shabir said darkly, 'the monkey-heads will be able to surround us at their leisure.'

Fraxinus had a defence ready to counter that argument, but Ereleth got in ahead of him. 'More fool them if they do,' she said. 'To draw a ring around us they'd have to spread themselves so thin that the dragomites could pick them off one by one.'

'The one with the damaged leg wouldn't be much use at that kind of work,' Merel pointed out. 'Aulakh seems to have set the limb well enough but the creature's lost most of its speed.'

'Vaca Metra's a warrior too,' Ereleth said. 'She was bred to work in the dark, and she's been riding just as you have so she should be able to remain alert. You might go with her if she calls for volunteers. Steal us a few more horses if you can.'

Vaca Metra came back to the wagon then, to report on the state of the surrounding ground. Fraxinus had picked the best spot he could but there were a great many flowing stones in the vicinity and it would not be easy to find places where those who had to stand watch could take up their stations. No one except Dhalla slept outside the wagon nowadays, and even the giant took great care selecting her places of rest.

Although he had been guiding the wagon for hours Fraxinus appointed himself to share the first watch. The others had been busier than he with various kinds of work. The dragomites delivered the results of their scavenging at a remarkably steady rate even though the injury it had sustained had forced one of them to cut its contributions by half. The produce kept Mossassor and Merel constantly busy; that which did not have to be cut up, cleaned and cooked had still to be inspected and stored. In the meantime, Aulakh Phar and Shabir had been forced to occupy themselves with a whole series of petty repairs and routine tasks of maintenance which had stretched Phar's genius for improvisation to the limit. Even Ereleth had been fully occupied in ministering to the horses and the giant.

It was not strictly necessary for anyone else to stand watch with Fraxinus, given that the two dragomites were patrolling arcs to either side of the camp which met at a point ahead of them, but Mossassor came out with him, claiming that it was not tired enough to sleep.

'Iss good, I ssink,' the Serpent said, when they had found a suitable station some ten or fifteen mets behind the wagon, looking out in the direction from which trouble was most likely to come. 'When ssun rissess will ssee living ground. Closse to gardenss now.' Fraxinus knew Mossassor well enough by now to know that it was trying to maintain its own morale; behind its impassive mask the Serpent knew exactly how bad things were, and how much worse they might yet become.

'Not close enough, alas,' Fraxinus said, keeping his own voice level and his tone matter-of-fact. 'On Myrasol's map the Gauntlet of Gladness which marked the way to Chimera's Cradle extended no more than a day or two's ride, but if I've judged it aright the shadow ahead is more than twice that distance from the Navel of the World. If it's the limit of the living ground the so-called dwellers in the deep must have grown a great deal since the maps were made. Even if the pathway through the Silver Thorns still extends to the limit of the new borderlands it might be a hard and dangerous road.'

287

'Every day ended iss good,' Mossassor insisted. 'Road hass been hard but sstill on it. Are sstrong, sstubborn, unsstoppable.'

'I'd like to think that's true,' Fraxinus admitted. 'Old and frail as some of us are, we're still alive and still fit to fight. I wish I could take heart from the fact that the monkey-heads haven't attacked a second time, but I can't help wondering why they seem so perfectly content to trail along in our wake. Perhaps they know something we don't.'

'Too sstupid to know *anyssing*,' Mossassor opined.

'Maybe so,' Fraxinus agreed. 'But they're still back there somewhere. They haven't forgotten us.'

'Sscared of dragomitess,' said the Serpent flatly. 'Will keep away.'

'Dragomites are pretty scary,' Fraxinus agreed. 'Your ability to make peace with them must be very useful. It's as well for all the other species with which they share the world that drago-mites spend most of their time fighting one another. If all the dragomites in the hills united into a single army they'd certainly be unstoppable. Shabir's ragged army held them back for two years because they came out of the hills a dozen at a time, weakened by hunger and fatigue. If three or four of those groups had combined their forces, they could have cleared a way through the narrow land with ease and established any number of new nest-sites, but they didn't. If they could make common cause with one another the way they've made common cause with us they could take over the world.'

'Not made ssat way,' was Mossassor's judgment.

Fraxinus didn't think the dismissal was adequate or conclu-sive. After all, a substantial minority of the nests had human mound-queens as well as the queens whose substance provided the walls of the nests. Their intelligence was borrowed but it was intelligence nevertheless. Even after the hills had been blighted the mound-queens must have had the means to raise invincible armies, if only they could have called a halt to the endless routine of nest-wars. By remaining divided they had effectively con-demned almost all their nests to piecemeal destruction. Perhaps General Shabir had been right in his insistence that the mound-women were slaves. They were not slaves of the dragomite queens in any simple sense, but it seemed that they were slaves to instinct and tradition – and that the chains which bound them could not be broken until the hive was effectively dead. *We are all of one mind here*, the mound-queen had told Ereleth, but the unity which she and her daughters had shared was based in implacable opposition to others of her own kind. He wondered whether the greater queens which clustered around Chimera's Cradle would be any different.

So far as Fraxinus could see, it wasn't clear that Serpents were very much better off than the humans who had united themselves with dragomite nests. Serpents knew too little about their own species and their own place in the scheme of things – even less, it seemed, than the Salamanders. At least the Salamanders had managed to acquire a measure of control over the living ground which produced their 'adult' forms; Serpents didn't even seem to know what their 'adult' forms looked like. As they were perversely fond of claiming, they were good at forgetting. According to Mossassor, that was because they *had to be* good at forgetting – but the Serpent didn't know why. It was just lore, cemented by endless repetition. Serpents too were slaves to instinct and tradition.

But humans are no different, Fraxinus reminded himself scrupulously. *We too have been adopted by the living ground, and we too are subject to its mysterious powers. The dwellers in the deep don't seem to care that we're the produce of another world; they deal with us as casually as they deal with Serpents and Salamanders, subjecting human flesh to all kinds of strange metamorphoses. All our species are in danger of supersession now, both individually and collectively. It's not enough that the Salamanders can control their own parent ground; if sentient creatures are to maintain our hegemony within the world we must take control of all the living ground – including that which comprises the vastness of the Dragomite Hills, and that which comprises the infinitude of the flowing stones. If we can't do that, the dwellers in the deep will eventually produce a species which can: a species compounded out of flesh and stone, Serpents and Salamanders, dragomites and men. Why did our forefathers abandon us to the mercy of such a world as this? Why did they not carry us all away, when they discovered the mistake they had made?*

He knew, of course, that there were three possible answers to the second question he had posed. Perhaps the forefathers believed that men could prevail against all the efforts of the dwellers in the deep. Perhaps they believed that the dwellers in the deep ought to be allowed to make what they could of human flesh, in combination with all the other kinds of flesh with which they worked. Perhaps it had simply been too late to undo what they had done, and they had had no option but to abandon their children to whatever fate awaited them.

The lore, of course, favoured the first answer. The purpose of human life, according to the *Lore of Genesys*, was to 'fight evil wherever it may be found'. But Fraxinus was sufficiently cynical now to see that the lore would have to say that, even if it were a lie. How else could it justify the actions of its makers?

Mossassor suddenly hissed. Fraxinus had spent long enough in the Serpent's company to recognise a warning and he took up the half-pike which he had brought for his defence.

'Where?' he asked.

Mossassor pointed to the north-west. 'Dragomite hass gone,' it said.

Fraxinus tried to remember whether the dragomite patrolling to the right was the one with the patched-up leg or the one that was fully fit, but he was still uncertain when he heard the sound of a cry.

It was as much a howl of anguish as a word, but the syllable contained within it was obviously: 'No!' It was followed by the clatter of iron-shod hooves.

Fraxinus knew that there was no way Mossassor could instruct the dragomite what to do at such a distance, and that Vaca Metra was asleep in the wagon. He had no idea how flexible the warrior's responses might be, or how sensitively Metra had instructed it. He could only wait to see what the dragomite brought out of the darkness.

It came, in the end, with a single body clasped in its jaws: a human body. It laid the body down, with surprising delicacy, at Fraxinus's feet. It was a man, apparently fully human; Fraxinus recognised him immediately even though he had been laid face down. It was ex-Sergeant Purkin of King Belin's citadel guard.

Fraxinus knelt and put his hand to the man's neck, feeling for a pulse. When he found one he checked the body for mortal wounds, rolling it over. Purkin was bleeding from a head wound and his right arm had been badly broken below the elbow, but both wounds had been inflicted some hours earlier. The dragomite warrior had exercised restraint, inflicting no further injury. Whether that was because it had learned the meaning of the word 'No', or because it had recognised Purkin's scent, or merely because it had been carefully instructed, Fraxinus didn't know. So far as he could tell, it wasn't likely to make a great deal of difference. The head wound was bad and the mangled limb was so filthy that it seemed certain to become infected. So far as Fraxinus knew, neither Phar nor Ereleth had the medical resources to treat a gangrenous limb and if Phar were to attempt an amputation the operation might well complete the job that the enemy had begun.

'Wass alone,' Mossassor said, as the dragomite scuttled off again. 'Wass trying to reassh uss.'

Fraxinus slapped the stricken man about the face, trying to rouse him. Purkin could not have been deeply unconscious, for he came round quickly enough. Fraxinus concluded that he had fainted, out of fright or shock.

'I thought you were bound for home,' Fraxinus said, unable to keep the harshness out of his voice.

'Was,' the sergeant replied thickly. 'With you, would have stood a chance.' He didn't seem in the least repentant, but he had the sense not to sound too resentful.

'Was it the things with animal heads?' Fraxinus queried.

The starlight was just bright enough to let him see Purkin's nod.

'If you'd joined us,' Fraxinus told him, 'you'd have been on the winning side in *our* battle.'

The supine Purkin managed to say: 'I know.' Fraxinus supposed that it was the nearest thing to an admission of error the sergeant was likely to make. After a pause, the stricken man added: 'How bad?'

'Bad,' Fraxinus confirmed. 'Phar will know better than I what might be done. Can you get up and walk to the wagon? If Mossassor and I have to carry you, it'll put more pressure on that mangled arm.'

Purkin muttered something more, but Fraxinus had to wait for him to repeat it before it became comprehensible.

'Don't wait till day,' was what the sergeant said. 'Too many, too close.'

Fraxinus looked out towards the shadowed horizon, wondering how many half-men there would have to be, and how close they would have to be, to force a man like Purkin to take the risk of confronting the dragomite patrol. It wasn't a comfortable thought.

'Are there any others still out there?' he demanded. 'Did anyone else survive?'

Purkin shook his head again, but Fraxinus didn't trust him enough to take it for granted that he was telling the truth, even if he knew for sure whether or not he was the sole survivor.

'Get up,' Fraxinus said, his voice hard-edged with bitterness. 'If you can walk to the wagon, you might live.'

Purkin made as if to shake his head again, but thought better of it. Instead, he said: 'A minute.'

When the minute had lapsed, though, Purkin signalled with his good hand that he couldn't get up again. Fraxinus had to suppress an urge to kick the man, but in the end he took the sergeant's shoulders as gently as he could and motioned to Mossassor, who obediently lifted his legs.

What use is he to us with an arm like that? Fraxinus thought, although he wasn't proud of himself for thinking it. *It would be better to leave him here for the scavengers than let him take a share of our food and water while he hovers at death's door.* All he said out loud was: 'If you'd shouted earlier you might have brought your horse in with you. The warrior can't have caught it or it'd be back by now.'

Purkin didn't apologise. Fraxinus and the Serpent began walking unsteadily towards the wagon, carrying the wounded man between them. Purkin blinked away the blood that had begun to flow from his reopened head wound but he didn't complain about the way he was being handled.

'I'd better tend to him,' Fraxinus said, with a sigh, as they bundled the sergeant over the backboard and into the wagon. 'No point in waking Aulakh up just yet. I know where the woundglue is.'

Mossassor stepped away from the wagon, scanning the horizon before looking up at the sky, which was rimmed with unmoving cloud to the north and west. 'Ssingss wiss sstrange headss won't come in dark,' it opined, although it was mere optimism rather than reasoned judgment. 'Sscared of dragomit-ess. *Very* sscared.'

'We're all very scared,' Fraxinus declared, wishing that he were not so confident of this judgment. 'The problem is that none of us knows what to do in response to our fear – and if we all end up doing the wrong thing, none of us will survive.'

16

L UCREZIA TRIED WITH all her might to remain fully conscious but she only succeeded in turning her ascent into the roof of the forest into a kaleidoscopic torrent of images without coherence or continuity. The threads which lifted her aloft and swallowed her up pinned her arms and swathed her legs, making all effective movement impossible. They coiled around her face too, but not as thickly or as tightly; as soon as they had her secure the choking sensation abated.

When coherency and continuity were returned to her sensations she found herself hanging in mid-air, some distance from the nearest lance-like pinnacle. The sun was setting, and even though the flamestars were bright the light was fading fast. She had no difficulty judging that she was high above the invisible ground, but her surroundings had already become a horrid confusion of glimmers and shadows.

The branches extending from the steepled dendrites were liberally festooned with slack structures like gigantic curtains of spidersilk. They were translucent but they obscured her vision nevertheless. They looked far too weak to hold up a body as heavy as hers but she knew that must be an illusion, for she was surely trapped by exactly such a web.

It proved possible, once she had turned her head this way and that with sufficient insistence, for Lucrezia to free her face from the restraint of all but a few of the clinging threads. She was able to look down then, to see that her body was, as she had suspected, so completely wound around and around that it was virtually cocooned. Her first instinct was to exert the power of her arms and legs to the end of breaking free, but as soon as she had tested the bonds which held her to the extent of being sure that they would not be impossible to break she was seized by a different anxiety. If the threads that held her suspended were as liable to tear as those that had imprisoned her face, it might be direly unwise to start thrashing about lest she should fall into the gloomy depths. She had no way of knowing how far above the ground she was, and she knew full well that whether the ground in question were very hard or very soft it would certainly be dangerous.

She looked up, to see how she was suspended, and from what. It was not an encouraging sight; the strings which extended from her shoulders looked perilously thin and their anchorage was lost in the filmy drapes.

There were still a few sticky threads impeding the movement of her jaw, and others crossing her lips, but she began to work her facial muscles carefully, in the hope of winning free of them. The ligature that had briefly choked her into unconsciousness was no longer in evidence about her neck – a fact for which she was initially profoundly grateful, until she began to wonder what its removal might signify. If it had choked her just sufficiently to render her unconscious and had then withdrawn its grip, that surely signified careful intent.

If that were so, then she must have been taken prisoner – but by what, and with what purpose?

After an interval of patient endeavour she was able to make space enough to speak, and immediately called out, 'Hyry!'

The reply came from above and behind. 'Don't move too rashly, highness! Don't even try to turn. I can see you, but if you struggle to see me you will only make the threads wind more tightly about you . . . and if you try too hard to break free you might fall.'

'Are you hurt, Hyry?' Lucrezia asked. 'Can you see Ssifuss?'

'I've no broken bones,' the trader replied. 'I think Ssifuss escaped, by virtue of being on foot and not on horseback.'

'Did you see what hauled us up here like fishes on a line?'

'All I saw and felt were more and more of those accursed threads falling from above – whole sheaves of them billowing in the air. I suppose they must be nets of a sort, but I couldn't see anything casting them. There are webs aplenty above and below us, presumably spun by creatures of some kind, but I haven't seen a spinner yet – not clearly, at any rate. I've caught glimpses of moving shadows, but I couldn't judge their size or shape. If they're spiders, or something similar, I'm certainly not enthusiastic to make their acquaintance.'

'So much for the wisdom of the Serpent's nose,' Lucrezia said. 'We should have gone the other way.'

'It led into the same forest of needles,' Hyry reminded her. 'These fishers of men are unlikely to restrict their lines to a single stream. If they're part of the great organism whose body lies below us, they presumably have the power to discriminate between their siblings and strangers. If they're opportunist invaders, the man-like things which use these roads presumably have some means of keeping them at bay.'

Lucrezia didn't follow this ominous argument as closely as she should have done. Her mind had become crowded with fearful thoughts of her own. *If these webs were made by spiders, how big must the spiders be? Are we only alive because they prefer their meat fresh?* She looked wildly about, scanning the web which hung above her, whose elements were distorted into a shallow cone by her weight – but there was no sign of any spider lurking at its edge ready to respond to the vibration of her struggles.

'Try to keep still, highness,' Hyry said. 'The webs seem to be alive and responsive to our movements. The individual threads are mostly frail and easily broken but the whole is surprisingly strong – and it's moved to action by every break.'

Perhaps there are no spiders after all, Lucrezia thought. *Perhaps it's only the webs with which we have to contend. But if so, what are they doing with us, and why? How shall we ever get free?*

'Be careful, highness,' Hyry said, her voice dropping to an urgent stage whisper. 'I can see something moving, nearer to you than to me. It's behind you and above you. Keep still, and it might pass you by.'

Lucrezia could think of nothing worse than being told that something was behind her but she mustn't turn round. She tried to do as she was told and keep perfectly still, but she could feel the threads which clustered about her shifting slightly as they strained beneath a moving mass. She couldn't bear it, and tried to turn her head to see what was coming, but she couldn't turn it quite far enough before the threads tightened. Whatever the thing was, it wasn't as big as she had feared; its body seemed no larger than a clenched fist, although there were long legs too, groping in every direction.

She felt a sudden touch at the back of her neck, and then another. She knew that the creature was reaching out to her with tiny feet, one of which was settling on each shoulder. It was steadying itself. She didn't want to meet its eyes, or even to know exactly what it was. She simply wanted to brush it off and get rid of it – to send it hurtling into the dark depths – but her arms were trapped.

She felt a slight prick at the back of her neck, and then a numbness which muffled all sensation. She imagined some obscene mouth-part drawing blood from her veins. She wanted to call out to Hyry, to ask what was happening, but her voice stuck in her throat.

This is the end, she thought. *I'm about to die, drained of my accursed Serpent's blood.*

Then there was a soft thud, and the things resting lightly on her shoulders were whipped away.

She tried to turn yet again, convinced that nothing could be worse than not knowing what was happening, but she couldn't see anything except a much huger shadow emerging from the gloom, and she could only see that from the very corner of her eye.

'Sstill,' hissed a voice that was definitely not Hyry's. 'Ssafe, if sstill.'

'Ssifuss?' she said, but she knew even as the word escaped her lips that it was not Ssifuss. The latter's hiss was far deeper in pitch.

'Sstill,' the Serpent hissed again, so close to her ear that she felt its breath. 'Musst cut, but musst not let you fall. Ssafe, if you trusst. Sstill now.'

The command to be still was not easy to obey. She knew that the Serpent must be cutting the thickest of all the bundles of threads which entwined her: the ones which bound her to the web and held her in position. She had no idea how it had avoided being caught itself, or how it had disposed of the creature which had come to suck her blood – nor, for that matter, had she any idea how it proposed to carry her safely to the ground – but she did know that her salvation would not be easily accomplished.

'Hyry!' she called uncertainly, in a thinner tone than she intended.

'It's all right, highness,' came a similarly faint reply. 'They're not enemies. They mean to set us free, if they can.'

The Serpent reached out an arm so that Lucrezia could see it. She was astonished by its slenderness. Mossassor and Ssifuss had been far from burly, but she judged that this individual must be almost as lean and lightly framed as the winged Salamanders she had seen in the Reef. She couldn't imagine that it could bear her weight, but it wasn't alone. Its companion approached from a different angle, and she was able to watch it sliding nimbly along one of the main threads of the web which hung above her. Once it arrived overhead, though, she was unceremoniously upended, her senses consumed by a sudden vertigo.

She thought for a moment that the two Serpents must have dropped her, and that she must be falling, but that was mere illusion. They held on to her easily enough, although their own positions must have been precarious. Her descent, though by no means without alarms and discomforts, was not unduly precipitous.

When she finally got to the ground she was laid down on her side while one of the slender Serpents attacked the bonds which still enveloped her. It clearly had a certain skill in dealing with them, for it freed her much more easily than she would have expected. The ground on which she had been set was hard and seemingly safe; she assumed that it must be the roadway. She was soon able to sit up and use her own hand to clear the remaining strands from her face.

Only then did she see Ssifuss, waiting nearby. 'Friendss,' it said, when she looked directly at it, but it sounded every bit as surprised and uncertain as Hyry had been. It had not summoned this assistance, and was doubtless astonished to have received it.

It was uncomfortably dark at ground level now that the sun was gone; the webs trailing between the spires cut out a good deal of the starlight. Her eyes had adjusted as well as they could, but it was difficult to see much. She only caught the merest glimpse of the two Serpents which carried Hyry Keshvara down, but she certainly heard them when they arrived on the forest floor, and immediately began chattering away in their own tongue. Ssifuss joined in, and she was left to her own devices, clearing away the remainder of the threads which had confined her.

She managed to get rid of most of them, but not all. Some of those which had attached themselves to her shirt and trousers were now so closely integrated with the loosening weave of the cloth that they seemed to be making a significant contribution to the work of holding the garments together. The remainder had not been so quick to attach themselves to her flesh, but when she ran her fingers over her cheeks she could feel tiny ridges, and she only had to look at the backs of her hands to see what they were; it was as if a number of tiny grey hairs had begun to grow along the surface of the skin.

She put her hand to the back of her neck and found that there was indeed a wound there, oozing blood. As soon as she touched it the protective numbness was lost, replaced by a burning sensation. She wondered what might have become of her had the thing which had started to feed on her been allowed to finish its meal.

She moved to Hyry Keshvara's side, and helped the older woman clear away the remnants of her own cocoon. The abstract pattern engraved by the threads which refused to be cleared was most marked on the trader's cheeks and chin. When Hyry inspected the backs of her own hands she made a small sound of disgust.

'It looks worse on me,' Lucrezia told her drily. 'You've been going grey for years.'

The Serpents – who were five in number, including Ssifuss – were still jabbering away. It was difficult to tell whether the newcomers were interrogating Ssifuss or giving him instructions, but he seemed to be having great difficulty finishing his own sentences without being interrupted.

The kneeling Lucrezia had barely begun to ask Hyry whether she had got a clear sight of her vampiric visitor when they were *all* interrupted. She couldn't make out the forms of the things which descended from the forest roof but she certainly heard the sound of their wings as they zoomed towards the clustered Serpents.

The Serpents scattered, but not in disarray. The four strangers moved purposefully to packs which they had left on the ground before beginning to climb. The whirr of wings built into a sudden storm when the creatures descending from the canopy began to wheel around their heads, but two of the Serpents were quick to strike lights. They each touched the tiny match flames to something which fizzed and spluttered, spraying violent orange sparks in every direction.

The flying sparks burned afterimages like shooting stars across the field of Lucrezia's vision, startling her darkness-accustomed eyes. The resultant confusion, coupled with the fact that she was determined to keep her head down, made it impossible for her to see with any certainty what was happening around her.

Afterwards, she was sure that there had been at least a dozen attackers, but she could not be certain whether they had been bats or giant insects, nor whether they had been the size of a man's head or merely the size of his fist. Whatever the things had been they had zoomed this way and that with bewildering speed, buzzing like angry wasps, swooping again and again at the heads of the Serpents – but the fierce fizzing lights had disturbed them, and made them veer away as quickly as they had come. By the time the fireworks had settled to a steadier glow they were gone again.

The Serpents immediately resumed their rapid speech. It didn't seem to Lucrezia that they were at odds; Ssifuss was nodding its head vigorously now. By the time there was a lull in the conversation Hyry was free and had tentatively regained her feet. Lucrezia stood up too, to find that one of the slender Serpents was looking at her appraisingly.

'From far away,' the Serpent said, looking into Lucrezia's eyes with what she took to be an inquisitive stare, although it had framed the sentence as a statement rather than a question. She looked back in the same appraising manner, noticing that the complexity of the markings dappling its scaly hide had been redoubled by all manner of recent embellishments, whose extent made her infection by a few thin stripes seem very slight indeed.

'Yes,' she answered. 'You too?'

'Musst take care,' the Serpent said. 'Osserss from outsside alsso here. Killerss. Big lissardss. Nassty.'

Lucrezia remembered that Ssifuss had identified some of the marsh herbivores as 'big lizards', but those had not been noticeably nasty. She looked at Ssifuss now, hoping for a fuller explanation.

'Horssess fine,' was all Ssifuss said, 'but besst not ride for now.'

Lucrezia turned back to the other Serpent that had spoken to her. 'Thanks for saving us,' she said. 'You're searching for the garden, aren't you?'

The Serpent nodded its head. 'Iss not good ground,' it said. 'Osserss worsse sstill. Killing, confussion . . . iss hard to get ssrough. Am Lississee. Name Lucressia, Ssifuss ssayss.'

'I'm Lucrezia,' she agreed, pronouncing it carefully although she knew the Serpent had made the best effort it could. 'This is Hyry Keshvara.'

'Why did you rescue us?' Hyry asked bluntly. 'You took quite a risk, making your way across those webs way above the ground.'

Lississee turned its head to face her. 'Are not like *ssem*,' it said, seemingly with considerable feeling. 'Are *friendss*.'

'Which *them* do you mean?' Lucrezia asked. 'The riders who go forth with giant Serpents to bring back captives?'

'Not ssem,' the Serpent replied. 'Mean *flierss* – lissard-massterss. Not like uss – besst forgotten.'

Serpents are supposed to be good at forgetting, Lucrezia recalled. *They have to be.* 'Were those things the fliers you mean?' she asked, waving her hand vaguely to indicate the recently departed creatures.

Lississee shook its head. 'Not *ssem*,' it said impatiently. It groped for the words to frame a better explanation. When it couldn't find them it looked at Ssifuss, but Ssifuss shook its head.

'Mossassor said that we should search for the garden together,' Hyry put in guardedly. 'Humans and Serpents together. Allies, not enemies.' She refrained from making any comment on Ssifuss's initial response to this proposal.

'Iss true,' the slender Serpent was quick to say. 'But ssiss not good earss. Iss *our* ground, but not good. Your earss may be better, even for uss. Wass *promissed*.'

'Mossassor said that, too,' Hyry said. 'Our lore says the same – but no one seems to know who promised what, or when or why.'

'Long time ago,' Lississee said. 'Not eassy to be ssure. Iss myss, but iss alsso truss, ssee? We ssink. Have sseen big flierss, know ssiss ground iss bad even ssough it iss ourss. Myss iss eassier to believe now. You ssearssh too, Ssifuss ssayss. You know about promisse – but ssiss *our* earss. Dangerouss. Besst turn asside, perhapss.' Having finished its long speech the slender Serpent raised itself up a further sem or so, as if it were swelling with pride occasioned by its mastery of the human language.

'We're also searching,' Lucrezia agreed. 'First and foremost, though, we're searching for our friend. He was brought to this ground some time ago. A big man, much bigger than us.'

Lississee shook its head. 'Bad ground here,' it said. 'Not ass bad ass earss ssat produssess flierss, but not good. Ourss, but bad for *uss*. Besst go to *your* ground, we ssink. Ssat iss our plan. Iss promisse – good for uss too.'

Lucrezia couldn't be absolutely certain that she had grasped what the Serpent was trying to get across with all its talk of *our* ground, but she thought that she could see the sense of it.

'If what we call Chimera's Cradle is what you mean by *our ground*,' Lucrezia said carefully, 'that's where we intend to go, eventually – but first we must look for our friend. If there's still a chance of saving him, we have to try.'

Lississee looked back at Ssifuss, who had presumably told it all this already. It shook its head with studious deliberation. 'Iss not ssafe,' it said. 'Killerss ahead of uss. Besst go osser earss.'

'Ssey are afraid,' Ssifuss put in unhappily. 'Have ssaid iss debt but we owe *ssem* debt now. Iss hard. Ssey ssay myss are true – all kindss Sserpentss besst forgotten are remembered here. Ssay *we* are disseasse now, worsse ssan humanss ssough humanss *brought* disseasse. Ssay musst go to besst garden – *human* ground, or ssomessing elsse. I ssay cannot, musst find Andriss. Will go alone, if musst. You tell Mossassor, if he reasshess garden.'

'We're not leaving you, Ssifuss,' Lucrezia said. 'I don't understand the way Serpents calculate their obligations, but Andris has saved my life more than once. I'm grateful to you, Lississee, and to your companions, but I have to go to *this* garden first, no matter how unsafe it might be. *Then* I'll go to Chimera's Cradle, if I can.'

She couldn't judge Ssifuss's reaction to this declaration, but

Lississee looked at all its companions with obvious uncertainty, trying to gauge their reaction. Two of them spoke; the other merely gestured. There didn't seem to be any fierce disagreement.

'Iss ssettled,' Lississee told her. 'Iss besst sstay togesser. All go to garden – but musst beware of killerss. If ground iss . . .' It stopped and looked at Ssifuss, waiting for the stouter Serpent to provide the missing words.

'*Corrupssion and corrossion*,' Ssifuss said, in a manner that was eerily reminiscent of Checuti, from whose lips the Serpent had presumably first heard the oath.

Lississee, of course, did not mean it as an oath. 'If *corrupssion* and *corrossion* iss in ground,' it repeated dubiously, 'ssen may be unssafer ssan before.' It had already turned away to retrieve its pack; its companions were also on the move.

'No way to know,' Ssifuss was quick to add, 'ssat *any* ground iss ssafe. *Your* ground may be jusst ass bad, Lucressia. Even if myss are true, nossing ssafe, nossing ssertain. Chaoss may take *everyssing*.'

It was not a reassuring note on which to continue their journey, but any prospect seemed good to Lucrezia by comparison with the fate she'd just escaped, and her step was as light as could be expected as she went to pick up the rein of her horse.

17

Aᴀs ᴛʜᴇ ʀᴇᴘᴛɪʟᴇs reached out to savage him with their teeth and the daggers they held in their hands, Andris acted. Wishing that he still had hands of his own, he made what efforts he could to grab and hold them both. His fingers had long since dissolved into branches and he had neither elbows nor shoulders, but he had made some progress in the art of coiling his new limbs and he was able to engage his enemy. The sensation of unreality that still haunted him, taunting him with the possibility that all of this was a dream, actually helped him now; in a dream, all things were possible and skills that had never been properly cultivated could nevertheless be feigned.

Alas, the signals which his captive brain sent forth were awkwardly confused. His useless instincts and reflexes had been preserved within his consciousness and the pressure of conflict brought them to the fore, so that his response to the dual assault was reduced to a mad and ill-directed thrashing of his thorny branches. He felt the impacts, and knew he was doing damage, but he also felt the slashing blades and the cutting teeth. He had been insulated from painful sensations for some time but pain surged through him now. Its assault was misinterpreted by his displaced brain, producing the illusion that his old body was being flayed, the skin torn from his arms in great strips while his joints were being levered apart.

The vicious beak-like snouts of his assailants stabbed at his face with reckless brutality. Had he been no greater in stature than his kindred on the slopes Andris might not have been able to defend his eyes but the tendency of his spreading boughs to hang down, by virtue of their weight, compensated in some small measure for his lack of pertinent command over their movement. The reptiles could not force a way through the heavy tangle; its sheer mass and complexity kept them at bay.

Although the pain was intense Andris continued to put what effort he could into the fight. It seemed that his flailing became gradually less random, and hence more effective. It was as if the agonised contact with the attackers called forth reflexes built into his new limbs, which required little in the way of conscious instruction. The growing points twisted and writhed, and the thorns they bore raked the soft tissues about the beasts' nostrils, threatening their madly staring eyes.

Andris tried to force the dangling branches lower still and to increase the violence of their thrashing. He could not tell whether his efforts made much difference to the efficacy of his defences, but he saw that the reptiles were in grave difficulties. Their kin had wrought such awful destruction upon the smaller tree-people that Andris had not expected to find them as small or as frail as they now seemed. He realised that his careless boasts had had more substance than he imagined; he had known that he was still a giant of his kind but had not fully appreciated what that signified. His attackers hurt him, but the wounds they inflicted on his new body were much slighter than the pain implied.

Had the two reptiles continued to act in concert they might have done more damage than they did, but they could not co-ordinate their movements, and they grew rapidly weaker beneath the crushing assaults of his limbs. Suddenly, one was gone altogether.

Andris could not tell whether Arilla had somehow contrived to attract attention away from him, or whether the monster had simply sought an easier target, but once it had departed the one that was left behind had little chance of withstanding the rain of blows. It continued to bite but both its arms were broken and its daggers were useless.

The reptile which had switched targets had no better luck. Arilla had far better command over her multitudinous limbs than Andris did, and as soon as the enemy was within the reach of her thorny tentacles she brought every atom of her strength to bear upon it. Within seconds she had the creature trapped in a compound noose. Both its arms were held fast and she began to draw it up into her lofty crown. It screamed very loudly.

Andris was glad to hear the scream, not least because there

were so many other screams sounding from the slopes below his station, all but a few of which were the screams of tree-people.

The attacker which continued to trouble Andris was in no danger of such expeditious destruction but it was doomed nevertheless. The innate reflexes of his trailing branches were still taking their toll, and the creature was being clumsily battered to death. His limbs paid a heavy price for their untutored tenacity, being badly torn by the teeth mounted in the thrashing jaw, and the bloody sap rained down upon the monster's head like the spray of a fountain.

As Andris's attempts to control his unaccustomed body grew even more frenzied, so did the actions of his assailant. It lost the sight of one eye to a scoring thorn, and then its neck snapped beneath a crushing blow from a heavier limb. No sooner had it fallen to the ground, though, than Andris saw two more closing in on him.

Andris was more confident now that he could repel attacks by creatures such as these, but he knew that they would undoubtedly do a great deal more damage to his new body as well as causing more pain. His first reaction on seeing them was to hope that help might arrive before they reached him. He thought of 'help' in terms of more giant Serpents or imitation men, thinking that the living ground might yet have reinforcements of that kind in hand. When relief quickly came his first thought was that something of this kind had occurred, but he was wrong.

The reptiles which were closing in on him were not drawn away by some counter-attack or struck down from the rear; they were *called* back, like hunting dogs. When he saw the creatures that had summoned the reptiles back, however, Andris knew that he had only been granted a stay of execution. Help had not arrived; the battle had simply moved into a new and nastier phase.

The newcomers must have entered the garden at their leisure, having let their shock troops clear the way for them, but they had moved swiftly enough once they were within it. They were as reptilian as their hounds, but they were much more obviously akin to Serpents. They were nearly as long in the body as Mossassor and Ssifuss but they were very much thinner and their tails were as slender as the whips plied by coachmen. The colours and patterns of their scaly hides were like those of

Serpents and their little loincloths were similar to the one which Ssifuss wore. There were, however, other aspects of their anatomy which were not at all Serpentine. Their heads were humanoid, albeit no bigger than the heads of newborn children. Their mouths were lipped like human mouths, but their snake-like eyes were not human at all and their noses were so flat as hardly to be there.

The most remarkable thing of all, however, was that they were zooming hither and yon like monstrous dragonflies, sustained in mid-air by fast-fluttering insectile wings.

Slim as they were, Andris could not believe that these creatures could fly very far. He observed that they had long legs, well-muscled in spite of their slenderness. He felt sure that they had not overflown the forest which ringed the garden, but it was easy enough to understand that the wings must be useful in the avoidance of the many traps that might be set by living ground.

They were darting about so quickly that it was difficult to estimate their number, but there were more than twenty. Nor was it easy, at first, to see exactly what they were doing while they were shuttling back and forth between the edge of the forest and the garden – and the task was made even more difficult by great gouts of dark grey smoke which were belching forth from at least a dozen of the lowest-situated tree-people. It was their screams which had risen in pitch to fill the air with anguish.

Andris realised, numbly, that the flying creatures were burning the inhabitants of the garden.

This was not an easy task, given that the delicate fliers could only carry small objects. They had also to be careful not to come within easy reach of the straining branches of their victims lest they be caught and their fragile wings instantly broken. Some had to prime their victims with flammable liquid, while others had to deliver the fire. The tree-people were not helpless in the face of such assaults; those which were uninjured could snuff out the flames or shield the flammable substance from them. Alas, it seemed that few of them remained uninjured.

So far as Andris could tell, no human or giant Serpent was still standing. Nor was there any sign of the Watcher, or any being like him. He knew that there were coverts in the rock where dozens of creatures of that modest size might have taken protective shelter, but he could not imagine that any of the garden's attendants would be hiding there while such terrible damage was being done to its sedentary population.

Andris felt both horrified and helpless. For the moment, at least, he was not overwhelmed by awareness of his own peril; it was simply the sight of so much wanton destruction that affrighted him. Even if he had been the Andris of old he would have been deeply affected by the screams of the creatures that were being burned alive; even then he would have known that they had voices and minds and feelings as keen as those of any other sentient creature. The fact that he was one of them now, and had been hurt himself, gave him a better sense of the exact degree of their anguish, but he would in any case have recognised the savage cruelty of the attacking fliers.

The horror did not prevent his being able to see that the fliers were not entirely occupied in destruction. When they had released their makeshift bombs and flew back to the forest edge to collect more they didn't go back empty-handed. Indeed, they imperilled themselves far more than was necessary by swooping very close to a few of the bushes that they had not yet fired, sometimes reaching beneath the lowest branches to snatch up objects from the ground.

He realised that what they were picking up was fruit dislodged from the boughs of the half-human and half-Serpent bushes by the reptiles which had launched the first wave of attacks. He supposed that must be the reason why the first wave of reptiles had not contented themselves with murdering the garden's guardians but had carried on with their frequently suicidal assaults on the tree-people – but it didn't make any sense. He didn't need to be the son of a fruit-farmer to know that the only reason trees produced fruit was to spread their seed; it was essential to a tree that its fruit be gathered and eaten, so that the hard seeds contained within might be distributed far abroad. There was no evident need for these marauders to destroy the trees that produced the fruit; if they wanted it, they would surely be allowed – indeed, gratefully encouraged – simply to gather it and take it away.

'Why?' he bellowed, hoping that Arilla could hear him above the noise. 'Why are they doing this?'

Her reply was partly lost in the general uproar, but he heard the words 'destroyers' and 'nature'. Then he remembered that his judgments of what made sense and what didn't were based on his understanding of earthly life, and that he was in a different world now, where the business of reproduction was far more complicated.

Perhaps, in this world, fruit had a different significance – but if that were the case, why had bronzes sold fruit from this garden to Hyry Keshvara, along with an elaborate account of the conditions required for its successful growth and maturation? Even a nightmare should make better sense than this.

The flying creatures were operating further up the slope now, but they were becoming careless of the methodical pattern of their advance. Andris judged that they were in a hurry to be gone, and that they knew full well that they couldn't destroy every tree in the garden. The fires they had started would not leap from tree to tree in the sullen breeze, and they must be running short of supplies by now. At least three of their number had been struck down by vengeful branches while reaching for fallen fruit – a cost which had to be added to the loss of three in every four of the bigger reptiles. Were they to continue too long with the attack they'd run the risk of reducing their numbers to a point at which they might well be unable to carry their plunder safely home.

This was, of course, a hopeful thought – but Andris soon saw that his own immunity from attack was by no means guaranteed. Indeed, now that the invaders were coming close to the limit of their endeavours their objective seemed to be changing. Instead of attacking the tree-people immediately above those they had most recently fired, several of the Serpentine creatures were now overflying the inhabitants of the upper slopes in order to come at Arilla and himself.

The first few came empty-handed, aiming to pick up fruit – and this purpose made them concentrate their attentions on Arilla, for Andris hadn't yet produced any fruit at all. Arilla's brief contest with the wingless reptile had only shaken loose a few of her overripe fruits, but the two Andris could see stood out starkly red against the mossy soil around her bole, and her lowest branches were so high above the ground that they seemed easy targets.

The appearance was deceptive; as the first of the fliers swooped, Arilla's supple branches struck downwards with

309

deadly effect, smashing the creature's brittle wings. Another followed immediately after, and met the same fate. The killing blows were delivered with such precision that Andris let loose a cry of exultation.

The third flier, which had initially aimed to follow its companions, abruptly changed direction, darting instead for the shadowed space which lay beneath Andris's crown. It was a foolish move, for there was nothing there to justify the risk. Andris struck out with all his might. It was a desperately clumsy blow, which succeeded more by luck than by judgment, but it did succeed. He felt the contact as his thorns ripped through the creature's wing, tumbling it upon the ground. The flier screamed, and he was glad to hear the sound, although its uncanny resemblance to a human scream caused a slight thrill of distress.

The next, alas, did not come empty-handed – and it had seen enough to know the more dangerous enemy. It hurled something deep into Arilla's crown. Andris didn't hear it break, but he knew that it was a fragile container of some kind and he knew what it contained. Another flier followed the first. Although he was awkwardly contorted, his bole corkscrewed around so that he could see what was happening to his companion, Andris tried to reach out with his longest branches. He was hoping to catch the trailing feet or tail of the newcomer, but it cast its flaming brand with deadly accuracy. The foliage with which Arilla sought to shield herself must have sustained damage of its own; the liquid in which she had ben doused caught fire.

Arilla immediately began to thrash her branches wildly, and would surely have been able to beat out the fire had not other fliers come with fresh supplies of the liquid.

Andris strained to reach them, but he couldn't do it until Arilla struck one a glancing blow and sent it careering into range, whereupon he slashed it across the neck and the tail. Such blows would not have troubled a more robust creature, but the flier's bones were so light and Andris's limbs so heavy that it fell to the ground, badly broken.

The rest turned and fled, leaving Arilla's produce untouched – but one picked up two of Andris's broken twigs as it zoomed away, complete with ruined flowers.

Within a minute the invaders had utterly disappeared; the

forest surrounding the garden had swallowed them up. The legacy of their visit was mapped out in a host of continuing screams uttered by a host of burning bushes, not one of which had yet been rendered silent.

The loudest scream of all was Arilla's, and it cut through Andris like a knife, not merely by virtue of its violence but also because it filled him with a sense of his own absolute helplessness. He was stronger now than he had ever been before – and no matter what Seth had said to him in the wilderness of his dreams, he had begun to entertain hopes and fantasies of authentic immortality – but he was rooted in the earth, unable to cross the twenty mets which separated him from his nearest neighbour . . . and he was utterly impotent to help her as the flames took hold of her all too frail flesh.

He could not even face her squarely, for the twist in his torso was becoming unbearable. He had no alternative but to turn away.

The pain was already departing from his strange new body, reflexively anaesthetised; he fought against the somnolence that replaced it, but it dragged him down regardless, further and further into the dark vortex of his reality-saturated dream, until he was utterly lost beyond sight and beyond hearing.

The only scream which echoed in him now was his own, and that one had never been voiced in actual sound. It was a private and secret thing, more phantom than actuality, more fugitive fancy than inner voice – but it was real, and it was honest.

18

THE BACK OF the wagon was now so unreasonably crowded, thanks to Purkin's arrival, that Fraxinus could not resist the temptation to saddle up one of the spare horses and ride ahead. After so many days stuck inside or on the driver's bench of the lumbering cart there was a delicious sense of freedom in the relative independence. He had the responsibility of scouting the way, warning Ereleth about possible pitfalls, but that was a small price to pay.

The broken cloud in the south-west had hardly moved at all and the day was as bright as the one before, but the rising sun was behind him and he was untroubled by the heat or the light. The two dragomites also moved in front of the wagon, but they kept their distance – the horse he rode was still very nervous of the warriors and became fractious if they came too close.

There was no sign whatsoever of the half-human horsemen who had been following the cart ever since they had been defeated in the skirmish; if they were still in attendance, Fraxinus supposed, they had either dropped back below the eastern horizon or hidden themselves in the glare of the early sun. In either case, he was no longer frightened of what they might do – it was what lay ahead that intrigued him now.

There was no mistaking the Silver Thorns. Like huge needles they extended high into the sky, taller by far than the upper limits of the coppery networks that were vaguely sketched around their bases. The tips of the Thorns caught the light in such a way that they appeared to be on fire. Even at this distance Fraxinus could see that there was a break in the curving line of the great palisade at the point where the Thorns were most densely clustered and he had already begun to think of it as a gate: the gateway to the Gauntlet of Gladness. No matter how vastly the Nest of the Phoenix had expanded, the Gauntlet was still there to be run, and he had every reason to hope that it still ran all the way to the site of Idun – to Chimera's Cradle and the Pool of Life.

Fraxinus was wary enough not to become overconfident, and anxious enough to fear that there might yet be trouble ahead and fighting to be done, but his determination remained unwavering. This was still the greatest adventure of his life, and in his reckoning it would be a triumph outmatching any achieved in Xandria for as many generations as were still remembered. He could have wished for a better-disciplined band of followers, but he wasn't altogether displeased with the ragged band he had. It included a queen, a giant and a general, all of whom could be relied upon to add spice to the tale if and when it could be told in awed tones in the corn exchanges of Xandria and the taverns on the waterfront beneath the citadel wall.

Fraxinus immersed himself in these pleasant fantasies to the extent that it was Vaca Metra and not he – although his station was slightly higher than hers – who first caught sight of the approaching riders. His eyes were better than hers in this kind of light and he should have been able to identify them before she did, but it was also she who sent up a cry saying that they were friends.

He watched in some surprise as the dragomite Metra was riding accelerated its pace to the maximum, while the one whose injured leg had been patched up by Phar struggled to keep up. A full minute passed before he realised that they had sensed a nest-sister; by that time he had recognised the second rider and had urged his own horse forward into a fast trot. Mercifully, the figured stones exacted no penalty for his hurry. His gladness waned, however, when he saw what condition the riders were in. They were not wounded in the way that Purkin had been wounded, but they had obviously suffered.

The last time Fraxinus had seen Checuti the thief-master's face had still been round and soft, his beard and curly hair adequately groomed. Now the man was positively lean, and his face was covered with scars and peculiar lesions; his eyes seemed to have sunk deeper into his head and his black hair had run wild. Jume Metra had never been anything but thin but when he had last seen her she had been stern and stubborn; now she looked like a mere phantom and her skin was mottled as if by

313

fungal hyphae. Her expression was unnaturally vacant, as if she were hardly conscious. Vaca Metra's condition had not deteriorated nearly as badly, and Fraxinus couldn't help wondering what judgment she would make as she ran to meet her sister, who had already dismounted to greet the limping dragomite.

Checuti saluted him with attempted flamboyance. 'The prince of thieves welcomes the prince of merchants,' he said, in a croaky voice, as the two mounts came together and drew to a halt.

Fraxinus extended his hand and Checuti took it; they were old friends now, although Fraxinus knew how probable it was that Checuti had grown rich in Xandria partly at his own expense. Fraxinus saw that the thief's hands were also damaged. Checuti noticed his reaction.

'It's not as bad as it looks,' the thief-master told him hoarsely. 'We were badly scratched while forcing our way through the Soursweet Marshes, and the scars flared up again as we travelled around the Reef. Wherever we went there were things avid to stick to our skin, but they don't hurt and they don't seem to be poisonous. I'm not the handsome youth I once was but I'm not yet a wreck of a man.'

'Are there no others?' Fraxinus was quick to ask. 'Did only two of you survive the journey through the Soursweet Marshes?'

'To the best of my knowledge,' Checuti assured him, a little less hoarsely, 'the only one who was certainly killed was the soldier Herriman. I fear the worst for Andris Myrasol, and I fear that those who went after him might have delivered themselves into dire danger, but when I saw them last the princess, Hyry Keshvara and the Serpent Ssifuss were all alive and as well as could be expected. Jume Metra and I have come by the route I deemed less dangerous, but it proved a little harder than I expected – I hope with all my heart that theirs was less daunting than it seemed. I don't suppose, by the way, that those creatures with the bodies of men and the heads of mocking apes are our friends?'

'What have you seen?' asked Fraxinus, seized by a sudden chill.

'Ah! So you *have* met them. They rode into the grand avenue little more than two hours ago, just as dawn broke. Fortunately, Metra and I were already in hiding, having been pursued by long-legged crocolids and menaced by giant snakes with scales like gems. If we could spare the time to collect them, a dozen snakeskins like that would probably a fetch a small fortune in Xandria – but the biggest of the monsters have fangs a foot long, and I didn't care to test the proposition that they might not be poisonous.'

'The creatures with ape-like heads, or others like them, were behind us,' Fraxinus said. 'They fell upon Purkin's men during the night. Perhaps they thought it best to get ahead of us, as soon as they were certain where we were heading, to set an ambush . . . but it's possible that they have business of their own. They rode into the grand avenue, you say? You're being sarcastic, I assume.'

'Only slightly,' Checuti said. 'Along the curve of the Reef the Silver Thorns grow singly, mingling with all manner of strange stony growths. Their coppery kin cannot seem to hold their branches straight at all, coiling in every direction with determined eccentricity. Along this strange road, however, the Thorns are unchallenged in their empire and they grow in measured lines, like ranks of guardsmen. There are other roads running towards the centre but they're winding and they follow the undulations of the crumpled ground. The road to Chimera's Cradle is different. It's by no means as straight as the arrow to which Prince Myrasol's map likened it, but its curves are gentle and it's flat. The Silver Thorns are arranged so neatly to either side of it that they form a kind of hedge – or perhaps I should call it a broken wall, for there's precious little thereabouts which bears the slightest resemblance to earthly vegetation.'

'The Spangled Desert is much the same,' Fraxinus told him. 'All its trees are made of stone, studded with gems – and for what it's worth, I've seen far too many jewelled snakes to think their skins worth gathering, no matter how big they might be. So the gap ahead really is a gateway, giving access to a road of sorts. There are other roads, you say?'

'Not built by any human hand,' Checuti was quick to say, 'nor any Serpent hand either – but yes, they're certainly roads of some sort. The living ground is replete with pitfalls and quicksands, and many of its stony hairs and spines are equipped with trawling nets, but it takes care to make safe passages across its face. The ground *intends* creatures like you and me – not to mention Ssifuss and Mossassor – to trek across it, provided only that we will go exactly where it wants to lead us. What do you read into that, O mighty merchant adventurer?'

'It's interesting,' Fraxinus admitted.

'Indeed it is,' Checuti replied. 'I've been some little way along the walled highway, and it seems as safe as any road in Xandria – although it has its fair share of bandits and scavengers, if I took the right inference from what I saw a little while ago. It's almost as if Chimera's Cradle were determined to make provision for its visitors, providing what protection it can from the incursions of rival ground. Alas, my long experience as a thief and patron of thieves tells me to beware of routes which are overly inviting; those who try hardest to tempt unwary visitors are usually those who have no intention of letting them leave again.'

'You and I have lived in different worlds,' Fraxinus told him. 'In mine, it is those with goods to trade who make great efforts to welcome visitors in – and see them from the premises politely, with effusive hopes that they will come again.'

'Have you met anyone who has come out of Chimera's Cradle with such generous invitations ringing in their ears?' Checuti asked. When Fraxinus made no reply, he added: 'Neither have I.'

The wagon had arrived now, and there were others anxious to talk to Checuti. Merel Zabio had already leapt down and was running towards him.

Perhaps, after all, this is a world made for thieves and not for merchants, Fraxinus thought. *It would be a tragedy, if so – for even thieves thrive best where merchants establish successful commerce.*

Merel Zabio was followed by Mossassor, as anxious for news of Ssifuss as Merel was for news of Andris Myrasol. Checuti had got down from his horse and Fraxinus dismounted too. He listened to the brief second-hand account which Checuti gave of Myrasol's heroism in the Soursweet Marshes and the Great Reef, and of the sterling support rendered by Ssifuss, but when he had heard enough he went to the place where Jume Metra and her sister were still locked in physical embrace. They drew apart as he approached, but they stayed between the two dragomite warriors, who seemed to be holding their massive jaws more proudly erect than they had for many a day.

'I'm glad to see you safe,' Fraxinus said to the mound-woman, although he wasn't sure that *safe* was an accurate judgment of her condition. 'Your warriors have saved our lives a dozen times; I only wish the whole troop had survived.' He was being slightly insincere, because he knew that if the whole troop had survived, and the workers with them, the warriors would have gone about their own business long ago. They were with him only because they had no nest, and he couldn't help being anxious that the situation might now have changed.

Whether Jume Metra guessed the underlying nature of his concern or not she was quick enough to give him the relevant information. 'All the eggs are gone,' she reported mournfully. 'All hope is gone with them.' There was no time for the first statement to put his mind at rest before the second disturbed it again.

'What will you do now?' he asked.

She met his gaze, in a way that neither she nor any of her sisters had ever done before. Her ravaged face and dazed expression still displayed a little of the haughty determination that he remembered. 'We are together,' she said. 'There is no nest, but we are together, and we are warriors still. We will fight together, die together. It is all that remains.'

'I still hope that we might not die,' Fraxinus said mildly. 'I still hope that we might reach the heart of the territory which lies before us and ride back out again, richer than before – if only in the currency of wisdom.'

'We are warriors,' Jume Metra repeated, although the faintness of her voice belied the import of the words. 'We do not lie down and die, like tired workers. We fight *until* we die. We are together, and we will go on together, until the end. You fought for us, and we do not forget.'

Fraxinus had a strange suspicion that she was rationalising: carefully converting her intentions into the jargon of the hive, the code of the warrior-women. Whether she was doing it for Vaca Metra's benefit or her own he couldn't tell, but felt certain that she was more human – and more ordinary in her humanity – than she cared to confess.

'Thank you,' he said. 'Had we not been on the same side, we'd all have failed, whatever happened at the bridge. While we're still together, I really do believe we have a chance. The road to

317

Chimera's Cradle lies open before us. If the half-humans have set a trap for us, we'll be ready for them. They can't stop us now.' He wished that he felt as brave and as confident as he sounded, or was trying to sound. The meeting was a happy one, but it would have seemed a better omen by far had the two of them not been so thin and so disfigured – and infinitely better had Hyry Keshvara and Princess Lucrezia been in the company. He knew that Ereleth would want a much fuller account of the princess's fate, and he couldn't help wondering how Keshvara and Checuti had ever consented to a parting of their ways – but for the time being, the thief-master was fully occupied.

Fraxinus returned to the wagon, leading Jume Metra's gladly abandoned horse. Intensive negotiations had already been carried out to decide who was going to ride in the wagon and who was going to take the horses, now that there were more mounts available. Shabir had claimed one, on the grounds that he was the most experienced cavalryman in the party – or, at least, the most experienced who still had the use of both his arms. Aulakh Phar had claimed another, simply because he wanted to be in a good position to observe the Silver Thorns. Fraxinus refused to give up the third, for the same reason.

When they finally set off again Fraxinus felt unexpectedly glad to be riding three abreast, with Phar on his right hand. It would have been even better had Hyry Keshvara been at his left – and he still couldn't quite figure out why she wasn't, although Checuti had added a few more details to his story – but for the time being he was prepared to settle for what he had, and to focus his attention on the road ahead.

'Now, at last, it begins,' he said to Phar. 'I had hoped to arrive here in far greater strength than this and with far better resources, but at least we're here.'

'There are others ahead of us,' Phar replied, in a darker and more contemplative tone. 'We're not the first to have come this way.'

'We've defeated them once, and at least we know they're there,' Fraxinus pointed out. 'If they've any sense, they'll leave us alone. For all they know, Dhalla is still invincible and we're stronger by three than we were before.'

'I didn't mean *them*,' Phar said. 'I meant all the Serpents and Salamanders, and all the other humans who've passed through that strange gateway in the last few years. We've come from the far north, and at least two years passed before the news reached us that the Dragomite Hills were passable. *We're* just beginning, but the Time of Emergence has already passed its climax and may well be running to its end. We'd be fools to think that we're the first to travel this wide-open highway, and Checuti's right to remind us that we haven't met a single soul who's travelled it in the other direction – unless it was those monkey-men. If *they* came from Chimera's Cradle, it wasn't wisdom they brought with them but blind and ugly bloodlust.'

'He's right,' said Shabir. 'This is suicide.'

'So why are you with us?' Fraxinus wanted to know. 'Why is Checuti with us?' Even as he asked the question, he knew what the answer would be; he'd already heard it, put in somewhat bolder terms by Jume Metra.

'It's like any other suicide,' the general said. 'Suicide is what you have left when all your other options are exhausted. We all know that we're never going to get back home – even those of us who still have homes to go to.'

'We don't know anything of the kind,' Fraxinus contradicted him. 'All we know is that we've come this far, and have a way still to go. We're not the kind of people who give up – not one of us. We're all warriors, each after his or her fashion.' He was obliged to say so, because he was the leader, but it wasn't a lie. Like Jume Metra, he *was* a warrior, in the best sense of the word. So were they all. They were together, and they would go on together, even if they came forth changed . . . or never came forth at all.

19

LUCREZIA WAS RELIEVED when she first saw bright daylight shining ahead. The density of the 'forest' through which they were walking had become oppressive. It was not completely dark in spite of the thickness of its tangled canopy, because there were extensive patches of luminous moss everywhere, but their light was not in the least comforting. It seemed to her to be a diseased light, reminding her of a phrase she had once heard quoted: the phosphorescence of putrescence.

Despite their vitreous hardness, all the elements of the forest seemed to be plastered with decay, like the crumbling walls of some long-abandoned hovel as decrepit as those she had seen in the northernmost reaches of the Narrow Land. Although she still thought of it as a 'forest', the region through which they were passing had come to resemble a network of tunnels hollowed out in some solid substrate – but it was not like a dragomite nest, whose tunnel walls had been smooth and warm. Nothing here was smooth, and nothing was warm. The body of the dragomite queen had maintained its duty of protection even as she sickened and died, but this place was as remote as it could be from the heart of whatever vast creature dwelt beneath her feet and decay was hardly kept at bay at all.

Where obvious signs of active life remained they were hazardous ones; two of Lississee's companions had been seized by pitfall traps and it had taken considerable exertion to free them. Had they not had Ssifuss and Hyry in their company they might have been lost or severely injured, but Ssifuss was far stronger than its slender cousins and Hyry was cleverer with her hands.

In view of all this, and the anxiety caused by the proximity of the threads which constantly threatened to add to the accumulation of their superficial parasites, it was hardly surprising that

Lucrezia felt her spirits lifting at the thought of stepping out into the sunlight again. Unfortunately, her pleasurable anticipation was short-lived. Almost as soon as she passed into the daylight she was rudely seized by a horror more urgent than any she had felt in the leprous depths.

There was still smoke drifting in the lazy air of the garden, although the fires had burned out long ago. The acrid dryness stung her nostrils but couldn't entirely suppress the sweeter taint of dead flesh.

She thought at first that the dead flesh in question belonged to the corpses that lay on every side, every one half reabsorbed into the patient ground as if slowly sinking in a viscous green sea, but then she realised that these were not the only casualties of whatever catastrophe had visited this place.

At the core of every burned-out tree a blackened trunk still stood upright, denuded of its foliage and all but a few of its branches – and within the cracked and charred bark there was flesh of a different kind: flesh which could still leak fluids, even now. Outlined in the blackened bark there were faces: human faces with mouths agape with interrupted agony, and a few Serpent faces with forked tongues dangling from narrower cavities.

Lucrezia knew that she should not have been so astonished. After all, she had seen such chimeras before and she had expected to see them here. She had known exactly what kind of a garden she was searching for – but nothing she had seen or known could have prepared her for the appalling sight of the burned-out trees, many of whose human parts still lived in spite of the injuries they had sustained. The eyes of the nearest one were still open, but they could not see; they had been burned blind. Even so, the eyes shifted slightly in her direction. The presence of newcomers had been sensed in some other way, but the stricken tree-creature made no sound; either its lungs had been seared and crisped or it was past caring.

Lucrezia stared at the blind eyes and blackened body for a minute or two, calculating the enormity of that individual tragedy. Then she lifted her head to look up the slope at the higher ground, multiplying the individual tragedy by ten, and then by fifty. The horror of it wasn't greatly ameliorated by the observation that there were as many trees still clad in resplendent green as there were blackened hulls, or that the proportion of living foliage was higher the further up the slope her eyes wandered. A few of the survivors still bore frail white flowers; others carried a fugitive cargo of bright red fruit.

She looked higher still, at the crown of the hill, where the tallest trees of all grew in a horribly ill-matched pair. The first was as black as charcoal, with dead branches protruding in every direction like a thistle's protective spines; the second was very green indeed, with a trunk paler than any other in the garden, the colour of newly minted brass. It was the colour that focused her attention; that was all she needed to see. It didn't matter that the awful knowledge which sprang into her mind was hardly credible, given the limited time that had elapsed since the battle in the Reef; she *knew*.

She immediately began to run, careless of any treachery of which the mossy ground might easily be capable. She hurdled the half-digested corpses of humans, giant Serpents and elongated crocolids. She didn't stop until she could position herself directly in front of his closed eyes and shout 'Andris!' at the top of her voice. She could see the cast of his features now, and in spite of the fact that they had been reconfigured and redistributed she could recognise him in them. The widened mouth was still *his* mouth, the massive brow *his* brow.

When he didn't respond she shouted his name again, and then again – and she kept on shouting, even when Hyry Keshvara tried to calm her.

In the end, the shouting had its effect. Whatever new senses he might have acquired, he still had hearing.

After his sleepy eyes had opened he stared at her blearily for thirty seconds or more – so long that she was forced to wonder whether he would be able to recognise her own strangely decorated features, or whether he were still capable of speaking her name.

In the end, though, he said: 'Lucrezia? Is that you?'

'Yes,' she said, 'I have a few extra lines in my face, but it's still my face.'

'I know *that*,' he said thickly. 'The question is, are you just another figment of my dream, or is it *really* you? It can't *really* be you, can it?'

'It's really me,' she assured him, although she wasn't sure what she could do to prove it if she were asked.

'Keshvara?' he said, looking past her. 'Is that Ssifuss coming up the hill?'

Lucrezia didn't bother to confirm these observations. She was looking down at the cadaver which was being sucked by painfully slow degrees into the ground beneath Andris's amazing crown. She could not see its face but its body looked like a Serpent's – albeit a Serpent much thinner than Lississee and equipped with crumpled wings. The fact that Lississee had said that they had seen 'big fliers' and that this was 'our ground' suddenly took on new significance.

'Lucrezia?' Andris said again. 'Why did you come here?'

'We came to rescue you,' she said, without any inflection in her voice. 'It seems that we came far too late. I'm sorry for that.'

Ssifuss had joined them now. Lississee and the other Serpents had stayed on the lower slopes, making some investigation of their own.

'Corruption and corrosion,' Hyry rasped. It seemed that she was letting out a breath which had been caught in her throat for a painfully long time. 'It's not possible. It takes a lifetime to grow a tree as huge as that.'

'Not if it's planted in living ground, apparently,' Lucrezia murmured.

'Ground full of sudden life, overanxious for expression,' Andris added, his voice strangely uncertain. It was as if his consciousness were wavering on the edge of delirium. 'Perhaps I brought this on myself, by robbing the garden of its other stock. Those battles we fought for Venerina's deists . . . in the end, they only made my dream more vivid, my metamorphosis more expansive. *You* must see the irony in that, princess. You've waited a long time to see me like this, but you're a princess after all – the world itself bows to your whims.'

'Don't,' Lucrezia said. She fought back tears: tears of anger; tears of bitterness; tears of pain. She hated herself for having wanted this. She hated the world for having pandered to her whim with such malevolent assiduity.

'Ssorry,' said Ssifuss. It had been long enough in human company to inject some manifest feeling into the word. 'Sshould have *tried*. Ssought besst to get help. Ssorry.'

'I think I'm sorry too,' Andris replied distantly, 'but I can't be sure. It's as difficult to separate the true feelings from the false ones as it is to separate reality from the dream. I'm not even sure it makes sense to try. I'm not what I was. I don't know what I *am* exactly, but I'm not what I was. This isn't just me as I was, imprisoned within the flesh of some magical tree as if by witchcraft – this is me as I'm becoming. Different body, different mind. I'd explain it to you, if you could only wait until I've explained it to myself.'

Lucrezia wanted to assure him that she'd wait, but she couldn't.

'What happened here?' Keshvara wanted to know.

'Ah,' said Andris. 'Start simple, get complicated later. Maybe I'll be able to explain that, too, when I've had time to gather my faculties. First the dancing crocolids came, cutting and biting – then the flying lizards, hurling firebombs. Considering that they don't make much use of fire in the ordinary way of things, Serpents' kin seem remarkably fond of deploying it as a weapon. Pity we never got to Salamander's Fire – *Serpents'* fire has done us some really bad turns of late. Not you, Ssifuss – not even your kin, in the narrower sense of the term. The kinds of kin you tried so hard to forget. Forgetting was probably a mistake, you know. My kind haven't done so well remembering, but forgetting wasn't the right course either. Maybe there's a balance to be struck, but I doubt that anyone's struck it yet. Not here . . . not on *this* ground.'

'He's raving,' Hyry whispered in Lucrezia's ear. 'This would have driven anyone mad.'

Andris's metamorphosis hadn't made his hearing any worse. 'I'm merely taking on my fair share of the *world's* madness,' he retorted. 'I'm not raving. It all makes sense, somehow. I don't say that we'll like the sense it makes, but there's a logic to it. Given the time, I'm sure I could figure it all out – and it's not impossible that I'll have the time, now. Even if the flying Serpents come back, or if others come in their wake – even if I'm chopped down and cut into firewood and burned to ash – I'm part of the dream now, a figment of the dweller's imagination. I'm not going to die. I'm not immortal in any simple sense, but I'm part of this now and I'll continue to be part of it, somehow. Even if the Serpents' war goes to the fliers and not to the giants,

324

I'll be part of it. So will you, princess. They may not plant a tree in your soft flesh, or suck you into living ground and devour you flesh and bone, but there was something in your blood not human long before the spiders began spinning webs about your lovely face.' His voice broke, perhaps because his lungs had caught a gout of acrid smoke drifting from his dead companion.

'Don't try to say more just now,' Lucrezia said, stepping forward and raising a hand in a gesture that seemed empty even to her.

He ignored her. 'We've never been *entirely* human,' he told her hoarsely. 'Not since the day our forefathers came into the world, nor for a long while before that. Before this tale began, though, we were *only* human. Not any more. This world's not like the one that gave us birth, and what the fugitive lore calls the world of dreams is actually the world outside the dream, the world not yet gathered *into* the dream. We're in it now. We're in the dream and in the game, and even though the deists have it inside out and upside down when they appeal to *thou who changest not*, they've sensed something of the *real* reality. I wish I could go to Chimera's Cradle now, but I can't. It can't be very far away from here. I'm sure that *you* can reach it now, given that you've come so far.'

'Iss not . . .' Ssifuss began, but Andris had built up momentum now and he wasn't about to be interrupted.

'I know you've done more than anyone could possibly have expected, simply by coming after me,' he went on, 'and I thank you all for that, but there's nothing to be done for me now, and there's an urgency in matters that I don't quite understand. It seems that the day of the gatherers is done and the day of the killers is here. If you're to get to the heart of the matter, you shouldn't delay. I wish you would, because I really would like to understand. If I'm to be a tree, and to live again, I'd rather be the Tree of Knowledge than any common thing. Always my trouble, you see – never able to forget that I was once a prince, never able to accept that my size was just an accident of fate. Always ambitions, always delusions . . . and now, the greatest delusion of all, capped by the greatest ambition. Dreaming, a man can be anything; dreaming, everything makes sense; dreaming, nothing is absurd . . . I'd like to ask one thing of you if I may? Will you

325

grant me one boon, princess, as princesses in travellers' tales always have the power and the grace to do?'

The torrent of words had been too much; Lucrezia had long since lost a firm grip on the sinuous thread of argument that might have connected it all together. All she could say was: 'What?'

'Come back and tell me what you found. I'd like to know. I can't pretend that I *need* to know, but I'd like to. Perhaps I *do* need to – for myself, at least.'

'This may be a stupid question,' Hyry Keshvara said, deliberately cutting across Lucrezia's half-formed answer, 'but is there any way the process can be turned back? Is there any way you can be changed back into what you were before?'

'No,' said Andris. 'The ground is capable of many things, and perhaps it would be capable even of that, if it had intelligence of its own to guide its energies, but it doesn't. It has a mind of sorts, and a purpose of sorts, but it has no voice and it can't answer pleas or questions. Perhaps I should regret that more than I do, but the nature of the dream makes it difficult. It's not really a dream, of course – it's just that my mind is changing along with my body – but I've no other way to think or talk about it. I do miss my old self, but I can't hate my new self as much as my old self would have done. I've been a wanderer all my life, you see. Essentially rootless. Going on and on without having any destination in mind, without having any goal to achieve. This is just one more step – one more leap into the unknown. Except, of course, that this time it really *is* the unknown, not just one more city and one more jail, one more infinity of rickety ceilings and rotting walls.'

'You don't have to say it all now,' Lucrezia said. 'There's time. We need rest. There's time.'

'There isn't,' Andris assured her. 'Whatever else there is, there isn't *time*. The climax is hurrying upon us. Fate is bearing down on us all. That's not as bad as it sounds, mind. Fate isn't capable of kindness, any more than the Serpents' nest into which I've strayed is capable of kindness, but it isn't vicious either. I think I can be what I'm becoming, and if I can't get to like it I can certainly get to a state of mind from which the whole notion and function of liking has been banished. You can do that in a dream, you see, and this is *the* dream. You don't have to cry for me, or agonise over the fact that you didn't save me from this. You don't owe me anything now and you never did . . . but if you'd like to do something for me, come back when you've been to Chimera's Cradle and tell me what's going on there. I really would like to know. Perhaps, then, I'll be able to explain to you exactly what the state of the world is, and what will become of it. I can so nearly see it all, but seeing isn't enough. You have to be able to *reason it through*. Sorry, Keshvara, you're right. I *am* raving. I shouldn't.'

Hyry was startled by that admission. 'Don't worry about it,' she replied defensively.

Lississee and the other Serpents arrived then, having completed their examination of the lower slopes.

'Iss not sso bad,' Lississee said. 'Not for uss. Not ssafe, but weak. Ssafe *enough*, if flierss do not return.'

'They got what they came for,' Andris said.

'What did they come for?' Lucrezia asked, before anyone else could.

'Fruit,' said Andris. 'Fruit, and wanton destruction. They don't want the fruit to reproduce the ground, of course; they want to appropriate its creativity for their own ground. It's Serpent against Serpent hereabouts – different elsewhere, I expect.'

'These winged things are the adult form of the Serpents, then?' Hyry Keshvara asked. 'Not the giant Serpents.'

'Boss,' said Lississee.

Lucrezia knew that it meant 'both'. She understood what it meant, now, when it referred to this place as 'our ground'. There was more than one kind of metamorphosis that the 'juvenile' Serpents might undergo; perhaps there were dozens. That was what Serpents had to be so good at 'forgetting': the urgings of their flesh which tried, at least on occasion, to seduce them into undesirable maturity – undesirable not merely by virtue of its stupidity but by virtue of the involvement of the adult forms in an eternally violent struggle for existence.

'Is there anything we can do for you now Andris?' she asked. 'Is there anything you want that we can provide?'

The expression in his eyes was hard to read, even though his face was still recognisable as his and was not as grotesque a caricature of his former self as she or Hyry would have been had they been transformed into trees. He had always had the capacity to be enigmatic, though; all ambers had that, at least in golden eyes.

'I don't know,' he said, after a slight pause. 'I know it seems absurd, but I really don't know. Dreaming is so easy, it's hard to focus on such trivial matters as desire.'

It could be worse, Lucrezia told herself. *He might be a blackened corpse. He might be consumed by anguish and terror. He might be genuinely mad, not capable of thought at all. Are we any better off, given that the alien ground is making inroads into our flesh too? In spite of everything, we're on the same side still . . . and in the same boat. He's right; when you're adrift in a world as strange as this, it's hard to focus on such trivial matters as desire.*

Had it not been so difficult, she might have desired to be anywhere else but here; as things were, it wasn't easy even to feel her own exhaustion.

'I'll come back if I can,' she promised, meaning every word. 'Whatever happens, when I've been to Chimera's Cradle I'll do everything I can to come back. Depend on it.'

20

ANDRIS DIDN'T KNOW how he ought to feel about the arrival of Lucrezia, Ssifuss and Hyry Keshvara in the garden. He still wasn't entirely convinced that they weren't mere figments of his imagination, conjured up to give him solace in the aftermath of the garden's devastation. In some ways, though, the possibility of their being real seemed even more ominous than the possibility that he was utterly lost in a fantasy.

He knew that he couldn't be sure that Hyry and Lucrezia would be safe here, even if he could provide a refuge of sorts within the shelter of his spreading crown. He had told the truth when he spoke of being reconciled to his new state of being, but he certainly didn't want them to suffer the same fate. On the other hand, he had a suspicion that if and when they went away they would be heading into even greater danger. He was convinced that the Time of Emergence had reached the crisis of its fever, and that this was the most dangerous interval of all. Then again, he was well aware of the fact that the marks engraved on their faces suggested that it might already be too late – that they had already been invaded by alien flesh whose gradual possession of their own might be irremediable.

Now that Arilla had been silenced, if not actually destroyed, Andris felt that he was effectively alone within the garden. Keshvara had counted sixty survivors among the tree-people on the slopes, but none was in a position to hold a comfortable conversation with him, and none showed the least inclination to try. According to Hyry, most of them seemed to have surrendered the habit of intelligent speech, perhaps having failed to retain it during their initial transmogrification; they could scream and they could mutter, but they did not talk sense.

The slender Serpents who had joined forces with Lucrezia and Ssifuss had found water and food that was safe to eat in the coverts where their giant kin had been accommodated, so they were in no distress. They had been able to make themselves comfortable lodgings in the caves, untroubled by any unwelcome company. If any of the garden's mobile servants had survived the massacre they had gone away before Lucrezia's party arrived.

While Lucrezia and her companions were making their temporary camp they left Andris to his own worries, but the princess returned soon enough. By then he had managed to bring his thoughts into a more orderly train and he felt as fully awake as he had been at any time since first being taken prisoner. He was determined to control the waywardness of his dream, to discipline himself so thoroughly that she would be able to believe that he was essentially unaltered and not to be pitied. He wasn't quite sure why he felt that he owed her that, but he did.

The princess told him about the wound she had sustained in the second battle, and how the combination of the woundglue and the doctor's treatment had put her into a deep but intermittent sleep for several days. She told him about her meeting with Jume Metra, her reunion with Checuti, and her delight in the discovery that Keshvara had been among the liberated prisoners. She told him that Checuti and Metra had gone to meet Fraxinus, having been assured by flying Salamanders that he was on his way. She also told him what Hyry Keshvara had told her about Merel Zabio's recovery from *her* wounds, and their journey to Antiar.

'Fraxinus still has two dragomite warriors and Dhalla,' the princess told him, by way of summation. 'It seems very probable that Jacom Cerri, Aulakh Phar and Merel were able to go south with the bronze Amyas, protected by his mercenaries, and that they rejoined Fraxinus. If it's still possible to reach Chimera's Cradle by the Gauntlet of Gladness, they will surely do it.'

'All good news,' Andris agreed. 'You are heroes, every one. Who could have imagined that we would see so much, and survive so much? What a tale you and Keshvara will have to tell when you return to Xandria!' He did not think it politic to say *if*. She was as reluctant to complain about the infection disfiguring her features as he was to weep and wail over his own metamorphosis.

'We have a way to go yet,' she said. 'Whatever Lississee says about Chimera's Cradle being better ground than this, we might not find a welcome there. If we do meet Fraxinus again, there'll be no question about our coming back to give you news. Fraxinus will want to see you himself, and so will Merel . . .'

She left it there, waiting for his reaction.

'Yes,' he said, with carefully calculated sobriety. 'It would be good to see Merel again. I ought to explain to her that this isn't the worst of fates. She might not be prepared to believe your assurances.'

'She might not agree even if she hears it from your own lips,' Lucrezia said.

'I dare say that she won't – and I certainly won't ask her to eat the fruit that would allow her to see for herself. She's more human than you or me.'

'Is she?'

'I think so. Whatever passengers she carries in her blood, they're not as strange as Serpent's blood or the Spirit of the Lake. They're the kind of passengers which work for her and not for themselves. She's probably safe from unearthly kinds of change, if she can only keep the bolder predators and more insidious parasites at bay.'

'But I'm not?' He could tell that Lucrezia was deliberately keeping her own voice neutral.

'Perhaps you are,' he replied judiciously. 'You can tell better than I exactly what might be working within you. Perhaps it's something left over from an earlier Time of Emergence, perhaps not. Either way, it's not corrupted you yet, except perhaps with restlessness. I've always had that – so much so that a season of immobility might do me the world of good.'

The expression on her ravaged face suggested that she didn't believe him. 'What happens if the fliers come back?' she asked. 'What happens if other warriors wander into the undefended garden?'

'I'm not helpless,' he told her. 'I'm unpractised, but I'm not helpless. I've grown uncommonly fast, but I can educate my new form if I work at it. I'll not be easily destroyed . . . and it may well be that I can't be destroyed at all, now that I'm united with something much more deeply buried in the mantle of the world.'

'All right,' she said, 'let's assume that no other enemies arrive,

331

or that they'll fail to harm you if they do come. What if you're still here when this strange season ends? What happens then?'

'I don't know,' he told her truthfully. 'I can only suppose that my dream will enter another new phase. Perhaps I'll sleep without dreaming, for a thousand years and more. Perhaps I'll never wake up – but why should I be afraid of that, when I could have died a dozen times these last few tendays? I've lost count of the times I've fallen into unconsciousness without knowing whether I'd ever awake. I don't say that I've got used to it, but it's life. I shouldn't be terrified by the thought that I've turned into some horrid chimera, and I shouldn't be frightened by the thought of any fate which might befall such a monster. I can still feel pain, but I have a new kind of tranquillity with which to overlay and soothe it. If this is what it's like to be a tree, perhaps I was a fool ever to have taken pleasure in being a man.' This declaration was far from sincere, but after he'd said it he realised that there might be more sense in it than he'd intended.

She pointed at the human head which swung from one of his many branches. 'Has it opened its eyes yet?' she asked. 'Have you renewed its life, as it asked you to do?'

'Not yet,' Andris told her. 'I've had some strange conversations with him in my dreams, but he's as unripe as all my other fruit. I'm not at all sure that this is the kind of life he wanted, even if borrowed blood will enable his brain to work again, but I dare say he'll take it if it's all he can get.'

'You won't be alone, at any rate,' she said, although she sounded a little dubious about the value of that kind of company. Andris was dubious about it himself; it was not a kind of intimacy that appealed to him, nor was Seth the person with whom he would have chosen to share it.

'I don't think loneliness will be a problem,' he said. 'Nor will hunger or thirst. Nightmares, perhaps, but I can live with nightmares. You ought to gather some fruit, by the way – not to feed to your enemies, but as an offering to take to Chimera's Cradle. You won't have to risk your life to gather it; the people on the slopes ought to part with it readily enough.'

'Are they really *people*?' Lucrezia asked, in a low tone. 'Are they people *still*?'

Andris thought that what he was really being asked was: Are *you* still a person?

332

'I'm not sure,' he answered, with scrupulous honesty. 'It's difficult to know where the limits of the word's meaning lie. Even if they can be called people, it doesn't necessarily follow that they're the same people they were before. Perhaps that kind of transformation is impossible to accommodate within our notion of *sameness*. Perhaps we're all dead, and this is the afterlife promised by the deists' God – a dream beyond death, sustained by some mysterious process we aren't equipped to comprehend. I don't know what I am, or who I am – but for the time being, at least, I remember my name and my history. I'm Andris Myrasol, exiled prince of Ferentina, and any fruits that ripen on my boughs will be *my* fruit, just as the thorns I bear are mine. Maybe they'll be poisonous, and maybe the seeds they carry will be the seeds of some unfathomable dweller in the deep, but they'll be mine too. This is my life, Lucrezia. This is what I have become. It's not so horrible that I can't endure it without going mad. I'm dreaming, but I'm not mad. If only I could talk with somebody who knew the words, and could slot the last few pieces of the puzzle into place, I think I could offer a perfectly rational account of what is happening here, and where creatures like me – not to mention creatures like you – fit into its scheme.'

'If your fruits are ripe by the time I come back,' she said, 'I'll take some with me – to Xandria, if that's where we decide to go.'

'That's good,' he said. 'But if you decide to grow another tree like this, please don't feed the fruit to some poor idiot thrown into your father's jail. Find someone desperate enough to give their informed consent – someone with an incurable disease.'

Hyry Keshvara was coming up the hill behind the princess. Lucrezia didn't notice at first, but she turned when she realised that Andris was looking over her shoulder.

'Food's ready,' the trader said.

Lucrezia thanked her, but didn't immediately turn away. 'I'll come back,' she said to Andris, as if she were fearful that he might think otherwise if she didn't say so.

'No hurry,' Andris said. 'Time moves more quickly these days – I suppose it's one of the privileges of my present condition. But you mustn't stay here too long – this ground isn't faring well in the war, and its enemies might sense the possibility of killing it off.'

333

She made no reply to that, but she raised her arm in salute as she walked away.

No sooner had she gone than Ssifuss came to take her place. It appeared that the Serpent had been anxious for a private word with him.

'Iss debt,' the Serpent said. 'Sstill owed.'

'No it's not,' Andris told it. 'All debts are settled now. It's Mossassor you should be thinking about. You owed him a debt too, as I remember.'

'Will be paid,' Ssifuss said. 'Lississee knowss promisse too – promisse made by humanss to Sserpentss like uss.'

Andris knew why the creature felt the need to specify that the contract forged in Idun was between humans and Serpents 'like us', but he couldn't imagine how it felt about the prospect of being caught up in a war between different adult forms of its own species.

'I think I know what that promise was,' Andris said. 'My forefathers promised yours that they would do what they could to preserve your kind against the temptations of your own flesh. They recognised that your kind had something precious in common with theirs, by virtue of your sentience and intelligence, and they borrowed something from your deep-dwelling parents which they used in an attempt to secure the future of their own children and of yours. We're still bound by that compact – not just you and I but all humans and all Serpents – in spite of the fact that the plan went awry, and in spite of everything that's happened since.'

'Ssink sso too,' Ssifuss agreed. 'Will come back, if can. Promisse.'

'Thanks.'

'Besst ever ssaw,' the Serpent added, extending a finger to indicate that it was talking about Andris. 'Giant Sserpentss, kill kill kill. Never believed it. Hero. Iss right word, no? Hero.'

'You too,' Andris assured it. 'I wouldn't have believed it possible either, if I hadn't seen you in action. We two fought a small army, and we won. We're both heroes.'

'Not hero later,' Ssifuss lamented. 'Too many. Had to get help. Too late.'

'There's no point in being a dead hero,' Andris observed. 'You were right. You did everything you could, and then some. You did bring help, and it's not too late. It's done me a great deal of good to see you again, and Lucrezia. I'm still alive and I'm still in the game – and we're still on the same side. I'll still be in the game when you've been to Chimera's Cradle and come back again.'

'Humanss are not disseasse,' Ssifuss said, contradicting his earlier opinion. 'Disseasse of world iss matter of sshansse. Know ssat now. Are all on ssame sside, ass Mossassor ssaid. Ssalamanderss too.'

'You're right,' Andris agreed. 'I know it sometimes seems that it hardly matters which side we're on, given that we can't make any meaningful contact with the dwellers in the deep or the tiny things that live inside us – but, at the very least, it matters to us. I think it matters in the grander context too. Sentience and intelligence are the prerogative of beings like us, and they remain ours even when the things inside us take control and when the dwellers in the deep swallow us up. We have to fight to keep sentience and intelligence alive, no matter where we find ourselves or what we become. That's what this is all about – I'm convinced of that. Can you follow what I'm saying? Do you understand what I'm getting at?'

It was obvious that the answer was no, but it was equally obvious that the Serpent was trying to make sense of it, trying to grasp the essence of the argument. That was a heroic struggle too, in its way. After all, they wouldn't have been able to speak to one another at all had they had to rely on Andris's understanding of the Serpent language.

'*Will* come back,' the Serpent said again. 'Iss promisse. Not debt – promisse.'

'I know,' Andris said. 'I understand. I'll be here. In fact, if it's *humanly* possible, I'll be here long after everyone else I ever knew is dead and gone. I don't know whether hopes and promises of immortality mean anything at all, but if effort is what it takes to bridge the gaps between these feverish times I'll do the very best I can. If I don't quite understand what's happening yet, I'll keep on trying until I do. That's what we're here for, after all.'

He carefully didn't specify what he meant by 'here', but he was even surer now than he had been before that he did understand what he was here for, or at least that he could, and eventually would.

335

Part Three

In the Cradle of the Future,
Instruments of Destruction and Destiny

Humans were made by a world other than the one they know, close kin to it but not the same. No man of the world will ever see the world which made him, and yet it can be glimpsed in dreams. No memory of the world which made the human race survives in this world, nor is there any account of it in the sacred lore, but what is written in the blood can never be wholly erased, and the flickering flame which lights the most intimate dreams can never be utterly extinguished. The tides which surge in human blood are greater by far than the petty tides which stir the world's shallow seas, because humans are children of other and unimaginably distant seas.

Humans were made by a world other than the one they know, and will remake the world because of it, but the world they make will be stranger by far than the world which made them and the world to which they came. The man shall not be born for a hundred generations who will see the world remade, and yet the manner of its remaking can be glimpsed in dreams. No record of the remade world exists in the world as it is, nor is there any account of it in the lore, but what is presaged in the blood of men will one day be inscribed upon the face and flesh of the world entire.

Humans were made by a world other than the one they know, but their being was not defined by that world alone. All worlds and all living beings are children of the great and fathomless abyss which is the dark between the stars, and all are kin no matter how different they seem to be. The living being shall not be born for a million generations who will see the story of life to its climax, and yet it can be glimpsed in dreams. No calculation of the destiny of life can yet be made, but the hopes and fears which eddy in our dreams are bound one day to swell into a greater tide, and the dream incarnate in the blood and flesh of men and worlds will become a glorious reality.

The Lore of Ultimogenesys

I

THE ROAD TO Chimera's Cradle did not run directly from east to west. It slanted towards the south, but only by a few degrees. Nor did the course of the sun run directly from east to west, because the Nest of the Phoenix was hundreds of kims south of the equator. The quality of the light which marked the way Fraxinus followed was gradually but markedly altered by the progress of the sun across the sky.

For a little while, early in the morning, the sun hovered between the vast silver lintels of the 'gateway' through which they had passed soon after dawn. While it was there, the way before him was astonishingly bright; the great palisades to either side of the route reflected the light back and forth between them, so that it seemed as though the expedition were drifting along a river of fire. It was impossible to look back while the sun was framed in that manner; if Fraxinus tried to glance over his shoulder he was dazzled. It was as if the river of fire were flowing from some infernal gorge.

Once the sun had moved far enough to be eclipsed by the northern pillar of the gateway everything changed. For an hour or two it passed out of sight and cast the road into shadow, although light reflected from the tips of the southern palisade sent scattered rays down into the shade. Now it was the ribbon of blue sky above the road which looked like a stately river of light.

Long before noon, however, the sun climbed high enough to peep over the tops of the Thorns distributed to the south, which did not crowd the road quite so narrowly. This made the light far more confusing, rippling around Fraxinus as he moved his horse forwards. It was no simple matter of moving from light to shadow and back again; the patterns of reflection were complex and ever-changing. It was as if he were now adrift in a stormy strait drawn upon a veritable sea of light.

The predominant colours were silver and white, but they were confused by all the familiar colours of stonerot: pastel greens, ochreous yellows, russet browns and faded mauves. Fraxinus didn't doubt for a moment that the road was alive beneath the surface, but the flat bed on which the wagon rolled so easily was quite inert. That surface and the irregular columns which fenced it in were but a single seam in the outer shell of an entity whose fluid tissues were buried very deep. They were home to countless competing parasitic growths.

Fraxinus had likened the Silver Thorns to the gaudtrees of the Spangled Desert, but now he was among them he was more sensitive to the differences than the similarities. The Spangled Desert had been vitreous through and through; its 'sands' were powdered crystal, its 'trees' gem-studded rhapsodies in stained glass, and its animal species were delicately jewelled with multitudinous tiny scales. The Silver Thorns and the road which they guarded were more like polished limestone. The bases of the Thorns were like stout stalagmites, and where they made a wall they often fused exactly as stalagmites did when arrayed beneath a crack in the ceiling of a cave, although there were no stalactites here reaching down like rows of filed teeth to meet them. It was only as they narrowed towards their sharp points that the Thorns became silver, and the silver that justified their name was more like the dull lustre of a fish's scales than the bold gleam of a mirror.

'It really is a wall, isn't it?' said Aulakh Phar. 'This might well be the native habitat of all the stonerots which afflict the structures our masons erect. The yeasts and moulds which human artisans use to harden rubble into neatly shaped blocks must have their analogues in the process by which this living ground shapes its tegument. Can that be coincidence, do you think?'

'I doubt it,' Fraxinus replied. 'Perhaps the technics which the first loremasters gave to our stonemasons were adapted from local materials and local processes rather than imported by the ship. Perhaps the forefathers merely showed their children a new way to use the resources which the world provided.'

'If that was what they did they must have known that every

structure we put up would be affected by the things which blight this curious corridor. It would have been infinitely more convenient had they offered us something different, which would not be corrupted so easily.'

'Had it been easy to give us incorruptible stone they would surely have done it,' Fraxinus pointed out. 'They promised that the Pool of Life would ultimately produce it, so they certainly recognised its importance. The ship which sailed the dark between the stars is said to have been free of corruption, but the city which its people built when they first set down must have proved more vulnerable than they expected. Perhaps it was a coincidence that what had not been corruptible before became so when it was imported into this world. Is it possible that the ship was free of lustrust and its kin as well as all the forms of stonerot, so that its metals and ceramics were effectively immortal?'

'I don't think so,' said Phar, shaking his head. 'Sterile iron kept free of lustrust remains vulnerable to the common kind of rust so long as air and water are present. On the other hand, the lore suggests that the kind of plastic we know was originally one of many – that there were stable plastics as well as unstable ones. We make plastic only to explode it, making use of its exaggerated tendency to decay, but the lore has hints that our remotest forefathers used other kinds for the opposite purpose: to *resist* decay. As I told Andris Myrasol not so long ago, the lore of various guildsmen confirms that our notions of decay are far too general, covering a whole series of processes which are very different in chemical terms even though they all have the same effect of weakening the power of human artifice. To the naked eye, stonerot seems very like the parasites which infest the trunks of trees and the planks of floors and ceilings, but what it actually does is quite different. Wood is *food* for the organisms which rot it; stone isn't.'

'It's eaten away just the same,' Shabir put in.

'No it isn't,' Phar persisted. 'We only call it *being eaten away* because it looks the same to the naked eye, whose vision is far too coarse to sense the reality of molecular events.'

'You can split hairs and invoke superstition if you wish,' Shabir countered, 'but it's all just talk. It doesn't matter what you call things. What really matters is where those men with monkey heads have got to. The wall formed by these columns has far too many holes in it for my liking – they could be lurking behind any one of them. *That*'s what we should be watching out for, not the rot that's either eating the walls away or doing something else which only looks like eating away.'

'What you mean,' Fraxinus said to Phar, ignoring the general as he would have ignored Jacom Cerri in the days when the captain was prone to make similar speeches about the necessity of paying attention to practical matters, 'is that stonerot's a kind of corrosion rather than a kind of corruption.'

'Yes and no,' Phar answered unhelpfully. 'I mean, yes, there's more than one process going on, but no, you can't account for the differences simply by having two words instead of one. It's far more complicated than that. And it does matter what we call things, and why we choose to give them the names we do. Of course we have to look out for the monkey-heads, who probably do intend to ambush us if and when they get the chance, but we also ought to wonder why Myrasol's mapmakers called this thing the Gauntlet of Gladness. They could have called it the White Road, but they didn't.'

'A gauntlet's just a fancy glove,' Shabir said. 'I don't see what sense that can possibly make, although some of those clustered columns do look like bunches of fingers.'

'*Running the gauntlet*'s an expression we use in Xandria,' Fraxinus explained. 'It means travelling a dangerous route – I have no idea why. That part of the name may be warning us that although the ground seems much better here than it was out on the plain of flowing stones it's not without its dangers. The monkey-heads may not be the only ones lying in wait for us. The lore asks us to return at intervals to Chimera's Cradle, but it also warns us that the land around it is poisoned. This road has been maintained even though the ring that Myrasol's map calls the Nest of the Phoenix is much bigger now than it used to be, but the fact that it's fenced in suggests that there are things which have to be kept at bay. Merchants have a saying, of which Checuti was kind enough to remind me a few hours ago: good roads attract avid robbers. Perhaps it holds good even here.'

'If it were robbers we had to worry about,' Shabir muttered, 'we'd not be in much danger. It's murderers, alas.'

'Now who's the one who wants to draw nice distinctions?'

Phar was quick to say. 'But you're right – they don't seem at all interested in stealing what we have; they simply want us dead. On the surface, they're no different from the army you led against us. You had an objective, mistaken though it was: you wanted to make absolutely sure that dragomite refugees couldn't establish nests south of the boundary you'd marked with scorched earth. They must have an objective too, even if they're merely pawns of some vastly magnified figured stone, but it certainly isn't clear what it is. Why should it matter to a half-man or a giant figured stone whether people follow this road or not? Why should it matter whether they continued to live in the Last Stronghold? If the monkey-heads aren't robbers, what do they stand to gain from our extermination? And let's not forget that the half-men Checuti encountered *were* robbers, who stole people – apparently in order to feed them to their monstrous master.'

'Monstrous *mistress*,' Fraxinus corrected him. 'Whatever else these vastly magnified figured stones may be, they're certainly maternal; they give birth more prolifically, and more variously, than a dragomite queen, albeit at intervals thousands of years apart. The Pool of Life must be one of them, else why would Chimera's Cradle be called a cradle, the Navel of the World a navel, or the Nest of the Phoenix a nest?'

'What's a phoenix?' Shabir wanted to know.

'A mythical bird,' Phar informed him. 'A bird which lays no eggs but builds a nest once in a thousand years. The nest catches fire and the bird burns, but is reborn from the flames younger and stronger than before. You see how much it matters what we call things? The mapmakers were trying to tell us something significant about Times of Emergence – about their rarity, and about the involvement of the kind of fire otherwise called Salamander's fire.'

'All of which is less helpful than it might have been, because the metaphors are mixed and the meanings horribly tangled,' Fraxinus pointed out. 'The trouble with words like *fire* is that they can mean all sorts of things . . . just like *corrosion* and *corruption*. On the other hand, a man's memory can only preserve a few thousand words and meanings – that's why we need loremasters to specialise in the maintenance of different areas of knowledge. If we had all the words we really needed, we

343

might need hundreds more different kinds of loremasters . . . and even the kinds we have often find it almost impossible to communicate with one another, let alone combine their multitudinous skills with reasonable efficiency in the making of a city-sized community. We Xandrians are proud of our possessions and achievements, but in the eyes of the forefathers we'd probably seem little or no better than the men of the Nine Towns.'

'Ebla is civilised,' Shabir said sharply. 'Don't judge a place you've never seen.'

Phar refused to be distracted by the interruption. 'The fact that some words can have several meanings isn't just a fault or the result of a shortage of supply,' he pointed out pensively. 'When a word means two different things the coincidence usually identifies some sort of connection between them. Which is to say that it's not really a coincidence at all. We have to bear the connections in mind as well as the distinctions. However different the rotting of corpses and the rotting of stones might be, there's probably some link between them that goes beyond mere appearances. Perhaps the forefathers *were* taken by surprise when they built a city whose fabric fell victim to the local stonerots, but I think there's more to it than that. They must have had some idea what the world was like before they built their city, even if they didn't know in the beginning that the figured stones had much bigger cousins. I think they were surprised by something much more awkward than mere stone-rot, and something much more challenging. They didn't simply turn round and go, they changed their entire plan . . . and the Serpents and Salamanders changed *their* ways of life too. Whatever kind of fire it was that started in the space our forefathers chose to call the Nest of the Phoenix, it was something that excited them as well as alarming them.'

Phar might have gone on, but he was forced to pause when Checuti rode forward to join them, anxious to be heard. Fraxinus wondered whether it was merely a trick of the light that made the thief-master's face look even worse than it had before, or whether the corruption planted there really was spreading out in its patient and inexorable manner.

'Purkin's raving,' Checuti reported. 'Ereleth says that his arm will have to be taken off soon, or it'll be too late. Dhalla says that we're being followed, albeit at a respectful distance, by a pack of big dogs – she says you've met their like before.'

Fraxinus couldn't help clasping his hands together, so that the fingers of one could run over the bite marks still engraved in the flesh of the other. The infection of the hellhound bite had been stilled at Salamander's Fire, but he had no wish to see it renewed.

'They're just scavengers,' Phar said dismissively.

'When scavengers cling hard to your trail,' Shabir pointed out, 'it means that they expect a meal – perhaps a better one than *that*.' He pointed at a set of scattered bones that lay to the side of the road. They weren't human bones, but those of a creature bigger and stronger than a man. It wasn't the first set they had passed; the others had been stripped with similar precision.

Fraxinus looked at the twin walls ahead of them, appearing to converge as they extended towards the horizon. Suddenly, they seemed more like a trap than a protection. The sun was high in the sky now, approaching the height and ferocity which caused civilised men to think in terms of sleeping through the noonday. The broken palisade on their right-hand side was dappled with deep shadows, especially where the stone columns didn't meet and fuse, while the one to the left was dazzlingly aglow. No matter how good a watch they might have kept, there was ample opportunity for a legion of enemies to remain hidden, biding their time while they waited for exactly the right moment to launch their assault.

'We'd better pause for a little while,' he said, reining in and raising his hand to signal to Ereleth. 'Aulakh, you'd better see to . . .'

He had no time to add Purkin's name. It was as if his signal had been long and impatiently awaited by clandestine observers, who responded with horrid alacrity.

There wasn't even time for General Shabir to say: 'I told you so.'

2

LUCREZIA HAD NEVER felt quite as strange as she did while she was climbing to the top of the tree that Andris Myrasol had become. She knew that she could never have climbed any other tree of the same kind, for the branches would have moved around and beneath her, if not to cage her in, strangle her and stab her with multitudinous thorns then at least to refuse support. Andris, by contrast, did his utmost to make her task easier, actually trying to lift her as far as he could and making every effort not to puncture her.

It was easy enough to imagine him as he had been, tall and amber-skinned, lifting her up in his strong arms and holding her aloft. This was a more delicate task, for he had now a hundred arms instead of two, and he had not yet learned to use them with facility. On the other hand, he was far taller now. If he could only could gain sufficient mastery of his new body he might be able to lift her higher than even Dhalla would have been able to do – but whether he could lift her high enough to see over the petrified forest which surrounded the garden remained to be seen.

In the meantime, she tried to make the best of her own way upwards, balancing on his thicker branches and moving very gingerly for fear of accidental stings.

Lucrezia's hope was that she might be able to see Chimera's Cradle. Hyry and Ssifuss had agreed that it must lie to the south, at the centre of the great circle formed by the Reef, and that it might be no more than two days distant if the ground were good enough to walk on. They had agreed that it would be far too optimistic to hope for a road like the one which had brought them here – indeed, that they were more likely to encounter a barrier dividing this living ground from its neighbour – but they felt free to hope that the way might not be impassable.

She was high enough now to look out over the nearer reaches of the forest canopy, which looked from this vantage more like a badly pitted roof precariously made from shattered slates. Unfortunately, she was not yet high enough to see over the tops of its tallest structures.

'Now it's your turn,' she said to Andris. 'You'll have to lift me up a couple of mets more. I'll cling to these two branches, with my feet lodged as they are now. Can you feel my boots?'

'I can feel them,' Andris assured her. 'Are your hands firmly clasped?'

She held the two branches just behind the growing points, where they were no thicker than her own slender wrists. 'I have them,' she confirmed.

'Hold tight,' he said, and began to lift.

The ascent was anything but smooth, but she didn't know whether it was her unsteadiness or his clumsiness that was primarily responsible for the way she wobbled and swayed. She had further to go than she thought and his reach was longer than she had imagined.

She had taken care to position herself in such a way that she was facing southwards, but it was not in that direction that she first caught sight of something beyond the protective forest. The top of a conical hill was visible away to her left, capped with a green that was as close to the colour of earthly vegetation as anything she had seen for days. She reported its existence and appearance to Andris, but if he heard her he made no reply.

'There *is* something on the southern horizon,' she continued, as she reached the limit of her upward course. 'More than one something, in fact. It's all rather blurred – the air's not as clear as it might be, and there's a haze if not an actual mist. There are at least three tips, but I don't think they're very close together – it's just that two of them are nearly in line. The nearest one is also the lowest and very hard to see, but it looks to be as neatly cut as any human artefact. It *looks* like the top of a four-sided pyramid, but I can't be sure. I don't think it can be more than a few kims away, but I can't see anything at all of the territory in between. If the Pool of Life really is a pool I wouldn't be high enough to see it.'

And if the Navel of the World really is a pit in its flesh, she thought, *I wouldn't be able to see that either. But if the pyramid*

347

really is a pyramid, it might indeed be within the bounds of Chimera's Cradle.

She glanced to the right, where she saw a purple expanse that she took to be the canopy of another exotic forest; then she looked over her shoulder very quickly, not daring to risk her balance with a fuller movement. She could just see the inner rim of the Reef, its coppery curls mingling with silver points with a few scattered gems glinting in the sunlight.

It didn't seem to be a substantial reward for the effort she and Andris had put in.

'Let me down now!' she shouted. She was still not certain that he had been able to hear the whole of her longer speech, or even to catch its gist. She swayed and wobbled again as he lowered her and she nearly fell into his thorny crown, but her handholds were safe. She was soon able to take up the task of safe navigation herself and she made her way down to the ground without collecting more than a few scratches.

'Well,' she said, 'we'll just have to find a southward route through the forest, and see what can be seen when we come out on the far side.'

'I wish I could provide a guide,' Andris said, 'but I seem to have lost all the human and Serpentine associates I had and I'm not sure that I could command them if they were still here.'

'Actually,' said Lucrezia, looking down the slope with a fluttering heart, 'I think you might have the chance to find that out.'

She stood to one side so that she wasn't blocking his view, although he had to turn to look where she was pointing. His entire crown rotated as he turned, and his leaves rustled in a most peculiar fashion.

The creature walking up the slope was not a human being, but Lucrezia was exceedingly glad to see that it wasn't a giant Serpent either. It was more like a frog that walked erect, wide-mouthed and bug-eyed. Its skin was patterned, not unlike a Serpent's, but its scales were much smaller and much smoother. It was naked, and – so far as she could tell, at least – sexless.

'Have you seen it before?' she asked, in a low tone.

'Not that one,' he replied. 'But there was another not altogether unlike it, which always seemed to be around in the

348

murkiest phase of my dream. I called it the Watcher – but I think the Watcher I saw was killed by the lizards. This must be . . .'

He left it at that, but she presumed that he was wondering whether this was something newly born from the living rock – a replacement for the creature that had been lost. Having reasoned as far as that, it wasn't hard to figure out why Andris had interrupted himself.

If such a thing as this could step from the bosom of the rock, fully formed and active, perhaps a legion could follow it. Perhaps a new host of false men and giant Serpents was in the process of hatching even while the last troop was being slowly reabsorbed into the fabric of its maker.

The frog-like creature didn't even glance at Lucrezia. First of all it went to stand before the blackened and immobile face of the burnt-out tree which Andris had called Arilla. It studied the inert features for a minute or more before turning to Andris, meeting the inquisitive gazes of the human and the tree with uncommonly steady eyes. The eyes didn't blink at all, but Lucrezia noticed a transparent nictitating membrane flick back and forth across the convex eye in a horizontal arc.

'Can you speak?' Andris asked.

'Yes,' said the other. There was no Serpentine hiss in its pronunciation, but the Y was unclear. It had evidently recognised the language in which the question was couched.

'Do you have a name?'

It said nothing to that. Lucrezia thought, uncharitably, that if its vocabulary didn't even stretch as far as 'No' their conversation was likely to be limited.

'I have seen creatures of your kind before,' Andris said, equally enough. 'Here, and in the Lake of Colourless Blood, and even in the depths of a dragomite nest. I don't know exactly *what* you are, but you're not unfamiliar. Do you understand what I'm saying?'

Perhaps it did and perhaps it didn't. Instead of replying, it looked from side to side, gesturing vaguely in the direction of the burnt-out tree. 'Bad,' it said.

'Not good,' Andris agreed. Lucrezia looked down the slope to where Hyry Keshvara was approaching, with a javelin in her hand. Lucrezia didn't bother to signal that there was no immediate cause for alarm. Hyry could see that much for herself.

When the creature said nothing more, Andris tried again: 'If you understand what I'm saying, I'd be glad of some indication. What are you? What's your purpose here?'

It wasn't easy to read the expression on the alien features but Lucrezia judged that it was perplexed and uncertain, as if it wasn't at all sure what it was or what its purpose might be, and wished that it did. She waited to hear what it would say, if anything. It shifted uneasily on the spot as Hyry arrived to take a stand beside Lucrezia, but it continued staring at the face set into the bole of the giant tree – the face that was still clearly recognisable, at least to someone who knew him as well as Lucrezia had, as the face of Andris Myrasol.

'Try to remember,' it said, in the end. It was more like a plaintive promise than an instruction. From what distant past, she wondered, might those memories have to be dredged up?

'I wish I could help you,' Andris said, with a studied formality which seemed almost macabre, 'but I'm a stranger here myself. My name is Andris Myrasol – or was when I was human – but what the purpose of bringing me here might have been I still can't tell. We are prisoners of one of the dwellers in the deep, it seems – a mother of Serpents which has branched out into many other kinds of progeny. Perhaps the dweller in the deep is no more than a creature of dull and simple instinct, which has gained no more reward from its investments than confusion and craziness, but we must hope not. We must hope that there is some kind of plan in all this, else we are both figments of a mad dream, monsters wrought for no more reason than to be the expression of nightmares. What you might wish for I can't tell, but if I'm condemned to be a tree, I'd far rather be a Tree of Knowledge than some stupid idle bush producing fruits that no herbivore will ever eat and seeds within them that will never grow.'

Lucrezia could see that the creature wasn't yet ready to take aboard ideas like this, if it ever would be, but she understood what Andris was trying to do. If it had to struggle even to remember the languages it knew, it required prompting.

'Think of a name,' she suggested softly, taking a step forward to bring herself more fully to the attention of the huge eyes.

'Think of a name, and take it as your own. That would be a beginning, would it not?'

It seemed to be a victory of sorts that the creature turned to look at her, and a greater one when it spoke again.

'Know what I am,' it said – and then, less certainly: 'Know what I was.'

'What are you?' Andris asked.

When no reply came forth, although the creature had turned to look at Andris again, Lucrezia asked: 'What *were* you?'

'Ghost,' the creature said. 'Was ghost.'

It seemed the most unlikely of replies, given that it was very obviously made of flesh and blood. Lucrezia was tempted to tell it that there was no such thing as a ghost, but she was no longer certain of that. If this creature really had been extruded from the face of a figured stone, then it really might be the echo of some former creature that had been sucked into the same face a thousand – or ten thousand – years ago. Perhaps all the creatures she had lately seen and fought, no matter how solid they might have been, were 'ghosts' of individuals who had once lived lives like hers. Was Andris now a ghost, she wondered, or was he merely fated to become one when this Time of Emergence faded away, leaving him to be reborn in some future cycle, as a chimera of the same or some other kind?

'What were you before you were a ghost?' Andris asked, evidently having followed a similar train of thought.

The question was too difficult.

'*Where* were you a ghost?' Lucrezia asked, on a sudden inspiration.

Again the creature condescended to meet her stare, quizzically. 'Nowhere,' it said, as if it found the prospect frightening.

'We have food,' Hyry Keshvara put in, presumably thinking that it might be better to stay with more elementary matters. 'Would you like food? Are you hungry? Thirsty? We have water too.'

That struck a chord. 'Yes,' the creature said. 'Hungry. Thirsty. Hungry ghost. Try to remember.'

'You'd better come this way,' Hyry said, aiming a tiny shrug at Lucrezia as she used the haft of her spear to point down the hill.

The creature meekly followed the direction of her pointed

finger, but it stopped after half a dozen paces when it saw Ssifuss coming to meet it. It said something full of clicks and hisses.

Ssifuss stopped too, astonished but not alarmed.

'What iss?' the Serpent asked.

'We don't know,' Lucrezia said. 'What did it say?'

'Ssayss it iss . . .' Ssifuss hesitated. 'Iss human word for dead thing come back?'

'Ghost,' said Lucrezia. 'It's telling you that it's a ghost. It told us the same thing – but it can't seem to remember what or where it was before it was a ghost.'

'*Rememberss*,' the Serpent said. 'Couldn't *ssay*. Nor can I. Can *draw* ssough.'

It would doubtless have been easier had Ssifuss really been able to draw, but it had nothing to draw with or to draw on save for its stubby finger and the empty air. It had to trace the three-dimensional design three times before Lucrezia finally realised what it was.

'It's a pyramid,' she said eventually. 'A four-sided pyramid. And you'll never guess what I just saw, almost due south of here, exactly where we expect to find Chimera's Cradle. That could be fortunate. I only hope that our friendly ghost can remember its way home.'

'You'd better hope as well that it wants to go,' Hyry put in. 'Not everybody does, you know.'

'No home,' said the frog-like creature, picking out the vital word with alacrity. 'Message. Criss cross. Voices must talk. Hope, not home. No home. Messenger. Am messenger.'

'That's what the winged Salamander told you,' Lucrezia said to Ssifuss. 'They were messengers too.'

'What message are you carrying?' Keshvara wanted to know. 'Who will receive it? Who has *sent* it?'

'Voices must talk,' the creature repeated. 'Silence is bad. Hope in voices. Watch and learn. Listen and say. Make links. Ground to ground, voice to voice. Criss cross. Always criss cross, no matter how long.'

Lucrezia realised that the creature was more like a Serpent than it seemed. It could pronounce the human words well enough but it wasn't thinking in the human language. It was translating, as best it could, but it didn't have the right concepts. Like Ssifuss, it was having trouble making its meaning clear –

but Ssifuss hadn't seemed to establish a readier rapport when it had spoken to the creature in its own tongue.

'If these things are the produce of Chimera's Cradle,' she said slowly, 'sent as emissaries to other grounds and other gardens, gathering intelligence, there must be people there capable of receiving that news. There must at least be *voices*. Perhaps there are people who are taking an active and considered part in this crazy war, trying to bring it to a planned conclusion – people who made these things to gather intelligence and carry messages.'

On another occasion, no one would have bothered to contradict her, but Andris was different now. 'There must be voices,' he agreed. 'In fact, there must be minds and voices – but they surely can't be *people*, or anything very like people. If they were, this creature would be much better able to tell us exactly what its purpose is.'

'But Chimera's Cradle is *our* ground,' Lucrezia said. 'Lississee says so. It's human ground, made by human beings.'

'This is Serpent ground,' Andris reminded her. 'A great deal has changed since the people of the ship took flight. Whatever lives in the garden of Idun now, the one thing of which we can be certain is that it's chimerical – as are we. Perhaps the Pool of Life has given birth to something better and wiser than human beings.'

On another occasion, the phrase he'd set to dangle from the end of the penultimate sentence wouldn't have seemed particularly ominous. As things were, it echoed in Lucrezia's mind like a deadly threat. She lifted her decorated hand to touch her decorated face.

As are we, she thought. *As are we*. She couldn't believe, though, that the Pool of Life had produced anything very much better or wiser than human beings. If it had, they'd surely have made their way into the world by now, even reaching Xandria. But if it hadn't, whose voices were trying to maintain a dialogue between the warring grounds, in spite of all the difficulties in so doing? What kind of links were they trying to forge by means of these absurd living instruments?

'If you want to go to the pyramid in Chimera's Cradle,' she said to the frog-like creature, 'you'd better come with us.'

She couldn't tell whether its failure to express any gratitude

353

was due to confusion or incapacity, but what it did say was ominous enough to send another thrill of anxiety creeping up her spine.

'All ghosts,' it piped, in a curiously singsong fashion. 'All ghosts now. Nearly finished. All ghosts now.'

3

IT WAS NOT until the visitation was over and the travellers had gone on their way – still led by Lississee and the lissom Serpents rather than the confused 'ghost' which had been produced by the garden's maternal earth – that Andris found the leisure to continue his intense examination of his new situation. While the others were there, he had felt a duty to put their mission ahead of his own. Lucrezia, Ssifuss and Hyry had come after him in the hope that they might save him from a fate worse than death, and to do that had required a kind of courage which none of them had ever mustered before. They had risked death, in a spirit of bold and reckless defiance. To some extent, that was a measure of their own desperation: a testament to the way they too had inherited a new and nightmarish state of mind from which familiar discretions and calculations of risk had been casually erased. Even so, they had done it, and they had done it for him. They had done it for a stranger, a foreigner, an alien, with whom they happened to have forged a temporary and coincidental alliance. He had had no alternative but to respond to such a gesture.

Hindsight allowed him to see, though, that the encounter had also been a trial of sorts, a challenge to his ability to communicate with his erstwhile kin. He had made every effort to 'awaken' and to be as fully human as he could in his conversation, and in so doing had tested the limits of his new identity in a rigorous manner. He could not have done that while he remained in solitude, or in such exotic company as was now his; it had been necessary for him to have others bear witness to what he was doing and to provide the context for it. No one could be fully human, or discover exactly how human he was, in the absence of other human beings.

Now he knew, and could take count of his discovery. He had

made what effort he could to re-establish intimacy with his own kind, and now had the opportunity to measure the limits of his success and failure.

Although Lucrezia did not feel the kind of affection for him that Merel had, she was an intimate nevertheless; she had been fully qualified to play the part of the person appointed to define and reflect the kind of being that he was and the kind of being he might yet try to become. Now that Lucrezia had gone, he was free to admit that he was no longer the kind of man he had been, or any kind of man at all. Whatever he might try to become now, he thought, the one thing he could not try to be was a man. The frog-like creature had helped him to see that by telling him exactly what he was and would be for ever: a ghost.

Even if some miracle of further mutation were to allow him to recover his original body, or something like it, Andris knew that he would not be the Andris Myrasol he had been before, nor anything *that* Andris Myrasol could ever have aspired to become. He would be an Andris Myrasol who had once been a chimerical tree and was still an outgrowth of a dweller in the deep.

He would still, in essence, be a product of the ground which had adopted him and fused its flesh with his. He was kin to giant Serpents now, and stupid half-men, and lonely ghosts; above all, he was kin to the tree-people on the slope and to dead Arilla.

For this reason, when Lucrezia and her companions had gone and he gave himself back to the dream Andris was content to give himself entirely. He knew that he belonged within the dream.

He hoped that he would have other opportunities to talk with individuals of Lucrezia's kind – with Lucrezia herself, if she were able to fulfil her promise – but he knew that things would be different then. He would not make any further effort to masquerade as his former self; from now on he would give himself over to the process of *becoming*. The person which spoke to Lucrezia, if and when she returned, would be the person he had become and not an echo of the person he had been.

He knew that he had to take the dream seriously now, and put aside the question of what was real and what was not. In a way, he had begun to take it seriously even while he was wandering deliriously in the Soursweet Marshes, but he understood now that the seriousness he had tried to impose upon it then had been the wrong kind of seriousness, more closely akin to the deists' faith than he had cared to recognise. Like them, he had looked to his delirium for some kind of magical revelation, as if it were an oracle speaking in the secret arena of his soul. Where they had looked for news of God he had looked for news of an intrinsically godless universe, but he had considered his dream as if it were a message, or at least a stream of sensations received by some inner organ of apprehension. He now accepted that it was not that – but as to what it *was* he was still trying to make up his mind, still searching for the best formulation.

In fact, he told himself, the dream had begun – when it was still the Spirit of the Waters – as a new way of ordering and organising the knowledge and streams of sensation he already had. Now that the produce of the garden's seed had been added to it, the dream had broadened out to include new streams of sensation and new stores of knowledge – new, at least, to him. Or was that too the wrong way round? Would it make more sense to say that 'he' was new to *them*?

He was now a chimera, part and parcel of the garden and of the creature whose organ the garden was, but he had always been a chimera of sorts. He had always had alien beings in his blood, passengers which were not mere parasites but creatures which shared his being, just as they shared the being of every other living species in the world. He couldn't even be sure that they had simply been sharers in his body, feeding on his blood; had they been sharers in his mind too he'd simply have accepted them as part of his own consciousness, elements of his own identity inextricably compounded with the rest. Now that his mind was changing, undergoing a profound metamorphosis in parallel with his body, he was sharply conscious of the difference between his present and former mental states – but that sharp consciousness would fade as time went by and he would become so deeply accustomed to his new state of mind that the old would fade from his memory, like the kind of dream which vanished utterly once wakefulness was fully restored.

Serpents are good at forgetting too, he thought. *They have to be. Any conscious being which is prone to metamorphoses has to be good at forgetting. Salamanders, it seems, have learned*

357

how to restrict their metamorphoses, though not to that bare minimum which has always seemed natural to humans. They have liberated themselves, at least to some degree, from the necessity of forgetfulness. If the lore can be trusted, humans learned the secrets of both tricks when they first came into the world, so that they were able to make use of Salamander's fire in making giants and Serpent's blood in the making of other kinds of chimeras – including the likes of Seth and Jume Metra as well as more deceptive kinds. Being party to those secrets, they were able to make Chimera's Cradle, a garden to replace a city, their own dweller in the deep . . . but that didn't work out as planned. There were dwellers in the deep already here, and they too began to learn, to penetrate the secrets which human beings thought they had reserved for themselves. So much has been learned, and so much forgotten, that the pieces of the puzzle have been scattered and jumbled, and no one can tell what kind of mind might be needed to put them all together again, if any can.

In the meantime, night came, and day, and night again. The mask which Andris wore, carefully preserving a recognisable representation of the features his former self had proudly worn, altered its lines by slow degrees. His eyes were more often shut than open, his ears routinely inattentive. His olfactory sense was no longer confined to the tissues within his nose; it was distributed far more widely. At first he continued to think of the signals it intercepted as 'odours' but in time he managed to forget that crude way of thinking. The sensations of touch were more widely distributed too, and materially altered. He continued to think in terms of 'pressure', 'pain' and 'heat', but these notions had already been reconfigured; the pain he knew now was a new pain, but he no longer knew precisely how it differed from the old. He was more acutely conscious of such new sensations as those associated with the wind in his branches, or the pollination of his flowers, but even they were fading into the background of consciousness, as taken-for-granted sensations which required no attention and provoked no wonder.

Seth, whose severed head was now fully integrated into his boughs, seemingly returned again to a state in which he could speak for himself, but he did not need to open his mouth – nor would it have done him any good if he could, given that he had no lungs to animate his vocal cords. When he spoke, he spoke as he had before, as a figment of a dream – but Andris believed that he could and did speak *for himself*.

'I asked you for a body of my own, *brother*,' he said, but not as bitterly as Andris had anticipated.

'I did what I could,' Andris told him. 'Would you rather I had left you in the entrails of the dragomite queen, to become mere food for the winners of the nest-war?'

'No. You did what you could, and I thank you for that. You'd have preferred a different fate for yourself, no doubt.'

'Perhaps,' Andris said.

'*Perhaps?* There speaks a man who had freedom of movement all his life, who walked in the sunlight and the starlight as a matter of course, who ate and drank what he wished, when he wished – and copulated with hundreds of women.'

'Not hundreds, alas,' Andris said. 'Not even scores.'

'It *could* have been hundreds – or scores, at least – if you'd taken the trouble.'

'It wasn't that easy. At least, it didn't seem so.'

'That's not important,' Seth said impatiently. 'The point is that you took it all for granted. If you had to have your time over again you wouldn't bother with any of that, because you've done it all. You've had it, and it's only natural that you should want to try something else, something different, because then you'll have had it *all*. You can contemplate the possible fates that might have befallen you and say, honestly enough, that *perhaps* you'd have preferred a different one. I had a different life; for me, everything you took for granted was the stuff of lore and legend. I never walked on legs; I never saw the sun or any other star.'

'You can see them now,' Andris said. 'The sun's the one you can't bear to look at, but I can't tell you the names of the flamestars, let alone their silvery companions; I never knew the first thing about astronomy.'

'That's not the point,' Seth insisted. 'You're being deliberately obtuse.'

'No I'm not,' Andris said. 'I'm making heroic efforts to understand *everything*, and I'm making progress. When I was in the dragomite nest, a creature came into the cell where I was held with Jacom Cerri, opening the wall as easily as if it were slitting a seam in a rotten shirt. *Come with me*, it said, over and over again. I'd always assumed that *you* sent it, that you *summoned* us to the chamber where we found you. I was wrong, wasn't I? You didn't send it at all.'

'How could I? How could I have known that you were there?'

'Nor is it any coincidence that there was one like it watching over me when I was fed the seed that turned me into this, or that another was produced while Lucrezia and Hyry Keshvara were here. When Philemon showed me the one in the lake I thought it was just another kind of unearthly creature, remote kin to Serpents and Salamanders, but I was wrong about that too. Do you know what those things call themselves?'

'Ghosts,' said Seth. 'They don't do much, and they're not very entertaining company, but they're harmless. More amusing, in their way, than workers and warriors.'

'They're the produce of Chimera's Cradle,' Andris said. 'Originally, that is – I suppose they're *reproduced* by all kinds of living ground, according to the promiscuous habit of the dwellers in the deep, but in the beginning they were born from Chimera's Cradle. I think they're part of the Genesys plan.'

'Isn't everything?'

'Yes it is – but some parts were there to begin with and had to be accommodated in the scheme whether the forefathers liked it or not. I think the ghosts are part of the *instrumentality* of the plan.'

'They're not very smart, or very talkative. In fact, they give the impression of being remarkably stupid.'

'They're not. Nor are they without initiative. If the one in the dragomite nest hadn't brought me to you, you wouldn't be here. In fact, if it hadn't brought the three of us out of the belly of the dragomite queen, I probably wouldn't be here either.'

'It wasn't being altruistic, let alone heroic,' Seth said dismissively. 'It was just following its instincts.'

'If it was,' Andris said, 'it was following instincts which are instrumental to the plan our forefathers sketched out. It brought the two of us together, and it did so for a reason, even if it didn't know what the reason was. The one which appeared when Lucrezia and Hyry arrived has gone with them to Chimera's Cradle – not as a guide in any vulgar sense, although it might turn out to know the way even if it can't spell it out, but as . . . well, as a guide in some more subtle sense, or at least as a witness and a messenger.'

'Which might not be a terrible destiny, all things considered,' the drone observed, 'especially compared with being a tree.'

Andris could see that point readily enough, but he knew it for the brutal simplification it was. He knew that he wasn't just a tree, nor even a tree that had once been a human being. He wasn't *becoming* a tree, or a mere hybrid of human and vegetable flesh. He was united with the flesh of one of the dwellers in the deep, which had once been a mere mother of Serpents – and perhaps of a few associated parasites – but now was something far more complicated and far more bizarre. And what he was *becoming* was stranger still.

'We're in the middle of a war,' he told his weary brother. 'It's a very violent war, in which a great deal of blood is being spilled and a great many individual lives are being lost, but it's not really about blood or individual lives and it's not really the kind of war which has winners and losers, conquerors and the vanquished. All wars, in the end, are processes of fusion; when the fighting is done, the conquerors settle down with the vanquished and interbreed with them, so that subsequent generations are descended from both. That's what this war is about, in the ultimate analysis: not destruction, but fusion.'

'I know all about fusion,' the drone assured him sarcastically. 'I've spent my entire life fused with the body of one host or another. It may seem an appealing idea to *you*, but I'd really like to try something different, if I had the chance.'

'I think that might be the heart of the matter,' Andris told him. 'I think that might be the key. After all, that's what metamorphosis is . . . something becoming what it wasn't before. Here, at least in Times of Emergence, *everything* tends to become what it wasn't before. It's all testing, trying, exploring . . . and in between, the results are counted, progress is measured, novelty is weighed in the balance of constancy.'

'Do you always talk like that?' Seth asked. 'It's a bit high-flown for my taste.'

'I certainly do,' Andris informed him. 'I'm a prince of Ferentina: an educated man invested with a wealth of hereditary arrogance. I may have become a vagabond – and, for that matter, a tree – but some things are ineradicable, even by the most profound of metamorphoses.'

'A simple *yes* would have sufficed.'

'No it wouldn't. For some creatures perhaps, but never for the likes of us. What else is all this for?'

'Search me,' said his self-appointed brother.

Perhaps, Andris thought, there would be time for that. For now, though, he was fully occupied in searching himself. He had decided that if messengers regularly passed back and forth between Chimera's Cradle and the other gardens, building a community of sedentary voices with their criss-cross movement, then he must play his part in that community and play it as well as he could. Why should he not aspire to be an *important* part of it, a *vital* part of it? He had been a prince, after all, and had found it a hard habit to break, even as a vagabond.

'I've seen as much of the world as any man alive,' he said aloud – although there was no figment of his dream to hear him now. 'I've as much wisdom in me as any other being, no matter how little lore I possess, or how little I choose to trust. If the future can be foreseen, I may yet see it; if the future is still to be made, I may yet play my part in making it. *There are seasons in the affairs of men, and always will be, despite that the men who live in the world we know were born and will be born again from Chimera's Cradle.*'

Those were words he had heard Carus Fraxinus quote, without understanding them. By the time he met Fraxinus again, he hoped to be able to tell the merchant exactly what they meant.

4

As the creatures with unhuman heads swarmed over the white walls to either side of him, Fraxinus realised that he had not distributed his forces to the best effect.

When he had last seen his enemies they were not so very numerous in number and all on horseback, and most of their arms had been long clubs and javelins. He had assumed that any attack they made would require them to bring their cavalry through gaps in the protective palisade, forgetting that these were not practised horsemen at all, and that they must have taken to horseback simply because that was by far the best way of traversing the plain. Now, back in what must have been more familiar territory – even though it was not the living ground that had spawned them – they had reinforced their numbers and reverted to their own tactics.

As they came over the walls they were already hurling their first weapons – not spears but voluminous nets which expanded as they were thrown, descending upon their various targets with awesome grace and seeming gentleness. The strands from which these nets were woven looked very light, as if a single slashing cut from a good knife would shear them from side to side, but it was immediately obvious that the matter wasn't so simple. The one which settled over Shabir, having been thrown with deadly accuracy, did not hang loose about him but immediately shrunk around his torso as if it were a living organism, avid to embrace his skin – as perhaps it was. Checuti avoided the one thrown at him, but Phar and Fraxinus were the only ones too near the centre of the highway to be unprofitable targets.

Fraxinus had placed both the dragomites in the van, setting them to walk some twenty or thirty mets in front of the three horses ridden by Phar, Shabir and himself – but when he had reined in they had continued on, unable to see his signal. They were now a full forty mets away, and each one had been caught by several nets thrown by enemies who had not yet descended from the tops of the walls. Jume Metra, who had been riding the healthy dragomite, was trapped between the spines of its crest, struggling to free her chitinous spear.

The wagon had been following twenty mets behind Fraxinus, while Dhalla and Checuti brought up the rear. The twenty-met gap had closed to something nearer ten, so that the central elements of the column were more tightly bunched, while Checuti's move forward had left Dhalla quite alone. Fraxinus knew that the awning over the wagon would protect Ereleth, Mossassor, Merel and Vaca Metra from the nets, but he knew that he had to get support to Dhalla as well as the dragomites.

'Back, Checuti!' he yelled. 'Aulakh – help the dragomites! Merel – get a bow and arrows – help Dhalla if you can.'

He had no time for further shouting, nor had he time to see whether Shabir could be assisted in his struggle against the thing which embraced him. Men with monkey heads were running at him, intent on unhorsing him.

He had freed his sword by now, and he immediately lashed out at the first attacker to come within range; the steel blade caught the creature across the face, blinding it. He would gladly have cut down two or three more but the one coming at him from the other side ducked low, aiming its own weapon – a quarterstaff of sorts – at the legs of his mount. It was the horse which had to take reflexive action, and it did, prancing with surprising skill. Alas, Fraxinus had no skill to equip him for thrusting from the back of a horse moving in such a fashion, and could not be surprised that the reckless swishes of his sword cut nothing but the air. Ironically, it was Shabir's horse that took care of the man with the quarterstaff, lashing out with a hind leg whose heavy iron shoe broke the creature's skull.

Somewhat to Fraxinus's frustration, no other enemies were close behind those first assailants. As he quieted his anxious horse he saw that the main thrust of the assault had been focused on the front and the rear, these being the positions of the most dangerous opponents. A human tactician would probably have concentrated his initial thrust on one or other of those targets, and followed it with a swift retreat no matter what the result. Given the nature of the forces at his disposal, and those of his adversaries, a thinking general would surely have settled for a war of attrition – a long series of cut-and-run skirmishes – but that was not the way the monkey-heads operated. This was a full-scale assault, launched with suicidal savagery.

Although they had divided their company, Fraxinus felt sure that the attackers had held nothing in reserve; they intended to put the dragomite warriors and the giant out of action as quickly as possible and then follow through with total determination, destroying everything in between.

Had the monsters had more bows and arrows – and the skill to use them – they would have done a great deal more damage than they actually contrived during the first few seconds of their hectic assault, while the men on horseback were still confused. On the other hand, had they only had the poor spears and clubs with which they had been armed in the last attack they might not have caused so much distress. As things were, a dozen of the creatures had as many half-pikes and metal-bladed swords as they had contrived to plunder from Purkin's men, and that made them fearsome, even though they came at the dragomite warriors on foot and not on horseback.

Fraxinus saw that both the dragomites had been seriously inconvenienced by the nets; both had the clinging stuff wrapped around their heads, and although their huge jaws could not be stilled by anything so fragile their eyes and antennae were tightly shrouded. They could not see and they had lost the most discriminating element of their sense of touch. Although they wheeled round, thrusting this way and that with their jaws, they could do no more than bowl their enemies over, and that by luck rather than by judgment.

The half-men with the best blades made no attempt to give the fearsome jaws a wide berth – they piled in five and six at a time, hacking at the dragomites' legs.

Fraxinus had told Phar to ride to their rescue but the older man had been unable to obey; there were equally determined half-men hacking at his horse's legs, and his mount was neither as quick nor as clever as the one Fraxinus had claimed. The monkey-heads brought it down, and Phar fell with what must have been bone-jarring force. Fraxinus hesitated for a fraction of a second, but loyalty drove all thought of tactics out of his mind. Forgetting the dragomites, he went to help Phar.

As one of the monkey-men raised its club to dash Phar's brains out Fraxinus cut it down with a brutal vertical slash of his blade. He cut another one too, though much more glancingly – but he had brought his own mount into danger again, and recklessly. The horse wasn't clever enough to evade the blows that were now aimed at its feet, and while it was trying its hoof swept up one of the nets that had fallen on to the ground, which immediately squirmed about its hock.

The horse stumbled. Fraxinus jerked his feet from the stirrups as it staggered, not daring to wait in case it might regain its balance. As it went down he jumped clear, using the tip of his sword to steady himself for just a second before swaying back on to his heels and whipping the blade up to protect himself. He was not an instant too soon – two of the creatures which had gone to finish Phar were on to him in a trice, and he had to muster all his strength to keep the blade moving between them. Had they been trained fencers they'd have swayed away and moved to increase the angle, even though their weapons were so crude – but they were mere toys of murderous instinct and they came at him together.

He slit both their bellies open with a single sweep of his blade, but he still had to finish them off else they'd have crawled to where Phar had fallen even while their guts spilled out all over the road. Fraxinus rammed the blade through the eye-socket of one and only just had time to haul it free again, with his booted foot wedged on the creature's pig-like snout, so that he could bring it down on the other's thrusting arm.

By the time he finished off the second creature his wrists were aching terribly with the strain – the blade was heavy and he was nearer to exhaustion than he had suspected.

He had a breathing-space then, because someone else was watching his back, laying about with a blade much thinner than his own. For a moment he thought it must be Merel, but when he actually turned to face his ally he found that it was Ereleth. He started back as the point of the slender foil whipped from left to right, because he knew that it was certain to be poisoned, but she only laughed at his alarm – and rightly so, given the margin there was between them.

'Two of a kind, Fraxinus!' she called, reminding him of a judgment they had agreed upon in much calmer circumstances.

366

'Thank you, majesty!' he called back, fully sincere in his gratitude. She had put three of the creatures down and all were doomed, if not yet actually dead.

He turned again to see how things were going with the dragomites, and there the news was not nearly so good.

Half-men with half-pikes still jousted with the massive jaws while nimbler combatants went for the warriors' legs, aiming to break them with deftly delivered blows. Neither of the warriors was wheeling now; neither would ever stand tall again. One had three legs broken, the other only two but both at the rear. Their jaws were thrusting feverishly, but also aimlessly; they had crippled or killed a full half dozen of their assailants, but more than that remained. Jume Metra had at last contrived to cut herself free from the net which had confined her, but she hesitated to jump down, seeing that she would be surrounded by enemies.

Fraxinus had no choice now.

'Watch Phar!' he yelled to Ereleth, and then he ran full tilt to the relief of the injured dragomites.

One half-man moved to meet him, but it was a silly mistake to come alone. Although it met the first thrust of Fraxinus's sword with a parry and then made a thrust of its own it had no skill at all, and the first riposte it had ever encountered was its last. Two came together then, one of them with a half-pike, but the creature had been wielding the heavy weapon so long that it could hardly get the head up off the ground. Fraxinus kicked the pike aside with his boot and slashed at the creature's soft belly with casual ferocity. The second actually landed a blow, but Fraxinus hardly felt it; his battle-fervour was now so great that he was incapable of responding to any ordinary pain. He struck the half-man down with the flat of his blade, then smashed its windpipe.

In the meantime, the flailing jaws felled two others, and Metra must have killed at least one more, because Fraxinus had already told himself that there were none left to harm him when he found himself falling over.

He realised, belatedly, that the wound he had taken was in the leg, and that the treacherous limb had ceased to support him. He fell more awkwardly than he could have wished, and more heavily too, but at least he didn't compound the damage that had already been done. He was already sitting up when Jume Metra came to help him, and he could see that it was just as well, for she certainly couldn't have hauled him to his feet. Although she was still standing she was in a worse state than he was, the already discoloured skin of her face awash with blood and her thin shirt soaked in gore.

He stopped her before she could try to make him rise. He looked back to see what was happening behind. Phar was still down and so was Shabir but Ereleth was standing. There were no more enemies ahead of the wagon; here, at least, the battle had been won.

He couldn't see clearly what was happening behind the wagon, but the action was still in full flow there. He could see one man backed up against the wall, defending himself against two monkey-heads, and knew that it must be Checuti, but he couldn't see Dhalla, nor even the tip of her massive spear lashing out to either side of the station she should have been holding. Perhaps for once, he thought, she had neither the time nor the space to whirl the weapon around her like a scythe and was using it more deftly – or perhaps she was no longer capable of using it at all.

There was still sound aplenty, but Fraxinus couldn't read the cacophony well enough to judge who was still alive and active. Steel clashed against steel or stone, stone or wood against wood. Voices were raised which must be human or Serpent, because the monkey-heads fought silently, but all was confusion.

Fraxinus got to his feet, balancing on one leg because the other was still slack and numb. He could see the blood flowing from a long gash in the front of his thigh but he couldn't feel it and couldn't believe that it was mortal.

That's not arterial blood, he told himself, with clinical formality. *It's too dull and too sluggish. I can't possibly die of a wound like that.*

Jume Metra cut to her left then, striking down another of the monkey-heads which had appeared from behind the body of an ominously still dragomite. Fraxinus limped to the mound-woman's right, intercepting the creature as it dodged the blow. His own steel met wood as a reprisal blow was aimed at his head, but that gave Metra time enough to thrust her chitinous blade into the side of the attacker, cutting through its entrails below

368

the bottom rib. The blade went in far more easily than it came out, but Metra had all the time she needed to work it loose, and Fraxinus finished off the twitching half-man for her, with a crude thrust whose callous brutality seemed entirely natural.

Fraxinus had been a clever fencer in his youth and he had fought in deadly earnest a dozen times in the course of his career as a merchant, but he had never been in a scramble as mad and violent as this one had been, and he knew that it was not skill but pure chance – and a total lack of any humane regard for the things he had been killing – that had brought him through it.

He looked back at the place where Checuti was still under attack. He saw a half-man try to take the thief-master's head off with a sweeping half-pike, and observed with unfeeling objectivity that the range was *just* too long. The weapon's blade whizzed past Checuti's chin, its momentum carrying it away so far and so comprehensively that the real human had no difficulty closing with the false. Checuti had sense enough to wait until the range was ideal before slashing with his own blade at the place where human skin met animal hide. Fraxinus watched the half-man fall, imagining that its throat must have been slit as bloodily as it might have been by a well-honed razor.

He was aware that there was something strange about his state of mind, but he wasn't sure exactly what it was.

Checuti was looking about for more adversaries now, but he couldn't seem to find one, and Fraxinus felt a sudden surge of triumph.

'It's over!' he said aloud. 'We've won!' But Jume Metra had already withdrawn from him; she was looking at the drago-mites, and it was obvious that she couldn't think of their fate as a victory. One was still alive, but it might as well have been dead. It hadn't enough legs left to lift its bulk.

Fraxinus remembered the pack of hellhounds that Dhalla had seen trailing in their wake. They could not have expected a meal as sumptuous as this one. He limped away, to see what had become of the remainder of his expedition.

Given that they had had no intention of getting away again, the half-men had chosen their moment well enough and they had planned their assault with sufficient guile. There was not one of them left standing, but they had done as much damage as they could reasonably have expected, and perhaps more.

Shabir was lying very still, enshrouded by tightly clinging threads. It was difficult to guess how much of the blood that covered the shroud might be his own. Vaca Metra was similarly outstretched, bloody and motionless. Aulakh Phar was sitting up with Ereleth in attendance, clutching a torn arm and bleeding copiously from a head wound. It was not until he passed the wagon, however, that Fraxinus's worst fear was confirmed.

Dhalla was down.

The giant was surrounded by bodies, some heaped two or three deep in a woefully untidy fashion, but she was down. Merel and Checuti were bending over her, and both seemed deeply concerned. They obviously did not expect the giant to rise again. Checuti was cut too, and he was swaying slightly; it would not have surprised Fraxinus had he fallen as well. Mossassor was huddled against the wall opposite the one against which Checuti had made his stand; the Serpent was obviously hurt but it was impossible to see how badly.

But we are still two days and more from Chimera's Cradle, Fraxinus thought, *and we have yet to discover why the mapmakers called it a gauntlet. All that is certain is that we have found no gladness here as yet, merely a superabundance of sorrow.*

In the distance, he could see the black dots which must be the hellhounds, moving against the dazzling white background like a swarm of lazy flies limned against a cloudy sky.

As the irresistible excitement of the battle vanished without trace, Fraxinus realised that he had not won any kind of victory. The monkey-heads had been slaughtered, but they had come far too close to achieving their purpose.

Is that the kind of war this is? he wondered. *Is that what we have come to find out – that there is nothing here but death and more death, destruction and more destruction? What fools we would be, to have left the comfort of our homes and the civilisation of our empire, if it should transpire that there is nothing here at all except a thousand different ways to die!*

5

L UCREZIA WAS VERY relieved to emerge from the dark depths
of the forest that surrounded Andris's garden. She knew that
her re-emergence into the sunlight was by no means an end to
their troubles – the unknown risks they had still to face might be
even greater than the partly known hazards which lurked in the
near-darkness – but she was grateful nevertheless. The prospect
of another encounter with the vampiric spider-things and their
clever webs had been one which felt particularly horrible.

Although she and her companions had not had a path to
follow they had not had too much difficulty forcing a way
through the thickets. Their once sharp blades were blunted now
but the forest had offered little in the way of active resistance to
their passage. Lucrezia knew that this tacit compliance was
probably a consequence of the fact that the forest's snares had
been deployed with the purpose of keeping enemies out rather
than in, but she couldn't help nursing the hope that Andris might
have been able to exert some subtle influence on the vast entity
with which his flesh had been fused. She wanted to believe that it
was indeed *his* garden now, changed for ever by virtue of his
recruitment, and that it might be disposed to obey his instruction
to favour his friends.

The terrain to the south of the forest was not much like that to
the north. Its predominant colours were much darker and its
lines somewhat smoother. The kinds of 'vegetation' which had
grown most prolifically in the territory within the rim were
much sparser here. Where there were structures growing
abundantly from the uneven ground they were not as precisely
shaped; it was almost as if the entire landscape had been melted
and then allowed to set again. The undulations of the terrain
could easily be likened to a turbulent sea whose waves and
whirlpools had become suddenly viscous before setting into

371

adamantine hardness – except, of course, that some of the surfaces which appeared to be hard were actually soft, or even fluid, ready to swallow anything which set foot upon their deceptive surface.

Lississee and its companions seemed far better equipped than Lucrezia or Hyry to plot a safe course across the alien landscape. Lucrezia wondered whether this was because they were particularly clever observers, or whether their senses had been adapted by millions of years of evolution to be sensitive to such projects. This was, after all, their ancestral ground, even though their more recent great-great-grandparents had shunned it while making their own reproductive arrangements.

Ssifuss had learned quickly since crossing the Reef, but was willing to concede that Lississee and its slim companions had the advantage in navigational skills. For this reason, Ssifuss walked with Hyry and Lucrezia, content to follow the course that its cousins piloted. The frog-like 'ghost' kept company with the slender Serpents, who seemed to find the task of trying to extract information from it just as vexatious as Hyry and Lucrezia had. It was almost as inarticulate in their language as it was in the human tongue.

'This must be a strange experience for you,' Lucrezia said to Ssifuss, as they carefully followed in the footsteps of the slimmer Serpents. 'To know that creatures like the one buried deep beneath our feet were once the sole progenitors of your own kind, before your more immediate ancestors won free of them.'

'Sstill bound to ssem,' Ssifuss replied, in a slightly embarrassed fashion. 'Not free yet. Ssosse born of falsse earss sstill have true earss in blood and boness. Underssstand Mossassor now. Ssingss besst forgotten not eassy to forget – forgetting hass prisse.'

Lucrezia furrowed her brow as she tried to follow the logic of this speech.

'What he means,' Hyry put in, 'is that although he and Mossassor hatched from eggs laid in the *false earth* of an improvised nest they're copies of copies of copies of individuals produced by dwellers in the deep. There may be a gradual diminishing of instinct as individuals reproduce themselves asexually for dozens of generations – that might be what Ssifuss means by *forgetting* – but it can't be eradicated entirely. Some presumably feel them more than others, but all Serpents must feel the subtle pressures of their earlier mode of existence. Things like the one we're walking on are still the only producers of Serpents which can chop and change the instructions built into those eggs and the Serpents still respond to that in some way – but the response is dangerous because it's not just the Serpents that have evolved since winning free. While the Serpents have been cultivating intelligence and technology, building a new kind of society, their ancient mothers have become much more prolific in their inventiveness. In the days when they were mothers of Serpents, the dwellers in the deep must have been much less ambitious in their chimerical endeavours than they are now.'

'Perhaps the defection of their best progeny gave them no choice,' Lucrezia suggested.

'Perhaps,' said Hyry sceptically. 'But if the lore can be trusted, the really *big* changes happened after *our* ancestors arrived – and they happened *because* our ancestors arrived. The mingling of earthly and unearthly life within the bodies of the dwellers instituted a whole new era in their productivity. We're all living with the consequences of that meeting – humans and indigenes alike.'

As she spoke, Hyry lifted her hand to her face to trace the lines which had been engraved there by the fusion of her skin cells with the strands that had briefly made her captive. None of them had escaped some such tainting, and Lucrezia knew that it would be optimistic to expect that her body's inner defences could expel such pollutants as easily as they overcame the trivial infections which the citizens of Xandria suffered as a matter of routine. The Serpents – who had acquired many more stigmata of this kind by virtue of exposing so much more of their flesh – were not yet showing any sign of debilitating sickness but that didn't mean the infestations were harmless.

'We're trapped, aren't we?' Lucrezia said soberly. 'We might have avoided every pitfall and quicksand, and fought free of the nets and their bloodsucking spinners, but we haven't escaped. If we'd stayed outside the Reef we might have kept the corruption of our bodies and minds to a manageable level, as Venerina's people have, but the living ground produces too many spores of too many different kinds. Most of the spores seem to be incapable of making a distinction between the surfaces of the living ground and the skin of our bodies. Are we all going to die, do you think? Or are we merely going to be changed, as Andris was?'

'I don't know,' Hyry told her grimly. 'All I'm sure of is that if there are any defences to be found against the kind of change which has us in its grip – and will one day have the entire world in its grip – the Nest of the Phoenix is where we must hope to find them. And whatever anyone tells us about Chimera's Cradle being no less dangerous than any of the other living grounds, we have to trust that our forefathers understood what they were doing well enough to give it the power to produce such defences. If that's asking for miracles . . . well, highness, what else do we have left to ask for?'

Lucrezia digested the implications of this judgment before saying, 'I wonder if that's what our ancestors promised the Serpents and the Salamanders: a miracle that would save all three species from being drawn back into the mindless wombs of their inventive mothers.'

'Who can tell?' said Hyry. 'Mossassor and Ssifuss must hope so – and Lississee too – or what they set out to do has no more purpose in it than what we set out to do. Do you understand what we've been saying, Ssifuss? Could you follow the argument?'

'Ssink sso,' the Serpent replied. 'Ssink iss right. For uss, next garden musst have ansswerss, elsse are losst. For osserss, may be hope elssewhere, but not for uss.'

The Serpent's long association with them had allowed it to become far better able to follow complicated discourses in the human language, but Lucrezia couldn't be sure that Ssifuss had understood everything she and Hyry had said.

'If all that's true,' she observed pensively, 'you were right, weren't you? Human beings and the other kinds of earthly life they brought with them to your world really could be thought of as a kind of disease. If Hyry's right, it's thanks to us that your ancient mothers became deranged and dangerous. If the forefathers hadn't arrived here, Serpents and Salamanders might both have succeeded in domesticating their peculiar kin, taking full control of their powers of mutation.'

'Perhapss,' was all Ssifuss had to say in reply to that.

374

'It can't have been intentional,' Hyry put in. 'The forefathers couldn't have known what would happen. They probably didn't even know that the dwellers in the deep existed. When things went wrong, they must have tried to put them right – we can be sure of that, even if we can't be sure that their efforts were successful.'

Lucrezia wondered what 'putting things right' might mean, in this context. The lore spoke of the region around Chimera's Cradle being tainted by its produce, but it didn't give the impression that the whole affair had been an unfortunate accident. The forefathers had made the garden of Idun to replace their crumbled city, and the lore suggested that they had known in advance that it would be a *garden of poisons*. Even the people sent by the forefathers to populate the world had complained of what the lore was content to call 'injustice', and the loremasters had replied that the cradle of the future *had* to give birth to evils in order that their ultimate purpose be served. That seemed a strange way to go about 'putting things right' – but there might have been no other.

'How much do these deranged mothers of Serpents differ from the ordinary kind?' Lucrezia asked, not really expecting Hyry or Ssifuss to be able to provide an answer. 'Are there any left that haven't been transformed by the disease that humans brought? The flowing stones must be much the same now as they have been for millions of years, and most dragomite queens seem to have retained their incapacity for radical innovation. Surely some of their bigger kin remain uncorrupted by earthly infections.'

'Don't know,' Ssifuss said tersely. 'Big world.'

Somehow, the absence of any hisses made the words seem more ominous than they were – but the world was, indeed, far too large for any one creature to say what might or might not be lurking in its farthest regions. If it really were the case, though, that all the living grounds which had been parent to Serpents had been deranged by earthly importations, Lucrezia could sympathise with Mossassor's insistence that humans owed Serpents a debt.

A cry of alarm went up then from one of Lississee's companions.

'Flierss!'

Having seen what fliers had done to the garden they had recently departed, Lucrezia had no wish to meet members of that species. She knew well enough by now that not all individuals which looked identical behaved in similar ways, but she dared not hope that these fliers would be different from the ones which had visited Andris's abode. She was grateful to see, when she looked in the direction in which Lississee was pointing, that the fliers were merely tiny dots on the threshold of perception, and that they didn't seem to be heading directly for her company.

For a second or two Lucrezia's eyes, being accustomed to the ways of a wholly earthly world, tried to insist that the fliers were tiny things quite close at hand – as if they were houseflies or elongated wasps no more than a few mets distant – but the error of perspective was corrected quickly enough. She soon saw how big they really were, and that allowed her to calculate their course more accurately. Her relief faded as she realised that although they were not heading directly for her or the slender Serpents their trajectory would take them slanting across the course that Lississee was following, no more than two hundred mets in front of them.

'I don't think they're hostile,' she said optimistically. 'They're not turning to attack us.'

'Not yet,' Hyry muttered apprehensively.

The fliers didn't change direction, but Lucrezia suddenly realised that her hopeful judgment of their lack of aggressive intent had been premature. They *were* hostile and they *were* attacking – but they were attacking another enemy, which had been hidden behind one of the larger 'waves' frozen in mid-surge upon the face of the vitreous sea and still couldn't be seen clearly.

Lississee was still hesitating, but two of its companions pressed on, moving faster than before. They wanted to get a clear sight of what was in front of them – because, whatever it was, they would soon have to contend with it themselves. Ssifuss moved after them, and Hyry moved after Ssifuss, baring the largest blade she had.

Lucrezia drew out the weapon she had chosen from the loot of the battles in the Reef. It was a long poniard with a sharp point and three dull edges arranged in triangular section. It was an ideal weapon for a witch, but she had no powerful poisons left

376

with which to anoint it. She ran after Hyry and the Serpents, determined to take her stand beside them, if a stand had to be taken.

She was hurrying so quickly to catch up that Hyry had to stop her when the Serpents had reached a position from which they could see what was going on – at which point Lississee suddenly decided that discretion was necessary. Hyry made Lucrezia duck down as well as pause, and her head was thrust down so abruptly that she failed to catch the least glimpse of what it was they were avoiding. She had to creep sideways to a place from which she could peep over the low barricade behind which they had regrouped.

All the others were jockeying for similar positions. Lucrezia observed that the frog-like creature seemed to be as inquisitive as any of its companions – an impression greatly enhanced by its large and seemingly innocent eyes.

There were five fliers, but they were – by necessity – very lightly armed. They had only two opponents, but those opponents were exceptionally fearsome in appearance. Lucrezia could not believe that fifty fliers could have killed them.

The two earthbound creatures had vividly striped bodies the size of horses – the weighty kind of horses that were bred to haul ploughs or laden carts rather than the light kind bred to carry riders – and they had heads even bigger than Dhalla's. They also had tails, each one as thick as one of Andris Myrasol's thighs and more than four mets in length. Each segmented tail ended in what looked like a huge thorn, and Lucrezia didn't doubt for a moment that the thorns were as poisonous as any actual thorns she had ever seen or heard of. The heads that were bigger than Dhalla's were as human as the giant's, but the cast of their features was definitely male.

'What are *they*?' she asked Hyry.

'I couldn't swear to it,' the trader replied, 'but I think they're manticores.'

Lucrezia watched the human-headed beasts rise up on their hind limbs, swatting the air with vast paws that seemed to be bristling in every direction with vicious claws. The fliers were very much faster, and they evaded the manticores' flailing limbs with apparent ease, but Lucrezia noticed that they gave the

377

claws a wide berth, being very wary indeed of the consequences of any collision.

Andris had told her how fliers which were probably of the same kind as these had bombed the tree-people, first with flammable liquid and then with lighted fuses. The five harassing the manticores were also hurling things but the objects they were hurling were too small to be clearly seen at this distance. Lucrezia guessed that they must be little darts. Whatever they were, though, the fliers ran out of ammunition very quickly, and as soon as they had no more left they zoomed away south-eastwards in tight formation. They did not stay airborne for long, alighting no more than two hundred mets away, but they kept running on their long, thin legs as if they expected fierce pursuit. They were lost to sight within a minute.

There was, in fact, no pursuit from the manticores. Both of them had sunk back to all fours, and it seemed to be distress rather than disdain that had discouraged them from chasing after their assailants. They were huddling face to face, as if comparing injuries. Some, at least, of the darts must have struck home, and they must have done more damage than had seemed likely when they were thrown. Lucrezia wondered whether some kind of witchery had been at work.

One of the manticores lay down, rolling over on to its side. Lucrezia couldn't tell whether it had been felled by pain or narcotic effect or whether it was simply sparing an injured foot the full burden of its weight. The other immediately left its companion and came straight towards the place where the humans, the Serpents and the batrachian ghost were crouching; their attempt to hide had obviously been ineffective.

'Can't outrun ssat,' said Lississee fearfully. 'Musst fight – all togesser, or all losst.'

Lucrezia could see the logic of the Serpent's assumption. If there was to be a fight their only hope was to surround the massive beast and close in from every side at once, hoping that those Serpents who were armed with spears could drive one or two of them home before that awful tail struck too many of them down.

'Wait!' said Lississee, meaning that they should wait for the command – but when Lucrezia looked over the smooth rim of the barricade again she saw that the manticore had stopped.

'Are there humans here?' the creature called, its voice as massive as its mouth. It was still fifty mets away, but its booming tones carried easily.

'Sstay down,' said Lississee, but Lucrezia had already rejected that course of action as futile. She stood up, so that the manticore could see everything above her waist. She kept her weapon in her hand, but she held it as low as she could.

'Yes,' she shouted. 'There are humans here. We only want to go on our way. We have no quarrel with you.' Hyry stood up alongside her; Lucrezia was glad of the support.

'We have no quarrel with you, either,' the manticore replied, 'and we have need of clever hands. Will you help us?'

'Iss trick,' said Lississee.

Lucrezia felt reasonably confident that it wasn't a trick. Creatures as powerful as the manticore had no need to play tricks on creatures as weak as she and her companions. She had faced too many alien beings by now to be terrified by mere size or strangeness.

'Gladly,' she said. She clambered over the barrier, sheathing her blade as she went. Hyry was only half a step behind. Together they walked towards the monster, neither one of them faltering in her stride. The manticore watched them come with an unfathomable expression in its huge eyes, but it turned away before they arrived in order to lead them to its recumbent companion.

'Thank you,' it said, glancing back over its shoulder.

Lucrezia couldn't quite bring herself to say 'It's no trouble', so she made do with a slight nod of her head. She was glad to see the manticore smile, and to see that its smile wasn't predatory at all.

379

6

ERELETH SAT BESIDE Dhalla's head, watching the slight
movement of the closed eyelids as the eyes beneath flickered
from side to side. She knew the giant must be dreaming but she
didn't know whether or not that was a good sign. She felt almost
as if she were dreaming herself, although she was certainly not
asleep.

Ereleth had not been badly cut by her assailants' knives but
the wounds she had sustained seemed to be having a strange
effect. The pain was by no means intense – indeed, it was muted
to the point at which it was almost pleasant – but she felt light-
headed. Considering that the expedition had just been through
their most hard-fought and most costly battle to date she
thought that her intoxication was inappropriate in the extreme,
and peculiarly ominous for that reason. Nor could she take
refuge in the hope that it was merely an aftermath of her battle-
fever, for a similar change had overcome Sergeant Purkin, who
had taken no part in the fight at all. Before the fight the
guardsman had been in obvious agony – to the extent that she
had decided that his gangrenous arm must be taken off whether
the operation killed him or cured him – but now his delirium was
very much quieter. He too seemed to be dreaming while awake,
and the infection in his arm had altered its appearance
dramatically. Ereleth had seen gangrenous limbs before but she
had never seen a gangrene develop like this, where the putridity
that was consuming the flesh seemed to be in the process of being
consumed in its turn by something as hard and vitreous as
bottle-glass.

Aulakh Phar and General Shabir were laid out beside the
sergeant, both of them unconscious but neither still; their eyes
too were roaming beneath their closed lids, and they were
muttering incessantly. Their condition was hardly less uncanny

380

than Purkin's, but Ereleth had neither puzzlement nor sympathy to spare for any of them while Dhalla was hurt. The giant's heartbeat was no longer erratic, but it remained to be seen whether it could tolerate another acceleration – even the moderate acceleration which would become necessary were she to awake and attempt to stand.

The only corpses they had been forced to leave for the hellhounds were those of Vaca Metra and the dragomites, but Ereleth knew that at least two of those deemed fit to ride or walk would have been consigned to the wagon had it not been so crowded. Like her, Checuti and Jume Metra had both sustained head wounds during the fight and the infections afflicting their skin had grown noticeably worse. Their wounds, like Purkin's, had quickly acquired a glassy patina. Fraxinus claimed to be fit and well, but in Ereleth's judgment the member of the expedition whose condition was most satisfactory was Mossassor, who had been bruised in the battle but not actually cut. Merel, who was driving the wagon, was nursing an ill-bandaged thigh wound and Fraxinus had taken a leg wound as well as sustaining a brutal battering about the head and shoulders.

'It's getting dark now,' Merel reported, looking back over her shoulder. 'We'll be able to continue easily enough. The pale colour of the rock catches the starlight, and the road's still hard and flat.'

Easily enough! Ereleth let the words echo ironically inside her head. It was evident that she and Merel attached very different meanings to 'easy' and 'enough'.

It would have once annoyed Ereleth to observe that Merel hadn't addressed her as *majesty*, or even *my lady*, but she had lost that kind of sensitivity. She had not forgotten that she had once been a queen while the girl had been a petty criminal but the difference seemed almost meaningless now. In Xandria there had been no more than a stone's throw of actual distance between the Inner Sanctum and the waterfront beyond the citadel wall but she and Merel had lived in utterly different worlds. So firm had been the barriers ordering their existence that they could never have met, let alone talked to one another, but that was all in the past now. Here, there was no recognisable or sustainable order at all, and there were no barriers left, even in the witch-queen's mind, to separate the two of them.

'If nothing else is lying in wait for us,' Merel added tiredly, 'we'll easily reach the centre the day after tomorrow. Just one more night after this one.' It wasn't news; the girl was simply uneasy, and felt the need to talk. Not long ago, Ereleth would have ignored her need in a casually disdainful manner, but she was more generously disposed now.

'We can only hope that nothing is lying in wait,' she said, 'but however clear the way to its heart may be, we must expect more surprises and difficulties in Chimera's Cradle.'

'Do your secret commandments tell you that?' the girl asked, not without a certain temerity.

'No,' the witch-queen answered, with only a slight hint of bitterness in her voice. 'They only told me to go there, and what to take with me if I could. If there is anyone or anything there to welcome me, I fear they'll be disappointed. I have a Serpent, but whether it's a Serpent of the right kind I have no idea. I *had* an apprentice with Serpent's blood, but she has gone her own way, like the Salamanders born of Salamander's fire. If other keepers of the secret commandments have come this way, I suppose I ought to hope that they have taken greater care.' She only *supposed* that she *ought* to hope, because she couldn't entirely avoid the contrary hope that she and only she had had the strength of mind and cunning to obey the age-old summons, and also because she had fallen increasingly under the sway of the awful suspicion that the secret commandments had betrayed her. She had begun to suspect – and her suspicion had been further nourished by the careful reasoning of Fraxinus and the flamboyant scepticism of Phar – that her commandments were false lore, not created by the forefathers at all. For a while she had tried to cling to the hope that at least they might have been invented by someone who had actually been to Chimera's Cradle during some earlier Time of Emergence, and had correctly understood what was to be found there, but lately she had lost faith even in that.

'I'm sorry about the princess,' Merel said, in a carefully neutral tone. 'She should have come with Checuti instead of going her own way. I'm surprised that she didn't.'

Ereleth judged that the last sentence was the only honest one. 'There's no surprise in it,' she replied. 'Lucrezia was never one to do what was expected of her. She was always stubborn through and through. Stubbornness can be an advantage to a witch-queen, but she could never moderate its practice. She always thought too much of Keshvara, and it seems that they haven't been together long enough to shatter her illusions. She's still trying to be what she thought Keshvara was: a great adventuress. And why not? I suppose it's what you and I are, whether we like it or not. Every step we take betrays our boldness and our recklessness.'

'I never had a choice,' Merel said, as if in apology. 'I never had a chance to settle down into any other way of being. I've always been a thief. Nothing so grand as a pirate – that's just one of Checuti's jests. For me, planning for tomorrow has always been a matter of one more dangerous adventure, risking the wall or the loss of a hand. Recklessness is my way of life, but I'm not really bold – I just got used to being scared, because there was hardly a moment when I wasn't. I've told myself a thousand times that I'll only die once, and that it might have happened a hundred times already, but the fear never dies. I can feel it still, although it's curiously numb just now. There's been too much trouble, too much death. I can't take it any more.'

'How's your leg?' Ereleth asked.

'It's stopped hurting,' Merel replied, evidently finding no particular cause for surprise in the fact. 'Do you think the princess and Keshvara had any chance of finding Andris? The Serpent must have thought that there was *some* chance, mustn't it?'

'There's always a chance,' Ereleth told her, although she didn't believe it. 'At least, we have to hope so. We've come too far to decide that there isn't. We gave away our last chance to go home when we sent Purkin packing – and it seems that we damned him too.'

Purkin stirred when his name was mentioned, but he didn't wake up.

'You're a lot braver than I am,' Merel told her ungrudgingly. 'If I'd had secret commandments handed down to me, I think I'd simply have ignored them. To leave the comfort and safety of the citadel's Inner Sanctum in order to travel halfway across the world, fighting all the way . . . well, that's *real* courage. Even if I knew I'd have a giant to help me, I'd have thought it over, then stayed exactly where I was.'

'You're evidently wiser than I was,' Ereleth said drily.

'That's not what I was trying to say.'

'I know. In fact, I was neither brave nor foolish. I was merely terrified of the pointlessness which threatened my existence. With my last pupil gone, I felt that I'd been abruptly reduced to nothing. I couldn't stay where I was . . . and everything I'd ever been, or pretended to be, was wrapped up in my secret lore, my *witchery*. If I'd ignored the demands of the secret commandments . . . what would I have had left? What would I have been?' *And what am I now?* she added silently.

Merel must have been surprised by that. At any rate, she hesitated before saying anything more. 'You don't have any idea what we're going to find when we get to Chimera's Cradle, do you?' she asked finally.

'No,' said Ereleth truthfully. 'I don't. I'm not even confident that there's a good reason for us to go looking. I tried to hold on to that conviction – not just because of the lore and the secret commandments, but because of everything Fraxinus and Phar have reasoned out – but I couldn't.'

'Fraxinus still thinks it's important,' Merel observed. 'If anything, he's more determined now than he ever was before.'

'He has to be. What else is there to keep him going?'

'No,' Merel said, 'it's more than that. He's tried to explain it to me. I'm not sure I understand it all, but I know he's no fool. He believes there's something important to be done, and he thinks he's got good reasons for believing it.'

'Perhaps he has,' Ereleth conceded, wishing that her head would cease swimming. She wondered if she could talk herself back to sobriety, and continued before Merel had a chance to say anything further. 'The land which gave birth to Xandria and her empire must have been insulated from the effects of earlier Times of Emergence by the natural barrier of the Dragomite Hills, but that won't always be the case. If Xandria isn't to go the same way as the Cities of the Plain and the Last Stronghold its loremasters need to be told what's happening here – and they must make far better lore than we inherited to prepare our descendants for the *next* Time of Emergence, and the one beyond that. We have to know where these changes are leading if we're to avoid them or learn to control them.'

'We'd better hope that you and Fraxinus stay alive, then,' said

Merel drily. 'Somehow, I don't think the loremasters of Xandria would listen to me, or to Checuti – or even to Aulakh Phar.'

It might be optimistic, Ereleth thought, *to imagine that the vainglorious loremasters of Xandria would listen to any of us. Perhaps the makers of the secret commandments had no alternative but to fall back on such an ingenious device, when all else had failed. Will they even listen to Fraxinus – or must we hope that Chimera's Cradle will give us the incorruptible stone on which we might inscribe our lesson?*

What she said aloud, however, was: 'I hope that we might all stay alive. We must hope that it's possible to penetrate the secrets of Chimera's Cradle and use them to our own advantage. We have at least one reason to think that it *is* possible.'

'What's that?' Merel wanted to know.

Dhalla stirred faintly in her sleep, disturbed by something in her dream. Ereleth reached out to place a soothing hand on the giant's forehead, hoping that the dream wouldn't turn into a nightmare. Even imaginary fears might overtax the giant's labouring heart. Purkin murmured something inaudible; Aulakh Phar and Shabir, as if in answer, redoubled their insistent but incomprehensible muttering.

'It's lying here beside me,' Ereleth said. 'The loremasters who make giants must have learned the secret somehow. It's probable that they took their inspiration from Salamander's fire, but I doubt that they were given a mother of Salamanders to use for their own purposes. If they stole living ground from the Nest of the Phoenix, and bent it to their own will, their example offers hope that humans might yet be winners in this strange contest.'

She would have gone on but she was interrupted. 'Majesty,' said Merel anxiously. 'You'd better take a look at this.' The use of her title told Ereleth that it was not a trivial matter, and she was quick to pull herself up to a standing position. She stooped slightly so that she could see under the wagon's awning. Merel had already reined the horses in, and they had stopped dead.

Mossassor and Jume Metra must have been behind the wagon; Ereleth could not see either of them. Fraxinus and Checuti had been riding together but Checuti had fallen back a little; his head was bowed and he seemed to be having considerable difficulty holding himself in the saddle. That didn't matter; Fraxinus was the one and only master of the expedition and it was his duty to go to meet whatever they might encounter, however fearful it might be.

Merel had been right to say that the paleness of the road along which they were rolling and the nearly continuous walls to either side were adept at catching the starlight. The things which were awaiting them were equally pale, and they too seemed to catch and trap the starlight in the glister of their skins. Ereleth could not help comparing their pallor to that of the marble figures which sat beside some of the ornamental doorways of Xandria's citadel. When the rot had been freshly scoured away from their baroque forms, they too seemed to gleam like awful phantoms.

The largest of the creatures that blocked their way were made on the same scale as Dhalla. They were every bit as tall as the huge horse the giant had ridden from the citadel and much more stoutly built. From the base of its forepaws to the temples of its humanoid head each one of the three must have measured at least four mets. Their catlike bodies were at least ten mets long, not counting their tails.

Their smaller companions, who were also three in number, were much less impressive but hardly less peculiar. They were batrachian humanoids, no taller than Merel or herself. Their wide faces and bulging eyes seemed oddly innocent.

'What are they?' Merel asked breathlessly, as she watched Carus Fraxinus move to meet them with admirable calmness. Ereleth tried to guess what Fraxinus was thinking, but she couldn't. They were two of a kind now, supposedly, but she couldn't imagine what kind of calculations were going on in his head. If the larger creatures attacked him, he was doomed, and so were his companions; if they did not care to let the wagon past, it would stay where it was. This time, Fraxinus had to hope that there was work for a skilful trader.

'The larger creatures are called sphinxes,' Ereleth said. She said it confidently because she had seen sphinxes before, carved into the murals that decorated the walls of Belin's Inner Sanctum. She even knew something of the mystery and symbolism of the sphinx – she was, after all, a queen among witches. She knew enough, at any rate, to perceive a certain propriety in the possibility that the masters of Chimera's Cradle had set sphinxes to guard the entrance to their realm – but she could only hope that she would have the chance to explain that propriety to Carus Fraxinus.

'And the others?' Merel said. 'Andris told me about something he met in the dragomite nest . . .'

'I remember,' Ereleth cut in. 'I couldn't make sense of his description, but it was more accurate than I gave him credit for. Why are they not true humans, if they come from Chimera's Cradle? Fraxinus was still hoping to find humans, of that I'm sure.'

Fraxinus had reined in now, no more than a dozen mets from the line of three sphinxes. Ereleth expected one of the frog-like humanoids to come forward, but they stayed close to their companions and it was one of the sphinxes that broke the tense silence.

'Don't be afraid,' it said sonorously. 'We mean you no harm. Have you come far?'

Fraxinus must have been slightly surprised by the question, but he was quick enough with an answer and Ereleth could hear the relief in his voice. 'We have. Nor has it been an easy journey. I fear there are things abroad which seem bent on preventing anyone reaching the Navel of the World and the Pool of Life.'

'I fear that there are,' said the sphinxes' spokesman. 'How is your party numbered?'

'Nine humans, one of them a giant. One Serpent. Four lie in the wagon, badly hurt; without help, they might not survive until we reach Chimera's Cradle.'

'Help is here,' the sphinx replied, as Fraxinus must have hoped that it would. 'If they have come so far alive, they will not die now. The Gauntlet of Gladness still lies before you, but you are safe from further harm.'

Safe from further harm! Ereleth echoed the words. That was more than Fraxinus could have hoped for, and more than she dared to believe.

'I had assumed that we had been following the Gauntlet of Gladness for a day and more,' Fraxinus said.

'No,' said the sphinx. 'It lies ahead, and cannot be avoided, but we will lead you through it. We cannot shelter you from its effects, but we can promise that no harm will come to you. Those who are hurt will be healed and you will be safe from further attack. We shall lead you to the womb of the world.'

It is a womb now, as well as a navel, a cradle and a nest, Ereleth observed privately. *Those who chose the names made the most of their options – or failed to find a satisfactory answer to the puzzle which confronted them.*

'What effects does the Gauntlet of Gladness have?' Fraxinus asked apprehensively.

'You will feel a certain intoxication,' the sphinx informed him. 'It is not unpleasant, but you might fall asleep or begin to dream while still awake. Don't be afraid.'

Ereleth was not in the least surprised by this answer; she had already made a tentative connection between the name and the condition of her patients – and, for that matter, her own.

'And what if we decide to turn back?' muttered Checuti, who had brought his horse to stand no more than three mets away from Merel and Ereleth. 'What difference will *that* make to your promises and prophecies?' His voice was thick and it was obvious that the foretold intoxication had already claimed him, but Ereleth judged from his tone that he was not finding it altogether pleasant.

The sphinx could not have heard what Checuti said, unless its hearing was preternaturally acute, but as if in reply it said: 'You will certainly die if you turn back. You have no need to fear us – and you have no alternative but to trust us.'

So it would seem, was Ereleth's unvoiced thought, but Fraxinus was more diplomatic. 'We shall be glad of your assistance,' he answered, after a slight pause. 'My name, by the way, is Carus Fraxinus. I am a merchant, and my home is in Xandria, a city on the shores of the Slithery Sea, several thousand kims to the north.'

The sphinx did not name itself or any of its companions. 'You are welcome,' it said. 'All of you, without exception. The hazard is the same for all; the reward is the same for all; while the scheme of which we are all a part runs straightly on its course, we shall all be partners in its deliverance.'

'Does he mean that we'll all grow to be as big as that, and walk upon all fours?' Checuti murmured, now looking directly at Ereleth with feverish eyes set in a face that was more mask than flesh.

'If we do,' Ereleth murmured in reply, 'we had better be careful of our hearts. We might easily outgrow their strength.'

She couldn't see the expression on Fraxinus's face, but she could imagine it. Safe passage to Chimera's Cradle was only the lesser part of what he wanted; an explanation of 'the scheme of which we are all a part'– and its powers of 'deliverance'– was the greater.

Alas, she was no longer prepared to place much credence in the sphinx's careful implication. She was more inclined to trust Checuti's instinct – which, had he been well enough to voice it, would surely have insisted yet again that a wise thief had to beware of open invitations.

7

O NCE LUCREZIA HAD grown used to their company she decided that meeting the manticores was the luckiest thing that had happened to her for some time. She was quickly convinced that they would have done her no harm even if she had not been able to assist them, but the fact that she had been in a position to help had worked to her advantage. In other circumstances, the creatures would probably have made their way to Chimera's Cradle at their own speed instead of condescending to join forces with the humans and the Serpents.

The service she and Hyry had rendered the two manticores – whose names were Vekoren and Kasabil – had been trivial enough, but it had saved Kasabil a good deal of inconvenience. The two darts which had stuck in Vekoren's hide would have caused no problems whether they were poisoned or not, because his hair grew so thick upon his hide that they had barely pricked the skin beneath, but one of those which had struck Kasabil had lodged in his paw, in the furrow which served as a sheath for his claw. The skin was unprotected there and the dart had been so nearly flush with the sides of the furrow that the manticore had been unable to pull it out with his teeth or dislodge it with his tongue, but Lucrezia's deft fingers had plucked it out readily enough.

Although Lucrezia could not identify the poison in which the dart had been dipped she had made a guess as to its effects, based on the appearance of the flesh around the wound and the manticore's report of his sensations. She had applied a palliative which ought to provide relief from the pain if nothing else. For this extra and unlooked-for service the manticores had been duly grateful.

'You should not be trying to reach your ground from here,' Vekoren had told her, when she had explained where they were going. 'There is a better way for humans and Serpents, where creatures like us provide protection against things like those.' By *those* he meant the waspish flying Serpents.

'Do you mean the Gauntlet of Gladness?'

Neither manticore knew that name, so she was quick to move on to the second matter of interest. 'Why should manticores stand guard there to offer protection to humans?'

'Not manticores,' Kasabil had told her. 'We belong to different ground. Perhaps our remotest ancestors were like the beasts that your ground makes, but it may be that their remotest ancestors were like us. What is the Gauntlet of Gladness?'

Lucrezia would rather have had answers to her own questions, but she had found it strangely comforting that the manticores were curious about her. It added a reassuring margin of uncertainty to the remarkable fact that the huge beasts were on their way to Chimera's Cradle. She was happy to take the coincidence as evidence that the war within the Reef might involve treaties as well as armies in conflict, and the curiosity was evidence that there might even be a part for beings such as her to play in the making of such treaties.

'According to our lore,' she had informed the manticores, 'it's a route which once extended from the eastern rim of the Nest of the Phoenix to the Navel of the World – although what now seems to be called the Great Reef is much further out than the circle marked on our maps. If that route's easier, why don't you use it?'

'It's the best way for humans,' Kasabil had repeated, 'but not for us. Its guardians are friendly to your kind, and Serpents too if they have human company, but even though the guardians are flesh-kin to manticores they're not ground-kin and their lore doesn't require them to let us pass. It's the same everywhere – manticores have to find their own ways.'

'Why should you want to go to Chimera's Cradle at all?' Lucrezia had asked.

'To see what there is to be seen and hear what there is to be heard,' Vekoren had told her. 'Ours wasn't human ground to begin with, but it has adopted human flesh more generously than others and our lore asks us to be interested in the human ground. We set out in company with a human and a newt but we met too many killers – both were lost.'

When Lucrezia had informed Vekoren that the creature he called a newt had identified itself to her as a ghost, Vekoren had replied: 'The human was a ghost too, but not the babbling kind. Our ground is very adept in the preservation of lore.' Every statement the creature made seemed to produce more questions than it answered.

Lucrezia had done her best to pursue the interrogation but Vekoren had advised that they make what haste they could in moving on, lest the fliers return with better weapons and the support of their reptilian kin.

It had required only minimal negotiation with Lississee and Ssifuss to decide that if the manticores were willing to tolerate their company they would be fools not to seize the opportunity to form a single party. One manticore looked to be worth half a dozen human cavalrymen; with two such beasts to guard them everyone agreed that they'd be better aided than they would by three dragomite warriors. When Lucrezia told Lississee that the manticores had already lost two bipedal companions Lississee merely observed that the territory they had already crossed must have been hazardous in the extreme.

Although Kasabil's injury would have slowed them a little anyway, the manticores had to sacrifice a good deal of speed in order to keep company with the humans and the Serpents. They made no complaint about that, however, and Hyry wondered aloud if they had some reason for wanting company. Lucrezia was prepared to assume that they simply felt an obligation to repay the service she had rendered but Hyry persisted in her scepticism.

'They must think that we might be useful,' the trader whispered, as they formed a column with Vekoren in the lead. 'Not as fighters, of course, nor even as clever hands, but in some other way. They obviously don't know what they'll find in Chimera's Cradle, but they do know that it's human ground and that its guardians are disposed to favour human beings – which I take to mean *true* human beings, not things like those who took me prisoner and all but burned you alive.'

'We shouldn't mind that,' Lucrezia replied. 'They'll certainly be useful to *us* if there are enemies hereabouts.'

Presumably there *were* enemies about, for when night fell they caught glimpses of movement to either side of their course.

Indeed, it sometimes seemed to Lucrezia that every shadow on the dark ground might be alive and fully mobile, but nothing threatened their company with teeth or claws, blades or darts. The manticores had an odour about them which was strong enough to be clearly manifest even to the feeble human sense of smell; it must have gone forth as a warning to every other kind of creature to steer well clear. Whenever a shadow large enough to be ominous moved, it quickly moved away.

The manticores carried no packs, evidently being used to hunting for food and taking water when they could find it – but this too proved fortunate for their new companions, because they were far cleverer at locating water than Lississee's Serpents. When they eventually paused beside a muddy pond to rest beneath the stars, Vekoren volunteered to go out and bring back meat for cooking.

While the Serpents lit a fire Lucrezia, intent on getting fuller answers to the questions which Vekoren had set aside, took Hyry back to the place where Kasabil had laid himself down.

'How is the foot now?' Lucrezia asked, by way of preparation.

'Numb,' the manticore replied, 'but whatever poison was on it has done no damage. Although the dart was tightly wedged in the furrow its head didn't go deep, and the salve you put on it has done some good. Sleep will help me heal.'

'We still don't understand why you're going to Chimera's Cradle,' Hyry said, with forthright impatience. 'In fact, we don't really understand exactly what you are. Your head and voice are human, but the remainder seems to us the design of a nightmare.'

Kasabil didn't seem to be offended by this, although he didn't seem to be amused. 'Why should you be surprised to find chimeras here?' he asked mildly. 'Your forefathers created this place, or caused its creation. What else should you expect? Have the Serpents not asked you why all this came to be?'

'I suppose we shouldn't be surprised,' Lucrezia agreed tentatively, 'but we come from the far north, where earthly life has entirely displaced the kinds of unearthly life which thrive outside the Reef, let alone those within it. Our lore tells us that we too are chimeras, and when we first met others they had human form – they were mound-women hatched from eggs laid by a dragomite queen. The warriors who brought us to the northern part of the Reef were outwardly human too. Since then we've visited a garden full of people who have been turned into trees, and you're certainly no stranger than they were – but the fact that we have seen these things doesn't mean that we understand them. We're grateful that you've allowed us to accompany you to Chimera's Cradle, but we'd be doubly grateful if you could tell us what we might find there.'

'Why are *you* headed for Chimera's Cradle?' Kasabil countered.

Hyry sighed, but Lucrezia could see that it was a fair question.

'For more generations than our lore has been able to count,' she explained, 'the nations of the north have been isolated from the south by the Dragomite Hills, which seemed impassable. When the hills were depopulated by a plague, the possibility arose that we might visit territories known to us only through our most ancient lore. The only descriptions we had were contained in maps passed down from such a remote era that they no longer fit the shape of the northern seas.

'We crossed the hills successfully and were making for Salamander's Fire when we were attacked. Hyry and I were separated from our friends and from one another. Winged Salamanders eventually brought us news to say that the remainder of our expedition is still on the move, trying to reach Chimera's Cradle by the road you described – but instead of going to meet them we went in search of one of our own party, who had been captured by things that looked like humans but weren't. He'd been take to a garden, and turned into a tree. Now we're going to meet up with our other friends, in Chimera's Cradle.'

The manticore listened to all this with evident interest. Lucrezia, conscious of all that she had left out of her account, wouldn't have thought it manifestly unjust if the creature had told her that if she had no inkling of what to anticipate when they reached their destination, she should not expect more of him. 'I haven't seen the garden where people become trees,' he said, 'but I've heard of it. No two grounds are alike, it seems. If there ever comes a day when there is but a single ground, with the whole world awaiting its dominion, that ground will be the survivor of a long and bitter contest in which a great deal will have been lost. Nothing is immortal, alas – not even the life set deep within the world's crust. You and I might be reborn, but there's no certainty about it and always a danger that we might be reduced to ghosts of the babbling kind.

'Vekoren and I are going to Chimera's Cradle for the same reason that some of our brothers have gone to other grounds and others have gone into the world beyond the Reef. We are searchers. We may look fearsome to humans – designs of nightmare, as your friend put it – but that's because we have to have the means to defend ourselves. The guardians of your ground are fearsome too, even though they leave the labour of searching to their weaker kin. New blood is more inclined to come to your ground, by virtue of the lore your forefathers left behind and the commands they made incarnate in your flesh. Serpents from the world beyond the rim also go more readily to your ground than to any of their own – and Salamanders will even serve as its messengers, it seems. I don't claim to understand these things, but we must all live with whatever understanding we have. Everything changes – even the reborn, and the grounds which give them birth – and those who refuse to play their parts in the endless flux will be lost.'

Again, there was a great deal in this speech that might give rise to further questions, but Hyry Keshvara had no difficulty in seizing one specific phrase for relentless pursuit. 'What do you mean, *you and I might be reborn*?' she asked bluntly.

'Exactly what I say,' Kasabil replied equably. 'Flesh which is taken in by the living ground may come out again, in a similar or different form, and minds may echo in the reborn flesh. Like you, I am a firstborn grown from infancy, and my mind is my own – but if I can take my mind into the living ground when I return, it might emerge again in the future, in part if not in whole. If you came here in search of some such rebirth, however, you must choose your ground very carefully and must risk its caprices. You must have seen many ghosts by now, but have you seen a single one which mirrors your own intelligence? Flesh is more easily recreated than memory, and nothing is reproduced without loss or alteration.'

Lucrezia followed the logic of his case easily enough, but Hyry still felt the need to be sure. 'You mean that if I cared to let myself be swallowed up by any one of these avid quicksands, I might one day be spat out again?'

'Yes. I thought that might be why you are here – that immortality might be the lure that your lore lays out, in order to tempt you back to Chimera's Cradle. It is a deceptive lure, if so; there are many more ways to oblivion than to rebirth, and many of the ways to rebirth are treacherous.'

'Our lore promises far less than that,' Lucrezia observed drily. 'It offers us the chance of finding incorruptible stone, and is dubious even about that. Deists believe in a sort of immortality, but they don't recommend that we should deliver ourselves into the heart of vast flowing stones in order to attain it.'

'Your lore is wise,' Kasabil opined, after a few moments' thought. 'There are many kinds of ground, and even the most generous are far from reliable. I would not trust any other than my own, and I have my doubts about my own. What we know about your ground suggests that it is more dangerous than ours, but if we were certain of what we knew we would not be here. Incorruptible stone, you say? Is that what your forefathers intended the ground to produce? We know the phrase, but we have never taken the notion seriously. All things are corruptible, in our belief, and always will be.'

Hyry was still interested in the other matter; she was a trader after all, who had set out in search of something for which the citizens of Xandria would pay good coin, and there was always a healthy market in ways and means of living longer. 'I'm not sure that it would count as immortality in any case,' she said. 'Whatever might emerge from a womb of stone after a hundred or a thousand years, even if it had my memories and called itself by my name, could hardly be reckoned to be *me*. Had I been digested by one of those shadowed pools, I'd be dead, and whatever it made in my image would be someone else, thrust into a world in which everything had changed.'

'Quite so,' said the manticore. 'And yet, you and I will lie down to sleep in a little while, when we have eaten our share of Vekoren's catch. When we awake again our flesh will have undergone some slight transformation and our memories will have been subtly altered by selective loss. Shall we say that those who awake will not be ourselves, but only other persons who bear our names and carry forward the lightened burden of our pasts?'

He is a philosopher! Lucrezia thought. *Even in this wartorn land, where the very ground is engaged in a ceaseless struggle for mastery, there are beings who think and wonder, consider and speculate. Perhaps there is a destiny to be sought here which is at least as good as any that might be sought in high-walled Xandria.*

'We shall not have been eaten in the meantime,' Hyry countered, stubbornly sticking to the point. 'Nor will the world in which we find ourselves have changed out of all recognition.'

It has done that already, Lucrezia thought, remembering how she had been stung by a drone in the Forest of Absolute Night and been restored to life in the depths of a dragomite nest. 'On the other hand,' she said aloud, 'the earthly maggot which immures itself in a chitinous cocoon and comes forth a fly is reckoned the same individual.'

'According to Aulakh Phar,' Hyry said, 'Serpents might be reckoned sentient maggots which can reproduce themselves without undergoing metamorphosis – and it seems to me they have learned to dread the possibility that they might undergo such metamorphoses precisely because they cannot think of the beings thus produced as *themselves*. Have we not deduced that the reason they have to be so accomplished in forgetfulness is that they must free themselves from the legacy of inducement which asks them to abandon their intelligence and society in order to become stupid giants or mindless fliers?' She turned to Kasabil again. 'Were I to go to your ground, and be swallowed up therein, might I be reborn as a manticore myself?'

'I doubt that,' said Kasabil. 'My brothers and I are all firstborns, although that may be a caprice of the day. In that way, we are more like you than the humans who were among our tutors. *They* were brought full-grown from the fluid rock, with mind and memory already in place.'

'The ghosts of men who lived long ago,' said Lucrezia thoughtfully. 'And were all your other tutors creatures like our ghost – the one you call a newt?'

'Most were like you,' said Kasabil. 'There were other kinds too, although our ground is less adventurous than some.'

'And to what end was this tutoring directed?' Hyry wanted to know.

There was a note of exasperation in her voice, but the manticore didn't seem to resent it. On the other hand, its answer was by no means straightforward. 'If I asked you the same question about your own tutoring,' Kasabil said mildly, 'what would the answer be?'

Hyry didn't have a reply ready.

'He's right,' Lucrezia said. 'What we have been taught is a mixture of many things, with no single end in view. We learn to survive and support ourselves, after a fashion – and beyond that, the world remains a mystery which we can investigate or let alone. We live because we discover ourselves alive, in a world which is as we discover it, and whether we have tutors or not we must decide for ourselves how we will make the most of life.

'It's useless to expect that anyone can tell us exactly what's going on in Chimera's Cradle or any of the living lands around it, or what the final outcome of all this turbulence will be. It's not just that nobody knows, it's that nobody *can* know. We all do what we choose, within the limits of what we are, and none of us can say what ends we ought to have in mind, let alone what the result of our choices might be. We're going to Chimera's Cradle because we're trying to find out, for ourselves and for others who might one day be interested to listen to our stories, what it contains – and so, it seems, is Kasabil.'

'Exactly so,' said the manticore. 'Like you, I have already merged my flesh with all kinds of tiny drifting spores. Like you, I am already condemned to imminent metamorphosis. Like you, I am afraid of what might happen. Like you, I dare to hope that it might be something better than mere extinction. Like you, I would be very interested to hear a better explanation of the world than the one I have to give.'

'And that's why we can be friends instead of enemies,' Lucrezia finished for him. 'That's why we're all on the same side.'

'It sounds to me,' Hyry observed drily, 'as if we're all on the same side because we're all damned in exactly the same way – all lost, with little or no prospect of ever getting home again.'

'What you call *home* is not a home at all,' the manticore observed, proving that he was not as similar to his interlocutors as his last speech had implied. 'Only living ground can provide a real home. If you have any real intelligence, you'll come home with us . . . always provided that any of us contrives to come away from Chimera's Cradle once we have set foot within it. That's your best chance of living again, when the long sleep is over.'

'You don't know that for sure,' Lucrezia said, uncertain whether she meant it as a statement or a question until she added: 'do you?'

'Not for sure,' the manticore admitted, 'but I think I'm in a better position to guess than you are . . . don't you?'

8

THERE WAS NO imposing gateway separating the path which Fraxinus and his companions had so far been following from the Gauntlet of Gladness, which they had presumably reached by now. Nor had there been any shift in direction, however slight. They had turned no corner and they had crossed no bridge. Even so, Fraxinus accepted that it was no longer the same highway.

The ground on which he rode was still hard, white and flat but the 'fence' which had been erected to either side of it – which had earlier been formed from elements which closely resembled the basal columns of the Silver Thorns – had now been replaced by a very different structure. Silver Thorns were still visible behind it, even taller than their counterparts further towards the rim, but the nearest of them was a hundred mets or more from the road's edge. The intervening space was occupied by a dense thicket whose principal component resembled magnified stalks of barley.

Had it not been for its lack of colour – all the elements were white or silvery grey even in the full glare of sunlight – this thicket might almost have been taken for earthly vegetation by a casual observer, but appearances were deceptive. Had they been as delicate as barley stalks the elements of the thicket would have swayed in the wind, but they were much too rigid. The dawn had been cloudy and the wind was fresher than any they had encountered for several days, but the seemingly delicate structures resisted its pressure. Fraxinus had reached out to touch some of them, and found them far from brittle but nevertheless very tough. They were not inflexible, but it would require more than mere wind to make them bend.

The dewy morning sunlight illuminated a strange kind of haze that lay upon the thicket. Although the wind was impotent to stir the stems of the strange plants its strength was more than adequate to dislodge dense clouds of dust, which Fraxinus would have taken for pollen had the grasses been earthly. The dust drifted across their path in lazy silvery swirls, and he could not help but breathe it in. This, he felt sure, was the Gauntlet of Gladness. He had undoubtedly breathed in a little of the dust before he reached the thickets, and a good deal more while the stars still shone, but it was only now that daylight had come that he realised how extensive the clouds were.

Fraxinus knew that the dust could not be harmless, although its immediate effects were by no means unpleasant, but he also knew that it would do no good to instruct his companions to improvise barriers against the infection. He bound a cloth about his own mouth and nose in order to prevent his mucous membranes being clogged with particles but he knew that no such token gesture could keep him safe. At best, he could hope that the mask might lessen the effect a little – sufficiently, at least, to allow him to remain awake and in reasonable possession of his faculties. He was not in the least astonished to find that the symptoms of his intoxication had grown steadily worse since he met the sphinxes, but he took some slight comfort from the fact that they clearly expected him to be able to carry on riding.

Checuti, having been starved of sleep for far too long, had fallen into a virtual trance while they kept doggedly on through the midnight and beyond, but the advent of daylight helped to rouse him a little, and Fraxinus was quick to encourage him. The thief-master's visage was a wreck now, the vitreous shell that had formed over his head wound having expanded to cover half his face, but he seemed blissfully unaware of his own monstrousness.

'We must stay upright and alert if we can,' Fraxinus advised his companion. 'The wagon's far too crowded already and I doubt that those delicate frog-creatures up ahead have the strength to carry a man of your bulk or mine, even if they'd be willing to bear a stretcher. I suppose one of the sphinxes might carry us in its jaws, but we'd find that less comfortable still.'

'It's been so long since I supped from a bottle of good wine that I could almost welcome this,' the thief muttered, in a slurred fashion, as he tied a protective kerchief behind his head in imitation of Fraxinus, 'but this is no mere alcohol. These are seeds we're taking in – the seeds of living ground.'

'I know,' Fraxinus agreed, 'but it's far too late to worry about it. I saw that your skin had been corrupted by spores as soon as I met you outside the Reef, but it was probably too late to turn back even then. Whatever harm these infections might do is already set in train.'

'Did you manage to obtain a better explanation from those creatures galloping impatiently ahead of us?' Checuti asked, although he would surely have asked before had he thought there was anything useful to be learned. It had been some hours since Fraxinus had given up on *that* unequal struggle.

'I think they had an enticing speech prepared and ready for delivery,' Fraxinus told him. 'Once they had said their piece they were eager to be off. They have graciously condescended to moderate their pace a little, but its hurried quality suggests that their insistence on our safety might not be as trustworthy as we could wish.'

Checuti made a visible effort to rouse himself, forcing himself to continue the conversation. 'So they haven't told you what this scheme is of which we're all a part, or what kind of deliverance they have in mind for us?'

'Not yet,' Fraxinus confessed. 'I suppose we might renew our pleas now that daylight has come. If the enemies they fear are more active by night, they may be in a better mood.'

Checuti coughed hoarsely, then had to tighten his kerchief again. 'Let me do that,' he said. 'You'd best see how the others are. There might be room in the wagon soon enough.'

Fraxinus nodded. If Checuti could get more out of the sphinxes than a stock answer to the effect that the visitors would see soon enough what lay ahead of them he would be content to hear it at second-hand. He reined in his horse and allowed the wagon to draw level. Merel was still clutching the reins; she had muffled herself against the drifting dust more comprehensively than anyone else, but Ereleth had not bothered with any mask at all. Merel's eyes were glazed and firmly fixed on the backs of the toiling horses; it was the witch-queen who acknowledged his presence. Fraxinus tied the rein of his horse to the arm of the driver's bench and hauled himself on to the wagon. Ereleth made room for him as he stepped over the back of the bench, placing his feet very carefully in the severely limited space.

'Are your patients quieter?' Fraxinus asked, looking down at Shabir, who was nearest to him.

'They're not dead yet,' she told him. 'If anything, they're all a little better – and if that makes them murmur in their sleep, who am I to complain? I feel better myself – I wouldn't call it *gladness*, but it certainly obliterates pain. My old bones were aching for more days than I could count, and all my witchery couldn't contrive to quell the ache – but here the very air is adequate to the task.'

'It's as well that we destroyed the monkey-heads before it began,' Fraxinus observed, making room to kneel down beside Shabir. 'Were I to fight now, I'm sure that I'd be far too slow, and careless of getting hurt. Alas, we've escaped one ambush only to fall into another far gentler and far less resistible. Perhaps I was a fool to lead us into it.'

'Perhaps you were,' Ereleth agreed, 'but our foolishness is equal to yours, given that we followed you willingly. What will be will be, and we shall all take a full measure of this dust into our bodies before we reach the road's end. It will have its way with us whatever we do.'

There was enough truth in this observation to tempt Fraxinus to tear his makeshift mask away, but he was cautious enough still to be interested in slowing down the effect. He looked back through the open flap of the rear awning. He could see Jume Metra riding behind the wagon, and noticed that she too had a borrowed cloth wound around the lower part of her face; Mossassor was hidden by the canvas.

'The sphinxes evidently believe that they can bring us safely to Chimera's Cradle,' Fraxinus said. 'We must be of some use to them, else they'd not be willing to guard us. I think we can be confident that we won't die yet, and that anyone who falls into a drunken stupor will awake again in due course.' He wished that he could sound more confident.

Fraxinus had allowed his hand to fall, so that the fingers rested on the planks of the wagon floor beside Shabir's outstretched body. Suddenly, his hand was seized by another. He saw that Shabir's eyes had flown open. He wasn't at all sure that the

403

general was awake, even when Shabir spoke his name and then repeated it, urgently.

'I'm here,' he said, in the most soothing tone he could contrive. 'Sleep, if you can. We'll soon be there.'

Shabir said something else, but even when he repeated it Fraxinus couldn't decipher the words. Ereleth, who had been listening to the dreamers' mutterings for far longer, made sense of it before he did.

'He says you're his friend,' the queen told him. 'He seems quite insistent.'

'Yes,' Fraxinus said to the general. 'I'm your friend. I always was, although you didn't know it. Don't worry about the past now – it's forgotten and forgiven. It's the future that matters.'

Shabir launched into a much longer speech, which Fraxinus found utterly incoherent.

'He wants to give you something,' Ereleth finally said, summarising what she had gleaned from the outburst. 'He wants you to take it to Ebla, if you can . . . to his family. Take it, Fraxinus. He's in no shape to hear prevarications, however well-intentioned.'

Shabir was already groping inside his torn and bloody singlet. What he fetched out was a metal amulet that he must have been wearing around his neck, suspended from a leather thong, ever since the wagon had taken him aboard in the Spangled Desert. It was obviously something of personal significance. The torrent of words continued, but Fraxinus had stopped trying to follow it, relying on Ereleth's practised ear for the best translation possible.

'He says that he was wrong to attack us,' Ereleth told him, with a wry twist to her mouth. 'He says that he regrets everything. He wants you to take the amulet to his family, to tell them that he did his very best, even to the end.'

Fraxinus didn't need telling again that this was no time for prevarication – and how could he possibly assure the man, in any case, that he wasn't about to die? He slipped the cord over Shabir's head and pulled it clear, then put the amulet in one of his pouches.

'Forgotten and forgiven,' he said again. 'You did what you thought you had to do. You were a brave man, and you never ceased to be a brave man. If I have the chance, I'll tell everyone who needs to know.'

He looked at Aulakh Phar then, half expecting the old man to make some final declaration of his own – but Phar was more deeply lost in his private dream.

'Checuti's signalling,' Merel said. 'You'd best see what he wants.'

Fraxinus stepped on to the bench, and then eased himself back into the saddle. He untied the rein and urged his reluctant mount to quicken its pace again. He caught up with Checuti a little way ahead, some twenty or thirty mets behind the striding sphinxes and their enigmatic companions.

'They say that we shall be safe,' the thief-master reported feverishly. 'Some may sleep and all may dream, they say, but they will see us safely to the womb of the world – which I take to mean the Pool of Life. As to what fate awaits us there . . . they are not overanxious to describe it. I think you're right – they had a pretty party piece to recite and they did it.'

'They know we have no option but to follow where they lead,' Fraxinus said grimly. He could hardly bear to meet Checuti's eye, so badly was the other man's face despoiled, but he forced himself to do it.

'I'd feel a great deal better about this if they were truly human,' Checuti muttered. 'If the living ground forged by the forefathers produces monsters uglier than all the rest, what hope is there for any of us?' He touched his head as he spoke, to show that he knew what was happening to him.

'We must take what little reassurance we can,' Fraxinus said. The news was no improvement on what their guides and guardians had earlier said to him, but he was glad to see that the self-styled prince of thieves was continuing the fight to shake off his drowsiness.

'Whatever comes, we must face it,' Checuti croaked. 'If we're to be transformed into sphinxes, the condition will not be without its advantages – but I'd hate to be reworked according to the other design. I've never liked toads.'

'A company of sphinxes would certainly create a stir as it marched northwards along the Great Spine Road to the gates of Xandria,' Fraxinus agreed. 'Were we to take them home with us Belin might even be persuaded to send his giants home and use sphinxes as guardsmen instead – but I doubt that the spores taking root within us have the power to make us into beings like that.'

'I doubt that sphinxes would recommend themselves as guardians of the Inner Sanctum,' Checuti said drily, 'given that they seem so obviously male.'

'Whatever filthy tales are told about giants and handsome guardsmen,' Fraxinus riposted, 'I doubt that satisfactory intercourse between them is actually possible. The same would certainly be true of beasts like that and Belin's forty wives, no matter how frustrated they might be.' He tried to laugh, but the joke simply wasn't good enough. He decided to be glad about the failure, on the grounds that inane laughter would only have provided proof of the dire effect that the tainted dust was having.

'If this is the way to death or horrid transfiguration,' Checuti said, his voice hardly above a whisper, 'at least it's a merciful way. Given that I've nothing to lose and everything to gain, I'm free to feel thankful that whatever we find at the far end of the road I can meet it without undue discomfort.' In the circumstances, it was a brave declaration.

Fraxinus imagined that he could feel a kind of spirit coursing through his veins, erasing all the petty pains which might otherwise have tormented and harassed him and filling him with glorious well-being. His limbs did feel unusually light, but the rest was his own confabulation and the fantasy crumbled as his head suddenly swam in a distinctly uncomfortable manner. Ereleth was right; there was more numbness in the drug than gladness.

'You ought to collect specimens of the plants which produce this dust, O mighty merchant prince,' Checuti suggested. 'Out of all the things we've encountered, this is the one most likely to generate a healthy profit . . . provided that its side effects are not always as severe as *this*.' The thief touched his glittering temple again, and Fraxinus could see the envy in his eyes as he measured the relative health of his companion's features.

'Perhaps I will,' said Fraxinus weakly. For the moment, it was the best reply he could contrive.

'We have to bear in mind, of course,' Checuti went on hoarsely, 'that many others have been here before us, and not one has found a way to make a fortune. This marvel must have been known, at least by repute, to Myrasol's ancient map-makers, but I doubt that it has ever been on offer in Xandria's marketplace. Perhaps the seeds won't grow in any ground but this. So far as I could observe, such plants haven't even made their way to the outer reaches of the land within the Reef. That might make sense, of course, if they were set here as a lure . . . or a reward reserved for the brave and the foolhardy.'

Fraxinus looked up then, to watch a flock of flying creatures moving overhead. They weren't birds and they weren't winged Salamanders; he couldn't put a name to them at all. They were heading southwards, but it seemed that when he caught sight of them they also caught sight of him, and they changed direction slightly, beginning an investigative descent. He watched them for more than a minute, half convinced that they intended to attack, but they veered away again to resume their original course. He wondered whether that was because they had seen the sphinxes.

'The sphinx advised us not to waste time,' Checuti said, seemingly anxious because Fraxinus had slowed his horse again. 'We have a long way yet to go.' The wagon had come abreast of them again and Jume Metra was gaining on it; when Fraxinus responded to Checuti's urging the mound-woman rode after them.

'Is something wrong with Mossassor?' Fraxinus asked, looking back at her.

'Still walking,' Metra reported dismissively. That was obviously not what had roused her from her former torpor.

'Are you all right?' Fraxinus asked, knowing that it was a faintly ridiculous question. She could hardly be significantly worse than anyone else who was still capable of riding.

She looked back at him with dull and corpse-like eyes. 'The nest is dead,' she said. 'It has been dead for a long time.'

'I know that,' Fraxinus replied diplomatically, 'and I regret it. Without the efforts of your warriors, we'd all be dead. I'm truly sorry about Vaca Metra.'

The warrior-woman was still staring at him, as if she were trying to recall to mind what it was that she had wanted to say. 'I . . .' she began. She paused immediately, but Fraxinus was astonished nevertheless. He knew how remarkable it was for a mound-woman to use the first person singular.

Metra pulled down the cloth with which she had swathed the lower part of her face, but it was not a gesture of defeat. Her face was not unblemished, but it was healthy by comparison with Checuti's. She was still looking at him with an intensity that recalled the way Shabir had gripped his hand. It appeared that more than one of his followers felt that the time had come to make what settlements were possible. 'I can't feel anything,' she told him. 'I can't feel anything at all.'

Fraxinus inferred that she thought her lack of sensation was a deficiency in herself rather than an effect of the dust they were all breathing in. She thought that she was changing because the last elements of the nest had died in the monkey-head attack, and had left her truly and absolutely alone.

She had not been in this condition while she had worked her way around the Reef with Checuti because she had been given reason to hope that she was coming to meet her sisters – as indeed she had, although their reunion had been tragically brief. She had lost the eggs she had brought out of the nest, but while she had sisters alive there had been a greater unit to which she might belong. Now, the horror of authentic isolation had awakened within her, and the anaesthetic dust had only served to magnify its strangeness. She had ridden forward because she wanted to be closer, not to him in particular but to *anyone* – and because he was the leader, whose duty it was to provide reassurance to all his followers, he felt obliged to reply.

'It's too late for fear,' he told her, raising his voice so that others might hear it too. 'It's too late for regret. Whatever comes, we must face it.' He felt a slight thrill of bravery and exultation as he said it but he knew that he wasn't entitled to any congratulation on that score. The dust was making it too easy. The dust was beginning to make everything too easy. He felt as if the world were becoming more distant from his fragile consciousness with every minute that passed. 'You ride with Checuti,' he said to Metra, thinking that she might be more intimately bonded to the thief than to anyone else. 'I'll fall back to keep Mossassor company.'

Metra nodded her head, although he wasn't sure whether it was a gesture of consent or a mere reflex. Checuti nodded too, in polite acknowledgment of the decision. Fraxinus let the wagon go past and waited for the Serpent.

Mossassor had no mask but it seemed relatively untroubled by the dust. 'Iss good,' it said valiantly, before Fraxinus even had time to ask a question.

'Is not so good, alas,' Fraxinus said, 'but whatever lies ahead of us, we'll find out soon enough. Nothing can stop us now. Nothing will attack us, nothing will deflect us from our course. We have no enemies left save those within.'

'Ssifuss ssaid would never reassh garden,' Mossassor observed. 'Wass wrong. Wass wrong about everyssing.' It didn't sound exultant, but it didn't sound disappointed either.

'We were all wrong,' Fraxinus said, in the grip of a sudden sourness. 'Whatever we expected, whatever we hoped for, it was nothing like this. I hoped to find humans, with whom I could talk and trade. You hoped to find humans who might repay a debt incurred in the distant past. What we have found is sphinxes, and frogs that walk on their hind feet, and living dust which is filling our lungs and our stomachs with who knows what corruption. We haven't even reached our destination, but it's already obvious why precious few of those who make this journey ever have the chance to return.' *But this isn't right,* he thought, as the words spilled out of him. *I'm the leader; I'm supposed to reassure him. He's a Serpent, but he's a member of my company.*

'Iss good,' was Mossassor's stolid reply. 'Iss *sstill* good. Ssearssh for garden togesser, ass lore ssayss. Ssomeone hass to do it. Iss nessessary. Iss uss. Near end now. Tomorrow, iss finisshed. Iss good. Iss *very* good.'

This time, Fraxinus had to stifle an utterly inappropriate laugh which rose unbidden to his lips, even though the Serpent's statement wasn't a joke at all. He thought about Checuti and Shabir, Ereleth and Jume Metra, Aulakh Phar and Merel, and about himself.

'You're right,' he said, wondering whether he could bring himself to believe it, even though it was the truth. 'Whatever happens now, we did what we set out to do. Whatever awaits us at the end of the road, *we didn't fail.*'

9

THE PYRAMID WHOSE apex Lucrezia had glimpsed from Andris's crown rose like the towers of Xandria's citadel from the heart of a vast complex of lesser edifices. There were cones and cubes, cylinders and toruses, hemispherical domes and ovoids. Each individual shape seemed to be stripped down to its elementary form but there was no discernible order in their distribution; they were as haphazardly clumped and as hectically crowded as the buildings of Xandria or the stony plants of the Great Reef.

Lucrezia assumed that the entities making up the 'garden' of Idun must be of the same general kind as those making up the Great Reef, although they were certainly not designed in imitation of fleshier forms. From a distance, the assemblage looked far more like a city than a garden, especially under the dull grey light of a heavily clouded sky, but she refused to submit to the illusion. The lore said that the people of the ship had built a city in Idun, but that they had been forced to replace it with a garden. If the garden had not changed in the intervening years, they had apparently elected to make the second construction resemble the first; if it had looked very different in the beginning then it had evidently made considerable progress in the attempt to recapitulate that which had been lost.

I suppose it is useless to wonder why, she thought. *The forefathers moved in mysterious ways, and any lore they left behind by way of explanation must have been lost in the long-distant past by their sinful descendants.*

In the approaches to the strange 'garden' the ground became much more treacherous. It was criss-crossed by deep crevices and jaggedly broken in between them. Lississee and its companions proved to be very nimble and remarkably agile jumpers, but their ankles and feet were cut in spite of the fact that the scales on their soles were as hard as bottle-glass. Lucrezia's boots had all but rotted away and Hyry's were badly holed, so they had to be very careful; without the help of the two manticores they would have had the utmost difficulty making their way across the last kim and would have shed far more blood in the process. Ssifuss was not as nimble as his fellow Serpents but he was tougher, and he came through without much injury at all, although he was very slow. The untalkative ghost seemed far more delicate in the flesh than any of them, and it was not as light as Lississee, but its limp lily-pad feet coped better with sharp edges than anyone else's and its frog-like legs were capable of a stride that almost put the manticores to shame.

Ironically, the nearest they came to losing a member of their patchwork expedition was when one of Lississee's friends slipped into a quicksand while balancing too precariously on its tender feet – but Lississee was quick to extend its tail as a lifeline, and with a little help from Ssifuss the Serpent pulled itself free.

While they were engaged in these troublesome manoeuvres it was difficult to make disciplined observations of the landscape which awaited them and quite impossible to carry forward a sensible conversation. It wasn't until they arrived on better ground that they were able to gather together and assess their situation. They took stock of their wounds and made what provision they could, but the supplies of woundglue which Lucrezia and Hyry had had were exhausted, and it seemed that some of them, at least, would be leaving bloody footprints wherever they went.

Lucrezia judged that such footprints would show up very clearly, because it was evident now that the pathways which wound between the various geometric shapes were the white of freshly exposed bone. There were plenty of footprints already to be seen, even from a distance.

The mute record of bloody traces served as a series of warnings; when Lucrezia and her companions came closer they were informed that there were hellhounds in the city, and crocolids too, and a dozen other things with slender feet and giant strides. As well as footprints, the pathways were strewn with litter, including bones accompanied by desiccated hides and ragged hanks of hair.

'Killers have been here,' Lucrezia said to Hyry. 'I dare say fliers came in their train.' They could see no fliers now, though, except for little insects that were here in unusual profusion. As soon as they were within the bounds of the garden 'butterflies' of the kind which had added their colour to the intricate patterns of the Serpents' scales fluttered towards them, and had to be driven off with flapping arms.

The protrusions which grew out of the garden's bedrock were mostly white themselves, although a few were shaded in pastel blues and purples and many were decorated with intricate patterns of black dots. Very few were less than two mets tall, although some of the globular structures were only half that. The cones extended their pinnacles five or six mets into the air, and a few of the ovoids were ten mets high even though they gave the appearance of having half their bulk buried beneath the surface.

So far as Lucrezia could see, there was not a portal in sight. If any of the structures nearby were hollow there was no obvious way to reach the interior. Lucrezia tested the texture of the nearest jutting forms and found them – as she had half expected – hard as stone. She didn't doubt that they were alive, or that something far beneath them was, but they had no perceptible warmth in them.

'I had expected a welcome of sorts,' she said, looking around. What she meant was that she had hoped to find human beings living here.

'Perhaps we would have been better received had we entered by the main gate,' Hyry suggested.

'We must still take care,' Kasabil warned them. 'The dark ground is behind us, but that doesn't mean that we're safe.'

The ghost had become impatient by now and wouldn't wait any longer; it was already marching off in the direction of the pyramid, but it glanced back over its shoulder once or twice, as if to reassure itself that the others would follow where it led. They did, although Kasabil was by no means the only one limping now, and when Lucrezia looked back she saw that the trail of blood they left behind them would give exact testimony to the course they followed to anything that cared to track them.

'Was it always like this?' Lucrezia asked Kasabil, who was looking around with evident interest.

'I doubt it,' the manticore replied. 'This is not what I expected.

The garden which our own ground made, for the use and comfort of our human siblings, is very different. I suppose I had imagined that your ground would make something similar – perhaps I took too much for granted. I dare say that this garden changes with every Time of Emergence – some of the masks which the dwellers wear go through a whole sequence of changes after each awakening, as if searching for some elusive perfection. If your lore is to be trusted, the evolution of this ground is working towards a definite goal.'

'Incorruptible stone for the purpose of inscription,' Lucrezia murmured, suspecting that the manticore was teasing her. 'Perhaps that function is perpetually under test – the black spots which decorate these shapes aren't any kind of stonerot I've ever seen, and those patterns seem to be calculated. It's not *writing* – not the kind of lettering we learn in Xandria, at any rate – but it's not random speckling either.'

'I can't believe that,' the manticore told her. 'In any case, if this or any other stone *were* incorruptible, we'd probably all have cause to regret it.'

'Why?' Lucrezia demanded. 'Our lore represents it as a great boon, and it always seemed obvious to me that it would be. The wall which surrounds my father's city requires the constant labour of hundreds of men to maintain its solidity; if it were built from incorruptible stone it wouldn't need constant renewal. Nor would the houses in which the people live – and the poorest would benefit most of all, for theirs are presently the most inadequate shelters. Writing sculpted in incorruptible stone would last for ever, relieving loremasters of at least a little of their burden. I dread to think of the extent of the stone face which would be required to inscribe the whole of human knowledge – it would certainly overfill the Great Wall of Xandria – but that which could be preserved in such a way would also become available to all rather than a few, as the lore of Genesys is supposed to be. I suppose the loremasters of the various guilds might oppose that, but my father's word is the law, and I'm sure that he would see the sense in it.'

'Humans are not the only beings in the world which build walls,' Kasabil observed. 'You are soft in the body and you have clever hands; your instruments are crafted for the use of those hands, carried in pouches and sacks. The beings which are at war here are made of different flesh, and they use all manner of materials in the creation of their own bodies. To them, incorruptible stone would mean the promise – or at least the hope – of invulnerability. Thus armoured, they might fight for ever, resisting further change.'

'Would that be a bad thing?' It wasn't Lucrezia who asked that question but Vekoren. Lucrezia was mildly startled to discover that the manticores were capable of disagreement, exactly as humans and Serpents were.

'I think so,' Kasabil said. 'Whatever the best end of this contest might be, we certainly haven't got near it yet. If we're to find better ways to be, we must preserve the power of change; it ought not to be stifled.'

'The existence of incorruptible stone would not forbid further change,' Vekoren said. 'Perhaps the secret of incorruptible stone is what we *all* came here to search for.'

'If it was, we've failed.' This time the intervention came from Hyry Keshvara. 'Look there, and there!' She was pointing to the higher parts of a cluster of upright cylinders. Lucrezia looked, and saw a generous abundance of the familiar tints of stonerot. 'You're looking at the newly emerged faces,' Hyry told them. 'You only have to look up, at that which has been exposed for some time to the air, and hence to drifting spores, to see that these walls are at least as corruptible as the Great Wall of Xandria. If these crude forms were raised in the hope that they could retain their geometric innocence, the hope has already been betrayed.'

Lucrezia couldn't help feeling a little disappointed, although she had not had the slightest reason to think that anything here might be free of the afflictions that ran riot through the world. For a moment or two it had been possible to entertain the notion that something new and miraculous *might be* here, and that she had been in the company of its discoverers, but mundanity had regained its empire easily enough. She wanted to hear more of the dispute that had begun between Vekoren and Kasabil, in the hope of discovering what possibilities concerned them, and what futures they had in mind, but they had already abandoned the quarrel and were moving after the retreating figure of the creature they called a newt.

Although their route was far from straight they were coming

closer and closer to the huge pyramid which was the centrepiece of this mute display of all too corruptible stone. *That is the true heart of the mystery,* Lucrezia thought. *These shabby edifices are merely the ragged edges of the living ground. If there are answers to be found, we will surely find them inside the pyramid.* She accelerated her pace slightly, thinking that nothing more would happen until they reached the centrepiece of the 'garden' – but that expectation was confounded as rapidly as most of her others had been.

They rounded one more corner, skirting a cubic formation which rose two mets above Vekoren's proud head, and came face to face with a creature that was even taller than the manticore. Its human face was three times as broad as Lucrezia's, and its lazily staring eyes seemed very big indeed. It moved towards the cavorting ghost so rapidly that Lucrezia's breath caught in her throat, but it didn't open its full-lipped mouth to swallow up the frog-like creature. Instead, it smiled a greeting.

The newt came to a halt before the quadruped, which was similar to a manticore except that its tail was not at all like a scorpion's and its body had no stripes. The batrachian piped a long sentence in some unknown tongue, but the newcomer's only response was to nod its head gravely.

The two manticores had come to a halt. Their attitude was very wary; their scorpions' tails stood up, swaying a little from side to side like two venomous snakes readying themselves to strike. Lississee and Ssifuss had stopped dead, and the other Serpents followed suit. Lucrezia felt that she ought to be rooted to the spot but in fact she was still moving, as if instinct impelled her to take the lead in dealing with this magisterial adversary. There was something about the creature's face that was oddly reassuring. It was a very handsome face – considerably more handsome than the faces of Kasabil and Vekoren, or even of Andris Myrasol or Jacom Cerri.

The ghost spoke again, in the language that Lucrezia had never heard before. She glanced back at Ssifuss, but the Serpent shook its head; it could not understand a word.

'Look!' said Hyry Keshvara. Lucrezia did as she was told, and saw that another figure had appeared behind the handsome quadruped: a second newt, moving as enthusiastically as the first. The one which had come with them from the garden of tree-people immediately left off its one-sided conversation and went to meet it. Both creatures widened their arms in readiness for an embrace.

The sight was so absurd that Lucrezia couldn't help laughing, but no one else joined in. The two newts did indeed embrace as they came together, but it was a far more intimate embrace than she had ever imagined possible. For a few moments they clung together as ardently as lovers – and then Lucrezia realised that their flesh had begun to flow and fuse. Her amusement turned to horror and her laughter froze.

She turned to Kasabil and said: 'Did you know . . .?' She broke off as Kasabil nodded; plainly, this aspect of newt behaviour was already familiar to manticores. She tried to remember exactly what the ghost had said when it was trying to explain itself in the garden of the tree-people. Like Kasabil and Vekoren it was a searcher, a gatherer of information – this, presumably, was one of the ways in which it communicated the information it had gathered. Lucrezia told herself that she had no reason to be surprised; humans had designed this creature, using what they knew of the properties and abilities of the living ground, for which such fusions were a matter of course.

The fusion of the two creatures was completed in less time than she would have imagined possible. For two or three minutes there was a heaving mass of flesh with too many arms, too many legs and too many eyes – and no obvious shape at all – but then a single individual began to emerge again: a newt that was twice as stout as either of its 'parents' but otherwise little different.

'Don't be alarmed,' Kasabil murmured. 'They never greet anyone that way but members of their own kind.'

'I think that other thing's a sphinx,' the princess remarked, for want of anything else to say. 'I've heard them described in some of the tales they tell in the Inner Sanctum.'

'I don't care what it's called,' Hyry retorted. 'I just want to know what it's going to do. If it summons a dozen of its friends to face the manticores . . .' She was becoming anxious because the sphinx had turned its eyes away from the newts and was studying them all.

'You must have had a hard journey,' it said eventually. 'There is a better way for humans and Serpents, had you only looked for it – but you are welcome.'

Hyry Keshvara was about to reply, but Lucrezia touched her on the arm and the trader accepted the instruction. Lucrezia walked forward and came to stand within reach of the sphinx's forepaw.

'My name is Lucrezia,' she said grandiloquently. 'I have come through the Forest of Absolute Night, crossed the Dragomite Hills and the Soursweet Marshes, fought battles to the north of the Nine Towns and on the northern rim of the Great Reef, and have visited a garden in which people have been swallowed up by trees. It has been a hard journey, but I followed the best route I could. These are my friends.' One by one she named them all, although she had to point rather vaguely at Lississee's companions because she still couldn't tell them apart. When she had finished with introductions she said: 'Kasabil and Vekoren helped us to reach the garden; I hope that you will extend to them the same welcome you have offered to us.'

The manticores had already lowered their stings. The sphinx seemed to be pondering the proposition. Lucrezia felt that it was best to continue. 'What it means I don't know,' she said, 'but I've been told since infancy that I have Serpent's blood in my veins, and that it somehow imposed a duty upon me to come here if I could. That's why I'm here.'

'You're safe now,' the sphinx assured her. 'Humans and Serpents are equally welcome, and we are glad to see the manticores. We have a message to deliver, if they will agree to serve as messengers. We may have need of something that their ground might have preserved, and we have something to offer in exchange.'

Lucrezia turned round to look back at the two manticores, who seemed every bit as surprised by this development as she was. It was Hyry Keshvara who said: 'Why do you need them to carry your message for you? If you have a message to send, you can surely deliver it yourself.'

The sphinx gave no sign of offence. It simply said: 'We never go beyond the boundaries of Idun, and we could not be sure that a newt would reach its destination. The awakening is near to its end, and time is pressing. Will you carry the message, Vekoren?'

Lucrezia assumed that it had named Vekoren because Kasabil was still walking less easily than his companion.

'What message?' Vekoren asked.

'If you come to the pyramid,' the sphinx said, 'it will be given to you there. No harm will be done to you by my kin, although you will be wise to avoid the produce of other grounds. Will you carry the message?'

'I came here to find what there is to be found,' the manticore replied. 'I suppose that a message will do as well as anything else, and perhaps better, but I can't promise a reply. What is it we might have that you might need?'

The sphinx raised its head a little higher. 'A memory,' it said – and added, before it turned away to lead them on their way: 'We had best not delay. This is not a safe place, for all that we have laboured hard to make it so. The enemies which have tried to keep you back are not impotent even here. The war is nearer to being lost than won – but the tide will turn. It must, and it will.'

It said no more, wheeling around with surprising grace in view of the limited space available for the manoeuvre. The compound newt had already turned, and was making its way towards the pyramid, moving with surprising facility considering that it had been two separate individuals only minutes before.

'Follow me,' the newt called, in a tone clearer and more robust than any its slimmer predecessor had used. 'Follow me, and all will be well. Safe now. Safe for ever.'

Lucrezia would have liked to believe it, but she didn't yet dare.

IO

BY THE TIME Fraxinus reached the end of the road he had almost lost contact with reality. He knew, vaguely, that he had not eaten for more than a day and that it was at least half as long since a drop of water had passed his lips, but so complete was the numbing effect of the Gauntlet of Gladness that he felt not the slightest hunger or thirst. He was aware of his utter exhaustion, but even that seemed to be no more than an extension of his lack of feeling.

He had not slept – and therefore had not dreamed, at least in any literal sense – but the meaning had been so comprehensively leached out of every sight and sound that he could easily have believed himself adrift in a bizarre but all-consuming hallucination. The road had become a kind of tunnel confining his whole existence and reducing existence itself to a prepared pathway without turnings, crossroads, choices or opportunities.

It would have been easy to give up the struggle and surrender to automatism: to let his body become a fleshy marionette, moving in mechanical fashion according to a set of programmed reflexes, while his mind sank gratefully into a passivity that was as devoid of responsibility as it was of feeling. There would have been a kind of relief in letting go of everything, and he had no doubt that if the Gauntlet of Gladness had been carefully designed that must be the purpose of its plan. For that very reason, though, he fought its deadening effect. He made what defences he could against the creeping death-in-life which sought to render his intelligence impotent.

'I am not a sheep content to be led to the slaughter,' he told himself sternly. 'It does not matter what intention these myth-borrowed creatures have, nor what purpose was integrated into Chimera's Cradle by its architects. I have my own reasons for being here, and my own ambitions. I must serve those ambitions

419

no matter what obstacles are put in my way. I owe these creatures nothing for their feeble welcome, and if their only reason for bringing me here is to feed me to the living ground I must gather every fibre of my strength in order to resist.'

Any hope he had conserved that the instruments of Chimera's Cradle had any other purpose in view than to give their visitors to their own particular living ground had disappeared when he discovered what the Gauntlet of Gladness was – but by the time he had reached that conclusion there was nothing to be gained by sharing it with his companions. There had been a very brief interval when he might have summoned up the strength of will to voice a warning sentence, but as soon as it had passed he realised that it would have done no good. Those capable of taking heed of warnings must also be capable of making their own calculations.

Once they had reached the end of the narrow road Fraxinus tried with all his might to concentrate his attention on his surroundings, but he had been too long on the narrow road and he was exhausted as well as drugged. The cubes and cones of the 'garden' which the sphinx had called the womb of the world seemed to his confused senses to be mere abstract designs sketched upon the walls of his inner self. They appeared to him as a substitute for the world rather than an aspect of it: a brutal theoretical reduction of its complexity. Its hues were mere echoes of colour randomly dashed upon a bleached backcloth; its shapes were caricaturish suggestions indicative of a much richer and more complex set of structures.

'It would be horribly ironic,' he said to himself, shaping every word with the utmost care, 'were I to achieve the destination I have sought so long without even being able to see it, let alone to establish any meaningful trade with its citizens. I must at least *see*; I must at least *know* what it is that I have attained at such dreadful cost.'

Alas, saying it was not enough; to do it would have required a better command over his senses than he now had.

His horse plodded on in the wake of the three sphinxes and their batrachian companions, as heavily drugged as he was himself, while he sat rigidly upon its back: a mote of frail and flickering intelligence adrift in a problematic void. Had he been able to lift his hand to his mouth he would have bitten it as hard

420

as he could, in the hope of restoring a bridge of sensation capable of connecting him to the world, but he simply could not do it.

When the horse finally came to a halt, Fraxinus couldn't step down. When the animal buckled at the knees and collapsed, released from the grip of mechanism only to perish, his left leg was trapped beneath its body, unable to feel the weight but tightly prisoned nevertheless. Two of the frog-like creatures had to drag him free, and then had to hold him upright because he couldn't stand unaided.

There were more of the batrachians now; he couldn't count them but there must have been dozens. They collected Checuti and Jume Metra, helping them down from their exhausted mounts. He saw that others were going to the wagon, some climbing up to the driver's bench while others went in at the back. There was not a single human still able to walk unsupported – but Fraxinus did see Mossassor, still alone, still upright, still moving. Mossassor only needed to be pointed in the direction of the pyramid; everyone else needed to be carried. Fraxinus supposed that everyone *was* carried – except for Dhalla, who was far too heavy – but he wasn't able to take any kind of census.

He was flanked by two of the frog-like creatures, each of which had him by an arm, but he was able to take a part of his weight on his own legs and he did his best to put up a show of walking. Indeed, as they drew him towards the portal in the base of the pyramid he convinced himself that a little sensation might be returning to his legs, and that if only he were walked far enough by his helpers he would recover the art of walking by himself. This impression was enhanced by the fact that as he passed through the portal into the shadowed interior of the pyramid the heat of the day was abruptly substituted by the cold of deep shadow. He couldn't shiver, but the clammy grip of his decaying shirt suddenly seemed much sharper.

Fraxinus tried to take notice of the internal architecture of the pyramid, but he could grasp no more than a few scattered impressions. The shadowy coldness of the floor was perceptible even through the soles of his boots and the walls seemed quite bare; they were certainly devoid of the spectacular figures which had dressed the 'walls' of the Crystal City. The dark corridor must have been at least thirty mets long, and it wasn't wide

421

enough for more than two people to walk abreast. He could see that the space beyond was better lit but when he passed through the second set of pillars he found that the illumination only added to his confusion; this wasn't the quiet bioluminescence of the Forest of Absolute Night but something more like the lens-guided light of Salamander's Fire.

When his batrachian guides stopped they intended to let him crumple to the floor, but he had recovered strength enough to fight against that. He wouldn't condescend to fall, and the determination which kept his legs straight strengthened the rest of him. His supporters accepted his assertion readily enough but they wouldn't speak to him; they simply stepped clear and left him to stand alone, but to his left and his right their siblings were laying his companions down and none of them seemed to be making any protest.

He saw that Checuti's whole skull was now covered by the glassy growth that had sealed his wound and then continued to extend its empire. When two more batrachians laid Purkin down Fraxinus saw that the sergeant's condition was even further advanced; the man was half petrified already. Had he been able to walk normally he would have gone to Aulakh Phar to see how badly *he* had fared but he had to concentrate all his effort simply to remain standing.

Above the flat apron where the bodies were being laid out there was nothing but a vague tent of light – but that was, in its way, the most amazing aspect of the space in which he found himself. He guessed that the pyramid must have been twice as tall as the towers of Xandria's citadel but its central chamber was uncluttered by pillars and arches, or by any horizontal divisions that might have served as floors and ceilings. Given that the slope of its four sides was gentle enough to permit a man to walk up or down in relative comfort, the enclosed space had to be vaster by far than any he had ever seen before.

Fraxinus forced himself to concentrate and to contemplate this particular wonder.

From the courtyard where Belin's stables were the great king's subjects could look up at the great wall and the tower of the Inner Sanctum, and at the segment of sky prisoned by their reach. Fraxinus had done that, dwarfed by the combined achievements of architect's vision and stonemason's ingenuity –

but this was a giddier experience by far. The vault was entirely enclosed, precisely shaped, and deftly lit. Fraxinus felt his head whirl as he tried to look up into the apex of the inner space: the vanishing point where all the lines met. He had to look down again immediately, and then had to fight against the gravity which tried to drag him down.

He won the fight, and looked around more carefully.

The space enclosed by the base of the pyramid was far bigger than any courtyard in Xandria's citadel but it didn't resemble a courtyard at all. Indeed, the greater part of the space was occupied by an artificial lake of some glutinous liquid whose unstirred surface nevertheless contrived to signify its fluidity. Fraxinus was not in the least astonished by this. He had been encouraged to expect something of exactly this sort; the lore referred to the Pool of Life, and here it was.

The straight sides of the lake were parallel to the walls of the pyramid; it would have been possible, had he been able to walk at all, to walk all the way around the pool on a terrace wide enough for five or six humans to walk abreast. The walls which formed the outer limit of the terrace were as devoid of figures as those in the corridor but they each had a neat array of doorless portals, which presumably gave access to smaller chambers.

Fraxinus was struck by the fact that there was no one to greet his party save for the batrachians, who had so far given the impression of being mere servants. No one had emerged from the inner portals to see what had been delivered to the pyramid: no human; no Serpent; no Salamander. The sphinxes had remained outside.

'There ought to be more ceremony than this,' Fraxinus said under his breath. 'We deserve that, at least. We have crossed thousands of kims to be here, and we are surely entitled to some ritual of reception.' He might have called out, but he wasn't sure that he could raise a whimper – and the thought of his voice echoing around that vast space, if it turned out that he could, was curiously intimidating.

It was not until he saw two of the frog-like creatures carrying one of his companions towards the pool, with the obvious intention of lowering the body into the fluid, that he found the necessary spur to action. Whatever else he could bear with passivity, he couldn't bear that.

'No!' he cried, although the cry came out as a strangled whisper. He took one step, and then another – and with each step he took the next became easier.

The batrachians turned when they heard him speak, and paused when they saw that he was coming towards them. They would have had plenty of time to complete their task had they been so inclined, but they waited. Fraxinus saw that the body they were carrying was that of Aulakh Phar.

'No,' he said again, as he came within reach of them. 'I won't allow it.'

Had they resisted he couldn't possibly have stopped it, given that he had so little control over his limbs, but the batrachians didn't try to hold him back.

'Must be done,' one of them said, in a reedy voice that sounded strangely plaintive.

'Not without a *reason*,' Fraxinus gasped. He would have used the word *explanation* had he been confident that he could navigate a course through its tangled syllables.

'He will not die,' said the second creature earnestly. 'He will *live*. It's the only way.'

'Must be done,' said the first again.

Impatient with his own incapacity, Fraxinus lashed out. He struck the creature across its absurdly wide mouth; it was a clumsy and open-handed blow but he was incapable of delivering any other.

The batrachian's arms were occupied in holding Phar's legs and it couldn't block the blow. It fell backwards, more surprised than hurt, and Phar's body tumbled to the floor. The creature came slowly to its feet again, but it made no move to retaliate.

'No!' Fraxinus said again, gritting his teeth momentarily in order to prepare for a longer sentence. 'First, you must *tell* us . . . *everything*.'

'No time,' said the more articulate of the two. 'No need.' Fraxinus couldn't help but construe the dismissiveness of the second statement as a blunt insult.

'*There's every need!*' he insisted again.

'Must be done,' recited the creature he had knocked down.

'Not murder,' the other amplified, staring at Fraxinus with its huge dark eyes as if he were some kind of fool. 'Is life – only life

424

here. Is everything. You are part of it now – always will be. Is life, not death. Don't be afraid. No need to be afraid.'

Fraxinus wanted to lash out again but he was ashamed of himself for wanting it. Had the drug not made him so stupid he felt sure that he could have thought of something better to do, something better to say, but all this was like some mad hallucination, some absurdly bad dream from which he only needed to awaken. In the meantime . . .

He took another lurching step forward, then knelt down beside Aulakh Phar's supine body. He picked the old man's head up, and forced the body into a sitting position – but Phar's head was covered by a strange patina, softer and crustier than the glassy tegument which decked Checuti's head but no prettier. The old man was deeply unconscious. It was difficult to imagine that he could ever wake up; there were too few signs of life left in him. Where his own flesh was still exposed it was cold to the touch; he hardly seemed to be breathing.

This is monumentally unfair, Fraxinus thought. *Aulakh's knowledge brought us here; all the explanations we have concocted for ourselves drew on his resources. He must be able to see what there is to see, to find what there is to find. He must!*

Fraxinus looked at the pool into which the frog-creatures had intended to lower the body. The glutinous surface gave off a faint glow and it was moving slightly: slow waves spread like lazy ripples from its centre. Fraxinus could see ghostly shapes within it: the bodies of humans and Serpents. Further out he could see thinner, vaguer forms which might have been winged Salamanders born of the brave heat of Salamander's Fire . . . and a few larger forms which might have been anything at all. The sluggish fluids of the pool moved around them, as if they were coursing through invisible veins and arteries.

What did I expect? Fraxinus asked himself. *We came to find the Pool of Life, and here it is . . . but we came to see it, not to surrender to it. We came in search of understanding, not to be told that there is no time and no need for explanations!*

Aloud, he said: 'I can't allow it.'

'You must,' was the only reply he received.

'I won't,' he repeated.

There was no way of knowing how long the game of contradictions might have gone on before he lost it – for he had not the power to win it – but he wasn't compelled to carry on. The batrachians were already looking past him, at someone else who had arrived to take a hand.

Fraxinus half expected to see Dhalla, who was the only member of the expedition not to have been carried in, but when he turned around he saw that the person standing there – who must have emerged from the corridor only a few moments before – was Princess Lucrezia.

To pile one miracle atop another, she seemed perfectly well able to walk and the expression in her eyes had not been dulled by long exposure to the Gauntlet of Gladness.

'Fraxinus?' she said. 'What's happening?'

He wished that he had the energy to explain, but he couldn't force himself to say anything at all.

'Is my mother here?' the princess asked, looking round at the fallen bodies and their patient attendants. All the batrachians were motionless; it seemed as if time itself had stopped.

'Yes,' Fraxinus said, when the silence had become unbearable. 'We're all here.'

'What's wrong with you?' she asked, but he could see that she already understood, partially at least. 'You came the easy way,' she added, when he made no reply. 'You came by the road marked on the map, and found it sown with poisons. I've followed roads of that sort myself. The ghosts mean to feed you to the living ground, and they prepared you in advance.'

Ghosts? Fraxinus thought, but he nodded his head.

'Unfortunately,' she said, looking round at the silent crowd, 'the ground is already within us. There's no escape. There never was. We've been damned for longer than we imagine . . . there's no way back. We can only go forward, and hope that we come *through*. It *is* possible to come through. There are ghosts and ghosts, you see – these aren't the only kind, or the best.'

Fraxinus did what he could to formulate an intelligent response, but all he could say was: 'Already dead.'

'From the viewpoint of the dwellers in the deep,' Lucrezia said, 'we've never been truly alive. In their terms, this is the beginning, not the end.'

Fraxinus wished that he'd been the one to say something as neat and portentous as that, but he was gracious enough to be glad that someone had. The unfortunate thing was that it still wasn't an explanation, or anything like an explanation. It was far too glib to qualify as any kind of answer. He hugged Aulakh Phar's head to his belly, as if the desire to protect his friend could conjure up some freak of chance that might make protection possible.

'Is he dead?' The question was voiced, fearfully, by Hyry Keshvara, who had come to stand beside the princess. Others were crowding in behind them now: Serpents all. One that was stouter than the rest immediately ran to the place where Mossassor had finally condescended to fall down.

'No,' Fraxinus said, although he was no longer sure. He was no longer sure that the dying man had ever been truly alive, or that there was any life at all beyond the rim of this fantastic war zone. Even in the midst of this awful confusion, however, he contrived to keep in mind the most important thought of all: that he had reached his goal, and that he had brought the greater number of his companions with him. The partnership he had forged with Phar and Keshvara was intact again, and Chimera's Cradle was all around them, waiting for them to begin their belated investigation of its mysteries.

Then the articulate ghost hurled itself upon him. It would not have been so bad had he been able to meet it hand to hand, as a fighting man might meet an almost-equal adversary, but that wasn't what happened.

Something soft and slimy smothered his waiting arms and flooded his face. The frog-like creature was producing the fluid in such astonishing quantities that it seemed to be turning all its flesh into a mass of protoplasmic liquid. It was as if the creature intended to drown him . . . or *dissolve* him. He couldn't have fought it whatever condition he was in; it would have been like fighting a cloudburst or a fog. Drugged or undrugged, it would have overwhelmed him with the utmost ease.

There's no escape, he thought – or perhaps the words only echoed in his mind, requiring no effort of repetition. *There never was.*

LUCREZIA MIGHT HAVE run forward in a vain bid to help Carus Fraxinus, even though she knew that there was nothing she could do, but she was given no chance. As soon as the ghosts made their move, surging forward in unison to secure their claim upon his living flesh, Hyry Keshvara grabbed her and hauled her backwards. The trader obviously feared that were they to stay where they were they would suffer the same fate as Fraxinus, and she pulled Lucrezia towards the narrow corridor through which they had come. Although she had to be forced to accept the initial impetus, Lucrezia soon consented to divert her own efforts to the same goal.

She knew, of course, that any thought of escape was frankly absurd, but there was reason to hope that help might be found outside; the two manticores ought to be there, and the sphinx which seemed to have a measure of authority over the newts. What sort of help it might be she didn't know, but like Fraxinus she felt an urgent need to claim a *delay*, until matters had been clearly explained. Perhaps, as the newts had said, there was no alternative but to deliver all visitors to the liquid flesh of the pool within the pyramid, but it certainly ought not to be done in this peremptory manner. Beneath this surface layer of rational thought, however, was a well of blind panic; it was really that which moved her. When she stepped outside the portal, the panic increased and its grip became even more insistent.

While she had been making her way to the pyramid Lucrezia had judged Chimera's Cradle to be a desolate place. The fugitive traces of hellhounds and crocolids that she had glimpsed in the littered 'streets' had only added to the impression of dereliction. Although faded tints of rot had tainted the underlying whiteness they had contrived to re-emphasise the impression that this whole place was a vast bone-heap: a sea of slaughterhouse waste picked clean by carrion birds. She had always known that it was alive, but it had not shown her the least hint of liveliness and she slipped into the habit of thinking of it as a flattened-out version of the Dragomite Hills.

Life had returned to it now, with a vengeance.

A sudden sweeping influx of colour had filled the air with dancing clouds. Nor were the clouds content to fill the air; they were painting the clinically delineated 'buildings' which clustered around the pyramid with broad and gaudy brush-strokes. It was as if the sullen sky had decided on a whim to disgorge a deluge of multicoloured snowflakes whose mission was to take triumphant possession of every exposed surface.

It was undoubtedly beautiful, but it was also terrifying. The five horses that were still standing – four of which were still hitched to Fraxinus's wagon – were wide-eyed with alarm. As flecks of colour settled on their backs and haunches they whinnied and bucked, but only a few of the flecks responded by dancing away into the air. The sphinx, the compound newt and the two manticores had already gone. There was no indication as to where – they certainly hadn't followed the humans and the Serpents into the pyramid.

Lucrezia knew that the clouds of colour were composed of 'butterflies' of a kind she had seen many times before, but she had never suspected for a moment that such profusion was possible. She had no idea what the significance of the invasion was, but she leapt readily enough to the conclusion that it would do her no good at all to surrender.

As the first few settled on her shoulders and clung to her hair, reflex insisted that she brush them off. It was impossible to clear them all – for every one she dislodged there were three more waiting to settle – but those she did make contact with were dissuaded easily enough. She knew by virtue of her previous observations that each one had four wings as earthly butterflies had, intricately patterned in all the colours of the rainbow, but that their bodies were like little black sticks with twelve very short legs. They had neither eyes nor mouth-parts nor antennae; in fact, they had no heads to speak of at all.

Hyry Keshvara sprang into action too, brushing the things from Lucrezia's hair and jogging her arm to dislodge the ones

429

that had been caught up in her ragged sleeve – but that only gave the ones which settled on her own flesh a better chance to cling.

The horses were becoming more agitated by the second; they were dislodging a lot of the multicoloured fliers but every one of them already had at least a hundred clinging to various parts of their bodies, mostly on the back and hindquarters. The butter-flies which had settled on the white walls of the ghost city were flattening out their wings, superimposing their own patterns on the monochromal ones beneath. The dull white background was disappearing, swallowed up by kaleidoscopic confusion. Hyry now began pushing Lucrezia back towards the portal from which they had only just fled, but Lucrezia had no intention of being pushed. She had climbed into the wagon for a few moments before entering the pyramid and she knew that it wasn't empty.

'Dhalla!' she called, as she evaded Keshvara's pressure and bounded down the slope to the 'forecourt' where the wagon stood. Hyry only hesitated for a moment before following her.

Vekoren and Kasabil had been waiting by the wagon with the sphinx and the compound batrachian last time she had seen them, but they hadn't taken refuge inside. There was no one in the wagon but the giant, who was still unconscious but by no means still. The canvas at the back of the wagon wasn't sealed and dozens of the butterflies were already inside; Dhalla wasn't incapable of reacting to their presence and she was tossing and turning as if in the grip of a dreadful nightmare.

The blankets with which Dhalla's body was draped had not been woven for the use of giants and there was a good deal of naked flesh on view, but the invaders showed no particular preference for one surface over another, so none had attached itself too firmly as yet. Lucrezia brushed off a couple of the creatures as she scrambled forward and began to strike Dhalla's heaving shoulders with her fists. Directed against anyone else such blows could only have been intended to injure, but Lucrezia had grown up with Dhalla. She knew that nothing less could be relied on to make an impression. While she struck out she also shouted.

'Dhalla! Dhalla! It's me! Lucrezia!'

Lucrezia had already tried to rouse the giant once and had failed. There was more than mere desperation in her shouting, though; the giant had been still before but was very agitated now. Furthermore, she still felt free to hope that Dhalla might react to the name Lucrezia, if she were capable of reacting to anything at all.

Dhalla's agitation increased, and the shadow of a frown appeared on her unrelaxed features, but the shouting must have seemed to her no more than a phase of her bad dream. She didn't open her eyes.

Lucrezia hit her harder, and shouted again: 'It's Lucrezia. Wake up, for corruption's sake! It's *Lucrezia*!'

The combination worked. The giant's eyelids flickered, and her jerky movements were calmed before they resumed in a more purposeful manner. 'Lucrezia?' she murmured, as her huge hands swept her forearms free of would-be parasites.

'Yes! We have to go inside! Now! We have to save Fraxinus and Ereleth – not to mention ourselves. No one can do it but you!'

The giant opened her eyes wide, and made as if to rise, but stopped when she had barely raised her head from the makeshift pillow. She seemed surprised that her body was so reluctant to obey her.

'Don't try to stand!' Lucrezia said impatiently. 'Just wriggle out of the wagon feet forwards. *Then* get on your feet. It's not far – three or four strides, for a giant.'

Hyry, meanwhile, was swiping away the things that settled on Lucrezia's head and back, as well as keeping her own body as clear as she could. Lucrezia knew that it probably wouldn't matter much if the things attached themselves to her clothing, and that they could probably be detached even if they gripped her with all those tiny legs – but she also knew that time was of the essence, and that they might have a great deal of work to do even when they got back to the pyramid's interior. The more fliers they dislodged now, the fewer they would have to dislodge later.

Lucrezia knew there could be no final victory over the demands of the living ground, but she wanted to claim every last second of whatever time remained to her present self – and she wanted to claim whatever time she could for Carus Fraxinus and Ssifuss, for Checuti and Mossassor, for Ereleth and anyone else

431

still capable of opening two eyes and seeing the mystery that was Chimera's Cradle.

With agonising slowness, Dhalla began to pull herself towards the back of the wagon. The hinged timbers which formed the rear flap weren't lowered, but Dhalla wasn't about to start clambering over – she smashed them with an unceremonious thrust of her booted foot and kept wriggling. Sacks and boxes tumbled from the back of the wagon, bursting on the hard ground, but no one paid them any attention.

Dhalla lowered her legs to the ground easily enough, but Lucrezia knew that the real test was still to come. Could the giant stand up?

She could – but not without difficulty. Had she not been so huge Lucrezia and Hyry could have helped her a little, but they were not tall even for human beings and the tops of their heads were no higher than the giant's navel. They used their hands to urge her in the right direction, but they couldn't help her walk.

The giant tottered drunkenly, but she stumbled the right way. Lucrezia and Hyry tried to clear the multicoloured blots which settled on her thighs and buttocks, and she flapped her own massive arms, scattering the clouds of colour which were already forming around her head and shoulders.

It was, as Lucrezia had said, only three or four giant's strides to the waiting portal, whose gloom now seemed welcoming in spite of the mayhem which must be waiting at its other end. In actual fact, it required seven steps before Dhalla actually reached the opening, and she nearly tripped twice as she negotiated the slope. In the end, though, Lucrezia and Hyry got her to and through the gap, and they followed her as soon as they had space to do it. They had no alternative now but to move in the same direction, brushing off butterflies and trampling them into the ground as they fell. When they came through the second portal, though, there were no other willing hands ready to help in the business of clearance.

The ghosts had contrived to deliver five of the recumbent bodies to the Pool of Life; Checuti, Purkin, Shabir, Jume Metra and Ereleth were already sinking into the protoplasmic fluid. By virtue of the interference of Fraxinus and Ssifuss, neither Phar nor Mossassor had yet been consigned to the living lake, but only one other human had roused herself sufficiently to resist the ghosts and that was Merel Zabio.

Alas, neither Merel's arousal nor the efforts of Fraxinus and Ssifuss had proved effective. All three had met the same reaction; each one of them was now encased in a capacious envelope of slime. Having seen two ghosts fuse with one another, Lucrezia had some notion of what must be happening; the batrachian creatures were evidently capable of emitting extraordinary quantities of the stuff, shrinking visibly as they did so. All three of the protoplasmic masses were still heaving as the individuals imprisoned within tried to throw off their glutinous encasements, but the task was impossible.

There was no sign of Lississee and the other slender Serpents; they had disappeared. If they had run away, they could only have run into the inner chambers of the pyramid. There were, however, at least a dozen newts awaiting the three newcomers, and they moved forward as one to intercept the giant. For once, Lucrezia realised, Dhalla was facing a battle that she couldn't possibly win. What use was her superhuman strength against an enemy which could dissolve its own flesh and drench her with liquid life?

Lucrezia knew that the ghosts could be killed. They could be crushed or cut in two – such had been the fate of the one that guided Andris through the dragomite hive and the one he had termed the Watcher. She also knew, though, that it would be futile to wreak such destruction here. They were too close to the heart of this dweller in the deep to resist its minions.

Lucrezia felt utterly helpless. Inside or outside the pyramid there seemed to be no available avenue of escape, however temporary. Like Fraxinus, however, she was unwilling in the extreme to submit tamely to ingestion and annihilation. Like Fraxinus, she wanted answers first; she wanted to be told what would become of her, and how, and *why*.

'Inside!' someone yelled, as Lucrezia tried to rake half a dozen of the creatures from her hair. It was Hyry who had spoken, and she meant *further* inside – into the darker portals let into the walls of the pyramid. It was an absurd instruction, but Lucrezia understood the panic that had produced it. Lississee and its fellows must have reacted in a similarly silly fashion.

Dhalla was staggering, trying to strike out sideways with her huge hands. She lurched one way and then the other in a futile attempt to swat the wary ghosts which moved around her. Lucrezia opened her mouth to howl a warning, but the words stuck in her throat as she saw how futile it would be. Dhalla staggered on, as if she were quite unable to stop herself now that she had built up momentum; the ghosts didn't have to draw her on or tempt her to take the path they wanted her to take. She hit one, and then another, sending them spinning away, but then she reached the edge of the great turbid pool, and took one step too many. Her leading leg sank into the pool, and her body tumbled in. She spread her arms wide, as if to break her fall, and Lucrezia winced in anticipation of a mighty splash, but no such splash came. It was as if the giant had fallen into a great vat of molasses.

The living lake received her gratefully, and sucked her down.

Dhalla made a few feeble movements, as though she were trying to swim, but she could make no headway at all. She must have lost consciousness even as she fell.

Lucrezia felt sick; it was as if she had seen her whole life vanish into that problematic mass. Numbly, she turned away and followed Hyry through a shadowed doorway.

She might have expected what happened next, but she wasn't thinking quickly enough or clearly enough. As she ran into the darkness, still groping absent-mindedly at her face and hair in the reflexive quest to get rid of the last half-dozen clinging butterflies, she tripped over something lying on the floor. She lurched to one side, trying to stop herself from falling, and collided with a wall.

Such a collision should have jarred every bone in her body, but this one didn't. This one was hardly a collision at all, because the wall yielded like a soft cushion, opening to receive her and grip her far more securely than any of the butterflies had. It was as if she, like Dhalla, had fallen into the surface of a viscous pool – except that her pool had somehow contrived to stand on end. She held her breath reflexively as the wall gripped her flesh and bore her imprisoned body away into total darkness.

She felt herself dragged downwards and carried sideways with remarkable rapidity, but she lost her bearings and couldn't tell whether she was going left or right, or how fast she was descending into the depths beneath the body of the pyramid. She had to let her breath out, even though she knew full well that she would be unable to take in more, but still she fought for consciousness.

It seemed that there was nothing left to fight for but one more useless second of her presence of mind, but still she fought.

As she was bound to do, she lost.

12

As THE DELUGE of glutinous fluid embraced him Fraxinus tried to move backwards. His fingers clawed at his face, trying to tear the horrid stuff away, but he couldn't get a grip on it at all. It swamped his face, cutting off his sight and blocking his nose and mouth. He fell down almost immediately, but he kept on fighting, opening a gap between his lips that was sufficient to let him draw breath. He rolled over and over, hoping that he might spread the stuff all over the chamber's floor and roll clear away from it, but there was no hope of that. It had him, and it couldn't be dislodged.

He heard Serpent voices shouting. Although he had learned no more than a dozen words of Mossassor's tongue he knew that Ssifuss was calling to its slimmer friends for help. Whatever they called back was not encouragement.

If the batrachian ghosts had come after him while he fought against the slowly solidifying cocoon they could easily have picked him up and carried him to the brink of the pool, but while he struggled they were content to let him alone. Fearing what might happen if and when he consented to be still, he continued to struggle with all his might, even though he knew full well that he was beaten. He was dizzy and exhausted but he was at least numb; he continued to kick out and he surprised himself by the protractedness of his efforts.

The fluid was leaking into his mouth now, and he couldn't seal his lips against it because he couldn't breathe through his nose. It was colder than his own internal temperature but not alarmingly so. Its taste was salty, but not offensively so. At first he tried not to swallow it, but he couldn't spit it out and in the end it came down to a straightforward choice between swallowing or being unable to draw breath – at which point he swallowed, and felt a treacly bolus flow down his oesophagus into his stomach.

436

Still he fought; still he managed to keep his limbs moving; still he achieved nothing but the postponement of his fate.

He felt a vibration in the floor as something – or someone – very large moved past him towards the Pool of Life. He heard a voice shout 'Inside!' and recognised it as Keshvara's. He might have been able to shout back had he concentrated all his effort on the task, but it seemed pointless.

He rolled over again, and then again, but the fluid was pressing him down with more than mere weight. It was actively trying to force him to be still, to force him flat against the floor – and the floor, meanwhile, was growing soft beneath him. It was as if the ground were opening a mouth of its own to swallow him up.

The pit into which he fell with such awful slowness didn't seem to be deep, but its sides were elastic; as soon as he was still – and the burden of the fluid had put a stop to his mad thrashing now – the sides oozed in around him to enshroud and entomb him. His arms and legs were so intimately enclosed that he could not move them at all, but he was able to breathe for at least a minute longer – until he felt the soft surface pressing on his face like a pillow borne down upon him by some irresistible hand.

He fought for breath but there was none to be had. The only effect of opening his mouth was to allow more of the fluid to surge into the orifice, reaching for the two passages behind his tongue. He couldn't stop it; it flowed in twin rivers down his gut and his windpipe alike.

He expected to lose consciousness then, but he didn't. After a moment's hectic giddiness, accompanied by a horrible feeling of invasion as his lungs filled up with cool liquid, his mind cleared again. He was blind and deaf, and his senses of taste and smell had been neutralised by the insipidity of the stuff that filled his mouth and nasal passages, but oxygen was still being fed into his bloodstream. He was still capable of thought and his brain – drugged though it was – had not yet given up that privilege.

He was sure that he was moving but he didn't know which way he was being carried. He suspected that it was down as well as along, but he had no real evidence to support the suspicion. The substance which surrounded him was now so uniform in its pressure and temperature that he seemed to have lost the sense of touch along with the other four.

Cut off from all external stimuli, Fraxinus tried to measure the passage of time by keeping track of his own heartbeats, which seemed regular enough to sustain the calculation. As the minutes elapsed it seemed that he became extraordinarily sensitive to the sensation of the blood surging through his veins – but he couldn't be sure that he wasn't magnifying the sensation subjectively, so as to fill the unprecedented void.

He wasn't afraid any longer. At least, he wasn't afraid of *dying*. Whatever held him evidently knew how to keep him alive and had every intention of so doing. For a little while, he hoped that he might be released into some secret and self-enclosed enclave of the pyramid, where he might be reunited with his fellows, but no such regurgitation occurred.

More time elapsed. He could no longer tell whether he was moving or not. He would have spoken if he could, but he couldn't. He would have struggled against his imprisonment, if only to enjoy the perverse pleasure of resistance, but no matter how much will-power he devoted to the task of tensing his muscles he could not increase or decrease the pressure on his limbs.

What now? he thought, framing the words carefully in case the invasion of his person might have been so absolute as to allow his private thoughts to be overheard.

There was no detectable response.

Somehow, he lost contact with his heartbeat. It was as if its awesome regularity had had the same ultimate effect as his prison's uniformity, allowing it to fade out of consciousness. He felt that a year might pass as easily as a minute, and that he would not know it. He tried to make his thoughts deliberate, so that their extent might provide a yardstick of sorts, but having nothing with which to compare the progress of their sluggish train he could not be sure that a sentence which would only have taken a few seconds to voice did not now require an hour to draw out in his thoughts.

As if by way of compensation, he felt that the deadening and soporific effects of the Gauntlet of Gladness were no longer so tangible. He felt that he was becoming more alert rather than less – and less exhausted too.

Perhaps I ought to try to sleep, he said to himself, *but were I to surrender consciousness in this condition, how could I be sure when I awoke that I wasn't still lost in a dream?*

He was prepared to assume that time was still passing in a reasonably familiar fashion, but he couldn't help wondering whether that might be an illusion. Perhaps he was already asleep, already lost in a dream. Perhaps a minute of objective time might be so unnaturally extended in his present state as to seem an eternity – or perhaps the converse was true, and years were passing in the world outside while he framed the thought. He wondered whether the reason that he could no longer sense his heart was that he was unnaturally suspended between two of its beats.

Can you feed me and give me water as well as air? he asked, knowing that there would be no answer. *I suppose you can. I might live the rest of my life in this kind of enclosure – if such an existence could be reckoned as a life. I'd go mad, wouldn't I? Or would I contrive to fill the awful emptiness of real experience with all manner of confabulations?*

No obvious dreams arose as yet to fill the void; there remained the hope of imminent release – and the dread that it might not come.

How I wish you might speak to me, he said, and would have spoken the words aloud if he could. *I cannot help but wish it, even though I have no real reason to suppose that you have a voice of any kind, or even a mind.* After a pause he added: *But Ereleth told me that even the dragomite queen had a voice, by virtue of her partnership with a human mound-queen, so I shall continue stubbornly to hope.*

His heart leapt as he received an answer of sorts, by courtesy of coincidence if not intelligent response. The darkness which entombed him was modified by a pink light which shone through his closed eyelids.

He wasn't certain that he could open his eyes but he tried, and eventually succeeded in pulling the lids apart.

The thickened fluid which had enclosed his eyes was still present, pressing in upon his eyeballs as gently and as firmly as it had pressed upon the closed lids, but it was already translucent and it was becoming authentically transparent. Whether this was due to a change of state in the suspension medium or to his continuing movement within it he couldn't tell, but the important fact was that he could see.

He could see what was happening to Chimera's Cradle, from a vantage point which must have been near to the apex of the pyramid.

The 'garden' of Idun was no longer drawn in shades of grey and pastel blue, stained with seams of stonerot and stippled with intricate patterns of black dots. The garden of Idun was a riot of colour now, and that colour was in its surfaces as well as in the living clouds which still swirled around them.

He guessed easily enough what those living clouds were; he had taken note of the 'butterflies' which had drifted across his path while he ran the Gauntlet of Gladness, and he had studied the things which had made themselves at home in Checuti's and Jume Metra's flesh while they followed the perimeter of the Great Reef. He could see larger and darker shapes moving in the clouds, however – shapes that were moving more steadily and more gracefully than the little butterflies could. Some were birds but some were bigger than birds; he supposed that some were merely feeding, but judged that others probably had more ambitious purposes.

In monochrome the structures of Idun had faintly resembled buildings: the garden had given the impression of harbouring the ghost of the city that had occupied its site before. Multicoloured, they seemed truly alive, not ghostly at all and not like any human-constructed edifice he had ever encountered. The ovoids and the cylinders now looked like the caps and stalks of giant mushrooms, while the cones and cuboids had lost their sharp definition in the riot of camouflage colouration.

For a while, that same camouflage effect concealed the reality of movement, making it seem a mere optical illusion, but as time went by Fraxinus realised that there really *was* movement within the body of the ghostly city.

New structures were growing; old ones were changing their form; creatures of many kinds moved, half hidden, between them. He convinced himself that he could see horses and sphinxes, but there were many other things which couldn't possibly belong to either species.

Fraxinus had assumed that the butterflies he had glimpsed during the last stages of his journey were invaders launched by some rival ground, and that their presence in the airspace above Chimera's Cradle was unwelcome. Now he wondered whether he might have been wrong. Grateful to know that he was capable of it, he followed the train of thought into the trackless wilderness of speculation. Perhaps the structures he had observed so closely while he and his companions had made their way to the pyramid were merely receptacles to which these coloured creatures served as pollen. Perhaps all this was merely a kind of pseudosexual reassortment, reproducing in the unearthly ground the kind of adventure that had been fundamental to the evolution of all but a few earthly life forms. Was it not to be expected, after all, that Chimera's Cradle would combine the fundamental attributes of both worlds: the world which he and his kind now inhabited and the world from which their forefathers had first set out?

If so, he wondered, where did he and his companions fit in? Did the sphinxes and the frog-like creatures think of human beings and Serpents as mere spores: grist to the mill of creativity that was Idun – which was, it seemed, no longer the mere *navel*, let alone the *cradle*, of a world newborn but the *womb* of one that was yet to take form. Were Aulakh Phar and Ereleth and all the rest no more than mere repositories of raw material, to be digested by the Pool of Life and broken down into their constituent parts? Was he anything more himself, in spite of the fact that he had been granted the gift of sight so that he might oversee the fate of the garden's ghostly growths?

The more Fraxinus pondered this final question, the more reason he found for optimism. It wasn't difficult to convince himself that he was being protected from the metamorphosis which was overtaking Chimera's Cradle, and that the reason he had been taken into the body of the pyramid was to preserve him, at least for a while, from the possibility of premature change. If he was eventually to be changed himself, the butterflies were certainly not to be the instrument of his metamorphosis.

He tried hard to extend this optimism to include his fellows. If he were being protected, why should the same not be true of Phar and Ereleth, Mossassor and Checuti, Purkin and Shabir? Perhaps the ghosts had told him the truth about what had to be done, although they had not had the time to explain why. Perhaps there might yet be a joyous reunion.

Alas, he couldn't quite bring himself to believe it.

If all of that were true, he thought, it would imply that the pyramid did have a conscious and clever mind directing its affairs . . . but he had seen no evidence of that, and even the sphinxes sent to greet him with their deceptive and sententious promises had not told him *that*.

He watched the garden of Idun grow into its new glory, studying with a clinical eye the patient flux of its maturing shapes.

The clouds of colour thinned and disappeared, taking their darker shadows with them. Rain fell from the grey sky, which turned to black before the true clouds dispersed, exposing the stars.

Now, with the riotous colours subdued by the paler light of the flamestars, the movements within the garden were more easily detectable. He saw sphinxes on the prowl, no longer white in their coats. He saw horses too, with multicoloured hides. When he looked for the wagon and the debris that had been strewn around it he saw no trace of it, but he wasn't sure which of the pyramid's faces he was overlooking, and he knew that it might simply be hidden from him. When he returned his attention to more distant ground he saw that there were smaller creatures moving between the fungoid shapes: a few kaleido-scopic hellhounds, and a number of bipedal creatures moving with the same gait as the batrachians which had consigned him to this strange prison.

He hoped to see more when the sun came up again, especially if it rose into a blue sky, but while he was waiting he drifted off into a strange series of dreams, in which he recovered movement as well as light.

Each time he discovered himself walking or riding, however, the pleasure of it was quickly overwhelmed by the guilty knowledge that it wasn't real. Such moments of uncomfortable realisation were always followed by the sensation of awakening, and a temporary sense of relief, but each seeming awakening was swiftly followed by a further realisation that what he had taken for life and freedom was merely another phantom of sleep. He soon became utterly confused, losing track of time over and over again, but he never quite surrendered to the dreams which seemed to be trying with all their insidious might to bear him away from sanity. As soon as any false reality threatened to take control of him he was able to extract himself from it sternly, condemning its seductions to the abyss of the unremembered.

It's as well that I can forget these temptations, he thought, on one occasion, *else any one of them might become a substitute for life – and then I would be mad, and my grip on reality permanently broken.* Unfortunately, actuality itself had come to resemble a dream – or a nightmare – far too closely for comfort. Lost in confusion, he had no way of knowing whether he slept for a few hours or a few days while the movements outside the pyramid faded into vagueness and seeming randomness.

Eventually, though, he felt that he was able to reassert the dominion of consciousness and continuity. The colours had begun to fade from the structures of the garden now, just as they had earlier faded from the atmosphere. They slowly leached out of the cones and the cuboids, leaving them stark and straight again, their lines sharply delineated and their angles precise.

Little by little, the garden returned to its former state. It was as if its flirtation with gorgeousness had itself been a kind of gaudy dream, succeeded now by a reluctant acceptance of dull sobriety.

Fraxinus didn't know whether this further change was cause for regret or exultation, but he did dare to hope that it might portend his imminent release. His optimism promised him that as soon as 'normality' was restored to Idun, he would be set free – and that he might then have the explanation he had sought in vain before.

Before that happened, though, there was another curious sequence of events to be witnessed.

Once the sphinxes had reverted to their ordinary whiteness he saw no more hellhounds and no more frog-like humanoids – at least for a while. As night fell again, though – perhaps for the fourth time, or even the fifth – he saw a new company of invaders. These were not skulking fugitives; they came proudly and purposefully, and the sphinxes politely made way for them.

The newcomers included creatures like sphinxes, but they had vividly striped bodies and tails like scorpions; Fraxinus had no difficulty in recognising them as manticores. They were six in number, and they were not alone. Every one of the six had a rider.

Five of the manticore-riders were batrachians of the kind Lucrezia had called ghosts, but the sixth one really *was* a ghost, in what Fraxinus thought of as the 'true' sense of the word: a man returned from the dead.

At least, the man gave every indication of being a man, in spite of the frank impossibility of his being the man he seemed to be. Fraxinus observed that he was even wearing tailored clothes, of a quality he had not seen anywhere south of the Dragomite Hills.

If I'm dreaming yet again, Fraxinus thought, *it is a more interesting and more compelling dream than any of those I contrived to banish in a trice. And if I am not, then it seems that fate has not yet done with surprises. I suppose I ought to be thankful for that. While fate still has surprises in store, there is hope, for myself and for everyone else.*

13

LUCREZIA WALKED BAREFOOT across the cold stone floor of the throne-room, passing between the massive and intricately carved pillars that helped to support the vaulted ceiling. The room had been designed to hold a company of several hundred people but it seemed unduly crowded now. The benches set into the walls for the use of the elderly and infirm were packed tight, as were the open spaces where the ordinary citizens took their stand. The enclosures where merchants and landowners congregated were overflowing, and the grand wooden pews where the aristocracy were supposed to be able to sit in comfort were overoccupied to the point at which no one had any elbow-room at all.

The room was not ill-lit but everything in it – including the people – seemed oddly vague. It was inconceivable that Belin's loyal subjects could really be a mass of blurred shadows, so Lucrezia concluded that something must be amiss with the air that filled the chamber. The atmosphere was indeed strangely thickened, like a dark and intangible vapour. In spite of the distortive effects of this thickening, however, she contrived to recognise a few of the nearer faces in the crowd.

The celebrated prince of thieves, Checuti, had somehow intruded himself into the box normally occupied by the Lord High Treasurer. Perhaps, she thought, it was because he now had a virtual monopoly on the capital's supplies of fresh coin.

The station usually occupied by the Prince-Commander of the Armed Forces was presently occupied by General Shabir of Ebla and the Convocation of the Nine Towns. She knew that it was the first time that a mere mercenary had ever risen to such a position, but had to suppose that he had earned it by his prowess in the dragomite campaigns.

The Chief Steward of the Citadel and his family were

accompanied by the grizzled physician and merchant adventurer Aulakh Phar, who was reputed to have brought the empire's stonemasons the precious secret of making incorruptible stone – although the guildsmen were keeping a tight hold on the secret, if so.

The shadowed alcove usually occupied by the man known to the favoured few as the Chief of the Secret Police was empty save for the slight presence of a woman. Surely, Lucrezia thought, that couldn't be Jume Metra? How could *she* possibly be here?

It made no sense. She knew that, but she wasn't quite sure where the awareness ought to lead. What inferences ought she to draw from the fact that it didn't make sense? Had it ever made sense?

The huge throne – the most ostentatious and brazenly ugly seat in the city, and hence in the entire world – could not possibly be occupied by anyone other than King Belin, but the lesser throne which was only brought out for particular ceremonial occasions had been given to the most mysterious of his many consorts: the witch-queen Ereleth.

The lesser throne was attended behind by the awesome figure of a four-met giant, and Lucrezia was glad to recognise her as Dhalla. Belin's own throne was attended in a much less conspicuous fashion by Sergeant Purkin of the citadel guard, who gave the impression of longing to be in the place that Jume Metra occupied.

There was a bleak hardness in Belin's eye which Lucrezia recognised and understood. She knew full well that whatever her father was, and however he might choose to appear to her, he was the centre of an unimaginably vast web of authority and intrigue, which extended throughout the Nest of the Phoenix and beyond. He was the heart and foundation stone of a political entity which the forefathers had declared impossible. 'In this world,' Goran was reputed to have said, 'there can be no empires, and the community of men, which is their strength and their glory, must be preserved in other ways.'

And yet, hadn't Goran and his fellows also said to the people of the world: 'You must go forth into the world and multiply. You must go to every region which will support you: to every forest, every plain and every seashore. You must build cities of your own wherever you can, and protect them as best you can against corrosion and corruption . . . *for the purpose of human life is to fight evil wherever it may be found.'*

Lucrezia knew that although corruption and corrosion were the primary evils, the ultimate evil was chaos. Everyone knew that.

'Are you well, daughter?' Belin inquired softly.

Lucrezia knew that she ought to say *Yes, thank you, majesty* but she didn't. When Belin had spoken she had heard another voice, like a gentle echo reverberating in the vault above her head, although it couldn't possibly have been an actual echo because the words it pronounced were not those that the king had spoken.

'One of you, at least,' the fugitive whisper had said, 'must become one with us.'

Lucrezia stared hard at Belin's face, and saw it dissolve momentarily into another set of features. In the same instant, she saw the king's plump body swell to far greater proportions and fuse with the body of the unreasonably grandiose throne. The fleeting image of two ill-matched dragomite drones was super-imposed on the faces of Dhalla and Sergeant Purkin. She knew then that this was all pretence: not mere illusion, but *pretence.*

We are supposed to be all of one mind here, Lucrezia thought, *but we're not. We're separate, and always will be, no matter what might happen to our flesh. We're free, no matter how securely we might be imprisoned.*

'I know what you are,' Lucrezia said to the creature on the throne. 'You can't delude me with all this show. You may be able to tap my memories but you can't touch *me.* I know where I am and I know what you are.'

It was Ereleth who answered. 'No, daughter,' she said, in her own voice. 'You don't.'

'You're not my house-mother,' Lucrezia said. 'You're just a simulacrum. My house-mother is a long way above us, drowned in the Pool of Life. Drowned and dead, corrupted and corroded by the subtle agents of the Gauntlet of Gladness. You're just a mask worn by the living ground. *All* of this is a mask worn by the living ground.'

'What am I?' Belin asked, in a silky tone which the real king could not have contrived. 'Tell me what you think I am.'

'You're the mound-queen of this fake mother of Serpents,'

Lucrezia said. 'You might think you're the voice of the ground itself, but you're not. You're just another instrument, like the sphinxes and the newts, the manticores and the imitation men dressed in Serpent-skin. You're not a monarch at all – you're just a slave set to work at the Wall until you can work no longer, then sent to the Inner Sanctum to be used by the witch-queen in demonstrating the power of her poisons. Metaphorically speaking, of course – I don't have the words to formulate a literal account.'

'Well done, princess,' said Checuti, almost as if he were proud of her. 'I could almost believe that you have the power to steal us all away.'

'You misunderstand,' said Aulakh Phar, although it wasn't clear whether he was talking to Lucrezia or Checuti. 'None of us ever understood. We were clever but not quite clever enough.'

Other murmurs rippled through the crowd: a thousand voices engaging in nearly half as many private arguments.

'Your subjects are unruly,' Lucrezia said to the false king. 'My true father always complained of the ingratitude of his own folk, who persisted in their ludicrous envy of his thirty-and-one wives and his hundred children . . . not to mention his lavish table and his wonderful wardrobe. They could never see him as he saw himself: as the overburdened man who maintained the order of their lives; the hero who laboured long and hard to keep chaos at bay. But that was why the forefathers built this place, isn't it? To keep chaos at bay. To fight evil wherever it might be found. To fight the evil of the newly empowered dwellers in the deep: the unexpected enemy that the forefathers discovered after they had built their city.'

'There are no subjects here,' her father told her. 'Even in a dragomite nest, humans may fight evil; no matter how hard the nest may strive to be *all of one mind*, it cannot in the end be done. It is the same for the mothers of Serpents; those which strive – unwittingly, but no less forcefully for that – to maintain uniformity of intention and purpose cannot in the end prevail. Even if their minions were to succeed in annihilating all competition, they would find themselves divided within. Chaos cannot be defeated by the imposition of unyielding order; chaos can only be answered by balance.'

'Balance?' Lucrezia echoed sceptically.

'You may think of yourself as a fixed entity,' her false father told her, dispassionately but very earnestly, 'almost as if you had been carved from incorruptible stone – but you're not. The molecules and cells which make up your body are in a constant state of flux, forever being discarded and replaced. You're in a perpetual state of renewal; the stability of your form is like the shape of a fountain, sustained by continuity of flow not by fixation. You're not so very different from the ghosts maintained and reproduced by the dwellers in the deep, nor from the dwellers in the deep themselves. *Order arises out of chaos*, Lucrezia; it's a continuity of flow rather than a process of fixation. An individual life is a moment of balance in the headlong rush of evolution, an aspect of change rather than a denial. Your life, my life and the lives of all those gathered here are moments in a continuum with no fixity at all.'

'It's true, daughter,' Ereleth said.

'It *is* true,' admitted Aulakh Phar, 'but it's not the whole truth.'

'It doesn't matter a damn whether it's true or not, highness,' said Checuti. 'The point is – can you get out of here? If you can work miracles too, you might bring us out with you.'

'You can't,' said Phar.

'You mustn't,' said Ereleth.

'But if you can, highness,' Purkin put in hurriedly, 'I'd be grateful if you'd take me too. You'll need me to see you safely home to Xandria.'

The last remark, as silly as it was bold, prompted Lucrezia to look at Dhalla, but Dhalla said nothing.

'This is just a dream,' Lucrezia said to the uncertain figure on the throne. 'I know that you're managing the dream very carefully, because you're inside my mind as well as my body, but it's still a dream. It can't be trusted.'

'It's the only thing that *can* be trusted,' the person wearing Belin's form assured her. 'This is as near as you or anyone can come to the heart of the mystery. You're right: I'm not the voice of Chimera's Cradle; I'm just one voice among a host. I can't explain every last detail of the past and I can't predict every last detail of the future – but if there's any understanding to be gained here, this is where you must gain it. This is the only voice you'll be given leave to hear. The ground is uncaring; it does what it does. The sphinxes and the newts are merely its instruments, as you say.'

'Are you human?' Lucrezia asked, knowing what the answer must be but wanting to hear it anyway.

'No,' said the voice, letting slip its fatherly mask. 'I'm not. I'm not even alive, according to your reckoning, and I never was. I'm just a machine: a memory machine – but in here, that's a distinction without a difference. In here, the boundary between the organic and the inorganic is as easily blurred and crossed as the boundary between the earthly and the unearthly, for much the same reasons. Aboard the ship which sailed the dark between the stars there were some who thought of all spacetime as a stage on which some kind of final battle would some day be fought between the organic and the inorganic, but they were foolish. All spacetime is a stage like *this*, where the organic and the inorganic will ultimately meet and inextricably merge, displaying their creativity in every possible way . . . but *in the end* achieving balance.'

This is a message for Andris Myrasol, not for me, Lucrezia thought. *He was the one who took aboard the Spirit of the Waters, which had shown lesser men a God as false as this father of mine, but which showed him a deeper and more enigmatic vision of the way of things.*

'What's the point of all this?' she asked. 'Why am I standing here, granted a special audience, while all my friends have been sucked into the decor of the dream, dissolved by the swamp into which we all had the misfortune to fall?' She realised as she said it, though, that some of her friends were conspicuous by their absence. Hyry wasn't here. Fraxinus wasn't here. Ssifuss wasn't here. Merel Zabio and Mossassor weren't here either, although they had certainly been with Fraxinus in the dark chamber that housed the Pool of Life.

'The truth needs ambassadors,' said the false Belin, in answer to her question.

'So you are going to let me go?' Lucrezia said, uncertain as to whether she had read that meaning aright.

'You'll always be here,' Belin told her, as if he were her father assuring her – hypocritically – that she would always have a place in his heart, even if she were to be sent across the sea to wed

450

the Prince of Shaminzara. 'We're part of one another now. In one sense, we always were.'

'Because I have Serpent's blood.'

'Because you're human, and because you belong to the world and not to the dark between the stars. We are kin, you and I. We are all kin, although we are bitterly divided.'

I am kin to machines now as well as Serpents, she thought. Aloud, she said: 'So I'm supposed to go back into the great wide world, carrying your seed within my body?'

For the first time in this peculiar drama Lucrezia looked down at her own body, and she saw that the raised scars inflicted by the web fragments that had fused with her skin had vanished. Her flesh had been cleansed – or perhaps *reclaimed*.

'Yes,' said Belin unambiguously.

'And what about these others?' Lucrezia wanted to know, meaning those whose faces were recognisable.

'Not yet,' said the figure on the throne.

'Not yet?' Lucrezia repeated sceptically.

'You mustn't be afraid,' the voice informed her earnestly.

'Yes you must,' said Checuti. 'Be afraid. Never stop. When you stop being afraid, you get caught. Believe me, I know.'

'Don't be any more afraid than you were before,' Phar put in. 'But don't be any less afraid either.'

'A little less wouldn't hurt,' Ereleth opined.

'You can't believe them, highness,' Purkin pointed out. 'You can't believe anything you see or hear while you're in this state. You're drowned in the pool, just as we are. You have to figure it out for yourself. Don't forget that you'll need me.' She had never had a good opinion of Purkin, who had always seemed to her to be a born traitor waiting for his opportunity, but she knew that what he said made sense – except, perhaps, the last sentence. She *did* have to work this out for herself.

'Dhalla?' Lucrezia said, looking the silent giant in the face. '*Do* I need him?'

'I'm afraid you do, highness,' the giant said. 'Him, or others like him. Find better ones if you can, by all means, but you'll always need men of *that kind*.'

'That's not true,' said Jume Metra. 'She believes it, but it's not true. Sisterhood is better; dragomites need no mercenaries.' Lucrezia knew that wasn't true; Carus Fraxinus and all his companions had served as mercenaries to dragomites, just as the dragomites had later served him.

'That doesn't matter,' Ereleth said, using her voice of authority to cut through the gathering dispute. 'What matters is that we've all reached our destination, at least for the time being. I've followed my secret commandments, and they haven't betrayed me quite as blatantly as I'd come to believe. Aulakh Phar has found a few of his answers, and a measure of life he had no right to expect. Dhalla went to the very brink of extinction, but didn't fall until there were safe hands to catch her. Jume Metra has a new nest. Checuti need no longer serve as a prince of thieves and may make himself a home at last. Purkin will never fail in his duty again. And you, daughter, have achieved your heart's desire. You're an adventuress now, with a world to roam – and you're a loremaster, with witchery to work that no one has ever worked before.'

This is a dream, Lucrezia reminded herself. *There's not a word of it that can be trusted, I have to figure it out for myself.*

She looked up at the wall behind the throne, whose lush drapes had been drawn aside to reveal a symbol and a legend. The symbol was a plus sign; the legend read: CHANGE AND DECAY IN ALL AROUND I SEE; O THOU WHO CHANGEST NOT, ABIDE WITH ME.

'You can't possibly be a deist,' she said to her false father.

'The plus sign means that no one is ever truly alone,' Belin told her, his voice again becoming soft and loving. 'We all exist as terms in an equation, in which the world within and the world without add up to the ultimate totality. Change and decay are eternal and nothing is immune, but within their ceaseless flow continuities are always appearing and extending, containing change and yet resisting it. There is order in chaos, child; there is balance in tumult; there is a universe, and we are all parts of it, all players in its story.'

'But we're not all on the same side,' she said, 'are we?'

'That remains to be seen,' said the figure on the throne. 'I believe that we might be, if we can only find the way to harmony – but that is what I was programmed to think. Some creatures, it seems, are programmed to think otherwise. There is no destiny; the future is *unmade* and *unfinished*, and perhaps it always will be. But we ought surely to hope that if we are not all on the same side yet, one day we can and will be.'

'It's not a bad hope,' opined Checuti, 'but it's certainly forlorn.'

'Aye,' said Purkin. 'Bad or not, it's wasted.'

'I can't accept that,' said Jume Metra.

'Nor can I,' Dhalla added.

'I could, but I won't,' said Aulakh Phar.

'And what do you say, mother?' Lucrezia asked, when a brief silence fell.

'I say that it doesn't matter whether this is a dream or reality,' Ereleth stated, using her authoritarian tone again. 'Nor does it matter who or what is speaking to you through that ridiculous parody of your father enthroned. All that matters is whether what is said *makes sense*. You don't have to decide that alone. You're not the only one appointed to play ambassador and loremaker. You'll have time enough to make up your mind, when you're free of this fleshy tomb.'

Lucrezia allowed the silence to last a little longer this time. 'I always was an apt pupil,' she said at last. 'I never liked you, but I always trusted you to tell me the truth.'

'I liked *you*,' her house-mother informed her, without taking any apparent offence, 'and I always tried to make sure that what I told you was true.'

Lucrezia knew that had to be the end of the message, and it was.

14

FRAXINUS WAS ROUSED by the sound of a voice. He knew that
it was a voice, although he couldn't make out the words and it
sounded impossibly deep. It was as if he were underwater and
the words, although spoken near at hand, were being distorted
out of all recognition.

When he tried to open his eyes he found that there was
something covering his face, gluing them shut. When he tried to
reach up with his hands to clear the obstruction he found that his
arms were anchored too, and when he tried to sit up he
discovered that his entire body was encased in an elastic
membrane of some kind. He struggled to free himself from the
strange tegument, and felt it tear as he forced his arms and legs
apart. Once the membrane had been breached it came apart; he
was able to pluck the remains away from his hands, and then
from his face. As soon as he could, he forced his eyelids apart.

The light which greeted his open eyes was dazzlingly bright,
but he had been forewarned as to what – or rather who – he
might see. He didn't need to be astonished by the fact that the
concerned face that hovered above him belonged to Jacom
Cerri.

'We thought you were dead,' he said, feeling proud that he
was able to say it so matter-of-factly. 'Purkin told us that the
monkey-heads had killed you.'

'He probably thought it was true,' Jacom said mildly. 'I was
hurt, and missed the worst of the battle, but I was saved.'

'By whom?'

'By a manticore. Have you encountered manticores within the
Nest of the Phoenix?'

Fraxinus remembered what he had seen, but he wasn't sure
that a vision counted as an encounter. He was still squinting into
the bright light but he could see now that he and Jacom weren't

out in the open. The walls which surrounded them and the ceiling above them were transparent; the shape of the space told him that they must be at the apex of the pyramid. 'Why did it bring you here?' he asked.

'It didn't, in the first instance,' Jacom told him. 'As soon as I was given a choice, though, I asked to be brought. I was certain that you would want to hear what I have to tell, and I wanted to see you again. While we were on our way we met messengers heading in the other direction. I dare say they'd have brought another ghost in my place had I not already started out.'

'Another ghost?' Fraxinus queried. 'But you're not a ghost – the monkey-heads didn't kill you.'

'I'm a ghost of sorts,' Jacom told him, glancing down as he spoke at the clothes he was wearing. They duplicated the colour and form of his old guard-captain's uniform, but Fraxinus knew that they couldn't actually be his old guard-captain's uniform. They were newly cut and newly sewn, showing not the slightest trace of decay or fraying. Having realised that, Fraxinus lifted his eyes again to study Jacom's face, and realised that it too was impossibly fresh – impossible even for a mature citizen of Xandria, let alone someone who had endured the avid pollutions of the Nest of the Phoenix. The soldier's face was as bright as the king's head on a newly minted coin.

In Xandria, coins could be refreshed but people couldn't; here, it seemed, different rules applied. Fraxinus touched his own face, searching with his fingertips for wrinkles and scars. He found none.

'I see,' Fraxinus said to the younger man. After a pause he added: 'If we're ghosts, we're ghosts of a very solid kind.'

'Indeed we are,' Jacom agreed.

Fraxinus was struck by a horrible thought. 'Do you mean to tell me that thousands of years have passed since the frog-man covered me with that deluge of slime? Is this a *new* Time of Emergence?'

'It's the same one,' Jacom assured him. 'You were captive for a matter of days, not centuries. Those who sleep for centuries, I'm told, are much more prone to forget who they were, and much more prone to alteration in form. It really was a kind of sleep that we experienced, not death – but we're not quite what we were before. We've been adopted.'

455

'You mean that we're chimeras – that the living ground has used its own substance to remake us.'

'We always were chimeras,' Jacom said. 'But we're chimeras of a different kind now: adopted sons of strange parents. Yours was made by humans, but it's not so very different from mine, which was . . .'

'A mother of Serpents,' Fraxinus supplied, anxious to demonstrate that he had deduced the greater part of the mystery of Chimera's Cradle. He was quick to regret his reflexive claim to the intellectual high ground, though; he was as desperate as ever to know more and he had taken note of the way that Jacom had said: *I'm told.*

The guard-captain was more than willing to overlook Fraxinus's rudeness. 'We've been purged of certain inconvenient passengers, most of which we picked up while crossing the living ground,' Jacom told him. 'We've acquired others to take their place which are far more obliging – but they have their own purposes. Not conscious purposes, you understand, but purposes nevertheless. We haven't been restored to our former state as a favour, or even by way of making a bargain. We retain our faculty of choice, but we're the instruments of other beings nevertheless – pawns in a greater scheme.'

'The Genesys plan,' Fraxinus said. 'The revised version, I mean – when the city of Idun was replaced by a garden.'

'It began as a plan,' Jacom agreed, 'but I think it's gone beyond that now. The forefathers did have an end in mind, it seems, but they couldn't direct the changes that the living ground would ordain.'

Fraxinus stood up, vigorously brushing off the last remnants of the cocoon in which he had been encased. He didn't need to go any closer to the transparent wall to see that the surfaces of Chimera's Cradle were dazzlingly white now, and that the mazy pathways which wound around its various edifices were clear and clean. The blaze of noonday presumably made a contribution to the brightness, as did the loftiness of his vantage point, but there had been a real change in its state since the wagon had toiled through the last few kims to reach the pyramid.

'Where are the others?' he asked. 'Are they alive?'

'I haven't seen anyone but you and him.'

Fraxinus turned to see what Jacom was pointing at, and saw a supine figure enclosed in a soft translucent membrane, as he had been himself a few minutes earlier. 'Mossassor?' he said, but he could see enough detail through the turbid encasement to recognise that the markings on the Serpent's scaly hide weren't Mossassor's. His next thought was that it might be Ssifuss, but he couldn't be sure of that – it was a long time since he'd seen Mossassor's sceptical companion. Fraxinus knelt down and reached out, as if to start tearing away the additional skin, but he thought better of it and stood up again.

'I was engulfed as soon as I stepped into the pyramid,' Jacom told him, by way of further explanation. 'I was expecting it, but I'd rather have had time to look round. I've been thoroughly explored, for the second time. I was regurgitated here. It's a peculiar experience, but I suppose we'll both get used to it, if we have to.'

'So the ground played fair with us after all,' Fraxinus murmured. 'It wasn't just avid to consume us. If only they'd explained. But where *are* the others?'

'Don't jump to any conclusions,' Jacom warned him. 'You and I were reproduced exactly as we'd have wanted to be, but that's not the fate of everyone who's brought here. Our bodies and minds have been given back to us, free will and all, but that's because this ground and the one to which I was delivered employ instruments of that kind. They employ others too, and I've no idea how the different fates are allotted. If the ground hadn't swallowed us we'd have been changed irrevocably by the tiny things that we'd already taken in . . . but we've also been changed by those that are within us now, and the ground might have destroyed us as easily as it saved us.'

'Who told you all this?' Fraxinus asked bluntly.

'Other ghosts,' Jacom answered, smiling a little at the partial evasion. 'I don't know how reliable they are, and nor do they, but they've kept their curiosity. They believe that there are no others like them – not even here, in the garden that humans made – but that may be just self-aggrandisement.'

'And these other ghosts have explained what's happening here?'

'They've told me what they think, and what they believe. I'm not sure that I understand it all, and I don't know how much of it to trust, but I think they must be right about how it all began.

457

Unless their memories are mere fantasies, they must know what happened in the distant past far better than we do. Their lore is a few generations old at the most; it can't have eroded and altered nearly as much as ours.'

'Tell me,' Fraxinus said. To say more, at that stage, would have been a waste. It was time to listen.

'Aulakh Phar must have told you everything that happened before we were attacked by the half-men,' Jacom said equably. 'If you've seen Purkin, you know about the attack too. After the battle, I was . . . well, I said *rescued*, but at the time it felt more like being taken prisoner. The manticore took me to the ground from which it had been born . . . and the ground took me. You know what that's like because you've been through it. Did you black out, or were you conscious throughout?'

'I was conscious, after a fashion,' Fraxinus said.

'So was I,' Jacom said. 'I felt the stuff pouring down my throat, like slimy mud, then into my lungs . . . I was more terrified than I ever thought possible, but that's not what matters. It needed to get inside me, but it wanted me alive and awake. It wanted the information in my head as well as my body. Few of the living grounds are as generous as that, it seems. Some extinguish all vestiges of intelligence from their active instruments, although instruments which retain a measure of cleverness and the power of communication ought to be reckoned more valuable.'

Fraxinus recalled the silent monkey-heads, the taciturn sphinxes and the enigmatic batrachians, but he made no comment.

'I think they were different even before the ship came, when there were no dwellers in the deep save for the mothers of Serpents and Salamanders,' Jacom went on. 'I think some of those were already engaged in a deadly competition, in which adult Serpents were their pawns. Anyhow, the manticores' ground took care to avoid too much interference with my inner being. It's always been clever that way, according to the ghost who took it upon himself to interrogate me. He told me that his name was Valeran. He claimed to be a reconstruction of a fourth-generation descendant of the people of the ship. He knew that he was a reconstruction, and that he hadn't actually been preserved in some kind of long sleep for thousands of years, and he admitted that he had no way of knowing how faithful a reproduction he was, or how accurate his memories might be, but . . . well, if all that he told me was a mere confabulation – if *he* was a confabulation – we'll never know any better. I told him my life story, and the story of the expedition – about you and Phar and Keshvara, Ereleth and the princess. I told him about Xandria. In exchange, he told me his story. I was honest; I hope he was too.

'He said that when the ship that brought our ancestors to the world first sent down its landing craft – the ship itself never landed – the people of the ship expected to be able to reproduce the elements of their own civilisation without much difficulty. They'd seeded worlds before, or their ancestors had. That's what they called it: *seeding*. The other worlds they'd seeded had all been inhabited by rich and varied forms of life. Without life, it seems, there can't be a life-sustaining atmosphere, so the only worlds they could seed were those which already had native life of a kind which was roughly similar to that of the world from which they'd come. They'd grown used to assuming that if a world had an atmosphere like their own its native life would be so similar to their own as to pose no insoluble problems. That's the way this world seemed, even after they landed the first immigrants and for some time to come thereafter.'

The soldier paused, long enough to prompt Fraxinus to say: 'What went wrong?'

'Apparently, the first people who came down to the surface brought millions of tiny machines with them: *nanomachines*, Valeran called them. They were *very* tiny – too tiny even to be seen. The yeasts that stonemasons use to make bricks and blocks of stone are machines of this kind, or descendants of them, and so are the pastes that make plastic . . . I always doubted Phar's talk about creatures too small to see – bacteria, and so on – but Valeran assured me that I didn't know the half of it . . . that there's far more beyond the scope of the naked eye than I ever could have dreamed . . .'

Fraxinus understood why Jacom sounded so uncomfortable. The captain had never been ashamed to trumpet his contempt for Phar's 'superstitious' explanations. His conversion must have been profound.

'Bacteria and viruses aren't machines,' Fraxinus pointed out. 'They're living beings.'

'That's where the problems started,' Jacom said darkly. 'As far as I can see, the distinction wasn't very clear even for the people of the ship. They had lots of these nanomachines inside them, keeping them healthy – they had no diseases, it seems, and they lived for a very long time because the nanomachines kept everything under control. They had other nanomachines which they could just *set free*: machines which would reproduce themselves like living organisms, and collaborate in awesomely complicated tasks of construction. These little machines could manufacture tools, clothes, buildings . . . even whole cities.

'All that the first people on the surface of a new world had to do, according to Valeran, was let loose a few million machines which already carried instructions for reproducing themselves until there were exactly enough of them – and exactly enough different kinds – to raise a whole city out of the dirt. They could isolate and recombine metals, break down and reconstitute rocks. That's how the city of Idun mentioned in the lore was built – just as other cities had been built on other worlds . . . except that on other worlds, the cities had stayed built.

'Like the people themselves, the city the forefathers built was filled with nanomachines that were supposed to maintain and preserve it: machines which were supposed to be *under control*. Whatever they were made out of – and some of them were certainly made out of the same kinds of things as living flesh, although most of them were made out of metals and stony substances – they were all controllable, all *programmed*. If ever anything went wrong with them, they could be stopped and wiped out – *deactivated* was the word Valeran used. Even the ones made out of fleshstuff were protected against change, against mutation. At least, they were supposed to be; they always had been in the past, on other worlds and in the dark between the stars.

'Valeran didn't understand all the details himself, and some of what he did understand he couldn't explain to me because I couldn't understand the words he needed to use. In brief, though, the controls which had been adequate to keep the nanomachines in line everywhere else weren't adequate here. On the ship, and on other worlds, the only things which violated the clear distinction between fleshstuff and stone-and-metal stuff were the nanomachines. They were built to cross that boundary, but their design and construction assumed that the boundary was always crystal clear *out there*, in the world where they had to do their work. Although the people of the ship didn't realise it to begin with, this world was different. This world had its own natural nanomachines, which weren't just fleshstuff – bacteria and all that – but also stony stuff. Here, there was *living ground*.

'The forefathers knew about the flowing stones, of course, and thought they were interesting. They found out soon enough that although Serpents and Salamanders were able to reproduce themselves they were also related to kinds of living stone, so that what the forefathers had assumed to be a normal cycle of reproduction was in fact a form of paedogenesis. Unfortunately, that kind of learning took time, and by the time they had figured out how it all fit together, the city of Idun was already rotting. The nanomachines were already out of control, because they'd already made their own contact with the living ground, and they'd already begun to mutate in ways the people of the ship hadn't thought possible. They were already beginning to be integrated into all the kinds of chimeras that the living ground could produce . . . and all that was long before the people of the world had a chance to witness the first Time of Emergence.

'At first, according to Valeran, the problem seemed to the forefathers to be a trivial nuisance. It seemed as if the problem could be contained easily enough, and control restored. Only a handful of the people newly arrived on the world were seriously worried from the beginning; the others still thought it was interesting, and potentially rewarding. The people of the ship thought of it as a chance to make their tiny machines even cleverer. They didn't realise that the fundamental rhythm of life here operated on a much grander scale than theirs; they thought the dwellers in the deep were always asleep, always slow. They didn't know about Times of Emergence . . . and when they were told by the Serpents and the Salamanders, they didn't realise the significance of it.

'It was difficult for them to learn the languages of the Serpents and the Salamanders, you see – and difficult for the Serpents and the Salamanders to learn theirs. The different species never had enough words in common, or enough ideas in common. The forefathers had no idea what would happen when the dwellers in the deep really started making use of what they'd taken in. They had no idea, either, what would happen to the living ground they made for themselves, incorporating the native biotechnology with their own.

'By the time the first Time of Emergence produced the hybrid monsters that the world had created, throwing them into conflict with the ones the forefathers had so carefully designed, the ship had already gone. The people of the world had to cope with the eruption themselves . . . and their descendants have been trying to cope with it ever since, modifying the lore to take account of what they learned but always losing far more than they gained.'

Jacom had built up such momentum by now that although Fraxinus tried to interrupt he was given no opportunity.

'The forefathers and their immediate descendants thought that it would be easy to conquer the world,' the captain went on, re-emphasising what he had already said. 'They still thought it would be easy even when they found out that the world was very different from any they had seen before. They weren't afraid of corruption or corrosion, because they thought that they could bring them under control . . . but they were wrong.

'Valeran was born in a time when they still hadn't realised the extent of the disaster which threatened them because they still hadn't encountered a Time of Emergence. The first one they did encounter was the one to which he fell victim – or the one which granted him the eternal life his unwitting cousins had thought to regain and preserve by very different means. *He* thought of it as *falling victim*, to begin with, but his ghost has come round to a different way of thinking. Even ghosts can learn, you see. Even ghosts can change. They have no choice, in fact; as the world changes around them, they can't possibly stay the same, in flesh or in thought.'

Fraxinus judged from Jacom's tone that the captain was no longer talking about Valeran or about ancient history.

'I suppose I'll live for ever now,' Jacom went on, winding down the torrent of words, 'at least in the sense that whatever happens to this body, others will wake up with my memories and my ambitions. I won't stay the same, though. We're immortal now, after a fashion, but we're not immune to change. I *can't* stay the same. Nor can you. Nor can the world. *Nothing* can.

'That's what we came here to find out, isn't it? We wanted to know how to hold back change, how to preserve the Xandrian empire for ever. Well, that's the answer: we can't. The dwellers in the deep can't be killed and they can't be confined; they've already adopted the nanomachines, and they've already adopted us. As Valeran says, we have no alternative but to accept what we are, and to help the dwellers complete the adoption of all life in the world – no matter how long it may take.'

15

JACOM PAUSED YET again in his narration, severely discomfited by the way that Carus Fraxinus was looking at him. He couldn't blame the man. He knew that he wasn't making matters as clear as the merchant would have wished. He wished that they were clearer to him. He knew that Fraxinus must be wondering how reliable his source of information was, and he wished that he had some way of determining that for himself.

Perhaps it was kindness that made Fraxinus turn away while he mulled over what he had been told. The merchant stared out over the vast white expanses of Chimera's Cradle and Jacom followed the direction of his gaze, studying the bizarre landscape whose strange symmetries were frankly displayed to their uniquely privileged viewpoint.

This dweller must have brought us here for exactly that reason, Jacom thought. *But how, given that it has no voice, no guiding intelligence of its own? How, given that it only has some kind of programme written into it by the forefathers? Even that must have suffered the corrosions and mutations of the centuries, so how can it be that the living ground still lays down a welcome of sorts for a chosen few among its visitors? How can it be that the sphinxes still send messengers back and forth between the gardens to trade memories?*

He wished, not for the first time, that he were not such a perfect replica of his former self. His body might be in better repair than it had been before but his mind was beset with all the same uncertainties, all the same anxieties, all the same inadequacies.

'Chimera's Cradle must have been made to be the protector of mankind,' Fraxinus said at last. 'The forefathers must have dedicated it, somehow, to the task of preserving the kind of society which exists on the far side of the Dragomite Hills. The lore makes us promises, even while it warns us against poisoned ground.'

'That was the intention,' Jacom confirmed. 'Valeran says that it was an impossible task – that Chimera's Cradle was bound to be corrupted just as the mothers of Serpents had been corrupted.'

'Has Valeran ever been here?'

'No,' Jacom admitted. 'But the manticores have; they're gatherers – gatherers of information as well as gatherers of new blood. The ground which adopted me has no mind of its own, but it's careful to preserve mindfulness in its instruments. Chimera's Cradle is careful too, but it takes men and Serpents for its instruments nevertheless – perhaps it's better ground than most, but it isn't different in any essential sense . . . so Valeran says.'

'I don't see how he can be sure,' Fraxinus objected. 'This is not a war of all against all – your coming here is proof of that. It may be a struggle for existence, but it's not a simple matter of kill or be killed, nor is it obvious that the only possible end to it is the adoption by the one surviving ground of every living thing in the world. If the dwellers in the deep eventually fuse into a single entity . . .'

The merchant had paused because the recumbent figure of the Serpent had begun to stir. It was awake, already testing the strength of the walls of flesh which held it captive.

Jacom couldn't help experiencing a slight sinking feeling as he contemplated the prospect of having to go through his entire story once more, in terms that a Serpent might be able to understand.

Fraxinus knelt down beside the Serpent again. As soon as the creature tore a hole in the membrane which confined it Fraxinus began peeling ragged strands of the stuff away.

'Ssifuss?' the merchant said. 'Are you Ssifuss?'

'Am Ssifuss,' the Serpent confirmed thickly. 'Iss Mossassor?'

'We don't know,' Fraxinus was quick to say. 'You and I seem to have been deposited in a chamber at the top of the pyramid, after a passage through the flesh of the living ground that had at least one earlier pause. Jacom came from another ground to find us. If any others have been released . . .'

Jacom understood why the merchant had left the sentence

465

dangling. There was no way to follow the 'if' through to any meaningful conclusion.

Ssifuss looked down at its own body. 'Am not . . .' it said, and then it too failed to complete the thought.

'Chimera's Cradle isn't a mother of Serpents,' Jacom said, hoping that it might be of some help. 'It doesn't produce adult Serpents of any kind. You're safer here than anywhere else within the rim, I suspect.'

Ssifuss didn't seem to find this news reassuring; it continued looking down at itself.

'The frog-like things aren't Serpent-descended, then?' Fraxinus asked.

'I don't know exactly what they are,' Jacom admitted, 'but the first ones were constructed from earthly flesh. They were designed to carry out several kinds of tasks. Like manticores, they gather information, but they have their own ways of storing and communicating it.'

Fraxinus helped Ssifuss to rise to its feet. 'Sshould be Mossassor,' it said ambiguously.

'You were with Lucrezia, weren't you?' Fraxinus said. 'I saw you just before that frog-thing jumped at me. You crossed the Soursweet Marshes with her.'

Ssifuss nodded its head. 'Wass wiss Andriss,' it said. 'Tried resscue . . . too late.'

'Andris is dead?' Jacom asked, wondering why the implication should seem so awkwardly painful.

Ssifuss shook its head again. 'Worsse, perhapss,' it said. 'Taken. Sshanged. Losst. All debtss sstill owed, all promissess unkept. Iss bad. Musst find Mossassor. All myss are true.'

Taken, Jacom echoed. *Changed. Not as fortunate as Fraxinus or I. How many others have been treated as gently as we have? Are we the only ones? Lucrezia!* 'I wish we had the power to make demands,' he said aloud, 'but we don't. If the dwellers in the deep have ears, and the power to respond to our pleas, they use that power so discreetly as to keep it perfectly hidden. We shall all be removed from here when your adoptive parent is ready, and not before. It will release you, I suppose, according to its whim. You might never be allowed to see Mossassor, whether he is alive or dead.' When he said *Mossassor,* though, he thought *Lucrezia.*

466

'What iss happening?' Ssifuss asked plaintively.

'It seems,' Fraxinus said, perhaps trying to make sure of his own conclusions, 'that we've all become pawns in a war between your original ancestors – the ancestors from whom your nearer ancestors tried to break free in the interests of conserving their intelligence and their society. You might have succeeded, as the Salamanders already had – or nearly had – but when our forefathers arrived from another world, your remoter ancestors received the unintended gift of a vast new armoury of weapons. The Salamanders seem to have kept control of Salamander's fire, and lore which instructs them to seal themselves away once its brave burning has released the tribute due to the dwellers within the Reef, but your kind and mine are more intimately caught up in the conflict. We can only hope that the friction between these vast flowing stones doesn't grind us into pulp – but we three seem to have been fortunate, so far.'

Whether this explanation was adequate or not – it sounded far from adequate to Jacom – it seemed to satisfy the Serpent for the time being. Ssifuss nodded slowly, while continuing to inspect the glossily refreshed scales patterning its body.

'Valeran said that I shouldn't think of the living ground as a kind of figured stone writ large, or even as a more complicated kind of dragomite hive,' Jacom said to both of them, by way of supplementing his earlier statements. 'He said that although the dwellers in the deep share a similar fundamental nature they're as different from one another as I am from a snake or a horse, and as different from dragomite nests and figured stones as I am from an ant or an invisible worm. He said that by virtue of its association with him and others like him the ground which adopted me had become closer kin to humans than all of the other grounds – and better kin to humans than Chimera's Cradle, or anything produced by Chimera's Cradle.'

'And why should it be reckoned *better* kin?' Fraxinus asked sceptically.

'Because it maintains so many fully human ghosts, I suppose.'

'A dragomite hive does as much,' Fraxinus countered.

Jacom wasn't certain that the mound-women counted as ghosts, being hatched from eggs as unformed infants, but he saw the point that Fraxinus was making. 'I didn't know whether to believe him,' he admitted. 'I still don't. I believe that I asked him

467

all the questions you would have asked. What is this war in which I have been caught up, and why am I a prize to be fought over? Why is the world suddenly beset by plagues and hordes of predators, spreading further northwards with every year that passes? What will be the end of it all? He couldn't answer them all – not simply or straightforwardly, at any rate – but I'm sure he did his best.'

'I'm sure he did,' Fraxinus agreed, 'and he was right to insist that the dwellers in the deep are very different from one another and from their humbler kin. But they're very different from humans, too, and I'm not sure that I can accept them as kin even now, let alone as valuable kin.'

'I don't think we have any choice in that matter,' Jacom told him. 'Your flesh is the ground's flesh now; it's inside you. It *is* you.'

'I'm still myself,' Fraxinus insisted. 'My conscious self, that is. That hasn't changed. My body may be tainted, but I can still choose what to do with it – and once I'm released from this glassy prison, I'll still be able to choose where it goes and why.'

Jacom had no reason to deny that, but he observed that Fraxinus was speaking defiantly, as if he half expected a contradiction to arise from somewhere.

'Are you sure that your will is still your own?' Jacom asked. 'Perhaps it would seem to be yours, even if it were secure within the dominion of the greater will of its adoptive parent?'

'I don't think any dweller in the deep possesses a *greater will* with which to dominate the lesser wills of its instruments,' Fraxinus said. 'If what you've told me is true, that's not the way they work. For beings like us – Ssifuss included – consciousness is a property of the whole; for the dwellers, it seems, consciousness is at best a property of certain parts.'

'I'm not sure I understand that,' Jacom said. 'I believe it, but I don't quite see how it can be the case. If a part of an organism has a conscious mind, ought that not to be reckoned the consciousness and mind of the whole? How could it possibly fail to become the intelligence of the whole, and hence the director of the whole? Or is it simply that where there are many conflicting parts, none can suppress the rest?'

'Think of it this way,' Fraxinus said, warming to his task. 'Creatures like us – I include Serpents and Salamanders with

468

human beings in this – consider the dominion of consciousness to be almost absolute, because we have the authority to direct the movement of our bodies. Even so, there is a great deal that happens within our bodies of which we are not conscious, and which we cannot control – and we mustn't forget that although we lose consciousness every time we sleep our bodies continue to function. The dwellers in the deep don't have the power of movement, and their equivalent of sleep lasts a very long time. A single overarching consciousness wouldn't be as useful to beings of that sort as it is to us.

'Consciousness and cleverness were never useful to the living grounds in the way that they were useful to some of the things that they produced – Serpents and Salamanders – so the living grounds never developed conscious minds of their own. When the Serpents and the Salamanders developed sentience they did so under the selective pressures of the intermediate phase of their existence – what Aulakh called the paedogenetic phase. That evolution offered them the possibility of permanent freedom from the living grounds.

'The living grounds continued to reabsorb individuals of both kinds, but their initial tendency must have been to erase that intelligence in the process of orchestrating further metamorphoses. A few – but certainly not all – had surely begun to make provision for the preservation of minds even before the forefathers arrived, but the new input of the tiny machines you've described presumably allowed greater versatility in that process, just as it did in others. The fact remains, though – even today – that the dwellers in the deep have no minds of their own. They play host to individual minds, but they don't combine those minds into a slavish instrument of the whole, in the way that dragomite nests seem to do – or try to do.

'The competition between the dwellers is still a competition of complexity and versatility, of invasion and absorption. The minds of the individuals associated with them are by no means mere bystanders, and some might in time come to be – or at least be parent to – the overarching consciousness of the wholes of which they are a part, but for the pr ent they remain peripheral, and problematic.'

This was too much for Jacom, who felt that he was incapable of following the intricacies of such a convoluted argument.

469

Ssifuss gave the impression of listening carefully, but Jacom couldn't imagine that the Serpent understood any more than he did. 'According to Valeran,' he put in, hoping that it might be helpful, 'it's not our minds and memories that are valuable to the living grounds. It's the nanomachines which are still inside us . . . not the ones our forefathers gave to us to keep us healthy, many of which proved far less efficient than they were intended to be, but the ones descended from the mutants to which the living grounds gave birth. In a way, he says, we're a testing-ground for those machines, which not only have to survive in competition with our protectors but have to become protectors themselves . . . and thus become useful as components of future generations of chimeras. That's why the lore says that we're chimeras ourselves, you see – because we're already united with legions of tinier beings, flesh-within-flesh.'

'In the beginning,' Fraxinus said, nodding in agreement as he sought to push his own chain of reasoning further, 'the grounds must have been able to implant instinctive commands requiring the offspring of their descendants to return to them during Times of Emergence – but the Serpents and the Salamanders learned how to modify or cancel those effects. They can't ever have been very effective in the human products of the grounds, and that must be why the dwellers in the deep now produce gatherers as well as destroyers, to recapture the descendant micro-organisms by harvesting their hosts.'

'As you and I have been harvested,' Jacom said, to show that he understood *that*.

'As we all were,' Fraxinus agreed. 'The remaining question is: what happens to us now that the harvest has been gathered in? If we three aren't to be delivered to the secret depths of the Pool of Life, what's to become of us? Are we simply to be set free, to carry whatever seeds – or nanomachines – have been planted inside us back to the lands of the far north? And if that's the intention, should we refuse, lest we unleash some dire infection upon our true kin?'

Jacom had no answer to that. So far as he knew, no one had. Valeran had no idea what happened to ghosts which were released into the world as Times of Emergence drew to their close.

'If humanss are disseasse,' Ssifuss said, 'iss not sso eassily sspread.'

'That's true,' said Fraxinus. 'If individuals like us have been released before, carrying a burden of Serpent's blood, they've not unleashed plagues capable of devastating the northlands or enlivening the ground on which our farmers grow crops. I thought that they hadn't brought back lore either, but now I'm not so sure. The *Apocrypha of Genesys* which helped to bring us here might be lore of exactly that kind.'

'But if the alien beings that have adopted us intend us to carry lore back to our homelands,' Jacom said, 'why do they not make the lore that we are to carry?'

'They can't,' Fraxinus said. 'They have no minds of their own, no voices of their own – and no intentions of their own. We're just hazards in a game of trial and error, one species of chimera among many.'

'*Two* sspessiess,' Ssifuss corrected him, but Fraxinus didn't make any gesture to concede the point.

'We might be getting ahead of ourselves,' Jacom said. 'I was set free by my own adoptive parent but yours has yet to release any of us. It has brought us to the top of the pyramid so that we might look through these remarkable windows, but the chamber has no door.'

Ssifuss looked around, as if to make sure that this judgment was sound.

'That's true,' Fraxinus conceded, allowing himself to be slightly deflated. 'We're still at the mercy of the unknown, and we have no way of knowing what alternatives may lie before us, if and when we're removed from here.'

'I wonder why the flesh of the pyramid took the trouble to carry us so high,' Jacom said, 'if it does indeed intend to set us free.'

Fraxinus frowned, and moved close enough to the transparent wall to reach out and touch it. 'You're right,' he murmured. 'The windows *are* remarkable. Even while I slept – or slipped into some alternative conscious state for which I have no name – I was given a window to look through. It wasn't to let in light, but to facilitate vision. If these have the same function, what is it that we are supposed to see?'

Even as he spoke, the answer became obvious.

'Ah,' he said, in the same murmurous tone. 'I thought the Time of Emergence had ended . . .'

But it hadn't, Jacom finished for him, although he didn't bother to say the words aloud. *Here, at least, it has one last phase to complete.*

Ssifuss, who had a more practical turn of mind than either of its companions, reached past them and smashed its clenched fist against the transparent wall, which instantly shattered into thousands of tiny fragments. Jacom ducked until the rain had ceased, and then looked up again, in order to watch the garden of Idun undergo yet another metamorphosis.

16

Hyry keshvara stepped out of the face of figured stone without any difficulty. The thin and brittle layer which had confined her simply crumbled away.

As soon as she had collected herself she looked back to see the cavity from which she had emerged. The chamber was ill-lit but she could see that it had already ceased to be Hyry-shaped. She judged that within an hour or so there would be no scar there at all. She inspected the twin figures set to either side of the closing gap, tracing their outlines with her fingers. Neither of them was Lucrezia; neither of them was even human.

Hyry observed that her hand was unmarked by any disfigurements; although she had no mirror with which to inspect her face she suspected that it had been similarly purged. Her sense of touch suggested that she had the appearance of an eight-year-old, but so far as she could remember she had never been beautiful, even at that age.

She came out of the doorway into which she had been driven by panic. The inner space of the pyramid was empty of butterflies, and almost empty of other creatures. When she had turned to run away in panic the chamber had been full of human and Serpent bodies, many of them erect and many more recumbent, but now there was only one individual standing up and two lying down. Even the ones that were lying down were covered over by lumpen masses that were certainly not blankets.

The Serpent turned to look at her as soon as she moved forward again.

'Kesshvara?' it said uncertainly.

'It's me,' she confirmed. 'Lississee?'

'Yess. Iss Sserpent here – ssat one iss human.' Lississee pointed first at the body over which it was standing, then at the other which lay some six or seven mets away.

473

Hyry went to the human body and knelt down to test the texture and the strength of the cocoon which had grown over it. For a moment she thought that it might be Lucrezia, but once she was able make a precise determination of the body's dimensions she realised that it was too tall. The confining membrane was leathery, and did indeed seem to be a mere cover; the woman's body was not let into a face of figured stone as Hyry herself had been.

'I think it's Myrasol's cousin,' she said. 'Merel Zabio. She was with Fraxinus.'

'Iss not Ssifuss,' Lississee said.

Hyry went to join the Serpent and knelt to make a second inspection.

'I can't be sure without a clearer sight of his markings,' she said, 'but I suspect that it's Mossassor. What can have happened to the others?'

Lississee pointed to the glowing surface of the living lake which all but filled the interior of the pyramid. Hyry went to the edge to look into its turbid but strangely illumined depths.

There was no mistaking the huge form of Dhalla, who was lying face down, suspended no more than a met beneath the surface.

'Well, we tried,' Hyry murmured. 'Had this been one of those romances the fond parents of Xandria love to tell their children, she'd have saved the day for us, with a little help from Lucrezia and myself. We'd have fled from the butterflies to confront some Dark Lord who was the embodiment of all the evil in the world – and having slain him, after a long and glorious battle, we'd have banished all evil from the world for ever, thus securing the future of love and laughter, beauty and bravery. As it was, we seem to have snatched the great lumpen brute from the frying pan only to have her stumble into the fire. This is supposed to be the Nest of the Phoenix, though – perhaps those cold flames will reignite the Salamander's fire that's supposed to burn in her heart.'

While she entertained herself with this private rhapsody, using its narrative flow to test the capability of her reawakened mind, Hyry's eyes probed the further depths of the pool, trying to put names to the other shadows that were slowly sinking into its depths.

She was confident that she could identify Aulakh Phar and

474

Checuti, but she wasn't certain of the others. One might have been Ereleth; two more were surely male . . . which meant that Lucrezia wasn't there, unless she had already sunk out of sight. Nor was Fraxinus, so far as she could tell – or, for that matter, Ssifuss. The only Serpent that was visible was as slender as Lississee, but which of Lississee's companions it was Hyry couldn't tell. There was no sign of the compound ghost or any of its simpler kin; nor were there any sphinxes to be seen.

Hyry turned to look Lississee in the eye. 'Why me?' she said, meaning *Why am I the sole survivor of my own kind?* It was a prospect which scared her more than it gladdened her, although she knew that the time would come when she would feel differently.

Lississee looked back to her, and said: 'Why anybody?'

In the absence of any treacherous sibilants, the sentence might have been spoken by anyone at all, human or Serpent. There was, Hyry thought, a certain aptness in that.

The recumbent Serpent began to stir within its confining blister and Lississee immediately returned to it. Inferring that Merel must also be alive, and possibly ready to emerge from her own confinement, Hyry went back to the other ugly lump. She began to test the leathery membrane, hoping to find a flaw. Her insistent fingers prodded the sleeper awake within a minute, and the struggling figure soon put sufficient pressure on the imprisoning skin to burst it asunder. After that, it was merely a matter of working the whole body free.

Like Hyry, Merel was wearing clothes exactly similar to those she had been wearing when the strange conflict had begun, save that they had been carefully refreshed and renewed.

'Keshvara?' Merel said.

Hyry didn't bother to confirm the identification; she knew what was coming next. 'Nobody else human, so far as I can tell,' she said. 'Just you and I, Lississee and . . . Mossassor.' She was now able to confirm that the second Serpent was indeed Mossassor.

Both Serpents were coming towards her and Mossassor seemed much more enthusiastic to greet her than Merel had been. 'Kesshvara!' it said, with what she would have liked to interpret as delight.

'Sure,' she said. 'We searched for the garden, if not quite together, and we found it. What now?'

Mossassor had no answer ready; it turned to speak to Lississee in its own language, presumably asking all the same unanswerable questions that had filled Hyry's mind a few minutes before. Hyry helped Merel to stand, then let go of the younger woman's elbow as it was rudely pulled away.

As soon as she had pulled free, Merel went to the edge of the luminous lake and started counting.

'Fraxinuss?' asked Mossassor, looking to Hyry for the answer.

'Not there,' Hyry said, shaking her head. 'Vanished. Lucrezia too. There's still hope for them, I guess.'

'And for Andris?' Merel said.

'Not for Andris,' Hyry said. 'He's not dead, but . . . well, there's no hope of the sort you mean.'

Merel opened her mouth to ask another question, but Hyry cut her off. 'Were this a romance of the kind fond parents tell their children within the safe compass of Xandria's walls,' she said, more brutally than she intended, 'you'd doubtless enjoy a joyous reunion with your beloved Andris, but it's not. Whether there'll be any further reunions at all remains to be seen – and it remains to be seen, too, whether we can even contrive an escape. Before we say or do anything else, I think we should try to find out what our chances are of getting out of here, don't you?'

She marched off without waiting to hear what Merel thought, perversely glad to be facing the dark corridor which led to the world outside rather than the questioning eyes of the younger woman or the newly awakened Serpent. She didn't feel ready, as yet, to attempt explanations, or even to offer an account of her recent adventures. Let Lississee try, if it thought the task worthwhile.

She was slightly heartened – or, at least, relieved – to discover that there was still light at the far end of the tunnel, and bright daylight at that. She didn't suppose that this was still the same day as the one on which she had helped the demented Lucrezia in her fatuous attempt to rescue Dhalla from the butterfly scourge, but she was glad that it wasn't night. At any rate, she was glad until she stepped out into the dazzling and empty arena that lay

476

before the pyramid and saw what had only just begun to happen there.

The newly cleansed surface of living stone that had given Chimera's Cradle the semblance of a ghostly city was cracking, not just in one or two places but everywhere. Like the brittle enclosure which had crumbled to dust as Hyry pulled herself free from the wall within the pyramid's inner chamber the vast cloak of white shell had already been pulverised by internal pressure. Bursting out of every ovoid and every distorted cone were the crowns of huge trees, already dressed in the most brilliant earthly green she had ever seen.

In the course of her career as a trader Hyry had spent a good deal of time in the Forest of Absolute Night and its fringe woodlands in Khalorn. She had also sailed to more than a hundred of the Thousand Isles, many of which had been lushly forested, but she had never seen trees like these before. There were trees like giant ferns and trees like monstrous stalks of green corn mingled with pines and oaks. The newly exposed leaves were moist; many which had been tightly furled were slowly expanding to their true forms while others gradually turned their faces to greet the bright sun.

She knew that it was nothing more than ordinary growth in the grip of some unusual generative energy, but it seemed so very eager and so utterly all-consuming that it put her in mind of raging flames. It seemed to her that a great green conflagration was consuming the arid grey face which the 'garden' must have worn for years.

When she and Lucrezia had led their ill-assorted party across the monochromatic landscape it had seemed dead and derelict, and unearthly through and through – but that had only been a mask, an alien layer which sheltered something else within, just as alien layers had sheltered Merel and Mossassor while they too were renewed and refreshed. The 'butterfly' spores which had settled on the greying faces, etching a riot of Serpentine colour into their superficial flesh, had achieved nothing more, in the end, than the similar spores which had wormed their way into her own skin. Their purpose had been dramatically subverted; the living ground had imposed its own new order.

'What's happening?' Merel asked breathlessly. She had been quick to pull away from the trader before, but she drew close

477

now, seeking the shelter of human company in order to face the unknown.

'The unearthly ground is giving birth to its earthly offspring,' Hyry told her. 'That was what the garden was designed to do, after all. The living ground that was mother to the Serpent race had begun to adopt earthly life forms, to subsume the patterns of earthly life within its own. This was the means by which the forefathers fought back: they made their own maternal ground, and set it to subjugate the patterns of unearthly life to an earthly template.'

'It doesn't look earthly to me,' Merel said, meaning that it didn't look like the meek cultivated woodlands of Xandria.

'But it is,' Hyry assured her. 'Earthly plus . . . plus whatever could profitably be borrowed from the unearthly. Exotic and chimerical, but earthly in its fundamental organisation.'

While she spoke she moved forward across the open space which still surrounded the pyramid, and came to stand beneath the crown of one of the nearest trees. There was nothing remotely human about the shape of its bole. She looked up at the rich foliage, which seemed to be rippling like the surface of a pond as the leaves bent in a dozen different directions before an eddying wind.

'That's why there's a war,' Hyry said wonderingly. 'I had begun to doubt that any of this made sense, because it seemed that all chimeras were chimeras, and that all absorption was merely fusion . . . that in the end the earthly and the unearthly would be so inextricably interwoven that it would no longer make sense to distinguish between them. But it isn't just a matter of tipping the two kinds of life into a single pot and stirring until they become homogeneous. The ultimate aim isn't uniformity or chaotic confusion: it really is a new order. Every one of these living grounds – every garden within the Reef – is tending by trial and error towards a different contract of conciliation, a different way of ordering the interwoven pattern.'

'But there's only one garden of Idun,' Merel said. 'There are dozens of rivals clustered around it. How can our tiny patch of living ground hope to win against an entire world?'

'Iss not ssat kind of contesst,' Mossassor said. 'Iss not human againsst Sserpent. Ssifuss wass wrong, myss right. Humanss and Sserpentss *togesser*.'

Hyry finally understood what Mossassor had been trying to get across to her since the time of their first meeting in the Forest of Absolute Night. 'He's right,' she said to Merel. 'It isn't just a matter of earthly against unearthly, a fight for domination of the world by one or the other. Within each pattern there are species in conflict with one another – species whose interests are diametrically opposed. Serpents and Salamanders had already begun to break free from their evolutionary heritage before humans arrived here. That's why they formed an alliance with us in the days of the forefathers. They had as much to gain as we did from the subjugation of the living ground – from control of its fecundity and its creativity.

'On the world which produced our species, long before the ship that sailed the dark between the stars, our remotest ancestors must have fought a battle to free themselves from the burdens of their own evolutionary heritage, setting aside instinct in favour of reason, cultivating intelligence and society in place of blind nature . . . and they won, because reason was their instrument as well as their aim.

'There's reason in this too, and it's Serpent reason and Salamander reason just as much as human reason. That's why being outnumbered doesn't matter. That's why others among the dwellers in the deep are being turned, imitating the evolutionary thrust of Chimera's Cradle instead of working to destroy it. That's why the manticores are on our side. That's why, in the end, the order which emerges from all this chaos – an order which will be neither earthly or unearthly – will contain the best of both and not the worst. Oh, Aulakh, you should be here to see this! You were the one who gave us all the means to understand it; it should be you standing here to bear witness, not me. Why should it be me?'

She meant, but dared not say: *And why this silly girl, who is probably the only one of us incapable of understanding?*

'Sstruggled,' said Lississee.

Hyry looked at the Serpent sharply, the fact that she hadn't the slightest idea what it meant subverting the heady rush of her intellectual arrogance.

'Why anybody,' Lississee reminded her. 'Iss answer. Ssome sstruggled. Fought hard. Osserss could not. Too weak or

479

assleep. Ssey went to pool. Lucressia, Ssifuss sstruggled hardesst. Musst be ssaved.' As it completed its speech it looked back
towards the pyramid, as if expecting to see Lucrezia and Ssifuss
come marching out of the shadowed portal to prove its point.

And Fraxinus too, Hyry thought. *He was struggling as hard as
anyone. He would never have given in. If that's what it took to
decide our fates, Fraxinus must have burst out of his imprisoning stone hours ago. Poor Aulakh! Too old, too weak . . . he was
the visionary of this mad adventure, but he couldn't open his
eyes to see the conclusion of his vision.*

'Can you hear voices?' Merel asked.

Hyry listened carefully, but the noise of so many rippling
leaves was like the roar of a stormy sea breaking on a shore; it
could have drowned out a hundred voices calling from a
hundred mets away.

'It's just the wind,' she said.

'I don't think so,' Merel persisted.

Hyry concentrated again, and her imagination immediately
began conjuring voices out of the confusion. She thought that
she could discern the voice of Aulakh Phar calling her own
name, and she guessed what Merel must be hearing.

'Andris isn't here,' she said gently. 'Andris is part of a different
forest. If we can find Ssifuss and Lucrezia, we'll take you there –
but you'll have to prepare yourself. If this were a romance . . .
but it's not.'

Merel must have been listening, but she was looking at
something behind Hyry: something that was coming through
the forest towards them. Mossassor and Lississee were looking
in the same direction. Hyry turned to see what they were looking
at. She was not unduly surprised to see the giant head and tawny
body of a sphinx. It met her curious gaze with its great liquid
eyes.

'You should not wait here, unless you intend to stay,' the
sphinx said. 'The forest is not safe, and the ground beyond is
becoming less so. If you intend to go, you should go soon.'

'Are we supposed to go?' Hyry asked. 'Is that *your* intention?'

'You are free to go or stay,' the sphinx replied carelessly, 'but
the way will not become easier.'

'Where are our friends?' Merel said. 'Are we the only ones, or
are there others?'

It was useless; the sphinx had said what it had come to say, and it was already turning away.

'Wait!' Hyry commanded – but she was surprised to see that the command had an effect. The sphinx stopped and looked back.

'When we came here,' she said, 'you or one of your kind told us that the war was closer to being lost than won. What did that mean?'

'It means that we cannot guard you from harm if you stay,' the sphinx told her, placidly enough. 'There are too many invaders, too many killers. The ground has taken in all that it can hold; it must sleep now. If you stay, you must sleep with it. If you want to go, go soon. There are horses in the forest; I will gather them for you. The newts took saddles into the pyramid, and other things. You must search, find what you need.'

'Where are our friends?' Merel demanded again. 'Have any others been set free?'

'Search,' the sphinx advised, before disappearing back into the forest. This time, Hyry didn't try to call it back.

'It was the same on the road which brought us here,' Merel muttered. 'The one which greeted us made its deceptive speech, and said no more. If this is human ground, why are there no people here? Why is there no one to meet us face to face and tell us what we need to know?'

'Dwellerss in deep have no voicess,' Mossassor said. 'Sseir time iss not our time, sseir sschemess not ourss. Will prosseed no matter what we do.'

'So what *do* we do?' Hyry asked again. 'We came, we saw, we served our purpose. What we know, we worked out for ourselves – the next step is up to us.'

'Musst ssearssh,' Mossassor said.

'We already found the garden,' Hyry pointed out.

'Ssearssh *pyramid*,' Mossassor said, as if it ought to have been obvious. 'If osserss ssere, musst find. If not . . .' The Serpent looked at the back of its hand, then slowly turned its forearm for inspection. Hyry took the inference readily enough. They already had what the living ground had consented to give them, although they didn't know exactly what the gift was worth. They had been renewed, ready to resume the journey of life with whatever goods had been carried into the pyramid by the helpful newts. As to what price had been exacted in return, they could only guess – except that they had lost Aulakh Phar and Ereleth, Dhalla and Checuti, Jume Metra and . . .

'You're right,' Hyry said. 'We have to search, as the sphinx advised. Given that the walls have only just let us go, I don't suppose they'll be inclined to take us back again so soon.'

'Is this the end?' Merel asked, waving a hand to indicate that she meant the forest. 'Is the Time of Emergence over now?'

'I don't know about the Time of Emergence,' Hyry answered, 'but it's certainly not the end of anything significant. That lies thousands of years in the future – and even then, it won't really be an end; it'll be . . .'

'A new beginning,' Merel said tiredly. 'I know that one. You might think that I'm stupid, but I'm not. Fraxinus talked to me. Phar too. You don't have to be so sharp. We're in this together, aren't we?'

Hyry remembered Merel lying half dead on the floor of the rickety haycart which had carried them both to Antiar, with an expression of perfect innocence on her face that was the perfect negative image of the wizened visage of Aulakh Phar. How much water had flowed under Shabir's blasted bridges since then?

'Sorry,' she said. 'You're right. We're in it together – equal shares of all profits and all losses. Let's go find out exactly how extensive our losses are.'

17

LUCREZIA COULDN'T UNDERSTAND why someone was slap-ping her face. It wasn't as if she were a child, and in any case she hadn't done anything wrong. She tried to move away from the offending hand but it wasn't possible; there was a solid wall behind her and nowhere to go – indeed, she seemed to be trapped in some kind of alcove which wouldn't even let her turn sideways.

She raised her arms, and felt brittle shards fall away from them as she did so.

'Lucrezia! Highness!' The sound of the words caused her to open her eyes. She recognised the voice but it took her some little time to bring the face into focus.

'It's all right,' she muttered thickly. 'I can hear you. You can stop hitting me now.'

Her assailant – Hyry Keshvara – obediently lowered her hand and stepped back. Lucrezia looked from side to side, identifying the older woman's two companions without difficulty. She wasn't surprised to see Lississee, but Merel Zabio's presence was less expected.

'Where are we?' she asked, tracking the contours of the gloomy space which confined them.

'In one of the inner chambers of the pyramid,' Hyry told her.

Lucrezia remembered. 'We ran away from the butterflies but we were seized by the walls.'

'That's right. That imprisonment doesn't appear to have done us any harm – quite the reverse, in fact.' Hyry touched her face to supplement her declaration.

Lucrezia took note of the amazing youthfulness of the trader's appearance but she didn't touch her own face. She was still remembering.

'I woke up a while ago,' Hyry went on. 'Mossassor's here too,

483

still searching for others. Fraxinus and Ssifuss don't seem to be in the living lake – we hope to find them cradled in a figured stone, as we were. We've been outside – the whole place has undergone a profound metamorphosis. A sphinx told us that we have to leave soon; it's rounding up horses for us. I've found four saddles and half a dozen waterskins but little else. We'll have to travel light, it seems.'

'I saw my house-mother,' Lucrezia said. 'I spoke to her.'

Hyry stepped back uncertainly.

'You can't have,' Merel told her. 'She's in the pool. So's Checuti.'

'And Shabir,' Lucrezia said. 'Jume Metra too, and Sergeant Purkin. I saw them all. They all spoke to me.'

'It was a dream, highness,' Hyry said tentatively. 'You were here all the time. I woke up in some kind of blister in the floor, but you haven't moved at all.'

'I was moved,' Lucrezia assured her. 'The walls are more fluid than you think. I've been down into the depths of the pyramid. I spoke to someone, or something, that's always been down there. It gave us all our voices, so that we could help one another to understand. I really did speak to my house-mother. She's alive. They're all alive.'

'Dying here isn't like dying anywhere else,' Hyry said flatly. 'Here, everything that normally gets lost is stored. Even the dead may dream – but they're all like Andris. Ereleth is part of something else now. They all are.'

'I know that,' Lucrezia said. 'So are we. We all have Serpent's blood now – or something of that kind.'

'Serpent's blood is near enough,' Hyry agreed. 'But it's not just *Serpent's* blood, any more than the fire which gave hectic birth to the forest outside is just Salamander's fire. This is our ground – designed, it seems, to be more versatile than all the rest.'

'All on ssame sside,' Lississee put in, repeating one of Mossassor's favourite assurances.

She allowed Hyry to draw her away from the wall then, and she looked back at the stony womb from which she had been reborn. It was inert now, like the broken shell of some hatchling bird. There were other figures to either side of her erstwhile station, but they were set deeper in the rock, their outlines reduced to mere impressions. One was a slender Serpent; the other was a manticore.

'Vekoren or Kasabil?' she asked, pointing at the manticore.

'Don't know,' Lississee replied. 'Are osserss in osser roomss. More ssan two. Ssingss ssat call ssemsselvess ghosstss too. Many of ssem. None . . .' It hesitated, groping for the right word.

'None in the process of re-emerging,' Hyry supplied. 'Only you, so far. Mossassor will find Ssifuss, if that's possible. There's still some kind of debt outstanding between them.'

'I remember,' Lucrezia assured her. She hesitated a moment over what to say next, but put aside the story of her descent into the depths where the dweller was; there would be time enough to tell it. Instead, she said: 'What did the sphinx say to you?'

'It told us that if we intend to go we'd best go quickly. The new version of the garden of Idun looks earthly – in fact, it looks beautiful – but the sphinx says it's still dangerous. I suppose the living ground has taken what it needs and now has no further use for us – but we've no reason to doubt the sphinx's advice. It looks as if we'll be leaving with little more than the clothes on our backs. We'll have to forage for whatever food we can find.'

Hyry delivered the latter part of her speech on the move as Lucrezia led the way into the interior of the pyramid. She didn't hesitate for more than a moment before turning her back on the glowing lake and heading for the outer portal. Once out in the open she stopped to study the new face of the Navel of the World. The sky was cloudy, but the forest seemed glorious nevertheless. The wind was fresh and it stirred the crowns of the trees with a vigour which seemed refreshing in itself; it was as if the trees were flexing their limbs, glad to have been let out into the world after a long confinement.

'The trees couldn't have grown from seeds so rapidly,' Hyry told her. 'They must have been preformed within the old structures, like any other emanation of the living ground. Now they're unfolding – stretching themselves just as a real butterfly struggling out of its chrysalis unfurls its wings. You can see flowers beginning to form already – and there are insects and birds among the branches. It's not like the garden where Andris is. Whatever else they may be, the trees aren't half-human.'

'I have to see Andris,' Merel put in. 'Keshvara says that you promised to return to where he is. I'm going with you.'

Lucrezia nodded to signal her consent while she continued to study the garden. The air was moist, and the odours produced by the forest were oddly familiar. The only earthly woodlands she had ever passed through were those to the north of the Forest of Absolute Night, but the apparent familiarity of the scented air was no mere memory of that. There was a more fundamental earthliness about it, even though the forest was the product of unearthly ground. She understood why Hyry had interrupted herself to say that the garden was beautiful; there was something about the combination of the many shades of green that was inherently pleasing to her eyes. There was a curious kind of recognition in her response whose origins were far more remote than her life in Xandria.

'We brought fruit from the other garden,' she murmured. 'One way or another, fruit from *all* the other gardens must find its way here – but this isn't a haphazard patchwork. This is something whole, intricately interwoven.'

'The pyramid has the fruit we brought,' Hyry said. 'The pyramid took *everything* we brought, not merely from our packs but from our skin and from our blood. It has the advantage of being in the centre of the great circle; everyone and everything that comes here brings a varied cargo. We brought gifts from other dwellers – more infections and poisons than we knew. They're all being nursed in Chimera's Cradle now – but you're right; this isn't a reckless mixture. There's a kind of order in it, brought out of chaos by design.'

'Balance in tumult,' Lucrezia quoted.

'The womb of the world,' Merel said. 'That's what the sphinx called this place, when we first moved into the Gauntlet of Gladness. I suppose this is what it's given birth to.'

'It has too many names,' Lucrezia opined. 'I can understand why, but it's a little confusing.'

'More than a little,' Hyry said, and might have gone on to explain what she meant, had she not turned abruptly to look at a group of moving figures who had just turned one of the corners at the base of the pyramid. They were led by Carus Fraxinus.

Lucrezia had never seen Carus Fraxinus within the walls of Xandria. Like everyone else involved in the expedition he had suffered a long and gradual degradation as he had travelled through the Forest of Absolute Night and endured the hardships of the Dragomite Hills. She had no memory of him as a thoroughly civilised and well-to-do man; when she had first encountered him his hair had been roughly cut by a makeshift barber and his beard had lost the sculpted precision that could only be conferred with the aid of a constantly refreshed razor. These factors had collaborated with the legacy of strain and fatigue to impress his image on her consciousness as that of a man for ever under pressure, fiercely resistant but sorely tried.

He didn't look like that now. There was still a certain failure of expertise about the cut of his hair but his beard had been carefully shaped and his skin was so clean and free of blemishes as to seem more extravagantly rejuvenated than Hyry's. His manner was relaxed; given better apparel he could have been taken for a courtier – and although his clothes were severely functional, they were well formed and not significantly worn or ragged.

His companions were a human, a Serpent and a manticore.

'Highness,' Fraxinus said, offering a slight bow in answer to her stare. He smiled more delightedly at Hyry and at Merel, but Lucrezia knew that he intended no slight to her; Keshvara had been his associate for many years, and Merel had been in his company since Salamander's Fire. The Serpent, who was Ssifuss, offered her a greeting that was even slighter, and she might have been offended by that in view of their recent adventures, but it meant no insult. It had turned abruptly aside as soon as it saw Mossassor emerging from the portal of the pyramid; that too was understandable.

Lucrezia was not particularly astonished to see Fraxinus or Ssifuss. She had already had reason to think that they might have been released by the dweller in the deep. The presence of the third member of the party was a different matter – and he had no one he would rather greet than her.

'Jacom Cerri,' she said, in frank disbelief.

He came to stand before her, as charmingly awkward as ever. The manticore came with him.

'Highness,' he said. 'I have a tale to tell that you will be very interested to hear, and a friend you will be glad to meet. This is Kasdeja, who saved me from near-certain death and brought me safely across the Nest of the Phoenix.'

Lucrezia was glad that she was able to look the manticore

casually in the eye and say: 'I have met brothers of yours named Vekoren and Kasabil. Do you know what became of them? Are they safe?'

'They're carrying a message to our parent ground,' the manticore informed her. 'They were well enough when we met.'

Jacom was looking at her closely. He had seen her several times in the roof garden atop the Inner Sanctum, but always from a distance. By the time they met again, in the Dragomite Hills, she had been somewhat dishevelled. This was the first time he had seen her at her best at such close range.

'I have a tale to trade for yours, captain,' she told him, 'and a crucial piece of the puzzle that might help us understand what is happening here, and what is happening to *us*.'

'We all have those,' said Merel Zabio. 'Even me.'

'How did you come to be here?' Hyry asked Jacom, with her customary lack of ceremony, as she briefly turned away from Fraxinus.

'I came riding on a manticore,' Jacom told her, with one eye still on Lucrezia and a self-satisfied smile on his face. 'And I have as much to add to our understanding as any of you, implausible as that might seem.'

'We're all the heirs of Aulakh Phar,' Keshvara told him. 'We all see with his vision now. I thought I heard his phantom voice when I stepped into the forest. It was an illusion, but it was what he taught me that enabled me to see what the forest was. He taught you too, did he not, while we trekked southwards with Amyas's makeshift army?'

Lucrezia was surprised by the fondness in the older woman's voice; it had never been there before when Hyry spoke about Phar – but it was no more strange that his was the loss that Hyry felt most deeply than it was that Lucrezia should feel the absence of her house-mother more keenly than the loss of Dhalla. She realised, however, that Phar was merely the temporary focal point of a more general grief, which had seized Hyry as soon as she realised that the people gathered here now were the only ones who would be able to leave this ground. The combination of joy and sadness in the trader's voice was odd, but far from inexplicable. When she had understood this, Lucrezia looked round too, measuring the extent of the fully assembled company as if she were seeing all those who were *not* gathered here as well as those who were.

'Is there no one else?' Fraxinus asked Mossassor, amplifying her awareness.

'No one,' Lucrezia answered, while the Serpent was still searching for the words to explain that it had searched the pyramid as best it could and found nothing but a few discarded goods. 'The others are all in the pool, and none of them will be released as we have been – but they're not entirely dead. The pool has their minds and their memories as well as their flesh.'

'But they *are* dead,' Hyry objected. 'Whether or not they live again as ghosts – and whether or not, if so, they have their true forms instead of being reshaped as languid sphinxes or horrid newts – they're dead *now*, casually murdered by the living ground.'

That brought an uneasy silence.

'The lore lied,' Hyry added, in a softer voice. 'Let's not forget that. However obliquely it told its lies, the trail it laid for us to follow was intended to lure us to death and destruction.'

It was Mossassor who contradicted her. 'Myss not liess,' the Serpent said. 'Missremembered, but not liess. Not ass ssimple ass ssat.'

'Lies,' said Hyry flatly.

'Ereleth told me that she felt betrayed by her secret commandments,' Merel put in. 'But I watched what happened to Checuti and Sergeant Purkin. The stuff that grew over their cuts was like living woundglue. Without it, they'd have died before we ever got here – and if we hadn't been healed by the pyramid, we'd all have died. If this place is murderous, it's also merciful, at least to some.'

Balance in tumult, Lucrezia thought. *The contest between death and life is sorely confused here, but it hasn't decayed into chaos. Corruption and corrosion may run riot every time the ground burns with Salamander's fire, but they're countered and contained.* 'Where were you?' she asked Fraxinus. 'Mossassor couldn't find you.'

'I was taken to a place where I could watch all this,' he answered soberly. 'I was taken up to the top of the pyramid – I don't know why. It was all a lottery, I suppose. Some were taken down, others lifted up.'

489

'Sstruggled,' Lississee put in. 'You, Ssifuss. Hardesst of all.'

'Perhaps that was it,' Fraxinus agreed cautiously. 'The most significant thing, I suppose, is that the process was displayed to an audience carefully placed to see it to its best effect. The living ground may have no voice, but it was designed to communicate, after its own fashion. The Gauntlet of Gladness isn't just a trap baited with lies. The ground plays fair with those who bring it what it needs; it dispenses rewards as well as staking claims.'

'It's not a matter of *fair play*,' said Hyry scathingly. 'If it weren't for the fact that the ground – or the plan according to which it was made – requires a few of us to go back into the world beyond the Reef, we'd all be drowned in that pool. We haven't been spared for *our* benefit. It's not a *reward*.'

Lucrezia knew that this must be true, and she could see in his expression that Fraxinus knew it too. The remade Genesys plan had never been intended to be forgotten or kept secret. The making and remaking of the lore was all a part of the plan, and that was why some of those who were taken by the living ground were returned again, refreshed and rearmed against the ravages of the lands within the Reef. Given that, she thought, what should those who were allowed to go tell the people who lived in nations like Xandria? Should they issue dire warnings, or should they try to communicate the far from simple truth? And would it matter what they decided, given that whatever they said would have to be handed down from generation to generation for thousands of years, subject to all manner of corruptions and corrosions? People had been here before, and had come away again – but all that now remained of *their* adventures was the fragmentary *Apocrypha of Genesys* and the secret commandments, and a handful of romances that had doubtless been reconfigured by every teller who had ever had charge of them, in the hope of making a more satisfactory story.

If only we could write down what we know, she said to herself, *in a form which wouldn't decay, this mad adventure wouldn't have been necessary. We'd have known what we were facing, and could have made our decision accordingly. Kasabil didn't believe it would ever be possible to preserve such knowledge perfectly. Everything's corruptible, he said. But while everything changes and creativity remains, whatever is possible will surely one day come to be – and that which is truly incorruptible, once made, can never be unmade.*

The crowns of the trees were still rippling in the breeze, each leaf bending to the pressure in its own way; the overall effect was that of great majestic waves surging through the canopy. There was no sign yet of the promised horses – nor, for that matter, of the sphinx that had spoken to Hyry. Lucrezia realised that she hadn't seen a single newt since awakening from her unnatural sleep; the only obvious chimera here now was Kasdeja, and he was no more native to this place than she was . . . but perhaps no less.

Jacom Cerri was still watching her, and still standing a little too close, as if to offer her his protection against all manner of unknown enemies. Fraxinus and Hyry Keshvara were still taking stock of their situation, while Mossassor and Ssifuss had moved aside to continue the settlement of their private affairs. Merel Zabio was standing close to Lississee, but the expression on her face said that she thought herself quite alone.

'We found nothing,' Hyry was saying to Fraxinus. 'We've nothing left of what we brought from Xandria, and we got nothing for it.' There was something in her tone, though, which gave evidence of a different system of accounting. Even Hyry thought they'd gained something.

Lucrezia met Jacom Cerri's eyes. 'No,' she said. 'You can't take me back to Xandria. We've come too far for that.'

'I know,' he said softly. 'Believe me, highness, I know.'

18

ANDRIS WAS GLAD TO have an audience again, because he had a good deal to say. His heroic intellectual efforts would not have been in vain even if he had not had the chance to communicate his conclusions, because he knew that the greatest battle of all was yet to come, and that the greatest prize of all was yet to be won, but he was nevertheless glad to have the opportunity to tell what he had discovered.

He knew that it was all speculation, all the product of dreams. He knew that the Spirit of the Waters and all its analogues could no more give him intuitive access to indubitable truth than it could give him inspirational knowledge of the mind of God – but he also knew that the rewards of speculation and inquisitive visions were not to be despised. They were what lay beyond the plus sign which was supposed to remind everyone, everywhere, that what they knew as everyday life was only the tiniest fraction of something much vaster – and that all the meaning and significance of everyday life depended on that which lay beyond the plus.

'What I've learned to recognise,' he told his hearers, 'is that there's a series of expanding scales in space and time, whose limits lie beyond the scope of our imagination. Within us there's a whole series of microcosms, each one contained within the other. We can only catch a few fleeting glimpses of the most immediate, while the rest – real though they are – exist only in the imagination. What we can know for sure of the world within ourselves is strictly limited, because its inhabitants are too tiny for us to see, but we can still appreciate its wonderful complexity. I can't tell how much truth there is in what Aulakh Phar told us all about cells and corpuscles, bacteria and viruses, atoms and molecules, let alone what Jacom's been told about nanomachines and the genetic systems which gave Genesys its name, but I do know that the world within me is so rich and so wonderful that no such account could do more than begin to do justice to its complexity.

'By the same token, we can only have the slightest grasp of the world of which we're very tiny parts. The world has an individuality of its own; seen from the perspective of the most immediate macrocosm it's more like a cell than a body but it's a whole of sorts nevertheless. We know that because of what we see in the sky when the sun goes down, but also because of what the lore tells us about ships that sail the dark between the stars. Life isn't just here, within and without the Nest of the Phoenix; life is everywhere.

'Everywhere, I dare say, there are places like Xandria, where life seems to be settled and stable, more or less at peace; and everywhere, I'm perfectly certain, there are places like the world within the Reef, where different kinds of life are engaged in a violent struggle for existence. Wherever there's settlement and stability, though, there's also change, because corruption and corrosion are everywhere too and nowhere is beyond their compass. But wherever corruption and corrosion run riot, even to the extent that chaos threatens to overwhelm everything, there's also creativity and the possibility – not the promise, but at least the possibility – of ultimate harmony.

'Life is universal; the games it plays are universal too. Everything, everywhere, is connected even though the connections may be invisible to the naked eye. All severance is temporary; in eternity, everything is part of everything else.

'The world of dreams – which is where we all live, if we could but step outside ourselves and look back – will always be frightening, because that's the nature of dreams. I don't think you can have any idea how frightened I've been, as I've been shifted from one dream into another, forced to realise in making the change that *both* lives were a kind of dream – but for the same reason, you can't imagine how little it seemed to matter, once I'd got used to the idea.

'Like you, I thought that what's happened to me would constitute a kind of ultimate horror, a fate worse than death – but it isn't. I dare say there *are* fates worse than death, but I can only think of two: unyielding pain and irreversible mental derangement. You might suspect me of the second, but it would

493

be poor judgment. I might not be the same as I ever was but I'm certainly as sane as I ever was. I am what I am, just as I was what I was, and the prospect I face is exactly the same, in its essentials, as the prospect facing all of you: I have to remain myself, for as long as I possibly can, returning from any sleep that overtakes me, no matter how long it may last.

'That's the final battle. That's the *only* battle.

'Remaining oneself isn't a matter of resisting all change, or even a matter of *taking charge* of change: it's a matter of accepting and accommodating change. In order to do that sensibly and well, we all have to remember that although we're children of the world we're also children of the world of dreams. The vividness of dreams contains the hope and urgency of our yearning hearts as well as the desperation of our fears of pain, madness and death.

'I think I've learned a lot about dreams since I realised that all conscious life can be seen as a kind of dream. I've learned that memories are subject to corruption and corrosion just like objects. I've learned that all the dreams and seeming memories which look back at any kind of paradise are untrustworthy – because there never was a paradise, only another world – but that we have to believe in them anyway, or believe that there's a kind of truth in them, in spite of their being lies, because they help us see where we might have been. Without that, it's much more difficult to see where we might want to be in future.

'The best dreams, I think, are those which look forward to the future. The art of prophecy is far more treacherous than the art of memory, if it can be called an art at all, but dreams of that sort can be treasured and kept safe from the worst ravages of corruption and corrosion.

'The lore's right when it insists that there's no such thing as destiny because the future's as yet unmade, but I'm certain that our dreams can play their part in its making, and that they're to be treasured on that account. Unless we dream the best dreams of which we're capable, the future will be poorer than it might be. I think the lore's also right to insist that conquest is always an illusion, and that the only kind of victory which means anything is reconciliation.

'I don't think anyone should be afraid or ashamed to dream; I think people who can't dream can't live – at least, not properly.

494

The future is the property of dreamers. So is the past. So is the universe.

'Does any of that make sense, do you think, or am I just fooling myself? Have I gone mad without realising it? Have I suffered a fate worse than death without knowing it?'

'It makes sense,' said Carus Fraxinus judiciously.

'You haven't gone mad,' Lucrezia assured him.

'If you say that it's not worse than death,' Merel answered, 'then it isn't. The question is . . .'

'You are what you are,' Andris told her. 'You have to fight for that, no matter what happens. We had what we had, but we couldn't make it last for ever. There's no shame in that. Look around you, Merel: the garden is dying, as all gardens do. Soon, it'll be still and silent. After that . . . I don't know. I suspect it will disappear into the bowels of the earth. If Fraxinus is right, it might not bloom again for eight thousand years. I intend to be here when it does, if I can.

'I intend to be here, *and to be who I am*, but only time will tell whether that's possible, and in the meantime . . . well, this phase of my life will end while you still have most of yours ahead of you. If you want to know what I want for you, I want you to be what you are and make as good a job of it as you can. That's what I intend for myself. Go with Fraxinus – but never forget that you've left a seed of yourself in Chimera's Cradle, and that you might live again as a ghost, just as I might. Remember too, if you will, that Lucrezia took my fruit to Chimera's Cradle, so that I could be there as well as here.

'Nothing's *finished*, Merel, not even when you die. You *will* die, but that's not the end. Whatever else may finish, the *story* never ends, and we're all part of the story . . . not just *our* story but *the* story. Worlds within worlds, change within chaos . . . all that stuff I just let out.

'I know you understand me – you were always as clever as I was, if not cleverer. Everyone can understand, if they only have the chance. Isn't that so?'

'Yes,' she said. 'It's so.'

He suspected that nothing he had said made a difference to the decision she had already made, but he hoped that the fact that he had said it might make all the difference to its consequences. He felt sure that she would remember every last detail of what he had asked her never to forget. She had loved him, after all, when he had been a man.

'Were sse besst,' Ssifuss told him. 'Besst ever. Sstupid giantss, kill! kill! kill!'

'I'm glad that you feel that way,' Andris told the Serpent. 'The world would be a peculiar place if human children felt the same way about adults, but I realise things work differently for you.'

'Are *not* sshildren,' Mossassor assured him earnestly. 'Are *true* adultss, true Sserpentss. Osserss are *not* true. Flierss, giantss . . . all bad.'

'Maybe so, for now,' Andris admitted. 'But things can change. Who knows what might be made of giant Serpents, if only they had the right guidance? Who knows what might be made of anything within the Great Reef, if only mind and intelligence can be preserved through the long generations? Jacom assures us that something can be done . . . it only remains to be seen how much.'

There were other conversations, of course, more intimate and more private, but once he had unburdened himself of everything that he felt he needed to say he found himself becoming slower and slower, descending further and further into the kind of dream that was entirely self-enclosed. He found it increasingly difficult to speak, or even to listen, but he made what efforts he could, lest his friends suspect him of meekly giving in to the woodenness of the alien flesh that had consumed him.

'I'm not going back with Fraxinus,' Lucrezia told him. 'I'm going in the opposite direction, into unknown territory. Jacom will follow me – he's always been mine to command. Hyry insists that she won't, but she will. She's always been mine to command too, although she'll never admit it. There are advantages to royal rank, and I'll always have that, no matter where I go or what I become.'

'Being a princess won't keep you out of jail,' Andris told her, still intent on communicating his laboriously accumulated wisdom, 'but it might help you to keep your head up while you're there. Always be kind to spiders – if you're not, you're sure to be plagued by flies.'

'I'll remember that,' she promised. Then she pointed at the head which was still suspended from his nearly leafless branches.

'He's not really alive, is he?' she said. 'He can't actually talk to you. When we leave, you'll be alone.'

'He's alive,' Andris assured her. 'He has no voice of his own, it's true, but he's alive. In the fullness of time, he too might be reborn as a ghost – and not the froggy kind. In the meantime . . . no, I'm not alone. The dweller in the deep has no voice either, but it can change. In time, anything's possible. That's what we ought to believe, at any rate.

'Our own remoter ancestors were voiceless once, every bit as stupid as giant Serpents. Perhaps there'll come a time when the ghost of my ghost can confront the intelligence of the ground itself, and say: We are *not* all of one mind here, nor should we make that our goal.'

'It might disagree,' Lucrezia pointed out.

'It probably will,' Andris agreed. 'But I'll be the expert, won't I? I'll be the one who knows that it really is possible for everyone to end up on the same side, no matter where they start out from and no matter what befalls them on the way.'

'That's true, I suppose,' she said. 'Even Mossassor and Ssifuss are on the same side now. Whatever debts they owed to one another are settled now. It doesn't seem to have been easy, though – and *they* started out in the same batch of hatchlings, products of the same nest.'

'Sometimes,' Andris said, 'the deepest and deadliest disputes of all are between the closest kin.' Because he was a prince of Ferentina he was an expert on that matter too – but because Lucrezia was one of Belin's many daughters, so was she.

'Ssifuss is right,' Lucrezia told him, shortly before she said goodbye. 'You are the best there ever was – but not because you killed so many giant Serpents.' It was just empty flattery, though, and he was too scrupulous to retaliate in kind.

It was, of course, Merel who said the last goodbye; she was entitled to that.

'I'll never forget,' she told him.

'Nor will I,' he promised in return. 'And when I say never, I hope I mean *never*.'

'So do I,' she said – and there was no empty flattery in that.

497

19

SO CAREFULLY HAD THEY been maintained it seemed that the walls of Xandria had not changed at all in three years. When his party passed through the Southern Gate Fraxinus was overtaken by an unexpected rush of familiarity. It was not that decay had not taken its customary toll of the city, but that the city had become so very adept at dealing with its ravages as to compensate for its effects reflexively. Although it had never ceased to renew itself, it was the same city he had left – and because it was the same city, he gradually fell back while he made his painstaking way through its crowded streets into the habit of being his old self. By the time he arrived at his house on the seaward side of Torc Hill he was almost ready to believe that he was the same man who had left it.

His son and daughter-in-law greeted him with all the astonishment and delight due to a man of his years who had been away so long – and a little more, because he seemed younger now than he had on the day of his departure. His grandchildren, who didn't even remember him, greeted him with all the wonder and excitement due to a man of whose exploits they had heard so many tales. The day was immediately declared a holiday, and servants were sent out at a sprint to plunder the markets of their very best produce while Fraxinus and his companion bathed themselves and put on the best fresh clothes that could be found.

It was obvious that business had been good while Fraxinus was away, as he had known full well that it would be. Xury was, after all, his well-trained son and heir.

Fraxinus deflected the many questions he was asked about his great adventure because he wanted to tell his story in his own way and in his own time, but it began to leak out anyway because his companion – who had shared so much of it with him – was seized so firmly by the high excitement of the day that she couldn't help attempting to answer any and all questions in whatever order they came, although she was scrupulous in obeying his injunction not to mention any names.

By the time midnight came and virtually everyone was falling asleep there had been a great deal said – but nothing really explained – about dragomites and manticores, men with the heads of monkeys and giant Serpents, gemsnakes and crocolids, figured stones and living ground. So much had been said, in fact, and in such a manner, that when Fraxinus and Xury were finally able to lock themselves away the very first question Xury asked was: 'How much of that was true?'

'You haven't heard the half of it,' Fraxinus assured him. 'Not even a quarter. What we saw and did wasn't just stranger than you imagine – it was stranger than you *can* imagine.'

Xury wasn't yet prepared to believe that, but he let it pass. 'Who is this Merel, anyway?' he wanted to know. 'She's certainly local, in spite of her pallid skin, but she wasn't with you when you set out.' What Xury really wanted to know was: *Are you intending to marry again?*

'Her surname is Zabio,' Fraxinus told him. 'She signed on in Khalorn.'

'I know that name from somewhere,' Xury said, furrowing his brow.

'That's a pity,' Fraxinus said. 'She'll have to change it, I suppose. Belin's officers have always had long memories.'

'What's she wanted for?' Xury asked, and then he remembered the coincidence of excitements that had casually eclipsed all the ceremony attached to his father's departure. 'She's one of Checuti's accomplices – one of only half a dozen still unaccounted for!'

'I can account for Checuti himself,' Fraxinus told him soberly.

Xury shook his head slowly. 'I don't suppose you know what became of the kidnapped princess and the disappearing witch-queen?' he asked, having no inkling of the truth.

'I don't want to have to explain it to Belin,' Fraxinus said. 'There's no way in the world I could make him understand. Neither of them will ever be found. The princess is alive and well, and so is the guard-captain who was sent to fetch her back, but they went south when we came north. If they ever return to

Xandria they'll have circumnavigated the globe in order to do it.'

'Circumnavigated the globe?' Xury echoed.

'Gone all the way around the world,' Fraxinus translated.

'I know what it means,' Xury said. 'I just didn't know that anyone had ever done it. I thought stories of that kind were just myths and fictions.'

'That's the crucial limitation of the lore,' Fraxinus observed. 'After a couple of generations, myth and memory become indistinguishable, and fiction and fact become so intricately entangled that no one can tell where one ends and the other begins. After half a dozen generations more the truth becomes so strangely mutated that no one could possibly figure out the limits of its meaning. It's a problem that's been preying on my mind for some time while I've been composing my own lore.'

'You mean the story of your journey to Chimera's Cradle?'

'I mean the myths and fictions that will guide a new band of adventurers in a few thousand years' time, when the Silver Thorns will draw back to open up the Gauntlet of Gladness for the sixth or the seventh time. Actually, I'm composing two sets of lore. One will be called *The Lore of Ultimogenesys*, the other *The Wisdom of the Tree of Knowledge*. I'm hopeful that even if one of them is lost or rendered useless the other might survive and retain a kernel of truth. Until the Pool of Life produces incorruptible stone that's the best we can hope for.'

Xury made no comment on the notion of a merchant inventing lore. All he said was: 'You didn't find any incorruptible stone, then?' – which, loosely translated, meant: *So the expedition was a complete washout, commercially speaking?*

'Keshvara's with the princess too,' Fraxinus told him gravely. 'She was genuinely torn, I think, between the two alternatives – but in the end she decided in favour of Lucrezia and Jacom Cerri.'

'That's the fruit-farmer's son, isn't it?' Xury said, but not because he didn't care what had become of Hyry Keshvara.

'Yes. Is Cerri still alive? Do we still have dealings with him?'

Xury nodded.

'I'll go to see him when I can,' Fraxinus said. 'He's entitled to know what happen to his son.'

'Whereas the king isn't entitled to know what happened to his daughter?' Xury countered.

'Kings can't be trusted not to blame the messenger for the content of the message. Fruit-farmers can. It's the way of the world.'

'And Aulakh?' Xury put in gently. 'I take it . . .'

'You take it wrong,' Fraxinus told him. 'I can account for him too – but his death wasn't quite as final as Belin's will be, or yours.'

'Or yours?'

'Or mine,' Fraxinus agreed, although he wasn't entirely convinced of that. He knew that his death would be perfectly ordinary, but he wasn't sure exactly how much the pyramid had taken from him. Nor was he absolutely sure that his 'real' body wasn't still there, drowned in the Pool of Life, while the one he now wore – including the consciousness that 'wore' it – was a duplicate.

Xury ostentatiously refrained from pressing him to explain.

'Anyhow,' Fraxinus said, with a sigh. 'You're not interested in any of that. These last three years have turned you into a true businessman. You want to know if I achieved anything worth-while. That's very sensible. Honest accounts first, frivolous embellishments later. Well, I've set up a trade route of sorts. It remains to be seen how strong it is, and how long it will endure, but while its links remain in place there ought to be a little money to be made.

'The core of the operation is in a place called Ebla. That's a city in a narrow strip of arable land south of the Dragomite Hills. It's in turmoil at present because the land is under invasion from the south, not by people – at least, not any more – but by various kinds of inconvenient unearthly life forms, especially a kind of tree with a very tough and very straight trunk. The Eblans' own tools are inadequate to cope with the trees, but Xandrian steel should allow them to take control of the new forests, and the timber is tougher and straighter than any species known in Xandria. The Eblan establishment is in the charge of a young amber named Koraismi, who's working in association with a local family called the Shabirs.'

'I suppose you must have more recent news than I do, having crossed them within the last few tendays,' Xury put in, 'but I had heard that the Dragomite Hills were recovering from the blight and were once again to be reckoned exceedingly dangerous.'

'So they would be,' Fraxinus said, 'were it not for the fact that there are people living there, in close community with dragomites. It wasn't easy to make contact with them, but it only required the courage to try and the tireless efforts of a Serpent named Mossassor, who'll be our linkman. The people of the Five Towns – there used to be nine but four have been abandoned – didn't reconcile themselves easily to the idea of making treaties with the dragomite-people, but when they were forced to accept that they couldn't continue to fight . . . well, suffice it to say that we have allies within the hills who'll do their best to guarantee the safety of convoys moving in either direction, in exchange for a toll that shouldn't prove *too* exorbitant. It's vitally important that we keep the road open if we can, Xury. If we could possibly put an end to the demonisation of dragomites, and create a new frontier in the southlands . . . but that's for the longer term.

'I've also established communication of sorts between Ebla and a curious community living on the shores of the Lake of Colourless Blood. They have some interesting medicines to sell – it's better to call them that than "witchcraft", at least until the day comes when a little underhanded advertisement is needed.

'More importantly, if more tentatively, I've opened a channel of communication between Ebla and Salamander's Fire. It involves a Serpent named Ssifuss, and a Salamander named Ixtlplt. They're both good men, and Ssifuss is kin to Mossassor, so I hope the link will remain solid. Salamander's Fire has regular commerce with the southern part of the Spangled Desert, and in particular with the Crystal City. There's unlikely to be any saving in respect of the kinds of goods we already import from the desert via the northern route, but I've already identified a dozen useful items which have never been traded in Xandria before. I think the Crystal City still has a great deal of promise as a source of merchandise; it requires more thorough investigation than I was able to carry out, but there's time for that now.'

'It's said that Serpents never act as agents for humans for very long,' Xury observed, although Fraxinus noticed that he was careful to keep a tight rein on his scepticism. 'Don't those who try experience problems with their own kind because too many of them think that we're invaders who've spoiled their world?'

'I don't think Mossassor and Ssifuss will have problems of that kind,' Fraxinus assured him. 'As for those who come after them . . . we'll just have to hope that the next generation will continue in their footsteps.'

'What about all this living ground?' Xury wanted to know. 'Did you set us up with representatives in the garden of Idun, who are busy bottling the water of the Pool of Life even as we speak?' His sarcasm was intended to be amusing rather than insulting, and Fraxinus took it in that spirit.

'The war that rages around Chimera's Cradle is returning to its quiet phase,' Fraxinus told his son. 'The dwellers in the deep are becoming passive again, and they probably won't return to fervent activity for several thousand years. The Nest of the Phoenix is falling into dereliction – but that doesn't make the ground any less dangerous. The forests within the Reef are becoming impassable, and the profits to be obtained by anyone brave enough to hack a way through would probably be slight.

'Having said that, though, I certainly intend to sow rumours of fabulous prizes that might be obtained by any who dares to go adventuring there. Whether people can actually establish homes on the Plain of Flowing Stones I don't know, and I doubt that there's any reward easy enough of attainment to make them try, but if humans can cling on to a foothold within or without the Great Reef it might be a very precious foothold in times to come. Some day, even if it's not for a hundred thousand years, humans will have to make their accommodation with the living ground, because there won't be any dead ground left to sustain the kind of home-from-home we have in Xandria. This is our world now, and we have to adapt to it.'

'It always was our world,' Xury reminded him. 'Wherever the people of the ship came from, they placed us here. Whenever the forefathers lived, it was so long ago that they might as well be products of imagination rather than memory. This is our world, and we've adapted it to suit us.' It was not the kind of speech he would have made three years ago, when he had been a much younger man; it was the first statement which made Fraxinus fully aware of the gap that had inevitably grown between them.

'That's one of the lessons my new lore will try to teach,'

Fraxinus said mildly. 'It's not a question of our adapting the world to our requirements, or the world adapting us to its own. Adaptation isn't a process which leads to a final settlement; it's something neverending. The old lore's right: there's no such thing as conquest. The consequence of every war is a fusion of the victors and the vanquished, a mutual dissolution which adds new impetus to change. We can no more remake the world in the image of another than the world can remake us in the image of Serpents and Salamanders, although it won't be for lack of trying on either side.

'In the end . . . well, there is no end, not here, not anywhere. The story will go on and on, and nothing will put a stop to it, neither the death of the world, nor the death of the sun. Every death, you see, is just a prelude to rebirth, and while there are ships to sail the dark between the stars – or spores to drift there – nothing can be truly lost.

'It doesn't matter how big or how small the circle is that's inscribed upon the map. The Nest of the Phoenix is without as well as within; it's just that the fire burns more bravely where its containment is most intense. Idun is everywhere and everywhen; it's just that it doesn't always show itself for what it is.'

'Somehow,' Xury said tenderly, 'I'd forgotten what an ardent philosopher you were, and how you loved to rhapsodise about the secrets of the lore and the secrets of the universe. I'm not Aulakh Phar, alas, but I'll try to take his place. I really will . . . if that's what you want.'

'Thanks,' said Fraxinus sincerely. 'A world like ours – and I doubt that it's different in any other – can't have too many philosophers, nor can they ever be too ardent.'

20

THOSE WHO HAD been summoned came in the end, one riding upon a manticore and another on a sphinx. Their journey had not been easy. Indeed, it had been fraught with perils at every step, but they came nevertheless. They did not know why they had been called, nor had they any way to be certain that they would be able to return whence they had come, but they came to stand before the Tree of Knowledge because they were inquisitive. They wanted to hear what it had to say, for their own benefit and that of others of their own strange kind.

They were not disappointed by the sight of their summoner, because he was a prince among trees, as glorious in his foliage as any that had ever been in the world before.

'Do you have a name?' asked the one who had ridden the sphinx, looking up at the face which studied him so carefully.

'No,' answered the tree. 'I am not the man whose name I once wore, and have no need of a name now. Do you have a name?'

'I have many names,' said the man who had ridden the sphinx. 'I dare say that I shall acquire many more, if I am only given the chance. I was once a prince of thieves, and the most cherished of habits die hardest of all.'

'I was a soldier once,' said the man who had ridden the manticore, 'but that was a long time ago. Do you, perchance, know how much time has passed since then?'

'The stars do not seem to have changed at all,' said the voice of the tree, 'but I was never an astronomer, so I cannot be absolutely sure of that. Does it matter? Who can count the fleeting days while the dwellers sleep? All that matters is that a new morning has dawned, and all the world is awake again. I am very glad to see you both, for we have plans to make.'

'Have we?' asked the man who had been a prince of thieves. 'I thought we had a war to fight. Everyone else that we have met seems to think so. I have a dear but tiresome friend – he was once a trader, a physician *and* a philosopher – who insists on explaining at great length to anyone who will listen that the war is merely an illusion, but no one seems to have communicated that fact to the killers which did their level best to put a stop to our adventure. What plans can possibly be made, in such a world as this?'

'There are schemes,' said the man who had been a soldier, 'but they are so much vaster than we are that I fear we can be nothing but their instruments. Are we not too tiny to hope that we might direct their course?'

'Soldiers and thieves might think so,' said the tree, 'but I was a mapmaker once and I am a mapmaker still, after my fashion.'

'As I remember the world before the world,' said the ghost of the prince of thieves, 'its maps had fallen into disuse because time and chance had moved on. The maps had become mere matters of legend, recalling realities long since changed.'

'It seems that way to me, also,' said the ghost of the soldier. 'I doubt that this is a time to follow maps. Is it not a time for exploration?'

'When I was Andris Myrasol,' the tree told them, 'I drew my maps as I had been taught to do, and protested at the evil of the world when its landscapes refused to match them. I am different now. Now, I intend to draw maps of the world as I desire it to be, and I have taken it as my mission to bring the landscape into conformity, no matter how arduous that work might be, or how long it might take.'

'When I was Checuti,' said the man who had ridden the sphinx, 'I would have thought that a foolish and hopeless aim, but I am different now. Now, I can assure you that it is foolish, but I certainly will not call it hopeless. The difference between a thief and a prince of thieves is that a prince of thieves believes the act of theft to be an end rather than a means; now that I am a ghost, I understand that there is nothing worth stealing but eternity. I cannot speak for those with whom I have slept through the long night, but I shall be willing to help you make your plans, as soon as I have rested.'

'When I was Jacom Cerri,' said the man who had ridden the manticore, 'I would have called you mad, but I am different now. I became a soldier then because I had a false idea of what it meant to be a soldier; I am a soldier now because I have discovered a far better meaning for the word. I shall be more than willing to help you both, when I have rested – and I am more confident than my friend that those who slept alongside me will give me a sympathetic hearing when I return.'

'I ask no more,' said the tree. 'Rest first, and then we will begin.'

While his guests rested, the Tree of Knowledge summoned creatures who looked like men, and sent them forth to cross the Dragomite Hills with seeds taken from his fruits, as testimony to the wonders that were now contained in Idun and the surrounding lands. Then he summoned the giant Serpents who were the first children of his Mother Earth, and sent them forth to guard the roads which led to the garden, instructing them to make all travellers welcome and protect them all from harm. Then he summoned the Watchers, and instructed them to range far and wide across the lands within the Reef, collecting what information they could and trading it according to their own methods. Only then did he consent to rest himself – and even then, he had to bear an interruption.

'We are not all of one mind here,' his brother said to him. 'Your promise to me is not yet fulfilled. You owe me better than this, and I still mean to have it.'

'I have not forgotten,' the Tree of Knowledge told him. 'Only be patient, and all our desires might be answered – but you must give me time. Now let me rest a while. There is much to be done, tomorrow and the next day and the day after that, now that my friends are here. If I am to play my part and play it well, I must dream a very particular dream – for there is much to be remembered and much more to be learned, while the world is still young.'

507

Author's Note

I OWE A CONSIDERABLE debt to my editor, John Jarrold, for commissioning this eccentric planetary romance and patiently seeing it through to completion. (I need hardly add that neither of us envisaged in the beginning that it would turn out to be 560,000 words long.)

I should also like to thank Jane Stableford and Teleri Beaty for their invaluable assistance in proof-reading the penultimate drafts of the three volumes.

The most useful assistant I had in the routine business of worldbuilding was the natural historian Pliny the Elder, to whom I shall of course be eternally grateful.

Brian Stableford, Reading, May 1996